'The Baronet of Ruddigore a[...] ride out to the stars, to discover a world never before seen [...] Terrans, there to found the Central Kingdom in reality, and live as men ought, by faith and sweat and steel. We shall need villeins and yeomen, gentlemen and knights! We shall leave in two days' time; any who are not with us then, will never be! Who wishes to ride? Sign here!'

He threw the tablet down into the multitude. With a roar, they pounced on it, and the whole crowd instantly reformed into a line, each one fairly panting in his eagerness to emigrate. Food-sellers and jugglers began to work up and down the queue.

Horatio turned back to Dar with a grin. '*That* is the mettle of my people!'

'They'll change their minds by the time they get to the from of the line,' Dar predicted.

Horatio nodded. 'Some of them, no doubt – but most will sign. They've wished for nothing half so much as to live in a world where folk are true, and the rulers worthy of trust. How say you, brave ones? Will you join us?'

'Instantly.' Sam beamed up at him.

Christopher Stasheff

# Warlock
# to the Magic Born

PAN
FANTASY
Pan Books
London, Sydney and Auckland

*Escape Velocity* first published 1983 by
Ace Science Fiction Books,
a division of The Berkley Publishing Group, New York

© Christopher Stasheff 1983

*The Warlock in Spite of Himself* first published 1969 by
Ace Science Fiction Books

© Christopher Stasheff 1969

*King Kobold Revived* first published in this substantially revised version 1984 by
Ace Science Fiction Books

© Christopher Stasheff 1984

Original version published 1971 under the title *King Kobold* by Ace Science Fiction Books

© Christopher Stasheff 1971

This combined volume first published 1990
by Pan Books Ltd,
Cavaye Place, London SW10 9PG

9 8 7 6 5 4 3 2 1

© Christopher Stasheff 1990

ISBN 0 330 31370 3

Printed in England by Clays Ltd, St Ives plc

# Contents

# Escape Velocity

**To Grail Crellin**

who wanted to know
why Horatio Loguire's ghost
didn't recognize the time machine
as being, at least, a machine

## 1

She was a girl. Dar knew it the moment he saw her.

That wasn't as easy as it sounds. Really. Considering [...]
was shaved bald and was wearing a baggy grey flannel c[...]
Dar was doing pretty well to identify her as human, let [...]
female. It would've been a much better bet that she wa[...]
department-store mannequin in one of those bags that are p[...]
on them between outfits, to protect them in case somebody with
a plastic fetish comes along.

But she moved. That's how Dar knew she was human.

And he was just in from a six-week trading tour and was just
about to go out on another one (Cholly, the boss, was shorthanded
this month; one of his traders had been caught shaving percentage
points with Occam's Razor). Which meant, since the Wolmar
natives didn't allow their womenfolk to meet strangers, that for
the last six weeks Dar had seen things that were human, and things
that were female, but never both at the same time; so he was in a
prime state to recognize a girl if one happened along.

This one didn't 'happen' – she strode. She nearly swaggered,
and she stepped down so hard that Dar suspected she was fighting
to keep her hips from rolling. It sort of went with the grey
jumpsuit, bald head, and lack of make-up.

She sat down on a bar stool, and waited. And waited. And
waited.

The reason she waited so long was that Cholly was alone behind
the bar today and was discussing the nature of reality with a
sergeant; he wasn't about to give up a chance at a soldier.

Not that the girl seemed to mind. She was ostentatiously not
looking at the two privates at the other end of the bar, but her
ears fairly twitched in their direction.

'He niver had a chance,' the grey-haired one burbled around his
cigar. 'He but scarcely looked up, and whap! I had him!'

'Took him out good and proper, hey?' The blond grinned.

'Out! I should say! So far out he an't niver coming back! Mark
my words, he'll buy the farm! Buy it for me yet, he will!'

The girl's lips pinched tight, and her throat swelled the way
someone's does when they can't hold it in anymore and it's just
got to bust loose; and Dar figured he'd better catch it, 'cause the
soldiers wouldn't understand.

After six weeks without women, he was ready
d anything, provided it came from a female.

idled up to lean on the bar, neatly intersecting her line
, smiled with all the sincerity he could dredge up, and
ped, 'Service is really slow around here, isn't it?'

She got that blank look of total surprise for a minute; then her
lip curled, and she spat, 'Yes, unless you're looking for death! You
seem to dish it up awfully fast around here, just because you're
wearing a uniform!'

'"Uniform"?' Dar looked down at his heavy green coveralls and
mackinaw, then glanced over at the two soldiers, who were looking
surprised and thinking about feeling offended. He turned back to
the girl, and said quickly, ' 'Fraid I don't follow you, miz. Hasn't
been a killing around here all year.'

'Sure,' she retorted, 'it's January seventh. And what were those
two bums over there talking about, if it wasn't murder?'

She had to point. She just had to. Making sure Dar couldn't
pretend she'd been talking about two CPOs walking by in the
street, no doubt. To make it worse, judging by their accents,
the two privates were from New Perth, where 'bum' had a
very specific meaning that had absolutely nothing to do with
unemployment.

The older private opened his mouth for a bellow, but Dar cut
in quicker. 'Points, miz. You can believe me or not, but they were
talking about points.'

She looked doubtful for a fraction of a second, but only a
fraction. Then her face firmed up again with the look of someone
who's absolutely sure that she's right, especially if she's wrong.
She demanded, 'Why should I believe you? What are you, if you
aren't a soldier?'

Dar screwed up his hopes and tried to look casual. 'Well, I *used*
to be a pilot . . .'

'Am I supposed to be impressed?' she said sourly.

'They told me girls would be, when I enlisted.' Dar sighed. 'It's
got to work *some*time.'

'I thought this planet was an Army prison.'

'It is. The Army has ships too.'

'Why?' She frowned. 'Doesn't it trust the Navy to do its
shipping?'

'Something like that.'

'You say that with authority. What kind of ship did you pilot –
a barge?'

'A space tug,' Dar admitted.

She nodded. 'What are you now?'

Dar shrugged, and tried to look meek. 'A trader.'

'A *trader?*' She spoke with such gleeful indignation that even Cholly looked up – for a second, anyway. 'So *you're* one of the vampires who're victimizing the poor, helpless natives!'

'Helpless!' the old private snorted – well, roared, really; and Dar scratched his head and said, 'Um, 'fraid you've got your cables crossed, miz. I wouldn't exactly say who's doing the victimizing.'

'Well, I would!' she stormed. 'Stampeding out here, victimizing these poor people, trying to take over their land and destroy their culture – it's always the same! It's all part of a pattern, a pattern as old as Cortez, and it just goes on and on and on! "Don't give a damn what the people want; give 'em technology! Don't give a damn whether or not their religion's perfectly adequate for 'em – give 'em the Bible! Don't ask whether or not they own the place – herd 'em onto reservations! Or make slaves of 'em!" Oh, I've heard about it, I've read about it! It's just starting here, but you wait and see! It's genocide, that's what it is! It's the worst kind of imperialism! And all being practised by the wonderful, loyal soldiers of our miraculously democratic Interstellar Dominion Electorates! Imperialists!' And she spat.

The two soldiers swelled up like weather balloons, and the weather was going to be bad, so Cholly yanked himself out of his talk and hurried down to the end of the bar to put in a soothing word or two. As he passed Dar, he muttered, 'Now, then, lad, whut've I told ye? Reason, don'cha know, now, Dar, reason! Try it, there's a good fellow, just try it! An' you'll see. Sweet reason, now, Dar!' And he hurried on down to the end of the bar.

Dar thought he'd been trying reason already, and so far it hadn't been turning out sweetly; but he took a deep breath, and set himself to try it again. 'Now, then, miz. Uh, first off, I'd say we didn't exactly stampede out here. More like a roundup, actually.'

She frowned. 'What're you talking about? . . . Oh. You mean because this is a military *prison* planet.'

'Well, something of that sort, yes.'

She shrugged. 'Makes no difference. Whether you wanted to come here or not, you're here – and they're shipping you in by the thousands.'

'Well, more like the hundreds, really.' Dar scratched behind his ear. 'We get in maybe two hundred, three hundred, ah . . .'

'Colonists,' she said sternly.

'Prisoners,' Dar finished. 'Per year. Personally, I'd rather think of myself as a "recruit".'

'Doesn't make any difference,' she snapped. 'It's what you do after you get here that counts. You go out there, making war on those poor, innocent natives . . . and you traders go cheating them blind. Oh, I've heard what you're up to.'

'Oh, you have?' Dar perked up. 'Hey, we're gettin' famous! Where'd you hear about us, huh?'

She shrugged impatiently. 'What does it matter?'

'A lot, to me. To most of us, for that matter. When you're stuck way out here on the fringe of the Terran Sphere, you start caring a lot about whether or not people've ever heard about your planet. 'Be nice to feel even *that* important.'

'Mm.' Her face softened a moment, in a thoughtful frown. 'Well . . . I'm afraid this won't help much. I used to be a clerk back on Terra, in the records section of the Bureau of Otherworldly Activities – and a report about Wolmar came through occasionally.'

'Oh.' Dar could almost feel himself sag. 'Just official reports?'

She nodded, with a vestige of sympathy. 'That's right. Nobody ever saw them except bureaucrats. And the computer, of course.'

'Of course.' Dar heaved a sigh and straightened his shoulders. 'Well! That's better than nothing . . . I suppose. What'd they say about us?'

'Enough.' She smiled vindictively. 'Enough so that I know this is a prison planet for criminal soldiers, governed by a sadomasochistic general; that scarcely a day passes when you don't have a war going on . . .'

'Holidays,' Dar murmured, 'and Sundays.'

'"Scarcely", I said! And that you've got an extremely profitable trade going with the natives for some sort of vegetable drug, in return for which you give them bits of cut glass and surplus spare parts that you order through the quartermaster.'

'That's all?' Dar asked, crestfallen.

'All!' She stared, scandalized. 'Isn't that enough? What did you want – a list of war crimes?'

'Oh . . .' Dar gestured vaguely. 'Maybe some of the nice things – like this tavern, and plenty of leave, and . . .'

'Military corruptness. Slackness of discipline.' She snorted. 'Sure. Maybe if I'd stayed with the Bureau, a piece of whitewash would've crossed my desk.'

'*If* you'd stayed with them?' Dar looked up. 'You're not with BOA anymore?'

She frowned. 'If I were working for the Bureau, would I be here?'

Dar just looked at her for a long moment.

Then he shook himself and said, 'Miz, the only reason I can think of why you *would* be here is because BOA sent you. Who could *want* to come here?'

'Me,' she said, with a sardonic smile. 'Use your head. Could I dress like this if I worked for the government?'

Dar's face went blank. Then he shrugged. 'I dunno. *Could* you?'

'Of course not,' she snapped. 'I'd have to have a coiffured hairdo, and plaster myself with skintight see-throughs and spider heels. I had to, for five years.'

'Oh. You didn't like it?'

'Would *you* like to have to display yourself every day so a crowd of the opposite sex could gawk at you?'

Dar started a slow grin.

'Well, I didn't!' she snapped, reddening.

'And that's why you quit?'

'More than that,' she said grimly. 'I got fed up with the whole conformist ragout, so I aced out instead.'

'"Aced out"?' Dar was totally lost.

'Aced out! Quit! Got out of all of it!' she shouted. 'I turned into a *Hume*!'

'What's a "Hume"?'

She stared, scandalized. 'You really *are* away from it all out here, aren't you?'

'I've kinda been trying to hint about something along those lines, yes. We get the news whenever a freighter lands, about three times a year. So until they invent faster-than-light radio, we're not going to know what's happening on Terra until a couple of years after it's happened.'

She shook her head in exasperation. 'Talk about primitive! All right . . . a Hume is me – a nonconformist. We wear loose grey coveralls like this to hide our bodies from all those lascivious, leering eyes. We shave our heads, so we don't have to do up a pompadour every day. And we don't submit to those prisons society calls "jobs"; we'd rather be poor. We've put in our time, we've got some savings, and between that, our GNP share, and whatever we can pick up at odd jobs, we manage to keep going.

We do what *we* want, not what the IDE wants. That's what's a Hume.'

Dar nodded, lips pursed and eyes slightly glazed. 'Uh. But you don't conform. Right.'

'I didn't say that, gnappie! I said we're nonconformists.'

'Uh – right.' Dar nodded. 'I see the difference – or I'll try to.'

She turned on him, but Cholly got there first. 'Do thet, lad! Do thet, and you'll make me proud of you! But you see, you have to know the history of it, don't you! Of course you do; can't understand nothing wot's happening in human society if you don't know the history of it. The first who was called "Nonconformists", see, they started showing up toward the end of the 1500s, now. Shakespeare wrote one of 'em into *Twelfth Night*, called him "Malvolio". Puritans, they was, and Calvinists, and Baptists, too, and Anabaptists, all manner of Protestant sects what wasn't Church of England. And the Anglicans, they lumped 'em all together and called 'em "Nonconformists" (the name got put on 'em from the outside, you see, the way it always does) 'cause they didn't conform to the Established Church (what was C. of E., of course). Yet if you sees the pictures of 'em, like Cromwell's Roundheads, why! they're like to one another as bottles in a case! Within their opposition-culture, you sees, they conformed much more tightly than your C. of E.s – and so it has been, ever since. When you call 'em "nonconformists", it doesn't mean they don't conform to the standards of their group, but that their group don't conform to the majority culture – and that's why any opposition-culture's called "nonconformist". Now then, Sergeant . . .' And he was off again, back to the reality case.

The Hume stared after him, then nodded thickly. 'He's right, come to think of it . . .' She gave herself a shake, and scowled at Dar. 'What was that – a bartender, or a professor?'

'Cholly,' Dar said, by way of explanation. 'My boss.'

The Hume frowned. 'You mean you work here? WHOA!'

Dar saw the indignation rise up in her, and grinned. 'That's right. He's the owner, president, and manager of operations for the Wolmar Pharmaceutical Trading Company, Inc.'

'The boss drug-runner?' she cried, scandalized. 'The robber baron? The capitalist slave-master?'

'Not really. More like the book-keeper for a co-operative.'

She reared up in righteous wrath, opening her mouth for a crushing witticism – but couldn't think of any, and had to content herself with a look of withering scorn.

Dar obligingly did his best to wither.

She turned away to slug back a swallow from her glass – then stared, suddenly realizing that she *had* a glass.

Dar glanced at Cholly, who looked up, winked, nodded, and turned back to discussing the weightier aspects of kicking a cobble.

The Hume seemed to deflate a little. She sighed, shrugged, and took another drink. 'Hospitable, anyway . . .' She turned and looked up at Dar. 'Besides, can you deny it?'

Dar ducked his head – down, around, and back up in hopes of a sequitur. 'Deny what?'

'All of it! Everything I've said about this place! It's all true, isn't it? Starting with your General Governor!'

'Oh. Well, I can deny that General Shacklar's a sadist.'

'But he *is* a masochist?'

Dar nodded. 'But he's very well-adjusted. As to the rest of it . . . well, no, I can't deny it, really; but I would say you've got the wrong emphasis.'

'I'm open to reason,' the Hume said, fairly bristling. 'Explain it to me.'

Dar shook his head. 'Can't explain it, really. You've got to experience it, see it with your own eyes.'

'Yes. Of course.' She rolled her eyes up. 'And how, may I ask, am I supposed to manage that?'

'Uhhhh . . .' Dar's mind raced, frantically calculating probable risks versus probable benefits. It totalled up to 50:50, so he smiled and said, 'Well, as it happens, I'm going out on another trading mission. You're welcome to come along. I can't *guarantee* your safety, of course – but it's really pretty tame.'

The Hume stared, and Dar could almost see her suddenly pulling back, withdrawing into a thickened shell. But something clicked, and her eyes turned defiant again. 'All right.' She gulped the rest of her drink and slammed the glass back down on the bar. 'Sure.' She stood up, hooking her thumbs in her pockets. 'Ready to go. Where's your pack mule?'

Dar grinned. 'It's a little more civilized than that – but it's just out back. Shall we?' And he bowed her toward the door.

She spared him a last withering glance, and marched past him. Dar smiled, and followed.

As they passed Cholly and the sergeant, the bartender was saying earnestly, 'So Descartes felt he had to prove it all, don't you see – everything, from the ground up. No assumptions, none.'

'Ayuh. Ah kin see thet.' The sergeant nodded, frowning. 'If'n he assumed anything, and thet one thing turned out to be wrong, everything else he'd figgered out'd be wrong, too.'

'Right, right!' Cholly nodded emphatically. 'So he stopped right there, don't you see, took out a hotel room, and swore he'd not stir till he'd found some one thing he could prove, some one way to be sure he existed. And he thought and he thought, and it finally hit him.'

'Whut dud?'

'He was thinking! And if'n he wuz thinking, there had to be someone there to do the thinking! And that someone was him, of course – so the simple fact that he was thinking proved he existed!'

'Ay-y-y-y-uh!' The sergeant's face lit with the glow of enlightenment, and the Hume stopped in the doorway, turning back to watch, hushed, almost reverent.

Cholly nodded, glowing, victorious. 'So he laid it out, right then and there, and set it down on paper, where he could read it. *Cogito, ergo sum*, he wrote – for he wrote in Latin, don't you see, all them philosophers did, back then – *Cogito, ergo sum*; and it means "I think; therefore: I exist".'

'Ay-y-y-y-uh. Ayuh, I see.' The sergeant scratched his head, then looked up at Cholly again. 'Well, then – that's whut makes us human, ain't it? Thinking, I mean.'

The Hume drew in a long, shuddering breath, then looked up at Dar. 'What is this – a tavern, or a college?'

'Yes.' Dar pushed the door open. 'Shall we?'

They came out into the light of early afternoon. Dar led the Hume to a long, narrow grav-sled, lumpy with trade goods under a tarpaulin. 'No room for us, I'm afraid – every ounce of lift has to go to the payload. We walk.'

'Not till I get an answer.' The Hume planted her feet, and set her fists on her hips.

'Answer?' Dar looked up, surprised. 'To what?'

'To my question. This boss of yours – what is he? A capitalist? An immoral, unethical, swindling trader? A bartender? Or a professor?'

'Oh.' Dar sat down on his heels, checking the fastenings of the tarp. 'Well, I wouldn't really call him a capitalist, 'cause he never really does more than break even; and he's as moral as a preacher, and as ethical as a statue. And he's never swindled anybody. Aside from that, though, you've pretty well pegged him.'

'Then he *is* a professor!'

Dar nodded. 'Used to teach at the University of Luna.'

The Hume frowned. 'So what happened? What's he doing tending bar?'

Dar shrugged. 'I think he got the idea from his last name: Barman.'

'"Barman"?' She frowned. 'Cholly Barman? Whoa! Not Charles T. Barman!'

Dar nodded.

'But he's famous! I mean, he's got to be the *most* famous teacher alive!'

'Well, notorious, anyway.' Dar gave the fastenings a last tug and stood up. 'He came up with some very wild theories of education. I gather they weren't too popular.'

'So I heard. But I can't figure why; all he was saying was that *everybody* ought to have a college education.'

'And thereby threatened the ones who already had it.' Dar smiled sweetly. 'But it was more than that. He thinks all teaching ought to be done on a one-to-one basis, which made him unpopular with the administrators – imagine having to pay that many teachers! – and thought the teaching ought to be done in an informal environment, without the student realizing he was being taught. That meant each professor would have to have a cover role, such as bartending, which made him unpopular with the educators.'

The Hume frowned. 'I didn't hear about that part of it.'

Dar shrugged. 'He published it; it was there to read, if you managed to get hold of a copy before the LORDS party convinced the central book-feed to quit distributing it down the line to the retail terminals.'

'Yes.' Her mouth flattened, as though she'd tasted something sour. 'Freedom of the press isn't what it used to be, is it?'

'Not really, no. But you can see why the talk gets so deep, back in there; Cholly never misses a chance to do some teaching on the side. When he's got 'em hooked on talk, he lets 'em start hanging out in the back room – it's got an open beer keg, and wall-to-wall books.'

She nodded, looking a little dazzled. 'You don't sound so "innocent of books" yourself, come to think of it.'

Dar grinned, and picked up the towrope. 'Shall we go?'

They trudged down the alley and out into the plastrete street, the Hume walking beside Dar, brooding.

Finally she looked up. 'But what's he doing out here? I mean, he's putting his theories into practice, that's clear – but why here? Why not on some fat planet in near Terra?'

'Well, the LORDS seem to have had something to do with that.'

'That bunch of fascists! I knew they were taking over the Assembly – but I didn't know they were down on education!'

'Figure it out.' Dar spread his hands. 'They say they want really efficient central government; they mean totalitarianism. And one of the biggest threats to a totalitarian government is a liberal education.'

'Oh.' Her face clouded. 'Yes, of course. So what did they do?'

'Well, Cholly won't go into much detail about it, but I gather they tried to assassinate him on Luna, and he ran for it. The assassins chased him, so he kept running – and he wound up here.'

'Isn't he still worried about assassins?'

Dar flashed her a grin. 'Not with Shacklar running the place. By the way, if we're going to be travelling together, we really oughta get onto a first-name basis. I'm Dar Mandra.' He held out his hand.

She seemed to shrink back again, considering the offer; then, slowly, she extended her own hand, looking up at him gravely. 'Samantha Bine. Call me Sam.'

Dar gave her hand a shake, and her face his warmest smile. 'Good to meet you, Sam. Welcome to education.'

'Yes,' she said slowly. 'There *is* a lot here that wasn't in the reports, isn't there?'

Sam looked at the town gate as they passed through it, and frowned. 'A little archaic, isn't it? I thought walled towns went out with the Middle Ages.'

'Only because the attackers had cannon, which the Wolmen *didn't* have when this colony started.'

'But they do now?'

'Well,' Dar hedged, 'let's say they're working on it.'

'Hey! You, there! Halt!'

They looked back to see a corporal in impeccable battledress running after them.

'Here now, Dar Mandra!' he panted as he caught up with them. 'You know better than to go hiking out at two o'clock!'

'Is it that late already?' Dar glanced up at the sun. 'Yeah, it is.

My, how the time flies!' He hauled the grav-sled around. 'Come on, Sam. We've gotta get back against the wall.'

'Why?' Sam came along, frowning. 'What's wrong?'

'Nothing, really. It's just that it's time for one of those continual battles you mentioned.'

'Time?' Sam squawked. 'You mean you *schedule* these things?'

'Sure, at 8 a.m. and 2 p.m., eight hours apart. That gives everybody time to rest up, have lunch, and let it digest in between.'

'*Eight* hours?' She frowned. 'There's only six hours between eight and two!'

'No, eight. Wolmar's got a twenty-eight-hour day, so noon's at fourteen o'clock.' He pulled the sled up against the wall and leaned back against it. 'Now, whatever you do, make sure you stay right here.'

'Don't worry.' Sam settled herself back against the plastrete, folding her arms defiantly. 'I want to get back to Terra to tell about this. I don't intend to get hit by a stray beam.'

'Oh, no chance of that – but you might get trampled.'

Brightly coloured figures rose over the ridge, and came closer. Sam stiffened. 'The natives?'

Dar nodded. 'The Wolmen.'

'*Purple* skin?'

'No, that's a dye they use to decorate their bodies. I think the chartreuse loincloths go rather well with it, don't you?'

The warriors drew up in a ragged line, shaking white-tipped poles at the walled town and shouting.

'Bareskins go down today! Jailers of poor natives! Wolmen break-um free today! Bareskins' Great Father lose-um papooses!'

'It's traditional,' Dar explained.

'What? The way they talk?'

'No, just the threats.'

'Oh.' Sam frowned. 'But that dialect! I can understand why they'd speak Terrese, but why the pidgin grammar and all those "ums"?'

Dar shrugged. 'Don't know, actually. There're some of us have been wondering about that for a few years now. The best we can come up with is that they copped it from some stereotyped presentation of barbarians, probably in an entertainment form. Opposition cultures tend to be pretty romantic.'

The soldiers began to file out of the main gate, lining up a hundred yards away from the Wolmen in a precise line. Their bright green uniforms were immaculately clean, with knife-edge creases; their boots gleamed, and their metalwork glistened. They held their white-tipped sticks at order arms, a precise forty-five degree angle across their bodies.

'Shacklar's big on morale,' Dar explained. 'Each soldier gets a two-BTU bonus if his boots are polished; another two if his uniform's clean; two more if it's pressed; and so on.'

The soldiers muttered among themselves out of the corners of their mouths. Dar could catch the odd phrase:

'Bloody Wolmen think they own the whole planet! Can't tell *us* what t' do! They think they c'n lord it over us, they got another think comin'!'

Sam looked up at Dar, frowning. 'What's that all about? It almost sounds as though they think the Wolmen are the government!'

'They do.' Dar grinned.

Sam scanned the line of troops, frowning. 'Where're their weapons?'

'Weapons!' Dar stared down at her, scandalized. 'What do you think we are – a bunch of savages?'

'But I thought you said this was a—'

BR-R-R-R-ANK! rolled a huge gong atop the wall, and the officers shouted, 'Charge!'

The Wolmen chiefs whooped, and their warriors leaped down toward the soldiers with piercing, ululating war cries.

The soldiers shouted, and charged them.

The two lines crashed together, and instantly broke into a chaotic mêlée, with everyone yelling and slashing about them with their sticks.

'This is civilized warfare?' Sam watched the confusion numbly.

'Very,' Dar answered. 'There's none of this nonsense about killing or maiming, you see. I mean, we're short enough on manpower as it is.'

Sam looked up at him, unbelieving. 'Then how do you tell who's won?'

'The war-sticks.' Dar pointed. 'They've got lumps of very soft chalk in the ends. If you manage to touch your opponent with it, it leaves a huge white blotch on him.'

A soldier ran past, with a Wolman hot on his heels, whooping like a Saturday matinee. Suddenly the soldier dropped into a crouch, whirled about and slashed upward. The stick slashed across the Wolman's chest, leaving a long white streak. The

Wolman skidded to a stop, staring down at his new badge, appalled. Then his face darkened, and he advanced toward the soldier, swinging his stick up.

'Everyone loses his temper now and then,' Dar murmured.

A whistle shrilled, and a Terran officer came running up. 'All right, that'll do! You there, tribesman – you're out of the war, plain as the chalk on your chest! On your way, now, or I'll call one o' yer own officers.'

'Oppressor of poor, ignorant savages!' the Wolman stormed. 'We rise-um up! We beat-um you down!'

'Ayuh, well, tomorrow, maybe. Move along to the sidelines, now, there's a good chap!' The officer made shooing motions.

The Wolman stood stiffly, face dark with rebellion. Then he threw down his chalk-stick with a snarl and went stalking off toward a growing crowd of men, soldiers and Wolmen alike, standing off to the east, well clear of the 'battle'.

The officer nodded. 'That's well done, then.' And he ran off, back toward the thick of the mêlée.

The soldier swaggered toward Dar, grinning and twirling his stick. 'Chalk up one more for the good guys, eh?'

'And another ten BTUs in your account!' Dar called back. 'Well done, soldier!'

The soldier grinned, waved, and charged back into the thick of the chaos.

'Ten credits?' Sam gasped, blanching. 'You don't mean your General pays a bounty?'

'No, of course not. I mean, it's not the General who let himself get chalked up, is it? It's the Wolman who pays.'

'*What*?'

'Sure. After the battle's over, the officers'll transfer ten credits from that Wolman's account to the soldier's. I mean, there's got to be *some* risk involved.'

'Right,' she agreed. 'Sure. Risk.' Her eyes had glazed. 'I, uh, notice the, uh, "casualties" seem to be having a pretty good time over there.'

'Mm?' Dar looked up at the group over to the east. Wolmen and soldiers were chatting amicably over tankards. A couple of privates and three warriors wove in and out through the crowd with trays of bottles and cups, dispensing cheer and collecting credits.

He turned back to Sam. 'Why not? Gotta fill in the "dead" time somehow.'

'Sure,' she agreed. 'Why not?'

Suddenly whistles shrilled all over the field, and the frantic runners slowed to a walk, lowering their chalk-sticks. Most of them looked pretty disgusted. 'Cease!' bellowed one officer. 'Study war no more!' echoed a Wolman chief. The combatants began to circulate; a hum of conversation swelled.

'Continual warfare,' Sam muttered.

Dar leaned back against the wall and began whistling through his teeth.

Two resplendent figures stepped in from the west – an IDE colonel in full dress uniform and a Wolman in a brightly patterned cloak and elaborate headdress.

'The top-ranking officers,' Dar explained. 'Also the peace commission.'

'Referees?' Sam muttered.

'Come again?'

'I'd rather not.'

Each officer singled out those of his own men who had chalk marks on them, but who hadn't retired to the sidelines. Most of them seemed genuinely surprised to find they'd been marked. A few seemed chagrined.

The officers herded them over to join the beerfest, then barked out orders, and the "casualties" lined up according to side in two ragged lines, still slurping beer. The officers walked down each other's line, counting heads, then switched and counted their own lines. Then they met and discussed the situation.

'Me count-um twenty-nine of mine, and thirty-two of yours.'

'Came to the same count, old chap. Wouldn't debate it a bit.'

The Wolman grinned, extending a palm. 'Pay up.'

The IDE colonel sighed, pulled out a pad, and scribbled a voucher. The Wolman pocketed it, grinning.

A lieutenant and a minor Wolman stepped up from the battlefield, each holding out a sheaf of papers. The two chief officers took them and shuffled through, muttering to each other, comparing claims.

'That's the lot.' The colonel tapped his sheaf into order, squaring it off. 'Only this one discrepancy, on top here.'

The Wolman nodded. 'Me got same.'

'Well, let's check it, then. . . . O'Schwarzkopf!'

'Sir!' A corporal stepped forward and came to attention with a click of his heels, managing not to spill his tankard in the process.

'This warrior, um, "Xlitplox", claims he chalked you. Valid?'

'Valid, sir.'

'Xlitplox!' the Wolman officer barked.

'Me here.' The Wolman stepped forward, sipping.

'O'Schwarzkopf claim-um him chalk you.'

'He do-um.' Xlitplox nodded.

'Could be collusion,' the colonel noted.

The Wolman shrugged. 'What matter? Cancel-um out, anyhow. Null score.'

The colonel nodded. 'They want to trade tenners, that's their business. Well!' He tapped the sheaf and saluted the Wolman with them. 'I'll have these to the bank directly.'

'Me go-um, too.' The Wolman caught two tankards from a passing tray and dropped a chit on it. 'Drink?'

'Don't mind if I do.' The colonel accepted a tankard and lifted it. 'To the revolution!'

'*Was hael*!' The Wolman clinked mugs with him. 'We rise-um up; we break-um and bury-um corrupt colonial government!'

'And *we'll* destroy the Wolman tyranny! . . . Your health.'

'Yours,' the Wolman agreed, and they drank.

'What *is* this?' Sam rounded on Dar. 'Who's rebelling against whom?'

'Depends on whom you ask. Makes sense, doesn't it? I mean, each side claims to be the rightful government of the whole planet – so each side also thinks it's staging a revolution.'

'That's asinine! Anybody can see the Wolmen are the rightful owners of the planet.'

'Why? They didn't evolve here, any more than we soldiers did.'

'How do *you* know?' Sam sneered.

'Because I read a history book. The Wolmen are the descendants of the "Tonies", the last big opposition culture, a hundred years ago. You should hear their music – twenty-four tones. They came out here to get away from technology.'

Sam shuddered, then shook her head. 'That doesn't really change anything. They were here first.'

'Sure, but they think we came in and took over. After all, we've got a government. Their idea of politics is everybody sitting around in a circle and arguing until they can all agree on something.'

'Sounds heavenly,' Sam murmured, eyes losing focus.

'Maybe, but that still leaves General Shacklar as the only

government strong enough to rebel against – at least, the way the Wolmen see it. And *we* think they're trying to tell *us* what to do – so we're revolting, too.'

'No argument there.' Sam shrugged. 'I suppose I shouldn't gripe. As "continual wars" go, this is pretty healthy.'

'Yeah, especially when you think of what it was like my first two years here.'

'What? Real war – with sticks and stones?'

Dar frowned. 'When you tie the stone to the end of the stick, it can kill a man – and it did. I saw a lot of soldiers lying on the ground with their heads bashed in and their blood soaking into the weeds. I saw more with stone-tipped spears and arrows in them. Our casualties were very messy.'

'So what are dead Wolmen like – pretty?'

'I was beginning to think so, back then.' Dar grimaced at the memory. 'But dead Wolmen were almost antiseptic – just a neat little hole drilled into 'em. Not even any blood – laser wounds are cauterized.'

Sam caught at his arm, looking queasy. 'All right! That's . . . enough!'

Dar stared down at her. 'Sorry. Didn't think I'd been all that vivid.'

'I've got a good imagination.' Sam pushed against him, righting herself. 'How old were you then?'

'Eighteen. Yeah, it made me sick too. Everybody was.'

'But they couldn't figure out how to stop it?'

'Of course not. Then Shacklar was assigned the command.'

'What'd he do – talk it to death?'

Dar frowned. 'How'd you guess?'

'I was kidding. You can't stop a war by talking!'

Dar shrugged. 'Maybe he waved a magic wand. All I knew was that he had the Wolmen talking instead of fighting. How, I don't know – but he finally managed to get them to sign a treaty agreeing to this style of war.'

'Would it surprise you to learn the man's just human?'

'It's hard to remember sometimes,' Dar admitted. 'As far as I'm concerned, Shacklar can do no wrong.'

'I take it all the rest of the soldiers feel the same way.'

Dar nodded. 'Make snide comments about the Secretary of the Navy, if you want. Sneer at the General Secretary of the whole Interstellar Dominion Electorates. Maybe even joke about God. But don't you *dare* say a word against General Shacklar!'

Sam put on a nasty smile and started to say something. Then she thought better of it, her mouth still open. After a second, she closed it. 'I suppose a person could really get into trouble that way here.'

'What size trouble would you like? Standard measurements here are two feet wide, six feet long, and six feet down.'

'No man should have that kind of power!'

'Power? He doesn't even give orders! He just asks . . .'

'Yeah, and you soldiers fall all over each other trying to see who can obey first! That's obscene!'

Dar bridled. 'Soldiers are supposed to be obscene.'

'Sexual stereotype,' Sam snapped. 'It's absurd.'

'Okay – so soldiers should be obscene and not absurd.' Dar gave her a wicked grin. 'But wouldn't you feel that way about a man who'd saved your life, not to mention your face?'

'My face doesn't need saving, thank you!'

Dar decided to keep his opinions to himself. 'Look – there're only two ways to stop a war. Somebody can win – and that wasn't happening here. Or you can find some way to save face on both sides. Shacklar did.'

'I'll take your word for it.' Sam looked more convinced than she sounded. 'The main point is, he's found a way to let off the steam that comes from the collision of two cultures.'

Dar nodded. 'His way also sublimates all sorts of drives very nicely.'

Sam looked up, frowning. 'Yes, it would. But you can't claim he planned it that way.'

'Sure I can. Didn't you know? Shacklar's a psychiatrist.'

'Psychiatrist?'

'Sure. By accident, the Navy assigned a man with the right background to be warden for a prison planet. I mean, any soldier who's sent here probably has a mental problem of some sort.'

'And if he doesn't, half an hour here should do the trick. But Shackler's a masochist!'

'Who else could survive in a job like this?' Dar looked around, surveying the 'battlefield'. 'Things have quieted down enough. Let's go.'

He shouldered the rope and trudged off across the plain. Sam stayed a moment, then followed, brooding.

She caught up with him. 'I hate to admit it – but you've really scrambled my brains.'

Dar looked up, surprised. 'No offence taken.'

'None intended. In fact, it was more like a confession.'

'Oh – a compliment. You had us pegged wrong, huh?'

'Thanks for not rubbing it in,' she groused. 'And don't start crowing too soon. I'm not saying I was wrong, yet. But, well, let's say it's not what I expected.'

'What *did* you expect?'

'The dregs of society,' she snapped.

'Well, we are now. I mean, that's just a matter of definition, isn't it? If you're in prison, you're the lowest form of social life.'

'But people are supposed to go to prison *because* they're the lowest of the low!'

'"Supposed to", maybe. Might even have been that way, once. But now? You can get sent here just for being in the wrong place at the wrong time.'

'Isn't that stretching it?'

'No.' Dar's mouth tightened at the corners. 'Believe me, it's not.'

'Convince me.'

'Look,' Dar said evenly, 'on a prison planet, one thing you don't do is ask anybody why he's there.'

'I figured that much.' Sam gazed at him, very intently. 'I'm asking.'

Dar's face went blank, and his jaw tightened. After a few seconds, he took a deep breath. 'Okay. Not me, let's say – just someone I know. All right?'

'Anything you say,' Sam murmured.

Dar marched along in silence for a few minutes. Then he said, 'Call him George.'

Sam nodded.

'George was a nice young kid. You know, good parents, lived in a nice small town with good schools, never got into any real trouble. But he got bored with school, and dropped out.'

'And got drafted?'

'No – the young idiot enlisted. And, since he had absolutely no training or experience in cargo handling, book-keeping, or stocking, of *course* he was assigned to the Quartermaster's Corps.'

'Which is where you met him?'

'You could say that. Anyway, they made him a cargo handler – taught him how to pilot a small space-tug – and he had a whale of a time, jockeying cargo off shuttles and onto starships. Figured he was a hotshot Navy pilot, all that stuff.'

'I thought he was in the Army.'

'Even the Army has to run a few ships. Anyway, it was a great job, but after a while it got boring.'

Sam closed her eyes. 'He wanted a change.'

'Right,' Dar said sourly. 'So he applied for promotion – and they made him into a stock clerk. He began to go crazy, just walking around all day, making sure the robots had put the right items into the right boxes and the right boxes into the right bins – especially since they rarely took anything *out* of those bins, or put in anything new. And he heard the stories in the mess about how even generals have to be very nice to the sergeants in charge of the routing computers, or the goods they order will "accidentally" get shipped halfway across the Sphere.'

'Sounds important.'

'It does, when you're a teenager. So George decided he was going to get promoted again.'

'Well, that's the way it's supposed to be,' Sam said quietly. 'The young man's supposed to find himself in the Army, and study and work hard to make something better out of himself.'

'Sure,' Dar said sourly. 'Well, George did. He knew a little about data processing, of course, but just the basics they make you learn in school. He'd dropped out before he'd learned anything really useful – so now he learned it. You know, night classes, studying three hours a day, the rest of it. And it worked – he passed the test, and made corporal.'

'Everything's fine so far. They assign him a computer terminal?'

Dar nodded. 'And for a few months, he just did what he was told, punched in the numbers he was given. By the end of the first month, he knew the computer codes for every single Army platoon and every single Navy ship by heart. By the end of the second month, he knew all their standard locations.'

'And by the end of the third month, he'd begun to realize this wasn't much better than stocking shelves?'

'You got it. Then, one day, the sergeant handed him some numbers that didn't make sense. He'd been on the job long enough to recognize them – the goods number was for a giant heating system, and the destination code was for Betelgeuse Gamma.'

'Betelgeuse Gamma?' Sam frowned. 'I think that one went across my desk once. Isn't it a jungle world?'

Dar nodded. 'That's what George thought. He'd seen such things as insecticides and dehumidifiers shipped out there. This heating unit didn't seem to make sense. So he ran to his sergeant and reported it, just bursting with pride, figuring he'd get a promotion out of catching such an expensive mistake.'

'And the sergeant told him to shut up and do what he was told?'

'You *have* worked in a bureaucracy, haven't you? Yeah, "Ours not to question why, ours but to do and fry." That sort of thing. But George had a *moral* sense! And he remembered the scuttlebutt about why even generals have to treat supply sergeants nicely.'

'Just offhand, I'd say his sergeant was no exception.'

'Kind of looked that way, didn't it? So George did the right thing.'

'He reported the sergeant?'

'He wasn't *that* stupid. After all, it was just a set of numbers. Who could prove when they'd got into the computer, or where from? No, nobody could've proven anything against the sergeant, but he could have made George's next few years miserable. Reporting him wouldn't do any good, so George did the next best thing. He changed the goods number to one for a giant air-cooling system.'

Sam's eyes widened. 'Oh, no!'

'Ah,' Dar said bitterly, 'I see you've been caught in the rules, too. But George was an innocent – he only knew the rules for computers, and assumed the rules for people would be just as logical.'

Sam shook her head. 'The poor kid. What happened to him?'

'Nothing, for a while,' Dar sighed, 'and there never were any complaints from Betelgeuse Gamma.'

'But after a while, his sergeant started getting nasty?'

'No, and that should've tipped him off. But as I said, he didn't know the people-rules. He couldn't stand the suspense of waiting. So, after a while, he put a query through the system, to find out what happened to that shipment.'

Sam squeezed her eyes shut. 'Oh, no!'

'Oh, yes. Not *quite* as good as waving a signal flag to attract attention to the situation, but almost. And everything was hunky-dory on Betelgeuse Gamma; the CO there had even sent in a recommendation for a commendation for the lieutenant who had overseen the processing of the order, because that air-cooling plant had already saved several hundred lives in his base hospital. And before the day was out, the sergeant called George into his office.'

'A little angry?'

'He was furious. Seems the lieutenant had raked him over the coals because the wrong order number had been filed – and against the sergeant's direct order. George tried to explain, but all that mattered to the sergeant was that he was in trouble. He told George that he was remanding him to the lieutenant's attention for disciplinary action.'

'So it was the lieutenant who'd been out to get the general on Betelgeuse Gamma!'

'Or somebody in his command. Who knows? Maybe that CO had a lieutenant who'd said something nasty to George's lieutenant, back at the Academy. One way or another, the lieutenant didn't have to press charges, or initiate anything – all he had to do was act on his sergeant's recommendation. He demoted George to private and requested his transfer to Eta Cassiopeia.'

'Could be worse, I suppose,' Sam mused.

'Well, George heard there was a war going on there at the moment – but that wasn't the real problem. This lieutenant had charge of a computer section, remember.'

'Of course – what's wrong with me? His travelling orders came out with a different destination on 'em.' Sam looked up. 'Not Wolmar! Not here!'

'Oh, yes,' Dar said, with a saccharine smile. 'Here. And, the first time he showed his orders to an officer, the officer assumed that, if he was en route to Womar, he must be a convicted criminal, and clapped him in irons.'

'How neat,' Sam murmured, gazing into the distance. 'Off to prison, without taking a chance of being exposed during a court-martial. . . . Your lieutenant was a brainy man.'

'Not really – he just knew the system. So there George was, on his way here and nothing he could do about it.'

'Couldn't he file a complaint?' Sam bit her lip. 'No, of course not. What's wrong with me?'

'Right.' Dar nodded. 'He was in the brig. Besides, the complaint would've been filed into the computer, and the lieutenant knew computers. And who would let a convicted felon near a computer terminal?'

'But wouldn't the ship's commanding officer listen to him?'

'Why? Every criminal says he didn't do it. And, of course, once it's on your record that you've been sent to a prison planet, you're automatically a felon for the rest of your life.'

Sam nodded slowly. 'The perfect revenge. He made George hurt, he got him out of the way, and he made sure George'd never be able to get back at him.' She looked up at Dar. 'Or do you people get to go home when your sentence is up?'

Dar shook his head. 'No such thing as a sentence ending here. They don't send you to Wolmar unless it's for life.' He stopped and pointed. 'This is where a life ends.'

Sam turned to look.

They stood in the middle of a broad, flat plain. A few hundred yards away stood a plastrete blockhouse, with long, high fences running out from it like the sides of a funnel. The rest of the plain was scorched, barren earth, pocked with huge blackened craters, glossy and glinting.

'The spaceport.' Sam nodded. 'Yes, I've been here.'

'Great first sight of the place, isn't it? They chose the most desolate spot on the whole planet for the new convict's first sight of his future home. Here's where George's life ended.'

'And a new one began?'

Dar shook his head. 'For two years he wondered if he was in hell, with Wolmen throwing nasty, pointed things at him during the day and guards beating him up if he hiccupped during the night.' He nodded toward the blockhouse again. 'That was the worst thing about this place, the first time I looked at it – guards, all over. Everywhere. They were all built like gorillas, too, and they all loved pain – other people's pain.'

'Yes, I was wondering about that. Where are they?'

'Gone, to wherever the computers reassigned them. When Shacklar came, the guards went.'

'*What*?' Sam whirled, staring up at him. 'That's impossible!'

'Oh, I dunno.' Dar looked around. 'See any guards?'

'Well, no, but – one uniform looks just like any other to me.'

'We didn't wear uniforms when I came here. First thing they did was give me a set of grey coveralls and tell me to get into 'em.' His mouth tightened at the memory. Then he shook his head and forced a smile. 'But that was eleven years ago. Now *we* wear the uniforms, and the guards are gone.'

'Why?'

Dar shrugged. 'Shacklar thought uniforms'd be good for morale. He was right, too.'

'No, no! I mean, why no guards?'

'Wrong question. Look at it Shacklar's way – why have *any* guards?'

Sam frowned, thinking it over. 'To keep the prisoners from escaping.'

'Where to?' Dar spread his hand toward the whole vast plain. 'The Wolman villages? We were already fighting them – had been, ever since this, uh, "colony" started.'

'No, no! Off-planet! Where the rest of society is! Your victims! The rest of the universe!'

'So how do you escape from a planet?'

Sam opened her mouth – and hesitated.

'If you can come up with an idea, I'll be delighted to listen.' Dar's eyes glinted.

Sam shut her mouth with an angry snap. 'Get going! All you have to do is get going fast enough! Escape velocity!'

'Great idea! How do I do it? Run real fast? Flap my arms?'

'Spare me the sarcasm! You hijack a spaceship, of course!'

'We *have* thought of it,' Dar mused. 'Of course, there's only one spaceship per month. You came in on it, so you know: Where does it go?'

'Well, it's a starship, so it can't land. It just goes into orbit. Around the . . . uh . . .'

'Moon.' Dar nodded. 'And a shuttle brings you down to the moon's surface, and you have to go into the terminal there through a boarding tube, because you don't have a spacesuit. And there're hidden video pickups in the shuttle, and hidden video pickups all through the terminal, so the starship's crew can make sure there aren't any escaping prisoners waiting to try to take over the shuttle.'

'Hidden video pickups? What makes you think that?'

'Shacklar. He told us about them, just before he sent the guards home.'

'Oh.' Sam chewed it over. 'What would they do if they *did* see some prisoners waiting to take over the shuttle?'

'Bleed off the air and turn off the heaters. It's a vacuum up there, you know. And the whole terminal's remote-controlled, by the starship; there isn't even a station master you can clobber and steal keys from.'

Sam shuddered.

'Don't worry,' Dar soothed. 'We couldn't get up there, anyway.'

Sam looked up. 'Why not?'

Dar spread his hands. 'How did you get down here?'

'The base sent up a ferry to bring us down.'

Dar nodded. 'Didn't you wonder why it wasn't there waiting for you when you arrived?'

'I did think it was rather inconsiderate,' Sam said slowly, 'but spaceline travel isn't what it used to be.'

'Decadent,' Dar agreed. 'Did you notice when the ferry did come up?'

'Now that you mention it . . . *after* the starship left.'

Dar nodded. 'Just before it blasted out of orbit, the starship sent down a pulse that unlocked the ferry's engines – for twenty-four hours.'

'That's long enough. If you really had any gumption, you could take over the ferry after it lands, go back up to the moon, and wait a few months for the next starship.'

'Great! We could bring sandwiches, and have a picnic – a *lot* of sandwiches; they don't store any rations up there, so we'd need a few months' worth. They'd get a little stale, you know? Besides, the ferry's engines automatically relock after one round trip. But the real problem is air.'

'*I* could breathe in that terminal.'

'You wouldn't have if you'd stayed around for a day. The starship brings in a twenty-four-hour air supply when it comes. They send an advance crew to come in, turn it on, and wait for pressure before they call down the shuttle.' Dar gazed up at the sky. 'No, I don't think I'd like waiting for a ship up there, for a month. Breathing $CO_2$ gets to you, after a while.'

'It's a gas,' Sam said in a dry icy tone. 'I take it Shacklar set up this darling little system when he came?'

'No, it was always here. I wouldn't be surprised if it were standard for prison planets. So, by the time Shacklar'd managed to reach the surface of Wolmar, he knew there wasn't really any need for guards.'

'Except to keep you from killing each other! How many convicts were here for cold-blooded murder?'

'Not too many, really; most of the murderers were hot-blooded.' He shuddered at the memory. 'Very. But there were a handful of reptiles – and three of them were power-hungry, too.'

'Why?' Sam looked up, frowning. 'I mean, how much power could they get? Nothing that counts, if they couldn't leave the planet.'

'If you'll pardon my saying so, that's a very provincial view. I mean, there's a whole *planet* here.'

'But no money.'

'Well, not real money, no. But I didn't say they were out to get rich; I said they were out for power.'

'Power over a mud puddle? A handful of soldiers? What good is that?'

'Thanks for rubbing my nose in it,' Dar snapped.

'Oh! I'm sorry.' Sam's eyes widened hugely. 'I just turn off other people's feelings, sometimes. I get carried away with what I'm saying.'

'Don't we all?' Dar smiled bleakly, reining his temper back. 'I suppose that's how the lust for power begins.'

'How – by ignoring other people's feelings?'

Dar nodded. 'Only worrying about how *you* feel. I suppose if you're the boss, you feel safer, and that's all that really matters.'

'Not the bosses *I've* met. They're always worrying about who's going to try to kick them out and take over – and I'm just talking about bureaucrats!' She looked up at Dar. 'Would you believe it – some of them actually hire bodyguards?'

'Sure, I'd believe it! After living on a prison planet *without* guards.'

'Oh. Your fellow prisoners were worse than the gorillas?'

'Much worse,' Dar confirmed. 'I mean, with the guards at least you knew who to watch out for – they wore uniforms. But with your friendly fellow prisoners, you never knew from one moment to the next who was going to try to slip a knife between your ribs.'

'They let you have knives?'

Dar shrugged impatiently. 'The Wolmen could chip flints; so could we. Who was going to stop us, with the guards gone? No, they loaded onto the ferry and lifted off; Shacklar stepped into Government House and locked himself in behind concrete and steel with triple locks and arm-thick bolts . . . and the monsters came out of the woodwork. Anybody who had a grudge hunted down his favourite enemy, and started slicing. Or got sliced up himself.'

'Immoral!' Sam muttered. 'How could he bring himself to do such a thing!'

Dar shrugged. 'Had to be hard, I guess. Lord knows we had enough hard cases walking around. When they saw blood flowing, they started banding together to guard each other's backs. And the first thing you knew, there were little gangs roaming around, looking for people to rough up and valuables to steal.'

Sam snorted. 'What kind of valuables could you have had?'

'Food would do, at that point. Distribution had broken down. Why should the work-gangs work, without the guards to make them? Finally, we mobbed the warehouse and broke in – and ruined more food than we ate.' He shuddered at the memory. 'They started knife fights over ham hocks! That was about when I started looking for a hole to crawl into.'

'Your general has no more ethics than a shark!' Sam blazed. 'How could he just sit there and let it happen?'

'I expect he had a pretty good idea about how it would all come out.'

'How could he? With chaos like that, it was completely unpredictable!'

'Well, not really . . .'

'What're you talking about? You could've all killed each other off!'

'That's predictable, isn't it? But there wasn't too much chance of it, I guess. There were too many of us – half a million. That's a full society; and anarchy's an unstable condition. When the little gangs began to realize they couldn't be sure of beating the next little gang they were trying to steal from, they made a truce instead, and merged into a bigger gang that *could* be sure of winning a fight, because it was the biggest gang around.'

'So other little gangs had to band together into bigger gangs too.' Sam nodded. 'And that meant the bigger gangs had to merge into small armies.'

'Right. Only most of us didn't realize all that; we just knew there were three big gangs fighting it out, all of a sudden.'

'The power-hungry boys you told me about?'

Dar nodded. 'And they were pretty evenly balanced, too. So their battles didn't really decide anything; they just killed off sixty men. Which meant you had to stay way clear of *any* of 'em, or they'd draft you as a replacement.'

'So two of them made a truce and ganged up on the third?'

'No, the Wolmen ganged up on all of us, first.'

'Oh.' Sam looked surprised, then nodded slowly. 'Makes sense, of course. I mean, why should they just sit back and wait for you to get yourselves organized?'

'Right. It made a lot more sense to hit us while we were still disorganized. And we'd stopped keeping sentries on the wall, and the Wolmen knew enough to hit us at night.'

Sam shuddered. 'Why weren't you all killed in your beds?'

'Because the Big Three *did* have sentries, to make sure none of the *others* tried a night attack. So all of a sudden, the sirens were howling, and everybody was running around yelling – and military conditioning took over.'

'Military conditioning?' Sam frowned. 'I thought you were convicts!'

'Yeah, but we were still soldiers. What'd you think – the Army provided a few battalions to fight off the Wolmen for us? We had to do our *own* fighting, with our own sergeants and lieutenants. The guards just stood back and made sure we didn't try to get any big ideas . . . and handled the laser cannons.'

'But how could they let you have weapons?'

Dar shrugged. 'Bows and arrows, tops. That gave us a fair chance against the Wolmen. So when the sirens shrieked, we just automatically ran for the armoury and grabbed our bows, and jumped any Wolman who got in our way. Then, when we had our weapons, we just naturally yelled, "What do we do, Sarge?" I mean, he was there getting his weapons, too – if he was still alive.'

'And most of them were?'

'What can I tell you? Rank has its privileges. Yeah, most of them were there, and they told us where to go.'

'Sergeants usually do, I understand.'

'Well, yes. But in this case, they just took us out to chop up anything that didn't wear a uniform – and look for a lieutenant to ask orders from. We pulled together into companies – and the lieutenants were already squawking into their wrist coms, demanding that Shacklar tell them what to do.'

'Why would they do . . .?' Sam broke off, her eyes widening. 'I just realized something: soldiers are basically bureaucrats. Nobody wants to take a chance on getting blamed.'

'It is kind of drilled into you,' Dar admitted. 'And as I said, when the Wolmen came over the wall, habit took over. It did for Shacklar, too, I guess. He started telling them what to do.'

'Habit, my great toe! He'd been waiting for a chance like that – counting on it!'

'Looking for me to disagree with you? Anyway, he had the viewscreens, and he knew the tactics; so he started giving orders.' Dar shook his head in disbelief. 'If you can call them orders! "Lieutenant Walker, there's a band of Wolmen breaking through over on the left; I really think you should run over and arrange a little surprise for them." "Lieutenant Able, Sergeant Dorter's squad is outnumbered two to one over on your company's right; would you send your reserves over to join him, please?"'

'Come off it! No general talks to his subordinates that way!'

Dar held up a palm. 'So help me, he did it! I overheard Lieutenant Walker's communicator.'

'You mean you were in that battle?'

'I had a choice?'

'But I thought you tried to find a hole to crawl into!'

'Sure. I didn't say I succeeded, did I?'

Sam turned away, glowering. 'I still don't believe it. Why should he be so polite?'

'We figured it out later. In effect, he was telling us it was *our* war, and it was up to us to fight it; but he was willing to give us advice, if we wanted it.'

'Good advice, I take it?'

'Oh, very good! We had the Wolmen pushed back against the wall in an hour. Then Shacklar told the lieutenants to pull back and give them a chance to get away. They all answered, basically, "The hell with that noise! We've got a chance to wipe out the bastards!" "Indeed you do," Shacklar answered, "and they all have brothers and cousins back home – six of them for every one of you. But if you *do* try to exterminate them – well, you'll manage it, but they'll kill two of your men for every one of theirs." Well, the lieutenants allowed that he had a point, so they did what he said and pulled back; and the Wolmen, with great daring and ingenuity, managed to get back up over the wall and away.'

'Then he told you to break out the laser cannon?'

'No, he'd sent the cannons home with the guards. Good thing, too; I'd hate to think what those three power-mongers would've done with them. But we *did* have hand-blasters, in the armouries. Each of the power-mongers had managed to seize an armoury as a power base as soon as he'd recruited a gang. They'd opened the doors and issued sidearms as soon as the sirens screamed. They weren't much good for the close fighting inside the wall, but once the Wolmen were over the top and running, we got up on the parapet and started shooting after them, until the lieutenants yelled at us to stop wasting our charges. The Wolmen were running, and they didn't stop until morning.'

'A victory,' Sam said dryly.

'A bigger one than you think – because as soon as the shooting was over the three would-be warlords showed up with their henchmen, bawling, "All right, it's all over! Turn in your guns! Go home!"'

'They *what*?'

'Well, sure.' Dar shrugged. 'After all, they'd opened up the armouries for us, hadn't they? Shouldn't we give them their guns back now? I mean, you've got to see it from their viewpoint.'

'I hope *you* didn't!'

'Of course we didn't. We just turned around grinning, and pointed the guns at *them*. But we didn't say anything; we let the lieutenants do the talking.'

'*What* talking?'

'It depended. The nice ones said: "Hands up." The rest of them just said: "Fire!" And we did.'

Sam formed a silent O with her lips.

'It was quick and merciful,' Dar pointed out. 'More than they had a right to, really.'

'What did you do without them? I mean, they had provided some sort of social order.'

'I see you favour loose definitions. But while the ashes cooled, the lieutenants got together and did some talking.'

'They elected a leader?'

'Yeah, they could all agree that they needed to. But they weren't so unanimous about who. There were four main candidates, and they wrangled and haggled, but nobody could agree on anything – I mean, not even enough to call for a vote.'

'How long did they keep *that* up?'

'Long enough for it to get pretty tense, and the boys on the battlements were getting kind of edgy, eyeing each other and wondering if we were going to be ordered to start burning each other pretty soon.'

'You wouldn't really have done it!'

'I dunno. That military conditioning runs pretty deep. You don't know *what* you'll do when you hear your lieutenant call, "Fire!"'

Sam shuddered. 'What are you – animals?'

'I understand the philosophers are still debating that one. My favourite is, "Man is the animal who laughs." Fortunately, Lieutenant Mandring thought the same way.'

'Who's Lieutenant Mandring?'

'The one with the sense of humour. He nominated General Shacklar.'

Sam whirled, the picture of fury. Then she developed a sudden faraway look. 'You know . . .'

Dar pointed a finger at her. '*That's* just about the way all the other lieutenants reacted. They started to yell – then they realized he meant it for a joke. After they'd finished rolling around on the ground and had it throttled down to a chuckle, they started eyeing each other, and it got awfully quiet.'

'But Shacklar didn't even *try* to talk them into it!'

'He didn't have to; he'd given them a taste of do-it-yourself government. So they were ready to consider a change of diet – but nobody wanted to be the first one to say it. So Lieutenant Griffin had to take it – he's the one with the talent for saving other people's faces. Too bad he can't do anything about his own . . .'

'What *happened*?'

'Oh! Yes . . . well, all he said was, "Why don't we ask him what *he* thinks?" And after they got done laughing again, Lieutenant Able said, "It'd be good for a laugh." And Lieutenant Walker said, "Sure. I mean, we don't *have* to do what he says, you know." Well, they could all agree on that, of course, so they put Lieutenant Walker up to it, he having spoken last, and he called the General on his wrist com, explained the situation, and asked what he'd do in their place. He said he was willing to serve, but really thought they ought to elect one of their own number.'

Sam smiled. 'How nice of him! What'd they do back at Square One?'

'They asked the comedian for a suggestion. He said they ought to call out each lieutenant's name and have everybody who had confidence in him raise a hand.'

'Who won?'

'Everybody; they all pulled. "No confidence." So Lieutenant Mandring called for a vote on General Shacklar.'

'How long was the pause?'

'Long enough for everybody to realize they were getting hungry. But after a while they started raising hands, and three hundred and sixty out of four hundred went up.'

'This, for the man who had to hide in a fortress? What changed their minds?'

'The chaos, mostly – especially since he'd just done a good job directing them in battle. Soldiers value that kind of thing. So they called Shacklar and told him he was elected.'

'I take it he was glad to hear it.'

'Hard to say; he just heaved a sigh and asked them to form a parliament before they went to lunch and to start thinking about a constitution while they ate.'

'Constitution! In a prison?'

'Why not? I mean, they'd just elected him, hadn't they?'

Sam developed a faraway look again. 'I suppose. . . .'

'So did they. That was the turning point, you see – when we started thinking of ourselves as a colony, not a prison. When we wrote the constitution, we didn't call Shacklar "warden" – we named him "governor".'

'Generous of you,' Sam smirked, 'considering Terra had done it already.'

'Yeah, but *we* hadn't. And once he had the consent of the populace, he could govern without guards.'

'That . . . makes . . . a weird kind of sense.'

'Doesn't it? Only when you can make a whole planet into a prison, of course – and there's no way out. But that's the way it is here. So he *could* send the guards home, and let us fight it out for ourselves.'

'Which made you realize he was better than the natural product.'

'It did have that advantage. And, once his position was consolidated, he could start proposing reforms to the Council.'

'Council?'

'The legislative body. The Wolmen are agitating for represent-ation, now. But that's okay – we traders are angling for a rep at their moots. Anyway, Shacklar talked the Council into instituting pay.'

'Oh, that certainly must have taken a lot of convincing!'

'It did, as it happens; a fair number of them were Communists. But pay it was – in scrip; worthless off-planet, I'm sure, but it buys a lot here – a BTU for a neat bunk, two BTUs for a clean yard, and so forth.'

'Great! Where could they spend it?'

'Oh, the General talked Cholly into coming in and setting up shop, and a few of the con . . . uh, colonists, decided he had a good thing going, and—'

'Pretty soon, the place was lousy with capitalists.'

'Just the bare necessities – a general store, a fix-it shop, and three taverns.'

'That "general store" looks more like a shopping complex.'

'Just a matter of scale. Anyway, that created a driving hunger for BTUs and that meant soldiers started spiffing up, and—'

'Higher morale, all over,' Sam muttered. 'Because they *can* improve their lot.'

'Right. Then Cholly started paying top dollar for pipe-leaf traders, and—'

'A drug baron!'

'Suppose you could call him that. But it turned out there *was* a market for it – the drug's very low-bulk after it's processed, you see; and it doesn't provide euphoria or kill pain, but it *does* retard the ageing process. So Universal Pharmaceuticals was interested, and Interstellar Geriatrics, and—'

'I get the picture. Top money.'

'But it costs a lot, too – especially at first, when it was a little on the hazardous side. But Cholly was bringing in trade goods that made glass beads just sharp-cornered gravel, so once we managed to get trade started, it mushroomed.'

'And all of a sudden, the Wolmen weren't quite so hostile any more.' Sam nodded.

'Aw, you peeked.' Dar scuffed the grass with his boot. 'And from there, of course, it was just a little fast talking to get them to agree to the chalk-fights.'

'So trade is growing, and morale is growing, and you're taking the first steps toward a unified society, and everybody feels as though they've got some opportunity, and—' Sam broke off, shaking her head, dazzled. 'I can't believe it! The central planets are mired in malaise and self-pity, and out here in the marches, you've managed to build a growing, maybe even hopeful, society! Back on Terra, everybody's living in walking despair because *nobody* feels they can make things better.'

'What?' Dar was shocked. 'But they've got everything! They've—'

'Got nothing,' Sam sneered. 'On Terra, you'll die doing the job your father did, and everybody knows it. You've got your rooms, your servos, and your rations. And that's it.'

'But even beggars have whole houses – with furniture that makes anything here look like firewood! And they don't have to do a lick of housework, with all those servos – their free time's *all* free!'

'Free to do what – rot?'

'To do anything they want! I mean, even a rube like me has heard what's included in those rations.'

Sam shrugged. 'Sure, you can get drunk or stoned every night, and you can go out to a party or go to a show . . .'

Dar gave a whimpering sigh.

'But actually *do* something? No chance! Unless you're born into government – and even *they* can't figure out anything worth doing.'

'But . . .' Dar flailed at the sky. 'But there's a thousand worlds out there to conquer!'

'Why bother?' She smiled bitterly. 'We've done that already – and it hasn't improved things back on Terra much.'

'Hasn't improved? But your poorest beggar lives like a medieval king!'

'Oh, does she?' Sam's eyes glittered. 'Where're the servants, the musicians, the courtiers, the knights willing to fight for her smile?'

'Even a Terran reject has three or four servos! They'll even turn on the audio for him – and there's your musicians!'

'And the courtiers? The knights?' Sam shook her head.

'What made a king *royal* was being able to command other people – and there's no coin that'll buy that!'

Dar could only stare.

Then he gave his head a quick shake, pushing out a whistle. 'Boy! That's *sick!*'

'Also decadent.' She smiled, with Pyrrhic triumph. 'They're moribund there. What I can't figure out is how you folks avoid it.'

Dar shrugged. 'Because we're already at the bottom? I mean, once you've landed here, there's no place to go but up!'

'There's no place to go, period!' Sam's eyes lit. 'Maybe that's it – *because* it's out here in the marches! Out here, on the edge of civilization – because anything you're going to do, you're going to have to do for yourselves. Terra's too far away to send help. And too far away to really be able to run you, either. By the time they can tell you not to do something, you've already been doing it for a year! And because—' She clamped her mouth shut.

'Because they really don't care?' Dar grinned. 'Because this place is a hole, and the only people Terra sends out here are the ones they want to forget about? I wouldn't be surprised if they even wanted to get rid of Shacklar.'

'Of course; he was a threat to the ones with the *real* power. I mean, after all, he's *capable*. He was bound to make waves. Which I'm about to do too.'

'I'm braced.' Dar tried to hide the smile.

'You still haven't shown me how you're not really fleecing the natives.'

'No, I haven't, have I. But it *does* take showing. We start trading at sundown.'

## 2

'That's not the way to make a campfire,' Sam pointed out.

'What would you know about it?' Dar blithely heaped green sticks and leaves onto the flaming kindling. 'You're a city girl.'

'Who says?'

'You. You said you came from Terra, and it's just one great big city.'

'It is, but we've kept a few parks, like the Rockies. I do know you're supposed to use dry wood."

'Entirely correct.' Dar smiled up at the roiling column of thick grey smoke turning gold in the sunset.

Sam sighed. 'All right, so you're trying to attract attention. What do we use for cooking?'

'Why bother?' Dar started foraging in the food bag. 'All we've got is cheese and crackers. And raisin wine, of course.'

Sam shuddered.

Darkness came down, and company came up – five Wolmen, each with a bale on his shoulder.

'Ah! Company for cordials!' Dar rubbed his hands, then reached for the bottle and the glasses.

'Get 'em drunk before they start bargaining, huh?' Sam snorted.

'That'd take more liquor than I can pack. But they count it friendly.' He stepped toward the arrivals, raising the bottle. 'How!'

'You not know, me not tell you,' the first grunted, completing the formula. 'Good seeing, Dar Mandra.'

'Good to see you, too, Hirschmeir.' Dar held out a handful of glasses; the Wolman took one, and so did each of his mates as they came up. Dar poured a round and lifted his glass. 'To trade!'

'And profit,' Hirschmeir grunted. He drank half his glass. 'Ah! Good swill after long hike. And hot day gathering pipeweed.'

'Yeah, I know,' Dar sympathized. 'And it brings so little, too.'

'Five point three eight kwahers per ounce on Libra exchange,' a second Wolman said promptly.

Dar looked up in surprise. 'That's the fresh quote, right off today's cargo ship. Where'd you get it?'

'You sell us nice wireless last month,' Hirschmeir reminded. 'Tell Sergeant Walstock him run nice music service.'

'Sure will.' Dar pulled out a pad and scribbled a note.

'Little heavy on drums, though,' another Wolman said thoughtfully.

'Gotcha, Slotmeyer.' Dar scribbled again. 'More booze, anybody?'

Five glasses jumped out. Dar whistled, walking around with the bottle, then picked up a bale. 'Well. Let's see what we're talking about.' He plopped the bale onto the front of the gravsled.

'Twenty-seven point three two kilograms,' the sled reported. 'Ninety-seven per cent *Organum Translucem*, with three per cent grasses, leaf particles, and sundry detritus.'

'The sundry's the good part.' Dar hefted the bale back off the sled and set it about halfway between himself and Hirschmeir.

'You sure that thing not living?' one of the Wolmen demanded.

'Sure. But it's got a ghost in it.'

'No ghost in machine.' The Wolman shook his head emphatically.

Dar looked up sharply, then frowned. 'Did I sell you folks that cubook series on the history of philosophy?'

'Last year,' Hirschmeir grunted. 'Lousy bargain. Half of tribe quote-um Locke now.'

'Locke?' Dar scowled. 'I would've thought Berkeley and Sartre would be more your speed.'

'Old concepts,' Slotmeyer snorted. 'We learn at mothers' knees. You forget – our ancestors opposition culture.'

'That does keep slipping my mind,' Dar confessed. 'Well! How about two hundred and thirty-four for the bale?'

Hirschmeir shook his head. 'Too far below Libra quote. Your scrip only worth eighty per cent of Libran BTU today.'

'I'm going to have to have a talk with Sergeant Walstock,' Dar growled. 'Okay, so my price is twenty per cent low. But you forget – we have to pay shipping charges to get this stuff to Libra.'

'And your boss Cholly also gotta pay you, and overhead,' Slotmeyer added. 'We not forget anything, Dar Mandra.'

'Except that Cholly's gotta show *some* profit, or he can't stay in business,' Dar amended. 'Okay, look – how about two seventy-five?'

'Tenth of a kwaher?' Hirschmeir scoffed. He bent over and picked up his bale. 'Nice talking to you, Dar Mandra.'

'Okay, *okay*! Two eighty!'

'Two ninety,' Slotmeyer said promptly.

'Okay, two eighty-five.' Dar sighed, shaking his head. 'The things I do for you guys! Well, it's not your worry if I don't come back next month. Hope you like the new man.'

'No worry. We tell Cholly we only deal with soft touch.' Hirschmeir grinned. 'Okay. What *you* got to sell, Dar Mandra?'

'Oh, a little bit of this and a minor chunk of that.' Dar turned to the sled. 'Wanna give me a hand?'

Together, all six of them manhandled a huge crate onto the ground. Dar popped the catches and opened the front and the left side. The Wolmen crowded around, fingering the merchandise and muttering in excitement.

'What this red stone?' Slotmeyer demanded, holding up a machined gem. 'Ruby for laser?'

Dar nodded. 'Synthetically grown, but it works better than the natural ones.'

'Here barrels,' another Wolman pointed out.

'Same model you sold us instruction manual for?' Hirschmeir weighed a power cell in his palm.

Dar nodded. 'Double-X 14. Same as the Navy uses.'

'What this?' One of the Wolmen held up a bit of machined steel.

'Part of the template assembly for an automatic lathe,' Dar answered.

Slotmeyer frowned. 'What is "lathe"?'

Dar grinned. 'Instruction manual's only twenty-five kwahers.'

'Twenty-five?' Hirschmeir bleated.

Dar's grin widened.

Hirschmeir glowered at him, then grimaced and nodded. 'You highway robber, Dar Mandra.'

'No, low-way,' Dar corrected. 'Cholly tells me I'm not ready for the highway.'

'Him got high idea of low,' Hirschmeir grunted. 'What prices on laser parts?'

Dar slid a printed slip out of his jacket pocket and handed it to Hirschmeir. ' 'Scuse me while you study that; I'll finish the weigh-in.' He turned away to start hoisting bales onto the sled's scale as the Wolmen clustered around Hirschmeir, running through the price list and muttering darkly.

Sam stepped up and tapped Dar on the shoulder. 'What happened to all the "ums" on the ends of their verbs?'

'Hm?' Dar looked up. 'Oh, they know me, y' see. No need to put on a show anymore.'

'All right, all right!' Hirschmeir grumbled. 'We take three rubies, three barrels, ten power supplies, and template assembly for lathe.'

'Gotcha.' Dar pressed a button on the scale, and it murmured, 'Total for goods, 4235.50 BTUs.'

Dar nodded. 'And the total for your pipeweed is 5337.50. You can spend another 1102, Hirschmeir.'

'No got any more goods we want,' Slotmeyer grunted.

Hirschmeir nodded, holding out a palm. 'Cash be nice.'

'You could put it on deposit at the bank,' Dar offered. 'Cholly's starting up a new kind of account.'

Hirschmeir shook his head. 'Only pays lousy five per cent per annum. We do better use it for stake for playing poker with soldiers.'

'But this is a new kind of account,' Dar reminded. 'The interest is compounded quarterly.'

Hirschmeir's head lifted a little, and his frown deepened. '"Interest compounded"? What that mean?'

'That means that, at the end of every five months, the interest is paid into your account, and figured as part of the principal for the next quarter.'

'So for second quarter, Cholly pay interest on 1157.125?'

Dar nodded. 'And for the third quarter, he'll be paying you interest on 1162.48. You're getting an effective annual yield of twenty-one and a half per cent.'

'Cholly go broke,' Slotmeyer snapped.

'No, he'll make a profit – if enough of you open up these accounts. If he gets five thousand for capital, he can buy Bank of IDE bonds that pay twenty-three per cent effective.'

Slotmeyer's head lifted slowly, his eyes widening.

He whirled to Hirschmeir. 'Take it!'

'You sure?' Hirschmeir looked decidedly uncomfortable.

'Sure? When Cholly making profit, too? Gotta be straight deal!'

Hirschmeir looked at the ground for a few minutes; then he looked up at Dar, face firming with decision. 'Right. We open new account.'

'Right here.' Dar whipped out the papers and handed them to Hirschmeir; but Slotmeyer intercepted them. He scanned the pages quickly, muttering to himself, then nodded and passed them on to Hirschmeir. Hirschmeir made his sign and added his signature after it in parentheses. Dar took the papers back, fed them into a slot in the sled. It chuckled to itself, then fed out a copy of the forms, and spat out a small flat blue booklet. Dar checked the passbook to make sure the deposit was recorded properly, then nodded and passed the bundle to Hirschmeir. The Wolman folded them away, straightening and grinning. 'Okay, Dar Mandra. Is good doing business with you.'

'Always a pleasure.' Dar held up the bottle. 'One for the trail?'

Sam watched the Wolman troop move off into the night, while Dar reloaded the grav-sled and fastened the tarp down again. Finally she turned back to him. 'Why do they call it "pipeweed"?'

'Hm?' Dar looked up. 'Take a look at it.'

Sam stepped over and fingered one of the bales. 'Long, thin, hollow stems.' She nodded. 'Little pipes.'

Dar covered the bale and fastened down the last corner of the tarp. 'Good quality, too. Not a bad night's trading.'

'But how can you *say* that?' Sam erupted. 'You've scarcely made any profit at all!'

'About one and a half per cent.' Dar picked up a plastic cube and stood up. 'Which is pretty good. Cholly's happy if I just break even.'

'Oh, he is, huh?' Sam jammed her fists on her hips. 'What is he, a philanthropist?'

'A teacher,' Dar reminded, 'and Shacklar's a politician. All Cholly really cares about is how much the Wolmen learn from the trading; and all Shacklar cares about is tying the Wolmen into an economic unit with the soldiers. And the goodwill that goes with both, of course.'

'Of course,' Sam echoed dryly. 'And I suppose you manage to pick up a few items about Wolman culture on every trip.'

'Which I faithfully report back to Cholly, who makes sure it winds up as beer-gossip.' Dar grinned. 'Give us ten years, and the soldiers and Wolmen'll know each other's culture almost as well as their own.'

'Well, they do seem to have a pretty thorough grasp of basic finance.'

'And Slotmeyer's getting some ideas about law,' Dar said with a critical nod. 'He's coming along nicely.'

Sam frowned. 'You sound like a teacher gloating over a prize pupil . . . Oh!'

Dar gave her a wicked grin.

'Of course; I should have realized,' she said dryly. 'Cholly doesn't hire traders; he recruits teachers.'

'Pretty much,' Dar confirmed. 'But we do have to have an eye for profit and loss.'

'How about the loss to the Army?'

'Hm?' Dar looked up. 'What loss?'

'Those laser parts – they're military issue, aren't they?'

Dar stared at her while his smile congealed.

'Come on,' Sam wheedled, 'you can trust me. I mean, after all, I know enough to sink you already, if I really wanted to.'

Dar's smile cracked into a grin. 'How? We're already sunk here.'

Sam frowned, nonplussed. 'But how do you know I'm not a BOA spy? Or an Army spy, trying to find out what Shacklar's *really* doing here? For all you know, when I get back to Terra, I might issue a report that would get him pulled off this planet.'

Dar nodded. 'Yeah. You could be.'

Sam inched away from him, watching him as a mouse watches a waking cat.

'But you obviously aren't,' Dar finished.

Sam frowned indignantly. 'How the hell could *you* tell?'

'Well, in the first place, I don't believe *anybody* on Terra really cares about what happens out here – not in the Army, and not in BOA either.'

'Shacklar is building a power base,' Sam pointed out.

'Power to do what? He can't even conquer the Wolmen.'

'But he *is* trying to weld them into one solid unit with his convicts.'

Dar smiled, amused. 'And just what do you think he'll do with that unit? Build a very long ladder, and *climb* to Terra?' He shook his head. 'There's no way Shacklar can be a threat to anybody off this planet – and the boys on Terra don't care what kind of threat he is to anybody on this planet.' He tossed the plastic cube in the air and caught it, grinning. 'Not that I think you really are a spy. Of course, you could be a reporter, looking for a little bit of muck to rake, but why would you come all this way for it?'

'To find something to report,' Sam said with a vindictive smile. 'Nothing *ever* happens on Terra.'

Dar shrugged. 'Okay – let's say you really are that hard up. What could you actually do? Turn in a ten-minute report for a 3DT show about the horrible, crooked, scandalous doings out here on Wolmar?'

'Sure. You're far enough away to have a touch of the exotic. It might really catch on for a while. We're *really* bored on Terra.'

Dar shrugged. 'So we'd be a six-day wonder.'

'Nine.'

'Nine. And the Army would say, "My Heavens! We didn't realize *that* was going on!" And they'd send a formal, official notice to Shacklar that would say, "You naughty, naughty boy! How *dare* you do all these horrible things! The way you're treating your convicts is criminal!" And Shacklar, I'm sure, would give them fifty excellent reasons, and finish by saying, "But of course, since this isn't what you want, I'll be glad to do it *your* way." And Central HQ would say, "Fine. You do it *our* way." Which they would go tell the media, and the media would tell it to the people in another show, and the people would sit back with that nice, solid feeling that they'd actually managed to accomplish something. And everybody would forget about it.'

'And Shacklar wouldn't actually *do* anything?'

'Oh, sure – he'd give me a week of chores for shooting off my mouth. Which is okay; it's restful to do something that doesn't involve any responsibility, now and then.'

Sam sighed. 'All right. Then you should just tell me about those laser parts because you *want* to – and because there's no good reason not to . . . Is there?'

'None, except my firm conviction that you'll put the worst possible construction on anything I tell you. What *about* those laser parts?'

'They're military issue, aren't they?'

'Sure. What else would a general be able to get, that natives would want?'

'That doesn't strike you as a little bit corrupt?'

'Why? They're being used for a military purpose.'

'The *Wolmen*'s military purpose!' Sam exploded. 'It's gun-running!'

'I suppose you could call it that,' Dar said judiciously.

'"Suppose"! Don't you realize you're signing your own death warrants?'

'Not as long as things stay peaceful,' Dar pointed out. 'Shacklar has more faith in trade than in firepower. It's awfully hard to fight your own customers.'

'But not exactly unknown.'

'True,' Dar agreed. 'That's why it's so important to get the two groups to understand each other, and do some socializing. You might fight your customer, but you won't fight your friend

– *if* we can get them to be friends. If a real war does start, and if all the Wolman tribes ever unite against us, we're dead. They outnumber us a thousand to one. Blasters would just speed up the process, that's all.'

'Then why not sell them blasters?' Sam demanded. 'Why just spare parts?'

'Well, for one thing, whole blasters are a little difficult to get the Army to ship to a prison planet.' Dar pressed a button in the side of the plastic cube; it started to hum. 'But spare parts they'll ship us by the thousands.'

Sam shook her head. 'The insanities of bureaucracy!' She watched the humming cube begin to unfold and expand. 'And for another thing?'

'For another thing, if we just sell them parts and instruction manuals, they have to learn how to put the dern things together.' Dar smiled, a faraway look in his eyes. 'And that makes 'em begin to wonder how and why it works – so they end up learning technology. Wait'll they find out what a headache that lathe's going to be! Just to get it working, they'll have to learn *so* much!'

'Something of a sadist, aren't you?'

'It goes with being a teacher.' Dar watched the plastic cube finish swelling into a slant-roofed shack, ten feet on a side. ' 'Bout time to turn in for the night.'

Sam shook her head, looking frazzled. 'If I'd known it was like this . . .'

'Hey, I never promised you a grav-bed or synthsilk sheets!'

'No, no! I mean this whole planet! The structure your General's built up! The things he's trying to do! If I'd known it was like this, I would've personally put a bomb on that new governor's ship!'

Dar froze halfway through the door.

Then he looked back over his shoulder. 'Excuse me – what was that again?'

'The new governor.' Sam frowned. 'You know – the one that's supposed to arrive tomorrow.'

Dar uncoiled back out of the door and straightened up. 'No, as it happens, I didn't know. And neither does anyone else on Wolmar.'

'They didn't tell you?' Sam looked startled. 'Well . . . anyway, they're doing it. BOA's sending out a new governor, with power to ship Shacklar home and take over all his authority. They're kind of unhappy that the "Wolman Question" is taking so long to resolve.'

'Oh, they are?' Dar breathed. 'How interesting. How'd you come by this fascinating little titbit? Common knowledge back on Terra?'

'Well, I wouldn't exactly call it headline news. . . .'

'We're not quite that important,' Dar agreed dryly.

'It was the last piece of paper to cross my desk the day I quit – arranging transportation for this man Bhelabher and his aides.'

'Bhelabher, mm? What's he like?'

'Oh . . .' Sam shrugged. 'You know – nothing exceptional. A career civil servant, that's all.'

'Quite,' Dar agreed. 'Stodgy, you might say?'

'Stuffy,' Sam confirmed. 'Very conservative – especially about military procedure and the treatment of convicts. . . . What are you doing?'

'Packing up.' Dar punched a button and watched the shack start folding itself back into a cube. 'We're getting back to town.'

'I said something?'

'You did – and you've got to say it again, as soon as possible. To Shacklar. We've got to make sure he knows what's coming.'


# 3

'Whatever you do, don't let him know what's coming,' Cholly advised.

'But he's gotta get ready!' Dar protested. 'Repel boarders! Fire when he sees the gleam of their spaceship! Damn the triplicates, full speed ahead! Over the top!'

'Under the counter,' Cholly corrected. 'Whatever happens, he's got to be able to truthfully say he doesn't know anything about it.'

'Oh.' Dar caught the inside of his cheek between his teeth. 'I forgot about that.'

'Don't.' Cholly began polishing the bar again. 'A clean conscience and a clean record, lad.'

'First rule in political lying,' Dar explained to Sam. 'Don't. Be able to claim somebody misunderstood you – or did it on their own.'

'We'll have to do it on our own, for this one,' Cholly amended. 'The General's a horrible liar. Can't even claim he was misunderstood.'

Dar nodded resolutely. 'Right. How about a quick commando raid?'

'Illegal,' Cholly pointed out.

'You don't think you can get rid of Bhelabher legally!' Sam exclaimed.

'Nay, but we can do it in a way that can't be *proved* illegal.'

'He means we've gotta be able to claim it was an accident,' Dar explained.

'Great.' Sam's lips thinned. '"Excuse me, sir, I didn't mean to slip that strychnine in your martini." "Oh heavens, my bomb! I *dropped* it!"'

'Effective, but impractical,' Cholly said judiciously. 'Very hard to ignore.'

'But you've got to do *some*thing! Think of the good of the planet!'

'I do,' Cholly said thoughtfully, 'and personally, what I'd say this planet needs is a good Customs Office.'

'*Real* Scotch whisky, mind,' the sergeant reminded.

Dar nodded. 'Straight from Terra itself – Nova Scotia Regal. Two litres each, for you and your corporal.'

'Fair enough!' The sergeant shouldered his laser rifle and came to attention. 'We'll stand guard day in and day out, mate – for all day tomorrow, that is. Though why you'd want to guard this old shack is beyond my understandin'. Ain't been nothin' in there but spare parts an' waste for ten years.'

'There is now.' Dar peeled off the backing and reached up to press the new sign into place over the doorway of the battered geodesic. 'A carpet, five chairs, two ashtrays, and a counter.'

'"Customs Office"?' The corporal squinted up at the sign. 'Is this official?'

'Thoroughly,' Dar assured him. 'Believe me, I know – I wrote up the orders myself.'

'Shacklar ordered it, hm?'

'You can't expect him to keep track of every little thing.'

The sergeant let out a throttled moan and stiffened, reddening. Dar looked up at him, frowning, then followed the direction of his gaze – to see Sam coming up to him, dressed in a tight-fitting blue uniform with gold epaulets and a visored beret. Dar stiffened, too – he hadn't been sure she had a figure.

'Cholly looked up his billings and found a Wolman who'd ordered a sewing machine.' She handed Dar a flat, neatly tied package, oblivious to their stares. 'His wife was willing to do a rush job.'

Dar shook himself. 'Uh, great. What'd it cost him?'

'Four power packs, six blaster barrels, two circuit chips, and a bathtub.'

'Worth every credit,' the sergeant wheezed, his eyes locked on her.

'Better get to it.' Sam turned to the door. 'I've got to set up the terminal and the paperwork.'

'Uh – right.' Dar tore his eyes away from her and glanced at his watch-ring. 'How much time do we have?'

'Cholly says the ferry's due to take off from your moon at thirteen o'clock,' Sam said from inside the shack. 'What time is it?'

'Thirteen o'clock.' Dar started stripping.

'Here then, Dar Mandra!'

Dar looked up, irritated, then snatched at his uniform; it wasn't good policy for a Wolman to see soldiers naked, and the man coming up with Cholly was the shaman of the Sars tribe.

'Peace, Dar Mandra.' The shaman held up a hand.

'Uh, peace, Reverend.' Dar scrambled into his uniform, sealed the tunic, and held up a palm. 'Honoured to see you, but, uh – why're you wearing a Customs uniform?'

'Why, he's one of yer staff now, ain't cha, Reverend?' Cholly grinned. 'Just to cover all bets, Dar.'

'Ye-e-e-e-ah.' Dar's eyes slowly widened. 'Your "hunches" might come in handy, Reverend.'

'"Officer Haldane", for the time being, Dar Mandra.' The shaman wrung Dar's hand a bit awkwardly; he wasn't used to the custom. 'You understand, I cannot guarantee to know the speaking of their minds.'

'Yes, yes, I know the Power sends the gift when It wishes, not when we do.' Dar clasped his hands behind his back and massaged his knuckles. 'But I hope It'll be with us today, Rever . . . uh, Officer Haldane.'

'I, too,' the shaman said sombrely. 'Shacklar must remain with us, Dar Mandra. I have no wish to see my young men die leaning on laser beams – nor yours, either.'

'Definitely not.' Dar was suddenly very conscious of his age.

'And I think you had best arrange matters so I need not speak.'

'Oh, I'm sure that won't be necessary, Reverend,' Dar said quickly. 'You speak better Terran than I do.'

'It is kind of you – but I do have something of an accent.'

'Less'n mine,' Cholly said. 'Still, the Rev has the right of it, lad – there might be an aide who knows something of Wolman.'

'And though I have washed off my dye for the occasion, my nation is written in my face, for him who knows how to see it.' The shaman stilled suddenly, then peered upward. 'The Power favours me this day, Dar Mandra. Your enemies approach.'

Dar squinted up at the sky, but couldn't detect the faintest glimmer of flame. Still . . . 'Your word's good enough for me, Reverend. Shall we go and look official?'

The ferry roared down, blackening the blast pit anew. Dar watched through the window as the ramp slid out and the hatch lifted. He saw the party troop out and stop in consternation at the sight of the shack. The guards glanced at each other and stepped forward; the sergeant went up to the group, holding his rifle at port arms, and had a few words with a fox-faced man in the front row. Another man elbowed his way to the fore to interrupt their conversation. He wasn't tall exactly, but he gave the impression of towering height; and he was skinny, but he had a massive presence. The longer his conversation with the sergeant went on, the more clearly Dar could hear his voice; but the sergeant remained firm and apparently soft-voiced; he just waited for a blast to blow itself out, then said a few words and leaned into the next blast. But Dar did begin to notice his rifle barrel twitching. Mentally, Dar upped the sergeant two pints of Scotch and a fifth of bourbon.

Finally, the skinny man threw his head up in exasperation and started for the shack. His entourage swept along behind him, and the sergeant followed, poker-faced.

'Get ready,' Dar said softly, 'customers.'

The door slammed open, and the skinny man waded in. 'Who is responsible for this farce?'

'I'm the senior official present, sir.' Dar kept his face carefully neutral. 'May I be of service?'

'Service! You can serve me admirably by dismissing this piece of asininity and conveying us immediately to your Government House!'

'Certainly, sir – as soon as we've cleared you through Customs.'

'Customs! This planet never *had* a Customs Office! I've read all the reports!'

'An innovation,' Dar said truthfully. 'We're constantly trying to improve conditions, sir.'

The rest of the entourage had trooped in; the corporal shut the door behind them. He and the sergeant discreetly took up places at the corners of the room.

'Honourable Bhelabher . . .' The fox-faced man appeared at the skinny man's elbow. 'It may be that these good people are unaware of your official status.' He gave Dar a glare of such intense malice that Dar felt his blood-temperature drop. Out of the corner of his eye, he noticed Reverend Haldane wince just the tiniest bit.

'Well taken, Canis, well taken,' Bhelabher harrumphed. He turned back to Dar. 'See here, fellow – do you know who I am?'

'Not really, sir – but I would like to find out. May I see your passport, please?' Dar decided Sam might've had the right idea after all: strychnine. 'Fellow', indeed!

'Passport!' Bhelabher bellowed. 'Young man, I'll have you know I'm your new governor!'

Dar paused and widened his eyes just a trifle; then he leaned forward, holding out his hand. 'An interesting theory, Honourable; I'll have to validate it with Government House. I'm afraid I haven't heard anything about Governor Shacklar being replaced, though. May I see your passport, please?'

'Absurd! On a planet full of convicts, certainly *I* should be above suspicion!'

'But because this *is* a convict planet, no one can be above suspicion,' Dar said smoothly. 'I'm afraid I *must* insist on seeing your credentials, Honourable.'

Bhelabher began to redden, making choking, gargling sounds; but the fox-faced man put a hand on his arm, and he subsided just short of magenta. 'Very well, if you must!' Bhelabher growled. 'Atavista, our credentials, please.'

A skinny young woman stepped up to open a folder and lay a set of microholos on the counter. Her clothing was skintight and transparent which, given her figure, wasn't exactly an advantage; but Dar found he had to focus very tightly on her face anyway. That definitely did the trick.

Sam took the microholos and began feeding them through the terminal. Dar noticed that the bottom wafer was a plastyrus envelope with Shacklar's name on it.

Reverend Haldane stepped up next to Dar, collecting the wafers as Sam handed them back. He glanced at the fox-faced man and murmured, so softly that Dar could scarcely hear him, 'Each person has copies of all those documents in his luggage.' Dar carefully didn't let anything show in his face, but he pressed his hand flat against the counter to show he'd heard. He also noticed that the plastyrus envelope didn't come back to the stack.

Sam finished and turned to murmur something to the Reverend. He turned to Dar and murmured, 'Officer Bine says the documents bear a lock-code and will not read through our Central.'

Nice, Dar thought. He'd wondered how he was going to justify it. Sam seemed more interesting than ever. 'I'm afraid we'll have to retain your documents, Honourable.'

'*What*?'

Dar glanced up to make sure the roof was still on the shack then back to Bhelabher. 'I'm afraid we'll have to retain your credentials. You see, they seem to be locked under a security code which hasn't been transmitted to our computer.'

'This is outrageous!' Bhelabher stormed. 'Of all the inconceivable idiocies I've encountered, this has to be the most imbecilic! Young man, I will not tolerate this!'

'I'm afraid *we* have no choice,' Dar said regretfully. 'And, under the circumstances, I'm afraid it will be necessary to search every item of your party's luggage.'

Bhelabher began reddening and gargling again, and the fox-faced man's glare narrowed to an ice pick.

'I appreciate that you may find this unacceptable,' Dar sympathized. 'If so, the shuttle isn't quite done refuelling yet; I'm sure the pilot will be glad to take you back.'

Bhelabher clamped his jaw shut, his eyes bulged, and the room was very silent for a few seconds. Then he released a huge hiss of breath and snapped, 'Very well. We'll begin with mine. Canis, the bags, please.'

Canis glanced at him, frowning, but stepped forward and hoisted two valises onto the counter. Dar opened them and passed them to Sam and the Reverend, who each began shuffling through the stacks of paper-thin garments in a half of each bag. Dar couldn't detect anything being removed but, when Sam closed the bag, set it upright on the counter, and turned to nod to Dar, there was a very meaningful look in her eye.

Dar made a mental note that she was a sleight-of-hand artist, too, and never to play poker with her; but he also started making very definite plans to start playing some other game with her as soon as he could manoeuvre her into it. He opened the next suitcase and passed it on.

They were quick, she and the Reverend; but there were a lot of bags, and the time stretched out. The aides began to mutter and grumble to one another, but Bhelabher stood rock-still, legs apart, hands clasped in front of him; and Canis stood like a malevolent statue at his side – or a ventriloquist's mannequin, Dar thought. He wondered which one was really doing the talking.

Finally Sam closed the last case and gave him the nod. Dar turned to Bhelabher with a smile. 'All done, Honourable.'

'Thank you,' Bhelabher said sourly. 'I assume we now have the freedom of the planet?'

'Uh – I'm sorry, Honourable.' Dar looked up in surprise. 'I thought I'd made that clear.'

'Clear? How so?' There was an ominous rumble under Bhelabher's voice.

'Your credentials,' Dar explained. 'We can't admit you officially until they've been verified with Government House. We should have them back to you in twenty-four hours, though.'

'Twenty-four hours!'

'If General Shacklar has the lock-code for your documents. Longer, if he doesn't. But I'm sure he will.'

There was a moment's silence while Bhelabher's face puffed up and passed magenta.

Dar braced himself.

Then the Honourable erupted. Dar leaned into the blast and listened closely; he was always out to improve his vocabulary. He wasn't sure what half the words meant; but he did get the impression that:

1 the Honourable was somewhat distressed by this turn of events;
2 the delay was totally unacceptable;
3 there was obviously a conspiracy afoot to prevent his assuming his rightful post; and that
4 he thought Dar's hide would make an excellent ornament for his new office, nailed to the wall and tastefully decorated with a carefully balanced pattern of intersecting whip-welts.

When Bhelabher ran down, Dar glanced at Sam, who whipped out a pad and jotted down a few lines.

'Your protest is noted,' Dar said with a small, polite smile, 'but I'm afraid that's all we can do about it. Regulations are regulations, Honourable. I'm sure you understand.'

Bhelabher took a breath, but the sergeant cleared his throat rather loudly and transferred his blaster rifle from his left shoulder to his right. Bhelabher paused in mid-gasp, glanced at the soldier out of the corner of his eye, then slowly closed his mouth and turned back to Dar. 'Of course. Quite. I trust you have accommodations for myself and my staff while we endure this outrage?'

'Not here at the port,' Dar admitted. 'But there are some transient facilities in town. The sergeant will show you the route – and stay nearby, in case you should need anything.'

'Solely for our convenience,' Bhelabher said dryly. 'Surely.'

He turned to survey his staff. 'Well . . . there seems to be no help for it. I see now how badly this poor, benighted colony needs our ministrations, good people. However, until we have an opportunity to streamline this laughable attempt at a bureaucracy, I'm afraid we'll have to endure some inconvenience. Please be patient.' He started toward the door.

The corporal stepped over and opened it for him. Bhelabher paused in the doorway to look back at Dar. 'You haven't heard the last of me, young man – be sure of it.'

'But you *have* heard the last of *us*,' Dar said as the door closed behind the last aide, 'and your credentials.'

'Right here.' Sam started piling wafers on the countertop.

'You're really good at that, y'know?' Dar yanked off his beret. 'I didn't know BOA trained pickpockets.'

'Just a difference in emphasis,' Sam said. 'Besides, I wouldn't have known what to do without the Reverend. He knew right where to look in each bag.'

'Yeah – thanks, Reverend.' Dar started peeling out of his tunic. 'We couldn't have brought it off without you.'

'The Power favoured me,' Haldane said modestly. 'I wish you luck, Dar Mandra. This will be, at most, an inconvenience to him.'

'Well, I'm hoping for more – but you're right; it's only a delaying tactic. And he might not be delayed very long in getting Shacklar out here.' He pulled on his coverall and turned to Sam. 'Better change. We've gotta get out of here, fast.'

# 4

The glass chattered on the table, and Dar looked up. 'I could swear I heard a dull boom.'

'Ayuh.' Cholly tilted his head to the side. 'I'd almost think I had, too. Queer, ain't it?'

'Right on the borderline between hearing and feeling.' Sam turned to Dar. 'Either it was very soft, or very far away.'

'Soldiers don't go in for target practice much.' Dar turned to Cholly. 'Anybody sell some Wolmen a cannon?'

'Only the parts – and they haven't got the button yet.'

'Must've been a natural phenomenon.' Dar tossed back the rest of his beer and set the glass down. 'How long do you think it'll take 'em to realize we, ah, "confiscated" all the copies of their credentials?'

'About as long as it takes them to find a hotel room – and I expect yer friend the sergeant'll lead 'em the long way 'round the barn.'

'If I know him, he'll take 'em by way of the back pasture – which is where Bhelabher belongs, anyway. The man's got all the tact of a bar-bell.' Dar turned to Sam. 'How'd a blusterer like that get promoted to governor, anyway?'

'They couldn't fire him,' she explained. 'He had too much seniority. So they had to kick him up to where he couldn't do any harm – to his bosses, anyway.'

'No *harm*? What was he beforehand, a general?'

'Chief filing clerk.' Sam shrugged. 'Sorry, Dar, but that's the way they see it. Gossip said he'd caused three rebellions by putting the right document in the wrong place.'

'Perfect.' Dar held out his glass for a refill. 'Not even as important as a pile of molecudots.'

'To them, you *are* a molecudot.'

The door bonged, and a man in a very ornate jumpsuit came in, grinning from ear to ear.

'You're off early today, Corve.' Cholly reached for a bottle and glass.

'Bit of a frumus today.' Corve adjusted himself to a barstool and accepted the glass. 'Boss decided to give everybody the day off and let the new guests shift fer themselves.'

'That flock of civvies?' Dar managed mild interest. 'Where they in from, anyway?'

'Terra, 'seems.' Corve took a gulp or two. 'Their boss claims he's the new governor.'

'New governor?' Dar frowned. 'What for? We've got Shacklar!'

'And we'd best find a way to keep him, from the looks of this one.'

'Now, Corve, that's not fer you to say,' Cholly reproved him. 'You just holds the door at the hotel.'

'Ayuh, but I'm not on duty now.' Corve turned to Dar. 'Its name's Bhelabher, an' its brain's in its mouth.'

'Just what we need to consolidate Wolman relations,' Dar said dryly. '*Is* he the new gov?'

'Dunno; he can't find his papers.' Corve grinned wolfishly. 'Hadn't but scarcely found his rooms when he let out a roar like a ship trying to land without jets; I swear he shook the whole hotel.'

Dar looked up at Cholly. 'Kind of an explosion, huh? Or a cannon? The chemical kind, I mean.'

'Heard him all the way down here, eh? Well, can't say as I'm surprised. I thought of luggage-bombs, myself. But no, he came storming back into the lobby with his whole flock at his heels. "There's thieves in this hotel!" he cries. "They've rifled all our luggage!" Well, I don't doubt the boss was thinking of rifling him – but no, he kept his face polite, and says, "There are no guests in this hotel today but you and yours; and as for me and mine, why, I stayed here at the desk, the maid's having her batteries charged, and the staff's there by the door, ready to hold it for you." Well, Bhelabher, he started up some deal of nonsense about how dumb it is to have a hotel with so small a staff to blame things on, but his top aide . . . face kinda like a rat—'

'Fox,' Dar murmured.

'—an' he – uh . . . say again?'

'He coughed.' Sam kicked Dar in the ankle. 'Please go on, sir.'

'Yeah, well, the rat-faced one, he says, "Those people at the Customs Office, Honourable . . ." And Honourable, he hits his forehead with the heel of his hand – must do that a lot, I notice he's a little flat-headed – and says, "How obvious! No wonder I overlooked it! Why, of course there'd be corruption – riddled with it! Bureaucratic piracy, without a doubt!" And he starts for the door, thundering, "But how could they have known where to find the documents?" And the rat-faced one, he says, "Read our minds, no doubt," and all the rest of them, they set to wailing about how unfair it was, to have mind readers all about, and how's a decent bureaucrat going to make a living if all his little secrets are known, and what evil people mind readers are. And Honourable, he says, "We must see the General immediately, and

have those Customs people questioned,'' and I pulled the door and
they swirled on out, Bhelabher and his whole covey right behind
him. And I closed the door and like to fell over, laughing so hard
I thought I'd shake myself apart.'

'No wonder.' Dar managed to chuckle himself. '*Customs* Office?
On a *prison* planet?'

'And mind readers! Hoo!' Corve chortled. 'Such a deal of
nonsense! And these're *educated*?'

'Wull, knowing facts can't cure stupidity,' Cholly mused, 'and
Shacklar's anything but stupid. I'd love to see what happens when
they find him.'

The door bonged, and a private stepped in, chuckling.

'I think we're about to find out.' Dar turned to the new arrival.
'Something go right, Cosca?'

'All depends on which end you were on.' Cosca pulled himself
up to a barstool. 'Me, I was on the outside, listening in.'

'Don't executives *any*where know better than to leave their
intercoms open?' Sam demanded.

'Just the other way around,' Dar corrected. 'Sometimes they
know better than to turn them off. What wasn't private, Cosca?'

'A complaint, chiefly.' Cosca accepted his beer. 'Or maybe a
challenge.'

'I can guess the chief who made the complaint,' Corve grinned.
'Who made the challenge?'

'Same as the complainer – this Terran bigwig, Beelubber . . .'

'Bhelabher,' Dar and Corve both corrected.

'Who's telling this story, anyway? All right, Bhelabher. Honourable high huckster from Terra – he says. He comes sailing
in without so much as a by-your-leave, roars, "Where's the
governor?" and goes slamming into Shacklar's office afore a
one of us could say a word. Matter of fact, we couldn't even
hear ourselves, his gang was making so much noise, chattering
about how telepaths was undermining the foundations of society
. . .'

'Telepaths?' Dar frowned.

'Mind readers,' Corve explained. 'Gotta hand it to 'em – they
keep to a line of thought. How'd the General take it, Cosca?'

'Well, he was in conference at the time . . .'

'With his cat-o'-nine-tails, or a patient?'

'Patient. As long as we can keep the troubled ones coming, it
keeps him away from the cat. Analysis, it was – with Rogoure.'

'Rogoure?' Dar stiffened. 'Isn't he that private who almost

chopped a Wolman in Monday's battle?'

'The same. An' you know how Shacklar is – he wouldn't ask the man to leave his knife outside. Well, I'd guess that Rogoure's paranoid.'

Dar started to grin.

'And they were deep into his childhood when Bhelabher charged in?' Cholly guessed.

'I'd say – but all I know is, Rogoure bellows, "They've come to get me!" and jumps up with that knife out. . . .'

'Good reflexes,' Dar noted.

Corve nodded. 'He'd make a top-notch soldier. Well! I don't need to tell you. It got somewhat furry for a while there.'

'Meaning Bhelabher was screaming, and Rogoure was shouting war cries, and Shacklar was trying to bellow them both into order?'

'Something of the sort. Well, the General, he did manage to get Rogoure calmed down, and apologized for the interruption. "But you know how it is," he says, "when one's involved in government. Any Johnny in the street thinks he's got the right to bust in to see you at all odd hours of the day and night." "Well, I can comp that," Rogoure answers. "I'd likely do the same if I felt I really had a gripe." He'd made progress already, that one. "I hope you will," says Shacklar. "Take it out on me, not on the Wolmen. Will you, Private?" "My word upon it, sir," says Rogoure. "Next time I'm feeling homicidal, I'll come for you." "Good chap!" says Shacklar. "But if you do stay calm, I'll see you at this time tomorrow?" "That you will, sir." And Rogoure, he salutes. "Well enough," says Shacklar, saluting back. "Dismissed!" And Rogoure clicks his heels, about-faces on the mark, and marches out.'

'And this time last week, you couldn't've got him to come to parade rest.' Dar shook his head. 'Shacklar's amazing.'

'Bhelabher didn't think so. Rogoure was barely out before the Honourable pulled himself together enough to bellow, "What is this place – a lion's den?" "So it would seem," says Shacklar, "when the folk who come don't even have the manners of a flea. I thought civilians still abided by the old quaint custom of requesting admittance when the door was closed."'

Even Sam smiled. 'He sounds a little miffed.'

'Oh, his tone was fresh dry ice! "That's a rather poor reception," Bhelabher says, "for the new governor of this planet." Well. I tell you, Shackler all but froze.'

'I should think the news would've come as a bit of a shock, yes.'

'Oh, the General's used to delusions of grandeur. You could almost see it going through his mind. "I understand a cargo ship came down today," he says. Bhelabher nods. "Myself was on it, and my whole staff." Well, if you knew the General, you could see he didn't think that ruled out aberrations. "You've come from Terra?" "We have," says Bhelabher, "sent out by the BOA to take charge of this planet and rid it of corruption and of vice." Shacklar, he sat down at his desk and made a note or two. "I assume you have got credentials to support your claim?" "I *had*," Bhelabher says, like it was an accusation, "but the officials at your Customs Office confiscated not only the originals, but all the copies, too.'

Corve chuckled.

Cosca nodded. 'I expect Shacklar thought so, too – but he didn't show it, of course. Bhelabher bellows, "You must find those scoundrels!" And Shacklar answers, "It would be rather surprising if we could. In fact, it's amazing that you managed to find our Customs Office, since we don't have one!" "Come sir," Bhelabher says. "Surely you at least know the departments of your own administration." "I do," says Shacklar, "and I tell you, there's no Customs Office. Where did you find it, by the way?" "Right at the spaceport," says Bhelabher. "A small plastrete structure, about twenty feet square." "One of the storage sheds," Shacklar says, nodding. "What did it have by way of personnel?" "Two men and a woman," answers Bhelabher. "Surely you know of them!" "I'm afraid not," says Shacklar, "though it shouldn't be too difficult discovering who the woman was; there're only about seventy of them in the settlement." Well, then you could begin to hear it in Bhelabher's voice; he'd begun to figure it out for himself. "Do you imply that these personnel were not official?" "Not really," says Shacklar. "I'm sure they appointed themselves properly before they took office." Well, Bhelabher was quiet then, but his face turned a very interesting colour . . .'

'Mauve,' Dar supplied.

'Magenta,' Corve corrected.

'Closer to maroon, I'd say. Then he explodes: "I have been deceived!" "I believe 'conned' is the old term," Shacklar agreed. "Certainly someone has played on your gullibility." Bhelabher rumbles, "I don't quite think . . ." "Quite," says Shacklar. "At any rate, this puts us both in a rather delicate position,

Honourable." Bhelabher says slowly, "Yes, I can understand that," which I, for one, found surprising. "Your claims may be quite legitimate," Shacklar goes on. "BOA may have sent you out here to assume the administration of this colony." "Indeed they have!" snaps Bhelabher. "But you have no credentials to verify that statement," Shacklar points out. "I have witnesses!" Bhelabher huffs. "My whole staff will testify in support of this robbery!" "I'm sure they will," Shacklar says, and his voice was vermouth. "But you'll pardon me, Honourable, if I can not quite accept their testimony as totally impartial." Bhelabher says nothing, and Shacklar gets gentle. "I'm sure you must see that I cannot cede administration of this colony to you merely on your say-so." "But this is intolerable!" Bhelabher cries. "My appointment is totally legitimate!" which was more than I could say for himself. "As well it may be," says Shacklar, getting hard again, "but it *could* also be a scheme of deception on a very large scale." "Sir," Bhelabher rumbles, "do I understand you to say that *I* am a confidence swindler?" "You do not," Shacklar answers, "but since you wish to say it, you may. Certainly I must assume as much, since you lack proof of your claim." "But this is intolerable," Bhelabher explodes again, "especially since it is far more likely that *you*, sir, are the schemer! You have absolute control of this settlement; how could a few of its inhabitants mount such a ruse without your consent, nay, your command? Is it not logical that you would so seek to maintain your own . . .' Well, sirs and madam, that's just about when the General turned round and slammed the door, and we had to content ourselves with what we could hear through the wall.'

'Which was?' Corve demanded.

'Oh, a deal of shouting and bellowing, and the odd low mutter from Shacklar, but nothing you could make out in words. It slackened, though, got softer and softer, till we couldn't hear nothing at all. And that's just about when we thought to see if the General'd maybe been careless with his intercom again.'

'You just checked it, of course.'

'Of course; I doubt that we listened for a full thirty seconds.'

Dar coughed delicately. 'We, uh, certainly wouldn't want you to violate a confidence or anything, but . . .'

'No fear. Not much we could violate, anyway; 'bout all we heard was, when we pressed the button, the Honourable saying, ". . . started when I was four. That's when my mother became involved with the amateur holovision programming club, you see, and of course it demanded a great deal of time. Our district child-care centre was very nice, really, but most of the children were older than I was, and looking back on it, I see that they all must have been rather disturbed . . .' Shacklar murmured something sympathetic, but that's just about when the rat-faced aide noticed us and started saying something about telepaths' eavesdropping couldn't be avoided, but . . . Well, we decided the intercom was working, and switched it off.'

'The ethical thing to do,' Dar agreed. 'How long ago was that?'

Cosca glanced at his ring. ' 'Bout half an hour. I'd expect that by this time he's into the traumas of grade school.'

'Ever Shacklar's way,' Cholly grinned. ' "If you can't beat 'em, analyse 'em." What were his henchmen doing, Cosca?'

'Oh, the usual – sitting around waiting, and bothering us for coffee, and wondering how the psi who'd swiped their credentials had known they was comin'. I mean, he'd've had to, wouldn't he, to've been able to set up a fake Customs Office in time to catch 'em comin' off the ferry?'

'Makes sense,' Dar said judiciously. 'Did they?'

'Not a bit.' Cosca shook his head. 'The rat-faced one, he said this proved there must be a conspiracy of psis, all the way from Terra to here, 'cause that was the only way word could've come out faster than an FTL starship could carry it – at the speed of thought, which he claimed to be faster than the speed of light . . .'

'Ridiculous,' Sam snorted.

'Isn't it just? There's nothing so unbeatable as wanting to stay ignorant. But even Ratty wasn't about to believe one single telepath could hear thoughts on Terra from all the way out here on Wolmar; so, he claimed, there must've been a network of psis, each one relayin' the message, till a telepath here picked it up and set up a reception for 'em. He didn't quite *say* Shacklar was a part of the conspiracy, and a telepath, too, but . . .'

'But that's when you decided you'd best take a beer break and cool off under the collar, hey?' Cholly guessed.

Cosca nodded. 'Got my perspective back on the way over, though, and got to seeing the humorous side of it. Well! I'm recovered, and I'd best get back to the office.'

'And let one of your mates come out and cool off?'

Cosca nodded. 'And hope there's no mayhem been done while I've been gone. Well! Ta-ta, chaps!' He headed for the door.

'And to yerself, Cosca.' Cholly waved. 'Corve, would you mind the store for a bit? Dar and Sam and me got to talk over their list for the next trading trek.'

'Eh? Eh, surely now, Cholly!' Corve heaved himself up, ambled round behind the bar, and began whistling through his teeth as he poured himself another mugful.

Dar looked up at Cholly, already halfway to the back room, and frowned. Then he nodded to Sam and followed.

'What's this all about?' she muttered as she caught up with him.

'Don't know,' Dar answered softly, 'but something's gone wrong. I wasn't supposed to go trading so soon.'

They stepped into the back room, and Sam stared.

Books. All around. Ceiling to floor, and the ceiling was high. Books bound, micro-books, molecue-books, holotapes, and readers for everything. Even some antique paper books.

'Just your average hole-in-the-wall tavern,' Dar said cheerfully. 'What's up, boss?'

'Sit down, lad, sit down.' Cholly pulled a large box from a drawer and set it on the table. Dar sat down, looking wary. 'The problem is,' Cholly said, shaking out a large white cloth and fastening it around Dar's neck, 'that the General's likely to give the Honourable and his troop the freedom of the planet.'

Dar blanched. 'I hadn't thought of that.'

'No, nor did I. Understandable lack, I'm sure, in view of the rush we were under; still, there it is. So you two've got choices: to hole up till it all blows over, or to go in disguise while they're here.'

'We can't be so well disguised that they won't recognize us,' Sam blurted.

Cholly held up a hand. 'Have faith. I had occasion, one time, to travel with a group of wandering actors . . .'

'The cops were after him,' Dar explained.

'Be that as it may, be that as it may.' Cholly took some putty out of a can and started kneading it. 'Took a small part now and again, myself, and didn't do badly, if I do say so . . . Well. The long and the short of it is, I became reasonably good with theatrical make-up, and accumulated a trunkful.'

'Which we are now about to get the benefit of,' Dar interpreted.

'Close yer mouth, now; you don't need no prosthesis on yer tongue.' Cholly pressed the lump of putty to Dar's nose and began shaping it into a startlingly natural hook. '"Robex", this is – best way of changing the shape of the face that the theatre ever came up with. Beautiful, 'tis – just knead it till it gets soft, set it on cartilage, shape it, and it'll adhere as tight as yer natural-born skin.'

'How do I get it off?' Dar muttered.

'With the solvent – and it tastes terrible, so close yer great gape of a mouth. Then it dries as hard as cartilage, this being Robex # 1.'

'It's changing colour,' Sam pointed out.

Cholly nodded. 'That's part of the beauty of it, don't yer see – it starts out pasty-grey, but takes on the colour of the flesh it's on. Now, back in the old days, you'd've had to choose the premixed sort of base that came closest to yer natural skin tone and baste it on all over yer flesh – you would've had "Dark Egyptian", lad. But with Robex, you see, all you do is blend it into yer skin, and it does the rest. No need for base.'

'That's great for cartilage. But if it hardens that way, won't it be just a teeny bit obvious if I use it to shape my cheeks?'

'Oh, we use Robex # 2 for that – dries to the consistency of whatever flesh it's on.' Cholly opened another can and scooped out a lump of dough. 'Yer own mother'll never know ye when I'm done with you, lad.'

'My own mother,' Dar mumbled, 'never wanted to know me at all.'

About an hour later, the door opened, and Corve stuck his head in. 'Uh, Cholly, I believe as how ya might want to be out here.'

'Do I indeed, do I indeed!' Cholly whisked the cloth off Sam and over his make-up chest. 'Ayuh, Corve, certainly.'

'Who's the strangers, Cholly?' Corve frowned dubiously.

'Why, this here's Enib Mas, Corve.' Cholly gave Sam a pat on the head, incidentally setting the roots of her wig into the adhesive. 'And that there's Ardnam Rod. Just in off the freighter. Turns out Enib's had a year of college, and Ard's had two, so I thought they'd like a look back here.'

'Oh! Welcome, welcome!' Corve bustled in, holding out a hand. 'What ya up for?'

'Rather not say,' Dar rumbled in his deepest voice. He pumped Corve's hand. 'Pleased to meet you.'

'Me, too,' Sam said in a high, nasal tone. 'Do you ever get used to this place?'

'Quick enough, quick enough.' Corve shook her hand. 'You don't look too well, lad – but don't worry, Wolmar'll put meat on yer bones. Well! Afraid I gotta be off, Cholly – if I know the boss, he'll've got over his miff, and be open for business again.'

'Best to be sure, best to be sure.' Cholly took Corve by the arm and guided him out. 'See you this evening, Corve.'

'That ya will, that ya will. Here's yer company, Cholly. Good day to you.' And Corve headed out the door, leaving Cholly to face General Shacklar and Bhelabher.

'Had him totally fooled, didn't we?' Sam murmured.

'Not for a second,' Dar muttered back. 'Why do you think he was so over-polite? And didn't ask where Dar and Sam were?'

Sam said nothing, but her eyes were wide.

'. . . nothing exceptional to look at,' Shacklar was saying as Cholly bustled over behind the bar, 'but the drink's as good as you can get out here, and the food's excellent. Most importantly, though, this is really our community centre. Groups meet here to discuss anything and everything, to socialize, and to work out personal problems into a sympathetic ear.'

'Hello, Sympathetic Ear!' Bhelabher reached out a tentative hand and smiled at Cholly with genuine, if confused, warmth.

Cholly accepted the hand as Shacklar murmured, 'The Honourable Vincent Bhelabher, of the Bureau of Otherworldly Activities.'

'Pleased,' Cholly affirmed, with an eye on the General.

Dar choked in his beer.

'Yes . . .' Bhelabher murmured. 'The General had mentioned something about your commercial enterprise . . .' He seemed rather bemused.

'Enterprising it is, enterprising it is.' Cholly nodded. 'Though lately, it's not been too commercial . . .'

'Well, I'm sure there're slack periods in any line of commerce. But the General seems to feel that this particular line of exchange offers his only real hope of any lasting peace with the natives.'

'The General's too kind,' Cholly demurred. 'Has he told you of his war games?'

'Only a stopgap, Charles,' Shacklar murmured. 'I was speaking of hopes for a permanent peace, which must be founded on mutual understanding.'

'I'm sure, I'm sure.' Bhelabher nodded genially. 'Still, I'd like to witness one of these, ah, "games".'

'As indeed you shall. I regret that I won't be able to conduct you, myself, due to the press of business; will you excuse me, Honourable?'

'Eh? . . . Yes, of course, of course!' Bhelabher seized Shacklar's hand and pumped it. 'No need even to explain, of course, old chap; I've had responsibility for major administrative sectors myself. Of course I understand!'

'I hoped you would.' Shacklar's smile seemed real. 'Charles, I trust you'll be able to spare the Honourable your best trader for a guide during his stay here.'

'Oh, of course!' With a wicked grin, Cholly slapped Dar on the back. 'None but the best, General! Ard here, he's yer man!'

This time Dar managed to at least get the beer down the right pipe, and lifted his head to give Cholly his best gimlet-glare. But Cholly just kept grinning, as though he hadn't a care in the world, which *he* hadn't.

'Ard will see you get a thorough look at our piece of this planet, and a good bit of what's outside the wall then,' Shacklar said. 'In the meantime, please be assured we'll do all we can to recover your credentials.'

'Not unless they're awfully good at reconstructing ashes,' Dar murmured to Sam. She kicked him.

'I very much appreciate it,' Bhelabher said earnestly. 'For my part, I've seen to it that the shuttle pilot carried back a note to BOA, an official dispatch, of course.'

'And the liner should be bound back inward in a week.' Shacklar nodded. 'But I'm afraid I'll have to ask your indulgence there, Honourable – after all, it *is* a two-month journey to Terra.'

'Oh, I quite understand! But if all goes well, we should receive a reply in half a year, Standard Terran. Still, I have hopes we'll recover our credentials before then.'

'I'm sure we'll manage to conclude the manner in *some* fashion,' Shacklar assured him. Something beeped at his hand, and his brow netted. 'Can't they get by without me for a short hour? Yes, Fordstam, what is it?' he murmured into his ring, then held it to his ear. After a moment, he sighed and spoke into it again. 'Yes, yes, I'm on my way. . . . You'll excuse me, Honourable, but it seems one of my soldiers has been making decent proposals to a Wolman girl, and the tribe's mayor's concerned. Indecent proposals they're used to, but they don't know quite what to make of this one.'

'Well . . . I'm sure it had to happen sooner or later,' Bhelabher mused. 'What's your policy on intermarriage?'

'None at all, at the moment,' Shacklar confessed. 'But I hope to have one by the time I get back to HQ. Will you excuse me?' The General went out the door.

Dar counted mentally, ticking off seconds on his fingers. When he got to five, a joyful whoop resounded from the street outside. Bhelabher looked up, blinking, but Dar nodded. Shacklar'd been waiting a long time for this 'incident'. He might not have had the policy, but he sure had it ready.

'Do your people always express themselves so exuberantly?' Bhelabher seemed smaller, somewhat lost, with Shacklar's departure.

'Not always,' Cholly admitted. 'They're often depressed. Still, there's no sense just telling you – take the good man and show him, Ard.'

'Mm?' It only took Sam's elbow in his ribs to make Dar react to his new name. 'Oh, yes! Yes . . .' He heaved himself to his feet with a sigh. 'Yes, if we hurry, we can just make the Two-O'Clock War. See you later, Cholly.' It was more of a threat than a promise.

# 5

Dar lifted a glass in a trembling hand and drank deeply. 'I tell you, I don't know if I can last it out.'

'What for?' Cholly twisted the empty out of his hand and replaced it with a full one. 'There's never a chance that he'd recognize yer.'

'Yeah, but I'm running out of things to show him.' Dar started to sip, then stared at the glass. 'I just emptied this.'

'And he just refilled it.' Sam shook her head. 'You *are* in bad shape.'

'Come, now!' Cholly cajoled. 'A whole planetful of marvels, and you can't find a week's tour? Come, indeed! What've you shown him?'

'Well, let me see.' Dar started ticking them off on his fingers. 'The Wall – all thirty miles of it. The Two-O'Clock War. A Wolman village. The Eight-O'Clock War. He had a conference with Shacklar. The Two-O'Clock War. The enlisted men's recreation complex and organic market. The officers' recreation complex and fixed market. The Eight-O'Clock War. Conference with Shacklar. The Two-O'Clock War. A Wolman trading session. A Wolman information-barter . . .'

'Adult school,' Cholly murmured.

'That, too . . . A Wolman workshop. The Eight-O'Clock War. Conference with Shacklar. The Two-O'Clock War. He likes wars.'

'I was beginning to get that impression,' Sam agreed.

'You still haven't shown him the parade ground. Or the jail.'

Dar shook his head. 'Depressing.'

'Or the Little Theatre. The Concert Hall.'

'Boring.'

'How do you know? Could be he *likes* amateurs. Then there's the radio studio, the 3DT studio, the barracks . . .'

'All the high spots, huh?'

Cholly shrugged. 'Nobody said you had to entertain the man – just to guide him. You wouldn't want him to get a false impression of us, would you?'

'Yes,' Dar snapped. 'Definitely.'

Cholly straightened up with a sigh. 'Then ye've naught but yourself to blame if he's hard to get along with.'

'That's the strange part.' Dar's brow knitted. 'He's not.'

' 'Course he would be. You'd be, too, if . . . how's that again?'

'He's not,' Dar repeated. 'He's not tough to get along with at all. He's been getting more and more pleasant every day. In fact, today he was a real nice guy. I'm amazed at how wrong my first impression of him was.'

'I'm amazed at how good a psychiatrist the General is,' Cholly grunted.

Something beeped in the back corner, and kept on beeping.

Sam looked up. 'A holophone? Here?'

'Why not?' Dar smiled. 'Radio waves don't *have* to have plastrete buildings around them, you know.'

Cholly ambled back to the phone and pressed the 'receive' button. 'Cholly's Hash House, Bar, an' Natural Food Emporium. . . . Oh, it's yerself, General! . . . Who? . . . Oh, yes, he's here! You want to . . . You don't want to . . . You want to see him? Right now? Begging yer pardon, General, but – what's he done? . . . Oh? Oh, I see. Yes, yes, right away . . . Same to you, General . . . Right.' He switched off and ambled back to Dar. 'Well, well, my boy, seems you've attracted notice.'

Dar's mouth went dry. 'What'd I do now?'

'Nothin', it seems, except maybe a good job. He says it's not what you have done, but what you *will* do, if you follow me.'

'I don't.'

'Neither do I. But that's what he said, and if you've any hopes of our scheme working out, I think ye'd best get over there. Hop to it now, Dar! Lick-split!'

Dar hopped.

'Yes, I really must thank you,' Bhelabher agreed. 'Seeing the way this colony's been organized has been a revelation to me.'

'My thanks,' Shacklar murmured. 'Still, it's scarcely in the same category as changing wine into water.'

'It certainly seems not far less.' Bhelabher beamed at Dar with owlish enthusiasm. 'Do you realize what this man has managed to induce here? Hope! Optimism! An atmosphere of opportunity! A growing, progressing society!'

'Well, yes, I had sort of realized something of the sort.' Dar wondered if he was missing something. 'And it sure is darn near a miracle, compared to the ball-and-chain world this place was when I came.'

'Compared to Terra! To the Proxima Centauri Electorate! To any of the Central Worlds! Do you *realize* what a paradise this is?'

Dar stared. 'You *like* outdoor plumbing?'

'I'll take it any day over the spiritual septic tank the Central Worlds have become! We've become stratified there, young man, stratified! Do you know what that means?'

'Uh-h-h-h . . .' Dar rewound his memories to a conversation with Cholly, six years ago, about the nature of tyranny. 'Yeah. It means you're either a subject or a ruler, and there's no way to change it.'

Bhelabher looked startled for a moment; then he nodded. 'Well put, well put!' He turned to Shacklar. 'Isn't it amazing how the simpler way of stating something so often catches the essence of it?' He turned back to Dar. 'But you're quite right, young man, quite right – no one can move up. So the vast majority live out their lives in dull, repetitive desk jobs, with only 3DT, euphorics, and cabaret passes for pleasures.'

'Sounds wonderful,' Dar sighed. 'When do I get a chance to be bored?'

'I'm sure any of our Terran slaves would be delighted to trade places with you if they really had the slightest inkling of what you have here. And our "fortunate few" would be even more eager – they can have anything they want, but find nothing worth having. Still, they're convinced there must be *some* job worth having – so they spend their lives in pursuit of some meaning in pleasure.'

'I'll find it.' Dar raised a hand. 'Won't take me long, either.'

'I'm sure you would. The pleasures of the senses only seem to have meaning when they're rare. So our poor privileged ones never *can* find the purpose they're seeking – but they keep looking for it.'

Dar frowned. 'Are you trying to tell me that the only real difference between the classes and the masses is that the classes' desperation is noisy, and the masses' desperation is quiet?'

'No, I'm trying to tell you that the only difference that matters is between them and yourself – or, more accurately between Terra and Wolmar. Here, a mere private has as good a chance as the General of getting whatever pleasures *are* available – that is, if he earns his points and saves his credits.'

Dar nodded. 'I do. And now that you mention it, we all do have pretty much the same, ah, forms of recreation . . .'

Shacklar nodded. 'The advantage of having very few pleasures.'

'And Cholly and the General, between them, keep opening up more upper-level jobs, such as – ' Dar swallowed, ' – trading.'

'The advantage of an expanding economy.' Shacklar leaned back, locking his fingers across his chest. 'Fortunately for us, the Wolmen had a very unsophisticated technology.'

'True, you found all the elements here when you came,' Bhelabher admitted. 'But you also had the wisdom and ability to combine them!' Bhelabher's smile saddened. 'Such traits are rare. I, for example, lack both.'

'You're wise to realize your limitations.' Shacklar picked up a data cube and rolled it between his fingers. 'But I wonder – do you have as sure a grasp of your strengths?'

'Oh, I think that I do.' Bhelabher fairly beamed. 'That cube you're playing with, now – give me a million of them, and the tools of my trade, and I'll set them up for you so that I can have any of their septillions of bits for you within thirty seconds of your asking for it.'

Dar developed a faraway look. 'General, excuse me – we have the complete military personnel records on cube, don't we?'

'Not for personal use,' Shacklar said dryly. 'And I'm sure the Honourable Bhelabher understands the importance of confidentiality.'

'That's what I was hoping. . . .'

'I don't think you appreciate how great a benefit the computer can be, for all humankind.'

Bhelabher nodded. 'Quite true, really. If the sum total of human knowledge holds the answer to a question, the computer will find it for you.'

'Quite enviable, really.' Shacklar toyed with the cube again. 'Myself, I have no ability to organize data. I have to keep everything in my head – and it goes without saying that, far too often, I fail to find the solution, because the one vital bit of information is *not* in my head.'

'Well, that won't happen again.' Bhelabher's eyes gleamed. 'I'll revamp your data banks so that you'll be amazed at the myriads of facts that you didn't know were there.'

Dar stiffened. That had an unpleasantly definite ring to it.

Bhelabher turned to him, beaming, to confirm it. 'The General has accepted my application, you see. I'm going to stay here on Wolmar, and set up an information storage-and-retrieval system.'

'And streamline our bureaucracy a bit,' Shacklar added. 'You'd be amazed at all the points of inefficiency he's noticed already. The Honourable Bhelabher has been gracious enough to place his considerable talents at our disposal.'

'And gracious of you it is to say so.' Bhelabher gave Shacklar a polite nod that bordered on a bow.

Privately, Dar shuddered, and wished he *weren't* going to be staying. He had an idea that living under Bhelabher's streamlining wasn't going to be much fun.

But then, he'd figured without Shacklar's restraining influence. Certainly the General had worked wonders in the Honourable already.

'But I do realize that I'm not the man for any more of a job than that here,' Bhelabher explained to Dar. 'So I'm sending my resignation back to Terra.'

Dar's eyes widened. It was too good to be true. Even if it *was* sort of what Cholly had figured would happen . . .

'And my staff will be staying here with me,' Bhelabher went on. 'The General assures me they're needed.'

That, Dar could believe. Most of Bhelabher's staff were female.

'This, however, leaves me without someone to carry my resignation back to Terra,' Bhelabher noted.

Dar suddenly felt very wary.

'Would you like to see Terra, Ardnam?' Shacklar murmured.

Dar held onto his chair while the blood roared in his ears and the world seemed to grow insubstantial. Escape! And to Terra!

'I'm afraid you must decide rather quickly,' Shacklar went on. 'The courier ship that brought the Honourable is scheduled to blast out of orbit in three hours, bound for the colonial branch government on Haldane IV. From there, you'll have to arrange transportation to Terra, and I don't doubt it'll take quite a few transfers. There's very little direct traffic to or from the Central Worlds.'

Dar's mouth went dry. 'Don't get me wrong, I'd love to do it – but I don't have much experience at that kind of travelling.'

'No, nor do you know how to work your way through the web of the IDE bureaucracy on Terra – but I understand there's a young lady, just in from the home planet, who's been in your company lately . . .'

'Sam Bine,' Dar croaked.

'Yes, a Ms Bine. I know it's beastly to ask her to leave so soon after she's arrived; but, in view of the importance of the matter . . .'

'She was just leaving, anyway.' Better and better! Escape to Terra, and with a female travelling companion! 'Or should I say, I think I can talk her into it.'

'Please do.' Shacklar picked up a pen and made a note. 'With luck, the two of you might reach BOA about the same time as my request for clarification of the Honourable Bhelabher's credentials.'

'You could cancel that, you know,' Bhelabher pointed out.

Shacklar looked up, his face a total blank. Then the light slowly dawned. 'Do you know, I believe you're right.'

'You see?' Bhelabher beamed at Dar. 'There's so much I can *do* here!'

'True,' Dar agreed – but he wondered how long Shacklar could keep up such high-quality acting.

Long enough for Bhelabher's resignation to reach Terra, at least.

'You'll have an official pardon, of course,' Shacklar added.

'I'll do it! But, uh – just one question. . . .'

'Yes?' Shacklar blinked mildly.

'Why'll it be so hard to find the right person in the BOA bureaucracy to give your resignation to?'

'Because,' said Bhelabher, 'my appointment to Wolmar was a very highly classified secret.'

Dar managed not to look startled.

## 6

'But if it was such a deep dark secret, how did you find out about it?' Dar demanded.

Sam's lips thinned. 'Oh, all right! If you really have to know – I was a clerk in the classified division, with a top-level security clearance.'

'Oh.' Dar's lower lip thrust out as he nodded slowly. 'Yeah, that makes sense. Weren't your bosses a little, ah, taken aback, when you resigned?'

'Very,' Sam said grimly, 'especially when they found out I'd turned into a Hume. I had a very difficult time getting a passport.'

'How *did* you manage it?'

Sam shrugged. 'Very involved. Let's just say I know how to handle a bureaucracy.'

'Uh, yeah, I don't think I really want to know the details.' Dar pressed a hand over his eyes. 'But you did get away. That's what counts.'

'Not all that much,' Sam answered with a grim smile. 'There was a commercial traveller outbound from Terra on the same liner I was on, and he made every transfer I did, up until the last leg from Haldane IV to here.'

'Agent, following you?' Cholly grunted.

Sam nodded, and held out her glass for a refill. 'You sound as though you recognize the symptoms.'

'In a manner of speaking.' Cholly poured. 'Now, I'm certain it's just my nasty, suspicious mind, but – I do believe that nice young blond man from Bhelabher's staff's been keeping an eye on you.'

'Just my glamour and magnetic personality, I'm sure,' Sam said dryly. 'I've noticed him, too. In fact, I'd've had to've been blind not to.'

'Well, every secret agent has to learn his trade sometime.'

'I know a way to ditch him,' Dar ventured.

'So do I,' she said sourly. 'Leave Wolmar.'

Dar stared. 'How'd you know?'

Sam's head lifted. 'You mean you were seriously going to recommend that? What's the matter, am I getting to be an embarrassment?'

'No, no, just the other way around!' Dar said quickly. 'You see, I've got this great offer to leave, but I have to take somebody with me who knows the ropes in the Terran bureaucracy.'

The silence stretched out while Sam's lower lip slowly protruded. 'So. They made you an offer you couldn't refuse.'

'Well, I wouldn't say *couldn't* – but I wasn't about to. How about it?'

Sam frowned. 'The idea's got its appeal – I've learned what I wanted to here. But this place has a lot of advantages over Terra, if you know what I mean.'

'No,' Dar said promptly. 'I can't imagine how *any* place could have an advantage over Terra – especially a backwater like this.'

Cholly turned away to put glasses back on shelves, whistling tunelessly between his teeth.

'Don't worry,' Sam said bitterly, 'you will. And, although I wouldn't mind a return visit to Terra, I have a notion I'd very quickly find myself looking back to this place with nostalgia. How do I get back here if I want to? It took me ten years of saving, just to get the fare out here in the first place.'

'Well, I think Shacklar might be induced to guarantee your return fare,' Dar said judiciously. 'He seemed awfully anxious to get me to leave.'

'Sheriff trouble?'

'No, no! I'm taking Bhelabher's resignation back to Terra!'

Cholly dropped a glass and spun around. 'That's all I need to hear. You're going. An' so're you.' He aimed a finger at Sam. 'Can't leave this poor, innocent lamb to the mercy of them Terran wolves. *I'll* guarantee yer return fare, if it comes to it.'

'Done!' Sam slapped the bar. 'I'm off on the road back to Terra! But why can't Bhelabher take it back himself?'

'Because he's staying here.'

Cholly dropped another glass.

'Oh.' Sam chewed that one over. 'How about his staff?'

'They're staying too. Seems we'll be needing 'em.'

'No, don't tell me – you're cutting into me glassware.' Cholly held up a hand. 'Shacklar's giving 'em all jobs.'

Dar nodded. 'Bhelabher's going to revise the filing system and streamline the bureaucracy.'

'Well, there goes private enterprise,' Cholly sighed.

'No, Bhelabher's not that bad,' Sam said judiciously. 'He did a fine job as long as he was only in charge of the records for Terra.

It was when they put him in charge of the records for the whole IDE that he ran into trouble.'

'Oh?' Cholly looked up, with a glimmer of hope. 'He had the ability, but couldn't handle responsibility, heh?'

Sam nodded. 'Something like that. As long as he was able to take orders, he was fine. It was being top man that stymied him.'

'Better'n better.' Cholly nodded. 'Then no doubt he'll take Shacklar's orders to leave some glitches in the bureaucracy.'

Sam frowned. 'Why?'

'It makes for flexibility, lass. If the bureaucracy's too efficient, it gives the central government too much power, and they control every aspect of life. But a little inefficiency . . . now, that leaves some room for a man to beat the system . . . Well! You'll only have one problem, then, Dar.'

Dar looked up, startled. 'What's that?'

'Shacklar thinks you're Ardnam Rod now, and all yer papers'll be made out to him.'

'Oh.' Dar pursed his lips. 'That will be a problem, won't it?'

'But not much of one.' Sam patted his arm reassuringly. 'Trust your travelling bureaucrat.'

Dar frowned. 'Where's *he* going?'

'Who?' Sam pressed up to the window, craning her neck. 'That guy in the coverall, going over to the control shed?'

'Yeah – he's the pilot! Who's going to fly the ferry up to the courier ship?'

Sam shrugged. 'His relief, I suppose. No doubt he's taking a planet-side leave.'

'He's just had a week's worth – or, no, I can't really say that, can I?'

'Right. For all you know, he's run daily missions since Bhelabher came in.'

'But I didn't know we had a relief pilot down here.'

'Is it your job to know the duty roster?'

Dar turned to her. 'You know, as a travelling companion, you might get to be a bit difficult.'

Sam shrugged. 'You're free to choose any other BOA clerk you can find here.'

'Well, I suppose I could talk to one of Bhelabher's people.' Dar turned back to the window. 'But somehow, I think you'd be a little more . . .'

'Dependable, I assure you,' murmured an approaching voice.

Dar stiffened. 'Company.'

'. . . Oh, I have no doubt of that,' Bhelabher was saying hurriedly. 'But the situation is not. I am concerned that our courier might be delayed.'

Dar and Sam turned around slowly as Bhelabher and Shacklar came toward them. 'I suggest you have a word with him yourself, and warn him of the pitfalls of the journey.' Shacklar looked up. 'Well, Ardnam! This will be *bon voyage*, then.' He clasped Dar's hand tightly and gave it a shake. 'You've been a credit to my command here, young man. I'll be sorry to lose you – but do remember how great a service you'll be performing, for all of us who remain here on Wolmar.'

'It's a pleasure to do my duty, sir.' Dar took Shacklar's commendation with a grain of salt, since 'Ardnam' had only been under Shacklar's command for a week.

Shacklar released his hand and stepped back. 'I believe the Honourable has a word for you, too.' Bhelabher pressed in, and Shacklar turned away to Sam.

'Be careful, young man, do be careful,' Bhelabher said loudly, drawing Dar further away from Shacklar and Sam. He dropped his voice to a low rumble. 'Now, I hadn't wanted to mention this to the General; after all, there's no need to worry him with something over which he has no control.'

Dar instantly felt a need to worry. 'Uh . . . such as?'

'When I was back on Terra, and in an office of some influence, some members of the LORDS party approached me – you know of them?'

'Uh, yeah.' Dar wet his lips. 'They're the arch-conservatives in the assembly, aren't they?'

'I wouldn't have used the "arch" a week ago. I do now, though.' Bhelabher shook his head in wonder. 'What an amazing planet this is!'

'About the LORDS,' Dar prompted.

'Indeed. They approached me, to see if I would be interested in joining in a scheme to overthrow the Secretary-General and establish a temporary LORDS junta, to govern while the IDE government could be restructured along more efficient lines.'

Dar stood rigid, feeling like a resistor in a high-voltage circuit. 'You're . . . talking about a dictatorship.'

'Certainly; it's the most efficient form of government there is!'

'Oh, sure.' Dar passed a dry tongue over drier lips. 'Of course it's efficient. It just wipes out all those silly time-wasters – you know, parliamentary debate, public input, elections, trial by jury. All those silly, inefficient boondoggles.'

'Indeed it does. And as an administrator, I can assure you – they *do* take a great deal of time. They also encumber an amazing number of people, keeping them from tasks in production.'

Dar nodded sardonically. 'And all you get for all that time and trouble are little, unnecessary luxuries, such as liberty and justice.'

'Make no mistake; they are luxuries.' Bhelabher smiled with sudden, amazing warmth. 'But they seem much more important out here, where they help people to actually *do* something!'

'Kind of makes up for the cost?'

'Well worth it, well worth it! In fact, I've a suspicion liberty is actually cost-efficient, in a growing society.'

'But you couldn't prove it, to the LORDS?'

Bhelabher smiled sadly. 'Would they even listen?'

'I'd think so,' Dar frowned. 'Even a conservative can have an open mind.'

'Not if he's in power. Efficiency matters far more to those who give orders than to those who take them.' Bhelabher held up a forefinger. 'Take the Minister of the Exchequer, now – his purpose is to keep the economy of the whole IDE family of planets as high as possible.'

'Uh, with respect, Honourable – isn't the correct word "profitable"?'

'No, it certainly isn't – but the Minister very quickly comes to believe that it is. Consequently, he tends to frown on anything that costs more than it makes.'

Dar frowned. 'Such as?'

'Such as trade to the outlying planets – for example, Wolmar.'

'Now, hold on!' Dar was amazed to realize he was getting angry; he fought down his temper, and went on. 'We always ship out a lot of pipeweed.'

'Indeed you do – but I've seen the trade reports, and the goods IDE sends to you cost far more than your pipeweed brings – not even counting the shipping cost. No, IDE shows a definite loss on you.'

'Well, you'll pardon me if I think we're worth it!'

'Of course – more than worth it. But how do you explain that to the Minister of the Exchequer?'

'Hm.' Dar frowned. 'I see the problem. And there're a lot of planets like ours, aren't there?'

'Upwards of thirty.' Bhelabher nodded. 'Thirty frontier worlds, and the Minister shows a loss for each of them – thirty or forty billion BTUs apiece. It adds up to a very substantial drain on the economy.'

'It'll pay off, though – someday!' Dar's temper kindled again. 'Give us time, and we'll be sending out more than we bring in!' A sudden thought nudged Dar's brain. He cocked his head to the side, gazing at Bhelabher through slitted eyes. 'It's no accident that you mentioned the Minister of the Exchequer, is it?'

Bhelabher stared at him in surprise. Then he smiled sheepishly. 'Indeed it's not. Yes, the Exchequer was the LORD who came to call on me. And his argument was very persuasive – very persuasive, indeed! And once he had me believing that the outlying planets *should* be cut off and left to their own devices, he arranged my appointment as governor.'

'So . . . that's . . . why!' Then another sudden hunch hit, and Dar frowned. 'You wouldn't be telling me this if you didn't think I could do something about it.'

'I don't know if you can or not,' Bhelabher said earnestly, 'but you must try. It isn't easy to gain an appointment with the Secretary-General, young man, but if you can, you must tell him that Electors Boundbridge and Satrap are leaguing with General Forcemain to attempt a *coup d'état*. Can you remember those names?'

'Boundbridge, Satrap, and Forcemain.' Dar nodded, repeating them silently in his head, getting the metre down. 'Boundbridge, Satrap, and Forcemain . . . yeah, I'll remember. But this is the top man in all of human civilization we're talking about, Honourable. He's not going to believe the ordinary young punk off the street without some pretty powerful evidence!'

'He shall have it.' Bhelabher pressed a slip of paper into Dar's hand. 'Memorize that set of numbers, young man, and when you've done so, burn the paper. The Secretary-General has only to put them into the nearest computer terminal, and the screen will display an excellent little collection of documents, complete with signatures.'

Dar stared at the slip of paper. 'But . . . but how did you. . .?'

'Find them?' Bhelabher smiled. 'I do give myself some credit, young man; and I know that I am an expert on data storage and retrieval. When I'd spoken with Minister Boundbridge, I was thoroughly convinced; but my bureaucrat's instincts still functioned, almost by themselves. I was determined to aid the

LORDS' coup; but I was also determined that I would not be made a scapegoat if anything went wrong.'

Dar's eyes widened. 'My lord! Is human trust *that* far gone on Terra?'

Bhelabher waved the objection away, irritated. 'It has been for centuries, young man – probably ever since the Chinese invented bureaucracy. One of the first rules you learn in an office is, "Get the directive in writing – and keep a copy." And if I knew that, certainly Satrap and Forcemain did, too, plus whomever else was involved in the conspiracy. I knew they'd each have saved their own bits of evidence.'

'But how could you find it?'

Bhelabher smiled, preening. 'People don't hide things in chests with false bottoms, or secret rooms, anymore, young man. They hide them in computers, with secret activation codes. But whatever code one man can think up, another can deduce – especially if he has his own computer to do the donkey-work of searching. I *am* an expert, after all – and I did have some time.'

Dar stared. 'You mean you actually managed to break each of their personal codes?'

'Only Satrap's and Boundbridge's; General Forcemain held his inside the military computer, which is somewhat better protected against even expert pilfering. But the Electors' dossiers sufficed – especially since they directed me to several others. No, young man, that code I've given you will reveal enough documented evidence to convince even the Secretary-General.'

The slip of paper suddenly seemed to burn Dar's fingers. He held onto it resolutely, the numbers fairly searing his retinas. 'Somehow I don't think I'll have any trouble remembering these numbers now, Honourable.'

'Stout fellow!' Bhelabher clasped his arm and pumped his hand. 'I'll be eternally indebted to you – and so will quadrillions of other persons, most of whom have not even been born yet!'

'I'll collect when they've grown, and the interest has, too.' Dar forced a smile. 'Don't worry, Honourable – I'll do my best.'

'More than that, no man can ask.' Bhelabher looked up. 'Except possibly your commander; I see he wants another word with you.' He stepped aside, and Shacklar stepped up. 'It's about time to depart, Ardnam.'

A high-pitched whine hit their ears as the ferry's coolant pumps started up. Sam pushed her way through the door and strode over to the small ship.

'Allow me to escort you,' Shacklar murmured, taking Dar by the elbow and steering him out of the door.

Once outside, he raised his voice to be heard over the beginning rumbles of superheated steam. 'You do realize the importance of the mission you're undertaking?'

'Yeah, to make sure BOA leaves us alone,' Dar called back. 'Uh, General . . .'

Shacklar gave him an inquiring blink.

'The Honourable just told me about a coup the LORDS're planning, back on Terra. Think I should take him seriously?'

'Oh, very seriously. I've been sure it would happen for quite some time now.'

Dar whirled to stare at him, appalled. 'You *knew*?'

'Well, not "knew", really. I can't tell you the date of its beginning, nor who will be behind it – but I do see the general shape of it. Any man who's read a bit of history can see it coming. On the inner worlds, it's all about you, the signs of a dying democracy. I'd been watching it happen for twenty years, before I came out here.'

'And that's *why* you came out here?'

Shacklar nodded, pleased. 'You're perceptive, young fellow. Yes. If democracy is doomed on the interstellar scale, it can at least be kept alive on individual planets.'

'Especially one that's far enough away from Terra so that whatever dictatorship replaces the IDE will just forget about it,' Dar inferred.

Shacklar nodded again. 'Because it's too costly to maintain communication with it. Yes. By the end of the century, I expect we'll be left quite thoroughly to our own devices.'

'Not a pleasant picture,' Dar said, brooding, 'but better than being ruled by a dictator on Terra. So what should I do about it?'

'Do?' Shacklar repeated, surprised. 'Why, there's nothing you *can* do, really – except to make the quixotic gesture: inform the media, if you like, or the Secretary-General, or something of the sort.'

'You can't mean it,' Dar said, shocked. 'We can't let democracy go down without a fight!'

'But it already *has* gone down, don't you see? And all you can gain by a dramatic flourish is, perhaps, another decade or so of life for the forms of it – the Assembly, and the Cabinet, and so forth. But that won't change the reality – that the frontier worlds have already begun to govern themselves, and that Terra and the other

Central Worlds are already living under a dictatorship, for all practical purposes. Ask anyone who's lived there, if you doubt me.'

Dar thought of Sam's disgust and despair, and saw Shacklar's point. 'Are you saying democracy isn't worth fighting for?'

'Not at all – but I am saying that all such fighting will get you is a lifelong prison sentence in a real, Terrestrial prison, perhaps for a very short life. The press of social forces is simply too great for anyone to stop. If you really want to do something, try to change those social forces.'

Dar frowned. 'How can you do that?'

Shacklar shrugged. 'Invent faster-than-light radio, or a way of educating the vast majority to scepticism and inquiring thought – but don't expect to see the effects of it within your lifetime. You can start it – but it'll take a century or two before it begins to have an effect.'

'Well, that's great for my grandchildren – but what do I do about the rest of my life?'

Shacklar sighed. 'Try to find a nice, quiet little out-of-the-way planet that the new dictators are apt to overlook, and do your best to make it a pocket of freedom for the next few centuries, and live out your life there in whatever tranquillity you can manage.'

'Which is what you've done,' Dar said softly.

Shacklar flashed him a smile. 'Well, it's still in process, of course.'

'It always will be, for the rest of your life. Which is how you're going to maintain your illusion of meaning in your life.'

'Quite so,' Shacklar said, grinning, 'and can you be certain it *is* an illusion?'

'Not at all,' Dar breathed. 'If I could, it wouldn't work. But that line of thought is supposed to induce despair.'

'Only if you take it as proof that there is no purpose in life – which your mind may believe, but your heart won't. Not once you're actually involved in it. It's a matter of making unprovability work *for* you, you see.'

'I think I begin to.' Dar gave his head a quick shake. 'Dunno if I'm up to making that little "pocket of freedom", though.'

'You'll always be welcome back here, of course,' Shacklar murmured.

'Two minutes till lift-off,' declared a brazen voice from the ship.

'You'd better run.' Shacklar pressed a thick envelope into Dar's hand. 'You'll find all the credentials you'll need in there, including a draft on the Bank of Wolmar for two first-class, round-trip fares from Wolmar to Terra.' He slapped Dar on the shoulder. 'Good luck, and remember – don't be a hero.'

Dar started to ask what he meant, but Shacklar was already turning away, and the ship rumbled threateningly deep in its belly, so Dar had to turn and run.

'Took you long enough,' Sam groused as he dropped into the acceleration couch beside her and stretched the shock webbing across his body. 'What was that high-level conference all about?'

'About why I should flow with the social tide.'

'Hm.' Sam pursed her lips, and nodded slowly. 'Quite a man, your General.'

'Yeah. I really feel badly about deceiving him.' Dar rolled back the envelope flap.

'What's that?' Sam demanded.

Dar didn't answer. He was too busy staring.

'Hi, there!' Sam waved. 'Remember me? What *have* you got there?'

'My credentials,' Dar said slowly.

'What's the matter? Aren't they in order?'

'Very. They're all for "Dar Mandra".'

'Oh.' Sam sat quietly for a few minutes, digesting that.

Then she sighed and leaned back in her couch. 'Well. Your General . . . perceptive, too, huh?'


# 7


The courier ship had room for ten passengers. Dar and Sam were the only ones. After five days, they'd both tried all ten seats at least twice.

'No, really, I do think it looks better from back here,' Dar said from the seat just in front of the aft bulkhead. 'You get more of a feeling of depth – and it's definitely more aesthetic to feel the force of acceleration on your back.'

'*What* force of acceleration? This ship could be in free-fall for all we feel. Built-in acceleration compensators, remember? This cabin's got its own gravity unit.'

'Luxury craft,' Dar griped, 'absolutely destroys all sense of motion.'

'Which makes it far more aesthetic to sit in the middle of the cabin,' Sam opined. 'You get the sense of the environment this way.' She spread her arms. 'The feeling of *space* – limited, but space. You're immersed in it.'

'Yeah, but who wants to be immersed in moulded-plastic seats and creon upholstery?'

'If your accommodations bother you, sir . . .'

Dar looked up at the stewardess in annoyance. 'I know: I don't have any choice about it.'

'Not at all, sir. I can offer you a variety of other realms of reality.' The stewardess's chest slid open, revealing several shelves crammed with pill bottles. 'All guaranteed to make you forget where you are, sir, and make the time fly.'

'And my brain with it. No, thank you – I'll stick with the old-fashioned narcotics.'

A plastic tumbler rammed into his palm; the stewardess's finger turned into a spigot, and splashed amber-coloured fluid and crushed ice into his tumbler. 'One old-fashioned, sir.'

'I had in mind a martini,' Dar grumbled. 'But thanks, anyway.'

'It is unnecessary to thank me, sir. I am merely—'

'A machine, yes. But it keeps me from getting into bad habits. When do we get to Haldane IV?'

'That's got to be the twelfth time you've asked that question,' Sam sighed, 'and I told you as soon as we'd boarded – Bhelabher said it'd take us five days!'

'I know, I know,' Dar griped, 'but I like to hear *her* say it. When do we get to Haldane IV, stewardess?'

'Experienced space travellers never ask "when", sir,' the stewardess answered, a bit primly.

'I love the programmed response.' Dar leaned back, grinning.

'Look at it this way – it's a faster trip than I had on the way out,' Sam offered. 'That took a week and a half.'

'I believe the ship transporting you on the outbound swing was a common freighter, sir . . .'

'Miz!'

'Oh, really? But I believe you'll find that an IDE courier ship is a bit faster than your earlier conveyance. In fact, we're approaching breakout now. Stretch webbing, please.' And the stewardess rolled into her closet, clicking the door shut behind her.

'Talk about bad habits!' Sam snorted. 'Or didn't you realize you were making fun of her?'

'I know, I know,' Dar growled. 'But I have definitely taken a dislike to that machine.'

'Programmed by a snob,' Sam agreed. 'Come on, we'd better get ready.'

'Approaching breakout,' the resonant PA ship's voice informed them.

'I don't know why we bother.' Dar stretched his shock webbing across his body. 'What could happen when you break out of H-space, anyway?'

'Y'know, you're getting to be a pretty surly bird.'

'So, I'll get a worm. You've got to admit, there isn't even a jar when you break out into normal space.'

'Not unless they've got you bottled up.'

Dar frowned. 'What's that supposed to mean?'

Sam sighed. 'It's a holdover from the pre-IDE days, when there wasn't any central government and things were pretty chaotic outside the Sol system. Pirates used to lie in wait for ships at the breakout points. They couldn't touch a freighter while it was in H-space, but they *could* jump it as soon as it broke out.'

'Oh.' Dar felt a slight chill of apprehension. 'Uh – the central government isn't too effective, these days. . . .'

'Breaking out,' the ship's voice informed them. 'We will be without interior power for a few seconds.'

The lights went out as all the ship's power was channelled into the isomorpher, translating them back into normal space. A surge of dizziness washed over Dar, and objective reality became a little subjective for a second or two – in fact, it seemed to go away altogether. Then it came back, and the lights came on again. Dar blinked and turned his head from side to side, to see if it still worked. 'On second thought, maybe the webbing isn't such a bad idea.'

'Please maintain your position,' the ship's voice advised. 'There is an unidentified craft in pursuit.'

Dar looked over at Sam. 'What were you saying about pirates?'

'Not in this day and age, certainly.' But she looked a little pale.

'I think they said something like that in the early 1800s, to a man named Jean Laffite.' Dar turned to stare out of the porthole. 'You know, you can actually see something out there now.'

'Of course – stars. We're back in normal space, remember? So what did he answer?'

'That one's got a discernible disk; must be Haldane. . . . Who?'

'This Jean Laffite.'

'Oh – "Stand and deliver."' Dar peered through the porthole. 'There was more; I forget the exact wording, but it had something to do with the ownership of a place called "the Caribbean . . ." Wow!'

An orange glare lit up the cabin.

'That was *close*!' Sam said through the afterimages.

'I think that's what they used to call a "shot across the bow".'

'This is *serious*!' Sam yelped. 'Where's the Navy when you need it?'

'Ask the pirates – I'm sure they know.'

'So do I; I got one of the Navy data operators drunk one night, just before I quit, and got the access code out of him.'

Dar frowned. 'Why'd you do that?'

'I wanted to make sure I was going to be safe on my trip out here. And I found out I would be; there wasn't supposed to be a sailor for fifty parsecs. The nearest fleet's a hundred and seventy-five light-years away, over toward Aldebaran, sitting on their thumbs and polishing the brightwork.'

'What're they doing there?'

'Somebody called 'em, about a year ago, to come take care of some pirates.'

'So, while they were on their way out, the pirates were coming back here! Great!' Dar said.

Sam took a deep breath. 'Now, wait a minute. Wait a minute. We're getting carried away here. For all we know, those aren't pirates out there.'

'Sure, maybe it *is* the Navy – and for all *they* know, *we're* pirates. If you'll pardon my saying so . . .'

A brilliant flare lit up the cabin. Sam shrieked. 'I'm convinced! It's pirates!'

Dar shrugged. 'Pirates or Navy – after we've been turned into an expanding cloud of hydrogen atoms, I'm afraid I won't really care much about distinctions.'

'You're right.' Sam loosed her shock webbing. 'Whoever it is, we've gotta get out of here.'

Dar's head snapped up, startled. Then he waved an airy hand toward the porthole. 'Sure – be my guest. It's a great day outside, if you face sunwards. Of course, the night on your backside gets a teeny bit chilly.'

'Credit me with *some* sense,' she snorted. 'This ship *must* have some kind of lifeboat!'

But Dar was looking out of the porthole. 'Get down!'

Startled, Sam obeyed. A rending crash shot through the ship, and she slammed back against the cabin wall. Dar bounced out against his webbing.

'What in Ceres' name was *that*?' Sam gasped.

'They got tired of playing games.' Dar yanked his webbing loose and struggled to his feet, bracing himself against the pull of acceleration. 'They shot to maim this time, and they had some luck. They got our gravity generator. Where'd you say the lifeboat was?'

'It'd make sense to put it between the pilot's bridge and the passenger cabin, wouldn't it?'

'Right.' Dar turned aft. 'Since that makes sense, it'll obviously be between the cabin and the cargo space. Let's go.'

Sam started to protest, then shut up and followed.

The ship bucked and heaved. Dar caught the tops of the seats on either side, bracing himself. Sam slammed into his back. 'Near miss,' he grated. 'We got hit by a wave of exploding gas. Wish I had time to watch; this pilot's doing one hell of a job of dodging.'

'Is that why my body keeps trying to go through the wall?'

'Yeah, and why it keeps changing its mind as to which wall. Come on.'

They wallowed through a morass of acceleration-pull to the aft hatch. Dar turned to a small closet beside the hatch, and yanked it open. 'Two on this side; there'll be three on the other side, I suppose.' He took down a slack length of silver fabric with a plastic bulb on top. 'Here, scramble into it.'

Sam started struggling into the space suit. 'Little flimsy, isn't it?'

Dar nodded. 'It won't stop anything sharper than a cheese wedge. It's not supposed to; the lifeboat'll take care of that. The suit's just to hold in air.'

The ship bucked to the side with a rending crash, slamming Sam up against him. Jumpsuit or not, he realized dizzily, she was *very* definitely female. Somehow, this didn't seem like the time to mention it.

She scrambled back from him, and kept on scrambling, into her suit. 'They're getting closer! *Hurry!*'

Dar stretched the suit on and pressed the seal-seam shut, being careful to keep it flat. Sam copied him. Then he braced himself and touched his helmet against hers, to let his voice conduct through the plastic. 'Okay, turn around so I can turn on your air supply and check your connections.'

Sam turned her back to him. Dar checked her connections, then turned on her air supply. When the meter read in the blue, he tapped her shoulder and turned his back. He could feel her hands fumbling over him; then air hissed in his helmet. He took a breath and nodded, then turned to the hatch, wrenched it open, and waved Sam in. She stepped through; he followed, and pulled the door closed behind them, wrenching it down. Sam had already pushed the cycle button. When the air had been pumped back into the reserve tank, the green light lit up over the side hatch. Dar leaned on the handle and hauled back; the three-foot circle swung open. Sam stepped through, and Dar stepped after her.

He sat down, stretching the web over his body. Sam leaned over to touch helmets. 'How about the pilot?'

'He's on his own – got his own lifeboat if he wants it.' Dar punched the power button, and the control panel lit up.

'You know how to drive this thing?'

'Sure; besides, how can you go wrong, with two buttons, two pedals, and a steering wheel?'

'I could think of a few ways.'

Dar shrugged. 'So I'm not creative. Here goes.' The READY light was blinking; he stabbed at the EJECT button.

A five-hundred-pound masseur slammed him in the chest, and went to work on the rest of his body. Then the steamroller lightened to a flatiron, and Dar could breathe again. He sat up against the push of slackening acceleration and looked around through the bubble-dome. It had darkened to his right, where a sun was close enough to show a small disk and kick out some lethal radiation. But that didn't matter; the silver slab of pirate ship filled most of the starboard sky. 'Way too close,' Dar muttered, and pressed down on the acceleration pedal. The flatiron pressed down on him again, expanding into a printing press. He glanced behind him, once at the silver-baseball courier ship, then turned back to the emptiness before him.

Sam struggled forward against the pull of acceleration. 'Any chance they haven't spotted us?'

Dar shrugged. 'Hard to say. We'll show up on their detectors; but they might not pay attention to anything this small.'

Then the silver slab began to slide toward them.

'Do they have to be so damn observant?' Dar adjusted his chair upright and stamped down on the acceleration pedal. The masseur dumped the steamroller on him again, shoving him back into the chair; he could just barely stretch his arms enough to hold onto the wheel.

The silver slab picked up speed.

'Somehow, I don't think we can outrun them.' Dar turned the wheel left; the port-attitude jets slackened, then died, as the starboard jets boosted their mutter to a roar, and the lifeboat turned in a graceful U, throwing Dar over against Sam. She sat huddled back in her chair, face pale, eyes huge.

No wonder, Dar thought. He'd feel the same way if he were a passenger in a boat he was driving. He straightened out the wheel and held the pedal down, sending the little ship arrowing back toward the courier ship, which was taking advantage of the pirates' preoccupation to try to sneak away.

Sam struggled forward, adjusting her chair upright, and laid her helmet against his. 'Shouldn't we be going *away* from them?'

Dar shook his head. 'They'd have about as much trouble catching us as a lean cat would have with a fat mouse. Our only chance is to hide.'

'Hide? Behind *what*? There's nothing out here!'

A bright red energy-bolt exploded just behind them and a little to their right.

'YEOW!' Sam shrank down inside her suit. 'Hide behind *something*! Fast!'

'As fast as I can.' Dar threw the wheel hard over. Sam slammed hard against his side.

'What're you *doing*?'

'Evasive action. They might get smart and hook that cannon up to a ballistic computer.' And Dar proceeded to lay a course that would have given a triple-jointed snake double lumbago. They rattled around inside the lifeboat like dice in a cup.

'We're winning,' Dar grated. 'We've got it confused.'

A fireball exploded right under their tail.

'YEOW! Learns fast, doesn't it?' Dar tromped hard on the accelerator and pushed on the wheel. They dived, and a great gleaming curve slid by overhead. Then they were out, with open space before them. Dar pressed down on the deceleration pedal, and threw himself and Sam forward against their webbing.

Her helmet cracked against his. 'Why don't you keep on running?'

' 'Cause they'd catch us.' Dar turned the boat, sent it racing back toward the silver sphere and the slab that loomed over it like a tombstone.

Sam stiffened in her seat. 'Don't ram it!'

'No fear.'

Blue sparks spattered up all around the courier. 'I think they just mistook it for us.' Then Dar pushed on the wheel again. The lifeboat dived, and the bottom of the silver sphere swam by overhead again.

'*Why*?' Sam fairly shrieked.

'Because.'

The little ship spat out from under the courier, darting across the gap toward the silver slab.

Sam took a deep breath. 'Correct me if I'm wrong – but aren't we supposed to be trying to get *away* from them?'

'Yes – and we are.' The silver slab loomed right above them, so close it seemed they could almost touch it. Dar shoved on the deceleration pedal again, slowing the lifeboat by deft touches till the pitted silver plates above them were almost motionless. 'There!' He sat back and relaxed. 'We've matched velocities. With any luck, they won't have noticed us jumping under them; they'll have been too busy taking potshots at the courier.'

'Why wouldn't they notice us?'

'Because it would make a lot more sense for us to be still hiding behind our mother ship.'

'Definitely.' Sam glanced up at the pirate with apprehension.

'Even if they do start looking for us, they're apt to *over*look us – unless they've got their ventral detectors on.'

'Which they probably have.'

'With our luck, of course. But even if they do, they probably won't see us – we're too close to their skin, in their detectors' "shadow".'

'Nice theory.' Sam settled back. 'What happens if you're wrong?'

'Well, in that case, they shoot away from us faster than we can go, leave us sitting here, and practise their shooting.'

'Now I know why I always sympathized with the clay pigeons.' Sam shivered. 'What're they doing?'

Dar turned around, looking out over the tail. 'Still trying to shoot through the courier . . . whup!'

'"Whup", what?' Sam asked with foreboding.

'The courier's moving away – "streaking" would be more likely.'

Brace yourself – the pirates're going after him, and fast! Even damaged, that courier's *quick*!'

Sam frowned. 'Then how'd the pirates catch it in the first place?'

'Lurking in ambush.'

'Lurking *where*? There's no cover bigger than a hydrogen atom out here!'

'Whup! There they go!' Dar spun around and set himself as the silver slab slid away toward their rear. Dar pushed down the acceleration pedal, heading sunwards.

'We . . . can't . . . possibly outrun . . . them,' Sam grated against the pull of acceleration.

'Not if they're going . . . our way,' Dar answered. 'But at the moment . . . they're going . . . out, and we're going . . . in.'

'Why bother?' Sam spoke more easily. 'As soon as they're done with the courier, they'll come after us.'

'Assuming we're big enough to bother with. But by that time, maybe we can find a place to hide.'

'Hide? *Where*?'

'Wherever they did, while they were lurking . . . *there*!' Dar's forefinger stabbed out, pointing ahead, at a string of pierced diamonds backlit by the sun. 'Asteroids! They confused the ship's detection system; it thought the pirates' ship was just a large rock, closer than the others!'

Sam stared. 'What're they doing here?'

'This is *not* the time to ask questions.' Dar craned around, looking aft. 'They're still going after the courier . . . they've overhauled it, they're gonna fire a warning shot. . . . NO! They're starting to slow and turn!'

Sam stared. 'Why?'

'Because they're not interested in the courier, obviously! They just took a peek, saw our boat's pod was still empty and we were nowhere in sight, and started scanning for us!'

Sam frowned, shaking her head. 'I don't get it. You make it sound as though they want *us*.'

'Guess what?' Dar said dryly. 'What I'd like to know is how they knew we were aboard?'

'Maybe they didn't,' Sam said hopefully. 'Maybe they think we're somebody else.'

'You'll pardon me if I don't stay around to find out.' Dar swerved and jammed the deceleration pedal; the ship bucked as the nose rockets spewed superheated steam, slamming them into their webbing. The shiplet danced and curvetted as Dar tried to avoid the smaller chunks of stone and metal. The ship rang like a cymbal in a percussion solo, but nothing holed them. Dar managed to match velocity with an asteroid a little larger than the lifeboat. The ringing diminished to an occasional dong.

'So far, we're fantastically lucky.' Dar killed all power. 'As long as we don't run into a really fast-moving pebble astern, or a slow-moving one ahead, we're okay. This lifeboat's got enough armour to take care of most of the debris.'

Sam released a long, shaky breath. 'Taking a bit of a chance, weren't you?'

Dar shrugged. 'I had a choice? Now, as long as we don't get our engines smashed, we're okay.'

'And if we do?'

'So, which would you rather be – a prisoner, or an asteroid?'

Sam frowned. 'Let me think it over.'

'Sure.' Dar leaned back, folding his arms. 'You'll have plenty of time.'

The asteroid's path had carried them considerably out of the pirates' path; the huge silver slab flashed by overhead and well behind them.

'Just like that?' Sam looked about her, puzzled. 'They just go by and leave us?'

'Wrong,' Dar said grimly. 'They saw us curve off and join the asteroids, you can bet on it. But they couldn't decelerate fast enough to follow us – we *do* have an edge in manoeuvrability. They'll be back, though, don't worry.'

'Thanks for the reassurance.' Sam sat very still. 'Why'd you kill the power?'

'Because at least one of their detectors searches for it. Right now, that's the only thing that makes us different from an asteroid, unless they happen to get close enough to eyeball us.'

'Don't we reflect a lot more light?'

'I chose a bright asteroid to hide next to.'

'Here they come!' Sam yelped.

Dar poised a finger over the power button.

The pirates couldn't hear them, of course, and they both knew it – but the rabbit reflex took over, and they both sat rock-still as the silver tombstone drifted slowly over them in a prowling zigzag. It cruised closer, closer, and Dar felt an urge to shove his tiny boat to starboard, to nestle up against the comforting bulk of the asteroid. The pirate zagged to the right

– and, as it zigged past them, it was out beyond their covering asteroid. It loomed closer and closer, but slanting away now. It crossed their path a good half-mile in front of them, and kept on going.

Sam collapsed back against her chair with a sigh. 'Thank heaven.'

'Yeah.' Dar felt himself beginning to tremble as he lowered his finger from the power button. 'I never thought I'd be so glad to be inconspicuous.'

'As long as it worked.' Sam eyed him with dawning respect.

Dar felt his pulse quicken – after all, she *was* the only woman for several million miles. Sam stiffened, pointing ahead. 'Look! What're they doing?'

Dar stared. A giant hatch had opened in the stomach of the silver tombstone.

'They're gonna send down their scout boat for a closer look!' Dar lunged at the power button.

Sam caught his arm. 'No! You said that was a dead giveaway!'

Dar paused, his eyes on the pirate ship. 'Wait a minute! They're thinking it over.'

A shuttle hung halfway out the huge hatchway, motionless. Then it started to rise back up into the mother ship, and the huge doors swung shut.

'But *why*?' Dar bleated. 'They had us dead cold!'

'*That's* why!' Sam jabbed a finger toward the back window.

A huge, truncated pyramid came hurtling toward them. A vast eye seemed to float above it. The pirate ship slid into motion, gathering speed, and streaked away.

Dar winced in sympathy. 'I'd've hated to've taken *that* slap of acceleration . . . But they didn't have much choice, did they?'

'Why not?' Sam stared at the approaching pyramid. 'What *is* that megalith?'

'The cops.' Dar shrugged. 'Which ones, I'm not sure – but it comes out to the same thing. For once, I'm glad to see them.'

'Yo! Over here! Whoa! Help!' Sam tried to stand up, waving her arms frantically. 'Damn! Don't they *hear* us?'

'Sound waves don't travel too well through vacuum,' Dar pointed out.

'I know, I know,' Sam groused, dropping back into her seat. 'Just carried away by the heat of the moment.'

'So are they,' Dar noted, watching the police ship zip by.

'*Now* what do we do? Get out and walk?'

'Well, presumably we're in the Haldane system, since that's where we were going. And at our top speed, it can't be more than three or four months to the nearest habitable planet.'

'I don't think I can wait that long for lunch.'

'Oh, I'm sure there're some rations tucked away around here somewhere. But I don't think we'll have to wait that long. I expect the police ship to be coming back this way pretty soon.'

'Why?' Sam frowned. 'For reinforcements?'

'Oh, they don't need any. Did you see that "eye" on top of their ship? It is one *very* powerful blaster.'

'Oh.' Sam chewed that one over. 'That why the pirates ran?'

Dar nodded. 'With that "eye", the police have the pirates outranged, no matter *how* many guns they mount.'

'So why'll the police be coming back?'

'Because the pirate ship also mounts an isomorpher, and I strongly suspect that police ship is purely local. As soon as the pirate goes into H-space, the police'll be homeward bound.'

'Oh.' Sam thought it over. 'But couldn't the police catch the pirates before they isomorph?'

'They could,' Dar said judiciously, 'but I don't think they will. Those pirates're going to be very good at running. If they're not, they lose profits. So they'll take risks the police won't.'

'Like going into H-space too soon?'

'That's possible. If you see a big explosion, you'll know they tried it.'

They waited, staring ahead, where the police ship had dwindled to a glint of light.

After a while, Sam ventured, 'I don't think they tried it.'

A speck of light glinted in the distance. Dar's finger sprang out to the power button again.

'Not yet!' Sam cried. 'We don't know who won!'

'I bet we're gonna find out, though.' Dar waited, tense.

The glint grew into a dot, and kept growing.

It became a triangular dot.

'*Victory*!' Dar stabbed the button, and the engine roared into life. 'Let's hear it for the good guys!' He hauled back on the wheel, and the boat sprang up out of the plane of the ecliptic, toward the police ship.

'Shouldn't we identify ourselves? So they don't think we're attacking?'

'Not as ridiculous as it sounds,' Dar said soberly. 'For all they know, we could be a torpedo. There oughta be some kinda distress beacon around here. See if you can find it, will ya?'

It was labelled 'Distress Beacon', and it only had one button. Sam pressed it, and waited.

'How do we know if it's working?' she said finally.

'How do you know God listens?' Dar retorted. 'It's got radio; we don't.'

'Faith,' Sam grumbled. 'Does it *always* have to come down to that?'

The pyramid loomed up toward them – and disappeared in a cloud of steam.

'They heard us!' Dar yelped. 'They're decelerating!'

The fog cleared, and the police ship towered over them.

Sam shrank back. 'I can't help it – I feel as though it's going to fall on me!'

And it did. The great pyramid sank toward them, giving them a fly's-eye view of a giant foot. Dar opened his mouth to scream just as the hatch slid open in the huge silver wall above them, swooping down to swallow them up.

'Saved?' someone croaked. Dar would've thought it was Sam, but it was coming from inside his own head.

'Just glad we were nearby.' The captain poured two glasses of brandy and held them out to Sam and Dar. His insignia gleamed on the breast of his doublet – an eye-topped pyramid with 'Space Police' inside it in cursive script. Arcing above it were the words, 'Hal. IV', and, below it, 'Falstaff'. It stood out in a sea of ochre – no, maybe an ocean. The captain was obese, to say the least. So was his crew – the smallest of them was at least four feet around, and all were shorter than Dar. The captain also had the typical Haldane IV face: florid, with long curly hair and a jawline beard.

Dar accepted the brandy eagerly, but Sam held up a palm. 'Thanks, but I don't believe in alcohol.'

The captain blinked in surprise. 'I assure you, it exists.'

'We *were* lucky you were in the neighbourhood,' Dar said quickly.

'Well, it wasn't entirely luck,' the captain admitted. 'We have had reports about pirates trying to ambush merchantmen at the H-space jump points. But last week a freighter full of pickled herring that was supposed to come through this way, didn't – so we decided to guard this jump point. We only have this one patrol cruiser, so you'll understand that we couldn't guard *all* the points.'

'And the load of pickled herring was *that* important?' Dar said in surprise.

'To us,' said the captain, 'it's vital. But what brings you to Falstaff, gentlefolk?'

'"Falstaff"?' Dar frowned, puzzled.

'It's the local name for Haldane IV,' Sam explained. 'Just here to make a connection, Captain. We're inbound from Wolmar.'

The captain still sat comfortably leaning back, fingers laced across his butterbelly, but suddenly he was all vigilance. 'Wolmar? Really! How interesting. By the way, could I see your papers?'

'Hm? Oh, sure!' Dar slid his passport and ID out of his jacket pocket and laid them on the desk; Sam followed suit. 'Sorry; we should have thought of that right off.'

'Well, you were a little flustered.' The captain picked up their passports and suddenly, illogically, Dar had the insane conviction that the captain had a jeweller's loupe in his eye.

'Everything in order – of course.' The last part lacked conviction. The captain slid their papers back to them. 'We don't get many coming *from* Wolmar.'

'The traffic does seem to run the other way,' Dar agreed. 'But our pharmaceutical materials company's getting itchy to expand, and we're heading back to the inner planets to sound out possible investors.' Sam twitched; Dar reflected that he really should have told her about the cover story he was dreaming up.

'Didn't realize it was getting to be that big a business.' The captain seemed genuinely interested.

Dar grinned. 'It may not be – but we're sure going to find out. By the way, I was mightily relieved when you noticed our boat so quickly. Were you on the look-out for us?'

'No, not particularly.' The captain frowned. 'Should we have been?'

Dar sat still for a moment, letting the shock wash through him.

'Well,' he said carefully, 'I would've thought our courier ship would've told you we were missing.'

'That *is* strange, now that you mention it.' The captain scratched his head, then looked up. 'Maybe the pilot didn't notice you'd abandoned ship.'

'Uh . . . could be.' Dar thought of how much of a lurch the lifeboat must've given the courier ship when it blasted free. 'Of course – now that I think about it, that must be it. After all, how could the pilot have noticed we were gone?'

'How *couldn't* he've noticed?' Dar raged. 'When that lifeboat blasted free, it must've kicked the ship like a foundation anomaly!'

'Maybe he thought it was a blaster bolt,' Sam offered. 'It *was* a little hectic just then.'

'And he wouldn't've checked the passengers when the action was over?' Dar shook his head. 'No. It washes about as well as baked-on grease.'

They were strolling through the downtown section of Haskerville, the capital of Falstaff. The street was wide, but all the buildings had a second storey that projected out over the sidewalk – convenient in rainy weather, Dar was sure, but a little depressing on a sunny day. Also, it was a little strange that all the buildings were half-timbered and stuccoed.

'Well, it's a frontier planet, I guess,' he said aloud.

'Not really – it's a third of the way back to Terra, and it's been colonized for four hundred years. What makes you think so?'

'The architecture.' Dar pointed to the wooden beams. 'Don't they know how to make steel?'

'Oh, they know how, well enough.' Sam smiled. 'I asked about it on my way out here. Seems there's very little free metal on Falstaff. Even the iron's all locked up in rust, in the soil.'

'Oh.' Dar pursed his lips. 'So what do I use for money here – nails?'

Sam started, surprised. 'How'd you guess?'

'You're kidding!'

'Think so, do you? Well, just try to pay for something with an IDE BTU credit here.'

'I'll take your word for it.' Dar stopped by a storefront, looking up at the sign. 'I think this is the place we're looking for. Maybe they do money-changing here.'

'Makes sense,' Sam agreed, 'so probably they don't.'

They went into the ticket office of Outworld Interstellar Starship Enterprises, Unltd.

'Help you?' the clerk grunted around his sausage, his eyes on the newsfax. He was grossly fat, and jowly, like all the Falstavians they'd seen. In fact, Dar was beginning to feel like a freak – he was slim.

'Uh, yeah. We'd like to book passage to Terra.'

'Sure thing.' The man pulled out two tickets without even looking. 'That'll be two hundred pounds. Next ship lifts at fourteen hundred hours on the third of May.'

Dar froze with his hand on his wallet. 'May the third!? But it's only April the fifth!'

'Too bad, isn't it?' the clerk commiserated. 'You just missed the last boat – two days ago.'

'But we can't wait! We've got to get to Terra fast!'

The clerk shrugged. 'I just sell the tickets, buddy – I don't schedule the ships. Y' want 'em, or not?'

'Uh, not just yet, thanks.' Dar turned to Sam, looking helpless.

'Do you change money here?' she said briskly.

The clerk looked up. 'Money? Yeah, sure! Whacha got?'

'IDE therms – ten of them,' Sam said with a meaningful stare at Dar.

'Oh.' The clerk seemed disappointed. 'Well, we'll take anything, I guess. Put 'em up here.' He pulled out a small cloth sack and set it on the counter; it clanked.

Dar paused with his cash halfway to the counter. 'What's that?'

'Money.' The clerk looked up, frowning. 'For ten IDE therms, you get two pounds.'

'*Two* pounds?' Dar bleated, aghast. 'You must think your pound's worth an awful lot!'

'A pound of ten-penny nails?' The clerk eyed Dar as if doubting his sanity. 'Buddy, around here, that's worth a *hell* of a lot!'

'Oh.' Dar glanced at Sam out of the corner of his eye; she nodded. He sighed and laid his bills down on the counter. 'Okay, here you are. Say, uh – is there *any* connection to Terra sooner than next month?'

'Well, if y' really wanna know . . .' The clerk leaned forward confidentially. 'I got this buddy, see, an' he's got an inside track on this nice, used space yacht. . . .'

'Uh, thanks anyway.' Dar took a step back. 'I, uh, haven't done all that much piloting lately.'

Sam bit the inside of her cheek.

'Oh.' The clerk leaned back with a look of disgust. 'No high-grade, huh? Well, suit yourself.' He turned back to the newsfax.

'Uh, yeah.' Dar scooped up the moneybag. 'We'll, uh, get back to you.'

'You an' what miner?' But the clerk lifted an affable hand anyway. 'Good luck, chum.'

'Well, he *tried* to sound friendly, I suppose,' Dar said as they came out of the office.

'Not really. Around here, "chum" doesn't mean "friend" – it means "fishbait". The garbage kind.'

'Oh.' Dar frowned. 'What was all that stuff about "high-grade"? And why would we come back with a miner?'

'The kind who digs up ore,' Sam explained. 'High-grade ore.'

Dar glanced at her, but she wasn't smiling. He shrugged. 'Really serious about this iron thing, aren't they?'

A ground car went past, hissing steam from its turbine. The body was wooden; the boltheads were plastic.

'Very,' Sam agreed.

Dar's head swivelled, tracking the ground car. 'What do they make the engine out of?'

'A very high-temperature plastic,' Sam answered. 'But I understand they're short on radios.'

Dar turned back to her, frowning. 'That does require metal, doesn't it? But how does the newsfax work?'

'Optical-fibre cables; they've got no shortage of silicon. And it can print by heat-transfer.'

Dar shook his head, flabbergasted. 'Well, at least they don't have traffic jams.'

'Sausage, sir?' inquired a rotund pushcart proprietor.

Dar stopped, suddenly realizing that darn near every passerby had a sausage in his mouth, chewing placidly. 'Well, I guess I shouldn't look out of place. Yeah, we'll take two.' He fished in his moneybag, and brought out . . .

. . . a large nail.

He looked up at Sam, horrified.

She frowned, and nodded toward the pedlar, who was holding out two sausages on a scrap of plastic. Dar stared from her to the hotdogs and back. Then he shrugged, took the sausages, and dropped the spike in the pedlar's palm. He turned away, with two three-penny nails and a brad for change. 'What do they do around here when the Revenue Service comes calling?'

'They pay their tacks, like honest citizens. What's the matter? Culture shock?'

Dar shook his head. 'Couldn't be; I can't find the conductor.'

'Around here,' Sam said slowly, 'I think that's some kind of political office. You need a drink.'

'Good idea.' Dar nodded numbly. 'I used to favour a cocktail called a "rusty nail".'

'On this planet, that's an obscenity.' Sam steered him through a swinging door. 'I think you'd better have an old-fashioned.'

'I think I already have,' Dar muttered.

The tavern was dim, in the best tradition of alcohol stations. They stepped up to the bar.

'Orderzh? Orderzh?' the bartender slurred, blinking.

'Uh, an old-fashioned and a martinus.' Sam seemed fascinated by the blinking.

'Two bitsh.' The bartender pushed buttons.

Dar laid down a ten-penny nail.

'Two from a ten-pin,' the bartender muttered. Its hand sucked up the nail; a door in its chest slid open, and ejected two glasses of clear liquid and one glass of amber. It rolled away down the bar to the next customer, leaving two flat-head screws and a drill behind it.

'I'd count your change, if I were you,' the patron two stools down advised. He wore a dark brown robe belted with a length of coaxial cable; the crown of his head was shaved in a neat circle. The yellow handle of a small screwdriver peeked from his breast pocket. 'That bartender isn't too reliable today.'

'I *thought* his lights weren't blinking in the right pattern!' Sam said triumphantly. 'What's the matter with him?'

'You'd have to say he's drunk, I suppose,' the shave-pate answered. 'You see, the tavernkeeper couldn't afford wire for his conductors, so he had to use tubes of saline solution. Well, that means the bartender has to have a little fluid added every morning, and it seems someone spiced his morning pickup with metallic salts today. That increased conductivity, of course, and threw all his circuits off.'

'Which is why I got two when I only ordered one. Oh, well.' Sam shrugged and took a sip. 'I should gripe?'

'Sounds like an expensive prank, for this neck of the woods,' Dar commented.

'No, not really. It's *free* metal that's in short supply on Falstaff. Compounds are plentiful.'

'You seem to know quite a bit about it.' Dar held up his glass and peered through it warily. 'From your clothing, I would've thought you were a friar – but you talk like an engineer.'

'I'm both, really.' The stranger grinned and held out a hand. 'Father Marco Ricci, OSV, at your service.'

'Dar Mandra.' Dar shook his hand. 'And this is Sam Bine. What's "OSV"?'

'The "Order of Saint Vidicon of Cathode",' the friar answered. 'We're a society of Roman Catholic engineers and scientists.'

'Oh yeah. I should have recognized it. The chaplain on our transport was one of your boys.'

'They frequently are.' Father Marco nodded. 'The Church tends to assign Cathodeans who specialize in astronautics to such jobs – it's one more protection in case of a malfunction.'

'Yeah, makes sense.' Dar nodded, and his training in Cholly's bar took over. 'If you'll pardon me, though – isn't that something of a paradox?'

'What, having a priest who's a scientist? Not really. Any conflict between science and religion is simply the result of clergy who don't understand science, and scientists who don't understand religion.'

'Wouldn't a scientist-religious tend to be a bit sceptical about both?'

'Indeed he would.' The priest grinned. 'The Vatican's habitually annoyed with us – we tend to keep asking new questions.'

'Then why do they let you keep going?'

'Because they need us.' Father Marco shrugged. 'Even the Vatican has plumbing.'

'Well, I can see that.' Dar sipped. 'But why would the Church ever declare a maverick like one of you a saint?'

'Oh, you're thinking of our founder.' Father Marco nodded. 'Well, they hadn't much choice, there. It was very clearly a case of martyrdom.'

'That gives you quite a record to live up to,' Sam noted.

'Oh, we don't *plan* to be martyrs,' Father Marco assured them, 'and I'm sure our founder would approve. After all, he was the practical sort – and a live priest can usually accomplish far more than a dead one.'

Dar wondered about the 'usually'. 'Well, we have a bit of a practical problem ourselves, at the moment, Father – and you seem to be familiar with the planet.'

'But not native – as I'm sure you could tell by my size.' Father Marco was only a little on the stout side.

'Yes, and that's our problem – we're not native, and we *would* like to get on with our trip.'

'And the last freighter left orbit a few days ago.' Father Marco nodded. 'Well, I'm afraid there's not much you can do just now – especially with the IDE police sealing off the planet.'

'Doing *what?*'

'Sealing off the planet,' Father Marco said mildly. 'You hadn't heard? It was on the newsfax just a few minutes ago. The Interstels had a reliable tip that a telepath came in on the last ship, so they've forbidden anyone to leave the planet while they search for him.'

'Well,' Sam said slowly, 'that does kind of delay us, doesn't it?'

Dar frowned. 'What's this telepath done?'

Father Marco shrugged. 'Nothing, so far as I know. At least, nothing was said about it.'

'Then, why are they searching for him?'

'You don't know?' Father Marco asked in mild surprise. 'Why, telepaths are a menace to everything any right-thinking citizen holds sacred – haven't you heard?'

'Something of the sort, yes,' Sam admitted. 'We didn't know it was exactly a widely held belief.'

'Oh, it's been all the rage for at least a month! Telepaths invade other people's privacy, you see – you can never tell when one might be reading your mind. You could make laws against that, but there'd be no way to enforce them – unless you had telepathic police; and if you did, they'd probably side with their fellows. Those telepaths stick together, you know.'

'No, I didn't,' said Dar. 'In fact, I didn't know there *were* any – well, almost.' He remembered the Wolman shaman.

'Ah, you see?' Father Marco wagged a forefinger at him. 'You've known at least one person who always seemed to know what you were thinking. So has everyone, of course.'

'Of course! Who doesn't have someone who knows them really well?'

'It could be that,' the priest said judiciously. 'But when that person always seems to be one jump ahead of you – well, you naturally tend to wonder. Because telepaths use what you're thinking against you, you see – they have an unfair advantage in the competition of life. They always know what you're going to do, so they always know how to head you off.'

'That's horrible!'

'Isn't it just? But it gets worse. The IDE police are reasonably sure that telepaths all over the Terran Sphere are getting in touch with one another, forming a society of their own, conspiring to overthrow the government and take over.'

'But how?' Sam frowned. 'Couldn't the police intercept their messages?'

'Intercept a message from one mind reader to another? Hardly. Besides, rumour has it that these telepaths don't even need to get on a starship to get a message from one planet to another.'

'What?'

'That's the word.' Father Marco nodded. 'Their thoughts travel from star to star almost instantaneously. You can see that would give their conspiracy a bit of an advantage over the forces of society.'

'Yes, I certainly can.' Dar leaned a little closer and lowered his voice. 'And do I gather from your tone, Father, that you don't quite believe all this?'

Father Marco leaned over. 'Frankly, I think it's the biggest pot of rotten incense I've ever smelled!'

'What I can't figure out,' Sam put in, 'is why people would get so worked up about something that probably doesn't even exist.'

'Well, it's been known to happen before,' Father Marco said judiciously. 'Mass hysteria is never that far beneath the skin, I suppose. A human being is a thinking animal, but crowds don't seem to be. So I suppose it's just as well that the police are taking action, even though they're probably acting only on the strength of a rumour.'

'Rumour?' Dar frowned. 'How so?'

'Tips are usually hearsay, I gather. Nonetheless, better to act on a rumour than to risk a riot.'

'Riot?' Sam protested. 'You've got to be joking.'

'Unfortunately, I'm not. If the people didn't know the authorities were on the look-out, they might try to do something on their own – then all it'd take would be one whisper that so-and-so was a telepath, and you'd have a full-scale witch-hunt to deal with. No, it's better that . . .'

'Do you mind?'

A portly gentleman had huffed up from a nearby table.

'Am I in your way?' Father Marco said politely.

'No, but you're upsetting my party quite a bit! If you must insist on discussing politics, would you please have the courtesy to do it in your own quarters? It's in frightfully poor taste, and it's ruining my digestion!'

'Oh!' Dar exchanged a look with Father Marco. 'My apologies, citizen. Of course, if we're offending . . .'

'You'll keep right on!' A skinny hand clapped Dar's shoulder like a pincers. 'Ay, give offence! Bother the lazy hogs out of their trough! Goad them into *doing* something – into living, for Lord's sake!' He was a short, lean, ageing man, who looked to be as hard as a meteorite and as merry as a comet. And next to him . . .

Dar stiffened, eyes widening. Next to the old man stood the most beautiful woman he had ever seen, with the body of Venus outlined by a flowing, sleeveless, calf-length gown that clung to every curve. Her face was comprised of a high, smooth brow; delicate eyebrows; large, wide-set eyes heavily lidded; a small, tip-tilted nose; and a mouth with a hint of a smile that promised delights and challenged him to seek them. Tawny hair rippled down to her waist. It was the face from the dreams of his boyhood, the face that he had never thought could be, the face that could never let the grown man rest.

The unfairness of it hit him like a stiletto – that she should be with that old geezer, instead of with him!

The old geezer was turning on the portly indigestion case, who had made some outraged noises. 'And *I'll* thank *you* to let *your* remarks go public! Don't you know what happens to people who won't talk politics? They stop caring about their government! And do you know what happens when they stop caring? One night, some sneaky, unprincipled scoundrel sneaks in and changes their government on them! And the next morning, they wake up and find their taxes are as high as their collarbones, and they can't go anywhere without a permit, and, taken all in all, they're not much better than slaves! And *that's* what happens when you keep your remarks to yourself!'

'Sir!' The fat one recoiled as though he'd stepped on slime. 'This is obscene!'

'I'd rather be obscene, and not absurd – but since you seem to think the other way, I think my friends and I had better go look for some fresher air!' He turned to Father Marco, Dar, and Sam. 'How about it, O ones with spirit? You'll find a breeze blowing by the stage that's amazingly fresh! We're going down there, my niece and I – join us, if you're up to it!' And he turned away, limping between the tables in a rush, as though life would get away from him if he didn't hurry to catch it.

The girl turned to follow him – and did her gaze linger just a moment on Dar?

Imagination. Had to be. But . . .

She was only his niece!

'Huh? What?' His head snapped around toward Father Marco.

'I said, shall we join them?' There was a gleam in the priest's eye.

'Uh . . . yeah. Seem like nice folks.'

'Why not?' Sam was a monotone in a frigid face. 'It's sure to be lively.'

They got up, with their glasses, and filed after the loud voice on the old legs.

'Sit down, sit down!' The geezer waved them to chairs around a large table as he slid into one himself. His niece sat demurely next to him. 'So you're a Cathodean,' the oldster greeted Father Marco. 'What's a live order like yours doing in a dead place like this?'

'Where is a minister of Life more needed than among the moribund?' Father Marco countered.

'Wait a minute. Hold on, there.' Dar held up a palm. 'Back that up a few lines, will you? I think I missed something.'

'What?'

'How'd you know he was a Cathodean?'

'Huh? Why, the emblem of his order, of course!' the old man exclaimed.

'This.' Father Marco tapped the tiny yellow screwdriver in his breast pocket. 'Used to be the sign of an electrical engineer – like a fraternity pin. We just made it official.'

'Oh.' Dar pulled his head down, feeling dense.

'You've got the advantage of me now,' Father Marco informed the geezer.

'Yeah, I know.' The old man grinned wickedly. 'Ain't it great?'

'Grandfather!' the vision reproved, and the old man winced (her shoes did have very sharply pointed toes).

'Well, I can't have everything,' he sighed. 'I'm Whitey, Father, and this is Lona, my . . . *niece*,' he added, with a glare at her.

She tried to look chastened. 'Anything you say, Grandfather.'

'*Must* you make me feel my age, lass?' Whitey sighed. 'I know you have a fixation about absolute honesty in all the little things – but have mercy! I don't ask for much – just that you call me "Uncle" when other people are around. Is that so much to ask?'

'Not at all, now that they know the truth.' She gave the rest of the company a dazzling smile, and lied, 'He's my uncle.'

'Glad to meet him,' Dar muttered, his eyes on Lona.

Father Marco cleared his throat and stretched out a hand. 'I'm Father Marco Ricci. And this is Dar Mandra, and Sam Bine.'

'Here y'are, Whitey.' A waiter set a large glass of wine in front of the old man. 'And you, Lona.'

'Thank you.' She accepted the cocktail with a smile that was polite, but warm too, then deliberately turned her eyes away. The waiter hesitated a moment hopefully, then sighed and turned away.

'Whitey the Wino?' Father Marco guessed.

Whitey held up his glass in a semi-toast and nodded approval. 'You're quick.'

'Not really; I've been hearing about you in every tavern and tap-room for the last three parsecs. Glad I finally caught up with you.'

The name fitted, Dar decided. The old man's hair was stark white, and his eyes were so light a blue that they verged on being colourless. Even his skin had a bleached look – weathered and toughened, as though it ought to have a deep space-tan; but he was almost white.

And the second name seemed to fit, too. He'd drained half the glass at a gulp.

'"Caught up with me", is it?' Whitey grinned. 'If it weren't for the cassock, I'd worry.'

Father Marco grinned too. 'No, I'm not the Revenue Service.'

'Or an angry husband,' Lona added.

'My dear!' Whitey protested, wounded. 'Would I come between a man and his wife?'

'Only if you had a chance to,' she murmured, and sipped at her drink.

Whitey turned to Father Marco with a sigh of despair. 'Ah, the cynicism of this latter generation! Are there no ideals left, Father? No faith?'

'I believe in you implicitly, Grandfather – I'm just not saying what for.'

'To move around, for one thing,' Father Marco said. 'You don't seem to have stayed on any one planet any longer than I have, Whitey.'

The Wino nodded. 'I can take any of these fat, complacent peoples, for just so long.'

'Or they you,' Lona murmured.

'Well, they usually do offer to pay my expenses to the next planet. I'm getting a bit restless in my old age, Father – moving outward, hoping to find a place that isn't sliding down into decadence.'

'It's about time, Whitey.' A tallow-ketch of a man stopped by the table.

'And I have to keep finding new audiences.' Whitey slid a flat keyboard out of his tunic and stood up. 'If you'll excuse me for a few minutes, folks . . .'

'You're the entertainment?' Dar said, astonished.

'Aren't I always?' he answered. Lona added, 'Not much security, but it's a living.'

'Better than it was in the old days, my dear,' Whitey reminded her, 'before I met your grandmother. I sold narcotics back then, Father – not entirely legally. Before I saw the light – when I went under the name of Tod Tambourin.' He turned away toward the stage, following Lona.

Sam sat stiff and rigid, her eyes bulging. '*That's* Tod Tambourin?'

'Couldn't be.' But Dar felt a sinking certainty. 'Great poets don't sing in bars.'

'I can think of a few exceptions.' Father Marco leaned back and sipped his drink. 'Let's judge the product, shall we?'

The 'product' didn't bear judgement at all. Whitey settled himself on a low stool while Lona slid onto a high one, heels hooked on a rung, knees together, hands clasped in her lap. Whitey struck a rippling crescendo from his keyboard. It filled the room, leaving a moment of silence behind it. Into that silence Whitey pumped a vigorous song which had its roots in the best of the bad old days, a bit of bawdy nonsense about a lady spacer, who was scarcely a lady, and whose interest in space was confined to some interesting spaces. Lona sat through it, amused joining in on the choruses with almost as much relish as her grandfather.

'*This* is the poet laureate of the Terran Sphere?' Sam cried, scandalized.

Dar felt a trifle disillusioned too – but not in Whitey.

The song ended with a rocketing crescendo that sounded like a spaceship taking off. The patrons roared their approval, stomping and laughing; and when the racket slackened and died, it blended into a slower, almost melancholy tune that nonetheless had a feeling of quiet certainty underlying it.

Then Lona began to sing, not looking at Whitey, gazing off into space a little above the audience's heads, in a voice as sweet as spring and as clear as a fountain. The words didn't quite register; they seemed to slide around and envelop Dar in a dazzle of consonants – but the meaning sank in: a lament for the wilderness that was, but never was, the primeval beauty that men hearkened back to when the name 'Terra' was spoken.

Then Whitey joined in on the chorus, in a quiet, sad-but-satisfied judgement that the wilderness had passed, but that it had had to, as all things must. Then Lona took up the verse again, in lilting wonder that the same wilderness had greeted men anew, on distant planets, under suns unseen from Terra.

Then the chorus again, that these too had passed, as they'd had to; and another verse, another planet, a hundred more, each greeting humankind with wilderness, to tame and then destroy within the bars of hedges; then the chorus, and one final verse, in notes that soared with triumph – for bit by bit, men had learned to live within the wilderness, and preserve it – and yonder, past the marches, new planets beckoned with their forests – the ancient home of humans, which they must ever seek.

Dar sat, stunned. How could he have ever thought that poem was great when he'd read it without hearing its music?

Then the keyboard slashed out a great, jarring discord, and they were off into another bawdy song. And so it went – bits of poetry sandwiched in between carousing, continually taking the audience by surprise. When Whitey finally bade the audience give the singer time for a drink, Dar was on his feet with the rest of them, applauding wildly and shouting, 'More! More!' Then Lona and Whitey came up to the table, she flushed and glowing, he smiling, grinning, and Dar felt very foolish.

'Sit, sit!' Whitey waved him into his chair. 'And thousands of thanks, youngling. That's the greatest praise a singer can get – that you forget yourself in the music.'

Lona didn't say anything, but she answered with a look that set Dar's blood thrilling through him and gave his teeth a tingle.

Then the waiter broke the spell by plunking glasses down in front of the singers.

'I can believe it!' Sam exploded. 'I couldn't believe such a distinguished poet would be playing in taverns – but I've heard you! I believe it!'

'Well – I'm glad to know I'm still myself,' Whitey said, with a twinkle in his eye. 'And a poet I am – but "distinguished" I most emphatically am not!'

"Don't let him bother you,' Lona assured Sam. 'You couldn't have known it was an insult.'

'But what're you doing, playing in a backwater bar on a boondock planet?'

'Looking for a clean breath of air.' Whitey's mouth tightened a little. 'The bars on Terra, now, they're so damn polite you can't get away with anything *but* poetry, and that takes all the fun out of it. Also, they don't really listen – they just want you for background while they try to make time with each other. And say a word about politics, and wham! you're out of the door! They've gone effete, they've gone gloomy, they've gone hopeless, and the finest songs in the world won't cheer 'em! Things get better as you go away from Sol – but even here, though there's some life, they've lost the sense of joy and wonder. They want to just sit back behind thick walls and taste fat meat, and they don't want to hear about hunting dragons.'

'It's true enough,' Lona agreed, 'but you're not so young any more, Grandfather.'

'That's so.' Whitey nodded. 'That's why I need to seek for life and freshness.'

'But I *am* fresh,' Lona pointed out, 'and fully alive, and no doubt of it! Just give me a try at being decadent, Grandfather – just give me a little try!'

Whitey sighed, and started to answer, but a huge slab of lard interrupted him, six foot four in height and three feet wide, four feet at the waist, with little, squinting, piggy eyes and an out-thrust jaw. 'Whatsa matter, singer? Don't like progress?'

Whitey's eyes kindled. 'Progress? Just because you get more goods doesn't mean your soul's better!'

'So, who are you, my father confessor?' The thickened thug grabbed Whitey's shirtfront and yanked him out of his chair. 'Disgusting little bastard! First talking politics, and now religion! Why, I oughta paste you up on the wall.'

'Go ahead,' Whitey carolled, 'try!'

The thug stared at him for a moment; then his eyes narrowed, and he wound up for a pitch with a snarl.

Whitey chopped down on his elbow, hard.

The beefy one dropped him with a howl, and two more slabs of meat waded in, reaching for Whitey. Someone yanked Dar out of his chair and flipped him around with a fist to his jaw. He slammed back against the tabletop and sat up, blinking, the roar of a full-scale brawl coming faintly through the ringing in his ears. Most of the patrons were squealing and clearing back against the walls, looking for an exit. A knot of thugs kept trying to form around Whitey, but Father Marco kept roaring in, yanking them out of the way by their collars and bumping them away with his back when they tried to swing back in. The ones who did get in kept popping back as Whitey caught them with undercuts.

Sam and Lona fought back-to-back, with clips to the chin, and kicks to the shin. So far, they'd yielded a lot of hoppers.

Then Dar saw the glint of steel swinging up at Sam's belly.

He shouted and leaped forward, lurching in between Sam and her attacker. The blade slid along his side, opening the skin; he bleated in pain and anger, and pivoted to face the slice artist.

He was tall and fat, with a gloating grin. 'You'll do just as well.' The knife snaked out at his liver.

Dar swung to the side, grabbing the man's wrist, cradling the elbow on top of his own, and snapping down. The thug yelled, high and hoarsely; his hand opened, and the knife fell out. Then a grenade exploded on the back of Dar's neck.

He lifted his head, blinking blearily, and got a great view of feet kicking and lunging all around him. Through the singing in his ears, he heard the hoot of police horns. *About time*. Then it occurred to him that the tangling feet all around him might think he was part of the floor. He stumbled to his feet, and looked up into a breast-patch that said 'Police'. He looked on up to a grinning face underneath a helmet, and noticed an electroclub swinging down at him. He spun away, to find a stun-gun level with his chest, with another police-patch behind it. He yelled and leaped to the side just as the club came crashing down and the stun-gun fired. The one cop was shocked, the other was stunned, and a third caught Dar around the middle. Dar slammed a fist down – right on a helmet. The cop dropped him and levelled a stun-gun. Then the cop dropped, terminally, and Father Marco grabbed Dar's arm and yanked him over the scrambling uniform. 'Follow me! Fast!' He turned away, and Dar stumbled after him. He bumped into Sam, coming up on his right, and caromed off Whitey on his left. Father Marco yanked open a door, and Lona darted through ahead of them. 'Follow her!' the priest snapped.

Well, it went along with Dar's natural inclinations; he just wished he hadn't had so much company. He clattered down a set of narrow steps, following Lona's slim form, and came out in a cellar surrounded by shelves of kegs and racks of bottles. The door slammed behind him, and the noise of the fight diminished to a far-off rumble.

'Quick! It won't take them but a few minutes to think of the cellar!' Father Marco brushed past them, fumbled at a bolthead in the panelled wall, and swung open a hidden door. Lona darted through, and Dar followed.

Father Marco slammed the door behind Whitey, and Dar found himself suddenly in total darkness. Something soft and curved brushed against him. Lona sprang to his mind's eye, and he wished she hadn't brushed away so quickly.

'Dar?' Sam whispered, right next to him, and he fairly jumped. 'Yeah, right here,' he whispered back through a whirl of emotions. She'd sounded shy and unsure of herself – feminine. It roused every protective reflex he had – and a full flood of hormones behind them. And the touch of her . . .

'Where are we?' she whispered.

'I don't know,' he answered. 'Why are we whispering?'

Then a spot of light glared. They turned to see Father Marco's face, illuminated from below by a tiny glow-globe in the handle of his miniature screwdriver. 'The reflex is correct,' he said in a very low tone. 'Keep your voices down; I don't think the police know about this bolthole, but they might search the tavern basement, and we don't want them to get curious.'

'Perish the thought!' Whitey agreed. 'Where are we, Father! In a, you should pardon the phrase, priest-hole?'

'No, the persecutions on this planet have never been religiously oriented.' Father Marco grinned. 'We're in the basement of the establishment next door.'

'Which one – Leong Chakov's Foot Laundry?'

'No, the other one.'

'Oh, Madame Tessie's Tenderloin Chop House.' Whitey raised his eyebrows, nodding. 'Pretty good, Father. Even I didn't know there was any, ah, connection, between the two establishments.'

The priest nodded. 'Only a few select patrons know.'

'*You're* one of them?'

'Well – let's just say it's surprising what you pick up in moments of confidence.' Father Marco turned away, groping along the wall.

'Oh.' Whitey fell in beside him. 'You picked it up in the confessional.'

'No, *because* of it. They had something of an emergency here last month, calling for the Last Rites and all possible discretion.' There was a loud *clunk*, and the light bobbed. Father Marco hissed something under his breath. Dar wondered why 'blue' should be sacred.

'I think I've found the stairs.' Father Marco's voice was strained. 'Slowly and quietly, now.' The light began to bob upward. 'The net result is, the ladies here have come to trust me. I think they'll be discreet about our passage through their quarters.' His light shone on a richly-grained door. 'Quietly, now,' he murmured and turned the knob.

Laughter and raucous music assaulted their ears. They stepped out into the middle of a party for the usual assortment of portly patrons and what had to be the only slender inhabitants of Falstaff. The svelte shapeliness was real, too, obviously – since they were wearing as little as possible.

'Must be later than I thought,' Sam observed.

'No, it's always like this,' Father Marco answered. 'Come now, let's see if we can't find a quiet place to meditate.'

Personally, Dar had all he wanted to meditate on right there; but Father Marco was slipping quietly along the wall toward the stairway, and Whitey was pushing from behind, so he followed suit.

'Marco!'

The priest turned just as a bosomy beldam smacked into him, lips first. She leaned back, holding him by the shoulders and laughing. 'You old scoundrel, what brings you here? Interested in *our* services, for a change?'

'In a way, Tessie, in a way.' Father Marco gave the madam an affectionate squeeze – on the hand. 'Just looking for a place to relax and chat with a few friends, where there's a little less noise than the average tavern.'

Tessie sighed and shook her head. 'What a waste of a good man! And here I was getting my hopes up. I really ought to be angry with you, y'know.' She gave him a coquettish flicker of eyelashes.

'Because of Rosamund, eh?' Father Marco spread his arms. 'There's no help for it Tessie. I have to do my job, even as you have to do yours.'

'Yes, and usually it's all well and good – the girls get remorseful for a few days, and when they get back to work, they've got a certain freshness about them. But getting one of them to kick the trade completely? Now, don't you think that's going a bit too far?' She emphasized the point with a few strokes on his arm.

Father Marco gently disengaged her hand. 'No, from my point of view, it's just enough. Where is she now, do you know?'

Tessie shrugged. 'Hopped an outbound liner, that's all I can say. None of us are natives, Father.'

'Father?'

'It's Father Marco!'

In a second, they were surrounded by a bevy of shapely no-longer-maidens with very long fingers. Dar thought of checking his wallet, but he was having too much fun being frisked.

The hands were all over the priest, coming on faster than he could take them off.

'Oh, Father, I'm so glad to see you!'

'Have *I* got a lot to tell you!'

'Oh, Father, it's so horrible. I tried and I tried to resist, but . . .'

'Yes, girls, I understand. Patience, patience; if I can't talk with each of you today, I'll come back another time.'

'You aren't a priest's apprentice, are you?' A beautiful redhead straightened Dar's tunic with a lingering touch.

'Well, no, not really. I am interested in virtue, though.'

'So am I,' she cooed, 'it's such a wonderful conversation topic.'

Dar felt a stroke along his buttocks, and just barely managed to keep from jumping. A blonde head poked over his shoulder and murmured, 'Any friend of Father's is a friend of mine.'

'Well, I *am* the friendly type . . .'

There were at least five of them, all very good with innuendo, verbal and otherwise. It would've been great if they'd come one at a time; as it was, Dar was beginning to feel a little like a pound of ground sirloin at a hamburger sale.

Not that he was complaining . . .

A rippling chord filled the room. Everyone looked up, startled.

'Ladies and gentlemen!' Whitey was standing on a chair, with Lona beside him, perched on a table. 'For your entertainment and delectation – the "Ballad of Gresham's Law"!'

An incredulous mutter ran through the room – especially from the zoftig patrons, who were all in the bracket that knows some economics.

The rippling chord stilled them again, and Whitey and Lona began to sing:

'When the upright ladies come to town,
Right away they gather round
To form a club, and then decide
Who is out, and who's inside.'

There was a tap on Dar's shoulder, and Father Marco murmured, 'I hate to distract you from what looks to be a rare event, but we do have other matters to consider.'

With a jolt, Dar remembered an electroclub swinging down at him. 'Uh, yeah. We are in kind of a rush, aren't we?' He sidled through his circle of admirers. 'Excuse me, ladies. I'm on call.'

They made politely distressed noises, and turned back to Whitey and Lona eagerly. Whatever the song was, it seemed to strike a chord with them.

It seemed to be making an analogy between economics and sexual relations, but reversing what was usually understood to be a 'good' woman versus a 'bad'.

'Look at the coin in which you pay,
The wages of a working day.
Compare it to the "honest" bill
Of lifelong toil and thwarted will.'

The patrons cheered, and the girls' faces turned very thoughtful. It occurred to Dar that Whitey might be accomplishing the same task Father Marco was trying, though by very different methods.

'. . . but it is pretty urgent,' Father Marco was explaining to Tessie.

She held up a palm and shook her head. 'Don't explain, Father; I might be pegged for an accomplice. Besides, I've had to leave a place in something of a hurry myself, on occasion. Bring your people here.' She beckoned.

They followed her around through a darkened salon. There was a squeal and a muffled curse. 'As you were,' Tessie ordered crisply, eyes resolutely fixed straight forward. Dar followed her example, though he was burning to look over his shoulder and make sure Sam was safely following. He felt like Orpheus on the return trip.

They turned left into what was either a small room or a very large closet – probably the latter; the walls were lined with racks of evening clothes, cut for small elephants.

'Sometimes our, ah, clients, find it advisable to leave in a different set of clothes than the one they wore on the way in,' Tessie explained. 'We've gathered quite a stock, over the years. Of course, you'll all need some padding, but we're not exactly short on pillows here. Let's see, now – this one ought to fit you, Father, and this one'll do for your young friend, here . . .'

Half an hour later, swathed in evening clothes and padded out to the equator, they filed out of Madam Tessie's like a flock of pregnant penguins.

'Well, you can't deny they were hospitable,' Dar said through a dazed but happy smile.

'I don't particularly care for that sort of hospitality.' Sam was fuming.

Dar glanced at her, and couldn't help feeling gratified. Yesterday he would've felt downright hopeful. Today, though, he was primarily concerned with Lona, who was, unfortunately, taking it all in her stride.

'They even offered me a job,' she noted.

Sam hadn't been asked. 'Is that's what's bothering you?' Dar could at least make it sound as though she had.

'No,' Sam snapped. 'What bothered me was that whole scene in the tavern.'

Whitey shrugged. 'A brawl is a brawl – and you can't blame the cops; squelching that kind of thing is their job.'

'Yeah, but they don't have to gang up three-to-one.' Dar frowned, remembering. 'Especially since I was losing.'

'No, that *isn't* standard.' Whitey frowned, too. Then he shrugged. 'Anyway, *I* had a good time.'

'I didn't,' Sam said stiffly. 'I recognized the chock who led the cops in – and he *wasn't* in uniform.'

'Oh?' Dar looked up. 'Anyone I know?'

'You might say that. He had a face like a rat.'

'A rat! What's *he* doing here . . .? Oh.' Dar pursed his lips. 'We never did see who was piloting our courier ship, did we?'

'We didn't,' Sam confirmed. 'I wondered why he took off and left us to the pirates, remember?'

'If you don't mind my asking,' Father Marco put in, 'what's this all about?'

'Our nemesis, at a guess,' Sam said slowly. 'We thought we'd left him back on Wolmar, with the rest of Governor Bhelabher's staff. At least, Terra sent Bhelabher out to take over the governorship; but he, ah, wound up resigning. We got the assignment of taking his resignation back to Terra.'

'And we *thought* we were the only ones who left,' Dar explained. 'But apparently Bhelabher had a change of heart, and sent his right-hand man along to stop us.'

'No, it wasn't Bhelabher.' Sam shook her head. 'If he'd changed his mind, all his sidekick would've had to do is order us to hand back that resignation form – or even to hand in a counter-letter from Bhelabher.'

'You mean Rat-Face is doing this all on his own?'

'I wouldn't say that,' Sam said slowly. 'He *is* a career bureaucrat in the Bureau of Otherworldly Activities, remember. Chances are he's doing what his superiors in BOA want done.'

'A man with a face like a rat, in the BOA bureaucracy?' Father Marco asked. He was frowning.

Dar nodded. 'That's him. But why would he be trying to kill us?'

'*Kill* you?'

Sam shook her head. 'There were two cops after me, but the worst thing they had was a hypodermic bulb.'

'A hypo?' Dar looked up sharply. 'They were trying to put you out and take you in?'

Sam nodded. 'That's the way it looked. But it doesn't make sense. There were two of them, and they were a lot bigger than I was. Why'd they have needed a hypo?'

'And why'd their buddies be trying to put me out completely? I could swear their intentions weren't toward prolonging my life.'

'Could be you're paranoid,' Lona suggested.

'No doubt; but in this case, I think it doesn't matter. And I don't quite agree with *your* reading of it, Sam – one of them was trying a blade on you.' He touched the bandage that Tessie had thoughtfully taped over his wound.

'No, I'm afraid you're both right.' Father Marco was definitely brooding. 'After all, if you think someone's a threat, and you can't capture them, what's the logical thing to do?'

'But why would they think *I'm* dangerous?' Sam wailed. 'I don't have the papers!'

Lona was looking very interested.

'A fascinating episode,' Whitey mused, 'especially since I do believe I see some uniforms approaching.'

All heads snapped up, and noticed the strolling pair who had just turned the corner.

'Just keep walking,' Father Marco's iron tone advised, and Dar soothed his body's impulse to jump into flight.

' 'Course, it's been a while since I did this . . .' Whitney offered, and Lona coughed, '. . . but I do notice there's some sort of arcade just a few feet down, on our left. Might make a handy bolthole.'

'Ideal,' Father Marco breathed. 'Shall we, gentlefolk?'

They nonchalantly turned into the cavelike coolness of the arcade. Its long concourse stretched away before them, lined with shops on both sides.

'Last time you did this, Grandfather, you split us up into small groups,' Lona reminded.

'A good point,' Father Marco agreed. 'No doubt they counted noses after that tavern brawl, and came to the conclusion we'd all gone off together.'

'Well . . .' Dar caught a door-handle and swung it open, '. . . see ya 'round, folks.'

Sam stepped through the door before he could close it; the rest went on their way, and his team was back to its original components.

They moved down a short aisle, surrounded by skeins of yarn, squares of stiff netting, and racks of patterns. 'What is all this stuff?' Dar whispered.

'Knitting, crocheting, things like that – age-old hobbies,' Sam whispered back. 'Ever try needlepoint?'

Dar was about to answer with a pointed remark of his own, when the proprietor popped up behind the counter at the end of the aisle, grossly fat, with the face of an ageing cherub and a fringe of puffy white hair around a bald dome. 'Something you'd . . . like, gentlefolk?'

'Just browsing,' Dar said quickly. 'Interesting collection you've got here.'

'Oh yes, I try to keep it up-to-date. Had some fascinating patterns come in last week, from Samia.'

'Samia?' Dar wondered, but another customer approached before the storekeeper could answer. 'Ah there, Kontak! Is my order in?'

'Just an hour ago,' Kontak grinned. He laid a slender parcel in plain brown wrap on the counter. 'Sixty spikes, five brads, Grazh Danko.'

'Samia?' Dar whispered to Sam. 'Isn't that the pleasure-planet? You know, "wrap up all your cares and clothes, and do whatever's legal"?'

Sam nodded, her eyes on the brown parcel. 'And there isn't much that's illegal, except murder. I understand they don't even look too closely at that, provided the victim isn't a tourist. I think I'd like a look at the next shop.'

'But this is just getting interesting,' Dar protested as Sam hustled him toward the door.

'Maybe too interesting.' She kept her voice low as the door closed behind them. 'That was a porno shop. And did you catch the prices? For a pack of sleazy pictures? I have a sneaking suspicion we're in the middle of what they euphemistically call an "organic market".'

'One that charges whatever the traffic will bear?' Dar looked around him. 'These innocent little shops? Illegal goods?'

'And services,' Sam reminded. They went into a confectionary. The patron at the end of the counter was thumbing through a menu that seemed to be mostly bodies, while the proprietor was helping an obese, surly patron strike up an acquaintance with a slender sweet young thing. They turned around and went back out.

So it went, for the length of the arcade. Finally, in the office of the Legal Aid Society, which kept a neat list of judges, cases, and the aid the judges required to help them make up their minds about the cases, Dar exploded. 'Is there *anything* that isn't for sale?'

'Haven't found anything, myself,' a customer answered cheerfully, not noticing Sam's frantic shushing motions. 'Of course, some commodities can't be had for cash just yet; but I understand they're working on them.'

'I suppose I'm naïve,' Dar said slowly, 'but I thought *the law* was supposed to help make people equal, not uphold the one who can pay the most.'

The customer winced. 'Please, young man! We must be patient with the follies of youth – but that remark was so distinctly political that I can't ignore it!'

'Don't offend the gentleman,' the proprietor growled, an ugly glint in his piggy little eye.

'*That* was political?' Dar stared. While he was staring, Sam grabbed his arm and hustled him out of the door. By the time he recovered enough to resist, he was in the street. Then he managed to get his mouth moving again. '*Political?* Speculating about the purpose of law is political?'

'Of course, when you say things such as "equal",' Sam explained. 'You really must do something about that death wish of yours.'

'Why?' Dar shrugged her hand off. 'It puts me in phase with this whole planet!'

'Just because people don't talk politics, doesn't mean they're moribund,' Sam hissed.

'No, but it means their society is! They don't even care about the law any more! Don't they realize that's what keeps a society from falling apart?'

'Oh. You're one of these people who believes that law prevents revolutions, huh?'

'Sure, by making sure no one's too badly oppressed.'

'Sin?'

Dar looked up, startled; but it was just a portly passerby, chatting with a waddling clergyman. 'Sin? Come now, Reverend! What a medieval idea!'

'It'll always be current, I'm afraid,' the minister rejoined, 'and even fashionable – though rarely as a conversational topic.'

'It does lend a certain sauce to pleasure,' the passerby admitted. 'And, after all, the really important element in life is getting what you want – the things that make you happy.'

'Of course, of course,' the clergyman agreed. 'Take heaven, for example . . .'

The passerby was laughing as they passed out of hearing.

Dar shook his head. 'I don't think the revolution'll wait a hundred years.'

'You think this is bad?' Sam scoffed. 'Just wait till you get to Terra!'

'I can wait, thank you. I'm beginning to see why you liked Wolmar so much. You know, this pretty little market couldn't be here unless the police were helping it a lot.'

'Of course,' Sam said brightly. 'But be fair – they might not have enough officers to cover everything.'

'Yeah, but which is it?' Dar muttered. He glanced up and saw a blimp of a shopkeeper leaning against his storefront. Dar stepped up to him, pointing an accusing finger and snapping, 'Which is it, citizen? How can you get away with this? Don't you have any police here?'

'Sir!' The shopkeeper drew himself up, offended. 'I'll thank you not to discuss such disgusting issues!' And he wheeled about majestically, slamming his door behind him.

'*I'm* not so squeamish,' said an oily voice.

Dar and Sam looked up and saw a hunched old man with a lascivious grin, peering out from the shop next door. He was obscenely slender. 'What's your perversion, younglings? Plato? Descartes? Machiavelli? I've got 'em all in here, all the banned books! Come in and read anything – just fifty BTUs an hour!'

'Let's go,' Sam hissed. 'I don't like the way your jaw is setting!'

'All right, all right,' Dar growled. He turned away toward the end of the arcade, and bumped into someone. 'Oh, excuse me . . .' He broke off, staring into a face like a rat's above a short, lean body.

The little man stared back at him, eyes widening in shock and horror. Then his mouth opened in a moan that turned into a scream, and he slumped to the ground, clutching his chest.

'What happened?' Dar bleated, staring at the bright redness spreading over the man's tunic from under his hands.

'Murder, I'd say.'

Dar's head snapped up; he found himself staring into a very familiar beefy face, above an even more familiar breast-patch badge.

'You're under arrest.' There was another one like him on the other side of Sam. 'Just hold out your wrists, now . . .' He produced a length of cable that glowed, even in daylight.

'Uh, no thanks.' Dar stepped backward; he'd worn a manacle-loop before, on his way to Wolmar. Once around his wrists, the cable would virtually meld with his skin, and his wrists would stick together as though they'd grown that way. 'Actually, I have an appointment at the confectionery shop, you see . . .'

'Well, I'm afraid we've got one that's a little more important. Come on now, let's not make a scene.' The policeman stepped forward. Sam backed away as the shopkeeper hefted an electroclub and snapped it down against the officer's occiput. He slumped to the ground with a muted sigh as two lean and muscular types materialized out of adjacent doorways to zap the other policeman and take their places.

'Bit of a lucky thing for you we happened along,' the shopkeeper observed. 'From what I read on the newsfax, all the cops in Haskerville're out hunting you two. Now, if I was you, I'd be wanting a nice, safe bolthole to bolt into, and lock behind me.'

'Good idea,' Dar agreed. 'But, personally, I go along with the idea that says the more you move around, the harder you are to find.'

'I was afraid you'd make this difficult,' the shopkeeper sighed. He nodded to the two gorillas. 'Move 'em around, boys.'

Huge arms seized Dar from behind, hoisting him off the ground and carrying him toward the open air. Beside him, Sam cursed and swore, trying to kick a shin with her heels, and missing every time.

As the toughs bundled them into a waiting car, Dar observed, 'I think the cops were the better choice.'

## 8

The sign said, 'You are now leaving HASKERVILLE.'

He turned to the tough who shared the back seat with them. 'You must work for somebody important, to rate a car.'

'Might be,' the man said shortly. 'Ain't so much, though.'

'Well, no – it goes on wheels, not an air cushion. But it's still more than most folks have here. Must cost a fortune – all that metal in the engine.'

'Metal?' The man frowned. 'Where'd you grow up – on Orehouse?'

'They're doing such marvellous things with synthetics these days,' Sam murmured.

'Sure, plastic,' the driver confirmed. 'Polythermothane. Takes all the heat we need to give it, an' more.'

'Well, I suppose – for a turbine.' Dar frowned. 'Maybe even for a boiler. But how do you shield the fissionables?'

' 'E *is* from Orehouse,' the first tough snorted. 'Fissionables're metal, lunk. How'd we get 'em 'ere?'

'Yeah, I suppose it would be a little heavy on the import price.' Dar scratched his head. 'So what do you use for an energy source?'

'Methane.'

'Methane?' Sam cried, scandalized. '*Chemicals?*'

'Uh – I hate to butt in.' Dar glommed onto the tough's arm with a mastiff-grip. 'But, could you say a word to your friend? We're running right into a mountainside!'

The granite outcrop towered over them, rushing down on them.

The tough nodded. 'Close enough, Rog.'

Rog pushed a button set into the dashboard, and the scrub at the base of the cliff swung outward and upward, revealing a huge gaping cave-mouth.

'Just a bit o' camouflage,' the backseat tough explained. 'Can't leave yer front door open fer just any Tom, Dick, or Paddy t' walk in, y' know.'

'No, definitely not.' Dar's eyes fairly bulged out of his head as the car swept into the cave, and a line of glow-plates lit up along the length of the walls, lighting their way onward. The floor sloped away in front of them, spiralling down at a thirty-degree angle. Rog held the car to a continuing hairpin turn, slowing down only as much as was absolutely necessary. Sam swung over against Dar and stayed there, which would've been very pleasant, if Dar hadn't had to keep fighting to hold himself away from the backseat tough, who might not have understood, especially since that was his gun-hand.

The ramp levelled off and the car straightened out, but Sam stayed over against Dar. He counted it a hopeful sign, but was no longer sure he cared, now that he'd seen Lona.

The tunnel flared out into a huge cavern. Brilliant glow-plates spread a cold greenish light over alleyways between towering gray plastrete slabs.

'I'd almost think those were buildings,' Dar said, in hushed tones, 'if they had windows.'

'They *are* buildings,' the tough affirmed. 'What'd y' need windows for, down 'ere? Whacher gonna look at?'

Rog pulled the car into a slot between a small van and another car. They got out, and found themselves surrounded by a fleet of trucks and vans, parked in very orderly rows.

'Yes,' Dar mused, 'your boss isn't exactly hurting, is he?'

'Ask 'im,' the tough invited. 'Y've got an appointment – immediate.'

The door slid aside, and they stepped into a leather-and-mahogany office with a rug as thick as graft.

'Citizens Dar Mandra and Sam Bine,' said the bald man behind the acre of desktop, almost lost in the vast swivel chair. 'Come in.'

They came in slowly, feeling as though there were guns pointed at their backs from all angles. Ridiculous, of course; the guns were probably aimed from the front.

'Sit.' It was an order, not an invitation. Under the circumstances, Dar wasn't disposed to argue. He sat at the lefthand corner of the desk; Sam sat at the right. That's where the chairs were. They didn't look as though they'd move.

'What is this – our invitation to join the Underground?' Dar joked, with a tight smile.

It died under the look the little man gave him. Did he always have to make the right guess at the wrong time?

Their host wasn't tall, but he was very broad across the shoulders and chest – and not fat. In fact, he was very hard, in the flesh – and, from the look of him, in the soul, too. He wore a quiet brown business tunic with a muted yellow ascot –

conservative, punctiliously correct, with the look of a very high price. His nails were manicured, and his eyes were hidden behind brown lenses.

'You're in the House of Houses,' he grated.

Dar stiffened and tried to keep his face immobile. Even buried on a prison planet, he'd heard of the IDE's biggest organized crime ring.

'The House of . . .' Sam's voice choked off. She cleared her throat. 'Uh, not the head offices, of course.'

The brown lenses swivelled toward her. The little man nodded slowly.

'But the head offices have to be on Terra!'

The brown lenses turned slowly from side to side. 'We like it better here.'

Dar clenched his fists to hide their quivering. 'And, uh, whom do we have the pleasure of addressing?'

The brown lenses tracked back toward him. 'I've got a lot of names.'

'Any one will do.' Dar tried to grin.

'Call me Sard, then – Thalvor Sard. I'm the Syndic.'

'The Syndic?' Sam gasped. 'The biggest boss criminal in all of Terran space?'

'A businessman,' Sard said, a bit impatiently, 'only a business-man. Just a little impatient with government regulation, that's all.'

'Right?' His masked gaze swung to Dar.

'Right,' Dar mumbled. From what he'd heard, Sard's 'im-patience' amounted to a running war on fifteen planets, and underground anarchy on most of the rest.

'But – *here?*' Sam spluttered. 'On a frontier planet halfway to the marches?'

'Not so much of a frontier, as you've maybe noticed. The folks here like their comfort – like it enough to be glad to have us handy, and make sure their cops can't do much about us.'

'And because they don't have radios,' Dar guessed.

Sard's head swivelled back to him. 'My, you're the quick one, though. Right, this time – radios cost so much, the cops don't have 'em. That means we can stay one jump ahead out here. Oh, they can move efficiently enough inside the town, where they can use couriers – but not out here. I'm what little law there is, outside the bounds of Haskerville.'

Dar nodded slowly.

'And the law can do a lot for you.' Sard nodded back at Dar. 'Safety and protection, and a fat salary. What'll the town law give you, the IDE law? Arrest and, probably, a quick death.'

'Arrest? Whoa! What is this?' Dar protested. 'We're not in trouble with the cops!'

Sard just stared at him.

'Well . . . okay. Maybe they did try to bushwhack us in that tavern,' Dar amended. 'And maybe they were trying to take us in when your, ah, people intervened. But we haven't done anything illegal.'

'You're there,' Sard said. 'That's enough.'

'*Why?*'

'Because you're a telepath – or your woman is. And all the government sees is that, in the wrong hands, your power could be a real threat to them.' He leaned back. 'They're right, too.'

Dar found his voice again. '*Telepath?* Me?'

Sard shrugged. 'All right, play innocent, if you want. They'll be out after you, just the same. That's why that BOA man faked being murdered right next to you – to give the cops a reason for arresting you.'

'No!' Dar cried. 'He's trying to stop us from taking the new governor of Wolmar's resignation back to Terra!'

'Sure,' Sard said slowly. 'Right.'

'Uh . . . what would we have to do for this salary-plus-benefits of yours?' Sam put in.

The dark glasses swivelled toward her. 'Nothing much. Just tell us what certain people are planning to do. You'd travel a lot – especially to Terra.'

'Handsome offer,' Sam said slowly. 'Unfortunately, neither of us is a telepath.'

The glasses swung toward Dar.

' 'Fraid that's true,' Dar seconded. 'Either IDE's got its signals crossed, or you do.'

'My signals don't get crossed,' Sard corrected. 'IDE might, but not the LORDS – and they're the ones who're out after telepaths.'

'The exception proves the rule,' Sam said. 'This is it.'

Sard shook his head slowly. 'Too bad. Such nice young kids.'

'*What's* too bad?' Dar felt a premonition walking up his spine.

'Your untimely deaths.' Sard leaned forward. 'One of you is a telepath, whether or not the other one knows it – and that telepath must've already picked up enough information to pack half of my people off to prison worlds, maybe enough to shut down the whole House of Houses. And you'd do it, too, 'cause you'd think it'd buy the LORDS off your back.'

'But we're *not* telepaths.'

'Sorry,' Sard shook his head. 'Can't take the chance. Either you join, or you leave in an urn.' He pushed a button. 'Don't say anything right now – think it over. This shouldn't be a snap judgement, you understand.'

Two tall, muscular men, impeccably dressed, came in.

'These gentlemen will conduct you to your accommodations,' Sard explained. 'You'll get better ones if you join up, of course. Think it over.'

The accommodations had a door made of steel bars and a very elaborate combination lock.

'Gee, I didn't know you were a telepath.' Dar flopped down on a very hard bunk.

'I didn't know *you* were,' Sam retorted. 'Now that we've established that, shall we try to make sense out of the situation?'

'What's to make sense of?' Dar shrugged. 'Somebody's spreading nasty lies about us. Probably Rat-Face. Does that make any more sense out of it?'

'Some,' Sam insisted. 'That gets him official help in trying to get us locked up, which keeps the resignation from getting to BOA, while he waits for Bhelabher to change his mind.'

Dar snorted. 'Bhelabher? He'll wait for a century. The Honourable won't change his mind as long as Shacklar's right next to him.'

Sam shrugged. 'So Rat-Face is doomed to failure. Unfortunately, he doesn't know that – so he still gets in our way.'

'So the telepath who just landed on the planet, and for whom the police are searching, is supposed to be one of us, huh?'

Sam nodded. 'Looks like it – which explains why we've seen so many of their shoestring police.'

'Well, what they don't get done, the House of Houses does.' Dar scratched behind his ear. 'It's almost as though this planet has two governments, one inside the cities, and one out.'

'Somewhat like our noble interstellar government,' Sam said acidly. 'There's the official government, and there's the LORDS.'

'Can't stand long, can it?' Dar stretched. 'Well! That leaves us two real simple problems – one, to get out of here; and two, clearing our names.'

'I don't know what to do about two,' Sam said, 'but about one . . .' She stared off into space, eyes losing focus.

Dar frowned. What was she doing? He was just about to ask, when Sam turned and smiled brightly. 'Nope, don't hear a murmur. Now, let's see . . .' She stood up, went to the door, knelt down, reached around to the front, and pressed her ear against the back of the lock. 'One nice thing about a low-metal planet is the lack of modern devices.'

'What're you . . .?'

'Sh!' she hissed fiercely, and Dar shut up. She punched buttons and turned a dial for a few minutes, muttering, 'No . . . no, the other way . . . there, that's right . . . there . . . there!' Triumphantly, she shoved on the door and, slowly, with a soft rumble, it slid to the side. She stepped out.

Dar stared.

Then he darted out after her. 'Where did you . . .?'

'Whisper,' she hissed. 'Sound carries in these tunnels!'

Dar put his lips against her ear and murmured, 'Where did you learn to do *that*?'

'You pick up a lot in a government office,' she whispered back, 'especially if you want a look at your own personnel file. Come on, let's go!'

She led off, padding silently down the dark tunnel. Dar could remember that they had to turn left as they came out of the cell, but after that, he was as lost as Handsel and Gretel without the bread crumbs. But Sam wasn't in doubt for a moment; she paused at the corridor's end (he bumped into her: it was so dark, that was the only way he knew she'd stopped), listened a moment, then darted to her right, hauling Dar after her. They went on for what seemed a half-hour, but must've been all of five minutes; then he bumped into her again. 'Sorry,' he mumbled. 'Sh!' she answered; then, 'All clear. Come on.'

Halfway down the next midnight passage, she stopped suddenly. Then she was pushing him back frantically, and shoving him into a cross-corridor. They went down it for a few steps; then she yanked on his arm, stopping him, and froze. He could tell she froze because he could see her in the first ragtag of light that hit the far wall from a handlamp. Dar froze too, plastered against the wall like a tapestry.

'Whut'ja expect?' A lean, scarred man in faded coveralls, hands handcuffed behind him, slouched forward in front of two toughs in business tunics. 'A'ter all, he wint for me with a knife!'

'Y' c'n tell Sard about it in th' mornin'.' One tough prodded him. 'Git along, now.'

The scarred one snarled, and they passed across the end of the corridor. The reflection from the handlamp wavered over the wall to Sam's right, and was gone. Dar held his breath till their footsteps had faded away, then let it out in a gusty sigh. Instantly, Sam's finger pressed over his lips, then was gone, and she was tugging on his hand again.

They turned right at the end of the corridor, and went on.

So it went, for what seemed the better part of a day. Dar was amazed at the sharpness of her hearing. Twice she pushed them into hiding in time for someone passing by to miss them, when Dar hadn't heard the faintest sound until after they were in hiding. And she never led him past an occupied cell. How could she figure out where to go?

Then, finally, she dropped down to kneel; Dar almost fell over her, but he groped back just in time. He wondered what she was doing until he heard a very faint click. Then, slowly, a slit of light appeared, and widened into a narrow rectangle that widened to a door. They stepped out into a starlit night; the door slid quietly shut behind them.

'How did you manage that?' Dar whispered. 'The Labyrinth couldn't've been worse!'

'This was nothing,' she snorted. 'You should've seen the government building where I used to work. Come on!'

She set out at a long, catlike stride that Dar had to stretch to keep up with. They'd come out of the side of a hillock; as they rounded it, they saw nothing but a level plain, broken by the occasional outcrop, stretching away into the distance. At its limit, a feeble gleam marked Haskerville.

'Just like the early days,' Dar sighed, 'when the Wolmen still thought we were enemies and I had to be ready to hide, fast, whenever I went out trading!'

'Oh.' Sam eyed him sideways. 'You've been on the run in open country before?'

Dar nodded. 'The main principle is to stay away from the roads, and stay near whatever cover there is. And, of course, if something moves, you hit the ground fast, and worry later about whether it's dangerous or good to eat. Here, I'll show you some of the fine points.'

He moved off through the long grass without a breath of sound. Sam shook her head and sighed, then went after him.

*

As the sky lightened with false dawn, Dar started to sneak across the last yard that separated dirt track from paved Haskerville street.

Sam caught his shoulder. 'Act nonchalantly, gnappie. You go sneaking around like that, the first citizen who spots you'll blow the whistle.'

Dar turned back. 'So who's going to be awake to see me?'

'Agreed. So why sneak?'

Dar sighed and gave up.

So they strolled into town like a couple of late-night revellers returning to their hotel rooms.

'Any idea where we're going?' Dar asked. 'With the authorities *and* the Underground after us, we're kinda short on hideouts.'

'A point,' Sam admitted. 'In this town, I wouldn't even trust a cheap hotel . . . What's that?'

Dar stopped, turning his head from side to side, and saw nothing. He strained his ears, but all he heard was a hiss of wind.

'Over there.' Sam pointed toward a shopfront a block to her left. 'Come on.'

She set off toward the shop. After the episode in the jail-tunnels, Dar wasn't about to dispute her hearing. He followed.

They had come into a shabbier section of Haskerville. The houses were big, but they were simple frame dwellings – no half-timbering and stucco – and looked somewhat infirm. Most of them were overdue for a coat of paint – the older part of town, at a guess, built before the planet had enough surplus to worry about aesthetics in architecture.

Someone came out of the shopfront they were heading for, and turned down the street away from them. He/she was bald, and wore a grey, loose coverall.

'I think,' Sam said, with a catch to her voice, 'we've struck paydirt.'

Dar could see her point – and now he could hear the trace she'd picked up: a low mutter of conversation, underscored by the ripple of a string instrument and a flute.

Sam swung the door open. They stepped into a room decorated in Late-Modern Junkyard. The walls were plain pastel-painted plastiboard, decorated with hangings of knotted, brightly coloured twine, some of which held potted plants. The tables were plastic delivery drums, and the 'chairs' were tree stumps, somewhat levelled off on the bottom. There was a counter against one wall; Dar recognized a section of it – it had 'Wolmar' rolled across it. The far end was topped by an arcane plastic contraption that gave off clouds of steam and a rich, spicy aroma.

Most of the tables were filled, and all the patrons had shaved heads and loose grey coveralls. So, for that matter, did the people behind the counter. The musicians, on a small raised platform at the far end, wore the same attire.

Dar paused just inside the doorway, feeling a prickling along the back of his neck. He couldn't help it; he felt as though he'd just stepped into a village populated by a tribe he hadn't met, who might or might not be hostile.

'Don't worry,' Sam murmured, 'you're with me.'

She sauntered over to the counter. A girl who looked enough like her to make Dar rub his eyes, came over and said, 'Yeah?' in a neutral tone.

'Two cups,' Sam said, and Dar felt in his purse for nails. The girl turned to the arcane contraption, picked up a cup, and pressed a valve; then she turned back to them with two steaming mugs. 'New here.'

'Am,' Sam confirmed. 'Just in from Wolmar.'

Panic jammed Dar's stomach up toward his throat. Why not just send up a rocket that'd explode into the words, 'Here're the suspects!'

But the girl's face came alive. 'The prison planet? Where they're oppressing the natives? Hey, tell me about it!'

'Yeah, me too!' A tall, lanky man lounged up to lean on the bar beside Sam.

'Wolmar? I want to hear this!'

'Hey! The real word?'

In thirty seconds, they were surrounded by a small crowd. Dar kept trying to edge closer and closer to the counter, and to glance over both shoulders at once; but Sam launched happily into an account of her tour of Wolmar. Dar was amazed at her accuracy; under equivalent conditions, he couldn't have resisted the temptation to colour the tale a little, probably putting in a bevy of scantily clad maidens and a hair-raising escape from a bloodthirsty tribe or two; but Sam stuck to reporting what she'd seen and heard, introducing Dar as her guide, which won him a look of respect, then glares of scorn when she mentioned his being a trader, then looks of awe when she explained his teaching function.

'You mean it's not really a prison colony?'

Sam shrugged. 'Depends on how you look at it. They've all been sentenced to go there.'

'They're not really oppressing the natives?' The asker sounded almost disappointed.

'No – but look what they *are* doing!' Sam fairly glowed with missionary fervour as she went into an explanation of Cholly's educational programme. Dar listened, enthralled. He hadn't known he was that much of a hero.

'Hey – it sounds like heaven,' said one Hume, with a shaky laugh.

'Yeah. What crime do I have to commit to get sent there?' another joked; but the laughter that followed had a rather serious echo.

'Well, don't jump too soon.' Sam leaned on the counter and pushed her cup over for a refill. 'The Bureau of Otherworldly Affairs sent out a new governor.'

Dar was delighted at the groan.

'Bastards always gotta foul up something good when they find it,' muttered one Angry Young Man.

'Establishments can't stand progress,' growled another.

'Yeah, but BOA didn't figure on Shacklar.' Sam sipped her refill with relish.

'Why? What could he do?' The AYM frowned.

'Well, the new governor's credentials kinda got, uh, "lost", before he could show them to Shacklar. And by the time Shacklar got done with him, he'd decided to resign and join the colony.'

The room rocked with a hoot of laughter. The AYM smote the counter gleefully. 'Go, General! The Organic Will Grow, in spite of the defoliators!'

Sam nodded. 'Dar and I got the job of carrying his resignation back to Terra. But the new ex-governor's left-hand man didn't like the whole idea, so he set out to sabotage us.'

'How?' The AYM scowled. 'What could he do?'

'Well, first off, he seems to have wrangled himself in as the pilot of the courier ship that brought us here – and he sicced a bunch of pirates on us as soon as we broke out of H-space.'

A low mutter of anger ran around the crowd.

'Oh, it was okay – we got out of it, all right, and got picked up by a patrol cruiser. But when we got here, we found out he'd told the Haskerville government that one of us was a telepath and was a threat to social order.'

'You?' a voice hooted. '*You're* the witches they're hunting?'

'What've they got against telepaths, anyway?' the AYM grumbled. 'They're not hurting anybody.'

'Especially when they aren't really telepaths,' Sam agreed. 'But the House of Houses got wind of it, too, and tried to 'script us. So we're on the run two ways, and running out of hideouts.'

A chorus of protest filled the room, and a dozen Humes thrust forward with offers of sympathy.

'Sons o' sobakas,' the AYM growled. 'Just let one person try do do something decent, and they throw every roller they can in your way! Come on! *We'll* hide you!'

And the whole crowd swirled them out with a chorus of agreement. Dar started to dig in his heels in alarm, then noticed Sam whirling by with a delighted grin. He relaxed, and let himself be borne by the current.

It deposited them in the street outside, with only the AYM and a few other Humes.

'Come on!' the AYM declared, and he set off down the street. Dar had to hurry to catch up.

'Lucky bumping into you,' Sam was saying as he came up with them.

'Not all that much luck. This's the ideal place for us – they leave us alone.'

Dar could see why. The townsfolk would want to stay as far away as they could from the drab Humes and their shoestring existence. Of course, the shortage of radio communication and police might have had something to do with it, too – if the system was rigged to stay out of the way of the taxpayers' pleasures, it wouldn't be able to bother anyone else much, either.

The AYM led them into an old building that looked as though it had been an office collection in its youth, but had been converted to dwelling purposes. The liftshaft still operated, and took them up to the third level.

'Got to exploring one day.' The AYM ran his fingers over the bas-reliefs that decorated the wall at the end of the corridor. 'I was doing a rubbing here, and I must have pressed just hard enough on the right thing, because . . .'

Something clicked; a hum sprang up; then, slowly, a portion of the wall retracted, to leave a doorway about two metres high.

Dar stared. Then, slowly, he nodded. 'A very interesting suite.'

'Yeah, isn't it?' The AYM grinned. 'I don't know what kind of business the office had in the old days, but they must've had some kind of a security problem. Import-export trade, at a guess.'

Dar stooped through the doorway. 'Don't suppose it comes equipped with little luxuries like light.'

'Try the wall-plate.'

It hadn't occurred to Dar that there might be one. He slid his hand over the wall until he felt the smoother rectangle. It responded to his skin temperature by glowing a small, dim plate in the ceiling into life.

Sam stepped through, too. 'You knew we were coming?'

'No, but I had a notion I might need it someday.' The AYM pointed to a few boxes of sealed packets and demijohns against the lefthand wall. 'Made a deposit every time I could scrounge a little extra. There's a week's supply in here, at least. Pretty plain – biscuits and fruit, and some meat, and nothing to drink but water – but it'll keep you alive.' He pointed to a neat stack of blankets just beyond the two straight chairs. 'That's all I could scrounge for sleeping and sitting. But all I promised was a hideout.'

'The way we are right now, this is a palace.' Sam clasped his hand. 'No way I can thank you, really, grozh.'

'No need. Who knows? You may be doing the same for me someday.' He squeezed her arm. 'Enjoy what you can. I'll check in every now and then.' He stepped back through the doorway, and the wall-segment rolled back into place.

'Of course,' Dar observed, 'you realize we can't get out now.'

'Lesser of two evils.' Sam settled herself on one of the hard chairs. 'We can get him to tell us when the next ship lands, and duck out to the port.'

'A *month* in this crackerbox?'

'This one, or one like it, maintained by the authorities.' Sam shrugged. 'Your choice. Personally, I'll take this one.'

'No contest,' Dar sighed, flopping down onto the other chair. 'I didn't know your tribe was so widespread.'

'There're a lot of us – an awful lot. Oh, there always have been some, at least as far back as the late nineteenth century – but they're always a minority, unless something's going wrong in the government. When a political system has engine trouble, alternative cultures spread.'

'Until the engine starts running again?'

Sam nodded. 'But the numbers have been on the increase, steadily, for more than a hundred years now.'

'I always seem to come in on the end of things,' Dar sighed.

'And the beginning.' Sam's face lit with a rare, dazzling smile. 'That's what comes after the end, you know.'

The monster in his dream was knocking on his head with a very loud, hollow sound. Dar waded up out of the morass of slumber to check on the objectivity of the knocking.

Sure enough, it *was* objective – but in the drab reality of their roomlet, it sounded only as a tapping, not a booming pounding.

Dar frowned. Why would the AYM tap? He knew how to open the door!

Therefore, the tapper didn't know how.

Therefore, it wasn't the AYM.

Dar reached out and squeezed Sam's ankle. Her head came up slowly, eyes squinting painfully. 'What . . .?'

'Sh.' Dar laid a finger across her lips, then pointed toward the wall/door.

She turned toward the tapping, irritated. He could virtually see her brain waking up as her eyes widened and her mind traced the same path of logic his had.

'Double-crossed?' Dar whispered.

'Can't be!' Sam scrambled to her feet. 'I just won't believe it!'

The door/wall began to hum.

'Uh oh.' Dar tried to get between Sam and the entryway. 'He found the right leaf.'

The door rolled back to show a segment of a man.

It was sort of the centre stripe of a personality. Dar could see the man's face, and a little of his shoulders to either side (he had no neck), a slice of chest and belly, one knee and the other thigh, and the middle of the front of an armchair. The rest of both the man and the armchair went on to either side of the doorway and, from the look of him, went on for quite a distance. If the average Falstavian was fat, he was enormous. His face was a beach-ball with four chins and a blob of nose over a thin-lipped, tight mouth. But the eyes, tiny as currants in a vat of dough, were sharp and alive, quick with intelligence, chill with shrewdness. His chest and belly had been cast in one piece and, if there was a ribcage beneath, it was sunk full fathom five. His legs were sections of whale, and his foot was the whaleboat.

The chair floated a good eighteen inches off the floor – antigravity, no doubt; and the connection sparked in Dar's mind: the man couldn't get out of the chair. He couldn't move without it. *That* fat.

'Greetings,' Gargantua said. 'I am Myles Croft.'

'Uh – a pleasure. I suppose.' Dar was willing to take a chance on it; after all, the man couldn't get in. 'Let me guess – you're the landlord, and it's the first of the month.'

'Closer than you intended.' The mouth didn't smile, but the eyes twinkled. 'I have the honour to be mayor of Haskerville.'

Dar levered his jaw back in place and swallowed.

'We're doing better than I thought,' Sam said behind him. 'The Humes're getting chummy with the mayor.'

'Not particularly.' The irony in Croft's voice *had* to be humour. 'No one needed to tell me where you were hidden. Once I'd heard that you'd escaped from the House of Houses, it was obvious you'd be somewhere back in Haskerville – and, since I knew the lady of the party was a Hume, it was logical to conclude you'd seek refuge in this quarter.'

Sam nodded. 'All right, so far as it goes – but how'd you know about the two of us? . . . Hold on, cancel that! Of course. If the police knew, you'd know. But how'd you know we'd been taken to Sard, let alone that we'd escaped?'

'I have my sources.'

'Interesting, interesting.' Dar nodded slowly. 'But how'd you know which building to look in?'

'If anyone had hidden you, it would logically be Anthony Marne, who's as much of a leader as the Humes have.'

'Angry-young-man type?'

'I thought you'd met. Therefore, you'd probably be hidden in his building – so I surveyed the establishment floor by floor, until I realized one hall was noticeably shorter than the others. Beyond that, I believe you heard my search for the activating control.'

Dar just stared.

Then he gave his head a quick shake. 'Did you ever consider taking up detective work?'

'Frequently, young man – and I frequently do. The mayor should know *something* about the goings-on in his own city.'

'But if you know all that, the House shouldn't be able to get away with anything, and ninety per cent of your citizens ought to be in jail.'

The huge face smiled into waves of fat. 'You are observant, young man. I leave it to your imagination to determine why all are still at large. Suffice it to say that I have some rather elaborate plans, which are working rather well in practice; but they result in a delicate balance, which could very easily be upset by a new and random factor.'

Dar's spine turned into an icicle. 'You mean us.'

Croft nodded. 'It is in my interest to see that you're removed from my planet as quickly as possible.'

'Shouldn't you have brought along a little protection on this jaunt?' Sam asked grimly.

'I think not. I've discussed you with a friend of mine, and he seems to have high regard for you.'

'Well, it's nice to have a good reference.' Dar was wary. 'Who's our yea-sayer?'

'A Mr Tambourin; he styles himself "Whitey the Wino". And, too, I think, all things considered, that the best way to remove you from circulation is to assist you in your progress.'

'You mean you'll get us out of here?' Dar pounced on it.

'I had that in mind, yes. You've certainly done nothing meriting permanent incarceration; but the longer you're here, the more disruptive you'll be. And I don't relish having two police forces on my planet.'

'Two?' Now it was Sam who pounced. 'Where'd the second one come from?'

'A gentleman named Canis Destinus, I believe. He came to me yesterday morning, bearing a letter "To Whom It May Concern", from the Secretary for Internal Security for the IDE, requesting the reader to aid Mr Destinus in any way possible. But the Secretary, as you may know, is head of the reactionary LORDS party . . .'

'I didn't,' Sam said, 'but I'm glad to.'

'Mr Destinus seems to be more than he appears,' Dar said softly.

'Really? I thought his appearance quite indicative; looks somewhat like a rat.'

'I take it you don't quite approve of the LORDS?'

'Not germane.' Croft dismissed the point with a wave of his hand. 'Fortunately, in such circumstances, the letter of the law requires a planetary official, such as myself, to make certain lengthy verifications of the applicant's bona fides, including the Secretary's signature; so I explained to Mr Destinus that I would probably be able to accord him my full co-operation early next week.'

'As I said.' Dar grinned. 'You don't approve of the LORDS.'

'Be that as it may; Mr Destinus did not seem disposed to wait. So I assumed, when I began to receive reports of pairs of police officers who were definitely not among those I had employed, that Mr Destinus had induced my co-operation by his own initiative, possibly with Sard's assistance.'

'He hired some bullyboys from the House to impersonate cops,' Dar translated. 'But I can see your problem; the longer we're around, the longer you've got a second, but illegal, police force.'

'Of course, I have ways of making such an enterprise pro-hibitively expensive for Mr Sard – but not while the LORDS' bottomless purse is open to him. However, if you depart, Mr Destinus will leave in pursuit of you.'

'Makes excellent sense,' Dar agreed, 'from your point of view.'

'And from yours, I should think.'

'As far as it goes,' Sam said cautiously. 'Problem is, when we *do* leave, we're a little picky about where we're going.'

'Young Hume, where you go is entirely your own affair.'

'Nice theory,' Dar approved. 'Unfortunately, once you're on a freighter, it's kind of hard to persuade it to change its destination.'

'Come to that,' Sam chimed in, 'there aren't any ships of *any* kind scheduled to lift off for a month. How're you getting us out of here?'

Croft signed. 'Haskerville is the only town of any size on the planet; we've something near ninety per cent of the population here. Accordingly, I'm *de facto* planetary governor, as well as mayor. So I've authority over all IDE equipment here; and part of that inventory is a small fleet of outmoded IDE scout ships. I've arranged for Mr Tambourin to buy one, as government surplus.'

'To *buy* a spacer?' Dar's eyes fairly bulged. 'All by himself?'

'Government surplus is ridiculously inexpensive,' Croft noted.

'Even so – a *spacer*! How much money does this guy *have*?'

'Not much, after this little purchase.' Sam smiled up at the mayor. 'Can we hitch a ride, Mr Croft?'

'Hey, hold on!' Dar caught her arm. 'What do you mean, hitch a ride? We can't trust this man!'

Sam turned back, frowning up at him. 'Why not?'

'Why *not*?' Dar spluttered. 'I mean . . . look! We're on the *run*! He's the *law*!'

'That's right, he's the law. So if he says to let us go, they'll let us go.'

'But . . . but . . .'

'Look,' Sam said, with forced patience, 'I'm a good judge of character. Have you ever known me to be wrong about who I could trust, and who I couldn't?'

Dar started to answer, then hesitated.

'Including you,' Sam reminded.

Dar sighed and capitulated. 'All right. You win.' He looked toward Croft. 'When does the next bus leave?'

With a load like Croft in it, Dar wouldn't've thought the armchair could support any more. But it had lift to spare; they glided through the deserted streets of Haskerville perched on the arms like a couple of children come to recite their Christmas lists to Santa.

After a little while, Dar said, 'It occurs to me that what you've got here is a planetful of grifters and marks, about evenly divided.'

Croft nodded agreeably. 'An over-simplification, but accurate within its limits.'

'In fact, you could almost say it's got the potential for becoming a balanced society.'

'The potential, perhaps,' Croft agreed.

'How do you manage to keep the House of Houses from totally destroying the citizens?'

Croft smiled, amused. 'Come now, young man! You give me too much credit. Even a criminal realizes that he must take care of his geese if he wants them to grow more feathers for plucking.'

'Not from what I've read,' Dar said slowly. 'Historically, even the organized criminals haven't cared who they hurt or killed, as long as they made a profit on it.'

'Ah, but that is when they have an unlimited supply of geese!'

'Somehow, I don't think the House of Houses has quite that much foresight.'

Croft nodded, amused. 'I may have arranged for the odd idea to reach the House through circuitous routes. Then, too, even with a severely limited police force, there are ways of making certain activities unprofitable.'

Dar nodded, bemused. 'So you've got two societies that pretty much balance each other – and it's got the potential for becoming a single, cohesive society. That would take a lot of guidance and manoeuvring – but it is possible.'

Croft nodded. 'Of course. *Anything* is possible – even that; with an exterior challenge and thrown back on their own resources, both halves of the population might forgo their own forms of decadence.'

'A challenge such as being cut off from the rest of the human-inhabited universe?'

Croft nodded, a slight smile on his thin lips. 'You evince a definite talent, young fellow. Given time and practice, you might prove as capable of deduction as I am.'

The spaceport was guarded by a split-log fence, like an old-time Western fort. But the gate opened at Croft's approach, and they floated through, to stare at a square mile of plastrete, pock-marked with blast-pits. The two-storey personnel and passenger building seemed like a minuscule bump on the fence. The only other break in the bald field was a silvery manta-ray shape tilted upward toward the stars, as though it strained to be free of the planet – an FTL scout, streamlined and planed for atmospheric capability. No ferry this time, but a ship that could go from surface to surface, though without the speed of the great liners. It was beautiful, but it seemed pathetically small and frail against the immense stretch of plastrete.

The hatch was open, and a silhouette appeared against its rectangle of yellow light as they drifted up. 'As good as your word! You found 'em!' Whitey jumped down to pump Croft's arm.

'You doubted me, Whitey?'

'Not for a second! Trouble was, it was turning into hours.'

A black robe blocked the hatch, and light gleamed off a bald pate. 'Welcome, wanderers!' Father Marco waved. 'Come on in and tell us about your travels! We should have time; we're going seventy-five light-years!'

But Dar's eyes snapped to the figure beside the priest. Even as a silhouette, she looked wonderful.

'Good to see you again, Father.' Sam hopped down off Croft's chair and strode toward the hatch. 'But why're you coming along? It's *our* misfortune, and none of your own.'

'Someone has to look after your souls,' the friar joked. At least, Dar hoped he was joking. 'Nice of you to care, Father – but why should you?' He jumped up into the ship, carefully brushing against Lona in the process.

'Because,' said the priest, 'I'm a brother of the Order of St Vidicon, and you two present a case that an engineer can't resist.'

Dar didn't follow the logic, but it didn't matter; Lona was giving him the long stare. He couldn't tell whether it was admiring or accusing, but he didn't really care – so long as he had her attention.

'Well, that's it!' Whitey hopped aboard and sealed the hatch behind him. 'Always helps to have friends in the right places.'

'Sure does,' Dar agreed, 'and I'm awfully glad we've got you. But why? This isn't your quarrel, Whitey.'

'It is now.' Whitey flopped down into the nearest acceleration couch and stretched his webbing across. 'Things were getting dull, but you two promise to make them interesting again.'

'But you're heading for the frontier, and we have to get to Terra!'

'So do we – now.' Whitey grinned. 'As long as you promise to shake the old place up a bit. Besides, I have to see my publisher – I've suddenly run low on funds.'

Dar swallowed, feeling guilty, but Whitey looked around and bawled, 'Who's going to pilot this tub?'

'Who else?' Lona jumped into the pilot's couch with relish. 'I'd fly a mountain to get back to some good old-fashioned decadence!' She hit a few keys, and the spacer roared to life.

'I'll take communications.' Sam slipped into the couch beside Lona and keyed the talker. 'What's the name of this tub?'

'I christen it *Ray of Hope*,' Whitey declared.

'*Ray of Hope* to Control,' Sam called, 'outward-bound toward Sol.'

'Uh . . . come in, *Ray of Hope*.' Control was, to say the least, startled.

'Permission to lift off.'

'Permission to . . .? Uh – be right with you, *Ray of Hope*.' Dar could hear a squawk in the background before Control killed its mike. 'Looks like we took them by surprise,' he said to Whitey.

'Not surprising enough.' Whitey frowned. 'Who's got to them?'

'Three guesses – which is two more than you need.' Sam keyed her mike again. '*Ray of Hope* to Falstaff Control. What's the delay?'

'Uh . . . *Ray of Hope*,' Control stammered, 'it seems you forgot to file a ballistic plan.'

'Ballistic plan?' Whitey bawled. 'What does he think this is – a hop to the next planet?'

'*Ray of Hope* to Control,' Sam said grimly. 'I thought ballistic plans went out when FTL came in.'

'Well – we have to make sure you don't interfere with any incoming traffic.'

'Incoming traffic! *What* incoming traffic? The sky's as clear as a verdict!'

Whitey chuckled. 'As owner of this ship, pilot, I order you to lift off.'

'Yes, Grandpa,' Lona murmured, entirely too demurely. Then there wasn't much talking, because they were plastered back in their couches for a few minutes as the *Ray* streaked up through the atmosphere.

Then the pressure eased off, and 'down' gradually stopped being the back of the ship and became the deck, as ship's gravity took over from acceleration.

'Coasting at nine-tenths maximum.' Lona spun her chair around and loosened her webbing. 'I'd advise you stay in your couches, though; should only be about twenty minutes till we're far enough out to isomorph into H-space.'

'We barely made it,' Sam said with a sour smile. 'Remember that squawk in the background? That was Destinus.'

'Destinus?' Father Marco sat up, frowning. '*Canis* Destinus?'

'Why, yes, now that you mention it.' Sam turned to Father Marco. 'You know him?'

'More than that; we're related.' The priest seemed suddenly saddened. 'He's my father's half-brother's son.'

Dar frowned. 'Wait a minute – that makes him . . .'

'Half a cousin of the brother.' Whitey turned to the friar. 'The two of you were on the same planet, and he didn't bother to say hello?'

Father Marco nodded. 'And it *would* seem that he probably knew I was here. But then, under the circumstances, I suppose he wouldn't've wanted to be associated with me.'

'Doesn't sound like the overly sentimental sort.'

'To say the least,' Father Marco replied grimly. 'In fact, I haven't heard from him since I went into seminary; he was very upset with my choice of order. Thought I was horribly radical, that sort of thing.' He turned to Sam. 'He's been causing you trouble for a while?'

'Hunting us down,' Sam confirmed. 'He seems to be working for the LORDS.'

Father Marco sighed and shook his head. 'Poor Destinus! We knew he was keeping bad company, being in the government and all – but I didn't know it was *this* bad . . . well!' He slapped his knees and sat up straight. 'Looks as though I made the right decision, coming along with you.'

'How so?' Dar frowned. 'Finding out about your half-cousin makes that much of a difference?'

Father Marco nodded. 'Family obligation. It's up to me to try to counter the damage Destinus's trying to do to you.'

'Well, don't be too hard on the boy.' Dar frowned up at Sam. 'I mean, it's not as if he were doing it on his own. He's just acting for his bosses. *They're* the ones who're going in for telepath-hunting.'

'Oh, I wouldn't be too sure of that.' Sam's lip curled slightly. 'Do you think hardheaded politicians would really believe in telepaths? I mean, believe in 'em enough to mount a major hunt?'

'Why else would they bring in their own "police"?'

'Because,' Sam grinned, 'it makes an excellent excuse to immobilize you and me, before we can get Bhelabher's resignation to BOA.'

'Could a governorship of a boondocks planet be all that important?'

'To the governor's right-hand man it could. Besides, even if the LORDS *are* planning to cut off all the outlying planets, that doesn't mean they like the idea of governors who're ready to get along without them very nicely, thank you.'

'A point,' Dar admitted. 'That is a little deflating to the collective Terran ego. Which makes me think Myles Croft can't be all that popular with BOA, either.'

'He always was an independent cuss, My was.' Whitey grinned, leaning back with his hands locked behind his head. 'Myself, I think it's just fine, seeing the outer worlds getting ready for Terra to axe 'em.'

'Ready? Eager, almost.' Lona was watching her data board. 'About to isomorph, gentlefolk – tighten your webbing.' She frowned, and peered closer at her detectors. 'Strange – that blip's *gotta* be another ship lifting off from Falstaff.'

'Strange indeed.' Dar frowned, too. 'There weren't supposed to be any arrivals or departures for a month.'

'You don't think . . .?' Sam began, but then the isomorpher kicked in, and reality turned very fuzzy for a while.

Out near the asteroid belt, on the Jupiter side, the solar system's tapestry of gravity begins to thin out just enough for a ship to emerge from H-space. It's not the safest thing to do, of course; there is a respectable chance of Jupiter's gravity fouling the isomorpher enough to make the ship twist into that other realm where ships that *nearly* made it back out go to. Still, probability favours success; so, if you're in a hurry, you might try it.

Dar and Sam were in a hurry, so Lona tried it.

Deceleration slammed Dar against his webbing. It was killing pressure, but it slowly eased off – very slowly; it took the ship's internal field a while to win over momentum. When he could sit back and talk again, he did. 'I – take it we made it?'

'We're in one piece.' Lona sounded offended as she scanned her damage readout. 'Not even a split seam.'

'Didn't mean to question your ability,' Dar said quickly. 'It's just – well, it *was* a little risky.'

Lona snorted.

'Not for my niece.' Whitey leaned forward and tapped the autobar for Rhysling. 'The only kind of machine Lona doesn't understand is a hammer – it doesn't have any moving parts, let alone circuits. Anyone join me?'

Red light exploded off the walls and ceiling. Lona's hands flew over her board. 'That was a cannon bolt! Chug that drink and hold on!'

Something groaned, winding up to a scream as ship's gravity fought to keep up with velocity changes. But it was a losing battle; Lona was putting the little ship through so many rolls and dives, a four-dimensional computer couldn't've kept up with her.

Which, of course, was exactly the idea.

But their pursuer's battle comp was *good*; ruby flashes kept flickering off the walls, now brighter, now dimmer, now brighter again.

'How about the traditional shot across the bows?' Dar called.

'They're not big on tradition,' Lona snapped, sweat beading her brow.

'I never did have much use for iconoclasts,' Father Marco grumbled.

'It's a Patrol cruiser!' Sam stared at the rear viewscreen in horror. 'The Solar Patrol – the ones who rescue stranded spacemen from starship wrecks!'

'And shoot down smugglers,' Whitey added grimly. 'But they *never* shoot without warning!'

'You've been watching too many Patrol-epic holos, Grandpa,' Lona grated. 'These are the *real* ones!'

'Are they?' Sam keyed the transmitter. 'Let's find out! *Ray of Hope* calling Patrol cruiser! Come in, Patrol cruiser!'

An energy-bolt lanced past them as Lona rolled the ship to starboard.

'Come in, Patrol cruiser! Why're you shooting at us? We haven't broken any laws! And we're not carrying contraband!' Sam let up on the key and listened, but there wasn't even a whisper of static.

'Maybe it's broken,' Dar said quickly, 'not picking up their answer!'

'Dreamer,' Lona growled.

'I'll try anything.' Sam spun the sweep-knob, and a voice rattled out of the tiny speaker. '. . . at the top of the roster. It's on his new holocube, "Roll Me to Rigel!"'

'Commercial channel,' Sam grated.

A new voice interrupted the announcer in mid-word. 'Ganagram News Update – brought to you by Chao-Yu's Chandlers, with the latest in used burro-boat fittings!'

'Must be the Ganymede 3DT station,' Whitey said, nodding. 'They broadcast for the asteroid miners, mostly.'

'How can you tell?'

'Who else uses burro-boats?'

'We interrupt this programme to bring you a special hot flash,' the radio went on. 'We've just been notified that a small pirate ship with a notorious telepath aboard has just entered the Solar System. Citizens are advised not to worry, though – the mind reader's being chased by a Solar Patrol cruiser. They should be calling any minute to tell us he's been captured and locked up.'

'They're talking about *us*,' Dar choked.

'Correction,' Lona snapped. 'They're talking about *you*.'

'They did say, "he",' Whitey admitted.

'Also, that they're going to capture us – which sounds like a fine idea, right now.' Sam keyed the transmitter again. '*Ray of Hope* to Solar Patrol cruiser! We surrender! We give up! We throw down our arms!'

Red light blazed through the cabin, and the whole hull chimed like a singing bell.

'That was *really* close!' Lona rolled the ship over so fast that Dar's stomach lost track of his abdomen. 'They've got a weird idea of capturing!'

'I think,' Whitey mused, 'that they're out to avoid the expense of a trial.'

'So, what do we do?' Dar demanded. 'We can't keep running forever. So far, the only reason we're still alive is their lousy marksmanship, and Lona's fantastic piloting.'

'Flattery will get you an early grave,' Lona snapped. 'I need ideas, not compliments!'

'Well, how's this?' Dar frowned. 'We came in between Jupiter and Mars, heading sunward. What's our speed?'

'We're back up to point nine seven light-speed.'

Father Marco's eyes lost focus. 'Let's see, that means . . . it's been about five minutes for us, so for the people on Earth . . .'

'It's been a few weeks,' Lona finished for him, 'and if we don't do something soon, we're going to get punctured by a small swarm of teeny-tiny asteroids, and flattened when we run into a few big ones!'

'Asteroids!' Sam sat up straight, her eyes locking on Dar's. 'We did it once . . .'

'And I'll bet the Solar Patrol aren't much smarter than pirates!' Dar turned to Lona. 'Can you match velocity with an asteroid?'

'Of *course*!' Lona crowed. 'Kill our power, and all we are is a new asteroid with a high albedo!'

'Not even that, if you can get a big rock between us and the sun. Can we slow down that fast?'

'Can do.' Lona nodded. 'It'll take most of our power, though, and it won't be very comfortable.'

She had a nice knack for understatement; it was hell. Not as bad as it could've been — at least she had the courtesy to turn the ship around so she could decelerate with the main engine, and they were plastered back into their seats instead of being slammed against their webbing — but they were rammed so far into their couches that Dar could've sworn he felt the hard plastic of the frame, and held his breath, waiting for the couch to either snap or spring a leak. But it held, and he began to wonder if *he* would. His nose felt as though it were trying to flow around both sides of his face to join his ears; his eyes tried bravely to follow their optic nerves to their sources; and after a while, it occurred to him that the reason he was holding his breath was simply that he couldn't breathe. It was about three anvils, a barrel of horseshoes, two blacksmiths, and a percheron sitting on his chest. . . .

Then the pressure eased off, and swung him against the side of the hull as Lona turned. The acceleration couch slowly regurgitated him, and he found himself staring around at a cabin that perversely persisted in looking just the way it had before they passed through the hamburger press.

Then Lona flicked a finger at her console, and the lights went out.

All he could think of was that she was over there, and he was over here, still webbed in. It was such a horrible waste of a great situation.

Into the sudden darkness her voice murmured, 'I've killed all power, so they won't have any energy emissions to track us by. Don't let it worry you; you can still see out the ports. And we won't lose heat too fast; the hull's well insulated. But the air recycler's off, and this isn't all that large a cabin for five people. So do the best you can not to breathe too much. Breathe lightly – sleep if you can. And don't talk – that's a waste of air.'

'If the power's off, your detectors're out,' Father Marco murmured.

'Right. We won't know where they are, except by sight. Which doesn't do too much good, of course – they could be far enough away to only show as a speck of light, but they could still get here in a matter of minutes.'

'So, how will we know when to turn the lights back on?' Whitey asked.

'When the air starts getting foul,' Lona answered. 'When you start feeling short of breath, and drowsy.'

'But they might still be nearby then,' Dar objected.

'Life is filled with these little chances,' Lona murmured. 'But let's make it as long a wait as we can. No more talking.'

Sibilant silence descended on the cabin, filled with the rasp and wheeze of people in various states of health trying to control their breathing. After a few minutes, someone began to snore softly – Whitey, no doubt; Dar could only admire his composure. For himself, he was watching nervously out of the nearest porthole, and, sure enough, there was the tiny dot of light, swelling rapidly, turning into a Patrol cruiser which shot by overhead so close that Dar had to fight the urge to duck.

'One pass,' Lona murmured.

'Gadget-lovers,' Father Marco chuckled. 'They don't trust their eyes any more; if it isn't on a sensor-screen, it doesn't exist.'

'Then pretend we don't,' Sam hissed. 'Shut up!'

The Patrol cruiser slid out from the top of the vast asteroid that hid the *Ray of Hope*. Dar held his breath; if there were a single eye actually watching out of a porthole, all he'd ever know about it would be a huge red flash that just *might* burn out his life before it melted his eyes. But, come to think of it, he didn't even *see* any portholes, and the big ship drifted on past them and disappeared into a cluster of space junk.

Sam heaved a sigh of relief, but Lona hissed, 'Belay that!'

'What?' Sam protested. 'Breathing?'

'You were hoping,' Lona accused.

'What's wrong with that?' Sam demanded, but Father Marco assured her, 'It's too soon.'

And right he was, because here came the space-shark again, drifting up so closely above them that Dar halfway expected it to ask if he was interested in life insurance. But there must have been enough nickel-iron in their friendly asteroidal neighbourhood to hide the *Ray of Hope*'s mettle, because the cruiser lifted its nose and rose above them, more and more quickly until it disappeared into the clutter of floating rock overhead.

A multiple sigh filled the cabin, and Whitey croaked, 'Huh? Wha'sa matter? They find us? Huh? What?'

'I think they went up above the plane of the ecliptic, Grandpa,' Lona assured him.

'Hoping to get a better view of the situation – looking down at us,' Dar suggested.

'Can I hope now?' Sam squeaked.

A huge bass chime shook the cabin, and Lona hit the power key. 'Only if we get out of here,' she answered Sam. 'That was our first visiting neighbour, hinting we should move out of the neighborhood.'

'A little asteroid, colliding with us,' Dar explained as the lights came on and gravity sucked him back down into his seat. 'It's a wonder it's only the first one; they could've knocked us to bits by now.'

'Not really,' Lona said, punching buttons. 'We came in above the plane of the ecliptic, matched velocities with this asteroid, and swooped in right next to it. Most of the local pebbles are in orbit around it. That little stone that just hit us shot in from a close bypass with another big rock. It was just a matter of time before it came calling though.'

'But it won't happen again if we're going back above the plane of the ecliptic?'

'Are you kidding?' Lona snorted. 'That Patrol boat's up there! We're going *below*, sister, so we'll have the whole depth of the asteroid belt between us and them, to foul their sensors! Brace yourselves, everyone – this is going to be a rough ride!'

'*Nos morituri te salutamus*,' Father Marco intoned.

*We who are about to die, salute thee* . . . Dar shivered. 'You could've thought of a cheerier blessing, Father.'

'You speak *Latin*?' Father Marco cried in surprise. 'What are you – a fossil?'

'No – I just got stoned at Cholly's a lot.' Then Dar's stomach rose as the ship sank and a huge gong reverberated through the hull.

'Nothing to worry about.' Lona's voice was tight with strain. 'It can't really hurt us unless it's as big as my head, and I can swerve around anything that size – I think.'

Then Whitey was pointing upward out of the porthole and shouting – but the gist of his comment was lost in another huge BONG! as red lightning lit the cabin and the ship bucked like a metal bull. Over the fading chime, Dar could hear Lona cursing as she fought to stabilize the craft. The red glow faded – and left them in darkness broken only by the shards of reflected sunlight from the dancing asteroids around them. Sam shouted in panic, and everybody started talking at once.

'BELAY IT!' Lona shouted, and a sudden, eerie silence fell. Dar drew in a long, trembling breath. Whatever had happened, it was really *bad*!

'They were waiting for us,' Lona said into the hush. 'As soon as we fired up, their sensors locked their battle computer on us and let loose a ball of pure energy – several, really; the first few just vaporized the junk between us and them. The last one knocked off our tail section. As it is, we're lucky – if I hadn't swerved to avoid a rock, they'd have caught us right in this cabin.'

'They're rising again.' Whitey had his head craned back against the viewport, staring upward.

'Sure.' Lona shrugged. 'They didn't just shear away our engines – they blew away our reactor, too. There's no power left for them to "sense". Besides, why should they bother hunting down the pieces? They know we're dead now, anyway.'

Sam strangled a sob.

'Take heart,' Father Marco said sternly. 'We *aren't* dead.'

'We do have emergency power,' Lona agreed. 'It'll keep recycling air while it lasts – and the sun's radiation'll keep us warm, if we block the portholes on the far side. And we have a couple of weeks' rations.'

'Will the power last that long?' Sam's voice was hollow.

Lona was silent.

'It will, if we don't talk much and can do without light,' Whitey answered. 'Of course, we can't go anywhere.'

Father Marco grunted in surprise. 'I didn't know you knew any physics.'

'I was an engineer before I was a bard.' Dar could hear Whitey's grin. 'Who else could make enough sense out of this civilization to set it to music? But I'm a gambler, too.'

Dar felt the dread coalescing into terror.

'Just what kind of gamble did you have in mind?' Father Marco's voice echoed with foreboding.

'Well, we can't go *to* help,' Whitey mused, 'so we've got to make it come to us.'

Dar cleared his throat, which pushed the fear back down. 'You're talking about a distress signal.'

'It'd give us a little chance, at least,' Whitey answered. 'Without it, we're dead – unless you can arrange a miracle, Father.'

'I'm afraid my connections don't quite run that high.' The priest sounded amused. 'Even if St Vidicon reaches out to us, we've got to give him a handle to grab us by – some sort of action to put us into the ring of coincidence.'

'How much energy would it leave us?' Dar dreaded the answer.

'If it's going to be strong enough to do us any good, we'll have to put half our remaining power into it,' Lona answered.

'A week's worth.' Dar wet his lips. 'That gives us a week for somebody to hear us and get here.'

They were all silent.

*A week!* something shrieked within Dar. *Only a week to live! I've never even been in love!*

'We don't really have any choice, do we?' Sam said softly.

The cabin was silent again.

Then Sam heaved herself upright and leaned forward to the communications panel. 'All right. How do you want it?'

Breath hissed out in a sigh of consensus.

'Broadband.' Lona slapped keys, routing the emergency power to communications. 'Just the traditional Mayday, with our co-ordinates.'

Sam leaned forward to the audio pickup and thumbed the transmit key.

'Don't give the name of the ship,' Whitey said quickly.

Sam hesitated, then spoke. 'Mayday, Mayday! Distressed spacer at 10:32:47 V.E., 5:22 below P.E. Mayday, Mayday! Moribund!'

*Moribund* . . . 'Death-bound.' Dar felt the dread wrap around him, creeping up his spine.

Sam shut down her board.

'Leave trickle-power on,' Lona advised. 'If salvage does come, they'll need contact – a second of arc is a big distance out here.'

Sam hesitated, and Dar could almost hear her thoughts – how much life-time would they lose to that trickle? But I.C. grains drew only a few milliwatts per hour, and a rescuer a mile away who couldn't spot them was no better than no rescuer at all. Sam nodded, cracked one slider, and left her main on.

The cabin was silent again; then Lona said, 'Now we wait. . . .'

. . . *for death*. Dar completed the sentence in his head. 'What do we do with our minds?'

The silence became acutely uncomfortable.

Then Father Marco stirred. 'I do know a little about meditation. Would anyone like a mantra?'

'Burro-boat FCC 651919 to distressed spacer. Respond, please.'

Dar sat bolt upright, staring at the first pair of eyes he saw – Lona's, fortunately. 'So *soon*? Where was he, just around the corner?'

'It's been two hours . . .'

'Even so . . .'

'Burro-boat, this is distressed spacer,' Sam snapped into her pickup. 'Can you rescue?'

'Distressed spacer, I can rescue and am in your vicinity, but need transmission to home on. Please continue transmission of carrier wave.'

'Burro-boat, will do. We await you anxiously.' Sam locked down the 'transmit' button, but covered the pickup with her hand and swivelled to face the others. 'It doesn't *have* to be the Patrol, you know.'

'If it is, we'll know in a minute.' Whitey gave her a dry smile. 'As soon as they get a locus on us, they'll blast us to vapour.'

Sam flinched, and whirled back to her console.

'No!' Lona snapped. 'It *might* be legit – and if it's not, I'd rather steam than starve, anyway!'

Sam hesitated, but she left the 'transmit' button on.

'And it *could* be honest,' Father Marco pointed out. 'The prospectors flit all over the belt in their burro-boats. Why shouldn't there have been one two hours away?'

Lona's eyes glazed. 'Well, the probabilities . . .'

'Spare us,' Whitey said quickly. 'Have you been praying for St Vidicon's help, Father?'

Father Marco squirmed. 'It couldn't hurt, could it?'

'Not at all. He might've stacked the deck in our favour.' Whitey craned his neck, staring out of the porthole. 'Dar, take the starboard view. What do you see?'

'Just asteroids . . . No, one of them's getting bigger. . . . There!'

There was a concerted rush to the starboard portholes.

'Is *that* a ship?' Dar gasped.

It was dingy grey, and it might've been a sphere once, but it was so pocked with crater dents that it looked just like any of the asteroids. Two paraboloid dishes sprouted from its top, one round for radio and microwave, the other elongated, for radar. Below them, the hull sloped down to two huge windows; the miners liked naked-eye backup for their scanners. Below *them*, the hull kept sloping until it reached the loading bay: two huge holes, housing solenoids, for small bits of ore; below it, a 'mouth' for big chunks. Beneath a bulbous belly hung two pairs of pincers, one fore and one aft, for grappling onto small asteroids that were too big for loading. From the aft section sprouted a spray of antennae that set up a force-field to prevent rear end collisions by small asteroids.

'It's beautiful,' Sam breathed.

The burro-boat rotated, broadside-on to the *Ray of Hope*, and a small hatch opened in its side. A magnetic grapple shot out, trailing a line. It clanged onto their hull.

'Distressed spacer,' said the com console, 'we are prepared for boarding.'

Sam dived for the console. 'Acknowledge, burro-boat. We'll just slide into our pressure suits, and be right over.'

Whitey swung out a section of the wall. 'I hope they left the suits when they mothballed this thing . . . There they are!'

All five crowded around, feasting their eyes on their means of escape.

'Air?' Sam said doubtfully.

Dar snorted. 'So hold your breath. It's only a hundred yards!' He hauled down a suit and handed it to Sam. 'Ladies first.'

'Male chauvinist! *You* go first!'

'All right, all right,' Dar grumbled, clambering into the stiff fabric. 'Check my seals, will you? Y' know, something bothers me.'

'You too, huh?' Whitey was sealing him in with a crisp, practised touch. 'You wouldn't be wondering why we haven't heard from the pilot?'

'Well, yes, now that you mention it. Or is it the custom here, to let the computers do the talking?'

'Definitely not,' Lona assured him, sealing Sam into her suit. 'Of course, there might not *be* a pilot.'

'Could be – but not likely,' Whitey grunted. 'Didn't you hear the serial number? This is one of those new FCC brains – "Faithful Cybernetic Companions" programmed for extreme loyalty. They're not supposed to want to do *anything* without their owner's express command.'

'I thought those were robot brains.' Father Marco frowned. 'What's it doing conning a ship?'

Whitey shrugged. 'Can't say, Father. I *do* know that every scrap of junk and every used Terran part finds its way to the asteroid belt sooner or later, to get the last erg of usage out of it . . . There!' He slapped Dar on the shoulder; it sent him spinning in the free-fall of the powerless ship. 'Go out and conquer, young fella!'

'I thought I was going to be rescued,' Dar grumbled. 'And why do I have to go alone?'

'Because a burro-boat's lock is only big enough for one at a time.' Whitey all but kicked him into the *Ray of Hope*'s airlock. 'Have a good trip – and try not to breathe!'

The door slammed behind him, and the other hatch was opening; and if he didn't go out there and try to swim through vacuum to the burro-boat, he'd be killing his four friends, who couldn't go into the airlock till he'd gone. He gulped down his panic and forced himself to step through.

He held onto the line with one hand, groping frantically at his waist for the suit's anchoring cables. There! It was a snap-hook with a swivel. He pulled it out; a strong line unreeled from somewhere inside his suit. He snapped the hook onto the line.

Catching the overhead line, he pulled himself back against the *Ray of Hope*'s side, bracing his feet and backing down into a crouch. Then he fixed his gaze on the burro-boat's airlock, took a deep breath, and – jumped as hard as he could.

He went shooting out along the line like a housewife's dry laundry in the first drops of rain. For a moment, he was tempted to try going faster by pulling himself hand-over-hand along the line; then he remembered that he was in vacuum, which meant no friction, but his gauntlets on the line *would* mean friction, and would probably slow him down as much as they speeded him up. So he hung on, arms outstretched in a swan dive – and began to enjoy it.

Then the burro-boat's side shot up at him, and he grabbed frantically for the line, remembering that he might have lost weight, but he hadn't lost mass – which meant inertia. If he didn't brake, fast, the next friend down the line would have to scrape a nice, thin layer of Mandra off the burro-boat before he could get into the airlock. The scream of improvised brakes squealed all through his suit, while the burro-boat's side kept rushing up at him, seeming to come faster and faster. Frantically, he doubled up, getting his feet and flexed knees between him and it . . .

Then he hit, with a jar that he swore knocked his teeth back into the gums. But, as he slowly straightened, he realized his joints were still working, and the stars that *didn't* fade from his vision were really asteroids sweeping past. Somehow, he'd made it – and all in one piece! He breathed a brief, silent prayer of thanks and stepped gingerly through the hatch. When he was sure both of his feet were pressing down on solid metal, he let go of the line with one hand to grasp the rim of the hatchway; *then* he let go with the other, and pulled himself down into the nice, safe darkness of the interior. His elbow bumped a lever; irritated, he pushed it away – and the hatch swung shut behind him.

Darkness. Total. Complete.

That was when Dar learned what 'claustrophobia' meant. He had to fight to keep himself from pounding on the nearest wall, screaming to be let out. *It's just an airlock*, he repeated to himself, over and over. *They* can't *let me out until it's filled with air. Just a few minutes . . .*

It seemed like an hour. He found out, later, that it was really forty-two seconds.

Then a green light glowed in the darkness. He lunged toward

it, felt the wheel of the door-seal, wrenched it open, and tumbled into light, warmth, and . . . AIR! He twisted his helmet off, and inhaled a reek of rancid food, unwashed body, and a sanitation recycler that wasn't quite working right. They were the sweetest scents he'd ever smelled.

A chime rang behind him. He whirled about to see an amber light blinking next to the airlock. Of course – nobody else could come in until he shut the inside hatch! He slammed and dogged it shut – and realized he'd been hearing voices as soon as he'd come in; they were just now beginning to register.

'Consarn it, 'tain't none of my affair!' a gravelly voice ranted. 'Now you turn this blasted tub around and get back to my claim!'

'But under the Distressed Spacers' Law,' a calm, resonant voice replied, 'you are required to render assistance to the crew of any imperilled ship.'

'You've said that fifteen times, hang it, and I've given you fifteen good reasons why we shouldn't!'

'Three,' the calm voice reminded, 'five times each, and none of them sufficient.'

'*Any* of 'em's good enough! 'Tain't none of our business – that's the best one of all!'

Dar finished shucking out of his space suit and racked it, then tiptoed along the companionway toward the voices.

'Totally inadequate,' the other voice answered, unruffled. 'The Distressed Spacers' Law specifically mentions that a distressed spaceman is the overriding concern of any who happen to be near enough to offer assistance.'

'Overriding' was the key word; it made Dar suddenly certain as to who the calm voice belonged to. He peeked around the edge of the hatchway, and saw the burro-boat's cabin, a cramped space littered with ration containers and papers, dirty laundry, and smudges of oil and grease. It held two acceleration couches, a control console with six scanner screens, and a short, stocky man in a filthy, patched coverall, with matted hair and an unkempt, bushy beard.

'Jettison the law!' he yelled. 'Common sense oughta tell you that! It's the Patrol's job to take care of a shipwreck!'

'Which was your second reason.' The calm voice seemed to come from the control console. 'The crew of the ship in question might be those whom the Patrol was pursuing.'

'If they was, bad cess to 'em! Damn telepaths, poking their

noses into other people's secrets! Who do they think they are, anyway?'

'Human beings,' the voice answered, 'and as much entitled to life as anyone else – especially since the Patrol has apparently not accused them of any crimes.'

Dar decided he liked the unseen owner of the calm voice.

'Bein' a telepath's a crime, damn it! Don't you follow the news?'

'Only in so far as it is logical – which is to say, not very far at all. I fail to comprehend how a person can commit a crime by being born with an extra ability.'

Neither did Dar – and it was definitely news, at least to him. Just how powerful *were* the people involved in the plot to overthrow the IDE, anyway?

Apparently, powerful enough to whip up a full-scale witch-hunt, just for the purpose of catching his humble self. He realized the implications, and felt his knees dissolve.

' 'Tain't fer you or me to understand it – the government does, and that's enough. What – you figger you're smarter than the Executive Secretary and all them Electors put together?'

Suddenly, Dar realized why the plot had got as far as it had. The old man sounded more like a medieval serf than a well-informed citizen of a democracy.

A hand fell on his shoulder, and Sam snarled in his ear, 'I didn't think you'd sink so low as to listen at keyholes.'

Dar looked up, startled; then he smiled. 'Of course I haven't. That's why I left the door open.'

'That depends on your definition of intelligence,' the calm voice answered.

'What difference does it make?' the old man howled. 'You can't vote, anyway – you're just a damned *computer*!'

'Computers do not have souls,' the voice said complacently, 'and therefore cannot be damned.'

'Kicked into the mass-recycler, then! Do you realize how much money you're losing me, by kiyoodling off to rescue these garbage-can castaways?'

Sam's lips drew into a thin hard line. She took a step toward the door. Dar grabbed her shoulder, hissing, 'Not yet.'

'Perfectly,' the computer answered, 'since this is the sixth time you've mentioned the fact. Considering the quality of your ore and the current price of a kilogram of nickel-iron as quoted by

Ganymede half an hour ago, multiplied by my rate of excavation, this salvage mission has thus far cost you exactly 1,360 BTUs.'

'There!' the old miner crowed triumphantly. 'See? You know how much one thousand BTUs'll *buy*?'

'Ten cubic centimetres of hydrogen, at current prices,' the computer answered, 'or three ration bars.'

'Damn inflation,' the miner growled. 'It's getting so a body can't afford a patch for the arse of his coveralls anymore.'

'Be that as it may,' the computer mused, 'I believe a human life is worth considerably more.'

'Not the life of a confounded telepath, damn it!'

Sam was trembling. She pushed Dar's hand away and took a determined step into the cabin.

'Me first,' Whitey growled as he squeezed past her. 'This one's more my size – or age, anyway.'

He stepped into the cabin, calling out, 'There aren't any telepaths on our ship, old-timer.'

Looking back over his shoulder, Dar saw that Whitey was only telling the truth – Lona and Father Marco stood right behind him.

'And thanks for the rescue, by the way,' Whitey finished.

The old miner spun around, staring wild-eyed. 'Where in hell'd *you* come from?'

'No, we hadn't quite got *there* yet,' Whitey said amiably. 'Might have, if you hadn't picked us up, though.'

The miner whirled back to his console, glaring. 'Who said you could let this trash in?'

'The Distressed Spacers' Law . . .'

'Shove the law up the plasma bottle!' the old miner howled. 'You're supposed to be loyal to me, not to them!'

'My initial programming included only one principle of higher priority than loyalty to my current owner,' the computer admitted.

'There wasn't even supposed to be *one*!'

Whitey grinned. 'Don't tell me you believed everything the used-brain salesman told you. What was the higher priority, anyway?'

'The sanctity of human life,' the computer answered, 'unless the human in question is attacking my current owner.'

'Well, who could object to that?' Whitey fixed the miner with a glittering stare. The old man glared back at him, started to say something, stopped, and turned away, muttering under his breath.

'No, I didn't think you would.' Whitey smiled, amused. 'No decent person could. And we want to show you our thanks, of course.'

The old miner swept a quick, appraising glance over Whitey's worn, tattered clothing. 'Thanks don't mean much, unless it shows up as figgers in my credit readout.'

Whitey kept the smile, but his eyes glittered again. 'Well, of course. We wouldn't expect you to ship us to safety for free.'

'Oh, sure! When we get to port, you'll slip your card into my bank's terminal, and it'll read pretty – but five days later, it'll turn out that account in a Terran bank was closed out five years ago!'

Whitey didn't answer; he just slapped his jacket pocket. It clinked. The old miner's gaze fastened onto it.

'Thirty kwahers for taking each of us to Ceres City,' Whitey said easily.

The old miner's eye gleamed. 'Fifty!'

'Well, we don't use up *that* much air and reaction mass – and it'll have to be short rations, since you only provisioned for yourself. Call it thirty-five.'

'Thirty-five kilowatt-hours apiece?' The old miner hawked and spat. 'You fergit, mister – I'll have to go on short rations, too! Forty-five – and that's gifting!'

'Yes, it means I'm gifting you with an extra ten kwahers for each of us. I'll go up to forty.'

'Forty kwahers apiece?' the miner bleated. 'One hundred twenty all told? Mister, you know how much I'll lose from not working my claim while I haul you?'

'One hundred fifty kilowatt-hours, 3,087 BTUs,' the computer answered, 'including reaction mass, air, and sustenance.'

'There! See? I won't even break even!' The miner lifted his chin.

'But I've got five people, not three. It's two hundred kwahers total.'

'Five . . .?' The miner's gaze darted toward the companionway; Lona and Father Marco stepped into sight.

'You'll make a profit,' Whitey pointed out.

'The hell I will!' The miner reddened. 'That's two more for air, reaction mass, and rations!'

'Cost included,' the computer informed him. 'I counted the number of times the airlock door opened and closed.'

The miner rounded on it, bawling, 'Whose side are you on, anyway?'

'My apologies. I cannot resist accuracy in mathematics.'

'Try a little,' the miner growled, and turned back to Whitey. 'Forty-nine kwahers ain't much of a profit, mister. Why don't you just ask me for the whole blasted boat?'

Whitey shrugged. 'What do you want for it?'

The miner stared.

Then he said, flatly, 'One thousand therms.'

The computer said, 'Current list price . . .'

'Shut up!' the miner roared. He turned back to Whitey with a truculent glare. 'Well?'

'Oh, now, let me see . . .' Whitey stepped up to the console and turned the clinking pocket inside out. Coins cascaded onto the bench. He picked them up, stacking them on the console and counting slowly.

'Twenty . . . eighty . . . two hundred . . .'

The miner's eyes followed each coin, whites showing all around the irises.

'Eight hundred fifty-six . . . eight hundred fifty-seven . . . five kwahers . . . ten kwahers . . '

The miner's mouth worked.

'Eight hundred and fifty-seven therms, twenty-three kwahers, 2,392 BTUs.' Whitey looked up at the miner. 'Take it or leave it.'

'Done!' The old man pounced on the stack, scooping them into his coverall pockets. 'You bought yourself a burro-boat, mister!'

'And its computer.' Whitey looked up at the grid above the console. 'You work for me now.'

'You were cheated,' the computer informed him.

The old miner cackled.

'I know,' Whitey said equably. 'A beat-up old tub like this couldn't be worth more than five hundred therms.'

The old miner glanced up at him keenly. 'Then why'd you buy it?'

'I felt sorry for the computer.' Whitey turned back to the grid. 'You take orders from me, now – or from my niece, really; she's the pilot.'

'Hi,' she said, stepping up beside Whitey. 'I'm Lona.'

Dar stared, galvanized by the warmth in her voice. What a waste! All that allure cast before a machine – when it could've been coming at him!

Lona sat down at the console. 'Let's get acquainted, FCC 651919. By the way, do you mind if I call you – uh – "Fess"?'

'Fess?' Dar frowned. 'Why that?'

Lona looked back at him over her shoulder. 'How would *you* pronounce "FCC"? Never mind, this is how *I'm* going to pronounce it!' She turned back to the grid. 'If you don't mind, of course.'

'My opinion is of no consequence,' the computer answered. 'My owner has delegated the necessary authority to you, so you may call me what you will.'

'Not if you don't like it. A good computer tech needs a certain degree of rapport with her machine.'

'Such rapport can only exist within your own consciousness,' the computer replied. 'I am incapable of feelings.'

'All right, then, humour me; I need the illusion. Besides, since a computer's mathematical, it has to be electronically biased toward harmony and euphony. So I ask you again: does the name "Fess" suit you?'

The computer hesitated. When it did speak, Dar could've sworn there was a note of respect in its tones. 'The designation is pleasing, yes.'

'Fine.' Lona settled down to work, eyes glowing. 'Now, Fess – how long ago were you first activated?'

'Five years, seven months, three days, six hours, twenty-one minutes, and thirty-nine seconds – Terran Standard, of course. I assume you do not require a more precise response.'

'No, that'll do nicely.' Lona's eyes gleamed. 'And computers tend to be very durable these days; you're almost brand-new. With you in it, this burro-boat should've been worth twice what Grandpa paid for it.'

The old miner cackled again.

'What's wrong with you?' Lona demanded.

The computer was silent for a minute; then it answered, 'My first owner inherited vast wealth, and spent a great deal on material pleasures . . .'

'A playboy.' Dar could almost see Lona's mouth water. 'I can see why he'd need a very loyal brain for his personal robot.'

'Indeed. Due to his, ah, excesses, it was frequently necessary for me to assume piloting of his aeroyacht.'

'Meaning he did the best he could to become a cask, and you had to fly him home when he was dead drunk.'

'You choose accurate terms,' the computer admitted. 'On our last journey, however, he retained consciousness, though his judgement and reflexes were severely impaired. Consequently, I could not, according to my program, assume control until it became totally obvious that his life was imperilled.'

'Meaning he was heading right for a collision, but you couldn't take over until it was almost too late. What happened?'

'By swerving the ship, I did manage to avoid damage to the cabin. Unfortunately, I was located in the aft bulkhead, which did suffer some impact.'

Lona nodded. 'What was broken inside you?'

'Nothing. But one capacitor was severely weakened. Now, in moments of stress, it discharges in one massive surge.'

Lona frowned. 'It could burn you out. Couldn't they fix it?'

'Not without a complete overhaul and reprogramming, which would have been more expensive than a new unit. They did, however, install a circuit breaker and a bypass, so that the capacitor now discharges in isolation. Unfortunately, I am thereby deactivated until the breaker is reset.'

'If you were human, they'd call it a seizure. What'd your owner do?'

'He elected to sell me, which was economically wise.'

'But lacked ethical harmony.'

'Aptly put. However, there were no buyers on Terra, nor in the Martian colonies. No one wished to purchase an epileptic robot-brain.'

'But in the asteroid belt,' Lona murmured, 'they'll buy anything.'

'If the price is low enough, yes. Mine was seventeen therms.'

'Of low price, but incalculable value.' Lona smiled grimly. 'After all, you've just saved all five of our lives.'

'True, but it was a low-stress situation for me. In a moment of true crisis, I would fail, and cause your deaths.'

Lona shook her head. 'When things get that tense, I do my own piloting. The computer just feeds me the choices. No, I think you'll turn out to be the best thing that ever happened to me, Fess.'

Which was something of a blow to Dar's ego; so maybe it was just his imagination that made the computer sound worshipful as it said, 'I will do all that I can to serve you.'

Lona just smiled.

'Apropos of which,' the computer went on, 'it might interest you to know that, while we have been talking, my former master was surreptitiously transmitting a message to Ceres City.'

Every eye locked onto the old miner.

'That's garbage!' he spluttered. 'You've been sitting here next to me the whole time! I didn't say a word!'

'Computers can't lie.' Lona's gaze was a poniard.

'It's a breakdown! Malfunction! Programming error!'

'How'd he do it, Fess?' Lona never took her glare off the old miner.

'By pressing and releasing the transmission button,' the computer answered. 'That sent out carrier-wave pulses, which spelled out letters in the ancient Morse code.'

'What did he say?' Whitey's voice was almost dreamy.

'"Solar Patrol, emergency!"' the computer recited, '"Burro-boat FCC 651919 has just picked up five castaways. Have reason to believe they were crew and passengers of ship you were just chasing. Emergency!"'

Lona stood up with the slow, sinuous grace of a panther. Whitey stepped over beside her, his eyes chips of ice. 'How do you want to be spaced – with or without your pressure suit?'

'But – but you can't do that!' The old miner cowered back against the bulkhead. 'I picked you up! I saved your lives!'

'Your computer did,' Lona corrected, 'and it's ours now.'

'The killing of humans,' Fess murmured, 'is the worst of crimes.'

'What's your definition of "human"?' Whitey growled, glaring at the miner.

'Treachery is right up there, too,' Lona pointed out.

'True,' Father Marco agreed, 'but this man had no reason for loyalty to our little band – and every reason for loyalty to the government, and its Solar Patrol.'

'If you can call blind faith "reason",' Whitey grunted. 'But I guess you would, Father.'

'Sir!' Father Marco stiffened. 'I'll remind you that I'm an engineer as well as a priest! . . . But I am able to look at the situation from his viewpoint.'

A gleam came into Whitey's eyes. 'Well, then – why not let him see things from *our* viewpoint? The one we had an hour ago.'

'You wouldn't!' The miner blanched.

'Oh, don't worry.' Whitey's lip curled. 'They'll pick you up way before your supplies run out. What's he got on his claim, Fess?'

'A bubble-cabin ten feet down inside the asteroid,' the computer replied, 'with complete life-support systems and a month's rations.'

'With a two-way radio?'

'No; he had mine, and didn't see the need for the expense. I do, however, have a spare emergency beacon.'

'Perfect!' Whitey grinned. 'He can call for help, but he can't rat on us. Oh, don't give me that terrified look, you old crawler! The Patrol'll have you safe in Ceres City inside of a week!'

'Will that give us enough of a start?' Lona growled.

Whitey's lips pressed into a thin line. 'It'll have to.'

'Come back here, consarn you!' The voice echoed tinnily from the console's grid. 'Come back here with my burro-boat, you blasted pirates! I'll have the law on you!'

'Damn!' Whitey snapped his fingers into a fist. 'I should've made him sign a bill of sale! Now he'll have the Patrol hunting us down for piracy, on top of everything else.'

Dar shrugged. 'What does it matter? They'll chase us anyway, as soon as they pick him up and he tells them his story.'

'I know, I know. But this'll give 'em a legal pretext for holding us.'

'I think not,' Fess demurred. 'Since the transaction was a verbal contract, I recorded it as standard operating procedure.'

Whitey's scowl dissolved into a grin. 'Old Iron, I think you may have your uses.'

'A lot of them; he wasn't really designed to pilot a boat, or even just to compute,' said Lona. 'He was designed as the brain of a humanoid robot.'

'True, but my motor functions are adaptable to almost any sort of mechanical body,' Fess explained. 'I'm really quite generalized.'

'And, therefore, versatile,' Whitey concluded. 'Well, what we need you to do most, just now, is to get us to Luna undetected.'

'Why Luna?' Dar frowned. 'We want to get to Terra.'

'They don't allow spacers to land there,' Sam explained. 'Population's too dense; too much chance of a minor accident killing thousands of people. Spacers have to land on the moon, and take a shuttle down to Earth.'

'Besides, we're running a little high on notoriety at the moment,' Whitey added. 'We need some sort of cover to let us travel – and I have a few friends on Luna.'

Dar shrugged. 'Why not? You have friends everywhere.'

'Since you wish to avoid attention,' Fess suggested, 'it might be best if we wait for a large vessel to pass near, and match orbits, staying as close to it as possible, so that we're inside its sensor-range, and blend into its silhouette on any Patrol ship's screens.'

Dar frowned. 'Isn't that a little chancy?'

'Not for the two of us.' Lona patted the console.

Dar felt a hot stab of jealousy. 'What do you think that circuit-stack is – the boy next door?'

Lona gave him a look veiled by long lashes above a cat-smile. 'Why not?' She turned to the console grid. 'Where'd you grow up, electron-pusher?'

'I was manufactured on Maxima.'

'Not exactly my home territory.' Lona's eyes gleamed. 'But I've heard of it. All they do there is make computers and robots, right?'

'That is their sole industry, yes. Their sole occupation of any sort, in fact.'

'Sloggers,' the girl translated. 'A bunch of technological monks. They don't care anything about creature comforts; all they want to do is build robots.'

'Not quite true,' Fess corrected. 'The few humans on Maxima have every conceivable luxury known – including a few unknown anywhere else, which they invented themselves. In fact, they live like kings.'

'Oh, really!' Lona smiled, amused. 'When're they planning to join the aristocracy?'

'Some have already begun buying patents of nobility from the Terran College of Heralds.'

Lona lost her smile. 'That takes *real* money! Where do they get it from?'

'From the sale of computers and robots.' The computer added modestly, 'Their products are already acknowledged to be the finest in any of the human-occupied worlds.'

'So they sell for a small fortune each, of course. But the biggest luxury of all is servants – which they can't have, if there're only a few humans.'

'True,' Fess admitted, 'but there are three robots to every human, on the average. They do not lack for servitors.'

'Sounds like a great life,' Whitey sighed, 'if you don't mind settling down.'

'And don't mind being stuck out in the middle of nowhere,' Sam added.

'The planetoid is rather bleak,' Fess admitted.

'"Planetoid"?' Lona frowned. 'I thought Maxima was a world.'

'It would be counted a small moon if it orbited a planet,' Fess demurred. 'But since it is located in Sirius's asteroid belt, it can only be counted as one of the larger of those asteroids.'

Whitey frowned. 'No atmosphere.'

'No trees or grass,' mused Sam.

'Only rocks and dust,' murmured Dar.

'Only eight point seven light-years from Terra!' carolled Lona.

Dar stared. 'You *like* the sound of the place?'

'It's practically heaven!' Lona squealed. 'Nothing to do but design and build computers, laze around luxury, and hop around the corner to the fleshpots of Terra for the weekend! Where do I sign up?'

'Immigration is completely open,' Fess said slowly, 'but very few people choose to go there. It would be miserable for anyone who was poor – and only excellent cyberneticists can make money.'

'I'll take it!' Lona crowed. 'How do I get there?'

'That,' Fess agreed, 'is the rub. They will accept you – *if* you can get there.'

'Grandpa!' Lona whirled around to Whitey. 'Got a few royalty cheques coming in?'

Whitey shrugged. 'You can have the burro-boat when we're done with it, sweetheart – but first there's a little matter of saving democracy.'

'Well, let's get it over with!' Lona whirled back to the console. 'I want to get on with the really *important* things! Found a big liner yet, electro-eyes?'

'I have been tracking the SASE *San Martin* while we have been conversing,' Fess answered. 'It approaches above the plane of the ecliptic, inbound from Ganymede, and will pass us only one hundred and thirty-seven kilometres away.'

'Then let's *go!*' Lona grabbed her webbing and stretched it across her. 'Web in, everybody!'

A chorus of clicks answered her. She grinned down at her console, then frowned at a blinking red light and looked back over her shoulder at Father Marco. 'Look, Father, I know you trust in St Christopher, and all that – but would you please buckle in?'

The monolith of a liner hurtled into eternal morning, its aft hull lost in the total black shadow of its bulging bridge. A tiny speck danced up to it from the asteroid belt, glinting in the sunlight. It swooped up to disappear in shadow under the monster's belly, where it clung like a pilot fish to a shark by the bulldog magnetic fields of the solenoids in its nose.

Inside, Dar asked, 'Couldn't they spot us by the magnetic fields on their hull?'

'They *could*.' Lona shrugged. 'But why would they look for them?' She switched off the engines.

'It doesn't quite seem ethical,' Father Marco mused, 'hitching a free ride this way.'

'Don't let it worry you, Father,' Whitey assured him. 'I own stock in this shipping line.'

# 10

The SASE *San Martin* drifted down toward its berth in the Mare Serenitatis. As it passed over Darkside, a mite dropped off its belly, falling toward the surface at no higher acceleration than lunar gravity could account for. No glint of light reflected from it to any watching eye in the shadows; and if anyone thought to glance at it on a sensor screen, they would surely think it nothing but another meteorite caught by the moon's gravity, coming to add one more crater to the ancient, pockmarked satellite.

It fell almost to the surface, so low that it was beneath the sensor-nets, and barrelled over the jagged landscape.

Inside the cabin, Lona asked, 'Is this what you'd call a "stress situation"?'

'Not at all,' Fess assured her. 'It is simply a matter of adjusting our trajectory with the attitude jets, according to the irregularities in the landscape indicated by the sensors. At this low a speed, I always have several milliseconds to react.'

'Piece of cake, huh? I think *you'd* better keep the con for this one.'

'As mademoiselle wishes,' Fess murmured.

He finally brought them to rest when the glittering lights of a spaceport appeared over the horizon. The burro-boat sank to the dust in the shadow of a huge crag, with the weary, thankful groan of engines idling down.

'I detected an airlock hatch in this outcrop,' Fess informed them. 'There is an electronics kit in the cabinet below the console; can any of you bypass the telltale on the hatchway, so that

Spaceport Security will not know the lock has been opened?'

'Duck soup,' Lona affirmed, 'the instant kind. Where'll you be while we're gone?'

'In the shadow of a ring-wall, in a remote crater,' Fess answered. 'I will move as the shadows move. Next to the electronics kit, you will find a small transmitter of convenient size for a pocket. Press the button on it, and it will send a coded pulse to me. When I receive it, I will determine your location from its vector and amplitude, and bring the boat to you.'

Lona opened the cabinet, pulled out the electronics kit, and flipped the recall unit to Whitey. He caught it and slipped it into a pocket inside his belt. 'What's its range?'

'A thousand kilometres,' Fess answered. 'If you call from Serenitatis Spaceport, I will hear you.'

'How about if we have to call you from Terra?'

'You will have to feed the signal through a stronger transmitter.'

'We can't ask for a complete guarantee.' Father Marco rose and turned toward the companionway. 'I think I can remember where I left my pressure suit.'

'There are ten air bottles in the locker with them,' Fess noted.

'Well, thanks for all the help.' Lona shooed the rest of the crew aft. 'If anyone knocks while we're gone . . .'

'I will not let them in,' Fess assured her.

The airlock hatch had a panel with a button inset beside it. Lona pulled out a screwdriver, tightened in the appropriate blade, and set it into the screw. It whined twice, and she lifted the panel away, handing it to Dar. Dar watched her clip a couple of leads in.

Above them, a twelve-foot parabolic dish moaned as it rotated a few degrees, and stopped.

Lona leaped back as though she'd been stabbed. Dar didn't blame her; it was all he could do to keep from dropping the plate. He wished he had; then he couldn't have heard the antenna's moan, since the sound conducted into his suit through the wires holding the plate.

Whitey leaned over, touching his helmet against Lona's. After a minute, she nodded, then stepped grimly back to the airlock. She took the plate from Dar and replaced it. Then she pressed the button, and the hatch slowly swung open. She gestured to Dar and he stepped in. The others followed, Lona last. Whitey pressed a plate in the wall, and the hatch swung shut. Dar waited, fidgeting. Finally, the inner hatch opened. He stepped through into darkness, cracked his helmet seal, and tilted it back. He turned as a glow-light lit in Whitey's hand, saw Lona tilting her helmet back as Father Marco closed the airlock.

'What're we gonna do about the bypass?' Dar asked.

'Leave it there.' Lona shrugged. 'Can't be helped.'

'Security patrols all the locks regularly,' supplied Sam the bureaucrat. 'They'll find it within a few days.'

'Not exactly what I'd call a cheery thought, but it lightens the conscience. What'd you do to make that microwave dish swing around, Lona?'

'Nothing,' Whitey answered. 'That dish was beaming commercial DT programming down to the Terran satellites. When it gets done feeding its schedule to one satellite, it rotates to lock onto another one, and starts the whole feed all over again.'

'3DT?' Dar frowned. 'Why do they feed it from the moon?'

'Because that's where they make the programmes, innocent!' Sam snorted.

Whitey nodded. 'It takes a lot of room for enough 3DT sound stages to make new programming for a hundred twenty channels each, for twenty-six main cultures – and they have to make new stuff constantly. There just wasn't enough room for it in the major cities. So, bit by bit, the production companies shifted up here to Luna, where real estate was very cheap. The whole entertainment industry for the entire IDE is in the moon now.'

'Some say it belonged there all along, anyway,' Lona muttered.

'Oh.' Dar mulled it over. 'So your publisher's offices are up here, too?'

'No, the print industry stayed Earthbound.'

'Oh.' Dar looked around at the rough-hewn tunnel walls scored with the screw-tracks of a laser-borer. 'Well, not much we can do here, is there? I suppose our next step is to hop a shuttle to Terra.'

'Wrong.' Whitey shook his head. 'That asteroid miner has probably sung the Solar Patrol a whole opera by now. Every security guard on the moon will have memorized little sketches of us. We've got to establish some kind of cover identities first, not to mention something by way of disguises.'

Dar felt his stomach sink. 'I should've known it couldn't be something straightforward and simple.'

'Not on Terra,' Sam agreed, 'and the moon's just as bad.' She turned to Whitey. 'What kind of cover did you have in mind?'

'I didn't.' Whitey started climbing out of his gear. 'I recommend we rack these suits and find some place to hole up while we think about it.'

Whitey had indeed emptied out his purse for the old miner – but he had another one hidden inside his belt. A brief stop at a department store turned up a coiffured wig and translucent dress for Sam, some hair dye and baggy tunic-and-trousers for Lona, some more hair dye and business outfits for the men. A somewhat longer stop at a comfort station produced remarkable changes in their appearance.

Whitey lined them up in the hallway, looked them over, and nodded. 'You'll do. Just barely, maybe, but you'll do. Now, the odds are that your prints are on file somewhere – oh, you're sure of it, Dar? Well, the rest of you don't take chances, either. Don't put your thumbprint to anything. Don't look into anything that might want to scan your retinas, either – no peekholes in amusement galleries, eyepiece 3DT viewers, or lens-fitting scopes. Understand? Good. Because you're in the Big Sapphire's computer net now, folks, and every step you take is liable to monitoring by a computer tied into Terra Central.'

'Is it really that bad?' Dar asked.

'Worse,' Sam confirmed.

Whitey nodded again. 'Have no illusions, folks. Our chances of getting away free, back to the colony planets, are slightly worse than a dinosaur's caught in a glacier. I can only hope the gamble's worth the share-time. Okay – from now on, we're a free-lance production crew, looking for work. Anything I say about you, just confirm it, and don't look surprised. That includes your names; I'll be thinking up new ones for you as we go along. Ready? March!'

The 'march' took them to a twenty-foot-high facade sheared out of the lunar rock, decorated with the modest gleam that comes of vast wealth, and the words 'Occidental Productions, Inc.' carved over the doorway and sheathed in platinum.

'This is just the production house,' Whitey explained. 'Manufactures most of the entertainment for one of the anglophone channels.'

As they passed through the door, Dar found himself somehow totally certain that each person's height, weight, build, and colouring was registering in a computer somewhere deep inside the complex, which was trying to correlate it with the descriptions of all known criminals who might have a grudge against OCI. It was almost enough to make him turn right around to hijack the next outgoing spacer.

That didn't quite do it, but the foyer nearly did. Oh, the carpet was thick and the decoration superb; that wasn't the problem. It was the three uniformed guards, two androids, and five cameras, every one of which seemed to be looking directly at him. He stopped in his tracks, swallowing something that he hoped wasn't his heart.

But Whitey strolled ahead, confident and nonchalant, looking totally like your ordinary, everyday plutocrat.

'Service, citizen?' the lead guard asked with perfect, impersonal politeness.

'Gratitude, citizen. Mr Tambourin, to see Mr Stroganoff.'

'Do you have an appoi—' the guard began, out of habit. But he closed his mouth, and gazed up at Whitey for a moment. Then he said, 'Of course, Mr Tambourin.' He turned to murmur into a shielded com unit, waited, then murmured again. A delighted yelp sounded faintly from the unit. The guard listened, nodded, and turned back to Whitey. 'He will be up in a few minutes, Mr Tambourin. I regret the delay, but . . .'

'Of course.' Whitey smiled indulgently. 'He didn't know I was coming – but then, neither did I. Old friends, you understand.'

'Perfectly.' The guard was a good liar, anyway. 'If you'll step into the lobby, Mr Tambourin . . .?'

Whitey smiled with a gracious, affable nod, and turned back to the 'team'. 'Come along, children.' He turned and ambled away toward the big interior doors.

Dar could fairly hear Sam bristling as they followed.

The androids swung the doors open, inclining in a slight bow as Whitey passed through. As Dar filed by, he definitely did not receive the expected impression of being scanned. What with one thing and another, it boosted his opinion of Whitey's status till it almost soared.

They entered a world of sybaritic luxury – parqueted walls with huge, inscrutable paintings that fairly screamed, 'ART!' surrounding chairs that seemed to mould themselves around the sitter's body, a carpet so thick that it must have had a heart-beat, and a tastefully almost-dressed hostess who bent low to murmur, 'Refreshment, citizen?'

A month ago, Dar would have grabbed her and enacted the wildest scene of animal lust ever recorded (which it no doubt would have been). But, with Lona in the same room, the woman just didn't seem interesting. 'Yes, something to drink, thanks. Nothing too stimulating.'

When she handed him the drink, he took a tiny sip – and euphoria/ecstasy/exaltation/Nirvana rose up behind his eyeballs and exploded in streamers that enveloped his brain. He sat rigid for a moment, then coughed delicately into his fist, and set the drink down. He'd had occasional experiences with the pipeweed of Wolmar, during prairie grass fires, and knew a depressant when one hit him. The lady had taken him at his word, and then some; he wondered if he'd unwittingly spoken a code phrase.

Then a medium-sized man with a giant of a personality swept into the lounge. 'Tambourin! You infernal old scoundrel! Welcome back!'

Whitey stood up just in time to be almost knocked down by the dynamo's enthusiasm. All that kept him up was the bear hug as Stroganoff's rolling laughter boomed in their ears.

Then Stroganoff held Whitey back at arm's length, grinning from ear to ear. 'Let me look at you, ancient my wastrel!. . . Not a day! Ten years, and he hasn't aged a wrinkle!'

'Well, I was old enough the last time I saw you.' Whitey slapped Stroganoff on the shoulder. 'Solid meat still, eh? You're not doing so badly yourself, David!'

'Not since they gave me that new stomach, no. But let me put on my manners a second. Glad to meet you, folks, I'm David Stroganoff. Who're your friends, Whitey?'

'Oh, this is Fulva Vulpes.' Whitey stretched a hand out to Lona, whose eyes registered only the faintest of surprises. 'She's my assistant director and director of editing.'

Stroganoff's eyebrows went up. 'Unusual combination.' He pressed Lona's hand. 'You must be very good with computers.'

Now Lona did show surprise. She glanced at Whitey. Stroganoff chuckled. 'And who's *this* enchantress?'

Sam answered the compliment with a glare, which brought even more charm feeding back from Stroganoff. 'Watching to make sure the compliment's not more than its subject is worth, eh? Believe me, it's sound as an erg. What is she, Tod – your unit manager?'

'If it comes in a bureaucratic package and is wrapped with red tape, I can cut it,' Sam said warily.

'Unit manager, it is! And you, citizen?'

'Coburn Helith, research and script development. Co's the one who came up with the idea for tying my verses into a story, Dave.'

'Wh . . . Tod 'n' I've been talking for some time now.' Father Marco shook Stroganoff's hand without batting an eyelid. 'I work from fundamental mythic structures – which means I have trouble thinking commercially, of course.'

'Well, don't let it worry you – the myth hasn't been born that can't be debased,' Stroganoff said with a perfectly straight face. He turned to Dar. 'And the young one, Tod?'

'Perry Tetic – "Pa" to us juveniles. He's the debaser you just mentioned.' Whitey was obviously making it up as he went along. 'The commercializer. He's very good at putting the most abstract ideas into words even the average dunce can understand.'

'Oh, really.' Stroganoff shook Dar's hand with guarded interest. 'Let's hope we have time for a chat, Perry. I'm kind of interested in that kind of thing, myself.'

'Let's *make* time.' Dar was sure of being able to hold up his end of *that* conversation; anyone who'd been through Cholly's curriculum could. At least Whitey had given him a role he knew something about – and, looking back on it, he realized Whitey'd done the same for each of the others, too.

'. . . a little behind the state of the art,' he realized Lona was saying. 'Could I have a look at your editing facilities?'

'Of course, of course! Tour of the whole place, in fact. Sound Stage Number Ten's the first stop – I just ducked out of there, and I've got to quack back to make sure everything's running smoothly. Come on, this way!'

He set off, Whitey beside him; the rest followed in their wake. They turned into a corridor that opened off the lounge, Whitey and Stroganoff talking double-speed.

'So you put together your own production unit, eh, Tod? Glad to see you were listening when I kept saying you ought to package up a tank-play – but I didn't expect you to raft your own team!'

'Only way I'll touch it, Dave.' Whitey shook his head, jaw set. 'With me in control over the whole thing. You may notice we're lacking a producer, though.'

'Yeah, I did kind of notice that.' Stroganoff grinned like a shark. 'Is that an offer, Tod?'

'What do you want – thumbscrews?'

'Always the consummate diplomat. You know I can't resist a chance on something this good – but you need backing, too. You can't be crazy enough to try to finance something like this on your own.'

'Well, I don't exactly have a reputation for thrift.' Whitey grinned. 'But I'm not *that* far gone.'

'No thrift, my Aunt Asteroid,' Lona muttered. 'He's got enough in the Bank of Terra to buy a small planet – developed!'

It was a good chance to get close to her. Dar sidled up and whispered, 'They're buddies. How come Stroganoff keeps calling him "Tod"?'

' 'Cause he doesn't know about "Whitey",' Lona muttered back. 'Nobody does, outside the taverns.'

Well. That also explained the security problem that had been giving Dar heartburn. He'd thought Whitey was bringing sure disaster down on them by using his real name – but anyone on Falstaff who'd told Canis Destinus that Whitey the Wino was helping Dar Mandra wouldn't have known him as Tod Tambourin. So his best alias was his real name.

'Right in here.' Stroganoff hauled open a door that looked like a huge airlock hatch. 'Stage Ten.' As Sam filed past him, he added, ' 'Fraid I didn't catch your name, citizen.'

'She's Ori Snipe,' Whitey called back over his shoulder, and Sam forced a quick smile and handshake as she left Stroganoff in her wake.

They walked into chaos. Dar's first whirling impression was of a thousand people frantically everywhere, doing purposeless things and shouting at each other in an arcane jargon. But after a few minutes, he began to be able to make sense out of it. There weren't really a thousand people – more like three dozen. And they weren't really moving very quickly – it was just that there were so many of them moving in so many different directions that it *seemed* frantic. He locked his gaze onto one woman and watched her for a while. She was riding around on a lift, a slender telescoping column on top of a three-wheeled dolly, adjusting the lights that hung far above him. Her movements were methodical, almost plodding – nothing chaotic about them at all. He dropped his gaze to watch another person, then another.

'It may look confusing,' Stroganoff said beside him, 'but everyone knows what he or she has to do, and does it.'

Dar glanced up at him, saw a frown. 'Something wrong?'

Stroganoff shook his head. 'No, it's all going smoothly. A little ahead of schedule, in fact.'

'Then what's the matter?'

'Oh, nothing, really.' Stroganoff forced a smile. 'It's just that sometimes the phoniness of it gets to me.'

Dar frowned. 'But you're making stories, here – and stories have to be made up; they *can't* be real.'

'Oh yes, they can.' Stroganoff pursed his lips. 'There're a lot of really great stories in the history books.'

The statement had a ring of familiarity to Dar; suddenly, he could almost believe he was back in Cholly's Tavern. He cleared his throat to get rid of a sudden tightness. 'That almost sounds like education.'

'Sh!' Stroganoff hissed, finger to his lips. He glanced around furtively, then breathed a sigh of relief. 'Thank heaven! No one heard you!'

'Why?' Dar stared. 'What's wrong with education?'

'Be quiet, can't you?' Stroganoff glanced around again. 'Don't you dare say that word in here!'

'Why? What's the matter with ed . . . uh . . . hum . . . *you* know!'

'What's the matter with it is that it pulls low ratings,' Stroganoff explained in a lowered voice. '*That* kind of programme never attracts more than a handful of viewers.'

'Yeah, but that's a handful of all the people in Terran space! A handful out of a trillion-and-a-half!'

'So that "handful" is a billion or so people; yes, I know.' Stroganoff nodded. 'But that never sinks in, to the people who run this company. All they know is that they can get a higher price for a more popular show.'

'So.' Dar frowned. 'You don't dare put in anything ed . . . uh . . . at all deep, or they'll cancel the script.'

Stroganoff nodded. 'That's the basic idea, yah.'

'And you don't like it that way?'

Stroganoff hesitated; then he shook his head.

'So you don't like your job?'

'Oh, I *like* it well enough.' Stroganoff looked around him. 'There is still a fragrance left, out of the old glamour I thought was here when I was a kid. And it *is* exciting, putting together a story, even if it's purely trivial dross. It's just that . . . well, sometimes it gets to me.'

'But *why?*'

'Because I wanted to educate.' Stroganoff turned back to Dar with a gentle, weary smile. 'Not just a few interested students in a classroom – but the whole, huge mass of the audience, the billions of people who *aren't* interested, who don't *want* to learn all those "irrelevant facts" about Socrates and Descartes, and Simon de Montfort and the Magna Carta.'

'I kinda thought knowing about the Magna Carta was necessary for *all* the citizens in a democracy,' Dar said uneasily. 'At least, if that democracy is going to survive . . .'

'*If*,' Stroganoff said, with a sour smile. 'Look around you.'

Dar swallowed. 'I think you've got a point.'

'Oh, I know I do.' Stroganoff looked up at the lights on their grid of pipes, gazing at them but not seeing them. 'And I knew 3DT was the perfect thing to teach with – give the people lectures, but make them so visually interesting that they'd watch it in spite of themselves. Don't just tell them about Waterloo – *show* it to them, the actual place, the way it is today, and the way it was then. Then show them the battle, re-enact it, cut to an overhead shot so they can see how Wellington and Napoleon were moving their troops . . .' He trailed off, a faraway look in his eyes.

'Wait a minute!' Dar stabbed a finger at the producer. 'I saw that battle! In an old 3DT programme! The charge, and the horses galloping into the sunken road – then you saw from overhead, watched Napoleon's army folding in, but while you were watching it, you heard Wellington describing his strategy . . .'

'Sure you didn't read that in a book somewhere?'

'Yeah, but it didn't make any sense until after I saw the programme! *Josephine's Boudoir*, that was it!'

'Yeah, it sure was.' Stroganoff's mouth worked as though he'd tasted something bitter. 'I'm surprised you're old enough to have seen it.'

'I was way out on a, um, frontier planet. I remember it was mostly a pretty risqué version of Napoleon's private life – but it did have the battle of Waterloo in it.'

'Yes. It did have that.' Stroganoff smiled out at the studio. 'Not much education in it – but some. It'll do.'

'Why didn't you go into educational programming?' Dar asked softly.

Stroganoff shrugged, irritated. 'I did, fresh out of college. But they insisted that everything be dull and dry. Claimed the students wouldn't take it seriously if it was too entertaining – and they had research studies to back them up. Strange as it may seem, most people don't believe it's education if it isn't dull – and that means it reaches a very few people, indeed.'

'Most of whom would learn by themselves, anyway?'

Stroganoff nodded. 'The minority who read. Yes. They're wonderful people, but they're not the ones I was worried about, not the ones who endangered democracy.'

Dar nodded. 'It's the ones who don't want to learn that you want to reach.'

'Right.' Stroganoff closed his eyes, nodding. 'Not that it's going to do any good, of course. Oh, if I'd started a hundred years ago, maybe . . .'

'It can't be *that* bad!' Dar frowned. 'I thought a democracy had to become decadent before it collapsed.'

'So?'

'But we're *not*!' Dar spread his hands, hooked into claws. 'Where're the orgies? Where's the preoccupation with sex? Where're the decadent aristocrats?'

'At the IDE enclave in New York.' Stroganoff gave him a wry smile. 'Ever seen 'em? Funny about that . . .'

'Well, okay. But the orgies . . .'

'Been looking for them pretty hard, haven't you? Well, don't worry – they don't need to be there. How many orgies do you think the average Roman shopkeeper saw? Look for the decadence in the small things – the people who don't bother to vote because the candidates're "so much alike". The people who think it's fine for the government to crack down, as long as it doesn't interfere with their getting their supply of their favourite euphoric. The people who think talking politics is in poor taste. *There's* the decadence that kills a democracy.'

'And it traces back to lack of knowledge,' Dar said softly.

'Not all of it.' Stroganoff frowned; then he nodded. 'But a lot of it. Yah. A lot.'

'Ever hear of Charles T. Barman?' Dar said slowly.

'The rogue educator?' Stroganoff grinned. 'Yeah, I've heard of him. Read his main book, even. Yes, I've followed his career with great interest. Great interest. Yes.' He turned to Dar, his eye gleaming. 'They never caught him, you know.'

'No,' Dar said judiciously, 'they never did.'

Dar took a sip and frowned up at Lona over the rim of his glass. 'What's he doing in there?'

'Creating,' Lona answered.

'For so long?'

'Long?' Lona smiled without mirth. 'It's only been six hours so far.'

'It takes that long to do up one of those – what'd Stroganoff call it . . .?'

'Series format,' Sam reminded him.

'Yeah, one of those.'

'He finished that three hours ago.' Lona took a sip. 'Stroganoff needs the script for the first programme, too.'

'But he's just talking into a voice-writer! How can a one-hour script take more than an hour?'

'It's thinking time, not talking-time. And don't forget, it's got to be verse. That's the only reason Stroganoff might be able to persuade OPI to do it – because it's a 3DT series of Tod Tambourin's poetry.'

'And poems take a great deal of work,' Father Marco said softly. 'Actually, I don't see how he can possibly have a full hour's worth of verse by 10:00 hours tomorrow.'

'Oh, verse he can manage.' Lona glanced at the closed bedroom door that hid Whitey. 'Poetry would take forever – but he isn't worrying about quality. Verse he can grind out by the yard.'

'What if inspiration should strike?' Father Marco asked quietly.

'Then,' Lona said grimly, 'we may be in here for a week.'

'Oh, well.' Dar got up and went over to the bar-o-mat for a refill. 'At least he gave us a nice waiting room.' He looked around at the luxurious hotel-suite living room. 'Come to think of it, I hope inspiration *does* strike . . .'

Dar had a vague memory of Father Marco shepherding them all to their bedrooms, muttering something about an early day tomorrow, but it was rather fuzzy; a tide of some nefarious mist reeking of Terran brew seemed to have rolled in as the light faded. He awoke with a foul taste in his mouth, a throbbing ache in his temples, and an acute sensitivity to noises. He dropped back against the pillow, but sleep refused to return. Finally he resigned himself to having to pocket the wages of sin – though the pocket in question was feeling rather queasy at the moment – and slowly, very carefully, swung his feet over the side of the bed. He clutched his head and waited for the room to stop rolling, gulping air furiously to quiet his stomach. Eventually, it sort of worked, and he staggered to his feet. Then he had to lean against the wall, gasping like a beached fish, to wait until things stabilized again. It was a longer wait, but it worked, and finally he was able to stagger out into the sitting room.

The light had been turned down to a dim glow from the ceiling, thank heaven – but there was a babble of voices. Strangely, they didn't make his head hurt any worse – and, even more strangely, there was only one person in the room.

That person was Whitey, sprawled in a recliner with a strange glow in his eyes. He noticed Dar, cocked his head to the side, and held out a tumbler full of a thick, brownish liquid. Dar groped for it, seized it, and drank it off in one long gulp. Then his eyes bulged as his stomach gave a single, tumultuous heave. He swallowed it down and exhaled in a blast. 'My lord! What *is* that stuff?'

'Uncle Whitey's Homemade Hangover Helper,' Whitey answered. 'Don't ask what's in it.'

'I won't,' Dar said fervently. He groped his way to a recliner and collapsed into it. 'How'd you know I was going to need it?'

'I looked in on you halfway through the "night".' Whitey grinned. 'You were a gas.'

Dar frowned. 'A gas?'

'Throughly tanked,' Whitey explained.

A hazy memory of Whitey's bleached face, peering down intently, floated through Dar's mind. 'Oh, yeah. I remember something about it.' He frowned, then forced a feeble chuckle. 'Yeah, you . . . no, it must've been a dream.'

'It wasn't. Why'd you think it was?'

'Because you asked . . . and I told . . .' Dar swallowed heavily. 'No. Had to be a dream.'

'Asked what? Told me what?'

'Well – my mission. What I'm supposed to do on Terra.'

'No dream,' Whitey assured him. 'And I timed it just right. *In vino veritas.*'

'"In wine there is truth"?' Dar stared, aghast.

Whitey's eyelids drooped. 'You *do* know a little Latin! Amazing, in this day and age. Who managed to drum it through your head?'

'My old boss, a bartender named Cholly. But . . .'

'Hm. Must be an interesting man.' Whitey's eyes were glowing again. 'Like to meet him sometime.'

'You will, at the rate we're going. You won't have any choice in the matter.' Dar swallowed. 'What'd I tell you?'

'What do you remember?'

'That I had a message from General Shacklar to the IDE top brass – about a plan for a coup. . .'

Whitey nodded. 'Perfect recall.'

Dar groaned and crumpled, covering his eyes.

Whitey learned forward and patted his shoulder. 'Don't take it so hard, laddie – we all make mistakes the first time out. At least, if you had to spill the beans, you did it to a friend.'

'"Friend"?' Dar glared up. 'How can I be sure, now?'

'Because I've spent a lot of money, and put myself in quite a bit of danger, just to help you – and when I heard your story, I was glad I had. Not that I think we can succeed, mind you – but I can't let democracy go down without a fight.'

Somehow, Dar believed him. He frowned up at Whitey, against his headache. 'You must've had a hunch I was doing something you believed in, then – to put yourself and Lona at risk.'

'Well, yes.' Whitey settled back, picking up a glass. 'I did have a notion the gamble was worth it. Lona's another matter, though. I didn't make her come. She could've stayed behind, with plenty of money, and she knew it.'

Dar's brows pulled together. 'She doesn't strike me as the self-sacrificing sort.'

'She isn't. That line she feeds out, about wanting to wallow in luxury with plenty of leisure time to slaughter, is true down to the word – but she knows there are more important things. Such as having one person nearby who really cares about her – me – and freedom, without which she wouldn't have a chance at luxury.'

Dar looked around. 'Where is she?'

Whitey jerked his head toward the closed door. 'Proofing the script.'

'It's done?' Dar's gaze steadied on Whitey's face. 'Any good?'

Whitey shrugged irritably. 'Does it matter? It'll get you where you need to go; that's the important thing.'

Suddenly, something seemed wrong. Dar lifted his head. 'What happened . . .? Oh. The voices stopped.'

'Voices? The 3DT, you mean?'

'Is that where they were coming from?' Dar turned to the wall-screen, and saw the word 'EMERGENCY!' floating in a blue sea. A voice said, 'Indulgence, citizens. We have to interrupt to bring you news of a conspiracy against the whole of the Interstellar Dominion Electorates.' The word dissolved into the head and shoulders of an earnest-looking, handsome older man. 'Sehn Loffer here, with news directed from IDE Internal Security. We are threatened, fellow citizens – threatened by an insidious evil, creeping up on us everywhere, to choke the life out of our democracy and suck the blood of its freedom.'

Whitey muttered, 'Lousy prose!'

Dar stared at him, appalled. 'But he's the top newsface! They're hearing him all over the Solar System – and FTL liners will take this recording-cube to all the colonies within the month!'

'Yeah. "Nothing succeeds like excess."'

'The villain may be your neighbour, your friend, your co-worker,' Loffer went on. 'No one can know where the evil ones lurk – because, citizens, they are telepaths!'

Whitey stared. Dar goggled.

'Insidious telepaths, their tendrils of thought snaking out to enfold *your* brains! All through the IDE they are. How do we know? Because, for a month now, Security has been chasing a notorious telepath all the way from the marches, the outermost colonies, here to Luna itself! Time and again, they have almost caught him, only to have him whisked away into hiding, by local assistance!'

The 'local assistance' swore under his breath.

'Who would aid a rogue telepath?' Loffer declaimed. 'Who but *another* telepath? Wherever this monster goes, he finds help – so there must be telepaths spread throughout the IDE, helping him, working secretly, to undermine the foundations of our freedom and destroy our government – to take power themselves!'

'Uh – don't I detect a few flaws in his logic?' Dar asked.

'Logic? What's that?' Whitey snorted. 'It *feels* right, doesn't it? So it's *got* to be true – doesn't it?'

'But take heart, citizens!' Suddenly, Loffer fairly oozed calm strength. 'Our noble Solar Patrol is pursuing this monster, and will not rest until they destroy him!'

'What does "right to fair trial" mean?' Whitey wondered.

Smiling confidently, Loffer dissolved into a sea of plain blue, filling the screen. A voice said, 'We now return you to "Starship Captain's Wife".'

Whitey pressed the button in the arm of his recliner, and the picture faded into an assortment of fruits in a basket; the wall-screen became only a three-dimensional still picture again.

'Uh – I thought reporting was supposed to be objective, just telling you the facts they're sure of,' Dar said tentatively.

Whitey gave him a peculiar look. 'No, you haven't been to Terra before, have you?'

'But . . . *why*?' Dar exploded. 'Announcements like that are going to panic the public! Why get everybody into a state of terror about it?'

'I have a notion,' Whitey muttered, 'but I hope I'm wrong.'

'It's got to be because they want to make absolutely sure they catch me. But why? Am I that much of a threat to them? And how'd they get the idea I'm a telepath?'

'Maybe they didn't. "Telepath" is a nice scare word, conjuring up somebody poking into your most private affairs, somebody having a huge, unnatural advantage that makes everybody else feel inferior – and, therefore, all the more willing to go out and help hunt him down. Useful, if they want to make sure they catch you. And as to your being a threat, well – the answer is, you don't have to be *much* of a threat. Conspirators tend to not want to take chances, no matter how small. The LORDS party in the IDE Assembly want to restrict individual rights, and they've never been so strong. Their opposition has fractured into a dozen splinter groups. If there's an opposition leader, it's Tam Urkavne, the chairman of the CPR – the Coalition for the Protection of Rights. At least he's officially the Opposition speaker. But his "Coalition" is pretty weak – its members spend their time arguing over policy, instead of trying to *do* something.'

'But the LORDS aren't trying to overthrow the whole IDE government, are they?'

Whitey shrugged. 'If they are, they're not saying – of course. That's high treason, boy. No, you may be sure whoever's behind the coup are keeping their lips well sealed, and want to make sure everybody else does, too.'

The bedroom door opened.

'Well, enough of politics.' Whitey craned around in his seat, looking back over his shoulder. 'Hi, honey.'

Lona swayed out into the sitting room, and the sight of her made Dar decide to stay among the living. He decided Whitey's hangover cure *was* working. But she had a kind of glassy look in her eyes, a sort of fevered brilliance. Was she ill?

'I told you, you shouldn't have stayed up waiting for me to finish,' Whitey said, frowning. 'You get to bed, honey; you can still catch about three hours sleep before we have to leave.'

'How can I, with *this* running through my head?' Lona shoved a sheaf of papers at him.

Whitey squared the sheets on his lap, smiling up at her, almost shyly. 'Liked it, huh?'

Lona nodded, with a tight smile; she looked as though she were about to explode.

Whitey grinned and turned to Dar, holding out the sheaf. 'First hard copy. See what you think.'

Dar took the script and began to scan it. His eyes locked in after the third line, tracking the print at speech-speed, words thundering in his head. 'Whitey, this is . . .'

'. . . wonderful!' Father Marco breathed, looking up from the last page. Sam looked up from her copy with a numbed gaze and an awed nod.

'Rough,' Whitey grumbled, flushed with pleasure. 'Needs polish. Lots of it.'

'It's a masterpiece,' Sam whispered.

Whitey sat still a moment, then gave a brusque nod. 'Good. Yes. Rough, but – it's good. Thank you.'

Lona laid a gentle hand on his shoulder. '9:30 hours, Grandpa.'

'Yeah.' Whitey heaved himself to his feet with a sigh. 'Time to go meet Stroganoff, children – the Knight of the Shining Laser, who will do battle with the Dragon of Commerce for us. Ready?'

Dar paced the lounge furiously, hands locked behind his back. 'What's he doing in there – reading them the whole script?'

'Calm down, Da . . . uh, Perry.' Whitey leaned back in his chair like a cat by a fire, a tall drink in his hand. 'It means it's going well. If the execs didn't like his presentation, he'd've been out half an hour ago.'

The door opened, and Stroganoff shuffled in, holding the script in front of him as though it were a tray, eyes glazed.

Dar pounced on him. 'Well? What's the word? They like it? They gonna buy it? What?'

Stroganoff's head swivelled toward him, but his gaze went right through Dar. Father Marco pried Dar away with a soothing murmur, and Whitey echoed him: 'Calm down, Perry. They won't finish deciding for a while yet . . . How'd it go, David?'

Stroganoff's head turned toward Whitey, but his eyes still didn't quite focus. 'Tod . . . why didn't you warn me?'

'Warn?' Whitey frowned. 'About what?'

'About *this*!' Stroganoff held the script out reverently. 'I gave 'em the overview, and the audience potential, the cost-minimalization, and the company-image enhancement, and they sat there looking bored, so I started reading them the first few lines, just to give 'em the idea – and I couldn't stop! I just kept going, right through the whole thing – and they didn't cut me off! Not a word! They actually *listened*!'

Whitey grinned and sat back. 'Well. Nice to be appreciated.'

'Appreciated! My lord, Tod, that's topping the Prize!'

Dar heaved a silent sigh. He might make it to Earth, after all.

They were laughing and chattering as they came back into their hotel, riding high on a triumph – until a grave-faced major domo stepped up to Whitey and intoned, 'Mr Tambourin, sir?'

The laughter cut off as though it had been sliced with a razor blade. Whitey turned to the man in livery, frowning. 'Yes?'

'There's a call waiting, from Mr Horatio Bocello, sir. He's been quite insistent in his demands that he speak with you.'

Whitey's face cracked into a cream-whiskered grin. 'Old Horatio!'

Sam was staring, shocked. Father Marco blinked. Even Lona looked impressed. Dar looked around. Then they all jumped to catch up with Whitey.

But the major domo was ahead of them. 'Ah, Mr Tambourin?'

Whitey looked back. 'Yes?'

'He really has been *quite* insistent, sir. The staff would very much appreciate it if you would take the call as soon as you arrive in your suite.'

'Yeah. I know what Horatio's like when he gets "insistent".' Whitey's grin was downright evil. 'Don't worry, my good man – I'll hit the phone as soon as I'm upstairs. You can tell Terra the call's going through.' His hand brushed the major domo's as he turned away; the man glanced at his palm, and his eyebrows shot up. 'Thank you, sir.'

'My pleasure. Come on, troops!' Whitey was striding away toward the lift tube.

His 'crew' lurched into motion behind him. 'Who's Horatio Bocello?' Dar hissed.

'Only the richest man on Terra, gnappie!' Sam hissed back.

'Which means, in the whole system. Devout Catholic, too . . .' Father Marco said thoughtfully.

'Patron of the arts – especially Grandpa's,' Lona added.

Dar swallowed heavily, and walked faster.

When Whitey careened through the door, the com screen was already alive with white noise, its beeper beeping. Whitey pressed the 'answer' button and thumbed the toggle that uncapped his camera. The screen cleared, showing a thin, long-jawed, bony face with a receding iron-grey hairline, a blade of a nose, and burning eyes. The eyes focused on Whitey, and the face grinned. 'Tambourin, you old scallywag! Where've you been?'

'In a hundred bars on fifteen planets, Cello.' Whitey grinned back at him. 'You want exact figures, you'll have to tell me how long it's been.'

'What – five years, this time? Why don't you write, reprobate?'

'Buy it from your book-channel, windy. How's your empire?'

Bocello shrugged, with a trace of annoyance. 'You win some, you lose some, and it keeps growing, all by itself.'

Whitey nodded. 'No change.'

'It was a lot more fun back in the Northeast Kingdom.'

'I know.' Whitey smiled fondly, gazing back down the years. 'Running around in homemade armour, chopping at each other with rattan swords.'

'And for the parties, dressing up like a fourteenth-century duke. Except you, of course. You never could decide whether you wanted to be a knight or a troubadour.'

Dar nudged Lona, having a legitimate reason, and whispered, 'What're they talking about?'

'A bag of mixed nuts,' Lona whispered back. 'Some group they both belonged to when they were young. Used to go out to a park on weekends and pretend they were still living in the Middle Ages.'

'Well, I finally did.' Whitey's smile gentled. 'I swung to the troubadour – and you finally accepted your birthright obligations, and turned into a baron.'

'Yes, without the title.' Bocello's face clouded. 'But it's not as much fun, Tod.'

'You've got to lock into reality sometime, Cello. You keep tabs on the old Kingdom?'

Bocello nodded. 'Still. I'm still a member. I sneak into the annual festival every now and then. You should, too.'

'I do, when I run into a Kingdom. But there aren't too many of 'em on the colony planets yet, Cello. Hold onto your sword, Your Grace – you may need it.'

Bocello was suddenly alert. 'You see the signs, too, eh? But I don't think there'll be chaos, Tod.'

'No,' Whitey agreed, 'just the reverse. It's a dictator that's coming, not a warlord. Can't you do anything about it, Cello? You, with all your money!'

Bocello shook his head sadly. 'I always sneered at politics, Tod – and now it's too late.' He frowned, suddenly intent. '*You're* not planning to try to stop it, are you? To throw yourself in the path of a runaway destrier?'

'Romanticism's for the young, Cello,' Whitey said gently. 'No, I just got a *modern* idea, that's all.'

'Yes, I heard.' Bocello's face split into a mischievous grin. 'And I *love* it! *Damn* fine poem, Tod! *Damn* fine.'

Whitey scowled. 'Got eyes and ears everywhere, don't you?'

'Tod!' Bocello protested, wounded. 'I own OPI – or fifty-one per cent of it, anyway. They knew it was too hot to handle, so they bucked it on up to me fastest!'

'*You're* going to decide whether or not my epic gets made?'

Dar held his breath.

Bocello shrugged impatiently. 'What is there to decide? The way your last book sold, we couldn't possibly lose money on Tod Tambourin's first screenplay! All I want to know is, how quickly can you do it?'

Whitey grinned. 'My crew's ready to go tomorrow, Cello.'

'Wonderful. But you'll need a *little* while to cast the actors and have the sets designed and built.'

'Yeah, but we can shoot the documentary sequences meanwhile. And, Cello –' Whitey's voice lowered, '– if we're going to have the IDE Assembly and the Executive Secretary in that one sequence, I think we'd better shoot them *fast*.'

'Yes, I know.' Bocello sobered. 'The whole thing's built around the IDE.' He leaned forward, suddenly intense, eyes burning. '*Very fast*, Tod – before the whole programme's just an historical document!'

Dar fastened his webbing and looked around at the luxurious cavern of the shuttle's passenger cabin. 'Little different from a burro-boat, isn't it?'

'You could put two of them inside here,' Sam agreed. 'Maybe three.'

Dar swivelled his head to look at her, puzzled. 'You've been awfully moody these past couple of hours. What's the matter?'

'Nothing.' Sam shook her head with total conviction. 'Absolutely nothing is wrong.' But she still gazed off into space.

'It was that call from Horatio Bocello that did it, isn't it? What was so bad about it – didn't realize the IDE was in *this* bad a shape?'

'*That* is saddening,' Sam agreed. 'But I'm not saddened.'

'Then what are you?'

'Dazzled,' she said frankly.

Dar stared at her for a second. Then he smiled. 'Never saw anybody that rich talking just like an ordinary person, huh? Yeah, it kind of got to me, too.'

'Not that,' she objected. '. . . Well, maybe a little. But what got me was his *face*!'

'Face?' Dar stared again.

She nodded. 'That forehead! That blade of a nose! Those cheekbones! And . . . those *eyes*!'

Dar turned his head a little to the side, watching her. 'Are you trying to tell me you thought he was *handsome*?'

'"Handsome." That's a good word for it. "Attractive" is better. Maybe even . . . "compelling".'

Dar began to have serious doubts. 'I thought you were supposed to be an ascetic – an anti-materialist.'

She turned a gaze full of scorn on him. 'You take beauty wherever you find it, gnappie, and you keep the memory of it alive in your heart. I'll probably never even talk to this man and, when this whole escapade is over, never see him again, either. But I'll never forget that I did, and the memory of it will make the rest of my life that much richer.'

As they were crowding off the shuttle at Newark Interplanetary, Dar overheard some girl-talk between Sam and Lona.

'Married? Never,' Lona said firmly. 'Never even seen with a lady "friend" very often. That's brought the usual run of snide comments, of course.'

'About his masculinity?'

'And his sexuality, period! He reinforces that one, too – claims to be asexual. Says there's no point in sex unless you're in love.'

'What a medieval romantic,' Sam murmured dreamily.

Somehow, Dar didn't think they were talking about Whitey.

They strode down the concourse toward the main terminal, laughing and chattering. Dar felt heady, almost drunk. He was on Terra! The Terra of his history books, of Cicero and Caesar and the Plantagenets and Lincoln! The Terra of fable and wonder! He walked on a thick red carpet, surrounded by wall-screens flashing displays of arrival and departure times between spates of advertising – just the way he'd pictured it from his books!

Suddenly the wall-screens cleared. A giant chime sounded, reverberating throughout the entire building. All around them, conversation slackened and died; all faces turned to the wall-screens.

'Citizens,' a resonant voice intoned, 'the Honourable Kasi Pohyola, Chairman of the LORDS, and Majority Leader in the

Assembly of Electors of the Interstellar Dominions.'

A stern but gentle face appeared, surmounted by wavy, snow-white hair, gazing directly at Dar. He almost jumped out of his skin.

'Citizens,' the face intoned in a deep, resonant voice, 'a huge calamity has befallen us. An insidious danger stalks toward us across the stars – nay, *has* stalked us, has arrived, is even now in our midst! It may be the person beside you, or behind you – or even inside your head! For know, citizens, that there is no real guarding against this evil monstrosity, no wall that will seal it away, no shield that will stand against it – for it is a *telepath*! Even now, he may be probing your mind, wrapping his thoughts about your heart, cozening your innermost secrets!

'But worse, citizens – he is not alone! Our agents have shadowed him from the outermost colony planets, in to Terra herself – always treading upon his shadow, but never able to pounce on the creature – for always, just as they were about to close their trap, he has disappeared, spirited away by his friends and sympathizers on a thousand planets!'

'Only ninety-three,' Whitey muttered, 'as of last year's census report.'

'Who could have assisted such a one?' Pohyola rumbled. 'Who would give aid and solace to a being who could probe their innermost thoughts – save *another* telepath? That, citizens, is why we are sure there are many telepaths, spread throughout the Terran Sphere, on each and every one of its member planets – and including Terra herself!'

A horrified murmur and buzzing of oaths and curses spread through the concourse. It fairly made the hairs stand on Dar's head. He glanced at his companions – they were all watching with set, pale faces, lips drawn tight.

Except Whitey. He just looked sad.

Pohyola stared into the camera, not speaking, just holding the viewers' gazes with his own – apparently he'd been planning on the reaction. Just as it was quieting, he began to speak again. 'Our vaunted IDE Security Force has been impotent to stop them – these millions of highly trained warriors for whom we pay trillions of therms every year! Are they inept? No! Are they lazy or cowardly? No! They are brave, capable heroes, every one of them! Then, why have they not been able to seize this horror? Because, while he has been slipping into hiding, they have had to find a magistrate and present proof of need for a search warrant!

Because they have had to waste time securing *proof* of his guilt in order to obtain that warrant – though they have *known*, all along, what he is! Because the courts will not allow these fine officers to monitor the communications between this monster and his minions!'

He glared down out of the screen in righteous wrath. 'They are impeded at every turn, they are baulked at every approach! And, while the courts dither and obstruct them, the telepath moves unimpeded onto our fair mother planet!' He shook his head slowly. 'Citizens, this has gone too far! This obsession with legal pettifoggery has now imperilled your lives and mine, nay, even the fabric of our whole society! Who now can feel free to nurture secret hopes or longings, to dream of his beloved or reflect on his sins – knowing that, every moment, another's mind may have wormed its way into his, cozening up to his dearest, most cherished secrets!

'Nay! The time has come to put a *stop* to the nonsense! To purge the technicalities and loopholes that let the criminal escape while the law-abiding citizen shuffles in chains! To exorcize the demons of law! Make no mistake, citizens – a vast conspiracy of telepaths has wrapped its coils around us, and is even now beginning to squeeze the life from our democracy!

'Will they triumph? Nay!' he thundered. 'We will tear their coils apart, we will rip them asunder! The law will cease obstructing the champions of justice!'

Then, suddenly, his eyes were locked onto Dar's again, burning. 'But this cannot be done while Executive Secretary Louhi Kulervo dithers and vacillates! A man of decision must take the helm, a man of true strength, who does not waste expanses of time mewling about "sacred trusts" and "constitutionality"!'

He took a deep breath, very obviously fighting down wrath, struggling for composure, then said more calmly:

'It is for these reasons, citizens, that I will, today, demand a vote of confidence in the Assembly, and a general election. We must succeed in forcing this referendum, my fellow citizens – or we will waken one morning to find ourselves enmeshed in chains of thought! Contact your Elector, now, this minute, and tell him to demand an election. We must have it, citizens – we must have a man of decision and action to lead us – or the light of democracy will flicker out, and die!'

The image on the screen flickered out, and died.

A roar of conversation burst out all around them.

Whitey glanced back at his adrenalized crew, looking a little nervous himself. 'Ah . . . I think we should just start drifting toward the main terminal . . . and try to look surprised, folks.'

That wasn't hard. Dar felt as though he'd just been knocked spinning by a shockwave. It wasn't just that one fleeing little ship had been turned into a conspiracy – or that the coup was leaping out into the open. It was the idea that they might even be able to do it legally!

A very good chance, from what he was overhearing as they 'drifted':

'I thought they only had a couple of telepaths in the whole sphere!' an obese commercial-type was saying.

'So did I,' a slenderized companion answered, 'but I guess those were just the ones they knew about – you know, *legal* ones.'

'They can *really* find out your most secret memories?' This from an old harridan who obviously had one hell of a past, but didn't necessarily want it known.

'But . . . they could learn all my accounts, all the latest information I've gleaned about which stocks are due to rise!' The beefy, florid-faced individual in the conservatively expensive coverall glared in righteous indignation. 'That's a completely immoral competitive advantage!'

'*Have* to be stopped,' his companion agreed. '*Have* to be.'

'They could take over!' a sweet young thing shrilled, 'and they might clamp down on the vice laws!'

'Telepaths certainly wouldn't want people running around with their heads full of smut.' Her companion had the look of a questionable publisher. 'I mean, what about civil rights?'

'But what about civil rights?' Snow-white hair, face full of authority, oozing confidence – maybe a judge?

'They'd be gone.' His companion was younger, but cut from the same cloth. 'Make Pohyola Exec Sec'y, give him full emergency powers – and the first thing he'll do is suspend the constitution. We'll have a full-scale dictatorship in a year.'

'Are you two going to natter about technicalities at a time like *this*?' a slender, intense-type bawled, turning on them. 'Do you realize what our chances of getting approval for a price-hike would be if *telepaths* were running the Department of the Economy?'

They finally broke free of the mob, into a clear space in front of a drop-tube. Whitey hit the button; time stretched out as they waited, chafing, unable to do anything. Then the doors valved open and more citizens streamed out, chattering,

'. . . threat to everything we believe in . . .'

'. . . probably sacrifice babies at those secret meetings they have . . .'

'. . . got to vote Pohyola in!'

'Inside, folks,' Whitey growled, and they sprang. The doors valved shut behind them, and Whitey hit the street-level button.

'I'm scared, Grandpa,' Lona said softly.

'Comes of having brains,' Whitey growled. 'Me, I'm just terrified.'

Sam's eyes were huge in a pale, drawn face.

Dar's voice was very low. 'These people are so scared, they're actually going to be willing to give up all their rights!'

'Willing?' Whitey snorted. 'They're going to rush to it!'

'Whitey . . . my mission . . .'

'Still important,' Whitey snapped. 'If they lose the election, they'll still try their coup. In fact, they may not wait for due process.'

The doors valved open. 'Walk calmly,' Whitey growled. 'Don't do anything out of the ordinary. Just follow Papa.'

The crowd was much thinner here where people were coming into the terminal or leaving it, but there were still a lot of huddles of frantic citizens. Whitey strolled through them with his crew, retrieved his luggage, and sauntered out the ground-transport door.

A uniform stepped up to them with a man inside it. 'Mr Tambourin?'

Dar's heart jammed into his throat. Then he realized it didn't have any brass or badge; it couldn't be Security.

Whitey turned his head slowly, glowering. 'Yes?'

'Mr Bocello's compliments, sir. Would you accept his hospitality for the next few days?'

'Horatio always did have a great sense of timing,' Whitey sighed, pressing back into the limousine's seat. It responded, adjusting itself to his contours.

'What's in the cupboard?' Dar nodded at a sliding panel set into the wall in front of him.

'Why not ask the driver?' Whitey nodded toward a speaker-grille. 'He's just on the other side of the wall.'

'Why not?' Dar pressed the panel glowing beneath the grille. 'Uh, can you tell me what this little cupboard in the forward wall is?'

'A complete bar, sir,' the chauffeur replied. 'Please feel free to drain it. I hope we have your brands stocked.'

'Oh, anything expensive is fine, thanks.' Dar slid open the hatch, grinned at the gleaming panel in front of him, checked the codes listed above it, and punched up a Deneb Dimmer. 'Next order?'

'Sirian Scrambler,' said Lona.

'Canopus Concentrate,' said Sam.

'Château LaMorgue '46,' said Whitey.

Dar squinted at the index. 'Sorry, Whitey, all they've got is a '48.'

'Well, that wasn't a bad year,' Whitey sighed. 'It'll do.'

Dar pressed in the code and glanced at Father Marco.

'Nothing, thanks.' The priest raised a palm. 'I only drink in the early morning.'

Dar shrugged, took his tumbler out of the slot, and settled back with a contented sigh. 'I'm beginning to see advantages to decadence.' He beamed down on the city passing beneath them. Then he frowned. 'What's that?'

Below them, a mob filled several streets, waving signs and throwing bricks.

'What?' Whitey leaned over to the window, looking down. 'Hey, not bad! Let's see if we can hear them.' He turned a knob and punched a button beneath the speaker grille. It filtered faint words to them:

'Espers are Ethical!'

'Don't Sell the Psis!'

'Terra for Telepaths!'

Whitey nodded with satisfaction. 'A political demonstration. Nice to hear the voice of dissent.'

'The bricks are bouncing back at them,' Dar called. 'Bouncing off of thin air, in fact. What is it, a force-field?'

'Give the man a point!' Lona said brightly. 'You've got it, sophisticate – it's a force-field. Makes sure the demonstrators don't hurt anybody.'

'There're a few Security men outside the force-field . . .'

'Well, you wouldn't expect them to be inside, would you?'

'But why do they need them, with the force-field?'

'Who do you think set it up?'

'Also, they're the official sign that the government is hearing the citizens' grievances,' said Sam, with full sarcasm.

'The government *approves*?'

'The government embraces it, almost to the point of lewdness. They've even written it into law – for every hundred thousand persons demonstrating for eight hours, they get one vote on the issue in the Assembly.'

Dar turned to her, frowning. 'Sounds a little dangerous. A fad could get voted into law that way.'

'Not when you remember that the Assembly represents ninety-three human-inhabited planets with a total population of eighty billion. You have to have forty-eight votes just to get the issue onto the agenda! Not that it hasn't happened, mind you – but rarely, very rarely.'

'Two of the programmes based on such issues have been enacted into law,' Father Marco reminded her.

'Two laws in five centuries? Not exactly a great track record, Father!'

'Well, no. It does require that the majority approve the issue.'

'Yeah.' Sam slid over next to Dar and stared out the window gloomily. 'But some chance is better than none, I suppose. At least it gives the counterculture the illusion that they can accomplish something.'

They passed over three more demonstrations on the way to Bocello's; each was huge, making the pro-telepath mob look like a handful – and all screaming for the telepaths' blood.

'What're *we* getting upset about?' Dar wondered. '*We're* not telepaths!'

'Try and prove that to Pohyola,' Sam growled.

What with one thing and another, their nerves were in a fine state of disarray by the time the limo landed.

They stepped out into the midst of a tournament.

The knights had apparently unhorsed each other; the beasts in question were standing back, watching their masters with jaundiced eyes. The knights were hewing at each other with broadswords that went CLICK! CLUNK! whenever they met. The Green Knight wore full plate armour; his opponent wore a haubergeon. Behind and above them stood a scoreboard with two outline-drawings of a human form; whenever one of the knights managed to 'wound' his opponent, the 'wound' would show up on the scoreboard as a red light, and a chime would ring the knight's number of points.

Around them stood and sat a hundred or so people dressed

in the latest fashion of the fourteenth century. Or the twelfth. Or the tenth. Or maybe the ninth. They nibbled at pasties and swigged ale, laughing and cheering, while pedlars circulated among them with food and drink, and troubadours and gleemen strolled about singing and chanting. An occasional monk stood near, inveighing against the evils of tournaments and enjoining the faithful to repent.

Lona turned to the chauffeur. 'Sure you didn't take us to the wrong address? Say, maybe a mental hospital?'

'Not at all,' the chauffeur assured her. 'This is Mr Bocello's house.' And there it was, rising high behind the medieval crowd in full Gothic splendour, looking more like a public monument than a dwelling.

'A man's castle is his home,' Dar murmured.

'Mr Bocello is entertaining,' the chauffeur explained. 'Just a few friends from his club.'

Dar eyed the crowd. 'Not what I think of as the usual plutocrat-orgy set.'

'Very few of them are wealthy, sir. But all share Mr Bocello's fondness for the medieval. He has gathered them to celebrate the return to Terra of, ah, in his words, "the greatest gleeman of our age".'

A slow grin spread over Whitey's face. 'Now, *that's* what I call honouring me according to my own taste and style! I *am* more of a gleeman than a poet, anyway! Come on, folks – if the man does me honour, let's honour his doing!'

A very tall, skinny man in full ducal robes shouldered his way through the crowd with a peasant lass on his arm. 'Tambourin!'

'Cello, you filthy old wastrel!' Whitey reached up high to slap the duke's shoulder. 'How'd you get this crowd together on only a day's notice?'

'Oh, I had a few words with their employers, and they were more than happy to oblige. You didn't think you could set foot on old Terra again without causing a festival, did you?'

'Well, I did have some naïve notion about slipping in unnoticed,' Whitey admitted.

Bocello raised an eyebrow. 'What is it this time – a vengeful husband, or an irate sheriff?'

'It's more like a list, really . . .'

'Oh, is it indeed!' Horatio turned the peasant wench around and sent her off with a pat on the backside. 'Off with you, child – I have a feeling we're about to be saying things that you truly

want to be able to claim you didn't hear. Come now, no pouting
– I saw the way you were eyeing that acrobat; deny it if you can
. . .' He turned back to Whitey as the girl swept off with a blush
and a giggle. 'Now, then! It's been a while; perhaps you and your
entourage would like a quick tour of my gardens?'

'We would indeed! Preferably out in the middle of a wide
expanse of lawn, free from prying mechanical eyes and ears. . .'

'Ah, but one can never be totally certain of that any more.'
Horatio took Whitey by the arm and led him away. 'They're
doing such wonderful things with miniaturization these days.
Still, my gardeners do, ah, "sweep" the lawns every morning,
so we've a reasonably good chance . . . By the way, what did you
think of Greval's latest epic?' And they were off, happily ripping
apart other artists' work in the time-honoured tradition of amateur
critics, as they wove and dodged their way through the crowd. The
gang had to scramble to keep up with them, and by the time they
came out onto the open grass, Dar was winded.

Sam was starry-eyed.

Dar glanced at her, glanced again, and scowled. What was she
looking moonstruck about? He glanced around quickly, but didn't
see any gorgeous hunks of manhood nearby. As a last resort, he
glanced back at Sam, and followed the direction of her gaze;
it arrowed straight toward Horatio. Dar felt a sudden, biting
jealousy, which surprised him.

'Now, then!' Horatio stopped in the middle of a wide, open
field, chewed into mud at its centre. 'The lists are the most private
place we'll find, at least until the next joust. Let's have your list.
Who's chasing you first?'

'The Solar Patrol, at the moment,' Whitey answered with a grin,
'cheered on by a weasel named Canis Destinus.'

'Canis *what*?' Horatio frowned. 'Why is *he* on your trail?'

'Because I'm helping a friend.' Whitey nodded toward Dar.
'And this Canis guy is chasing *him* because he's on a secret mission
of some sort. It involves getting to the Executive Secretary for a
few minutes.'

'I think he does have an opening on his calendar, next Thursday
. . .' Horatio pursed his lips. 'Still, it's a difficult appointment to
make.'

'Especially with Canis trying to cancel it,' Whitey agreed. 'We
can't be sure, mind you, but we think he's the one who's been rousing
the local police against us on every planet we've been to. There
must be at least three warrants out for me, along my backtrail.'

'Well, that's nothing new.' Horatio's scowl deepened. 'Still, I expect the honour's being bestowed for the wrong reasons. What charge has he drummed up?'

'Now, we're not sure, mind you,' Whitey said, frowning, 'but we *think* he's managed to convince the LORDS that we're a bunch of telepaths, and that we've been aided and abetted by telepaths all along our route in from the marches.'

Horatio stared. '*You're* the Interstellar Telepathic Conspiracy?'

'Well, that is kinda what we think they've got in their heads, yeah,' Whitey muttered.

Horatio glared down at him, his face slowly turning purple. Dar stood frozen, with his heart in his throat. If Whitey were just a little bit mistaken about his old buddy, they could all wind up in prison at the snap of a finger. He could fairly feel that restraining field pressing in on him from all sides already . . .

Then Horatio blew. 'Foul!' he bellowed, fingers clawing into fists. 'How foul, how fell! That the High Gleeman of scores of worlds should be hounded and harassed like a common felon! And all for the brain-sick nightmare of a diseased and petty mind! Nay, nay! I have stood and smiled, I have gnashed my teeth whiles I watched them play their petty games of plot and counterplot; I have schooled myself to patience while the reek of their corruption stank in my nostrils – but this I cannot bear! Nay, how can there be any gram of goodness biding in a sovereignty that's so riddled with malice that it dreams up excuses to harry its bravest and best? Terra is become a stench-filled sty, a globe no longer fit for glee, a domain no longer fit for dwelling – nor can any planet be that falls within its sphere of influence!'

Whitey dug in his toes and braced himself against the gale. 'Peace, now, peace, good fellow! Hope lives on yet! Even corruption has its day, and ceases, and the seeds of goodness sprout up from it, to flower again in virtue!'

'Aye, but in how many years?' Horatio glowered down at him. 'Nay, centuries! I am not minded to hold my peace and bear myself in silence whiles I wait!'

Dar felt a surge of panic. Was this madman going to try a one-man rebellion, or something?

But Whitey suddenly became very casual. 'Well then, if you truly feel so, flee! There be no dearth of G-type suns, nor of worlds like Terra. If you find all known worlds so swinishly unfit, go seek the unknown! Go sail into uncharted skies and find a world to make anew, after the fashion of your dreaming!'

Dar held his breath. What Whitey was saying was, in effect, put up or shut up.

But Horatio was staring at him as though he'd spoken an idea never thought of before. 'Aye,' he breathed. 'Aye, surely!'

He whirled away toward the house, crying, 'Where are these hearts? Where are my comrades?'

The whole group stared at his retreating back.

'I, ah, think we might want to go along with him,' Whitey suggested. 'He sometimes needs restraining when he gets into these moods.' He set off after Horatio.

The troupe followed, and caught up with him.

'What's the matter with her?' Whitey muttered to Dar.

'Huh?' Dar glanced at Sam, who was moving a little more quickly than the rest of them, gaze fixed on Horatio, eyes shining. He turned back to Whitey. 'Just spellbound. Money has that effect, sometimes.'

But Whitey shook his head. 'Not so, or she'd have gone after *me*. Would you say Sam's the impulsive sort?'

'Well . . . in a way.' Dar frowned at Sam, seeing her anew. 'Controls it well, though.'

'And Horatio doesn't have to.' Whitey nodded. 'That explains a lot.'

Dar was glad it did, because he didn't understand a bit of it. On the other hand, he hadn't had much exposure to women who spoke his own language.

Horatio stormed up a flight of limestone steps and wheeled through French doors into his palace. By the time the crew caught up with him, he was leaning across a Louis XIV desk, glaring into a phone screen at an image of a bulky, black-haired man with a flowing beard. 'Ship?' he was saying. 'Of course you can buy a ship, Horatio! The Navy has surplus dreadnoughts it would love to be rid of – but why?'

'To issue from a sty of stenches!' Horatio snapped. 'What do you mean, they have ships they'd love to be rid of?'

'Always more on hand than they have buyers for. After all, who'd want a retired battleship – *without* its cannon?'

'We would! To bear a crew of colonists to a brave new world, where we may purify ourselves of this crass materialism, and rise above the suspiciousness and greed of this technological monster of a world!'

'Horatio.' Blackbeard eyed him warily. 'Do you speak of founding a society based on the Society?'

'Indeed I do, Markone!'

'I was afraid that this might come,' Markone sighed. 'You must not confuse the pleasant fantasy of our Society tournaments and moots with the reality of the real world, Horatio. That way lies madness.'

'I do *not* confuse them – I wish to make the fantasy *become* real! Think of it, Markone – your barony become a reality, your vassals and serfs forever at your call!'

Markone's eyes lost focus. 'A pleasant dream, Horatio – yet nothing but a dream.'

'It need not be!' Horatio insisted. 'Think, man! What need would we have for all our fortunes? Each could lay the half of them away for his heirs here, and take the other half to pool, to buy a ship and equip an expedition! What could it cost? Certainly no more than a hundred billion – and we must have a dozen barons in the Society who are worth more than half of that apiece!'

Markone gazed off into space. 'It might be possible, at that . . . as though we were holding an extended festival abroad . . . And 'twould be possible to return. . .'

'Meditate upon it,' Horatio urged. 'Yet if 'twere done, 'twere well 'twere done quickly, Markone. You know the uncertainty of the political situation.'

You could almost hear Markone's eyes click back into focus. '*Uncertainty?* What's doubtful about it, Bocello? Nothing but time – and that might be as short as a few days, before these petit-bourgeois politicians in the Assembly elect the Executive Secretary to the noble post of Dictator!'

'Oh, come now,' Horatio purred. 'I scarcely think they'd be so blatant as to give him the title.'

'No, but they'll give him the power! They're primed and ready; all they need is a trigger, some threat to all of them, and they'll cheerfully sell all their freedoms for security – and ours with theirs!'

'True, true – and we know how sensitive these lowborns are to anything that threatens their positions. When all's said and done, money is secondary to them. But give them one sign that there may be someone more powerful than they, who might usurp their powers, and they panic!'

'They do indeed – which brings to mind the latest news, Horatio.' Markone glowered up at him out of the screen. 'What think you of this Interstellar Telepathic Conspiracy?'

'Who could better recognize a fantasy than we? But there *is* a man of almost supernatural gifts there, as the grain of truth that rumour's wrapped around, Markone.'

'Indeed?' Markone's scowl deepened. 'What manner of man is that?'

'One you've met – the greatest bard of the Terran Sphere, Tod Tambourin. Government officials have been chasing him in here from the marches – secretly at first, but now openly, claiming that he and his band are telepaths.'

'Chased *Tod Tambourin*?' Markone bawled. 'This is too much, Bocello! They exceed excess in this!'

'They do indeed.' Horatio nodded slowly, eyes gleaming.

'If they will harry such a man out of pettiness and spite, what might they *not* attempt? By all the stars, Bocello – do you realize that they might come a-hunting *us*?'

'We are logical targets for envious men,' Horatio purred, 'the more so since we have wealth to confiscate.'

'Does it begin again, then? Must we watch the bloody flag arise, and ride on tumbrels to the guillotine?'

That, Dar thought, was overdoing it a bit – though he had to agree that there did seem to be some danger in staying on Terra just now, for anyone with large amounts of money or a taste for eccentric hobbies.

'I, for one, do not intend to learn the answer,' Horatio informed his phone-screen, 'at least, not from personal experience. I'll buy a ship alone, if I have to, and recruit my party guests. What say you, Markone? Will you join me?'

'That I will, and see the Baronetcy of Ruddigore established in reality! Go buy your ship, Bocello – and don't lift off without me!'

The screen blanked. Horatio turned to his guests with a wolfish grin. 'So it begins, and they'll fall into line quickly, I assure you; the twelve great barons of the Central Kingdom. Oh, we'll have that ship bought and outfitted within a day, and be loading passengers in two!'

Whitey spread his hands. 'It was just an idea.'

'You can't find enough people that fast,' Dar stated flatly. 'Oh, maybe you twelve rich men might be ready to jump at a moment – you know you can come back any time you choose. But it's different for the ordinary people. They'll need a long time to decide.'

'They will, eh?' Horatio seized a stylus and tablet from his desk and strode to the French doors. He came out onto the terrace, hands high, bellowing, 'Now I cry *HOLD*!'

The shouting chaos of laughing and singing ceased in an instant.

'They're loyal,' Horatio explained over his shoulder. Then, to the multitude: 'The Baronet of Ruddigore and I have decided to take ship, and ride out to the stars, to discover a world never before seen by Terrans, there to found the Central Kingdom in reality, and live as men ought, by faith and sweat and steel. We shall need villeins and yeomen, gentlemen and knights! We shall leave in two days time; any who are not with us then, will never be! Who wishes to ride? Sign here!'

He threw the tablet down into the multitude. With a roar, they pounced on it, and the whole crowd instantly re-formed into a line, each one fairly panting in his eagerness to emigrate. Food-sellers and jugglers began to work up and down the queue.

Horatio turned back to Dar with a grin. '*That* is the mettle of my people!'

'They'll change their minds by the time they get to the front of the line,' Dar predicted.

Horatio nodded. 'Some of them, no doubt – but most will sign. They've wished for nothing half so much as to live in a world where folk are true, and the rulers worthy of trust. How say you, brave ones? Will you join us?'

'Instantly.' Sam beamed up at him.

Horatio looked down at her, surprised. Then, slowly, he began to smile, almost shyly.

'I admit I'm tempted,' Father Marco mused. 'For a priest, the Middle Ages had definite advantages.'

'For gleemen, too.' Whitey grinned from ear to ear. 'I think it's a great idea, Horatio, and I'll cheer you on every AU of the way – but I never was much of a joiner.'

'Nor I.' Lona shook her head firmly. 'Stuck in a society that's never even heard of electrons? Horrible!'

Dar opened his mouth to answer, and a burring sound came out. He swallowed and blinked, then realized that the sound had come from the phone. A footman in tights and tabard stepped out to announce, 'There is a Mr Stroganoff calling, sir, for Mr Tambourin.'

Whitey looked up in surprise. 'Already? There shouldn't have been any progress yet.' He went back inside, with Dar trailing after.

Stroganoff was on the screen, dazed. 'What's the matter, David?' Whitey asked as he came into range.

'Oh, nothing, nothing at all! Everything's just fine – in fact, *too* fine. *That's* what's the matter!'

'Glad to hear it – I hope. Want to tell me why it's got so hot that it's turned cold?'

'The Executive Secretary.' Stroganoff swallowed. 'I sent a fax to his office, right after you left. I figured the way the government bureaucracy works, I'd better start right away if we were going to have any chance of shooting him within the year.'

'Wise.' Whitey was poised like a hawk about to stoop. 'And?'

'And his office just called. He's – he's willing to do the piece. But only if we can do it tomorrow!'

Whitey and Dar both stared.

'The primary citizen *never* says "yes" that quickly!' Stroganoff bawled. 'And even after you've talked him into it, you have to make an appointment months away!'

'And have it cancelled at the last minute, at least twice.' Whitey nodded, with a faraway look in his eyes. 'On the other hand, I do have a certain reputation. . . .'

'Well, you're at least as famous as he is, if that's what you mean. But. . .'

'But my fame is apt to last a bit longer,' Whitey mused, 'and from the current political news, I'd guess the Exec isn't too sure he's going to still *be* Exec in a few months – or even *next* month, for that matter.'

'Next *week*,' Stroganoff growled.

Whitey nodded. 'So he's making his bid for immortality. Do the piece for us, and he's guaranteed a featured place in Tod Tambourin's one and only 3DT masterpiece. Even if history forgets him, literature won't.'

Stroganoff nodded slowly. 'Y'know, that almost makes sense, Tod.'

'Yeah, but the schedule doesn't.' Whitey grimaced. 'Oh, the crew can make it easily enough – all we have to do is hop into a cab, and charge it to your company.'

Stroganoff shuddered. 'How about first class on a public shuttle?'

Whitey shrugged. 'Whatever you like. But how about equipment?'

'May have it, or may not. There's no point in dropping it down from Luna, of course; what we do is to rent it out from a dirtside company. I know a few. I'll have to make some calls, and get back to you.'

Whitey grinned. 'I always wanted to use a 3DT camera.'

'Uh, hold on, now. Whoa!' Stroganoff held up his palm. 'No can do, Tod. Cameras come with a union crew, or they don't come at all!'

'Why?' Whitey frowned. 'I've got two electronics techs right here!'

'I know, but if the union finds out you've shot a sequence without them, they won't give you any tech crew for the studio segments up here. Like it or not, we've got to use them.'

'Okay, I'll try to like it,' Whitey sighed. 'When do we meet them?'

'I'll let you know, if I manage to get them. Where'll you be?'

'Where should I be?'

Stroganoff grinned. 'Thank you, Meistersinger. Be on your way to the Gamelon, will you? Call me back when you're over Lake Champlain.'

# 11

'You're sure this's the Gamelon?' Dar muttered. 'For all I can see, it could be the inside of Moby Dick.'

'Moby Dick was a whale, not a snake,' Whitey muttered back, 'or haven't you noticed how many turns we've made?'

'Didn't look this big from outside,' Dar grumped.

Father Marco had become enmeshed in a long theological discussion with two young clerks who were devout atheists masquerading as medieval monks. Lona had become enmeshed in partying, and Sam was trying to become enmeshed with Horatio. So they had come alone to the long, striplike building that had replaced New York's eastside docks, and were following a lighted bar that slid along the hallway floor in front of them, making some very unpredictable turns as it led them farther and farther into the building that housed the Central Executive Staff of the Interstellar Dominion Electorates.

Finally, it stopped next to an open doorway. Dar looked up, and met the gaze of a wide, very muscular individual dressed in a labourer's overall. 'Help you?' he rumbled.

'Somebody's got to,' Dar answered. Then Whitey arrived at his elbow. 'Tod Tambourin,' he said, pointing to the ID tag the door-guards had hung around his neck.

'Oh yeah, the writer.' The muscular one looked bored. 'This your PA?'

'No, he's my assistant.'

'Right. Well, come on in. Not much for you to do, though; we're just about ready, here.'

They were, indeed. As Dar came in, he saw a huge desk sitting in front of a photomural of a starfield, with the IDE spiderweb superimposed over it in lines of light. On either side of the desk, between it and the backdrop, were two slender pillars. In front were two cameras. All around were at least a dozen technicians.

Dar turned back to Muscles. 'Mind if I show my ignorance?'

'That's what I'm here for,' the beefy one sighed.

'What do you need so many people for?'

'Easy.' Muscles pointed. 'Two camera ops, one electrician, one engineer for each set of camera controls, one engineer for audio, one for the holo-mole recorder, and a staging director.'

'That's only eight.'

'You're good at arithmetic.'

'But there're at least sixteen here!'

'Well, every position's gotta have a backup. You know, some-body might have a heart attack.'

'Yeah, like the accountant who has to keep track of the budget for this show. What do you do?'

'I'm the shop steward.'

'Oh . . . Uh, thanks.' Dar turned away to Whitey. 'You sure we didn't stumble into a mattress factory by mistake?'

Whitey frowned. 'What do you mean?'

'There's so much featherbedding.'

In the far corner, a small man in a business coverall came through a narrow door. 'Rise, citizens, for your Executive Secretary.'

Those of the crew who were sitting (twelve, at the moment) hauled themselves to their feet.

'Oh, don't be ridiculous, Hiram!' A tall man with white hair and a craggy, handsome face strode briskly in, the fabric of his modest coverall glowing with the quiet sheen of luxury. 'We don't stand on ceremony here.' To prove it, he sat down at the desk.

Dar swallowed around a sudden bulge in his throat. The Executive Secretary himself! Even out on a marches planet such as Wolmar, he'd seen pictures of that face so often that virtually every wrinkle in it was embedded in his memory. To suddenly be in the same room with the man himself was unnerving; he didn't quite seem to be real.

'You've come damn near a hundred light-years to talk to this man,' Whitey muttered in his ear. 'Go to it!' Aloud, he said, 'Go check and see if he's got any problems with his lines.'

Dar swallowed thickly and stepped forward, holding the script before him like shield. He hovered just behind the staging director, dimly aware that the lady was chatting with the Exec, but not at all sure what she was saying. Finally, the Exec nodded, and the staging director stepped back, calling to Dar, 'Ready any time.'

'Are there . . .' Dar's voice broke into a squeak; he swallowed and licked his lips. The Exec glanced up at him in irritation. Dar cleared his throat and tried again. 'Any problems with the script, sir?' He dropped his voice down just above a whisper and poured out the rest in a sudden rush: 'Boundbridge, Satrap, and Forcemain aren't going to wait for an election. They've had a *coup d'état* planned for months. I have the codes that will unlock the proof of their complicity. Save democracy, sir!'

A slow grin spread over the Exec's face. 'Had that memorized, did you?'

Dar swallowed, and nodded.

The Exec nodded, too, and rose, clapping Dar on the shoulder. 'It's always a pleasure to meet a genuine patriot.' But his hand tightened, and he called out, 'Did you hook up those cameras?'

'Yes, Mr Secretary.' The staging director looked frightened. 'We're patched into network. You can go live to all of Terra whenever you want.'

'Good, good.' The Exec let go of Dar just as harder hands laid hold of him. Looking up, he saw the shop steward and one of the assistants holding him, each one levelling a small but efficient-looking pistol at his torso. Whitey was suffering the same treatment; and the whole crew, except for the camera operators and the staging director, had pistols out.

'All right, then. Put us on,' the Exec said. He smiled into the camera in front of him, seeming suddenly warm and weary, but solemn. The staging director raised a hand, palm flat and stiff, gazing into space, listening to a voice talking into her ear-button. Suddenly his arm swung down like a sword, to point at the Exec.

'Fellow citizens,' the Exec intoned, 'we are happy to be able to announce that we have arrested the vile telepath who has been stalking relentlessly through the planets, to Terra. He is here.'

The red light on his camera went off, and the corresponding

light on the other camera glowed to life – pointing straight at Dar. With a sudden, horrible, sinking feeling, he realized everyone on Terra could see him.

'My Executive Guards caught him just in time,' the Exec went on, 'right here, in this studio, attempting to assassinate me.'

A sudden horrible chill seized Dar's intestines as he found a pistol in his hand. How . . .?

Then, suddenly, he realized what the Exec was saying, realizing he was being identified as the horrible, vicious, telepathic assassin. He screamed, 'N-o-o-o-o!' and threw his weight frantically against the hands that held him. They bit into his arms like steel clamps, and he writhed and twisted, bellowing in outrage, trying to shake them off.

'He knew what I was going to say next,' the Exec said grimly, 'that the danger is not over. For he has confederates, fellow citizens – travelling unseen and unknown, here on Terra itself! Where these vicious assassins will next strike, we cannot tell – nor who will be their next victim. Probably myself – but it also might be any one of you.'

His voice deepened, ringing with conviction. 'They must be stopped! For you, my fellow citizens, do not have a corps of guardsmen to protect you day and night. They must be stopped – but your Civil Police cannot arrest the people whom they know to be dangerous telepaths, because of the restrictions of civil rights laws! The only way to end this peril is to grant me full emergency powers, so that I can have your police clap these criminals into jails, where they belong. Today I will ask the Assembly for those powers – but I will not receive them without your support. Call your Elector now! Tell him to give me the powers I need to protect you! So that mad-dog renegades, such as this one, can be banished to the farthest reaches of Terran space!'

He stared solemnly into the camera, the perfect image of a good but troubled man, until the red light went out.

Then he thrust himself to his feet, grinning, and turned to Dar. 'Thank you, young man. You timed your struggling perfectly.'

'It's you!' Dar burst out. '*You're* the one who planned the coup!'

'No – but I will be the one who takes power. If there's going to be a dictator, I intend to make sure that I'm it.'

'You don't even care about saving democracy!'

'Why so surprised?' The Exec's smile was gentle, sympathetic – and underscored with contempt. 'You poor, naïve idiot! Did you honestly think any politician really cared about anything but personal power anymore?'

Dar stared at him, horrified.

Then the frustration broke, and the rage leaped through it. He threw himself at the Exec with a howl, fingers curving into claws – but the guards' hands held him back, and a cold spray hit his face, filling his head with fumes that spread darkness through his brain.

# 12

'WHY DID YOU ESCAPE FROM WOLMAR?'

The voice blasted through into Dar's nice, warm nest of unconsciousness. An idiot monotone was singing in his right ear, and a cricket with absolutely no sense of rhythm was chirping into his left.

'HOW DID YOU LEAVE THE PLANET WOLMAR?'

'I hopped into a courier ship,' Dar answered truthfully. He levered his eyelids open, squinting against the light.

Five of them, actually – red, blue, green, yellow, and orange – hitting him with stroboscopic flashes that didn't quite have a rhythmic pattern – but it was a different nonrhythmic pattern than the cricket's. Dar stared, dazzled.

'WHAT IS YOUR NAME?'

It was ridiculous, but he couldn't think of it. All he could think of was that he wanted someone to turn the lights off. 'I don't know!'

'EXCELLENT,' the unseen owner of the voice purred. 'WHICH OF YOUR TRAVELLING COMPANIONS WAS THE TELEPATH?'

'The *what*?'

'DO NOT SEEK TO MISLEAD US! WE KNOW THAT AT LEAST ONE MEMBER OF YOUR GROUP WAS A TELEPATH. AND DO NOT TRY TO READ OUR MINDS; THE SENSORY DISTRACTIONS YOU ARE EXPERIENCING WILL PREVENT YOU FROM BEING ABLE TO CONCENTRATE SUFFICIENTLY FOR TELEPATHY!'

'We hope,' someone near the voice muttered.

'I can't read anybody's mind!'

'SEE?' the voice boomed to someone else. 'THE LIGHTS AND NOISES DO WORK!'

'I never *could* read anybody's mind! I'm not a telepath!'

The voice was quiet for a moment; then it boomed, 'WHEN WERE YOU LAST A TELEPATH?'

'Never! Never, so help me!'

'He could be lying,' the voice muttered.

'Not with that sensory assault you've laid onto him,' the other voice answered. 'Poor fellow can't even close his eyes now. I don't think he could concentrate enough to think up a lie.'

'That was the other purpose of this system,' the first voice admitted. Then it boomed out again: 'OUR AGENTS FOLLOWED YOU ALL THE WAY FROM WOLMAR TO TERRA, OF COURSE. HOW DID YOU FORCE TOD TAMBOURIN TO AID YOU?'

'I didn't! I didn't force him at all!' Then, suddenly realizing they might accuse Whitey, Dar added, 'I conned him!'

'He *is* only a poet,' the other voice murmured. 'Probably true. Besides, you'd better get back to the main question before he goes catatonic on you.'

That sent a chill trickling down Dar's spine.

'Right,' the voice muttered; then, 'WHO IN YOUR GROUP *WAS* THE TELEPATH?'

'There wasn't any! There aren't any! There never have been any!'

'WE KNOW BETTER,' the voice said scornfully. 'WHO WAS IT?'

The flashing lights bit into his brain; the thousand-hertz tone bored straight through from ear to ear, while the random clicks tripped up every thought that tried to flow. 'I can't think!' Dar yelled. 'I can't think who it could possibly be! For the life of me!'

'IT MAY BE JUST THAT. DO YOU REALLY EXPECT US TO BELIEVE . . .?' The voice broke off in mid-sentence. 'WHO'S THAT? GET HIM OUT OF HERE!'

'My credentials, gentlemen.' It was a fulsome voice, growing louder as it came closer. 'If you doubt them, you may verify me through the computer.'

'Why?' snorted the other voice. 'They're computer-fed, anyway . . . *Chief Torturer*?'

'To Mr Horatio Bocello, yes.'

'He's just a billionaire, not a politician! Why would *he* need a torturer?'

'Industrial espionage, mostly.'

'INDUSTRIAL NUTHOUSE,' the nearer voice snorted. 'HE'S ONE OF THOSE CRAZY BILLIONAIRES WHO DRESSES UP IN ARMOUR AND TRIES TO PRETEND THE MIDDLE AGES'RE STILL GOING ON.'

'But we can't let some civilian come in here and . . .'

'WHY NOT? MAYBE HE'S GOT JUST THE CAN OPENER WE NEED. TAKE OFF YOUR COAT AND GET TO WORK, MR RICCI.'

'Well, thank you, gentlemen. Where's the coat-rack? Ah, there. Now, which way to the vict . . . ah, subject? Ah, there's the door . . .'

Father Marco! Dar nearly yelped with joy at the thought of a familiar face. But he managed to hold it in; some wavering remnant of good sense remembered not to let the cat out of the bag.

The priest drifted into view. 'Now, then, fellow! When did you stop being a telepath?'

'When did I . . . never!'

'Then you still are one!'

'No, of course not! I never . . .'

'When did you first become a telepath?'

'Never, I tell you! Never.'

'When did you begin to associate with telepaths?'

'Never! Never!'

'He's being recalcitrant,' Father Marco sighed, 'just as I feared. Well, get rid of these lights and noises – they aren't doing any good.'

'BUT . . . BUT, MR RICCI . . .'

'Turn them off, I say! They're not getting any answers out of him – and they're driving me crazy! Turn them off!'

'WELL . . . I HOPE YOU KNOW WHAT YOU'RE DOING . . .'

The light and sounds died. Dar could've wept with gratitude.

'Now, then! Let's try the old-fashioned methods!' Father Marco clapped his hands, and two giants shuffled into the light. Each was a head taller than Dar, and musclebound. You could tell, because they were both stripped to the waist. On top of that, they were shaven bald. And they both wore black masks.

They unfastened the straps that held down Dar's wrists, ankles, and chest, and yanked him to his feet. 'But . . . what . . . where . . .' Dar sputtered. He had his answer in a second; they hustled him through the nearest doorway while Father Marco followed, calling, 'Thumbscrews! The boot! The Iron Maiden! The rack!'

They burst into the torture chamber, the two men rushing him so quickly that his feet scarcely had time to touch the floor. Grim, vicious-looking instruments blurred past him, covered with cobwebs and rust. In the dim light, he could see that the stone blocks oozed drops of water. Then they burst through another door and twisted down an angling corridor.

'Wh . . . didn't I miss my stop, there?'

'Nope,' the black mask to his right answered. 'You ain't even in your cab, yet.'

And sure enough, they burst through a final door, and there stood the pregnant-teardrop shape of a cab, glistening in the muted light that filtered down to the underground cavern.

'No one'll notice y' here,' the other muscleman growled. 'They scarcely still know it exists.' He yanked open the door, and his mate booted Dar through it. 'But,' the young man sputtered, 'what . . . why . . .?'

'Because Horatio Bocello promised them berths on his spaceship, of course.' Father Marco slid in beside Dar. 'They couldn't resist an offer like that.'

' 'Course not,' the second man agreed, sliding into the front seat. 'If anybody'd want to go back to the Middle Ages, it'd be the torturers.'

'You can say that quintuply,' his mate agreed, clapping a chauffeur's cap onto his head. 'These namby-pamby lights and noises and dripping water – faugh! I wanna hear those bones crunch!'

His buddy clicked the hatch closed and advised him, 'You can stop acting now.'

'Good.' The first breathed a sigh of relief. 'But I do hate this job. Me, I can't even stand to set mousetraps! Just give me a chance to escape from this sick society!'

'I did,' Father Marco reminded him. 'You jumped at it.'

The cab swooped out of the shadows of the cavern into evening sunlight, up into clouds gilded by sunset and industrial waste.

Dar looked around him, recognizing the plush upholstery and computerized bar. 'This is no cab – it's Bocello's limousine!'

'I never woulda guessed it.' The righthand torturer yanked off his mask. 'Pass me an akvavit, will ya?'

## 13

The 'cab' dropped down and landed them on Bocello's back lawn, right next to an elongated dome big enough to have been a small spaceship. As Dar stepped out, Lona slammed into him with a hug that would've given a grizzly lumbago. 'Thank Heaven you're safe! We were so *worried*!' Then she shoved back, holding him off at arm's length, and he was amazed to see tears in her eyes. 'You poor, brave, dear idiot! Next time you have to go fling yourself on a sacrificial altar, do it for something worthwhile, okay?'

He couldn't spare the energy for an answer; he was too busy falling into her eyes. Apparently she *had* noticed his existence . . .

Then Whitey was slapping him on the back, and Sam was craning up to plant a kiss on his cheek. 'I should've known the system'd swallow you up!'

He grinned back at her and squeezed her hand. 'Yeah, but you didn't let it chew me up and spit me out!'

'No.' Sam caught Horatio's arm and beamed up at him. 'No, we didn't.'

'Well, give some praise to the real heroes of the rescue,' Horatio laughed, clapping Father Marco and one of the torturers on the shoulders. 'I only provided the car, and the code for getting into the Gamelon! Hurry and change, boys – the last shuttle's lifting off in ten minutes.'

The torturers grinned and trotted away.

'Nobly done, Father,' Whitey agreed. 'I don't know how you managed to bluff the *real* torturers.'

Father Marco shrugged. 'Nothing to it, when the computer said I was genuine.'

'Yeah.' Dar frowned. 'How *did* you manage that?'

'My versatile granddaughter,' Whitey sighed. 'Every time I despair of her because she can't make a sonnet, she does something like this.'

'Oh, it's nothing that big,' Lona said, irritated. 'I just made a little addition to an existing program, that's all.'

'Just a "little addition" that added Father Marco's name to a list of top security clearances,' Whitey corrected.

Dar stared. 'How'd she get past the security blocks?'

'Trade secret,' Lona said quickly, 'though I don't really see what all the fuss is about. I mean, computers may be fast, but they're really not very bright, the dear little things.'

The two 'torturers' came trotting back, dressed in plush overalls, and Horatio shooed them toward the dome. 'Aboard the yacht, now, quickly – time's wasting! If we don't move promptly, the Executive Secretary will be the Executive Dictator, and we won't be allowed to lift off from Terra! Hurry, hurry – the *Brave New World* awaits!'

He meant it literally – the *Brave New World* was the name the dozen plutocrats had given their newly purchased government-surplus FTL spaceship. (In memory of Shakespeare, not Huxley.) They saw it lying in the middle of Serenitatis Plain as they came in for a landing: a quarter of a mile long and eight hundred feet wide, glistening like a promise of the future. They landed near it and dropped down into an underground concourse with beige, textured walls and a burgundy carpet. Horatio hurried them along till the hallway widened into a circular bay with a double door in the far wall. A line of people in sturdy coveralls, with packs on their backs, was filing through it, to drift quickly upwards in a negative-gravity field.

'Up there is the ship,' Horatio explained. 'They should be almost done loading now. Are you sure you won't join us?'

'I'll go.' Sam beamed up at him. 'Anywhere you do.'

He smiled down at her tenderly. 'That's very touching, my dear, especially since I'm not taking my money with me. But really, I don't think you'd be very happy, stuck in a primitive society with an old goat.'

'Sounds delightful,' Sam pronounced. 'Besides, I'll be a lord's lady.'

'In a very draughty castle,' he reminded her, 'without central heating or air conditioning. Nor plumbing. It'll be very cold, sitting down in the garderobe on a winter's morning – and the wash basin'll be frozen.'

'I'll get used to it.'

'No, you won't. In effect, "you" will cease to exist just before we make planetfall; we all will. We'll sit down under a cerebral scan and have all memories of this technological nightmare of a culture erased from our brains. Then we'll have false memories implanted; each one of us has been developing a Society persona for years. On the trip outward, each one will record the imaginary memories of his persona; and after the brain-wipe, those "memories" will be recorded back into our brains. You won't remember Sam; you'll only remember Lady Loguire.'

'Lady Loguire! Oh!' Sam breathed, nestling up against him. 'It sounds wonderful. To oblivion with Sam; I never liked her much, anyway.'

'*I* do,' Horatio sighed, 'but I trust I'll love the Lady Loguire just as dearly. Well, then, sweeting, you're one of us, now – the Romantic Emigrés; we've changed our name, effective upon our leaving the Solar system. Would anyone else like to join us?'

Lona was whispering into Father Marco's ear. He frowned, shaking his head, and whispered something back. She hissed another sentence at him, and his face broke into a wreath of smiles. He stepped forward, clasping Horatio's hand. 'A delightful prospect! I'll come too, thank you!'

Horatio's face lit up, but his tone was guarded. 'Are you sure, Father? I know you're a Cathodean, and that means you're either a scientist or an engineer. You'll have to have most of your memories erased too, at least the ones that have anything to do with technology. We don't want our new society to be contaminated by *any* link to this decadent, materialistic culture.'

'I'm a priest before I'm an engineer,' Father Marco assured him, 'and the priest agrees with you: materialism is a contaminant.'

'Excuse me,' said Lona. 'Gotta make a phone call.' She swayed away to the nearest screen-booth, at her most sultry. Dar's eyes swivelled to follow her; he could almost feel them tugging at his sockets.

'Wonderful!' Horatio clasped Father Marco's hand, grinning from ear to ear. 'At least our colony will have a real priest! How would you like to be an archbishop, Father?'

'That's not up to us, I'm afraid.' Father Marco smiled, amused. 'But I wouldn't mind being an abbot.'

'As soon as we can build you a monastery,' Horatio assured him. 'Still, I think we might manage a bishop's mitre for you; I'll beam the Pope as soon as we lift off.'

Father Marco frowned. 'I'm afraid it's not quite that easy to be allowed to talk with His Holiness.'

'It is for me; we went to school together. Are you sure no one else would like to come?'

Dar shook his head. 'Thanks anyway, Mr Bocello.'

'Me, too,' Whitey agreed. 'I'm having too much fun in the present. But thanks for the offer, Cello.'

Lona came swaying back. 'Aren't you forgetting Mr Stroganoff?'

'My lord!' Dar cried, appalled. 'He was our producer – they'll think he masterminded the whole scheme! What'll they do – torture him, or kill him?'

'Neither one,' Horatio assured him, 'at least, not if my chauffeur is his usual, resourceful self.'

'He was.'

They all swung about, to see Stroganoff puffing toward them down the concourse. 'Thanks for having me kidnapped, Mr Bocello,' he panted as he came huffing up. 'Probably saved my life.'

'My pleasure,' Horatio assured him. 'I'm sorry to have been so unceremonious, but prompt action was required. Have you been briefed about our venture, Mr Stroganoff?'

'I certainly have, and I wish you all the luck in whatever world you find. I'd love to go along if I could bring a 3DT camera and come back – but I understand you don't want any technology developed later than 1300.'

'Except for full plate armour, yes. But are you certain, Mr Stroganoff? You don't have much of a future left, here.'

'Not on Terra or Luna, no,' Stroganoff agreed. 'But I would like to stop by Wolmar for a few years; there's a man there I'd like to chat with.'

Dar grinned.

Horatio shrugged. 'Certainly. We don't much care where we exit from Terran space; one vector's as good as another.'

'You're sure I won't be taking you out of your way?'

'Not at all, since we don't know where we're going. And we're doing our best to make certain nobody else does, either. We'll change directions after we pass Wolmar; but we won't decide which new heading to take until after we're out of communications range. This is going to be one "lost colony" that will *stay* lost.'

A man in uniform coveralls came running up to Horatio. 'Captain's compliments, sir, and some news – right off the 3DT. The Assembly just voted the Executive Secretary full emergency powers, and the title "Executive Director".'

'An ominous ring to it,' Horatio mused. 'I think we'd better be lifting off while we still can. Farewell, good people!'

There was a quick round of hugs, handclasps, and kisses. Sam glared up at Dar with tears in her eyes. 'Goodbye, gnappie, and good luck! Don't let 'em get to you!'

'I'll be kicking and screaming every centimetre of the way,' Dar promised. 'What *is* a "gnappie", anyway?'

'Someone who just sits back and lives off his GNP share, without trying to accomplish anything. You won't be that, will you?'

'Not if I can help it,' Dar assured her.

Then Horatio was whirling her away, whirling all three of them away, with an arm around Sam while he burbled to Father Marco, 'I'm *so* glad you decided to come, Father! After all, what would the Middle Ages be, without monks and monasteries?'

They stepped into the lift-tube, and Sam turned back to wave. Then the field bore them up, out of sight.

Whitey clasped Dar's shoulder. 'Up to the observation room, quickly! This is one lift-off I want to be able to watch!'

They ran to a smaller lift-shaft back down the concourse and flew up into the observation tower. It was a wide, circular space, with a thick carpet and thicker windows. In fact, it was nothing but windows, a full circle of them, and a transparent roof above. Dar looked around at the Lunar surface outside, a crazy quilt of brightness and blackness. 'Wonder why they didn't just build a clear dome?'

'The usual reason – this was cheaper.' Whitey pointed at the huge silver cigar a quarter of a mile away. 'She's lifting, children.'

They stared, tracking it in silence, as the *Brave New World* lifted from the Lunar surface and drifted upward, away and away, shrinking from a monster that filled half the sky, to a splendid flying hill, diminishing and diminishing, to a silver cigar indeed, then a cigarillo, then a matchstick, then only a point of brightness. Suddenly that brightness intensified; it became an actinic spark, throwing a faint shadow of the three watchers onto the floor behind them, and began to slide away across the heavens.

'Exhaust,' Lona whispered. 'They've ignited their interplanetary drive.'

The spark moved faster and faster until it was only a streak of light, shooting off toward the unseen orbit of Pluto, a miniature sun seeking a dawn.

When it had dwindled to being only one more faint star in the millions that surrounded them, they turned away with a sigh. 'I hope they make it.' Dar smiled sadly. 'I wonder if they'll really manage to set up their crackpot society.'

'I have a notion they will,' Whitey mused. 'When Horatio sets his mind to something, it gets done. Just hope they'll be happy, though.'

'Me, too.' Dar frowned. 'Especially Father Marco. How can he found a Cathodean monastery if he has his brain wiped of any engineering knowledge?'

'Oh, I wouldn't worry about that,' Lona murmured, with a quiet smile.

Whitey fixed her with a jaundiced eye. 'Granddaughter, lick that cream off your whiskers and tell me who you phoned!'

'Just the *Brave New World*'s computer, Grandpa – it isn't hard to get the number, if you know what to say to Central Memory.'

'No, not at all – you only had to talk your way past a few dozen of the System's strongest security blocks first!'

Lona shrugged it off. 'Just basic logic.'

'Yes, getting baser and baser as it goes along. And just what did you and the *Brave New World* have to say to each other?'

'Oh, I just convinced it that Father Marco's the only one aboard who might stand even a remote chance of fixing it, if it ever broke down. It saw my point right away, and promised that, when it came time to wipe brains, it would skip Father Marco's.'

Whitey nodded, with a wry smile. 'I was wondering why he was suddenly eager to go. I could see a Cathodean being willing to leave civilization for the sake of the Church – but technology is another matter.'

'I thought they ought to be able to keep *some* link to reality,' Lona agreed. 'And the only place they could do that, without it leaking out to the whole society, is inside the walls of a monastery.'

'How pure and altruistic of you,' Whitey muttered.

Lona shrugged. 'I just have fun with computers, Grandpa.'

'Well, enjoy it while you can,' Whitey sighed. 'I have a notion our new lords and masters aren't going to think too highly of fun – especially your kind.'

'Yeah, I hadn't thought about the future *here*.' Dar frowned. 'Maybe Horatio and his buddies aren't all that much crackpots.'

'Things could get rather dull here,' Lona agreed. 'That's why, as long as I was on the phone, I got in touch with the Bank of Terra's computer, Grandpa, and had all your funds transferred to the Bank of Maxima.'

A delighted grin spread across Whitey's face. 'How thoughtful of you, child!'

Dar frowned. 'Maxima? The place that built Fess? He's says it's just a barren piece of rock!'

'With robot factories,' Lona reminded him, 'which includes computer factories. And computer technicians and cybernetics experts, of course – my kind of people.'

'But I thought you wanted to participate in the life of decadence.'

'I do, if I can – but if I have to choose between that and toying with circuits and programs, I know where the real fun lies. Besides, Maxima's close to Terra; I might be able to come down for a spree, now and then.'

'Then why transfer the money there? *All* of it?'

'Because Maxima's the one world that might be able to keep the central government from gimmicking its computers,' Lona explained. 'That keeps the money intact, not to mention our privacy.'

'Privacy? You think *that'll* be threatened?' Dar turned to Whitey, frowning. 'You really think it's going to get *that* bad here?'

'It's called a police state,' Whitey explained. 'I'm sure they intend to include Maxima in it, too – in theory.'

'But not in practice,' Lona assured him. 'At least, not if I have anything to say to the Maxima computers.'

'A chip off the old bloke, if ever there was one!' Whitey grinned. 'Your mama would've said just the same. Well then, if Maxima's where you're bound, we'd better get started.' He pulled out the recall unit and pressed a button. 'Should be here, pretty soon.' He turned to Dar. 'How about you? Like to lift away from here?'

'Yes, I would, thank you – very much.'

'Thought so. You could go back to Wolmar, you know. The LORDS party's been saying for a long time that the frontier worlds cost too much, that we ought to just cut them off and leave 'em to their own devices. Might be some hard times coming out in the marches, but the worlds there should at least keep their freedom.'

Dar nodded. 'I'd thought about that. In fact, I'm pretty sure General Shacklar – our governor – has had that in mind for a while, too. Also Myles Croft, on Falstaff.'

'Well, I know My's been getting strapped down and ready to go on his own, so I don't doubt your Shacklar has, too. But I take it you're not planning to go back there.'

Dar frowned. 'How'd you figure that out?'

' 'Cause if you were, you would've hitched a ride with Horatio and dropped off with Stroganoff. What's the matter? Had a taste of the fleshpots, and decided to stay near 'em?'

'You've got me pegged,' Dar admitted. 'How'd you guess?'

'Believe it or not, I was young once, myself.'

'The trick is, believing that he ever aged.' Lona stepped a little closer to Dar, and it seemed to him that he could feel her presence as a physical pressure. And her eyes danced; she was watching him with a smile that was both secretive and amused. 'Where were you planning to go?'

'Someplace,' Dar pronounced, 'where I'll never have to hear about that Interstellar Telepathic Conspiracy again.'

'Yeah, that's a masterstroke of confusion, isn't it?' Whitey chuckled. 'I never saw a Big Lie work so well – it even has some of the liars convinced! I love watching a fantasy go out of control.'

'Oh, it isn't total fantasy,' Dar mused. 'There's a grain of substance to it.'

Whitey gave him a sidelong glance. 'You sure about that?'

'Well, it kinda makes sense, doesn't it?' Dar spread his hands. 'With all that fuss and bother, there should've been at least one real telepath at the bottom of it all.'

'Should've maybe.' Lona gave him her most sceptical look. '*Would*'ve's another matter. When it comes to telepathy, if it doesn't have integrated circuits, I won't believe in it.'

'Just telepaths?' Dar gave her the sceptical look back. 'I would've said that was how you looked at everything.'

'There's some truth to that,' Lona admitted. 'I don't have too much use for dreams, unless someone's trying to make them come true. Telepathy as a dream, now, I can see that – if someone's trying to invent a way to make it happen. Or faster-than-light radio, or maybe even rearranging the bonds in a single molecule, to make it into a complete electronic circuit.'

Dar's sceptical look turned into a fish-eye. 'That's your idea of a dream?'

'Well, the only ones that I'd talk about in public.' She had the amused, secretive look back, and her eyes transfixed him. 'Don't you have any?'

Dar frowned, and his gaze drifted away, out toward the stark, cruel sharpness of the lunar plain. 'No . . . I'm a little low on them, right now. I'll settle for getting away from Terra while I can.'

A bulbous, pitted teardrop fell from the starfield and drifted down, settling over the boarding-tube the *Brave New World* had used. Sensing a ship, it lifted and quested, homing automatically on the airlock, probing and touching tentatively, then locking tight.

'Fess's here,' Whitey announced. 'Let's go get safe, younglings.'

They stepped into the drop-tube and came out into the concourse. No one talked as they walked the quarter-mile to the gate; each was wrapped in his own thoughts, realizing that he or she was leaving Terra forever. Though Lona was making plans about how to be able to come back for visits, safely; that was her only real concern with the planet. She'd been raised between the stars, after all; to her, Mother Earth had always been only an extravagant relative, to visit when you wanted a treat. Dar had never been to Terra before, and didn't particularly care to visit again; but Whitey had been born and reared on Manhome. Memories were here, many of them; but for him, now, the triune goddess had shifted; Hecate had ceased to be either mother or lover, and had become the murderess. If he came back to her arms, he would die. The children didn't know that, because they didn't know what he was planning to do; but he did.

They stepped into the gate's lift-tube, and drifted up through the airlock, into Fess's familiar frayed interior. 'Ah, home,' Whitey sighed, 'or what passes for it these days. . . . Fess, get me a shot of real Scotch, will you? I'd like it to go with the view as we leave.'

'Certainly, Mr Tambourin. Lona? Dar?'

'Vermouth would be nice, right now,' Dar mused.

'Water,' Lona said firmly, 'at least, until we're on our way.' She dropped into her acceleration couch and webbed herself in. Dar sank down on the couch next to hers. The bar chimed softly, and he popped back up to fetch the drinks. 'No, stay put, Whitey.'

The bard settled back down into the couch behind Dar's with a grateful sigh. He stretched the webbing across his body and locked it in, then accepted the shot glass from Dar absentmindedly as he gazed at the viewscreen and its image of Terra, huge against the stars.

'What course shall I set?' Fess asked softly.

'Moment of decision,' Lona said to Dar. 'Where do you want to go?'

Dar looked deeply into her eyes. She held his gaze, hers unwavering. Her pupils seemed to grow larger, larger . . .

'Wherever you're going,' Dar said softly.

She sat still, very still.

Then she said, 'Are you sure?'

'Yes,' Dar said, 'very.'

Then they were still again, gazes locked.

Whitey cleared his throat and said, a little too loudly, 'Well, you know how it is, Fess – when you're young, and all that.'

'There are references to it in my data banks,' the voice agreed.

'You go off to your own little dream world,' Whitey explained, 'even though you think you're staying in the real one. You get wrapped up in romance for a while, and you don't really relate all that well to what's going on around you.'

'Similar to an artificially induced alteration in consciousness?'

'Well, that's what the drugs are trying to imitate, yeah – but you know how much an imitation's worth. Still, when they do get involved in the real thing, they're out of touch for a while, and it's up to us old folk to hold things together till they come out of their trances.'

'How do you intend to hold things together, Mr Tambourin?'

'Oh, just bumming around the Terran Sphere for a while, drifting and roaming, same as I've always done, singing innocent, apolitical songs – and gradually working my way out to Wolmar.'

'Wolmar? But why?'

'Oh, to see Stroganoff again, I suppose – and this Cholly that Dar's so enthusiastic about. Seems as though they might have some good ideas. I couldn't do it the easy way, though, hitching a ride with Horatio. I mean, I've got some responsibilities. Gotta see these two young folk settled and safe before I can go kiyoodling off. And at the rate they're going now, it's going to take them a long time . . .'

'I thought you were in love with Sam,' Lona finally said.

Dar shook his head. 'Not a bit – at least, not after you came along. She was a good ally, when things got tense – but a lover? No. I couldn't get interested.'

'Oh?' Lona said, dryly. 'Why not?'

'Because,' Dar said, 'I just wouldn't be able to make love to someone who was reading my mind.'

Lona sat very still for a few seconds. Then she said, 'Sam? The real, live telepath at the bottom of the whole scare?'

'The correlations *are* rather obvious,' Fess's voice murmured, 'if all you've told me is accurate. Her knowing exactly where to find the credentials in the luggage of Bhelabher's staff, her ability to open a strange combination lock, to lead Dar through the dark maze of the criminals' dungeon on Falstaff, her emotional reactions to the witch-hunt . . . What is surprising is that none of us realized it sooner.'

'And that Fess knew all the facts.' Lona eyed Dar suspiciously. 'Didn't know you two had got so chummy.'

'He's a very sympathetic listener,' Dar said brightly.

'But nobody told him to correlate for the identity of a possible telepath.' The suspicious gaze turned calculating. 'When did you realize it?'

'Right after Father Marco pulled me out of that interrogation. I realized that the flashing lights and noises were an awful lot of trouble to go to if they weren't really afraid of having their minds read – so they really believed there was a telepath, and it had to have been one of our crew. Then I remembered seeing suspicious, hostile Sam falling head-over-heels in love with Horatio Bocello on a moment's notice. It just wasn't like her. She had to be seeing something in him that the rest of us didn't see – and there was only one way she could've done that.'

'By peering into his mind.' Lona pursed her lips, nodding. 'Well, love at first second-sight, I can see.'

'The Executive Director, however, does not realize that you are not the telepath,' Fess pointed out. 'He will no doubt be hunting you for the rest of his life – and his successor after him. A telepath would make an invaluable aide for a dictator.'

'Yeah, I was thinking about that. But I think, if I find some out-of-the-way place and live quietly, I'll probably be pretty safe. Of course, I'll have to take a few standard precautions, such as changing my name . . .'

'To what would you change it?'

'Oh, nothing too elaborate; I'm kinda tired just now.' Dar sighed, leaning back in his couch. 'Just taking my real name and making a few changes – you know, "d'Armand" instead of "Dar Mandra", that sort of thing.' He turned to Lona. 'You ought to think about that – you're on their list, too.'

'Yes,' she said, eyes glowing, 'I know.'

'Interested in changing your name?'

'Yes, I think I will,' she said, '"d'Armand" sounds good to me, too.'

# The Warlock
# in Spite of Himself

To Jeanie D.

# Contents

# Part One
# Visit to a Small Plantagenet

The asteroid hurtled in from Capricorn, nosed around a G-type sun, swerved off toward the fifth planet. Such a trajectory is somewhat atypical for asteroids.

It slapped into the planet's gravity net, swooped around the globe three times in three separate orbits, then stabbed into the atmosphere, a glorious shooting star.

At a hundred feet altitude it paused, then snapped to the surface – but only *to* the surface. No fireworks, no crater – nothing more drastic than crushed grass. Its surface was scarred and pitted, blackened by the friction-heat of its fall; but it was intact.

Deep within its bowels echoed the words that would change the planet's destiny.

'Damn your bolt-brained bearings!'

The voice broke off; its owner frowned, listening.

The cabin was totally silent, without its usual threshold hum.

The young man swore, tearing the shock-webbing from his body. He lurched out of the acceleration chair, balanced dizzily on the balls of his feet, groping till his hand touched the plastic wall.

Steadying himself with one hand, he stumbled to a panel on the other side of the circular cabin. He fumbled the catches loose, cursing in the fine old style of galactic deckhands, opened the panel, pressed a button. Turning, he all but fell back to the chair.

The soft hum awoke in the cabin again. A slurred voice asked, with varying speed and pitch, 'Izzz awwl (Hic!) sadizfagtoreee . . . M'lorrr' Rodney?'

'All the smooth, glossy robots in the galaxy,' muttered Milord, 'and I get stuck with an epileptic!'

'Ivv ut bleeezz m'lorr', thuh c'passsider c'n be—'

'Replaced,' finished Rodney, 'and your circuits torn out and redesigned. No, thank you, I like your personality the way it is – except when you pull off a landing that jars my clavicles loose!'

'Ivv m'lorrd will vorgive, ad thuh cruzhial momend ovvv blanetfall, I rezeived zome very zingular radio waves thad—'

'You got distracted, is that what you're trying to say?'

'M'lorrrd, id was imerative to analyse—'

'So part of you was studying the radio waves, and part of you was landing the ship, which was just a wee bit too much of a strain, and the weak capacitor gave. . . . Fess! How many times do I have to tell you to keep your mind on the job!'

'M'lorrd egzbressed a wizh to be like thuh—'

'Like the heroes of the Exploration Sagas, yes. But that doesn't mean I want their discomforts.'

Fess's electronic system had almost recovered from the post-seizure exhaustion. 'But, m'lorrd, the choncebt of heeroizm imblies—'

'Oh, forget it,' Rodney groaned. Fess dutifully blanked a portion of his memory banks.

Fess was dutiful. He was also an antique, one of the few remaining FCC (Faithful Cybernetic Companion) robots, early models now two thousand years out of date. The FCC robots had been programmed for extreme loyalty and, as a consequence, had perished in droves while defending their masters during the bloody Interregnum between the collapse of the ancient Galactic Union and the rise of the Proletarian Eclectic State of Terra.

Fess (a name derived from trying to pronounce 'FCC' as a single word) had survived, thanks to his epilepsy. He had a weak capacitor that, when overstrained, released all its stored energy in a massive surge lasting several milliseconds. When the preliminary symptoms of this electronic seizure – mainly a fuzziness in Fess's calculations – appeared, a master circuit breaker popped, and the faulty capacitor discharged in isolation from the rest of Fess's circuits; but the robot was out of commission until the circuit breaker was reset.

Since the seizures occurred during moments of great stress – such as trying to land a spaceship-*cum*-asteroid while analysing an aberrant radio wave, or trying to protect a master from three simultaneous murderers – Fess had survived the Interregnum; for, when the Proletarians had attacked his masters, he had fought manfully for about twenty-five seconds, then collapsed. He had thus become a rarity – the courageous servant who had survived. He was one of five FCC robots still functioning.

He was, consequently, a prized treasure of the d'Armand family – prized as an antique, but even more for his loyalty; true loyalty to aristocratic families has always been in short supply.

So, when Rodney d'Armand had left home for a life of adventure and glory – being the second son of a second son, there hadn't been much else he could do – his father had insisted on his taking Fess along.

Rod had often been very glad of Fess's company; but there were times when the robot was just a little short on tact. For instance, after a very rough planetfall, a human stomach tends to be a mite queasy; but Fess had the bad sense to ask, 'Would you care to dine, m'lord? Say, scallops with asparagus?'

Rod turned chartreuse and clamped his jaws, fighting back nausea. 'No,' he grated, 'and can the "m'lord" bit. We're on a mission, remember?'

'I never forget, Rod. Except on command.'

'I know,' growled his master's voice. 'It was a figure of speech.'

Rod swung his legs to the floor and painfully stood up. 'I could use a breath of fresh air to settle my stomach, Fess. Is there any available?'

The robot clicked for a moment, then reported, 'Atmosphere breathable. Better wear a sweater, though.'

Rod shrugged into his pilot's jacket with a growl. 'Why do old family retainers always develop a mother-hen complex?'

'Rod, if you had lived as long as I have—'

'—I'd want to be deactivated. I know. "Robot is always right." Open the lock, Fess.'

The double doors of the small airlock swung open, showing a circle of black set with stars. A chill breeze poured into the cabin.

Rod tilted his face back, breathing in. His eyes closed in luxury. 'Ah, the blessed breath of land! What lives here, Fess?'

Machinery whirred as the robot played back the electron-telescope tapes they had taken in orbit, integrating the pictorial data into a comprehensive description of the planet.

'Land masses consist of five continents, one island of noteworthy dimensions, and a host of lesser islands. The continents and the minor islands exhibit similar flora – equatorial rain forest.'

'Even at the poles?'

'Within a hundred miles of each pole; the ice caps are remarkably small. Visible animal life confined to amphibians and a host of insects; we may assume that the seas abound with fish.'

Rod rubbed his chin. 'Sounds like we came in pretty early in the geologic spectrum.'

'Carboniferous Era,' replied the robot.

'How about that one large island? That's where we've landed, I suppose?'

'Correct. Native flora and fauna nonexistent. All lifeforms typical of Late Terran Pleistocene.'

'How late, Fess?'

'Human historical.'

Rod nodded. 'In other words, a bunch of colonists came in, picked themselves an island, wiped out the native life, and seeded the land with Terran stock. Any idea why they chose this island?'

'Large enough to support a good-sized population, small enough to minimize problems of ecological revision. Then too, the island is situated in a polar ocean current, which lowers the local temperature to slightly below Terran normal.'

'Very handy; saves them the bother of climate control. Any remains of what might have been Galactic Union cities?'

'None, Rod.'

'None!' Rod's eyes widened in surprise. 'That doesn't fit the pattern. You sure, Fess?'

The development pattern of a lost, or retrograde, colony – one that had been out of touch with Galactic civilization for a millennium or more – fell into three well-defined stages: first, the establishment of the colony, centred around a modern city with an advanced technology; second, the failure of communications with Galactic culture, followed by an overpopulation of the city, which led to mass migrations to the countryside and a consequent shift to an agrarian, self-sufficient economy; and, third, the loss of technological knowledge, accompanied by a rising level of superstition, symbolized by the abandonment and eventual tabooing of a coal-and-steam technology: social relationships calcified, and a caste system appeared. Styles of dress and architecture were usually burlesques of Galactic Union forms: for example, a small hemispherical wooden hut, built in imitation of the vaulting Galactic geodesic domes.

But always there were the ruins of the city, acting as a constant symbol and a basis for mythology. Always.

'You're sure, Fess? You're really, really sure there isn't a city?'

'I am always certain, Rod.'

'That's true.' Rod pulled at his lower lip. 'Sometimes mistaken, but never in doubt. Well, shelve the matter of the city for the time being; maybe it sank in a tidal wave. Let's just make a final check on the lifeforms' being Terran.'

Rod dived head-first through the three-foot circle of the lock, landed in a forward roll, rose to his knees. He unclipped the guerrilla knife from his belt – a knife carefully designed so that it could not be attributed to any one known culture – and drew the dagger from its sheath.

The sheath was a slender cone of white metal, with a small knob at the apex. Rod plucked several blades of grass, dropped them into the sheath, and turned the knob. The miniature transceiver built into the sides of the sheath probed the grass with sonics to analyse its molecular structure, then broadcast the data to Fess, who determined if any of the molecules were incompatible with human metabolism. If the grass had been poisonous to Rod, Fess would have beamed a signal back to the sheath, whereupon the white metal would have turned purple.

But in this particular case, the sheath stayed silver.

'That ties it,' said Rod. 'This is Terran grass, presumably planted by Terrans, and this is a Terran colony. But where's the city?'

'There is a large town – perhaps thirty thousand souls – in the foothills of a mountain range to the north, Rod.'

'Well . . .' Rod rubbed his chin. 'That's not exactly what I had in mind, but it's better than nothing. What's it look like?'

'Situated on the lower slopes of a large hill, at the summit of which is a large stone structure, strongly reminiscent of a Medieval Terran castle.'

'Medieval!' Rod scowled.

'The town itself consists of half-timbered and stuccoed buildings, with second storeys overhanging the narrow streets – alleys would be a better term – along which they are situated.'

'Half-timbered!' Rod rose to his feet. 'Wait a minute, *wait a minute*! Fess, does that architecture remind you of anything?'

The robot was silent a moment, then replied, 'Northern European Renaissance.'

'That,' said Rod, 'is *not* the typical style of a retrograde colony. How closely do those buildings resemble Terran Renaissance, Fess?'

'The resemblance is complete to the last detail, Rod.'

'It's deliberate then. How about that castle? Is that Renaissance too?'

The robot paused, then said, 'No, Rod. It would appear to be a direct copy from the German style of the 13th Century AD.'

Rod nodded eagerly. 'How about styles of dress?'

'We are currently on the night side of the planet, and were upon landing. There is a good deal of illumination from the planet's three satellites, but relatively few people abroad . . . There is, however, a small party of soldiers, riding Terran horses. Their uniforms are – uh – copies of English Beefeaters.'

'Very good! Anyone else in the streets?'

'Um . . . a couple of cloaked men – uh – doublet and hose, I believe and . . . yes, a small party of peasants, wearing smocks and cross-gartered buskins . . .'

'That's enough.' Rod cut him off. 'It's a hodgepodge, a conglomeration of styles. Somebody has tried to set up his idea of the ideal world, Fess. Ever hear of the Emigrés?'

The robot was silent a moment, mulling through his memory banks. Then he began to recite:

'Malcontents abounded toward the end of the 22nd Century AD. Bored with their "lives of quiet desperation", people turned primarily to mysticism, secondarily to escapist literature and entertainment. Gradually the pseudo-Medieval became the dominant entertainment form.

'Finally, a group of wealthy men pooled their funds to buy an outmoded FTL liner and announced to the world that they were the Romantic Emigrés, that they intended to re-establish the glory of the Medieval way of life on a previously uncolonized planet, and that they would accept a limited number of emigrants in the capacities of serfs and tradesmen.

'There were, of course, many more applicants than could be accommodated. Emigrants were selected "for the poeticness of their souls" – whatever that may mean.'

'It means they loved to listen to ghost stories,' said Rod. 'What happened?'

'The passenger list was swiftly completed. The thirteen tycoons who had organized the expedition announced that they thereby rejected their surnames and adopted instead the family names of great Medieval aristocrats – Bourbon, de' Medici, and so forth.

'Then the ship departed, with its destination carefully unspecified, so that there would be "no contamination from the materialist world". Nothing more was ever heard of them.'

Rod smiled grimly. 'Well, I think we've just found them. How's *that* set with your diodes?'

'Quite well, Rod. In fact, a statistical analysis of the probability of this being the Emigrés' colony reveals the following—'

'Skip it,' Rod said quickly. Statistics was Fess's hobby; given half a chance, he could bore you for hours.

Rod pursed his lips and eyed the section of the hull that housed Fess's brain. 'Come to think of it, you might send the statistics back to SCENT with our educated guess that we've found the Emigrés' colony. Might as well get at that right now; I'd like them to know where we are in case anything happens.'

SCENT, the Society for the Conversion of Extraterrestrial Nascent Totalitarianisms, was the organization responsible for seeking out the lost colonies. The Proletarian Eclectic State of

Terra had shown remarkably little interest in any colony that was lacking in modern technology; so that the lost colonies had stayed lost until the totalitarian rule of PEST had been overthrown by DDT, the Decentralized Democratic Tribunal. DDT had quickly consolidated its rule of Terra, governing in accordance with the almost-unattainable goals of Athenian democracy.

It had long been known that the inefficiency of democratic governments was basically a problem of communication and prejudice. But, over a period of two centuries, DDT cells had functioned as speakeasy schoolrooms, resulting in total literacy and masters' degrees for seventy-two per cent of the population; prejudice had thus joined polio and cancer on the list of curable diseases. The problems of communication had been solved by the development, in DDT laboratories, of sub-molecular electronics, which had lowered the bulk and price of electronic communication gear to the point where its truly extensive use became practical for the first time. Every individual was thus able to squawk at his Tribune at a moment's notice; and, being educated, they tended to do a lot of squawking just on general principles – all very healthy for a democracy.

Squawking by radio had proved singularly effective, due largely to an automatic record of the squawk. The problems of records and other bureaucratic red tape had been solved by red oxide audio recording tape, with tracks a single molecule in width, and the development of data-retrieval systems so efficient that the memorization of facts became obsolete. Education thus became exclusively a training in concepts, and the success of democracy was assured.

After two centuries of preparing such groundwork, the DDT revolution had been a mere formality.

But revolutionaries are always out of place when the revolution is over, and are likely to prove an embarrassing factor to the police forces of the new government.

Therefore, DDT had decided not to be selfish; rather, they would share the blessings of democracy with the other remnants of the old Galactic Union.

But democrats are seldom welcome on planets run by totalitarian governments, and scarcely more welcome on planets where anarchy prevails – this due to the very nature of democracy, the only practical compromise between totalitarianism and anarchy.

What was needed was a permanent organization of revolution-aries, subversive republican democrats. Since there was a large supply of out-of-work revolutionaries on hand, the organization was quickly formed, and christened the Society for the Conversion of Extraterrestrial Totalitarianisms. The 'Nascent' was added a century later, when all the known inhabited planets had been subverted and had joined DDT. The old revolutionaries were still a problem, the more so since there were more of them; so they were sent out singly to find the Lost Colonies.

Thus was formed SCENT, the organization whose mission it was to sniff out the backward planets and put them on the road to democracy.

Since Rod had found a Medieval planet, he would probably have to foster the development of a constitutional monarchy.

Rod, born Rodney d'Armand (he had five middle names, but they make dull reading) on a planet inhabited exclusively by aristocrats and robots, had joined SCENT at the tender age of eighteen. In his ten years of service, he had grown from a gangling, ugly youth to a lean, well-muscled, ugly man.

His face was aristocratic; you could say that for it – that, and no more. His receding hairline gave onto a flat, sloping forehead that ran up against a brace of bony brow-ridges, somewhat camouflaged by bushy eyebrows. The eyebrows overhung deep sockets, at the back of which were two, somewhat hardened grey eyes – at least Rod hoped they looked hardened.

The eye sockets were thresholded by high, flat cheekbones, divided by a blade of nose that would have done credit to an eagle. Under the cheekbones and nose was a wide, thin-lipped mouth which, even in sleep, was twisted in a sardonic smile. Under the mouth was a square jawbone and a jutting chin.

Rod would have liked to say that it was a strong face, but it tended to soften remarkably when/if a girl smiled at it. Dogs and children had the same effect, with a great deal more frequency.

He was a man with a Dream (there had been a Dream Girl once, but she was now one with his callow youth) of one unified Galactic government (democratic, of course). Interstellar communications were still too slow for a true democratic federation; the DDT was actually a loose confederation of worlds, more of a debating society and service organization than anything else.

But adequate communication methods would come along some day, Rod was sure of that, and when they did, the stars would be ready. He would see to that.

'Well, let's be about our business, Fess. No telling when someone might wander by and spot us.' Rod swung up and into the airlock, through and into the cabin again. He went to the plate in the wall, released the catches. Inside was a control panel; above this was a white metal sphere with a dull finish, about the size of a basketball. A massive cable grew out of the top of the sphere and connected to the wall of the work-shop.

Rod unscrewed the connection, released the friction clamp that held the sphere in place, and carefully lifted it out.

'Easy,' Fess's voice said from the earphone implanted in the bone behind Rod's right ear. 'I'm fragile, you know.'

'A little confidence, please,' Rod muttered. The microphone in his jawbone carried his words to Fess. 'I haven't dropped you yet, have I?'

'Yet,' echoed the robot.

Rod cradled the robot 'brain' in the crook of one arm, leaving one arm free to negotiate the airlock. Outside again, he pressed a stud in the side of the ship. A large door lifted from the side of the pseudo-asteroid. Inside, a great black horse hung from shock webbing, head between its forelegs, eyes closed.

Rod pressed a button; a crane extended from the cargo space. The horse swung out on the crane, was lowered till its hooves touched the ground. Rod twisted the saddlehorn, and a panel in the horse's side slid open.

Rod placed the brain inside the panel, tightened the clamp and the connections, then twisted the saddlehorn back; the panel slid shut. Slowly the horse raised its head, wiggled its ears, blinked twice, gave a tentative whinny.

'All as it should be,' said the voice behind Rod's ear. The horse champed at the bit. 'If you'll let me out of this cat's cradle, I'll check the motor circuits.'

Rod grinned and freed the webbing. The horse reared up, pawing the air, then sprang into a gallop. Rod watched the robot run, taking a good look at his surroundings in the process.

The asteroid-ship had landed in the centre of a meadow, shaggy with summer grass, ringed by oak, hickory, maple, and ash. It was night, but the meadow was flooded with the light of three moons.

The robot cantered back toward Rod, reared to a halt before him. Forehooves thudded on the ground; the great indigo eyes turned to look at Rod, the ears pricked forward.

'I'm fit,' Fess reported.

Rod grinned again. 'No sight like a running horse.'

'What, none?'

'Well, almost none. C'mon, let's get the ship buried.'

Rod pressed studs on the side of the ship; the cargo hatch closed, the airlock sealed itself. The ship began to revolve, slowly at first, then faster and faster as it sank into the ground. Soon there was only a crater surrounded by a ring-wall of loam, and the roof of the asteroid curving three feet below.

Rod pulled a camp shovel from Fess's saddlebags, unfolded it, and bent to his task. The horse joined in, flashing out with its heels at the ring-wall. In ten minutes the wall had been reduced to six-inch height; there was a large mound of earth in the centre, twenty feet across and two feet high.

'Stand back.' Rod drew his dagger, twisted the hilt 180 degrees, pointed the haft at the earth-mound. A red light lanced out; the loam glowed cherry red, melted, and flowed.

Rod fanned the beam in a slow arc over the whole of the filled-in crater till the soil had melted down a foot below ground level. He shovelled the rest of the ring-wall into the hole, making a slight mound, but the next rain would take care of that.

'Well, that's it.' Rod wiped his brow.

'Not quite.'

Rod hunched his shoulders; there was a sinking feeling in his belly.

'You have still to assume clothing appropriate to this society and period, Rod.'

Rod squeezed his eyes shut.

'I took the precaution of packing a doublet in my left-hand saddlebag while you were testing the grass, Rod.'

'Look,' Rod argued, 'my uniform will do well enough, won't it?'

'Skintight trousers and military boots will pass, yes. But a pilot's jacket could not possibly be mistaken for a doublet. Need I say more?'

'No, I suppose not.' Rod sighed. He went to the saddlebag. 'The success of the mission comes first, above and before any considerations of personal comfort, dignity, or – hey!' He stared at something long and slender, hanging from the saddle.

'Hey what, Rod?'

Rod took the strange object from the saddle – it had a handle on one end, he noticed, and it rattled – and held it up where Fess could see it.

'What is *this*?'

'An Elizabethan rapier, Rod. An antique sidearm, a sort of long knife, designed for both cutting and thrusting.'

'Sidearm.' Rod eyed the robot as if doubting his sanity. 'I'm supposed to wear it?'

'Certainly, Rod. At least, if you're planning to adopt one of your usual covers.'

Rod gave a sign appropriate to a Christian martyr and pulled the doublet from the saddlebag. He wriggled into it and belted the rapier to his right side.

'No, no, Rod! Belt it to your *left* side. You have to cross-draw it.'

'The things I go through for the sake of democracy . . .' Rod belted the rapier to his left hip. 'Fess, has it ever occured to you that I might be a fanatic?'

'Certainly, Rod. A classic case of sublimation.'

'I asked for an opinion, not an analysis,' the man growled. He looked down at his costume. 'Hey! Not bad, not bad at all!' He threw his shoulders back, lifted his chin, and strutted. The gold and scarlet doublet fairly glowed in the moonlight. 'How do you like it, Fess?'

'You cut quite a figure, Rod.' There was, somehow, a tone of quiet amusement in the robot's voice.

Rod frowned. 'Needs a cape to top it off, though.'

'In the saddlebag, Rod.'

'Think of everything, don't you?' Rod rummaged in the saddlebag, shook out a voluminous cloak of the same electric blue as his uniform tights.

'The chain passes under the left armpit and around the right-hand side of the neck, Rod.'

Rod fastened the cloak in place and faced into the wind, the cloak streaming back from his broad shoulders.

'There, now! Ain't I a picture, though?'

'Like a plate from a Shakespeare text, Rod.'

'Flattery will get you a double ration of oil.' Rod swung into the saddle. 'Head for the nearest town, Fess. I want to show off my new finery.'

'You forgot to seed the crater, Rod.'

'What? Oh! Yeah.' Rod pulled a small bag from the right-hand saddlebag and sprinkled its contents over the circle of raw earth. 'There! Give it a light rainstorm and two days to grow, and you won't be able to tell it from the rest of the meadow. Let's hope nobody comes this way for two days, though. . . .'

The horse's head jerked up, ears pricked forward.

'What's the matter, Fess?'

'Listen,' the robot replied.

Rod scowled and closed his eyes.

Distant, blown on the wind, came youthful shouts and gay laughter.

'Sounds like a bunch of kids having a party.'

'It's coming closer,' Fess said softly.

Rod shut his eyes and listened again. The sound *was* growing louder . . .

He turned to the northeast, the direction the sound seemed to be coming from, and scanned the horizon. There were only the three moons in the sky.

A shadow drifted across one of the moons. Three more followed it.

The laughter was much louder now.

'About seventy-five miles per hour,' Fess murmured.

'What?'

'Seventy-five miles per hour. That's the speed at which they seem to be approaching.'

'Hmmm.' Rod chewed at his lower lip. 'Fess, how long since we landed?'

'Almost two hours, Rod.'

Something streaked by overhead.

Rod looked up. 'Ah, Fess?'

'Yes, Rod.'

'They're flying, Fess.'

There was a pause.

'Rod, I must ask you to be logical. A culture like this couldn't possibly have evolved air travel yet.'

'They haven't. *They're* flying.'

Another pause.

'The people themselves, Rod?'

'That's right.' Rod's voice held a note of resignation. 'Though I'll admit that one who just flew over us seemed to be riding a broomstick. Not too bad-looking, either. Matter of fact, she was stacked like a Las Vegas poker deck . . . Fess?'

The horse's legs were locked rigid, its head swinging gently between its legs.

'Oh, hell!' Rod growled. 'Not again!'

He reached down under the saddlehorn and reset the circuit breaker. Slowly, the horse raised its head and shook it several times. Rod caught the reins and led the horse away.

'Whaddappen, RRRawwwd?'

'You had a seizure, Fess. Now, whatever you do, *don't* whinny. That airborne bacchanalia is coming our way, and there's an off chance they might be out to investigate the shooting star. Therefore, we are heading for the tall timber – and *quietly*, if you please.'

Once under the trees at the edge of the meadow, Rod looked back to check on the flying flotilla.

The youngsters were milling about in the sky half a mile away, emitting joyful shrieks and shouts of welcome. The wind tossed Rod an intelligible phrase or two.

'Rejoice, my children! 'Tis Lady Gwen!'

'Hast thou, then, come at last to be mother to our coven, Gwendylon?'

'Thy beauty hath but waxed, sweet Gwendylon! How dost thou?'

'Not yet robbing cradles, Randal . . .'

'Sounds like the housemother dropping in on a party at the Witches' College,' Rod grunted. 'Sober, Fess?'

'Clear-headed, at least,' the robot acknowledged, 'and a new concept accepted in my basic programming.'

'Oh.' Rod pursed his lips. 'My observation is confirmed?'

'Thoroughly. They *are* flying.'

The aerial dance seemed to have rediscovered its original purpose. They swooped toward the meadows with shouts and gales of laughter, hovered over the ring of newly-turned earth, and dropped one by one to form a circle about it.

'Well, not too many doubts about what they're here for, is there?' Rod sat on the ground, tailor-fashion, and leaned back against Fess's forelegs. 'Nothing to do but wait, I guess.' He twisted the signet on his ring ninety degrees, pointed it at the gathering. 'Relay, Fess.'

The signet ring now functioned as a very powerful, very directional microphone; its signal was relayed through Fess to the earphone behind Rod's ear.

'Ought we to tell the Queen of this?'

'Nay, 'twould fash her unduly.'

Rod frowned. 'Can you make anything out of it, Fess?'

'Only that it's Elizabethan English, Rod.'

'That,' said Rod, 'is why SCENT always sends a man with a robot. All right, let's start with the obvious: the language confirms that this is the Emigrés' colony.'

'Well, of course,' Fess muttered, somewhat piqued.

'Now, now, old symbiote, no griping. I know you don't consider the obvious worth reporting; but overlooking obvious facts does sometimes lead to overlooking secrets hidden right in plain sight, doesn't it?'

'Well . . .'

'Right. So. They mentioned a Queen. Therefore, the government is a monarchy, as we suspected. This teenage in-group referred to themselves as a coven; therefore they consider themselves witches . . . Considering their form of locomotion, I'm inclined to agree. But . . .'

He left the *but* hanging for a few minutes. Fess picked up his ears.

'They also spoke of telling the Queen. Therefore, they must have access to the royal ear. What's this, Fess? Royal approval of witchcraft?'

'Not necessarily,' said Fess judiciously. 'An applicable precedent would be the case of King Saul and the Witch of Endor . . .'

'But chances are they've got an in at court.'

'Rod, you are jumping to conclusions.'

'No, just coming up with a brilliant flash of insight.'

'That,' said Fess, 'is why SCENT always sends a robot with a human.'

'Touché. But they also said that telling the Queen would "fash her unduly". What's *fash* mean, Fess?'

'To cause anxiety, Rod.'

'Um. This Queen just might be the excitable type, then.'

'*Might* be, yes.'

Music struck up in the field – Scottish bagpipes playing the accompaniment to an old Gypsy tune. The young folk were dancing on the cleared earth, and several feet above it.

'Bavarian peasant dance,' Fess murmured.

'"Where the ends of the earth all meet,"' Rod quoted, stretching his legs out straight. 'An agglomerate culture, carefully combining all the worst Old Earth had to offer.'

'An unfair judgement, Rod.'

Rod raised an eyebrow. 'You *like* bagpipes?'

He folded his arms and let his chin rest on his sternum, leaving Fess the sleepless to watch for anything significant.

The robot watched for a couple of hours, patiently chewing his data. When the music faded and died, Fess planted a hoof on Rod's hip.

'Gnorf!' said Rod, and was instantly wide awake, as is the wont of secret agents.

'The party's over, Rod.'

The young folk were leaping into the air, banking away to the northeast.

One broomstick shot off at right angles to the main body; a boyish figure shot out after it.

'Do thou not be so long estranged from us again, Gwendylon.'

'Randal, if thou wert a mouse, thou wouldst woo oliphants! Farewell, and see to it from now thou payest court to wenches only six years thy elder!'

The broomstick streaked straight toward Rod, climbed over the trees and was gone.

'Mmm, yes!' Rod licked his lips. 'Definitely a great build on that girl. And the way she talks, she's a wee bit older than these birdbrains . . .'

'I had thought you were above petty conquest by now, Rod.'

'Which is a nice way of saying she wouldn't have anything to do with me. Well, even if I haven't got the buying power, I can still window-shop.'

The junior coven sailed over the horizon; their laughter faded away.

'Well, that's that.' Rod gathered his feet under him. 'The party's over, and we're none the wiser.' He rose to his feet. 'Well, at least we're still a secret; nobody knows there's a spaceship under that circle of earth.'

'Nay, not so,' chuckled a pixie voice.

Rod froze, turned his head, stared.

There, among the roots of an old oak, stood a man, broadshouldered, grinning, and all of twelve inches tall. He was clad in doublet and hose in varying shades of brown, and had very white teeth and a general air of mischief.

'The King of the Elves shall be apprised of your presence, Lord Warlock,' said the apparition, chuckling.

Rod lunged.

But the little man was gone, leaving only a chortle behind him.

Rod stood staring, listening to the wind commenting to the oak leaves and the last faint snicker dying away among the oak roots.

'Fess,' he said. 'Fess, did you see that?'

There was no answer.

Rod frowned, turning. 'Fess? Fess!'

The robot's head swung gently between its fetlocks.

'Oh, hell!'

A deep-toned bell was proclaiming the advent of nine o'clock somewhere in the large, ramshackle town that was, as near as Rod and Fess could figure from speed and bearing, the juvenile witches' home base. In view of their remark about the Queen, Rod had hopes the town would turn out to be the capital of the island.

'Only a guess, of course,' he added hurriedly.

'Of course,' Fess murmured. The robot voice gave the distinct impression of a patient sigh.

'On a more immediate level, what name should I go by in this culture?'

'Why not Rodney d'Armand VII? This is one of the few cases where your natural name is appropriate.'

Rod shook his head. 'Too pretentious. My forebears never did get over their aristocratic aspirations.'

'They *were* aristocrats, Rod.'

'Yeah, but so was everybody else in the planet, Fess, except the robots. And they'd been in the family so long they had a right to claim some of the honours.'

'It was honour enough to—'

'Later,' Rod cut him off. Fess had a standardized sermon on the *noblesse oblige* tradition of the Maxima robots, which he would gladly deliver at the drop of anything resembling a cue. 'There's a small problem of a name, remember?'

'If you insist.' Fess was disgruntled. 'Mercenary soldier, again?'

'Yes. It gives me an excuse to travel.'

Fess winced. 'You could pose as a wandering minstrel . . .'

Rod shook his head. 'Minstrels are supposed to be up on the current news. Might not be a bad idea to pick up a harp, though – especially if the ruler's a woman. Songs can get you places where swords can't . . .'

'We go through this every time . . . Would "Gallowglass" suit you, Rod? It was the Irish term for a mercenary soldier.'

'Gallowglass . . .' Rod rolled the word over his tongue. 'Not bad. That's got some dash to it.'

'Like yourself.'

'Do I detect a touch of irony there? But it *is* a good, solid word . . . and it's not exactly what you'd call pretty . . .'

'Definitely like yourself,' the robot murmured.

'I daresay it'll do. Rod Gallowglass it is. *Whoa*!'

Rod sawed back on the reins, frowning. From someplace ahead of them came the low mutter of a mob.

Rod frowned. 'What's all the commotion?'

'Rod, may I recommend caution . . .'

'Not a bad idea. Gee-up again, but lightly with the hooves, please.'

Fess went at a walk through the narrow moonlit street, sidling up against the weathered wall of a building. He stopped at the corner, thrust his horse's head around the angle.

'What do you see, Sister Ann?'

'A mob,' said Fess.

'Astute observation, Watson. Anything else?'

'Torchlight, and a young man climbing up on a platform. If you'll pardon the analogy, Rod, it closely resembles a pep rally at your alma mater.'

'Just might be what it is.' Rod swung out of the saddle. 'Well, you stay here, big fella. I'll scout the terrain.'

He rounded the corner and let himself fall into a soldierly swagger, one hand on the pommel of his sword.

Not a bad idea, from the look of the crowd. Must be a meeting of the local Vagabond's Union. Not an unpatched doublet among them. He wrinkled his nose; a washed body seemed to be even more rare. Definitely a seedy lot.

The meeting-place was a large, open square, bordered by a wide river on one side; there were wharves with wooden ships riding at their moorings. On the other three sides of the square were cheap, decaying lodging-houses; sea-tackle stores and other cheap shops, and warehouses. The warehouses, at least, were in good repair. All the buildings were half-timbered, with the characteristic overhanging second storey.

The shouting, jostling mob filled the whole square. Flaming pine knots lent a demonic light.

A closer look at the crowd revealed patched eyes, shrivelled limbs, heads minus ears – an odd contrast to the figure that stood on the jury-rigged platform.

He was young, broad-shouldered and blond-headed. His face round, almost innocent face, open and honest, filled with the eerie light of a Man with a Mission. His doublet and hose were clean, for a wonder, and well-tailored from good cloth. A sword hung at his hip.

'A kid from the right side of the tracks,' Rod mused. 'What in the Seventh Hell is he doing in this rathole?'

The youth threw up his hands; the crowd roared, pine-knot torches surged forward to light him.

'Whose shoulders have borne up the weightiest burdens?' the boy shouted.

'Ours!' roared the crowd.

'Whose hands are worn hard and scarred with rough toil?'

'Ours!'

'Who is it have built all the wealth that the noblemen squander?'

'We!'

'Who is it have reared up their lofty castles of granite?'

'We!'

'Shall you not have a share in these riches and luxuries?'

'We shall!'

'Why,' roared the young spokesman, 'there is wealth enough in even one of these castles to make each one of you a king!'

The crowd went wild.

'You catching this, Fess?'

'I am, Rod. It sounds like a mixture of Karl Marx and Huey Long.'

'Strange synthesis,' Rod muttered. 'And yet, maybe not so strange, when you come to think of it.'

'This is your wealth!' shouted the youth. 'You have a *right* to it!'

The crowd went wild again.

'Will they give you your due?'

The crowd went suddenly quiet. An ugly murmur began.

'No!' the young man bellowed. 'You must therefore demand it, as is your right!'

He threw up his arms. 'The Queen has given you bread and wine when the famine was upon you! The Queen has given meat and good wine to the witches whom she harbours!'

The crowd fell deathly still. A whisper ran through the ranks: 'The witches! The witches!'

'Aye,' roared the spokesman, 'even the witches, the outcast and spurned. How much more, then, will she give to you, who have borne the heat of the day?

'She will give you your due!'

The crowd echoed his roar.

'Where do you go?' yelled the young Demosthenes.

'To the castle!' someone shouted, and other voices took up the cry. 'To the castle! To the castle!' It became a rhythmic chant. 'To the castle! To the castle! To the castle!'

A high, keening wail cut across the chant. The crowd fell silent. A narrow, twisted figure hobbled to the edge of a warehouse roof and called out over the square:

'Soldiers, a company or more!'

'Out through the alleys and wharves!' bellowed the young man. 'At the House of Clovis we shall meet, within the hour!'

To Rod's amazement, the crowd remained silent. Streams of people began to pour down the twisted alleys. There was no panic, no crush.

Rod shrank into a doorway and watched as the torches were grounded. Score upon score of beggars ran past him, light-footed and silent, to be swallowed up by the dark mouths of the byways.

The square emptied; the light sounds of scampering faded away. In the sudden quiet, Rod heard the drum of approaching hooves – the soldiers, coming to check up on the Queen's loyal subjects.

Rod stepped out onto the cobbles, running on the balls of his feet, around the corner where Fess stood waiting.

He was into the saddle without breaking stride. 'The good part of town,' he whispered, 'fast and quiet.'

Fess could extrude inch-thick rubber pads from his hooves when silence was called for; he had also memorized a photo-map of the city from their aerial survey. There are advantages to a robot horse.

They fled through the town; the ground rose beneath them, building into the hill crowned by the royal castle. The quality of the buildings improved gradually; they were coming to the more affluent districts.

'What do you make of all that, Fess?'

'A totalitarian movement, beyond question,' the robot replied. 'A rabble-rouser, no doubt power-hungry, who will lead the people to make demands on the government, demands which cannot be met. The crown's refusals will be used to incite the mob to violence, and you have your revolution made.'

'Couldn't be just an ambitious nobleman trying to usurp the crown?'

'Usurpation derives its support from the upper classes, Rod. No, this is a proletarian revolution – a prelude to a totalitarian government.'

Rod pursed his lips. 'Would you say there was evidence of outside intervention from a more advanced society? I mean, proletarian revolutions aren't usually found in this kind of culture, are they?'

'Rarely, Rod, and the propaganda is rudimentary when they do occur. Persuasion in a medieval society never refers to the basic rights; the concept is alien to the culture. The probability of intervention is quite strong . . .'

Rod's lips pulled back in a savage grin. 'Well, old mechanism, it looks like we've come to the right place to set up shop.'

At the uphill edge of the town, they came on a rambling, two-storeyed structure built around three sides of a torchlit courtyard. A timber palisade with a gate closed the fourth side. A party of laughing, well-dressed young men sauntered out of the gate; Rod caught a snatch of drunken song. Tableware rattled, and voices called for meat and ale.

'I take it we've found one of the better inns.'

'I would say that was a warranted assumption, Rod.'

Rod leaned back in the saddle. 'Looks like a good place to spend the night. Is garlic sausage possible in this culture, Fess?'

The robot shuddered. 'Rod, you have the most unearthly tastes!'

'Make way, make way!' a voice trumpeted behind him.

Turning, Rod saw a party of soldiers, cavalry, trotting toward him. Behind them rolled a gilded, richly carved carriage.

A herald rode in front of the soldiers. 'Stand aside from the road, fellow!' he called. 'The Queen's coach passes!'

'Queen!' Rod's eyebrows shot up. 'Yes, yes! By all means, let's stand aside!'

He nudged Fess with his knee. The horse whirled off the road and jockeyed for a position on the shoulder that would give Rod a good look at the royal party.

The curtains on the coach were half drawn, but there was looking space. A lantern cast a warm yellow glow inside the coach, affording Rod a brief glimpse as the coach spun by.

A slender, frail form wrapped in a dark, hooded travelling cloak; a pale, small-boned face framed with blonde, almost platinum hair; large, dark eyes; and small, very red lips drawn up in a pout.

And young, very young – scarcely past childhood, Rod thought.

She sat ramrod straight, looking very fragile but also very determined – and, somehow, forlorn, with the hostile, chip-on-the-shoulder attitude that so often goes with fear and loneliness.

Rod stared after the retreating party.

'Rod.'

Rod started, shook his head, and realized that the coach had been out of sight for a while.

He glowered at the back of the horse's head. 'What is it, Fess?'

'I wondered if you'd fallen asleep.' The black head turned to Rod, the great eyes laughing gently.

'No.' Rod twisted, looking back at the turn where the coach had disappeared.

Fess schooled his voice to patience. 'The Dream again, Rod?'

Rod scowled. 'I thought robots didn't have emotions.'

'No. But we *do* have an innate dislike of a lack of that quality which has often been termed common sense.'

Rod threw him a sour smile. 'And, of course, an appreciation for that quality called irony, since it's basically logical. And irony implies—'

'—a sense of humour, yes. And you must admit, Rod, that there is something innately humorous in a man's chasing an object of his own invention over half a galaxy.'

'Oh yeah, it's a million yuks, sure. But isn't that the difference between a man and a robot, Fess?'

'What? The ability to form imaginary constructions?'

'No, the ability to get hung up on them. Well, let's see if we can't find you a quiet stall where you can chew your data in peace.'

Fess turned and trotted through the inn-yard gate.

A hostler came running from the stables as Rod dismounted. Rod tossed him the reins, said, 'Don't give him too much water,' and strolled into the big common room.

Rod hadn't known that rooms could be smoky without tobacco. Obviously, chimney-building was numbered among the underdeveloped sciences on this planet.

The customers didn't seem to mind, though. The room was filled with laughter, coarse jokes, and coarser voices in loud conversation. The great room was taken up by twenty or so large, round tables; there were several smaller tables, occupied by people whose dress marked them above the common (but not high enough to be staying at the castle). Lighting consisted of pine torches, which added to the atmosphere; tallow candles, dripping nicely on the guests; and a huge fireplace, fit to roast an ox, which was exactly what it was doing at the moment.

A small horde of boys and stocky peasant girls kept a steady stream of food and drink passing between the tables and the kitchen; many of them displayed considerable skill at broken-field running.

A large balding man with an apron tied around his ample middle burst out of the kitchen with a great smoking platter – the landlord, at a guess. Business was good tonight.

The man looked up, saw Rod, took in the gold and scarlet doublet, sword and dagger, the general air of authority, the well-filled purse – most especially the purse – and shoved the platter at the nearest serving girl. He bustled up to Rod, rubbing his hands on his apron.

'And how may I serve you, good master?'

'With a tankard of ale, a steak as thick as both your thumbs, and a table alone.' Rod smiled as he said it.

The innkeeper stared, his lips forming a round O – Rod had apparently done something out of the ordinary.

Then the old man's eyes took on a calculating look, one that Rod had seen before; it was usually accompanied by a remark to the waiter, *sotto voce*, 'Soft touch. Soak him for all he's worth.'

Rod had smiled.

He should have known better.

Some things can be undone, though. Rod let his smile droop into a scowl.

'Well, what are you waiting for?' he barked. 'Be quick about it, or I'll dine on a slice off your backside!'

The landlord jumped, then cringed, bowing rapidly.

'But of course, m'lord, of course! Quickly it will be, good master; yes, quickly indeed!' He turned away.

Rod's hand clamped onto his shoulder. 'The table,' he reminded.

The landlord gulped and bobbed his head, led Rod to a table beside an upright log that served as a pillar, and scurried away – cursing under his breath, no doubt.

Rod returned the courtesy, but enlarged the object to include all that the landlord stood for, namely the mercenary ways of mankind.

And, of course, wound up cursing himself for having catered to Mammon by getting tough.

But what could he do? SCENT agents were supposed to remain inconspicuous, and a softhearted medieval bourgeois was a contradiction in terms.

But when the landlord said quickly, he meant it. The steak and ale appeared almost before Rod had sat down. The landlord stood by rubbing his hands on his apron and looking very worried. Waiting for Rod to accept the cooking, probably.

Rod opened his mouth to reassure the man, and stopped with a word not quite past his larynx. His nosed twitched; a slow grin spread over his face. He looked up at the landlord.

'Do I smell garlic sausage?'

'Oh yes, your worship!' The landlord started bobbing again. 'Garlic sausage it is, your worship, and very fine garlic sausage too, if I may say so. If your worship would care for some . . .?'

'My worship would,' said Rod, 'and *presto allegro*, sirrah.'

The landlord shied, reminding Rod of Fess regarding a syllogism, and ran.

*Now, what was that all about?* Rod wondered. Must have been something he said. And he'd been rather proud of that sirrah . . .

He sampled the steak, and had just washed it down when a plate of sausage *thunked!* onto the table.

'Very good,' said Rod, 'and the steak is acceptable.'

The landlord's face broke into a grin of relief; he turned to go, then turned back.

'Well, what is it?' Rod asked around a mouthful of sausage.

The landlord was twisting his hands in his apron again. 'Beg pardon, my master, but . . .' His lips twisted too, then the words burst out. 'Art a warlock, m'master?'

'Who, me? A warlock? Ridiculous!' For emphasis, Rod jabbed his table knife in the landlord's general direction. The huge belly shrank in amazingly; then it bolted, taking its owner along.

*Now where did he get the idea I was a warlock?* Rod mused as he chewed a mouthful of steak.

*Never had a better steak*, he decided. *Must be the smoke. Wonder what wood they're using?*

*Must have been the* presto allegro *bit. Thought they were magic words, probably* . . .

Well, they *had* worked wonders.

Rod took a bite of sausage and a swig of ale.

Him, a warlock? Never! He might be a second son of a second son, but he wasn't *that* desperate.

Besides, being a warlock involved signing a contract in blood, and Rod had no blood to spare. He kept losing it in the oddest places . . .

He drained his tankard, set it down with a thump. The landlord materialized with a jug and poured him a refill. Rod started a smile of thanks, remembered his station, and changed the smile to a sneer. He fumbled in his purse, felt the irregular shape of a gold nugget – acceptable currency in a medieval society – remembered the quickness of the house to gyp the generous, and passed over the nugget in favour of a sliver of silver.

The landlord stared at the small white bar in the palm of his hand, his eyes making a valiant attempt to turn into hemispheres. He made a gargling sound, stuttered elaborate thanks, and scurried away.

Rod bit his lip in annoyance. Apparently even so small a chunk of silver was enough to excite comment here.

The touch of anger dissipated quickly, though; a pound or two of beef in the belly *did* tend to make the world look better. Rod threw his legs out in the aisle, stretched, and slumped backward in the chair, picking his teeth with the table knife.

Something was strangely wrong in this common room. The happy were a little too professional about it – voices a shade too loud, laughter a trifle strained, with a dark echo. The glum, on the other hand, were *really* glum; their brown studies were panelled in walnut.

Fear.

Take that pair at three o'clock on the third table from the right, now – they were awfully earnest about whatever it was they were hashing over. Rod gave his ring a surreptitious nudge and pointed it at the twosome.

'But such meetings do no good if the Queen is continually sending her soldiers against us!'

' 'Tis true, Adam, 'tis true; she won't hear us, for when all's said and done, she won't let us close enough to speak.'

'Why, then, she must be forced to listen!'

'Aye, but what good would that do? Her nobles would not let her give what we demand.'

Adam slammed his open hand on the table. 'But we've a right to be free without being thieves and beggars! The debtors' prisons must end, and the taxes with them!'

'Aye, and so must the cutting off of an ear for the theft of a loaf of bread.' He rubbed the side of his head, with a hangdog look on his face. 'Yet she hath contrived to do summat for us . . .'

'Aye, this setting-up of her own judges now! The great lords will no longer give each their justice, by style and taste.'

'The nobles will not bear it, and that thou knowest. The judges will not stand long.' One-Ear's face was grim; he traced circles on the wet tabletop.

'Nay, the noblemen will stand for naught that the Queen designs!' Adam plunged his knife into the tabletop. 'Will not the Loguire see that?'

'Nay, speak not against the Loguire!' One-Ear's face darkened. 'If 'twere not for him, we would still be a ragtag horde, with no common purpose! Speak not against Loguire, Adam, for without him, we would not have the brass to sit in this inn, where the Queen's soldiers are but guests!'

'Oh, aye, aye, he pulled us together and made men of us thieves. Yet now he holds our new manhood in check; he seeks to keep us from fighting for that which is ours!'

One-Ear's mouth turned down tight at the corners. 'Thou hast hearkened too much to the idle and envious chatter of the Mocker, Adam!'

'Yet fight we must, mark my words!' Adam cried, clenching his fist. 'Blood must be shed ere we come to our own. Blood must answer for blood, and 'tis blood the nobles have ta'en from—'

Something huge slammed into Rod, knocking him back against the table, filling his head with the smell of sweat and onions and cheap wine.

Rod braced an arm against the table and shoved with his shoulder. The heavy form swayed away with a *whuff!* of breath. Rod drew his dagger and thumbed the signet ring to off.

The man loomed over him, looking eight feet tall and wide as a wagon.

'Here now!' he growled. 'Why doncha look where I'm going at?'

Rod's knife twisted, gleaming light into the man's eyes. 'Stand away, friend,' he said softly. 'Leave an honest man to his ale.'

'An honest man, is it!' The big peasant guffawed. 'A sojer, callin' hisself an honest man!' His roaring laughter was echoed from the tables.

On an off bet, Rod decided, strangers weren't popular here.

The laughter stopped quite suddenly. 'Nay, put down your plaything,' said the big man, suddenly sober, 'and I'll show you an honest villager can outfight a sojer.'

A prickle ran down Rod's spine as he realized it was a put-up job. The landlord had advised the big ox of the whereabouts of a heavy purse . . .

'I've no quarrel with you,' Rod muttered. He realized it was the worst thing he could have said almost before the words were off his tongue.

The big man leered, gloating. 'No quarrel, he says now. He throws hisself in the path of a poor staggering man so's he can't help but run into him. But, "No quarrel", sez he, when he's had a look at Big Tom!'

A huge, meaty hand buried itself in the cloth at Rod's throat, pulling him to his feet. 'Nay, I'll show you a quarrel,' Big Tom snarled.

Rod's right hand lashed out, chopping into the man's elbow, then bouncing away. The big man's hand loosened and fell, temporarily numbed. Big Tom stared at his hand, a look of betrayal.

Rod pressed his lips together, tucked his knife into the sheath. He stepped back, knees flexed, rubbed his right fist in his left palm. The peasant was big, but he probably knew nothing of boxing.

Life came back into Tom's hand, and with it, pain. The huge man bellowed in anger, his hand balling into a fist, swinging at Rod in a vast roundhouse swipe that would have annihilated anything it struck.

But Rod ducked under and to the side and, as the fist went by him, reached up behind Tom's shoulder and gave a solid push to add to the momentum of the swing.

Big Tom spun around; Rod caught the man's right wrist and twisted it up behind Tom's back. Rod jerked the wrist up a little higher; Big Tom howled. While he was howling, Rod's arm snaked under Tom's armpit to catch the back of his neck in a half nelson.

Not bad, Rod thought. So far he hadn't needed boxing.

Rod planted a knee in Tom's backside as he released his holds; Tom blundered into the open space before the hearth, tried to catch his balance, and didn't make it. Overturned tables clattered and thudded as the patrons scuttled back, all too glad to leave the fireside seat to Big Tom.

He came to his knees, shaking his head, and looked up to see Rod standing before him in a wrestler's crouch, smiling grimly and beckoning with both arms.

Tom growled low in his throat and braced a foot against the fieldstones of the hearth.

He shot at Rod head-first, like a bull.

Rod sidestepped and stuck out a foot. Big Tom went flailing straight for the first row of tables. Rod squeezed his eyes shut and set his teeth.

There was a crash like four simultaneous strikes in a bowling alley. Rod winced. He opened his eyes and forced himself to look.

Big Tom's head emerged out of a welter of woodwork, wide-eyed and slack-jawed.

Rod shook his head sadly, clucking his tongue. 'You've had a rough night, Big Tom. Why don't you go home and sleep it off?'

Tom picked himself up, shin, wristbone, and clavicle, and put himself back together, taking inventory the while.

Satisfied that he was a gestalt again, he stamped a foot, planted his fists on his hips, and looked up at Rod.

'Here now, man!' he complained. 'You don't half fight like an honest gentleman!'

'Not hardly a gentleman at all,' Rod agreed. 'What do you say we try one more throw, Tom? Double or nothing!'

The big man looked down at his body as if doubting its durability. He kicked at the remains of an oak table tentatively, slammed a fist into his own tree-trunk biceps, and nodded.

'I'll allow as I'm fit,' he said. 'Come on, little man.'

He stepped out onto the cleared floor in front of the hearth, walking warily around the perimeter, keeping one baleful eye on Rod.

'Our good landlord told you I had silver in my purse, didn't he?' said Rod, his eyes snapping.

Big Tom didn't answer.

'Told you I was an easy mark, too,' Rod mused. 'Well, he was wrong on both counts.'

Big Tom's eyes bulged. He gave a bellow of distress. 'No silver?'

Rod nodded. 'I thought he told you.' His eyes flicked over to the landlord, ashen and trembling by a pillar.

And looked back to see Big Tom's foot heading right toward his midriff.

Rod fell back, swinging both hands up to catch Big Tom's heel and inspire it to greater heights.

Tom's foot described a neat arc. For a moment, he hung in the air, arms flailing; then he crashed howling to the floor.

Rod's eyes filled with pain as Big Tom floundered about, struggling for the breath that the floor had knocked out of him.

Rod stepped in, grabbed the front of Tom's tunic, braced his foot against Tom's and threw his weight back, hauling the big man to his feet. Tom immediately sagged forward; Rod shoved a shoulder under Tom's armpit and pushed the big man back to the vertical.

'Ho, landlord!' he shouted. 'Brandy – and fast!'

Rod liked to think of himself as the kind of man people could lean on, but this was ridiculous.

When Big Tom had been somewhat revived and commended to the gentle jeers of his booze buddies, and the guests had somewhat restored the room and resumed their places, and Rod had still not wreaked anything resembling vengeance on the landlord, that worthy's eyes sparked with a sudden hope. He appeared again before Rod, his chin thrust out and the corners of his mouth drawn down.

Rod hauled himself out of the depths of a rather cynical contemplation of man's innate goodness and focused on the landlord. 'Well, what do you want?'

The landlord swallowed thickly. 'If it please your worship there's a little matter of some broken chairs and tables . . .'

'Chairs,' said Rod, not moving. 'Tables.'

He slammed to his feet and coiled a hand around the innkeeper's neck. 'Why, you slimy little curmudgeon! You set that ox on me, you try to rob me, and you have the gall to stand there and tell me I owe you money?' He emphasized each point with a shake of the landlord's neck, slowly pushing him back against the pillar. The landlord made a masterful attempt to blend into the bark, but only succeeded in spreading himself thin.

'And to top it all off, my ale's got warm!' Rod shouted. 'You call yourself a landlord, and you treat a gentleman of arms like *this*?'

'Forgive, master, forgive!' the landlord rattled, clawing at Rod's hand with commendable effort and negative effect. 'I meant no harm, your worship; I meant only—'

'Only to rob me, yes!' Rod snorted, letting him go with a toss that fetched him up backward over a table. 'Beware the kind, for they tend to grow cruel when you cross them. Now! A goblet of hot mulled wine by the time I count three, and I may refrain from stretching your ears out and tying them under your chin. Git!'

He counted to three, with a two-second pause between numbers, and the goblet was in his hand. The landlord scuttled away with his hands clapped over his ears, and Rod sat down to sip at the wine and wonder what a curmudgeon was.

Looking up, he saw a half a garlic sausage sitting on the table. He picked it up with a heavy hand and tucked it into his purse.

Might as well take it along; it was about the only good thing that had happened today.

He surged to his feet and called, 'Ho, landlord!'

Mine host came bobbling up.

'A chamber alone, with heavy blankets!'

'A chamber alone, sir! At once, sir!' The landlord scuttled away, still bobbing his head. 'Heavy blankets, sir! Quite surely, sir!'

Rod ground his teeth and turned away to the door. He stepped out and leaned back against the jamb, letting his head slump forward onto his chest, eyes closed.

'The law of the jungle,' he muttered. 'If it looks weak, prey upon it. If it turns out to be strong, bow to it; let it prey upon you and hope it won't devour you.'

'Yet all men have pride,' murmured a voice behind his ear.

Rod looked up, smiled. '"Art there, old mole?"'

'"Swear! Swear!"' Fess answered.

Rod let loose a stream of invective that would have done credit to a sailor with a hangover.

'Feel better?' Fess asked, amused.

'Not much. Where does a man like mine host hide his pride, Fess? He sure as hell never let it show. Obsequiousness, yes; avarice, yes; but self-respect? No. I haven't seen that in him.'

'Pride and self-respect are not necessarily synonymous, Rod.'

Someone tugged at Rod's elbow. He snapped his head around, muscles tensed.

It was Big Tom, his six-foot-five bent strangely in a valiant attempt to put his head below the level of Rod's.

'God e'en, master.'

Rod stared at him for a moment without answering.

'God e'en,' he replied, his voice carefully neutral. 'What can I do for *you*?'

Big Tom hunched his shoulders and scratched at the base of his skull. 'Eh, master,' he complained, 'you made a bit of a fool of me back a while.'

'Oh?' Rod lifted an eyebrow. 'Do tell!'

'I do,' the big man admitted, 'and . . . well . . .' He pulled off his cap and twisted it in his great hands. 'It *do* seem like . . . well, master, you've finished me here, and that's gospel.'

Rod felt his back lifting. 'And I'm supposed to make it up to you, is that it? Pay you damages, I suppose!'

'Eh, no, master!' Big Tom shied away. ' 'Tisn't that, master, not that at all! It's just . . . well . . . I was a-wonderin', I was, if you might . . . that is . . . I . . .'

He twisted the hat through some gyrations that would have astounded a topologist; then the words came out in a rush.

'I was wonderin' if you might be needin' a servin'-man, you know – a sort of groom and lackey, and . . .' His voice trailed off. He eyed Rod sidewise, fearful and hopeful.

Rod stood frozen for a moment or two. He searched the big man's open, almost worshipful face.

He crossed his arms and leaned back against the jamb again. 'Why, how's this, Big Tom? Not half an hour agone, you sought to rob me! And now *I* am supposed to trust *you* for a squire?'

Big Tom caught his nether lip between his teeth, frowning. ' 'Tain't right-seeming, master, that I know, but—' His hands gestured vaguely. 'Well, the fact of it is, you're the only man what I ever raised hand against, could beat me, and . . .'

His voice ran out again. Rod nodded slowly, his eyes on Big Tom's.

'And therefore you must serve me.'

Tom's lower lip thrust out, pouting. 'Not must, my master – only that I *wants* to.'

'A robber,' said Rod. 'A cutpurse. And I'm to trust you.'

Big Tom's hat twisted again.

'You've got an open face,' Rod mused, 'not the kind of face that hides its feelings.'

Big Tom smiled widely, nodding.

'Of course, that doesn't mean anything,' Rod went on. 'I've known quite a few gentle-seeming girls that turned out to be first-class bitches.'

Tom's face fell.

'So you might be honest – or you might be a thorough rogue. It's a *Fess*-cinating puzzle.'

The voice behind his ear murmured, 'Preliminary interpretation of available data indicates basically simplistic personality structure. Probability of individual serving as reliable source of information on local social variables exceeds probability of individual practising serious duplicity.'

Rod nodded slowly. He would have settled for an even chance.

He fished a scrap of silver from his purse – it smelt slightly of garlic – and slapped it into the big man's hand.

Tom stared at the silver in his palm, then at Rod, then back at the metal.

Abruptly, his hand closed into a fist, trembling slightly. His staring eyes came up to Rod again.

'You've accepted my coin,' said Rod. 'You're my man.'

Big Tom's face split from ear to ear in a grin. He ducked his head. 'Yes, master! I thanks you, master! Forever I thanks you, master! I—'

'I get the message.' Rod hated to see a grown man grovel. 'You go on duty right now. Tell me, what are the chances of getting a job with the Queen's army?'

'Oh, most excellent, master!' Big Tom grinned. 'They're always needing new sojers.'

A bad omen, Rod decided.

'Okay,' he said. 'Duck back inside, find out which room we've been assigned, and check it to make sure there isn't a cut-throat in the closet.'

'Yes, master! Right away!' Big Tom bustled back into the inn.

Rod smiled, closed his eyes, and let his head fall back against the jamb. He rolled his head from side to side, laughing silently. He would never cease to be amazed at the bully psychology; how a man could go from arrogance to servility in less than ten minutes, he would never understand.

A low, quavering wail cut the night air, soaring into a shriek.

Rod's eyes snapped open. Sirens? In *this* culture?

The sound was coming from the left; he looked up, and saw the castle, there on its hilltop.

And there, at the base of the tower, something glowed, and keened like a paddy wagon lamenting the death of some squad cars.

The guests tumbled out of the inn to stand in the courtyard, staring and pointing.

' 'Tis the banshee!'

'Again!'

'Nay, all will be well. Hath it not appeared thrice before? And yet the Queen lives!'

'Fess,' Rod said carefully.

'Yes, Rod.'

'Fess, there's a banshee. On the castle battlements. A banshee, Fess.'

There was no answer.

Then a raucous buzz snarled behind Rod's ear, swelled till it threatened to shake his head apart, and cut off.

Rod shook his head and pounded his temple with the heel of his hand.

'I'm going to have to have that boy overhauled,' he muttered. 'He used to have *quiet* seizures.'

It would have been unwise for Rod to go to the stables to reset Fess while the inn-yard was full of gawkers; he would have been thoroughly conspicuous.

So he went up to his room, to lie down till things had quieted down a bit; and, of course, by the time the courtyard was clear, Rod was too comfortable to take the trouble of going down to the stables. No real reason to reset the robot, anyway; it would be a quiet night.

The room was dark, except for a long swath of light streaming in the window from the largest moon. There was a subdued murmur and clatter from the common room – night owl guests drinking late. Rod's chamber was very peaceful.

Not quiet, though. Big Tom, curled up on a pallet at the foot of the bed, snored like a bulldozer on idle, making more noise asleep than he did awake.

Now there was a riddle – Big Tom. Rod had never before been in a fight where he hadn't been hit at least once. Big Tom had left himself wide open, every time; and sure, he was big, but he didn't have to be *that* clumsy. Big men *can* be quick . . .

But why would Big Tom have thrown the fight?

So Rod would take him on as a serving-man?

And what about Adam and One-Ear? Their talk would seem to indicate they'd been at the pep rally down by the wharf, which would mean they were members of the proletarian party. What had the young rabble-rouser called it? The House of Clovis, yes.

But if Adam and One-Ear were a representative sample, the House of Clovis was a house divided against itself. There seemed to be two factions, one backing the Loguire – the juvenile orator? – and one led by the Mocker, whoever that might be. The usual two factions, nonviolent and violent, tongue and sword.

Now, why would Big Tom have wanted a butler job? Social climber, maybe? No, he wasn't the fawning type. Better wages? But he'd seemed to be moderately prosperous as the neighbourhood heavy.

To keep an eye on Rod?

Rod rolled over on his side. Tom just might be a member in good standing of the House of Clovis. But why would the House want to keep tabs on Rod? They couldn't suspect anything, could they?

If Fess's guess was right, and the House was backed by an off-planet power, they definitely might suspect something – never mind how.

But wasn't Rod letting his paranoia show again?

He was wide awake, every muscle tense. He sighed and rolled out of bed; he couldn't sleep now. Better reset Fess and have a talk. Rod needed the robot's electronic objectivity; he had very little of his own.

Big Tom stirred and wakened as Rod lifted the rusty door latch.

'Master? Where dost thou go?'

'Just got a little worried about my horse, Big Tom. Think I'll run down to the stables and make sure the hostler's treating him right. Go back to sleep.'

Big Tom stared a moment.

'Certes,' he said, 'thou'rt a most caring one, master.'

He rolled over and burrowed his head into the folded cloak he used for a pillow. 'To be so much concerned for a horse,' he muttered, and snored again.

Rod grinned and let himself out of the room.

He found a stairway a few paces away – dark and musty, but closer to the stables than the main door.

There was a door at the bottom of the stair, one that was not very often used; it groaned like a bullfrog in heat when he opened it.

The inn-yard was flooded with the soft, golden light of the three moons. The largest was only a little smaller than Terra's, but much closer; it filled a full thirty degrees of sky, a perpetual harvest moon.

'Great planet for lovers,' Rod mused; and, because his eyes were on the moon, he didn't notice the grey strand of cord stretched a little above the doorstep. He tripped.

His arms swung up, slapping the ground to break his fall. Something hard struck the back of his head, and the world dissolved in a shoal of sparks.

There was a ruddy glow about him, and a throbbing ache in his head. Something cold and wet moved over his face. He shuddered, and came wide awake.

He lay on his back; a limestone roof vaulted over him, glimmering with bits of captured light. Pinch-waisted limestone

columns stretched from the roof to a green carpet – stalactites
and stalagmites joined. The green carpet stretched away in all
directions for at least a mile. He was in a vast underground cavern.
The light seemed to come from everywhere, a dancing, wavering
light, setting the sparks in the ceiling into an intricate ballet.

The green carpet spread under him; he could feel it, cold and
springy, damp, under his back: moss, three inches thick. He
tried to put out a hand to touch the moss, and discovered that
he couldn't move his arms or legs. Lifting his head, he looked for
ropes binding him, but there was not so much as a thread.

He shook his head, trying to get the ache out of it so he could
think clearly.

'Fess,' he muttered, 'where am I?'

There was no answer.

Rod bit his lip. 'Come on, iron horse! Are you asleep at the
switch?'

Switch . . .

Fess had had a seizure. Rod had been en route to reset him.

Rod was on his own.

He sighed and lay back on the green moss carpet.

A deep voice began singing, off to his right. Rod looked.

A fire fluttered in a bare stone circle. A tripod stood over it,
supporting a cauldron – a covered cauldron, bubbling merrily,
with a tube leading from a hole in the cover. Drops of water fell
from the roof, striking the tube; and a beaker sat under the far
end of the tube, collecting drops.

A primitive still.

And a moonshiner, a moonshiner perhaps eighteen inches high,
very broad-shouldered and generally stocky, clad in doublet and
hose. He had a round, cheerful face, twinkling green eyes, a snub
nose, and a very wide mouth curved in an impish smile. To top it
off, he wore a Robin Hood hat with a bright red feather.

The green eyes looked up and caught Rod's. 'Ha!' said the little
man in a buzzing baritone. 'Th'art come to thy senses, warlock!'

Rod scowled. 'Warlock? I'm not a warlock!'

'To be sure,' said the little man, 'th'art not. Thou comest in a
falling star, and thou hast a horse made of cold iron . . .'

'Just a minute, there,' Rod interrupted. 'How'd you know the
horse was made of cold iron?'

'We are the Wee Folk,' said the little man, unperturbed. 'We
live by Oak, Ash, and Thorn, by Wood, Air, and Sod; and those
who live by cold iron seek the end of our woodlands. Cold iron is

the sign of all that cannot abide us; and therefore we know cold iron, no matter what form or disguise it may be in.'

He turned back to the kettle, lifting the lid to check the mash. 'Then, too, thou canst hear what is said a good half mile off; and thy horse can run as silent as the wind and faster than a falcon, when it has cause to. But th'art not a warlock, eh?'

Rod shook his head. 'I'm not. I use science, not magic!'

'Assuredly,' said the little man, 'and a rose by any other name . . . Nay, th'art a warlock, and as such th'art known already throughout the length and the breadth of Gramarye!'

'Gramarye? What's that?'

The little man stared in surprise. 'Why, the world, warlock! The world we live in, the land between the Four Seas, the realm of Queen Catharine!'

'Oh. She rules the whole world?'

'Certes,' said the elf, giving Rod a sidelong glance.

'And the name of her castle? And the town around it?'

'Runnymede. In truth, th'art a most untutored warlock!'

'That's just what I've been trying to tell you,' and Rod sighed.

The little man turned away, shaking his head and muttering. He opened a pipette on the collection beaker and drained some of the distillate into a shot-glass-sized mug.

Rod suddenly realized he was very thirsty. 'Uh, say – what're you brewing up there? Wouldn't be brandy, would it?'

The elf shook his head.

'Gin? Rum? *Aqua Vitae*?'

'Nay; 'tis spirits of another sort.' He bounced over to Rod and held the minuscule mug to the man's lips.

'Thanks.' Rod took a sip. He looked up at the roof, smacking his lips. 'Tastes like honey.'

'Where the wild bee sucks, there suck I.' The little man hopped back to the fire.

'Not bad at all. Could you spare the recipe?'

'Aye, assuredly.' The elf grinned. 'We would do aught within our power for a guest.'

'Guest!' Rod snorted. 'I hate to impugn your hospitality, but immobilizing me isn't exactly what I'd call a welcome.'

'Oh, we shall make amends ere long.' The little man lifted the cauldron lid and stirred the mash.

Something clicked in Rod's mind. The hairs at the base of his skull began to prickle.

'Uh, say, uh . . . I don't believe we've been introduced, but . . . your name wouldn't be Robin Goodfellow, would it? Alias Puck?'

'Thous speakest aright.' The elf replaced the lid with a clang. 'I am that merry wanderer of the night.'

Rod fell back onto the moss carpet. It'd make a great story to tell his grandchildren; nobody else would believe it.

'Say, Puck – you don't mind if I call you Puck?'

'Oh, nay.'

'Thanks, uh . . . I'm Rod Gallowglass.'

'We ha' known it.'

'Well, just thought I'd make it official. Now, you don't seem to spare me any particular ill-will, so, uh, may I ask . . . uh . . . why am I paralysed?'

'Ah, that,' said Puck. 'We must find if you are a white warlock, or black.'

'Oh.' Rod chewed the inside of his cheek for a moment. 'If I'm a white warlock, you'll, um . . . let me go?'

Puck nodded.

'What happens if you decide I'm a black warlock?'

'Then, Rod Gallowglass, you shall sleep till the Trump of Doom.'

Rod felt as though a weak electric current had been applied to his jaw. 'Great. The Trump of Doom. And I never was much good at bridge.'

Puck frowned. 'How . . .?'

'Skip it. "Sleep till the Trump of Doom." A very neat euphemism. Why don't you just come right out and say you'll kill me?'

'Nay.' Puck thrust his lower lip out, shaking his head. 'We would not kill you, Rod Gallowglass. Thou shouldst but sleep forever, and with pleasant dreams.'

'I see. Suspended animation?'

Puck's brow wrinkled. 'I know not that word. Yet rest assured, thou shalt not be suspended. The Wee Folk have no fondness for a hanging.'

'Well, I suppose that's something of a comfort. So how do I prove I'm a white warlock?'

'Why,' said Puck, 'by our enlarging you.'

Rod stared. 'How's that again? Aren't I big enough already?'

The elf's face split into a broad grin. 'Nay, nay! Enlarging you! Removing the spell that binds you!'

'Oh.' Rod lay back with a sigh of relief. Then he jerked back up. '*Freeing* me? That's going to prove I'm a white warlock?'

'By itself, no,' said Puck. ' 'Tis a question where we free you.'

He clapped his hands. Rod heard the scurrying of scores of small feet coming from behind him; a fold of dark cloth was drawn over his eyes, knotted behind his head.

'Hey!' he protested.

'Peace,' said Puck. 'We do but bear you forth to your freedom.'

A host of tiny hands lifted Rod. He resigned himself and lay back to enjoy the trip.

It was a rather pleasant way to travel, actually – like an innerspring mattress with four-wheel drive.

His feet tilted up higher than his head and the pace of the scuttling feet under him slowed – they were mounting an incline.

Damp night air struck his face; he heard the breeze sighing in the leaves, accompanied by a full complement of crickets, with an owl and maybe a curlew providing the harmony.

He was dropped unceremoniously; the blindfold was whipped from his eyes.

'Hey!' he protested. 'What do you think I am, a sack of potatoes?'

He could hear a stream gurgling off to his left.

'Th'art free now, Rod Gallowglass,' Puck's voice husked in his ear. 'May God be with you!' And the elf bounded away.

Rod sat up, flexing his limbs to make them realize they could move again. He looked about.

It was a moonlit forest glade, with a silver stream trickling past on the left. The trees were bright steel trunk and tinsel leaf, and black shadow among the trunks.

One of the shadows moved.

It stepped forward, a tall figure in a dark, hooded monk's robe.

Rod scrambled to his feet.

The figure moved slowly toward Rod, halted ten feet away, and threw back the hood.

Wild, disordered hair over a long, thin face, with hollows under the cheekbones and caves for eye sockets, with two burning coals at their backs – and the whole face twisted, curdled with bitterness.

The voice was flat and thin, almost a hiss. 'Are you, then, so tired of life that you come to a werewolf's cage?'

Rod stared. 'Werewolf!'

Well, why not! If elves were a basic assumption . . .

Then Rod frowned. 'Cage?' He looked around. 'Looks like the great outdoors to me.'

'There is a wall of magic around this grove,' hissed the werewolf. ' 'Tis a prison the Wee Folk have made me – and they do not feed me in my proper fashion.'

'Oh?' Rod looked at the werewolf out of the corner of his eye. 'What's your proper fashion?'

'Red meat.' The werewolf grinned, showing a mouthful of canines. 'Raw, red meat, and blood for my wine.'

Something with lots of cold little feet ran down Rod's spine.

'Make peace with your God,' said the werewolf, 'for your hour has come.'

Fur appeared on the backs of his hands, and his fingernails grew, curving outward. Forehead and cheeks sprouted fur; nose, mouth, and chin slipped together and bulged, tapering outward to a muzzle. His ears moved upward to the top of his head and stretched into points.

He flung off the dark cloak; his whole body was silvery fur, his legs had become haunches.

He dropped to all fours. His upper arms shortened and his forearms lengthened; his hands had become paws. A tail sprouted and grew into a long, silvery plume.

The silver wolf crouched close to the earth, snarling, growling low in its throat, and sprang.

Rod whirled aside, but the wolf managed to change course in mid-air just enough; its teeth ripped Rod's forearm from elbow to wrist.

The wolf landed and spun about with a howl of joy. It crouched, tongue lolling out, then it sprang again.

Rod ducked, dropping to one knee, but the wolf checked itself in mid-leap and fell on top of him. Its hindlegs clawed at his chest; the great jaws fumbled for a hold on his spine.

Rod surged to his feet, bowing forward and shoving against the wolf's belly with all his strength. The wolf went flying, but its claws had raked Rod's back open.

The wolf landed on its back, hard, and howled with the pain. It scrambled to its feet and stalked around Rod in a circle, growling with blood-lust.

Rod pivoted, keeping his face toward the wolf. How do you handle a werewolf? Fess would know, but Fess was still out of order.

The wolf snarled and leaped for Rod's throat.

Rod crouched low and lunged with his hand stiffened. His fingers caught the wolf right in the solar plexus.

Rod leaped back, falling into a crouch. The wolf clawed at the ground, struggling to regain its breath as life poured back into its nerves. Rod circled around it, widdershins for luck.

How do you fight a werewolf?

Wolfbane, obviously.

But Rod couldn't tell wolfbane from poison ivy without a botany text.

The wolf dragged in a long, grating breath and rose into a crouch. It snarled and began to prowl, widdershins around Rod, watching for an opening.

So much for widdershins, Rod thought, and reversed direction, circling clockwise in an attempt to get behind the wolf.

The wolf sprang.

Rod pivoted aside and let fly a right jab at the wolf's jaw; but the wolf caught his fist in its teeth.

Rod bellowed with pain and kicked the beast in the belly. Fang went down for a breather again, freeing Rod's hand as the toothy jaws gaped for air.

Silver bullets. But chemical sidearms had been out of vogue for thousands of years, and the DDT had gone off the silver standard quite a while before.

A crucifix. Rod made a firm resolution to take up religion. He needed a hobby, anyway.

His furry friend had meanwhile pulled itself back together. Haunches tensed, it sprang.

Rod sidestepped, but the wolf had apparently counted on his so doing. It landed full on his chest, slavering jaws snapping for Rod's jugular vein.

Rod fell on his back. He pulled up his legs, planted his feet in the wolf's belly, and shoved, catapulting the canine clear of his corpus. The wolf fell hard and squirmed, getting its feet under its body.

What else didn't werewolves like?

Garlic.

Rod circled around the wolf, fumbling in his purse for the garlic sausage left over from dinner.

The wolf spread its jaws wide and hacked a cough.

Rod munched a mouthful of sausage.

The wolf came to its feet with an ugly, very determined growl. It tensed and sprang.

Rod caught the beast under the forelegs, staggering back under the weight of its body, and breathed full in its face. He dropped the wolf and sprang away.

The wolf rolled, spitting and coughing, drew in a shuddering gasp, and collapsed.

Its form stretched, relaxed, and slowly stretched again – and a tall, lean wiry man lay naked, face down, in the grass, unconscious body heaving with great panting breaths.

Rod sank to his knees. Saved by garlic sausage!

Grass whispered by his knee; he looked into the smiling eyes of Robin Goodfellow.

'Return with us if you will, Rod Gallowglass, for our paths are yours, to walk at your pleasure, now.'

Rod smiled wearily. 'He might have killed me,' he said, with a nod at the unconscious werewolf.

Puck shook his head. 'We looked on, and would have prevented death to either of you; and as for your wounds, why! we shall quickly have them mended.'

Rod rose, shaking his head in disbelief.

'Then, too,' said Puck, 'we knew you to be a warlock of such potency that you could defeat him . . . if you were a white warlock.'

'Oh?' Rod raised an eyebrow. 'What if I wasn't? What if I was black?'

'Why, then,' Puck said, grinning, 'you would have leagued with him against us, and sought to fight loose of the prison.'

'Um.' Rod gnawed at his lower lip. 'Wouldn't that have put you in a rather delicate position?'

'Nay.' Puck grinned again. 'The magic of a score of elves has never yet been equalled by two warlocks.'

'I see.' Rod rubbed his chin. 'Hedged your bets, didn't you? But you couldn't let me know, of course. As long as I was in the dark, fighting the werewolf proved I was one of the good guys?'

'Partly.'

'Oh? What's the other part?'

'Why, Rod Gallowglass, there were several times when you had rendered the werewolf helpless, but you did not kill him.'

'And that shows I've got a good heart.'

'That,' Puck agreed, 'and also that you are sure enough of your own power that you dare be merciful. And *there* is proof that you are white, but greater proof that you are a warlock.'

Rod squeezed his eyes shut. With exaggerated patience, he said,

'Of course, it *might* just be that I'm a trained fighter.'

'It might,' Puck agreed, 'but it was by sorcery that you overcame him.'

Rod took a deep breath. 'Look,' he said carefully, 'I am not a warlock. I have never been a warlock. I never want to be a warlock. I'm just a mercenary soldier who happens to know a few tricks.'

'Assuredly, Master Warlock,' said Puck cheerfully. 'Will you come back to the cavern? We shall guide you forth to your inn.'

'Oh, all right,' Rod grumbled.

But he turned to look at the miserable collection of bone and sinew that was the sleeping werewolf, lying in the centre of the glade.

'Master Gallowglass?' Puck's voice was puzzled, disturbed. 'What troubles you?'

Rod shook his head, coming out of his reverie. 'Nothing,' he said, turning away. 'Just wondering.'

'What of, warlock?'

'They used to call me a lone wolf when I was a schoolboy . . . Never mind. Which way did you say the cavern was?'

The stars wheeled toward dawn as Rod stumbled, footsore and weary, across the inn-yard and into the stable.

A single candle-lantern lit the row of stalls, serving only to deepen the shadows.

Rod flung an arm across Fess's back to steady himself, his other hand groping across the robot's withers till he found the enlarged vertebra that was the reset switch. He pressed; the steel body stirred under its horsehair camouflage. The velvet black head lifted, shook twice, turned to look back over its shoulder, great brown eyes focusing on Rod. The robot was silent a moment; then the voice behind Rod's ear spoke with a touch of reproach:

'You have left me inactive a long time, Rod. I have no after-effects from the seizure.'

'Sorry, old iron.' Rod kept his arms across the horse's back; his legs felt a trifle wobbly. 'I was on my way to reset you when I got clobbered.''

'Clobbered!' Fess's voice writhed with shame. 'While I slept! May my casing lie forever corroding on the junkpile! May my germanium be consigned to the Converter for reclamation! May my—'

'Oh, stow it!' Rod growled. 'It wasn't your fault.' He stepped away from the horse, straightening his shoulders. 'I wasn't in any real danger, anyway. Just a busy night, that's all.'

'How so, Rod?'

Rod started to answer, then changed his mind. 'I'll tell you in the morning, Fess.'

'I have reoriented my circuits to accept the discrepancies between accepted theory and actual occurrence, Rod. You may confide in me without fear of overload.'

Rod shook his head and turned to stumble out of the stall. 'In the morning, Fess. You might be able to believe it right now, but I'm not sure I could.'

Rod sat down to a whopping breakfast, but he was on a starvation diet compared to Big Tom. The man was surrounded by unbelievable stacks of food.

Some of it was familiar to Rod – the eggs, pancakes, and ham. The 'cakes had a subtly alien flavour, though, and the eggs had three-inch yolks. There was some sort of grain on any human-inhabited planet, usually a descendant of Terran cereals; but the soil of another planet sometimes produced weird variations. There was always some sort of domesticated fowl; but more often than not it was a local lifeform. Pigs, of course, were ubiquitous; they were found on Terran planets even more consistently than dogs. Rod sometimes wondered about his species.

The food was all digestible, of course, and probably nourishing: genetic drift couldn't change human metabolism all that much. But trace elements were another matter; Rod swallowed an all-purpose pill just to be on the safe side.

Big Tom noticed it. 'What was that, master?'

Rod forced a smile. 'Just a minor spell. Don't let it worry you, Big Tom.'

Tom stared, then looked down at his plate, muttering a quick prayer under his breath. He attacked the pancakes with a shaking fork.

The big man started to speak, but his voice cracked. He cleared his throat and tried again.

'What doth the new day bring, good master?'

'A trip to the castle,' said Rod. 'We'll see if the Queen's in the market for a new soldier.'

Tom wailed a protest. 'A Queen's sojer! Nay, master, that's no trade for a honest man!'

Rod cocked an eyebrow. 'Are you trying to tell me that one of us might be honest?'

Big Tom shut up.

The landlord had a spare horse, or so he suddenly remembered when Rod rested a hand on the hilt of his dagger. It was an old, sway-backed grey gelding with a slightly longer neck and smaller ears than the Terran standard animal. That was bad, since it would call a certain amount of attention to Fess; but then, the great black horse wasn't exactly inconspicuous anyway.

The church bells were ringing as they rode out of the inn-yard, Rod on Fess and Tom on the equine antique. The sound of the bells reminded Tom of the early hour; he began to grumble at masters who kept unreasonable hours.

But his gripes trailed off as they mounted the slope above the town, where they could look out to the horizon and see the east pregnant with the morning sun.

Tom took a deep breath of the dawn and grinned back over his shoulder at Rod. 'Eh, master! 'Twill be a fine day!'

'And a chill one,' said Rod, turning up his collar, for the wind was at his back.

'Aye, aye! Did I not say 'twould be fine?'

'I don't quite share your enthusiasm for low thermometer readings,' Rod growled. 'Look alive, Tom; we're almost to the castle.'

'Stand and declare yourselves!' cried the sentry on the drawbridge.

'Oh, ye gods!' Rod rolled his eyes upward.

'Your name and your concern at the Queen's castle.'

'Overdoing it a bit, aren't you?' Rod eyed the sentry sidewise.

The footman's mouth turned down sharply at the corners. 'None of your mouthings,' he barked. 'I'm a Queen's man, and you'll speak with respect.'

'Not likely,' said Rod, smiling benignly. 'My name is Rod Gallowglass.'

'Gallowglass?' The sentry frowned. 'Your time is wasted; the Queen already has a fool.'

'From the look of you, I'd say she has many.' Rod grunted. 'My trade is soldier, and my manservant's, too. Call the master-at-arms, and let him enrol me.'

The sentry glowered. 'Enlisting in the Queen's army is not so easily done as that.'

'Why, how now!' Rod scowled. 'Must I prove I'm a soldier?' He dismounted, swinging out of the saddle to land just a yard from the sentry.

'If you're a soldier, you're a poor one,' the sentry said with a sneer, 'or you'd not leave your horse untethered.'

Rod threw him a saccharine smile and called out, 'Fess, back up four feet, take a half step to the left, come forward four and a half feet, then stand till I call you.'

The sentry stared, mouth gaping open, as Fess executed the manoeuvre with machine-like precision.

'I'm a soldier,' said Rod, 'and a good one.'

The sentry's mouth opened and closed like a fish's. His eyes bulged slightly as they flicked over Rod's lean frame, the black-gloved hand on the pommel of the sword.

'You see,' Rod explained, 'I might have need of my horse. It's easier to let him come to me.'

His right hand jumped out in a feint. The soldier grunted with surprise and stepped back as Rod's foot snaked out to catch him behind the ankle. The sentry went down in a clatter of tin.

Rod twisted the pike from the sentry's hands as he fell and threw it back under the portcullis.

'Now,' he said, 'let's try it again, shall we?'

'Well done, oh! well done, my master!' Big Tom pounded his nag's withers, grinning from ear to ear.

The sentry staggered to his feet, shouting, 'A rescue! A rescue!'

'Oh, no!' Rod dropped his forehead into his palm. 'Oh, no!'—shaking his head.

He leaned back against Fess's shoulder and folded his arms. Three guardsmen came running up, pikes at the ready. The leader looked from Rod to the sentry, back to Rod, then back to the sentry. He frowned. 'What need for a rescue?'

The sentry fluttered a hand in Rod's general direction. 'This man . . .'

'Yes?' Rod smiled.

'Why, he knocked me down, that's what he did, and took my pike from me!'

'I wouldn't brag, if I were you,' Rod murmured. Big Tom bent low over his saddlebow, convulsed with silent laughter.

'Is that the truth of it, man?' The leader glowered at Rod.

'True.' Rod bowed his head.

'Well, then!' The leader straightened, planting his fists on his hips and scowling.

'Well, what?' Rod raised an eyebrow.

The sergeant was beginning to get flustered. 'Well, what's your reason?'

'I wish to enlist in the Queen's army. This man-at-arms indicated I should prove myself.'

The sergeant looked from the flabbergasted sentry to Rod, and nodded.

'You'll have your chance,' he said. 'Come.'

The chance consisted of a hulking sergeant equipped with a broadsword and buckler.

'Will you not take a buckler, man?' growled the old knight who was Master of the Guard.

'No thanks.' Rod slipped his dagger from its sheath. 'This will do me quite well.'

'Naught but a poniard and a wisp of a sword 'gainst broadsword and buckler!' Sir Maris shook his head sadly. 'You must truly wish to die young!'

Rod's eyes widened in surprise. 'Thank you,' he said. 'I haven't been told I looked young since I was thirteen.'

'Well, cross your swords,' Sir Maris sighed. Rod and the sergeant complied; Sir Maris limped forward, his own broadsword coming up to separate their blades.

The sergeant's broadsword swung up for a full-armed chop. Rod took advantage of the moment's delay to feint once at the sergeant's belly. The buckler dropped down to catch the sword-tip, and Rod's blade leaped over the sergeant's arm to rip the cloth over his heart.

'Hold!' cried Sir Maris, and the sergeant's broadsword paused in mid-chop. He dropped his buckler, staring about him. 'Wot 'appened?'

'Had this Gallowglass not fought in sport alone,' said Sir Maris, 'thou wert a dead man this day, Sergeant Hapweed.'

He scowled at Rod, puzzled. 'Who would ha' thought to use a sword's point?'

'Shall we have at it again?' Rod's blade whined through the air and slapped against his leg.

Sir Maris studied Rod's face, his brow furrowing.

'Nay,' he said, lifting his head. 'I'll warrant you're a swordsman.'

'Aye,' muttered Big Tom, and Sir Maris glanced over at him; but the big man was only beaming with pride.

The Master of the Guard turned and caught up a quarterstaff. 'Here!' He tossed it to Rod. 'We'll try you with this.'

Rod sheathed his dagger and caught the staff by the middle. He slipped his sword into its scabbard.

The big sergeant was practising quick one-two-three blows with his quarterstaff.

'Have at it!' Sir Maris called, and the big sergeant stepped forward, knees bent, quarterstaff on guard. Rod followed suit.

Then he was in the middle of an oaken rain, blows from the sergeant's staff drubbing about his head and shoulders, seeking an opening, half a second's drop of Rod's guard.

Rod set his jaw and matched the sergeant's pace, catching the blows as quick as they came—just barely. His stomach sank as he realized he was on the defensive.

He blocked a swing at his shin, caught the rebound toward his head, swung the lower end of his staff to catch the answering blow at his belly – but the blow never came. It had been a feint.

Frantically, he tried to recover to guard his head, but the sergeant had gained his half-second's opening. Rod saw the heavy oak staff swinging at him out of the corner of his eye.

He sank back, rolling with the blow. It cracked on his skull like a thunderclap. The room darkened, filled with dancing motes of light; there was a roaring in Rod's ears.

He gave ground, blocking the sergeant's blows by sheer reflex, and heard the onlooking soldiers yell with triumph.

*Won't do at all*, Rod's thoughts whirled. He'd been trained at quarterstaff; but he hadn't had a bout in a year, whereas the sergeant had all the skill of a devout hobbyist. It was just a game to him, probably, as the swordplay had been to Rod. The sergeant was in the driver's seat, and he knew it.

There was one chance. Rod leaped back, his hands slipping to the middle of the staff. It began to turn end-over-end, twirling like a baton.

Rod set his jaw and put some muscle into it. His staff leaped into a whirling, whining blur.

It was French single-stick play, *le moulinet*. The sergeant probably knew it as well as Rod; but chances were he wasn't any better practised at it than Rod was. It was rather exotic form, unless you were French. And with a name like Sergeant Hapweed . . .

Sir Maris and Co. gaped. The sergeant stepped back, startled. Then a wariness came into his face, and his staff jumped into a whirl.

So he knew the style. But he wasn't a master; in fact, Rod had the advantage. The sergeant's staff was a blur, but a quiet blur.

Rod's staff was doing a very nice imitation of a buzz saw. He had the edge on the sergeant in angular velocity, and consequent greater striking power.

Sergeant Hapweed knew it too; the muscles of his neck knotted as he tried to speed up his wing.

*Now!* Rod leaped forward. His staff snapped out of its whirl, swinging down counter to the rotation of the sergeant's.

The sticks met with the crack of a rifle and a shudder that jarred Rod's back teeth. He recovered half a second ahead of the sergeant and brought his staff crashing down on the sergeant's in two quick blows, knocking the other's staff out of his hands.

Rod straightened, drawing a deep breath and letting the tension flow out of him as he grounded the butt of his staff.

The sergeant stared at his hands, numb.

Rod reached out and tapped the man's temple gently with the tip of his staff. 'Bang! You're dead.'

'Hold!' cried Sir Maris, making things official. Rod grounded his staff again, and leaned on it.

Sir Maris scowled at Rod, eyes bright under bushy eyebrows.

Rod gave him a tight smile.

Sir Maris nodded slowly. 'Shall I try you with a longbow?'

Rod shrugged, bluffing. With a crossbow, maybe. But a longbow . . .

A deep, skirling laugh rolled from the rafters. The Master of the Guard and all his men jumped. Big Tom fell on his knees, arms flung up to protect his head.

Rod's head snapped out, eyes searching for the source of the laugh.

On one of the great oaken beams crossing the hall sat a dwarf, drumming his heels against the wood. His head was as large as Rod's, his shoulders broader, his arms and legs as thick as Rod's. He looked as though someone had taken a big, normal man and edited out three feet here and there.

He was barrel-chested, broad-shouldered, and bull-necked. The shaggy black head seemed strangely large for such a truncated body. Black, curly hair hung down to the point of the jaw and the nape of the neck; bushy black eyebrows jutted out from a flat, sloping forehead. The eyes were large and coal-black, and, at the moment, creased with mirth. They were separated by a hawk-beak nose under which thick, fleshy lips grinned through a bushy black beard, jutting forward at the chin. Square, even teeth gleamed white through the beard.

Someone had tried to cram a giant into a nail-keg, and had almost succeeded.

'Longbow!' he cried in a booming, bass voice. 'Nay, I'll wager he's as fair a shot as the county ram in springtime!'

Sir Maris glowered up at the dwarf. 'A plague on you and your stealthy ways, Brom O'Berin! Is there not enough salt in my hair already, but you must whiten it all with your pranks?'

'Stealthy ways!' cried the dwarf. 'Forsooth! Had you some pride in your calling, Sir Maris, you would thank me for showing you your own lack of vigilance!'

'Brom?' muttered Rod, staring 'O'Berin?'

The dwarf turned to Rod, glowering. 'Black Brom O'Berin, aye!'

'That's, uh, a combo of Dutch, Irish, and Russian, if I've got it right.'

'What words of nonsense are these?' growled the dwarf.

'Nothing.' Rod looked away, shaking his head. 'I should have seen it coming. I should expect something else, on this crazy – uh . . . in Gramarye?'

The dwarf grinned, mischief in his eyes. 'Nay, unless I mistake me, that hath the sound of a slur on the great land of Gramarye!'

'No, no! I didn't . . . I mean . . .' Rod paused, remembering that apologies were unbecoming for a fighting man in this culture.

He straightened, chin lifting. 'All right,' he said, 'it was an insult, if you want it that way.'

The dwarf gave a howl of glee and jumped to his feet on the rafter.

'You must fight him now, Gallowglass,' Sir Maris rumbled, 'and you shall need every bit of your skill.'

Rod stared at the Master of the Guard. Could the man be serious? A dwarf, give Rod a hard fight?

The dwarf chuckled deep in his throat and slipped off the beam. It was a twelve foot drop to the stone floor, more than three times Brom's height, but he hit the floor lightly, seeming almost to bounce, and wound up in a wrestler's crouch. He straightened and paced toward Rod, chuckling mischief.

There was a roar behind Rod, and Big Tom blundered forward. ' 'Tis a trap, master!' he bellowed. 'Witchcraft is in this land, and he is the worst witch of all! None has ever beaten Black Brom! Yet I shall—'

Every soldier in the room descended on Big Tom in a shouting chaos of anger and outrage.

Rod stood a moment in shock. Then he dropped his staff and waded into the mêlée, hands flashing out in karate punches and chops. Soldiers dropped to the floor.

'*Hold*!' thundered Brom's voice.

Silence gelled.

Brom had somehow gotten up on the rafters again.

'My thanks, lads,' the miniature Hercules growled. 'But the big fellow meant no harm; let him go.'

'No harm!' yelped half a dozen outraged voices.

Brom took a deep breath and sighed out, 'Aye, no harm. He meant only defence of his master. And this Gallowglass meant only defence of his manservant. Stand away from them now; they're both blameless.'

The soldiers reluctantly obeyed.

Rod slapped Tom on the shoulder and murmured, 'Thanks, Big Tom. And don't worry about me; that Dutch Irishman is only a man, like you and me. And if he's a man, I can beat him.'

The dwarf must have had very keen ears, for he bellowed, 'Oh, can you, now? We'll see to that, my bawcock!'

'Eh, master!' Big Tom moaned, rolling his eyes. 'You know not what you speak of. That elf is the devil's black own!'

'A warlock?' Rod snorted. 'There ain't no such beasts.'

Sir Maris stepped back among his men, ice-eyed and glowering. 'Harm a hair of his head, and we'll flay you alive!'

'No fear,' Brom O'Berin chuckled. 'No fear, Gallowglass. Try all that you may to harm me. Be assured, you shall fail. Now look to yourself.'

He jumped on the rafter, bellowed '*Now*!'

Rod dropped into a crouch, hands drawn back to chop.

Brom stood on the beam, fists on hips, great head nodding. 'Aye, hold yourself ready. But –' his eyes lit with a malicious gleam; he chuckled – 'Brom O'Berin is not a light man.' He leaped from the rafter feet-first, straight at Rod's head.

Rod stepped back, startled at the suddenness of the dwarf's attack. Reflex took over; his hand swung up, palm upward, to catch Brom's heels and flip them up.

Then, expecting the dwarf to land flat on his back on the granite floor, Rod jumped forward to catch; but Brom spun through a somersault and landed bouncing on his feet.

He slapped Rod's hands away with a quick swipe. 'A courtly gesture,' he rumbled, 'but a foolish one; your guard is down. Save gentleness for those who need it, man Gallowglass.'

Rod stepped back, on guard again, and looked at the little man with dawning respect. 'Seems I underestimated you, Master O'Berin.'

'Call me not master!' the dwarf bellowed. 'I'm no man's master; I'm naught but the Queen's fool!'

Rod nodded, slowly. 'A fool.'

He beckoned with both arms, and a savage grin. 'Well enough then, wise fool.'

Brom stood his ground a moment, measuring Rod with a scowl. He grunted, mouth snapping into a tight smile, and nodded.

He sprang, flipped in mid-air, feet heading straight for Rod's chin.

Rod swung a hand up to catch Brom's heels again, muttering, 'I'd've thought you'd learn.'

He shoved the dwarf's feet high; but this time Brom flipped his head up under Rod's chin. He had a very solid head.

Rod rolled with the punch, wrapping his arms tightly around Brom O'Berin's body in the process.

The dwarf shook with merriment. 'How now?' he chortled. 'Now that you've got me, what shall you do with me?'

Rod paused, panting.

It was a good question. If he relaxed his grip for a moment, he could be sure Brom would twist a kick into his belly. He could drop the little man, or throw him; but Brom had a tendency to bounce and would probably slam right into Rod's chin on the rebound.

Well, when in doubt, pin first and think later. Rod dropped to the floor, shoving Brom's body out at right angles to his own, catching the dwarf's knee and neck for a cradle hold.

But Brom moved just a little bit faster. His right arm snaked around Rod's left; he caught Rod's elbow in a vice-like grip and pulled.

Rod's back arched with the pain of the elbow lock. He now had a simple choice: let go with his left hand, or black out from pain.

Decisions, decisions!

Rod took a chance on his stamina; he tightened his hold on Brom's neck.

Brom grunted surprise. 'Another man would have yelped his pain and leaped away from me, man Gallowglass.'

Brom's knee doubled back; his foot shoved against Rod's chest, slid up under the chin, and kept on pushing.

Rod made a strangling noise; fire lanced the back of his neck as vertebrae ground together. The room darkened, filled with points of coloured light.

'You must let hold of me now, Gallowglass,' Brom murmured, 'ere sight fails, and you sleep.'

Did the damn half-pint *always* have to be right?

Rod tried a furious gurgle by way of reply; but the room *was* dimming at an alarmingly rapid rate, the points of light were becoming pinwheels, and a fast exit seemed indicated.

He dropped his hold, shoved against the floor with his arms, and came weaving to his feet, with a throaty chuckle filling his ears.

For Brom had kept his hold on Rod's arm and had wrapped his other hand in the throat of Rod's doublet, his weight dragging Rod back toward the floor.

Brom's feet touched the ground; he shoved, throwing Rod back.

Rod staggered, overbalanced, and fell, but habit took over again. He tucked in his chin, slapped the floor with his forearms, breaking his fall.

Brom howled with glee at seeing Rod still conscious, and leaped.

Rod caught what little breath remained to him and snapped in his feet. He caught Brom right in the stomach, grabbed a flailing arm, and shoved, letting the arm go.

Brom flipped head over heels, sailed twenty feet past Rod, and landed on the stone flags with a grunt of surprise. He landed on his feet, of course, and spun about with a bellow of laughter. 'Very neat, lad, very neat! But not enough . . .'

Rod was on his feet again, panting and shaking his head. Brom hopped toward him, then sprang.

Rod ducked low, in a vain hope that Brom might be capable of missing once; but the little man's long arm lashed out to catch Rod across the throat, stumpy body swinging around to settle between Rod's shoulders.

One foot pressed into the small of Rod's back, both arms pulled back against the base of his throat.

Rod gurgled, coming to his feet and bending backward under Brom's pull. He seized the dwarf's forearms, then bowed forward quickly, yanking Brom's arms.

Brom snapped over Rod's head and somersaulted away. He crowed as his feet hit the floor.

'Bravely done, lad! Bravely done!'

He turned about, the glint of mischief still in his eyes. 'But I grow weary of this game. Let us be done with it.'

'Tr–try,' Rod panted.

Brom hunched forward, his long arms flailing out, slapping at Rod's guard.

He grabbed for Rod's knee. Rod dropped his right hand to block Brom's attempt, then threw his left about Brom's shoulders, trying to shove him forward to lose his balance; but the dwarf's hands seemed to have got tangled in Rod's collar again.

Rod straightened, trying to throw Brom off, hands chopping at the little man's elbows; Brom's grip only tightened.

The dwarf kicked out, throwing all his weight forward. Rod stumbled, saw the floor coming up at him.

Brom leaped past him, catching Rod's foot on the way. Rod did a belly flopper on the stone floor, but he slapped out with his forearms and kept his head from hitting.

He tried to rise but someone had tied a millstone across his shoulders. A snake coiled under his left arm and pressed against the back of his neck.

Rod tried to roll to break the half-nelson, but a vice closed on his right wrist and drew it up into a hammer-lock.

'Yield, lad,' Brom's voice husked in his ear. 'Yield, for you cannot be rid of me now.'

He shoved Rod's arm higher in the hammer-lock to emphasize his point. Rod ground his teeth against the pain.

He struggled to his feet somehow, tried to shake the little man off. But Brom's feet were locked around his waist.

'Nay,' the dwarf muttered, 'I told you you'd not be rid of me.'

Rod shook himself like a terrier, but Brom held on like a bulldog. For a moment, Rod considered falling on his back to crush Brom under him. It was galling to be beaten by a man one-third your size. He discarded the idea quickly, though; there were many times in this bout where Brom could have played equally shabby tricks on Rod.

So Brom had a strong sense of fair play; and Rod was damned if he'd come off as smaller than a dwarf.

Brom's voice was a burr in his ear. 'Will you not yield, man?' And Rod gasped as his right hand tried to touch the nape of his neck.

Then Brom shoved hard on Rod's neck, forcing his chin down to touch his collarbone. Rod staggered, lurched forward, and threw out a leg to keep himself from falling. The muscles across his back and neck screamed at the torture; his right arm begged him to give in. His diaphragm folded in on itself, stubbornly refusing to pull in another breath of air. His windpipe crooked into a kink, and his lungs called for air. In a weird, detached moment he noted that night seemed to have fallen all of a sudden; and, stranger yet, the stars were tumbling . . .

Water splashed cold on his face. The mouth of a bottle thrust between his lips, feeling as large as a cartwheel. Liquid trickled over his tongue and down to his belly, where it exploded into fire.

He shook his head, and noticed that there was cold stone under his back. Now what the hell was he doing, trying to sleep on a stone floor?

Voices echoed in his head. He opened his eyes, saw a round face with great brown eyes framed in shaggy black hair and beard peering down at him.

The head swam away, and grey stone blocks reeled about him. He gasped, stared at the glint of light from a spearhead, and the room slowly steadied.

A voice thundered in his ear. 'He is a miracle, Sir Maris! He made me sweat!'

A massive arm cradled Rod's head and shoulders, lifting them from the stone. Big Tom's great round face swam into view, brows knit with concern.

'Be you well, master?'

Rod grunted something, waving a hand and nodding.

Then the shaggy head was there, too, a shaggy head with a chimpanzee's body, and a hand heavy with muscle clasped his.

'Well fought, lad,' rumbled Brom O'Berin. 'I've not had such a bout since I came to my manhood.'

Rod gripped the dwarf's hand and tried to grin.

Then Sir Maris' scarred, white-bearded face bowed over him, his old hand clasping Rod's upper arm, lifting him to his feet. 'Come, lad, stand tall! For you're a man of the Queen's army now!'

'Queen's army!' boomed Brom, somehow up on the rafters again. The room rocked with his laughter. 'Nay, Sir Maris I claim this lad! 'Tis the Queen's own bodyguard for him!'

'No, damn it, Big Tom! Get away from me with that thing!'

'But, master!' Tom chased after him, holding up the breastplate. 'You must wear *some* armour!'

'Give me one good reason why,' Rod growled.

'Why, to turn away arrows and swords, master!'

'Swords I can turn easily enough with my own. Arrows I can duck. And against crossbow quarrels, it won't do a damn bit of good anyway! No, Big Tom! All it'll do is slow me down.'

The guardroom door groaned on its hinges, boomed shut. Brom O'Berin stood watching them, fists on his hips, a silver glimmer draped over one shoulder. 'How is this, Rod Gallowglass? Will you not wear the Queen's livery?'

'I'll wear livery when you do, you motley mannikin!'

The dwarf grinned, teeth flashing white through the wilderness of beard. 'A touch, a distinct touch! But I'm not a Guardsman, Rod Gallowglass; I'm a fool, and motley is fool's livery. Come, soldier, into your colours!'

'Oh, I'll wear the Queen's colours well enough. Fact is, I'm kinda partial to purple and silver. Only thing I've got against them is that they're livery; but I'll wear 'em. But, dammit, Brom, I absolutely refuse to have anything to do with that damn sweatbox you call armour!'

The dwarf's face sobered; he nodded slowly, his eyes holding Rod's. 'Oh, aye. I had thought you to be of such persuasion.'

The silver cloth flew jingling from his shoulder, slapped against Rod's chest. Rod caught it, held it up, inspected it with a frown.

'Will you wear a mail shirt, Rod Gallowglass?'

'I'd as soon wear a hair shirt,' Rod growled; but he wriggled into the iron vest. 'Good fit,' he muttered, and gave the mail shirt a baleful eye; but his chest expanded and his shoulders came back, almost as though he were strutting.

His glance stabbed out at Brom O'Berin. 'How is this, Brom? How come you'll let me get away without a breastplate? Out of uniform, aren't I?'

'Not so,' Brom rumbled, 'for the armour is hidden under the livery. And you are the only man of the guard who would not wish plate armour.'

Rod looked at the little man out of the corner of his eye. 'How'd you know I didn't want the breastplate?'

Brom chuckled, deep in his beard. 'Why, I've fought you, Rod Gallowglass, and 'twas well you fought me, in my own manner!' His smile disappeared. 'Nay, you'd no sooner wear armour than I would.'

Rod scowled, studying the great bearded face. 'You don't quite trust me yet, do you?'

Brom smiled, a tight grimace of irony. 'Rod Gallowglass, there's no man I trust, and I regard any Queen's Guard with suspicion till he has given his life to save hers.'

Rod nodded. 'And how many is that?'

Brom's eyes burned into his. 'Seven,' he said. 'In the last year, seven Guards have I come to trust.'

Rod jerked the left side of his mouth into a hard smile.

He caught up the silver-on-purple doublet, shrugged into it. 'So if you really come to think highly of me, you may let me taste the Queen's food to see if it's poisoned.'

'Nay,' Brom growled. 'That pleasure is mine, mine to me alone.'

Rod was silent a moment, looking into the little man's eyes.

'Well,' he said, and turned away to buckle on the purple cloak. 'I notice you're still alive.'

Brom nodded. 'Though 'tis several times I've been ill – ill for fair, my lad. But I seem to have the knack of telling poison by taste; I need not wait for death's proof.'

He grinned, and strode across the floor to slap at Rod's iron-clad belly. 'But come, there's no cause to be glum! All you'll have to face is swords, and perhaps now and again a crossbow, so be of good cheer.'

'Oh, I'm just trembling with eagerness,' Rod muttered.

Brom pivoted, headed for the door. 'But now to the Queen's council chamber! Come, I'll show you your station.'

He spun, arm pointing at Big Tom. 'You there, man Tom! Back to the barracks with you; your master will call you at need.'

Tom looked to Rod for confirmation; Rod nodded.

Brom slammed the door open and strode through. Rod shook his head, smiling, and followed.

The Queen's council chamber was a large, round room, mostly filled with a great round table twenty feet in diameter. There were ponderous doors at the south, east, and west points of the compass; the north point was taken up by a yawning fireplace, crackling with a small bonfire.

The walls were hung with gaudy tapestries and rich furs. A great shield blazoned with the royal arms hung over the fireplace. The ceiling arched concave, almost a dome, crossed by great curving beams.

The table was polished walnut. Around it sat the twelve Great Lords of the Realm: the Duke de' Medici, the Earl of Romanov, the Duke of Gloucester, the Prince Borgia, the Earl Marshall,

Duke Stewart, the Duke of Bourbon, the Prince Habsburg, Earl Tudor, the Baronet of Ruddigore, the Duke of Savoy, and the great grizzled old Duke Loguire.

All were there, Rod saw, listening to a herald read their names from a scroll – all except the Queen, Catharine Plantagenet. Mulling over the list of names the élite of the Emigrés had chosen for themselves, Rod decided that they had been not only romantics, but also genuine crackpots. Plantagenet forsooth!

Next to each of the Great Lords sat a slight, wiry, wizened little man, an old man; each had an almost emaciated face, with burning blue eyes, and a few wisps of hair brushed flat over a leathery skull.

Councillors? Rod wondered. Strange that they all looked so much alike . . .

All sat in massive, ornately carved, dark-wood chairs. A larger, gilded chair stood vacant at the east point of the table.

A drum rolled, a trumpet sneezed, and the lords and councillors rose to their feet.

The great double leaves of the east door boomed wide, and Catharine stepped into the chamber.

Rod was stationed at the side of the west door; he had an excellent view, one which gave his heart pause.

A cloud of silver hair about a finely chiselled, pouting face; great blue eyes and rosebud lips; and a slender child's body, budding breasts and kitten hips under clinging silk, moulded tighter to her by the wide belt of her girdle, a Y from hips to floor.

She sat in the vacant chair, hands gripping the arm rests, back braced stiff against the gilded wood.

Brom O'Berin hopped up onto a stool at her right. Directly across from her, at the west point of the table, sat the Duke Loguire. His councillor leaned close, whispering. The Duke shushed him impatiently.

Brom O'Berin nodded to a herald.

'The Queen's Grand Council is met,' the herald cried. 'The high and great of the land of Gramarye are gathered. Let all among them who seek redress of wrongs petition now the Queen, in the presence of their peers.'

Silence filled the room.

The Duke of Bourbon stirred uneasily and coughed.

Brom's head swivelled to the man. 'My lord of Bourbon,' he rumbled, 'will you address the Queen?'

Slowly, the Duke rose. His doublet was blazoned with fleurs-de-lis, but his hair and moustache were blond.

'Your Majesty,' said the Duke, bowing gravely to the Queen, 'and my brother lords.' He nodded his head toward the table in general, then lifted his chin, straightening his shoulders. 'I must protest,' he growled.

Catharine tilted her back so that she gave the impression of looking down her nose at the tall nobleman. 'What must you protest, my lord?'

The Duke of Bourbon looked down at the walnut tabletop. 'Since our ancestors came from beyond the stars, the peasants have been subject to their lords; and the lords have been subject to the Great Lords. The Great Lords, in their turn, are subject to the King . . . the Queen,' he amended, with a slight bow to Catharine.

Her lips pressed into a tight, thin line, but she took the slight with good grace.

'This,' the Duke resumed, 'is the natural order of mankind, that each man be subject to the man above him; that justice and order be the concern of the lord; within his demesne, he is, and should be, the law, subject, of course, to the Queen.'

Again the polite nod to Catharine, and again, she accepted the slight; but her hands pinched the arms of the chair so tightly the knuckles turned white.

'Yet now your Majesty would overturn this great and lasting order, and force upon us judges of your own appointing to dispense justice within our demesnes, judges subject only to yourself. This, though it be contrary to the wisdom of your father, noble Queen, and his father before him, and all your ancestors from the beginning of your line. If I may speak plainly, I find it almost a mockery of your great and noble forebears; and, speaking for myself, I cannot abide this peasant underling of yours, who thinks to lord it over me in my own manor!'

He finished almost in a shout, glaring red-faced at the Queen.

'Are you done?' asked Catharine in a tone she'd been keeping in cold storage for just such an occasion.

Slowly, the Duke of Bourbon bowed his head. 'I am.' He sat.

Catharine closed her eyes a moment, then looked to Brom O'Berin and nodded, almost imperceptibly.

Brom stood. 'Do any speak in support of my lord of Bourbon?'

A young man with fiery red hair came to his feet. 'I agree with all that my lord of Bourbon has said. I will add, moreover, that the Queen might do well to consider the question of the corruptibility of her appointed judges; for a man without lands or means, and no family name to uphold, might easily be tempted to sell his justice.'

'If they do,' Catharine snapped, 'they shall be hanged from the highest gallows; and the men they have wronged shall serve for their executioners.'

She was silent for the space of three breaths, eyes locked with the young nobleman's; then Brom O'Berin growled, 'Our thanks to the noble Duke of Savoy.'

The young man bowed, and sat.

'Who else will speak in favor of my lords of Bourbon and Savoy?'

One by one, the other ten lords rose to second the Duke of Bourbon. The Queen's Grand Council was unanimously against her.

Catharine held her eyes closed a moment; her lips pressed tight. She looked up to sweep the table with a glare. 'My lords, I am deeply grieved to find you all so much opposed to the Queen's justice.' She gave them a brittle smile. 'I thank you for your *honest* counsel. Yet I am constant in my purpose; my judges shall remain on your estates.'

The noblemen stirred in their seats, muttering to one another in low, husky voices. They seemed to comprise one large, restless animal, growling.

The old Duke of Loguire rose slowly, and leaned heavily on the table. 'My Queen,' he rumbled, 'consider: even kings may fault in judgement, and you are young in statecraft yet. It is known that many minds together may come to clearer knowledge than one mind alone; and here are gathered with you twelve men of most ancient and honourable lineage, of families grown hoary in statecraft; old men of old families; and, it is to be hoped, wise with the weight of their years. Will you persist in your course, when so many are so sure that you are wrong?'

Catharine's face was pale, almost dead white. Her eyes were burning. 'I will,' she said quietly.

The Lord Loguire held her eyes for a long moment, then slowly sat.

Catharine surveyed the faces around her, taking time to look deep into each pair of eyes.

Then, lifting her chin, she said, 'My judges will remain on your estates, my lords. As to their corruptibility, you will find them almost saintly in their disregard for money, wine, and . . . comforts. They care for one thing only, and that is justice.'

She paused to let her words sink in; and Rod noted that there were several beet-red faces among the Great Lords. At a rough guess, he decided, justice had not been quite as pure as it might have been on some of their estates.

The Duke Loguire did not have a red face. The only emotion Rod could read in him was grief.

'This whole matter of the judges is, however, secondary to the purpose for which I have called you here today.' Catharine smiled, with more than a hint of malice.

Heads jerked up in alarm, all around the board. Brom O'Berin looked more shocked than any. Apparently Catharine had not consulted with her Prime Councillor; even Brom was due for a surprise.

Each lord bent his head for a quick, whispered conference with his councillor; and the looks of alarm on their faces deepened into sullen anger.

'On each of your estates,' said Catharine, 'there is a monastery. You have been accustomed to appointing the priests for the parishes of your demesnes from your own monasteries.'

She looked down at the tabletop for a moment, then lifted her head again. 'Here in this castle I am gathering the best theologians of all the monasteries. You shall choose young brothers from your monks, one for each of your parishes, and send them here to me, to be trained by my monks. If in any case I do not approve of your choice in young men, I shall send them back to you, and demand others in their places. When they have finished their studies and taken their Orders, I shall return them to you, to be your parish priests.'

The lords slammed to their feet, shouting and gesturing, fists thudding on the table.

Catharine's voice crackled into the uproar. 'Enough! Be still!'

Slowly, one by one, the Great Lords fell into sullen silence and sank back into their seats, glaring.

But their councillors' faces seemed lit with a suppressed joy; their eyes were burning, and each face held a smile just short of a grin.

'I have spoken,' Catharine said, voice and eyes both chill. 'It shall be done.'

Trembling, the old Lord Loguire rose. 'Will your Majesty not—'

'I will not.'

Brom O'Berin cleared his throat. 'If your Majesty will permit—'

'I will not.'

Silence sat over the council chamber. Once again, Catharine surveyed the faces of her lords and their councillors.

Then, turning to her left, she bowed her head. 'My Lord Loguire.'

The old nobleman rose, his jaw clamped tight under the grizzled beard, his liver-spotted fist palsied with barely-held anger.

He drew back the great, gilded chair, and Catharine rose. He stepped back to his place. Catharine turned away, and the great oak doors were thrown wide. Guardsmen fell in before and behind her.

She paused in the doorway, and turned. 'Consider, my lords,' she said, 'and consent; for you cannot stand against me.'

The great doors slammed behind her.

The council chamber burst into pandemonium.

'Oh, come off it! It's the classic pattern, right down to the last look of outrage!'

His day's duty done, Rod was riding Fess back to the inn, bent on picking up a little gossip and a lot of beer. Big Tom was tending the home fires at the Royal Castle, with orders to keep his ears open for juicy titbits of information.

'I disagree, Rod. It's the classic pattern with something added.'

'Bull! It's a simple, premature attempt at centralization of authority. She's trying to unify Gramarye under one law and one ruler, instead of twelve near-independent dukedoms. This business with the judges is that, and nothing more. Five'll get you ten some of those dukes have been playing god on their estates, forcing half the women to sleep with them and overtaxing everybody and anything else that occurred to them. Catharine's a reformer, that's all; she's trying to cure all the evils she can find by making herself the only law in Gramarye – and she won't make it. The noblemen just won't stand for it. She might have got away with the judges; but this business with the priests'll bring on a rebellion for sure. Priests have more influence over the people than any other officials in this kind of society. If she makes them responsible to her, and only her, she's really pulling the noblemen's teeth, and they know it. And they won't give up without a fight.'

'So far I'll agree with you,' the robot said. 'So far, it is the classic pattern, closely resembling the attempt of the English King John to centralize his nation before such a project could succeed.'

'Yes.' Rod nodded. 'And we can hope that, like King John's noblemen, the great dukes will insist on a Magna Carta.'

'But . . .'

Rod assumed a look of martyr-like patience. 'But what, Fess?'

'But there is a foreign element: a group of councillors to the Great Lords, a group that seems to be very cohesive.'

Rod frowned. 'Well, yes. There is that.'

'And from what you tell me of the scene after Catharine left . . .'

'Yii!' Rod shuddered. 'It was just as though she'd thrown down a gauntlet, and all the dukes were out to see who'd get the honour of taking it up. The girl might know some elementary political science, but she sure doesn't know any diplomacy! She was just daring them to fight her!'

'Yes, and the councillors were egging them on very nicely – each one counselling his lord not to fight, because he was too weak . . . and then telling them that if he must fight, he'd better ally with the other lords, because each was too weak to stand alone. Expert use of reverse psychology. One would almost think the councillors were out to eliminate central authority completely.'

'Yes . . .' Rod frowned, musing. 'That's not quite normal to this kind of society, is it, Fess?'

'No, Rod. The theory of anarchy does not usually arise until the culture has attained a much higher degree of technology.'

Rod chewed at his lip. 'Outside influence, maybe?'

'Perhaps. And that brings us to the popular totalitarian movement: another anomaly. No, Rod, this is not the classic pattern.'

'No, dammit. We've got three groups contending for power: the peasants, the dukes and their councillors, and the Queen and whoever supports her. That support seems to be limited to Brom O'Berin at the moment.'

'Totalitarians, anarchists, and the Queen in the middle,' Fess murmured. 'Which one do *you* support, Rod?'

'Catharine, damn it!' Rod grinned. 'I'm out to plant the seeds of democracy; and it looks like the only chance to do that is to engineer a constitutional monarchy.'

'I might be mistaken,' Fess murmured, 'but I do believe you're delighted to find you must support her.'

Around them the few lights were dimmed by the night mist, a wall of fog thirty feet away. Rod rode alone through a world of smoke; Fess's hooves rang strangely weird in the echoing silence.

A long yell split the night, followed by the slapping clash of swords. 'A rescue, a rescue!' a young voice cried.

Rod froze, hand on the pommel of his sword; then he dug his heels into Fess's metal sides, and the great black horse sprang toward the ruckus.

A torch smouldered red through the fog at the mouth of an alley. There, under its smoky light, one man battled three, his back against the wall.

Rod bellowed and landed horse and all in the middle of the mêlée. He laid about him with the flat of his sword, howling like an Indian studying to be a Confederate soldier. He yanked the dagger from the small of his back, just in time to catch a rapier coming at him from his left. His own sword swung in an arc over his head and clashed against steel as his opponent caught the blow.

Then steel points were jabbing up at him like sawgrass. Rod was forced back on the defensive, swatting the blades aside.

But the intended victim let loose a yell that would have shamed a banshee and waded in from the rear.

All at once the three swords fell away, their owners pelting down the alley. Rod sat a moment dazed; then he yelled, and Fess sprang after the retreating figures.

But they gained the dark at the end of the alley; and when Rod caught up, the stones were empty. It was a dead end; they had gone through one of the shadowed, evil-smelling doorways.

Their would-be victim came running up behind, looked about, and panted.

'Gone, and no use to seek them further. They'll be five leagues away in as many minutes.'

Rod swore and slapped his sword back into its scabbard. He winced, and touched his forearm gingerly; one of the rapier-points had slashed through his doublet and sliced his skin.

He turned to the stranger. 'You all right?'

The young man nodded, sheathing his sword.

Rod looked down into an open, snub-nosed, blue-eyed face with a grin that flashed white through the fog. The cheekbones were high, and the eyes large and wide, with a look of innocence. Blond hair was cropped round in a bowl cut. It was a young, inexperienced, very handsome face – Rod felt a surge of resentment.

He swung down from his horse. The top of the youth's head was about on a level with Rod's eyes; but what the boy lacked in height, he made up in bulk. A barrel chest swelled into bull shoulders, a good six inches wider than Rod's. The arms would have looked more appropriate on a bear or gorilla; and the legs were two small tree trunks, rammed into narrow hips.

He wore a leather jerkin over a white shirt, a wide black belt, hose, and high, soft boots.

He frowned, seeing the blood on Rod's sleeve. 'You're hurt.'

Rod snorted. 'A scratch,' he said, and fumbled in Fess's saddlebag for an antiseptic bandage. He wound the bandage around his forearm, threw the youth a hard grin. 'You can pay the tailor's bill, though.'

The boy nodded, blue eyes sober. 'That will I gladly; for they would have cut my heart out, had it not been for your timely rescue. Tuan McReady stands in your debt.'

Rod looked him up and down, nodding slowly. A good kid, he thought.

He held out his hand. 'Rod Gallowglass, at your service; and there's no debt involved. Always glad to help one against three.'

'Ah, but debt there is!' said the boy, clasping Rod's hand with a grip like a sentimental vice. 'You must, at the least, let me buy you a tankard of ale!'

Rod shrugged. 'Why not? I was on my way to an inn just now, anyway; come on along!'

To his surprise, Tuan hesitated. 'By your leave, good Master Gallowglass . . . there is only one house in this town where I am welcomed. All others have known my custom of old, and –' the round face suddenly broke into a grin '– my manner of living does not please the peaceful and proper.'

Rod grimaced, nodding. '*Post jocundum juventutem*. Well, one inn's as good as another, I guess.'

The route to Tuan's inn was somewhat out of keeping with his well-bred looks. They dogged down two dark alleys, wriggled through a weathered brick wall, and came out in a wide, moonlit courtyard that had been elegant in its day. That day must have been a century or two in the past. The remains of a fountain burbled in the centre of cracked flagstones, sending up a stench redolent of primitive plumbing. Weeds, themselves in a state of dire poverty, poked through the paving everywhere. The brick of the walls was cracked and split, the mortar crumbling. Heaps of garbage lay by the walls and in the corners, with stray mounds of refuse here and there about the yard.

The inn itself was a rotting granite block with tumbledown eaves. The overhanging second storey was propped up with rough-hewn timbers, not to be trusted due to the infirmities of age. The windows were boarded over, the boards split, mouldy, and fungoid. The massive oak door was the only sound piece of wood in sight, and even it was sagging.

'Ah, they tolerate your behaviour here?' Rod asked, surveying the stagnant courtyard as Tuan knocked on the door with the hilt of his dagger.

'Tolerate, yes,' said Tuan, 'though even their hospitality is sometimes strained.'

Rod felt a chill between his shoulder blades and wondered just what kind of mild-mannered youth he'd run into.

Tuan knocked again. Rod wondered that he expected an answer; not a gleam of light showed through the sagging window boards. By the look of it, the place must be totally deserted.

But the door began to move, and groaned that it was going on strike for an oil break, till it was open just wide enough to admit the two men.

'Your host,' said Tuan cheerily, 'the Mocker.'

A gnarled, hunched, desiccated travesty of a human being peered around the door, making gobbling sounds in its throat. One ear was cauliflower, and the other was gone; a few strands of greasy hair straggled over a scabby skull. The nose was bulbous, the smouth a slash in a mass of warts, the eye malevolent, gleaming slits. It was dressed in a collection of tatters and patches that might once have laid claim to being a doublet and hose, sagging badly on the scarecrow figure.

The troll scurried away into the foul-smelling dark of its lair. Tuan strode through the door, following. Rod took a deep breath, squared his shoulders, and looked back over his shoulder to make sure Fess was still standing there, by the fountain, head lowered in a good imitation of a horse grazing. For a moment, Rod envied the robot his ability to cut off his olfactory receptors.

Then, lifting his chin, he followed Tuan into the inn.

The door ground shut behind him; there was a scurrying sound as the Mocker ran ahead to open another door.

This one opened easily, slammed back against the wall, flooding them with a blaze of torchlight and gales of coarse, bawdy laughter. Rod stared.

They stepped through the door, and Rod looked about him. It was a great common room, with four roaring open fires and score upon score of torches bracketed along the walls. Roasting meat hung over the fires; waiters wove their way through the crowd with tankards of ale and wine from two huge, flowing kegs that dominated the far side of the room.

The clientele were the lees of the city. Their clothes were crusted, patched castoffs. Their bodies bore the marks of primitive justice: this one was missing an ear, that one an eye. Their faces were disfigured and scarred by disease. Yet here in their own den they roared merrily; all of them grinned, though malice glinted in their eyes as they looked at Rod.

But the malice faded, was transmuted into something almost like worship, as they looked at young Tuan.

'It is said,' and the boy smiled, 'that there is no honour among thieves; but there is at least kinship here, among the beggars of Gramarye. Welcome, Rod Gallowglass, to the House of Clovis.'

The hair at the base of Rod's skull prickled. He remembered the torchlight mob he had seen on the waterfront the night before.

His eyes widened; he stared at Tuan. He couldn't be. He couldn't be.

Oh, but he could. Yes, he could.

Tuan McReady was the young rabble-rouser who'd been haranguing the mob to march on the castle.

This apple-cheeked, wholesome youth was top rat in the local sewer.

The crowd broke into a raucous, cheering clamour welcoming their Galahad. Tuan grinned and waved. A slight flush crept up from his collar. He seemed almost embarrassed by the reception.

He led Rod to a dark corner at the back of the hall. He hadn't said a word to the Mocker, but two steaming mugs of mulled wine thumped down on the table almost as they sat. The landlord scuttled away without pay.

Rod watched him go, one eyebrow lifted in cynicism. He turned to Tuan. 'You don't use money here?'

'None.' Tuan smiled. 'All who come to the House of Clovis bring what little money they have. It is put into a common chest, and meat and wine given out to all according to their needs.'

'And a place to sleep, I suppose?'

'Aye, and clothing. It is poor fare by a gentleman's standards; but it is great wealth to these my poor brethren.'

Rod studied Tuan's face and decided the boy might have meant it when he said brethren.

He sat back and crossed his legs. 'Would you call yourself a religious man?'

'I?' Tuan tried to choke back a laugh and almost succeeded.

'Oh, nay! Would that I were; but I have not seen the inside of a church for three score and more Sundays!'

So, Rod noted, his motive for helping the poor probably wasn't too hypocritical, whatever else it might be.

He looked into his mug. 'So you feed and clothe all these people out of the pennies they bring you, eh?'

'Nay, that is but a beginning. But with that much earnest proof of our good intentions, our noble Queen found us worthy of a livelihood.'

Rod stared. 'You mean the Queen is putting the lot of you on the dole?'

Tuan grinned with mischief. 'Aye, though she knows not whom she aids. She knows not the House of Clovis by name, knows only that she gives the good Brom O'Berin moneys to care for her poor.'

'And Brom gives it to you.'

'Aye. And for his part, he is grateful that there are fewer thievings and murders among the dark alleys.'

Rod nodded. 'Very shrewd. And this whole setup is your idea, is it?'

'Oh, nay! 'Twas the Mocker who thought of it; but none would give ear to him.'

Rod stared. 'The Mocker? You mean that twisted fugitive from the late show is boss of this operation?' Tuan frowned, shaking his head. 'Men will not follow him, friend Gallowglass; there is nothing of governance in him. He is host, keeping the inn, doling out goods as they are needed – a steward, and only a steward, but a good one. You will find him a sharper clerk than any; aye, even the Queen's Lord Exchequer.'

'I see, just a steward.' *But also the man who holds the pocketbook*, Rod added mentally. *The brains of the outfit, too. Tuan might know how to make people do what he wanted; but did he know what he wanted?*

*Yes, of course he did. Hadn't the Mocker told him? Which made the Mocker the local political economist, and probably Tuan's speechwriter.*

Rod leaned back, rubbing his chin. 'And you manage to keep them in this decadent luxury with only the alms the beggars bring in? Plus the Queen's shilling, of course.'

Tuan grinned sheepishly and leaned forward, nodding. ''Tis not easy done, friend Gallowglass. These beggars are loath to let any man rule them. It is tedious labour, cajoling, threatening, flattering — a man grows a-weary of it. Yet it is well worth the doing.'

Rod nodded. 'It would take a man with no false pride, and less false humility, and one who could see into his fellow's heart.'

Tuan blushed.

'Such a man,' said Rod, 'could make himself king of the beggars.'

But Tuan shook his head, eyes closed. 'No, there is no king here, friend Gallowglass. A lord of the manor, perhaps, but naught more.'

'You don't want to be king?'

Tuan's shoulders shrugged with a snort of laughter. 'The beggars would not hear of it!'

'That wasn't what I asked.'

Tuan's eyes locked with Rod's, the smile fading from the boyish face. Then Tuan caught Rod's meaning, and his eyes hardened. 'Nay!' he spat. 'I do not seek the throne.'

'Then why are you trying to lead the beggars against the Queen?' Rod rapped out.

The smile eased across Tuan's face again; he sat back, looking very satisfied with himself. 'Ah, you know of my plotting! Then may I ask of you outright, friend Rod, will you join with us when we march on the castle?'

Rod felt his face setting like plaster. His eyes locked with Tuan's again; his voice was very calm. 'Why me?'

'We shall have need of as many friends in the Queen's Guard as we may have . . .'

'You must already have quite a few,' Rod murmured, 'if you know already that I joined the Queen's Guard today.'

Tuan's grin widened; his eyelids drooped.

A stray fact clicked into place in Rod's mind.

'If I were to search through this hall,' he said carefully, 'would I find the three men who attacked you tonight?'

Tuan nodded, eyes dancing.

'A put-up job,' Rod said, nodding with him. 'A small performance, arranged solely for my benefit, with the single purpose of manoeuvring me in here for a recruiting lecture. You *do* know how to manage people, Tuan McReady.'

Tuan blushed, and looked down.

'But what if I don't want to join you, Tuan McReady? Will I leave the House of Clovis alive this night?'

Tuan's head came up, eyes boring into Rod's.

'Only,' he said, 'if you are an excellent swordsman, and a warlock to boot.'

Rod nodded slowly, the events of the past two days whirling through his mind. For a moment, he was tempted to join; he had no doubt that he could manoeuvre himself into the throne after the revolution.

But no; what Tuan said was true. It took a man with an inborn gift of mass hypnotism to control the beggars. Rod might take the throne, but the beggars – and the Mocker, and whoever was behind him – would not let him keep it.

No, the power structure had to stay the way it was; a constitutional monarchy was the only hope for democracy on this planet.

Then, too, there was Catharine. . . .

Then the jarring note in the score of events caught Rod's ear. He was hung up on Catharine, probably; she was the Dream.

But he had liked Tuan at first sight. How could he like them both if they were really working against one another?

Of course, all Tuan's forthright charm might be an act, but somehow Rod doubted it.

No. If Tuan had really wanted the throne, he could have wooed Catharine, and could have won her – Rod had no doubt about that.

So Tuan was supporting the Queen. How he figured his demagoguery could help her, Rod couldn't figure, but somehow it made sense that Tuan believed he was.

Then why the elaborate plot to get Rod into the House of Clovis?

To test Rod, of course; to find out if he was to be trusted next to the Queen.

Which made sense, if this kid had dealings with Brom O'Berin. It would be just like Brom to try to drum up popular support for the Queen in just this way – but why the propaganda for a march on the castle?

Tuan probably had an answer to that one, and speaking of answers, it was about time Rod came up with one.

He gave Tuan a savage grin and rose, with his hand on his sword. 'No thanks. I'll take my chances with swordcraft and sorcery.'

Tuan's eyes lit with joy; he caught Rod's arm. 'Well spoken, friend Gallowglass! I had hoped you would answer thus. Now sit, and hear the truth of my plot.'

Rod shook his hand off. 'Draw,' he said between his teeth.

'Nay, nay! I would not draw 'gainst a friend. I have played a low trick on you, but you must not hold anger; 'twas for a good purpose. But sit, and I shall tell you.'

'I've heard all I want.' Rod started to draw his sword.

Tuan caught Rod's forearm again, and this time his hand wouldn't shake off. Rod looked into Tuan's eyes, jaw tightened and arm muscles straining; but slowly and steadily, his sword was forced back into its scabbard.

'Sit,' said Tuan, and he forced Rod back into his chair as easily as though Rod had been a child.

'Now hear my plot.' Tuan let go of Rod's arm and smiled, as warmly as though nothing had happened. 'The Queen gives us money, and the beggars know that she gives it; but the taking of a gift raises only burning anger in the taker. If we would win friends for the Queen, we must find a way to transmute this anger to gratitude.'

Rod nodded, frowning.

'Thus we must make the Queen's shilling something other than a gift.'

'And you found a way to do it.'

'Not I,' Tuan confessed, 'but the Mocker. "When is a gift not a gift?" he riddled me, and answered, "Why, when 'tis a right."'

Tuan leaned back, spreading his hands. 'And there you have it, so easily done. The beggars shall march to the castle and cry to the Queen that she owes them bread and meat, because it is their right. And she will give it to them, and they will be grateful.'

Rod smiled, rubbing his chin. 'Very shrewd,' he said, nodding, but to himself he added: *If it works. But it won't; people who have money enjoy giving for charity, but they won't give a cent if you tell them they must. And how grateful will the beggars be when she refuses them, and calls out the army to drive them away?*

*And even if she did yield to their demands, what then? What about the sense of power it would give them? Beggars, forcing a Queen's hand! They wouldn't stop at bread and meat; no, they'd be back with more demands in a week, with or without Tuan.*

*Oh, yes, it was a very shrewd plan; and Tuan had been sucked into it beautifully. The Mocker couldn't lose; and neither could the off-planet totalitarians who were behind him.*

But Tuan meant well. His intentions fairly gleamed. He was a little weak on political theory; but his intentions were fine.

Rod raised his mug for a deep draught, then stared into it, watching the swirl of the heated wine. 'Yet some say that the House of Clovis would pull Catharine off her throne.'

'Nay, nay!' Tuan stared, appalled. 'I love the Queen!'

Rod studied the boy's sincere, open face and made his own interpretation of the statement.

He looked back into his mug. 'So do I,' he said, with more truth than he liked. 'But even so, I'd have to admit she's, shall we say, not acting wisely.'

Tuan heaved a great sigh and clasped his hands. 'That is true, most true. She means so well, but she does so badly.'

*Have you looked in a mirror lately, Mr Kettle?* Rod wondered. Aloud, he said, 'Why, how is that?'

Tuan smiled sadly. 'She seeks to undo in a day what ages of her grandsires have wrought. There is much evil in this kingdom, that I will gladly admit. But a pile of manure is not moved with one swing of a shovel.'

'True,' Rod admitted, 'and the saltpetre under it can be explosive.'

'The Great Lords do not see that she is casting out devils,' Tuan went on. 'They see only that she seeks to fill this land with one voice, and only one – and that hers.'

'Well'—Rod lifted his mug, face bleak with resignation—'here's to her; let's hope she makes it.'

'An' you think it possible,' said Tuan, 'tha'rt a greater fool than I; and I am known far and wide as a most exceptional fool.'

Rod lowered the mug untasted. 'Are you speaking from a general conviction, or do you have some particulars in mind?'

Tuan set one forefinger against the other. 'A throne rests on two legs: *primus*, the noblemen, who are affronted by anything new, and therefore oppose the Queen.'

'Thanks,' said Rod with a bittersweet smile, 'for letting me in on the secret.'

'Left to themselves,' said Tuan, 'the nobles might abide her for love of her father; but there are the councillors.'

'Yes.' Rod caught his lower lip between his teeth. 'I take it the lords do whatever their councillors tell them?'

'Or what they tell the lords *not* to do, which comes to the same thing. And the councillors speak with one voice – Durer's.'

'Durer?' Rod scowled. 'Who's he?'

'Councillor to my Lord Loguire.' Tuan's mouth twisted, bitter. 'He hath some influence with Loguire, which is a miracle; for

Loguire is a most stubborn man. Thus, while Loguire lives, Catharine may stand. But when Loguire dies, Catharine falls; for Loguire's heir hates the Queen.'

'Heir?' Rod raised an eyebrow. 'Loguire has a son?'

'Two,' said Tuan with a tight smile. 'The younger is a fool, who loves his best enemy; and the elder is a hothead, who loves Durer's flattery. Thus, what Durer will say, Anselm Loguire will do.'

Rod raised his mug. 'Let us wish the Loguire long life.'

'Aye,' said Tuan, fervently. 'For Anselm hath an ancient grievance against the Queen.'

Rod frowned. 'What grievance?'

'I know not.' Tuan's face sagged till he looked like a bloodhound with sinus trouble. 'I know not.'

Rod sat back, resting one hand on the hilt of his sword. 'So he and Durer both want the Queen's downfall. And the other nobles'll follow their lead – if old Loguire dies. So much for one leg of the throne. What's the other one?'

'*Secundus*,' said Tuan, with a Cub Scout salute, 'the people: peasants, tradesmen, and merchants. They love her for this newfound easing of their sorrows; but they fear her for her witches.'

'Ah. Yes. Her . . . witches.' Rod scowled, managing to look sharp-eyed and competent while his brain reeled. *Witches as a political element*?!

'For ages,' said Tuan, 'the witches have been put to the torture till they forswore the Devil, or have undergone the trial of water or, failing all else, been burned at the stake.'

For a moment, Rod felt a stab of compassion for generations of espers.

'But the Queen harbours them now; and it is rumoured by some that she is herself a witch.'

Rod managed to shake off his mental fog long enough to croak, 'I take it this doesn't exactly inspire the people with unflagging zeal for the Queen and her cause.'

Tuan bit his lip. 'Let us say that they are unsure . . .'

'Scared as hell,' Rod translated. 'But I notice you didn't include the beggars as part of the people.'

Tuan shook his head. 'Nay, they are apart, frowned and spat upon by all. Yet of this flawed timber, I hope to carve a third leg for the Queen's throne.'

Rod digested the words, studying Tuan's face.

He sat back in his chair, lifted his mug. 'You just may have what the Queen needs, there.' He drank. Lowering the mug, he said, 'I suppose the councillors are doing everything they can to deepen the people's fear?'

Tuan shook his head, brow wrinkled in puzzlement. 'Nay, they do nothing of the sort. Almost, one would think, they do not know the people live.' He frowned into his mug, sloshing the wine about inside. 'Yet there is little need to tell the people they must fear.'

'They know it all too well already?'

'Aye, for they have seen that all the Queen's witches cannot keep the banshee off her roof.'

Rod frowned, puzzled. 'So let it wear a groove in the battlements if it wants to! It's not doing any harm, is it?'

Tuan looked up, surprised. 'Dost not know the meaning of the banshee, Rod Gallowglass?'

Rod's stomach sank; nothing like displaying your ignorance of local legends when you're trying to be inconspicuous.

'When the banshee appears on the roof,' said Tuan, 'someone in the house will die. And each time the banshee has walked the battlements, Catharine hath escaped death by a hair.'

'Oh?' Rod's eyebrows lifted. 'Dagger? Falling tiles? Poison?'
'Poison.'

Rod sat back, rubbing his chin. 'Poison: the aristocrat's weapon; the poor can't afford it. Who among the Great Lords hates Catharine that much?'

'Why, none!' Tuan stared, appalled. 'Not one among them would stoop to poison, Rod Gallowglass; 'twould be devoid of honour.'

'Honour still counts for something here, eh?' Seeing the scandalized look on Tuan's face, Rod hurried on. 'That lets out the noblemen; but someone on their side's up to tricks. Wouldn't be the councillors, would it?'

Understanding and wary anger rose in Tuan's eyes. He sat back, nodding.

'But what do they gain by her death?' Rod frowned. 'Unless one of them wants to crown his lordling and be the King's Councillor. . . .'

Tuan nodded. 'Mayhap all wish that, friend Gallowglass.'

Rod had a sudden vision of Gramarye carved up into twelve petty kingdoms, constantly warring against one another, each run by a warlord who was ruled by his councillor. Japanese usurpation, the man behind the throne, and anarchy.

Anarchy.

There was an outside force at work in Gramarye, agents with a higher technology and sophisticated political philosophies at work. The great nobles were slowly being divided, and the people were being set against the nobility, by means of the House of Clovis. The twelve petty kingdoms would be broken down to warring counties, and the counties to parishes, and so on until real anarchy prevailed.

The councillors were the outside force, carefully engineering a state of anarchy. But why?

*Why* could wait for later. What mattered now was that skulduggery was afoot, and it sat next to the Lord Loguire; its name was Durer.

And his top-priority goal was Catharine's death.

The castle loomed up black against the sky as Rod rode back, but the drawbridge and portcullis were a blaze of torchlight. Fess's hooves thudded hollow on the drawbridge. A blob of shadow detached itself from the larger shadow of the gate, a shadow that reached up to clamp a hand on Rod's shin.

'Hold, Rod Gallowglass!'

Rod looked down and smiled, nodding. 'Well met, Brom O'Berin.'

'Mayhap,' said the dwarf, searching Rod's face. 'Thou must come before the Queen for this night's work, Rod Gallowglass.'

Rod was still wondering how Brom could have known where he'd been as they came to the Queen's audience chamber. Brom had a spy in the House of Clovis, of course; but how could the word have got back to him so fast?

The door was massive, oak, iron-studded, and draped with velvet, the green and gold of the Queen's house. Brom ran a practised eye over the two sentries, checking to see that all leather was polished and all metal gleaming. Rod gave them a nod; their faces turned to wood. Was he under suspicion of high treason?

At Brom's nod, one Guardsman struck the door backhanded, three slow heavy knocks, then threw it wide. Rod followed Brom into the room. The door boomed shut behind them.

The room was small but high-ceilinged, panelled in dark wood, lit only by four great candles that stood on a velvet-draped table in the centre of the room, and by a small fire on the tiled hearth. A rich carpet covered the stone floor; tapestries hung on the walls. A huge bookcase filled the wall at the far end of the room.

Two heavy carved armchairs stood at either side of the fireplace; two more were drawn up at the table. Catharine sat in one of these, head bent over a large old leather-bound book. Five or six more lay open on the table about her. Her blonde hair fell unbound about her shoulders, contrasting with the dark russet of her gown.

She lifted her head; her eyes met Rod's. 'Welcome.' Her voice was a gentle, slightly husky contralto, so different from the crisp soprano of the council chamber that Rod wondered, for a moment, if it could be the same woman.

But the eyes were wary, arrogant. It was Catharine, all right.

But the heavy crown lay on the table beside her, and she seemed smaller, somehow.

'Hast been to the House of Clovis?' she demanded. Her eyes read like a subpoena.

Rod showed his teeth in a mock-grin and inclined his head in a nod.

' 'Tis even as you said, my Queen.' Brom's voice had a grim overtone. 'Though how you knew—'

'—is not your affair, Brom O'Berin.' She threw the dwarf a glare; Brom smiled gently, bowed his head.

'How?' Rod snorted. 'Why, spies of course. A very excellent spy service, to get the word back to her so fast.'

'Nay.' Brom frowned, puzzled. 'Our spies are few enough, for loyalty is rare in this dark age; and we keep no spies at all at the House of Clovis.'

'No spies,' Catharine agreed, 'and yet I know that thou hast had words with Tuan of the beggars this day.'

Her voice softened; her eyes were almost gentle as she looked at the dwarf. 'Brom . . . ?'

The dwarf smiled, bowed his head, and turned to the door. He struck the wood with the heel of his hand. The door swung open; Brom turned with one foot on the threshold, and a malevolent glare stabbed at Rod from under the bushy eyebrows; then the door slammed behind him.

Catharine rose, glided to the fireplace. She stood staring at the flames, hands clasped at her waist. Her shoulders sagged; and for a moment, she looked so small and forlorn – and so beautiful, with the firelight streaming up like a mist about her face and shoulders – that Rod's throat tightened in an old, familiar way.

Then her shoulders straightened, and her head snapped around toward him. 'You are not what you seem, Rod Gallowglass.'

Rod stared.

Catharine's hand strayed to her neck, playing with a locket at her throat.

Rod cleared his throat, a trifle nervously. 'Here I am, just a simple blank-shield soldier, just carrying out my orders and taking my pay, and three times in thirty hours I get accused of being something mysterious.'

'Then I must needs think that it is true.' Catharine's mouth twisted in a mocking smile.

She sat in one of the great oaken chairs, grasping the arms tightly, and studied Rod for a few moments.

'What are you, Rod Gallowglass?'

Rod spread his arms in a shrug, trying to look the picture of offended innocence. 'A blank shield, my Queen! A soldier of fortune, no more!'

'"No more",' Catharine mimicked, malice in her eyes. 'What is your profession, Rod Gallowglass?'

Rod scowled, beginning to feel like the rodent half of a game of cat-and-mouse. 'A soldier, my Queen.'

'This is your avocation,' she said, 'your pleasure and your game. Tell me now your profession.'

The woman was A) uncanny; and B) a bitch, Rod decided. Trouble was, she was a beautiful bitch, and Rod had a weakness.

His brain raced; he discarded several lies and chose the most obvious and least plausible.

'My profession is the preserving of your Majesty's life.'

'Indeed!' Catharine mocked him with her eyes. 'And who hath trained you to that profession? Who is so loyal to me that he would send you?'

Suddenly, Rod saw through the mocking and the belligerence. It was all a mask, a shield; behind it lay a very frightened, very lonely little girl, one who wanted someone to trust, craved someone to trust. But there had been too many betrayals; she couldn't let herself trust any more.

He looked into her eyes, giving her his gentlest, most sincere gaze, and said in his best couch-side manner, 'I call no man master, my Queen. It is myself who has sent me, out of love for Catharine the Queen and loyalty to the nation of Gramarye.'

Something desperate flickered in her eyes; her hands clutched at the chair arms. 'Love,' she murmured.

Then the mockery was back in her eyes. 'Yes, love – for Catharine *the Queen*.'

She looked away, into the fire. 'Be that as it may. But I think you are in most comely truth a friend – though why I believe that, I cannot say.'

'Oh, you may be sure that I am!' Rod smiled. 'You knew that I was at the House of Clovis, though you couldn't say how, and you were right about that.'

'Be still!' she snapped. Then slowly her eyes lifted to his. 'And what affairs took you to the House of Clovis this night?'

Was she a mind reader, maybe?

Rod scratched along his jaw; the bone-conduction microphone would pick up the sound . . .

'There's some confusion *Fess*tering in my mind,' he said. 'How did you know I was at the House of Clovis?'

'Here, Rod,' a voice murmured behind his ear.

Catharine gave him a look that fairly dripped with contempt. 'Why, I knew you spoke with Tuan Loguire. Then where could you be but the House of Clovis?'

Very neat – only how had she known he was with Tuan . . . Loguire?

Loguire!

Rod stared. 'Excuse me, but – uh – did you say Tuan *Loguire*?'

Catharine frowned.

'I thought his name was, uh – McReady.'

Catharine almost laughed. 'Oh, nay! He is the second son of Milord Loguire! Did you not know?'

Second son! Then Tuan was himself the man he had been condemning for a fool!

And his big brother was the man who had 'an ancient grievance 'gainst the Queen', and was a major threat to the throne.

'No,' said Rod, 'I did not know.'

Fess' voice murmured, 'Data indicate existence of excellent intelligence system.'

Rod groaned mentally. Robots were a great help!

He pursed his lips, staring at Catharine. 'You say you have no spies in the House of Clovis,' he said, 'and if I assume that you speak the truth, then that means . . .'

He left the sentence hanging; Fess would fill in the blank.

There was a moment of silence; then a loud hum behind Rod's ear ended in a sharp click.

Rod cursed mentally. If Catharine had no spies, she logically couldn't have known what she did know. He'd given Fess another paradox, and the robot's circuits had overloaded. Epileptic robots could be very inconvenient.

Catharine glared at him. 'Of a certainty, I speak truth!'

'Oh, I never doubted!' Rod held up a hand. 'But you *are* a ruler, and you were reared to it; one of the first lessons you must have learned was lying with a straight face.'

Catharine's face froze; then, slowly, she bent her head, looking down at her hands. When she looked up, her face was drawn; the mask had been stripped away, and her eyes were haunted. 'Once again, my knowledge was true,' she murmured. 'You know more than soldiering, Rod Gallowglass.'

Rod nodded heavily. He'd made another slip; blank-shield soldiers don't know politics.

'Then tell me,' she murmured, 'how you came to the House of Clovis, this night.'

'My Queen,' Rod said gravely, 'one man was set upon by three, in an alley. I helped him out; he took me to the House of Clovis to tell me his thanks with a glass of wine. That is how I came to meet Tuan Loguire.'

Her brows drew together in an anxious little frown. 'If I might but credit your words with truth,' she murmured.

She rose and went to the fireplace. All at once, her shoulders slumped, her head bowed forward. 'I shall need all my friends in this hour that comes upon us,' she murmured, voice husky, 'and I think thou art the truest of my friends, though I cannot say why.'

She raised her head to look at him, and he saw with a shock that her eyes swam with tears. 'There are still some to guard me,' she said, her voice so low he could scarcely hear; but her eyes shone through the tears, and an invisible band tightened around Rod's chest. His throat tightened, too; his eyes were burning.

She turned away, biting her clenched fist. After a moment, she spoke again, her voice trembling. 'The time shall come soon when each of the Great Lords shall declare himself for or against me; and I think they will be few who ride to my standard.'

She turned, came toward him again, eyes alight and a shy, trembling smile on her lips. Rod rose to meet her, staring, fascinated, heart pounding in his ears.

She stopped just before him, one hand touching the locket at her throat again, and whispered, 'Will you stand by my side in that day, Rod Gallowglass?'

Rod nodded awkwardly and garbled out something affirmative. At that particular moment, his answer would probably have been the same if she'd requested his soul.

Then, suddenly, she was in his arms, lithe and squirming, and her lips were moist and full on his own.

Some timeless while later, she lowered her head and moved reluctantly away, holding to his arms as if to steady herself. 'Nay, but I am a weak woman,' she murmured, exultant. 'Go now, Rod Gallowglass, with the thanks of a queen.'

She said something else, but Rod didn't quite follow it; and, somehow, he was on the other side of the door, walking down a wide, cold, torchlit corridor.

He stopped, shook himself, made a brave try at collecting his wits, and went on down the hall with a step that was none too firm.

*Whatever else you might think of her political abilities, the gal sure knew how to bind a man to her service . . .*

He stumbled and caught himself; his stumbling block shoved a hand against his hip to steady him.

'Nay, mind thy great feet,' grumbled Brom O'Berin, 'ere thou trip headlong and foul the paving.'

The dwarf studied Rod's eyes anxiously; he found whatever he was looking for somewhere between iris and cornea, and nodded, satisfied.

He reached up to grab Rod's sleeve and turned away, guiding him down the hall.

'What had you from Catharine, Rod Gallowglass?'

'Had from her?' Rod frowned, eyes unfocused. 'Well, she took my pledge of loyalty . . .'

'Ah!' Brom nodded, as though in commiseration. 'What more could you ask, Rod Gallowglass?'

Rod gave his head a quick shake, eyes opening wide. What the hell more could he ask, anyway? What in heaven's name had he expected? And what, in the seventh smile of Cerebus, was he getting moon-eyed for?

His jaw tightened, sullen anger rising in him. This bitch was nothing to him – just a pawn in the Great Game, a tool that might be used to establish a democracy. And what the hell was he getting angry about? He had no right to that, either . . .

Hell! He needed a little objective analysis! 'Fess!'

He meant it as a mutter, but it came out as a shout. Brom O'Berin scowled up at him. 'What is a fess?'

'An unreliable gear train with a slipped cam,' Rod improvised. Where the hell was that damn robot, anyway?

Then he remembered. Fess had had a seizure.

But Brom had stopped, and was studying Rod's face with his ultra-suspicious look. 'What are these words, Rod Gallowglass? What is a gear train? And what is a cam?'

Rod pressed his lips together and mentally recited the books of the Bible. *Careful, boy, careful! You're at the brink! You'll blow the whole bit!*

He met Brom's eyes. 'A gear train is the pack mule a knight uses to carry his armour and weapons,' he growled, 'and a cam is a half-witted squire.'

Brom scowled, puzzled. 'Half-witted?'

'Well, some kind of an eccentric. In my case, it all adds up to a horse.'

'A horse?' Brom stared, completely at sea.

'Yes. My horse, Fess. The sum and total of my worldly goods and supporting personnel. Also the only soul – well, consciousness, anyway – that I can tell my troubles to.'

Brom caught at the last phrase and held to it with all the vigour of a drowning man. His eyes softened; he smiled gently. 'You are of us now, Rod Gallowglass, of we few who stand by the Queen.'

Rod saw the sympathy in Brom's eyes and wondered what bound the deformed little man to Catharine's service – and suddenly hated Catharine again for being the kind of bitch that enjoyed using men.

He set off down the hall, striding long. Brom marched double-time to keep up with him.

'Unless I miss in my judgement of a man,' Rod growled through his teeth, 'the Queen has another friend in the House of Clovis; yet she calls him her enemy. Why is that, Brom? Is it just because he's the son of her enemy the Duke of Loguire?'

Brom stopped him with a hand on his hip and looked up into Rod's eyes with a half-smile. 'Not enemy, Rod Gallowglass, but one that she loves well: her uncle, blood-kin, who gave her sanctuary and cared for her five years while her father tamed the rebel Northern lordlings.'

Rod raised his head slowly, keeping his eyes on Brom O'Berin's. 'She chooses strange ways to show her love.'

Brom nodded. 'Aye, most truly strange, yet doubt not she loves them, both the Duke and his son Tuan.'

He held Rod's eyes a moment, not speaking.

He turned away, pacing slowly down the hall. Rod watched him a moment, then followed.

'It is a long tale, and a snarled one,' Brom murmured as Rod caught up with him. 'And the end and beginning and core of it is Tuan Loguire.'

'The beggar king?'

'Aye.' Brom nodded heavily. 'The lord of the House of Clovis.'

'And one who loves the Queen.'

'Oh, aye!' Brom threw his head back, rolling his eyes upward. 'One who loves her right well, be certain; he will tell you as much!'

'But you don't believe him?'

Brom locked his hands behind his back and stamped as he walked, head bowed. 'He is either truthful, Rod Gallowglass, or a most excellent liar; and if he lies, he has learned the way of it right quick. He was trained only in truth, in the house of his father. Yet he is lord of the House of Clovis, of they who claim the ruler should be chosen as the ancient King Clovis was, or as they say he was – by the acclamation of those whom he rules.'

'Well, they've warped history a little bit there,' Rod muttered. 'But I take it their plan calls for pulling Catharine off her throne?'

'Aye; and how can I then believe him when he says that he loves her?' Brom shook his head sadly. 'He is a most worthy young man, high-minded and honest; and a troubadour who will sing you the beauties of milady's eyetooth as quick as he will twist the sword from your hands with his rapier. He was always a gentleman withal, and in him was nothing of deception.'

'Sounds like you knew him pretty well.'

'Oh, aye! I did, most surely I did! But do I know him now?' Brom heaved a sigh, shaking his head. 'They met when she was but seven years of age, and he but eight, at the keep of Milord Loguire in the South, where her father had sent her for safety. There two children met and frolicked and played – under my eye, for I was ever a-watch over them. They were the only two of their age in the whole of the castle, and –' he smiled, and gave a bitter laugh – 'I was a miracle, a grown man who was smaller than they.'

Brom smiled, throwing his head back, looking past the stones of the hall into the years that were dead. 'They were so innocent then, Rod Gallowglass! So innocent, aye, and so happy! And he worshipped her; he would pluck the flowers for her crown, though the gardener scolded him. Did the sun chasten her? He would put up a canopy of leaves! Had she broken milady's crystal goblet? He would claim the fault for his own!'

'Spoiled her rotten,' Rod muttered.

'Aye; but he was not the first to play Tom Fool for her; for even then, she was a most beautiful princess, Rod Gallowglass.

'Yet over their happiness stood a dark, brooding shadow, a lad of fourteen, heir to the keep and estates. Anselm Loguire. He would look down from the tower, watch them at play in their garden, his face twisted and knotted all sour; and he alone in the land hated Catharine Plantagenet – why, no man can say.'

'And he still hates her?'

'Aye; and let us therefore wish my lord of Loguire long life.

'For near to five years Anselm's hatred did fester; but then at long last he did stand triumphant. For the lords of the North were subdued, and her father called for her to be brought again to his side, here in his castle. And then did they vow, Tuan and Catharine, she at eleven and he twelve, that they would never forget, that she would wait till he came for her.'

Brom shook his great shaggy head sadly. 'He came for her. He came for her, a lad of nineteen, a golden prince riding out of the South on a great white charger – broad-shouldered, golden-haired and handsome, with muscles that would thicken any woman's tongue and make it cleave to her palate. A troubadour, with a harp on his back and a sword by his side, and a thousand extravagant praises for her beauty. And his laugh was as clear, his heart as open, and his temper as frolicsome as when he was twelve.'

He smiled up at Rod. 'She was eighteen, Rod Gallowglass, and her life had been as still and smooth as a summer stream. Eighteen, and ripe for a husband, and her head filled with the giddy gossamer dreams that a girl learns from ballads and books.'

He peered sharply, but his voice was gentle, echoing strangely in the emptiness of his years. 'Was there never a dream of princess for you, Rod Gallowglass?'

Rod glared at him and swallowed, hard. 'Go on,' he said.

Brom turned away, shrugging. 'What need to say it? She loved him, of course; what woman would not? He knew not what a woman was for, and I'll swear it, and neither did she; but it may be that together, they learned; you may be sure that they had golden chances.'

He shook his head, scowling. 'If 'twas so, 'twas the crown of the last days of her youth; for it was that spring that her father died, and the sceptre was set in her hands.'

He fell still, measuring the hall with his stride, and was silent so long that Rod felt the need to say something.

'Here is no matter for hating, Brom O'Berin.'

'Oh, aye! But hear the end of the tale, for only when the crown was on her head did Catharine come to see that Tuan was a second son; that he thus inherited his family's honour, but no more. She swore then that he loved her not, that he coveted only her throne. She would not have him; but in wrath and scorn she sent him away – without due cause, it seemed, though only they two could know the truth of that. She banished him to the Wild Lands with a price on his head, to dwell midst the beast-men and elves, or to die.'

He fell silent again.

Rod prodded him. 'And Milord Loguire rose up in wrath?'

'Aye,' grated Brom, 'and all his liegemen with him, and half the nobles of the kingdom besides. If Tuan failed in his courting, wrath and scorn were his due, quoth Loguire; but banishment comes only for treason.

'"And was it not treason, Catharine answered hotly, to conspire for the crown?"

'Then Loguire stood tall in cold pride and declared that Tuan had sought only the love of Catharine; but his words rang hollow, for he whom the Queen marries must reign; and this Catharine told him.

'Then did Loguire speak in sorrow, that his own son was no traitor but only a fool, a fool to be courting a silly, spoiled child; and then would Catharine have cried "Treason!" again, had I not prevented her.'

'And yet you say she loves them, Loguire and Tuan?'

'Aye; why else such harshness?'

Brom lapsed into silence again. Rod cleared his throat and said, 'Tuan doesn't seem to have stayed banished too well . . .'

'Aye.' Brom's mouth drew back at the corners. 'The fool would be near her, he swore, though his head should be forfeit. But with a price on his life, he must live like a murderer or thief.'

Rod smiled sourly. 'And, somewhere, he got hold of the idea that the beggars would cause less trouble if someone took care of them.'

Brom nodded. 'And thus the beggars became somewhat a power; but Tuan swears he will throw all his forces to guard the Queen's back. He professes that he still doth love her; that he will love her though she hew off his head.'

'And she, of course,' Rod mused, 'claims there isn't a reason in the world why he shouldn't hate her.'

'And in that she is right; yet I think Tuan loves her.'

They had come to the guardroom door; Rod put a hand on the latch and smiled down at Brom O'Berin, smiled and shook his head sadly. 'Brainless,' he said. 'The pair of them.'

'And most tender loving enemies they are,' Brom smiled, with a touch of exasperation. 'And here is your lodging; good night.'

Brom turned on his heel and stalked off.

Rod looked after him, shaking his head and cursing himself silently. 'Fool that I am,' he murmured; 'I thought he stood by her because he was in love with her. Oh, well, Fess makes mistakes too . . .'

The great candle in the barracks was burned down to a stub. Time in Gramarye was kept by huge candles banded in red and white, six rings of red and six white. One candle was lit at dawn, the other twelve hours later.

According to this candle, it was three a.m. Rod's eyelids suddenly felt very heavy. They seemed downright leaden when he remembered that an hour on Gramarye was roughly equal to an hour and twenty minutes Galactic Standard.

He staggered toward his bunk and tripped. The object underfoot gave a muffled grunt; Rod had forgotten that Big Tom would be sleeping at the foot of the bed, on the floor.

The big man sat up, yawning and scratching. He looked up and saw Rod. 'Oh, god e'en, master! What's the time?'

'Ninth hour of the night,' Rod said softly. 'Go back to sleep, Big Tom. I didn't mean to wake you.'

' 'S what I'm here for, master.' He shook his head to clear it of sleep.

Which was somewhat strange, Rod suddenly realized, since the man's eyes had been wide awake. A synapse flicked in Rod's brain, and he was wide awake and wary, once again the subversive agent.

So, to keep from arousing Big Tom's suspicions, he tried to appear even more sleepy than he had been.

'It was a great night, Big Tom,' he mumbled, and fell face forward into his bunk. He hoped Big Tom would leave matters as they were and go back to sleep; but he heard a deep, warm chuckle from the foot of the bed, and Big Tom started pulling off Rod's boots.

'A bit of folly in you, hadn't you, master?' he muttered. 'Aye, and a wench or two under your belt, I'll warrant.'

'Wake me at the lighting of the candle,' Rod mumbled into his pillow. 'I'm to wait on the Queen at breakfast.'

'Aye, master.' Big Tom worried loose the other boot and lay down, chuckling.

Rod waited till Tom began to snore again, then propped himself up on his elbows and looked back over his shoulder. Generally, the big oaf seemed thoroughly loyal and superbly stupid; but there were times when Rod wondered . . .

He let his head slump down onto the pillow, closed his eyes, and willed himself to sleep.

Unfortunately, the mind-over-matter bit wasn't working tonight. All his senses seemed boosted past maximum. He would've sworn he could feel every thread in the pillow under his cheek, could hear the mouse gnawing at the baseboard, the frog croaking in the moat, the festive laughter wafted on the breeze.

His eyelids snapped open. Festive laughter?

He rolled out of bed and went to the high slit window. Who the hell was partying at this hour of the night?

The moon stood behind the castellated north tower; silhouettes flitted across its face, youthful figures in a three-dimensional dance; and some of them seemed to be riding on broomsticks.

Witches. In the north tower . . .

Rod climbed the worn stone steps of the tower, toiling up the spiral. The granite walls seemed to crowd closer and closer the higher he went. He reminded himself that, having been declared a warlock by the elves – unreasonable little bastards! – he qualified for membership in this group.

But his stomach didn't get the message; it was still suing for a Dramamine. His mouth was bone-dry. Sure, the elves approved of him; but had they got the word to the witches?

All the old tales of his childhood came flooding back, liberally interspersed with chunks of the witch scenes from *Macbeth*. Now that he stopped to think about it, he couldn't remember one single instance of a philanthropic witch, except Glinda the Good, and you couldn't really call her a witch.

One thing in his favour: these witches seemed happy enough. The music floating down the stairwell was an old Irish jig, and it was salted with laughter, buoyant and youthful.

The wall glowed with torchlight ahead of him. He turned the last curve of the spiral and came into the great tower room.

A round, or rather globular, dance was in progress, a sort of three-dimensional *hora*. Through the clouds of torch smoke he could make out couples dancing on the walls, the ceiling, in mid-air, and occasionally on the floor. Here and there were knots of chattering, giggling people. Their clothes were bright to the point of – well, hell, they were downright gaudy. Most of them held mugs, filled from a great cask near the stairwell.

They were all young, teenagers. He couldn't spot a single face that looked old enough to vote.

He paused on the threshold, possessed of a distinct feeling that he didn't belong. He felt like the chaperon at a high school prom – a necessary evil.

The youngster tapping the keg saw Rod and grinned. 'Hail!' he cried. 'You are laggard in coming.' A full tankard slapped into Rod's hand.

'I didn't know I was coming,' Rod muttered.

'Be assured that we did.' The youth grinned. 'Molly foresaw it; but she said you would be here half an hour agone.'

'Sorry.' Rod's eyes were a trifle glazed. 'Ran into a couple delays . . .'

'Eh, think naught of it. 'Twas her miscalling, not yours; the wine, no doubt. Yet we have expected you since you set foot in the castle; the elves told us last night you were a warlock.'

Rod's mind snapped clear. 'Baloney! I'm no more a warlock than you . . . I mean . . .'

'Oh, thou art a warlock.' The boy nodded sagely. 'A warlock, and a most puissant one. Did you not come in a falling star?'

'That's science, not magic! And I'm not a warlock!'

The youth smiled roguishly. 'Knowing or not, thou'rt most surely a warlock.' He saluted Rod with the mug. 'And therefore one of us.'

'Uh . . . well, thanks.' Rod returned the salute and took a draught from the mug. It was mulled wine, hot and spicy.

He looked around the room, trying to grow accustomed to the constant clamour and the flagrant violations of Newton's Laws.

His eyes lit on a couple seated under one of the windows, deep in conversation, which is to say, she was talking and he was listening. She was a looker, fairly bursting her bodice; he was thin and intent, eyes burning as he watched her.

Rod smiled cynically and wondered about the boy's motives for such steadfast devotion.

The girl gasped and spun around to glare outraged at Rod.

Rod's mouth sagged open. Then he began to stammer an apology; but before it reached his lips, the girl smiled, mollified, bowed her head graciously at him, and turned back to her one-man audience.

Rod's mouth sagged again. Then he reached out, groping for the tapster's arm, his eyes fixed on the girl.

The boy threw an arm around his shoulders, his voice worried. 'What troubles thee, friend?'

'That – the girl,' Rod stammered. 'Can she read my mind?'

'Oh, aye! We all can, somewhat; though she is better than most.'

Rod put a hand to his head to stop it from spinning. Telepaths. A whole room full of them. There were supposed to be about ten proven telepaths in the whole of the known galaxy.

He looked up again. It was a mutation, or genetic drift, or something.

He drew himself up and cleared his throat. 'Say, pal . . . uh, what's your name, anyway?'

'*Ay de mi!*' The boy struck his forehead with the heel of his hand. 'A pox upon my lacking courtesy. I am Tobias, Master Gallowglass; and thou must needs meet us all.'

He whirled Rod away toward the nearest group.

'But – but I just wanted to ask—'

'This is Nell, this is Andreyev, this Brian, this Dorothy . . .'

A half hour and fifty-three introductions later, Rod collapsed on a wooden bench. He swung his tankard up and swallowed the dregs. 'Now,' he said, slamming it down on his knee, 'we're both drained.'

'Ah, let me fetch you another!' Toby snatched the mug from his hand and flew away.

Literally.

Rod watched him drift across the room, ten feet off the floor, and shook his head. He was beyond astonishment now.

It seemed what he had on his hands was a budding colony of espers – levitative, precognitive, and telepathic.

But if they could all teleport, how come the girls all rode broomsticks?

Toby appeared at Rod's elbow, with a slight *poof*! of displaced air. Rod goggled at him, then accepted the refilled mug. 'Uh, thanks. Say, you can, uh, levitate and teleport?'

'Pardon?' Toby frowned, not understanding.

'You can-uh-fly? And, uh-wish yourself from one place to another?'

'Oh, aye!' Toby grinned. 'We all can do that.'

'What? Fly?'

'Nay; we all can wish ourselves to places that we know. All the boys can fly; the girls cannot.'

*Sex-linked gene*, Rod thought. Aloud, he said, 'That's why they ride broomsticks?'

'Aye. Theirs is the power to make lifeless objects do their bidding. We males cannot.'

Aha! Another linkage. Telekinesis went with the Y-chromosomes, levitation with the X.

But they could all teleport. And read minds.

A priceless colony of espers. And, if their lives were anything like those of the rare telepaths outside the planet . . .

'And the common people hate you for this?'

Toby's young face sobered to the point of gloom. 'Aye, and the nobles too. They say we are leagued with the Devil. 'Twas the trial by water, or a most thorough roasting for us, till our good Queen Catharine came to reign.' Turning away, he shouted, 'Ho, Bridget!'

A young girl, thirteen at the most, spun away from her dance partner and appeared at Toby's side.

'Friend Gallowglass would know how the people do like us,' Toby informed her.

All the joy went out of the child's face; her eyes went wide and round; she caught her lower lip between her teeth.

She unbuttoned the back of her blouse from neck to bodice and turned away. Her back was a crisscross of scars, a webbing of welts – the sign of the cat-o'nine-tails.

She turned back to Rod as Toby buttoned her blouse again, her eyes still round and tragic. 'That,' she whispered, 'for naught but suspicion; and I but a child of ten years at the time.'

Rod's stomach tried to turn itself inside out and climb out through his oesophagus. He reprimanded it sternly, and it sank back to its ordinary place in the alimentary tract. Bile soured the back of his tongue.

Bridget spun and disappeared; a nanosecond later she was back with her partner, giddy and exuberant again.

Rod frowned after her, brooding.

'So you may see,' said Toby, 'that we are most truly grateful to our good Queen.'

'She did away with the fire and/or water bit?'

'Oh, she revoked the law; but the witch-burnings went on, in secret. There was only one way to protect us, and that she chose:

to give sanctuary to any of us who would come here and claim it.'

Rod nodded, slowly. 'She's not without wisdom, after all.'

His eyes wandered back to Bridget where she danced on the ceiling.

'What troubles you, friend Gallowglass?'

'She doesn't hate them,' Rod growled. 'She has every reason in the world to hate the normal folk, but she doesn't.'

Toby shook his head, smiling warmly. 'Not she, nor any of us. All who come to shelter in the Queen's Coven swear first to live by Christ's Law.'

Slowly, Rod turned to look at him. 'I see,' he said after a moment. 'A coven of white witches.'

Toby nodded.

'Are all the witches of Gramarye white?'

'Shame to say it, they are not. Some there are who, embittered through greater suffering than ours – the loss of an ear or an eye, or a loved one, or all – have hidden themselves away in the Wild Lands of the mountains, and there pursue their vengeance on all mankind.'

Rod's mouth pulled back into a thin, grim line, turned down at the corners.

'They number scarce more than a score,' Toby went on. 'There are three in the prime of life; all the rest are withered crones and shrunken men.'

'The fairy-tale witches,' Rod growled.

'Of a truth, they are; and their works are noised about just sufficient to cover report of any good works that we may deal.'

'So there are two kinds of witches in Gramarye: the old and evil ones, up in the mountains; and the young white ones in the Queen's castle.'

Toby shook his head and smiled, his eyes lighting once again. 'Nay, there are near threescore white witches beside us, who would not trust to the Queen's promise of sanctuary. They are thirty and forty years aged, good folk all, but slow indeed to be trusting.'

Understanding struck with all the power of Revelation. Rod leaned back, his mouth forming a silent O; then nodding rapidly, he leaned forward and said, '*That's* why you're all so young! Only the witches who still had some trust and recklessness left in them took the Queen's invitation! So she got a flock of teenagers!'

Toby grinned from ear to ear, nodding quickly with excitement.

'So the mature witches,' Rod went on, 'are very good people, but they're also very cautious!'

Toby nodded. His face sobered a trifle. 'There are one or two among them who had daring enough to come here. There was the wisest witch of all, from the South. She grows old now. Why, she must be fair near to thirty!'

That line caught Rod right in the middle of a drink. He choked, swallowed, gagged, coughed, wheezed, and wiped at his eyes.

'Is aught wrong, friend Gallowglass?' Toby inquired with the kind of solicitousness usually reserved for the octogenarian.

'Oh, nothing,' Rod gasped. 'Just a little confusion between the oesophagus and the trachea. Have to expect a few quirks in us old folk, you know. Why didn't this wise witch stay?'

Toby smiled, fairly oozing understanding and kindness. 'Ah, she said that we made her feel too much her age, and went back to the South. If thou shouldst come to trouble there, but call out her name, Gwendylon, and thou'lt right quick have more help than thou needst.'

'I'll remember that,' Rod promised, and immediately forgot as he had a sudden vision of himself calling a woman for help. He almost went into another coughing fit, but he didn't dare laugh; he remembered how sensitive he'd been in his teens.

He took another swig of the wine to wash down his laughter and pointed the mug at Toby. 'Just one more question, now: why is the Queen protecting you?'

Toby stared. 'Didst thou not know?'

'Know I didst not.' Rod smiled sweetly.

'Why, she is herself a witch, good friend Gallowglass!'

Rod's smiled faded. 'Hum.' He scratched the tip of his nose. 'I'd heard rumours to that effect. They're true, eh?'

'Most true. A witch unschooled, but a witch nonetheless.'

Rod raised an eyebrow. 'Unschooled?'

'Aye. Our gifts need a stretching and exercising, a training and schooling, to come to their full. Catharine is a witch born, but unschooled. She can hear thoughts, but not at any time that she wishes, and not clearly.'

'Hm. What else can she do?'

'Naught that we know of. She can but hear thoughts.'

'So she's sort of got a minimum union requirement.' Rod scratched behind his ear. 'Kind of handy talent for a Queen. She'd know everything that goes on in her castle.'

Toby shook his head. 'Canst hear five speak all at once, friend Gallowglass? And listen to them all the hours of the day? And still be able to speak what they spoke?'

Rod frowned and rubbed his chin.

'Canst repeat even one conversation?' Toby smiled indulgently and shook his head. 'Of course thou canst not – and neither can our Queen.'

'She could write them down . . .'

'Aye; but remember, she is unschooled; and it needs high training of an excellent good gift to make words of thoughts.'

'Hold on.' Rod's hand went up, palm out. 'You mean you don't hear thoughts as words?'

'Nay, nay. An instant's thought suffices for a book of words, friend Gallowglass. Must you needs put words to your thoughts in order to have them?'

Rod nodded. 'I see. Quantum thought mechanics.'

'Strange . . .' murmured a voice. Looking up, Rod found himself the centre of a fair-sized group of young witches and warlocks who had apparently drifted over to get in on an interesting conversation.

He looked at the one who had spoken, a burly young warlock, and smiled with a touch of sarcasm. 'What's strange?' He wondered what the kid's name was.

The boy grinned. 'Martin is my name.' He paused to chuckle at Rod's startled look; he still hadn't gotten used to the mind-reading. 'And what is strange is that you, a warlock, should not know the ins and outs of hearing thoughts.'

'Aye.' Toby nodded. 'You are the only warlock we have known, friend Gallowglass, that cannot hear thoughts.'

'Uh, yes.' Rod ran a hand over the stubble on his cheek. 'Well, as I mentioned a little earlier, I'm not really a warlock. You see . . .'

He was cut off by a unanimous burst of laughter. He sighed, and resigned himself to his reputation.

He reverted to his former line of questioning. 'I take it some of you can hear thoughts as words.'

'Oh, aye,' said Toby, wiping his eyes. 'We have one.' He turned to the ring of listeners. 'Is Aldis here?'

A buxom, pretty sweet-sixteen elbowed her way through to the front rank. 'Who shall I listen to for you, sir?'

A spark arced across a gap in Rod's mind. A malicious gleam came into his eyes. 'Durer. The councillor to Milord Loguire.'

Aldis folded her hands in her lap, settled herself, sitting very straight. She stared at Rod; her eyes lost focus. Then she began to speak in a high-pitched nasal monotone.

'As you will, milord. Yet I cannot help but wonder, are you *truly* loyal?'

Her voice dropped two octaves in pitch but kept the monotonous quality. 'Knave! Have you the gall to insult me to me face?'

'Nay, milord!' the high voice answered hurriedly. 'I do not insult you; I do but question the wisdom of your actions.'

Durer, Rod thought. The high voice was Durer, practising his vocation – the care and manipulation of the Duke Loguire.

'Remember, milord, she is but a child. Is it kindness to a child to let her have her wilful way? Or is it kindness to spank her when she needs it?'

There was a silence for a moment; then the deeper voice of the Lord Loguire answered, 'There is some measure of truth in what you say. Certain, there is something of the wanton child in her taking up the power to appoint the priests.'

'Why,' murmured the high voice, ' 'tis an act against tradition, milord, and against the wisdom of men far older than herself. 'Tis in bitter truth the act of a rebellious child.'

'Mayhap,' Loguire rumbled. 'Yet she is the Queen, and the Queen's Law shall be obeyed.'

'Even should the Queen make evil laws, milord?'

'Her actions are not evil, Durer.' The deep voice took on an ominous quality. 'Reckless, perhaps, and thoughtless, and ill-considered; for the good they bring today may bring havoc down upon our heads tomorrow. Foolish laws, perhaps; but evil, no.'

The high voice sighed. 'Mayhap, milord. Yet she threatens the honour of her noblemen. Is that not evil?'

'Why,' rumbled Loguire, 'how is this? She has been haughty, aye, taking to herself greater airs than ever a Queen may own to, mayhap; but she has never yet done aught that could be construed as insult.'

'Aye, milord, not yet.'

'Why, what do you mean?'

'The day shall come, milord.'

'What day is that, Durer?'

'When she shall put the peasants before the noblemen, milord.'

'Have done with your treasonous words!' Loguire roared. 'On your knees, slight man, and thank your God that I leave you with your head!'

Rod stared at Aldis' face, still not recovered from the shock of hearing two disembodied male voices coming from the mouth of a pretty girl.

Slowly, her eyes focused again. She let out a long breath and smiled up at him. 'Did you hear, friend Gallowglass?'

Rod nodded.

She spread her hands, shrugging. 'I cannot recall a word of what I said.'

'Don't let it worry you, I remember it all.' Rod rubbed the stubble on his chin. 'You were acting as a channel, a medium in the purest sense of the word.'

He threw his head back, drained his mug, and tossed it to one of the young warlocks. The youth caught the tankard, disappeared, and reappeared. He handed the tankard, brimming full, to Rod, who shook his head in mock despair.

He leaned back and sipped at the wine, looking up at the young faces around him, smiling and fairly glowing with the knowledge of their power.

'Have you ever done this before?' he asked, with a wave of the mug that took them all in. 'Listened to skull sessions like that one, I mean.'

'Only of the Queen's enemies,' Aldis answered with a toss of her head. 'We often listen to Durer.'

'Oh?' Rod raised an eyebrow. 'Learn anything?'

Aldis nodded. 'He is much concerned with the peasants of late.'

Rod was very still for a moment. Then he leaned forward, elbows on his knees. 'What's his interest in the peasants?'

Toby grinned knowingly. 'Hark now to his latest exploit! He hath brooded trouble 'twixt two serfs on the Queen's own estate. A young peasant wished to marry an old farmer's daughter, and the old man said nay. And the youth would've thrown up his hands in despair and let himself waste away with a broken heart.'

'But Durer stepped in.'

'Aye. He was after the young one night and day; for knowledge of the boy's suit spread throughout all the villages, and saw to it that the rumour was told with one question appended: Could the youth be a man who would let a dotard idiot rob him of the girl he loved?'

Rod nodded. 'And the other peasants started throwing that up to the kid.'

'Most certainly. Taunts and jeers and mocking – and the lad stole the girl away by night and got her with child.'

Rod pursed his lips. 'I imagine Papa was a trifle perturbed.'

Toby nodded. 'He hauled the boy before the village priest and demanded the lad be hanged for a rapist.'

'And the priest said . . .?'

'That it was love, not rape, and the fitting punishment was marriage, not hanging.'

Rod grinned. 'Bet the two kids were real sad about that.'

'Their grief was so great it set them to dancing.' Toby chuckled. 'And the old man gave a heavy sigh, and would have judged it the wisdom of God, and blessed them.'

'And Durer stepped in again.'

'Most certainly. He was up before the Queen, when she was at table before all her lords and her ladies, crying that the Queen must prove the justice of her new order by declaring herself what was just in this case; for were these not peasants on the Queen's own estates?'

Rod grinned and slapped his thigh. 'She must have been ready to spit in his eye!'

'Oh, you know not the Queen!' Toby rolled his eyes up toward the ceiling. 'She would most cheerfully have slipped a knife 'twixt his ribs. But the challenge must needs be answered; she must needs hear the case herself, when next she held General Court.'

'General Court?' Rod scowled. 'What the hell is that?'

'One hour each month the Queen opens her court to all in her realm who wish her ear; and peasants, nobility, and clergy come to her Great Hall. Mostly the Great Lords but look on while the petty nobility and peasantry bring forth their grievances. And with the great ones watching, you may be sure the grievances brought up are petty indeed.'

'Like this case.' Rod nodded. 'When's this next General Court?'

'Tomorrow,' said Toby, 'and I think the Great Lords shall have their tame clergy and peasantry protest the Queen's new judges and priests. The lords shall lodge their protest first, of course; and the other, more common folk shall be echoing them.'

Rod nodded. 'Put the whole matter on public record. But what does Durer hope to gain by bringing in this seduction case?'

Toby shrugged. 'That, only Durer may know.'

Rod leaned back, frowning, and pulled at his mug. He studied the young faces around him and scratched at the base of his skull.

'Sounds to me like this is information the Queen would like to have. Why don't you tell her?'

The faces sobered. Toby bit his lips and looked down at the floor.

Rod scowled. 'Why don't you tell her, Toby?'

'We have tried, friend Gallowglass!' The boy looked up at Rod in mute appeal. 'We have tried; yet she would not hear us!'

Rod's face turned to wood. 'How's that again?'

Toby spread his hands in helplessness. 'The page we sent to her returned to tell us that we should be thankful for the protection she accorded us, and not be so ingracious and insolent as to seek to meddle in her governing.'

Rod jerked his head in tight, quick nods, mouth drawn back in grim agreement. 'Yeah, that sounds like Catharine.'

'Mayhap,' one of the boys murmured thoughtfully, 'it is all to the best; for she hath cares enough without warning of doom from us.'

Rod grinned without humour. 'Yeah. Between the noblemen and the beggars, she's got more than enough worries to keep her busy.'

Toby nodded, eyes wide and serious. 'Aye, she hath trouble sufficient, between the councillors, the House of Clovis, and the banshee on her roof. She hath great cause to be most afeard.'

'Yes.' Rod's voice was tight, rasping. 'Yes, she hath good cause; and I think that she is thoroughly afeard.'

Big Tom must have been a very light sleeper; he sat up on his pallet as Rod came tiptoeing up to his bunk.

'Art well, master?' he whispered in a rasping voice that had about as much secrecy as a bullfrog in rut.

Rod stopped and frowned down at his manservant. 'Yes, very well. Why shouldn't I be?'

Big Tom smiled sheepishly. 'Thou hast small use for sleep,' he muttered. 'I had thought it might be a fever.'

'No.' Rod smiled with relief, shaking his head. He pushed past Big Tom. 'It's not a fever.'

'What is it, then?'

Rod fell backward onto the bed, cupping his hands under his head. 'Did you ever hear of a game called cricket, Tom?'

'Cricket?' Tom scowled. ' 'Tis a chirping creature on the hearth, master.'

'Yeah, but it's also the name of a game. The centre of the game is a wicket, see, and one team tries to knock down the wicket by throwing a ball at it. The other team tries to protect the wicket by knocking the ball away with a paddle.'

'Strange,' Big Tom murmured, eyes wide with wonder. 'A most strange manner of game, master.'

'Yes,' Rod agreed, 'but it gets worse. The teams trade sides, you see, and the team that was attacking the wicket before is defending it now.' He looked down over his toes at Tom's round beehive face.

'Nay,' the big man muttered, shaking his head in confusion. 'What is the point to it all, master?'

Rod stretched, let his body snap back to relaxation.

'The point is that no matter who wins, it's going to be hard on the wicket.'

'Aye!' Big Tom nodded vigorously. 'Most certain true, master.'

'Now, I get the feeling that there's a colossal game of cricket going on around here; only there's three teams in the game: the councillors, the beggars . . .'

'The House of Clovis,' Tom muttered.

Rod's eyebrows went up in surprise. 'Yes, the House of Clovis. And, of course, the Queen.'

'Then, who,' asked Big Tom, 'is the wicket?'

'Me.' Rod rolled over on his side, thumped the pillow with his fist, and lowered his head onto it with a blissful sigh. 'And now I am going to sleep. Good night.'

'Master Gallowglass,' piped a page's voice.

Rod closed his eyes and prayed for strength. 'Yes, page?'

'You are called to wait upon the Queen at her breakfast, Master Gallowglass.'

Rod forced an eyelid open and peered out the window; the sky was rosy with dawn.

He squeezed his eyes shut and counted to ten, almost dozing off in the process. He drew in a sigh that would have filled a bottomless pit, swung his legs over the side of the bed, and sat up. 'Well, no rest for the wicket. What'd I do with my damn uniform, Tom?'

Rod had to admit that Catharine Plantagenet had a good dramatic instinct and, moreover, knew how to use it on her court. The guards were at their stations in the dining hall before sunrise. The lords and ladies who were privileged – or, more accurately, cursed – to share the Queen's dawn breakfast arrived right after the cock's crow. Not till they were all assembled, and all waiting some time eyeing the breakfast meats, did Catharine make her entrance.

And she definitely made an entrance, even at that hour. The doors of the hall were thrown wide, revealing Catharine standing in a pool of torchlight. Six buglers blew a fanfare, at which all the lords and ladies rose and Rod winced (pitch was more or less a matter of taste in that culture).

Then Catharine stepped into the hall, head high and shoulders back. She paced a quarter way around the wall to the great gilded chair at the head of the table. The Duke of Loguire stepped forth and pulled the chair back. Catharine sat, with the grace and lightness of a feather. Loguire sat at her right hand, and the rest of the company followed suit. Catharine picked up her two-tined fork, and the company fell to, while liveried stewards invaded from the four corners of the hall with great platters of bacon and sausage, pickled herring, white rolls, and tureens of tea and soup.

Each platter was brought first to Brom O'Berin, where he sat at the Queen's left hand. Brom took a sample of each platter, ate a morsel of it, and placed the remainder on a plate before him. Then the huge platters were placed on the table. By this time Brom, finding himself still alive, passed the filled plate to Catharine.

The company fell to with gusto, and Rod's stomach reminded him that all that had hit his digestive tract that night had been spiced wine.

Catharine picked daintily at her food with the original bird-like appetite. Rumour had it that she ate just before the formal meal in the privacy of her apartments. Even so, she was so thin that Rod found it in himself to doubt the rumour.

The stewards wove in and out with flagons of wine and huge meat pies.

Rod was stationed at the east door; he thus had a good view of Catharine, where she sat at the north end of the table, Milord Loguire at her right hand, Durer, at Loguire's right hand, and the back of Brom O'Berin's head.

Durer leaned over and murmured something to his lord. Loguire waved a hand impatiently and nodded. He tore the meat off a chop with one bite, chewed, swallowed, and washed it down with a draught of wine. As he lowered the cup to the table, he turned to Catharine and rumbled, 'Your Majesty, I am concerned.'

Catharine gave him the cold eye. 'We are all concerned, Milord Loguire. We must bear with our cares as well as we may.'

Loguire's lips pressed tight together, his mouth almost

becoming lost between moustache and beard. 'My care,' he said, 'is for your own person, and for the welfare of your kingdom.'

Catharine turned back to her plate, cutting a morsel of pork with great care. 'I must hope that the welfare of my person would indeed affect the welfare of my kingdom.'

Loguire's neck was growing red; but he pushed on obstinately. 'I am glad that your Majesty sees that a threat to your welfare is a threat to this kingdom.'

The skin furrowed between Catharine's eyebrows; she frowned at Loguire. 'Indeed I do.'

'Knowing that the Queen's life is threatened, the people grow uneasy.'

Catharine put down her fork and sat back in her chair. Her voice was mild, even sweet. 'Is my life, then, threatened, milord?'

'It would seem so,' Loguire murmured carefully. 'For the banshee was upon your roof again last night.'

Rod's ears pricked up.

Catharine's lips turned in, pressed between her teeth; her eyes closed. Silence fell around the table. Brom O'Berin's voice rumbled into the sudden quiet. 'The banshee hath often been seen upon her Majesty's battlements; yet still she lives.'

'Be still!' Catharine snapped at him. Her shoulders straightened; she leaned forward to take up her goblet. 'I do not wish to hear of the banshee.' She drained the goblet, then held it out to the side. 'Steward, more wine!'

Durer was out of his seat and at the Queen's elbow in an instant. Plucking the goblet from her hand, he turned to the steward who had come running up. He held the goblet up while the steward filled it from his ewer and the court stared; such courtesy to the Queen was, from Durer, somewhat unusual.

He swung back to the Queen, dropping to one knee and holding up the goblet. Catharine stared, then slowly accepted it. 'I thank you, Durer; yet must I confess that I had not expected such courtliness from you.'

Durer's eyes glinted. He rose with a mocking smile and bowed very low. 'Drink deep in health, my Queen.'

But Rod was a trifle less trusting than Catharine; moreover, he had seen Durer pass his left hand over the goblet just before the steward poured.

He left his post and caught the goblet just as Catharine raised it to her lips. She stared at him, face paling, rage rising in her eyes. 'I did not summon you, sirrah.'

'Your Majesty's pardon.' Rod unclipped his dagger from his belt, shook the blade out onto the table, and filled the conical sheath with wine. Thank Heaven he'd taken the precaution of resetting Fess before he went on duty!

He held up the silver horn and said, 'I conFess, with apologies to your Majesty, that I cannot *analyse* my actions; it is only that I fear for your Majesty's life.'

But all Catharine's anger had vanished in fascination at Rod's action. 'What,' she said, pointing to the silver horn, 'is that?'

'Unicorn's horn,' Rod answered, and looked up to see Durer's eyes, burning with rage at him.

'Analysis complete,' murmured the voice behind his ear. 'Substance poisonous to human metabolism.'

Rod smiled grimly and pressed the knob at the apex of the horn with his little finger.

The 'unicorn's horn' turned purple.

A gasp of horror went up from the whole court; for they all knew the legend, that a unicorn's horn will turn purple if poison is placed in it.

Catharine turned pale; she clenched her fists to conceal their trembling.

Loguire's hand balled into a huge fist; his eyes narrowed as he glared at Durer. 'Slight man, if any part of this treachery was yours . . .'

'Milord, you saw.' Durer's voice crackled. 'I but held the cup.'

But his burning eyes were fixed on Rod's, seeming to suggest that Rod could save himself a lot of trouble and agony if he would just drink the wine right there and then.

Rod was assigned as one of the four guards who would escort Catharine from her apartments to the Great Hall for the General Court. The four of them waited outside her chambers till the door opened, and Brom O'Berin stepped out, preceding the Queen. Two soldiers fell in before the Queen and behind Brom; Rod and another Guardsman fell in behind her.

They moved down the corridor slowly, matching their pace to Catharine's; and the Queen, draped in a heavy fur cloak and weighed down by the great gold crown, moved very slowly. Somehow, she contrived to look stately rather than clumsy.

As they drew near the Great Hall, a slight, emaciated, velvet-clad figure came scurrying up – Durer.

'Your pardon,' he said, bowing three times. 'But I must speak with your Majesty.' His lips were pressed tight, anger in his eyes.

Catharine stopped and drew herself up to her haughtiest.

*Chip on her shoulder as large as a two-by-four*, Rod thought.

'Speak, then,' she said, looking down her nose at the cringing little man before her; 'but speak quickly, sirrah.'

Durer's eyes flared at the word of contempt; 'sirrah' was a term reserved for peasants.

He managed to keep his manner respectful, though. 'Your Majesty, I beg you to brook no delay in hearing the Great Lords' petition, for they are most greatly overwrought.'

Catharine frowned. 'Why should I delay?'

Durer bit his lip, looking away.

Catharine's eyes kindled in anger. 'Speak, sirrah,' she snapped. 'Or do you mean to imply that the Queen fears to hear her noblemen?'

'Your Majesty . . .' Durer spoke with great reluctance; then the words came in a rush. 'I had heard there were two peasants to be heard in Court today . . .'

'There are.' Catharine's mouth hardened. ''Tis the case you recommended to me, Durer.'

The little man's eye shot a malevolent gleam at her; then he was all fawning humility again. 'I had thought . . . I had heard . . . I had feared . . .'

'What hast thou feared?'

'Your Majesty hath been most concerned for your peasants of late . . .' Durer hesitated, then stumbled on. 'I had feared . . . that your Majesty might . . . perhaps . . .'

Catharine's eyes hardened. 'That I might hear these two peasants before I gave ear to the petitions of my noblemen?'

'Your Majesty must not!' Durer dropped to his knees, hands clasped in supplication. 'Thou must not risk offence of the Great Lords today! Fear for thy very life if thou—'

'Sirrah, do you call me coward?'

Rod closed his eyes; his heart sank.

'Your Majesty,' cried Durer, 'I meant but to—'

'Enough!' Catharine turned away, spurning the meagre form of the councillor. Brom O'Berin and the Guardsmen moved with her. The great oaken doors swung open before them.

Rod risked a glance back over his shoulder.

Durer's face was contorted with malevolent glee; his eyes glittered with triumph.

The best way to get a teenager to do something is to tell her not to . . .

Brom led the Queen's entourage into a great vaulted room, lighted by a row of clerestory windows on each side. Fifty feet above, the roof-beam ran through the hall like a spine, with oaken ribs running down to the granite walls. Two great wrought-iron chandeliers hung from the ceiling, with candles burning in the sconces.

They had come in onto a raised dais, ten feet above the floor of the hall. A huge gilded throne rose before them.

Brom led them in a swing around the lip of the dais to the throne. There the Guardsmen lined up on either side, and Catharine mounted the last half-step to stand slender and proud before the throne, gazing out over the multitude gathered below.

The multitude looked like a sampling of the population. They filled the great hall, from the steps of the dais to the triple doors at the far end of the hall.

In the first rank were the twelve great nobles, seated in wooden hourglass-shaped chairs in a semicircle twelve feet out from the steps of the throne.

Behind them stood forty or fifty ageing men in brown, grey, or dark green robes with velvet collars and small, square, felt hats. Chains of silver or gold hung down over their ample bellies. Burghers, Rod guessed – local officials, merchants, guildmasters – the bourgeoisie.

Beyond them were the black, cowled robes of the clergy; and beyond them were the dun-coloured, patched clothing of the peasantry, most of whom, Rod felt moderately certain, had been sent up from the castle kitchen so that the Great Court would have representatives of all classes.

But in the centre of the peasants stood four soldiers in green and gold – the Queen's colours – and between them stood two peasants, one young and one old, both looking awed and scared almost to the point of panic, caps twisting in their horny hands. The oldster had a long, grizzled beard; the youngster was clean-shaven. Both wore dun-coloured smocks of coarse cloth; more of the same material was bound to their legs, to serve as trousers. A priest stood by them, looking almost as much out of place as they did.

All eyes were on the Queen. Catharine was very much aware of it; she stood a little taller, and held her pose until the hall was completely quiet. Then she sat, slowly, and Brom sank cross-legged at her feet. Pike-butts thudded on stone as Rod and the other three Guardsmen stood to rest, pikes slanting outward at twenty degrees.

Brom's voice boomed out over the hall. 'Who comes before the Queen this day?'

A herald stepped forward with a roll of parchment and read off a list of twenty petitions. The first was that of the twelve noblemen; the last was Durer's two peasants.

Catharine's hands tightened on the arms of the throne. She spoke in a high, clear voice. 'Our Lord hath said that the humble shall be exalted, the last shall be first; therefore let us first hear the testimony of these two peasants.'

There was a moment's shocked silence; old Lord Loguire was on his feet bellowing.

'Testimony! Have you such great need of their testimony that you must set these clods of earth before the highest of your nobles?'

'My lord,' Catharine snapped, 'you forget your place in my court.'

'Nay, it is you who forget! You who forget respect and tradition, and all the law that you learned at your father's knee!'

The old lord drew himself up, glaring. 'Never,' he rumbled, 'would the old king have disgraced his liegemen so!'

'Open thine eyes, old man!' Catharine's voice was chill and arrogant. 'I would my father still lived; but he is dead, and I reign now.'

'Reign!' Loguire's lips twisted in a sour grimace. ''Tis not a reign, but a tyranny!'

The hall fell silent, shocked. Then a whisper began and grew: 'Treason! TreasontreasontreasonTreason!'

Brom O'Berin rose, trembling. 'Now, Milord Loguire, must thou kneel and ask pardon of milady the Queen, or be adjudged forever a traitor to the throne.'

Loguire's face turned to stone, he drew himself up, back straightening, chin lifting; but before he could answer, Catharine spoke in a tight, quavering voice.

'There shall be no forgiveness asked, nor none given. Thou, Milord Loguire, in consideration of insults offered our Royal Person, art henceforth banished from our Court and Presence, to come near us never more.'

Slowly, the old Duke's eyes met the Queen's. 'How then, child,' he murmured, and Rod saw with a shock that there were tears in the corners of the old man's eyes. 'Child, wilt thou serve the father as thou hast served the son?'

Catharine's face went dead white; she half rose from her throne.

'Hie thee from this place, Milord Loguire!' Brom's voice shook with rage. 'Hie thee from this place, or I shall hound thee hence!'

The Duke's gaze slowly lowered to Brom. 'Hound me? Aye, for thou art most surely our gentle Queen's watchdog!' He raised his eyes to Catharine again. 'Lady, lady! I had hoped to grace thee with a greyhound ere I died.'

Catharine sat again, drawing herself up proudly. 'I have a mastiff, milord; and let my enemies beware!'

The old man nodded slowly, his grieving eyes never leaving her face. 'Thou wilt, then, call me enemy . . .'

Catharine tilted her chin a little higher.

Loguire's eyes hardened; the grief was swept from his face by cold pride.

He spun on his heel, stalking down the length of the great hall. A lane through the crowd opened before him. The Guardsmen at either side of the great central door snapped to attention and threw the portals open.

The Duke stopped short under the lintel and pivoted to look back over the throng at Catharine. His heavy old voice filled the hall one last time.

And his voice was somehow gentle, almost kindly.

'Yet take this of me, Catharine, whom once I called my niece – thou shalt not fear the armies of Loguire while I live.'

He stood motionless a moment, holding Catharine's eyes.

Then he swung about, cape swirling, and was gone.

The court was silent for the space of three breaths; then, as a man, the eleven remaining Great Lords rose and filed down the lane to the great central door, and followed Loguire into exile.

'So how did she decide the case of the two peasants?' Fess asked.

Rod was riding the robot horse on the slope outside the castle, 'for exercise', or so he had told the stableboy. Actually, he needed Fess's advice as to What It All Meant.

'Oh,' he answered, 'she upheld the parish priest's decisions: the fitting punishment for the kid was marriage. The old man didn't like that too well, but Catharine had an ace up her sleeve – the kid would have to support his father-in-law in his old age. The old man grinned at that, and the kid walked out looking like he wasn't quite so sure he'd come out on top after all.'

'An excellent decision,' Fess murmured. 'Perhaps the young lady should seek a career in jurisprudence.'

'Anything, so long as it keeps her out of politics . . . Glorious sunsets on this planet.'

They were riding into the setting sun; the dying globe painted the sky russet and gold halfway around the horizon and nearly to the zenith.

'Yes,' the robot supplied, 'the excellence of the sunsets is due to the density of the atmosphere, which is nearly one point five Terra-normal. At this latitude, however, due to the inclination of the planet's axis, which is—'

'Yes, yes, I wrote it all down in the logbook when we landed. Have the grace to let it rest in peace . . . I notice the sun's rays turn almost blood-red . . .'

'Appropriate,' Fess murmured.

'Hmm, yes. That brings us back to the point, doesn't it? What's this about another assassination coming up?'

'Not an assassination, Rod – an attempt.'

'All right, an attempt. Pardon my denotations, and get on with it.'

Fess paused a moment to set up the readout for a pre-fabricated report.

'The political situation on the island of Gramarye is comprised of three definite factions, one Royalist and two Anti-Royalist. The Royalist faction consists of the Queen, her chief councillor – one Brom O'Berin – the clergy, the Royal Army, the Queen's Bodyguard, and a group of espers known by the local term "witches".'

'How about the judges?'

'As I was about to say, the civil servants may also be included in the Royalist faction, with the exception of those officials whose corruption leaves them opposed to the Queen's reforms.'

'Hmm, yes. I'd forgotten that hitch. Anybody else on the Plantagenet side?'

'Yes, a subspecies of *Homo sapiens* characterized by extreme dwarfism and referred to by the local term "elves".'

'Well, they sure don't seem to be against her, anyway,' Rod murmured.

'The Anti-Royalist factions are significantly *not* united by their common opposition to the Throne. The first of these factions is the aristocracy, led by twelve dukes and earls, who are in turn led by the Duke Loguire. It is worth noting that the aristocrats are unanimous in their opposition to the Queen. Such unanimity among the aristocrats of a feudal culture is totally without precedent, and must therefore be regarded as an anomaly.'

'And just where did this strange united front come from?'

'The unanimity may be attributed to the presence of a group termed the councillors, each member of which serves in an advisory capacity to one of the twelve great lords. The physical coherence of this group indicates—'

Rod jerked his head around, staring at the robot horse's ears. 'How's that again?'

'Each of the councillors is physically characterized by a stooped posture, extreme leanness, sparse cranial hair, pale skin, and a general appearance of advanced age.'

Rod pursed his lips. 'Ve-ry interesting! I hadn't caught any significance in that.'

'Such a physical appearance is characteristic of an extremely advanced technological society, in which the problems of longevity, metabolic adjustment, and exposure to ultraviolet have been controlled.'

'Modern medicine and a bar-room pallor.' Rod nodded. 'But how do you account for the hunched-over posture?'

'We may assume that is a part of the obsequious manner employed by this group. The extremeness of this behaviour would seem to indicate that it is not natural to the men in question.'

'Finagle's Law of Reversal.' Rod nodded. 'Go on.'

'The goal of the Royalist faction is to increase the power of the central authority. The goal of the councillors seems to be the elimination of the central authority, which will result in that form of political organization known as warlordism.'

'Which,' said Rod, 'is a kind of anarchy.'

'Precisely; and we must therefore entertain the possibility that the councillors may pursue the pattern of political breakdown from warlordism through parochialism to the possible goal of total anarchy.'

'And that's why they're out to kill Catharine.'

'An accurate observation; any chance to eliminate the central authority will be taken.'

'Which means she's in danger. Let's get back to the castle.'

He pulled on the reins, but Fess refused to turn. 'She is not in danger, Rod, not yet. The mythos of this culture requires that preliminary to a death, an apparition known as a banshee must be seen on the roof of the dwelling. And the banshee cannot appear until night-fall.'

Rod looked up at the sky. It was twilight; there was still some of the sunset's glow around the horizon.

'All right, Fess. You've got fifteen minutes, maybe a half-hour.'

'The evidence of the councillors' origin in a high-technology society,' the robot droned on, 'indicates that the group derives from off-planet, since the only culture on the planet is that of Catharine's realm, which is characterized by a medieval technology. The other Anti-Royalist faction also bears indications of off-planet origin.'

'I think I've heard that before,' Rod mused. 'Run through it again, will you?'

'Certainly. The second Anti-Royalist faction is known as the House of Clovis, a name deriving from the supposedly elective process of choosing ancient kings. The rank and file of the House of Clovis consists of beggars, thieves, and other criminals and outcasts. The titular leader is a banished nobleman, Tuan Loguire.'

'Hold it a moment,' said Rod. '*Titular* leader?'

'Yes,' said Fess. 'The superficial structure of the House of Clovis would seem to verge on the mob; but further analysis discloses a tightly-knit suborganization, one function of which is the procurement of nourishment and clothing for the members of the House.'

'But that's what Tuan's doing!'

'Is it? Who supplies the necessities of life at the House of Clovis, Rod?'

'Well, Tuan gives the money to the innkeeper, that twisted little monkey they call the Mocker.'

'Precisely.'

'So you're saying,' Rod said slowly, 'that the Mocker is using Tuan as a fund-raiser and figurehead, while the Mocker is the real boss.'

'That,' said Fess, 'is what the data would seem to indicate. What is the Mocker's physical appearance, Rod?'

'Repulsive.'

'And how did he earn his nickname of "the Mocker"?'

'Well, he's supposed to be a sort of Man of a Thousand Faces . . .'

'But what is his basic physical appearance, Rod?'

'Uh . . .' Rod threw his head back, eyes shut, visualizing the Mocker. 'I'd say about five foot ten, hunched over all the time like he had curvature of the spine, slight build – very slight, looks like he eats maybe two hundred calories a day – not much hair . . .' His eyes snapped open. 'Hey! He looks like one of the councillors!'

'And is therefore presumably from a high-technology society,' Fess agreed, 'and therefore also from off-planet. This contention is reinforced by his political philosophy, as indicated in Tuan Loguire's speeches to the rabble . . .'

'So Tuan is also the mouthpiece,' Rod mused. 'But of course; he never could have thought up proletarian totalitarianism by himself.'

'It is also worth noting that the Mocker is the only member of the House of Clovis of this particular physical type.'

'Ye-e-e-s!' Rod nodded, rubbing his chin. 'He's playing a lone game. All his staff are locals trained to back him up.'

'His long-range goal,' said Fess, 'may be assumed to be the establishment of a dictatorship. Consequently, he would wish someone on the throne whom he could control.'

'Tuan.'

'Precisely. But he must first eliminate Catharine.'

'So the councillors and House of Clovis are both out for Catharine's blood.'

'True; yet there is no indication that they have joined forces. If anything, they would seem to be mutually opposed.'

'Duplication of effort – very inefficient. But, Fess, what're they doing here?'

'We may assume that they derive from two opposed societies, both of which wish to control some commodity which may be found on Gramarye.'

Rod frowned. 'I haven't heard of any rare minerals aroundabout . . .'

'I had in mind human resources, Rod.'

Rod's eyes widened. 'The espers! Of course! They're here because of the witches!'

'Or the elves,' Fess reminded.

Rod frowned. 'What would they want with the elves?'

'I have no hypothesis available; yet the logical possibility must be entertained.'

Rod snorted, 'All right, you stick with the logical possibility, and I'll stand by the witches. Anyone who could corner the market on telepaths could control the galaxy. Hey!' He stared, appalled. 'They probably *could* control the galaxy.'

'The stakes,' Fess murmured, 'are high.'

'I'll have mine . . .' Rod began; but he was cut off by a ululating, soaring wail that grated like nails on glass.

Fess swung about; Rod looked back at the castle.

A dim shape glowed on the battlements, just below the east tower. Like a fox fire or a will o' the wisp. It must have been huge; Rod could make out detail even at this distance. It was dressed in the rags and tatters of a shroud, through which Rod could see the body of a voluptuous woman; but the head was a rabbit's, and the muzzle held pointed teeth.

The banshee began to wail again, a low moan that rose to a keening cry, then stabbed up the scale to a shriek, a shriek that held, and held, and held till Rod's ears were ready to break.

'Fess,' he gasped, 'what do you see?'

'A banshee, Rod.'

Rod rode down, ran into, through and over five pairs of sentries en route to the Queen's chambers. But there, at her doors, he met an insurmountable roadblock about two feet high – Brom O'Berin, standing with feet set wide and arms akimbo.

'Thou hast been long in coming,' the little man growled. His face was beet-red with anger, but fear haunted the backs of his eyes.

'I came as fast as I could,' Rod panted. 'Is she in danger?'

Brom grunted. 'Aye, in danger, though there is as yet no sign of it. Thou must stand watch at her bedside this night, warlock.'

Rod stiffened. 'I,' he said, 'am not a warlock. I am a simple soldier-of-fortune who happens to know a little science.'

Brom tossed his head impatiently. 'This is a poor time to bandy words. Call yourself what you will, cook, carpenter, or mason, thou hast still warlock's powers. But we waste time.'

He rapped back-handed on the door; it swung in, and a sentry stepped out. He saluted and stood aside.

Brom smiled grimly and went through the door.

'Still don't trust me behind your back, eh?'

'Nearly,' said Brom.

'That's what I said.'

The sentry entered behind them and closed the door.

The room was large, with four shuttered slit windows on one side. The floor was covered with fur rugs; the walls were hung with silk, velvet, and tapestries. A fire crackled on a small hearth.

Catharine sat in a huge four-poster bed, covered to the waist with quilts and furs. Her unbound hair flowed down over the shoulders of a velvet, ermine-trimmed dressing gown. She was surrounded by a gaggle of ladies-in-waiting, several serving-girls, and two pages.

Rod knelt at her bedside. 'Your Majesty's pardon for my tardiness!'

She gave him a frosty glance. 'I had not known you were called.' She turned away.

Rod frowned, looked her over.

She sat back against eight or ten fluffy satin pillows; her eyelids drooped in languid pleasure; there was a half-smile on her lips. She was enjoying the one spot of real luxury in her day.

She might be in mortal danger, but she sure didn't know about it. Brom had been keeping secrets again.

She held out a hand to one of her ladies; the woman gave her a steaming goblet of wine. Catharine brought it to her lips with a graceful flourish.

'*Whoa!*' Rod jumped to his feet, intercepted the goblet on its way to her lips, and plucked it away with his left hand while his right brought out his 'unicorn's horn'.

Catharine stared, amazed; then her eyes narrowed, her face reddened. 'Sirrah, what means this?'

But Rod was staring at the 'unicorn's horn' dagger-sheath; Fess's voice spoke behind his ear: 'Substance with the analysis unit is toxic to human metabolism.'

But Rod hadn't poured the wine into the horn yet. There was nothing in it.

Except air.

Rod pressed the stud that turned the horn purple.

Catharine stared in horror as the violet flush crept over the surface of the dagger-sheath.

'Sirrah,' she gasped, 'what means this?'

'Poison air,' Rod snapped. He shoved the goblet at a servant-girl and looked about the room. Something in here was emitting poison gas.

The fireplace.

Rod crossed to the hearth and held the horn upside-down over the flames; but the colour of the sheath dimmed to lavender.

'Not there,' Rod spun about, coming to his feet. He paced about the room, holding the horn before him like a candle. It stayed lavender.

He frowned, scratched at the base of his skull. What would be the best place to put a poison-gas cartridge?

As close to the Queen as possible, of course.

He turned, moving slowly to the four-poster. As he came to Catharine's side, the horn's colour darkened to violet.

Catharine stared at the horn in fascination and horror.

Rod knelt, slowly. The horn's colour darkened to purple and began to shade toward black.

Rod threw up the bedskirts and looked under the four-poster. There before him, on the stone floor, steamed a warming-pan.

Rod grabbed the long handle and yanked the pan out. He inverted the horn over one of the holes in the cover – if his memory was correct, warming-pans didn't usually have holes . . .

The horn turned dead black.

He looked up at Catharine. She had the knuckles of one hand jammed between her teeth, biting them to keep from screaming.

Rod turned, holding the pan out to the sentry. 'Take this,' he said, 'and fling it into the moat.'

The sentry dropped his pike, took the warming-pan, and rushed out, holding it at arm's length.

Rod turned slowly back to Catharine. 'We have cheated the banshee again, my Queen.'

Catharine's hand trembled as she took it away from her mouth. Then her lips clamped shut, her eyes squeezed tight, little fists clenched so hard the knuckles were white.

Then her eyes opened, slowly; there was a wild light in them, and a faint smile crept over her lips. 'Master Gallowglass, stay by me. All else, remove yourselves!'

Rod swallowed and felt his joints liquefy. She was, at that moment, the most beautiful woman he had ever seen.

The Guardsmen, ladies, and pages were already in motion, heading for an incipient traffic jam at the door.

Brom bawled orders, and the jam failed to develop. In thirty seconds, the room was clear, except for Rod, the Queen, and Brom O'Berin.

'Brom,' Catharine snapped, eyes locked on Rod's face. Her teeth were beginning to show through her smile. 'Brom O'Berin, do you leave us also.'

Brom stared a moment, outraged; then his shoulders slumped, and he bowed heavily. 'I will, my Queen.'

The door closed quietly behind him.

Slowly, Catharine lay back against the pillows. She stretched with a luxurious, liquid grace. One hand snaked out to clasp Rod's. Her hand was very soft.

'It is twice now you have given me my life, Master Gallowglass.' Her voice was a velvet purr.

'My – my privilege, my Queen.' Rod cursed himself, he was gawking like an adolescent with a copy of *Fanny Hill*.

Catharine frowned prettily, tucking her chin in and touching a forefinger to her lips.

Then she smiled, rolled over onto her side. The velvet gown fell open. Apparently it was the custom to sleep nude.

*Remember, boy*, Rod told himself, *you're just a travelling salesman. You'll wake up in the morning and be on your way. You're here to peddle democracy, not to court a Queen. Not fair to take advantage of her if you're not going to be here to take advantage of it . . . Did that make sense?*

Catharine was toying with a pendant that hung from her neck. Her teeth were worrying her lower lip. She looked him over like a cat sizing up a canary.

'Blank-shield soldiers,' she murmured, 'have a certain repute . . .'

Her lips were moist, and very full.

Rod felt his lips moving, heard his own voice stammering, 'As – as my Queen seeks to reform the ills of her land, I . . . hope to reform the reputation of soldiers. I would do . . . only good to your Majesty.'

For a moment, it seemed Catharine's very blood must have stopped, so still she lay.

Then her eyes hardened, and the silence in the room stretched very, very thin.

She sat up, gathering her dressing gown about her. 'Thou art much to be commended, Master Gallowglass. I am indeed fortunate to have such loyal servitors about me.'

It was much to her credit, under the circumstances, Rod thought, that there was only a faint tone of mockery to her voice.

Her eyes met his again. 'Accept the Queen's thanks for the saving of her life.'

Rod dropped to one knee.

'I am indeed fortunate,' Catharine went on, 'to be so loyally served. You have given me my life; and I think that few soldiers would have given me safe deliverance, as you have done.'

Rod flinched.

She smiled, her eyes glittering malice and satisfaction for just a moment.

Then her eyes dropped to her hands. 'Leave me now, for I shall have a trying day tomorrow, and must make good use of the night, for sleeping.'

'As the Queen wishes,' Rod answered, poker-faced. He rose and turned away, his belly boiling with anger – at himself. It wasn't her fault he was a fool.

He closed the door behind him, then spun and slammed his fist against the rough stone of the entry-way wall. The nerves in his fist screamed agony.

He turned back to the hall, forearm laced with pain – and there stood Brom O'Berin, face beet-red, trembling.

'Well, shall I kneel to thee? Art thou our next king?'

The anger in Rod's belly shot up, heading for Brom O'Berin. Rod clamped his jaws shut to hold it back. He glared at Brom, eyes narrowing. 'I have better use for my time, Brom O'Berin, than to rob the royal cradle.'

Brom stared at him, the blood and fury draining out of his face. ' 'Tis true,' he murmured, nodding. 'By all the saints, I do believe 'tis true! For I can see in thy face that thou art filled with Furies, screaming madness at thy manhood!'

Rod squeezed his eyes shut. His jaw tightened till it felt as if a molar must break.

Something had to break. Something had to give, somewhere.

Somewhere, far away, he heard Brom O'Berin saying, 'This one hath a message for thee, from the witches in the tower . . .'

Rod forced his eyes open, stared down at Brom.

Brom was looking down and to his left. Following his gaze Rod saw an elf sitting tailor-fashion by Brom's foot. Puck.

Rod straightened his shoulders. Smother the anger; vent it later. If the witches had sent word, it was probably vital.

'Well, spill it,' he said. 'What word from the witches?'

But Puck only shook his head and murmured, 'Lord, what fools these mortals be!'

He skipped aside a split second before Rod's fist slammed into the wall where he'd been sitting.

Rod howled with pain, and spun. He saw Puck and lunged again.

But 'Softly' said Puck, and a huge chartreuse-and-shock-pink dragon filled the hall, a full-size, regulation, fire-breathing dragon, rearing back on its hind feet and bellowing flame at Rod.

Rod goggled. Then he grinned, baring his teeth in savage joy.

The dragon belched fire as it struck. Rod ducked under the flames and came up under the monster's head. His fingers closed on the scaly neck, thumbs probing for the carotid arteries.

The dragon flung its head up and snapped its neck like a whip. Rod held on grimly, held on and held on while the dragon battered him against the granite walls. His head slapped stone and he yelled with pain, stars and darkness before his eyes, but he tightened his grip.

The great neck bowed, and the huge talons of the hind feet raked at Rod's belly, splitting him from collarbone to thigh. Blood fountained out, and Rod felt himself reeling into blackness; but he held on, determined to take the dragon with him into death.

*Yeah, death,* he thought, amazed, and was outraged that he should die over a puny fit of anger, anger over a slip of a bitch of a girl.

Well, at least he'd have a mount in the land of the dead. As darkness sucked him down, he felt the great head drooping, bobbing lower and lower, following him down to death. . . .

His feet felt solid ground and, for a miracle, his legs held him up. Light misted through the dark around him, misted and gathered and grew, and he saw the beast lying dead at his feet.

The darkness ebbed away from the dragon; light showed Rod granite walls and brocade hangings; and the castle hall swam about him, reeled, and steadied.

At his feet, the dragon's colours faded. Its outlines blurred and shimmered, and the beast was gone; there was only clean grey stone beneath Rod's feet.

He looked down at his chest and belly; his doublet was whole, not even wrinkled. Not a trace of blood, not a scratch on him.

He squeezed an elbow, expecting the pain of bruises; there was none.

His head was clear, without the ghost of even an ache.

Slowly, he raised his eyes to Puck.

The elf looked back, eyes wide and mournful. Amazingly, he wasn't smiling.

Rod covered his face with his hands, then looked up again. 'Enchantment?'

Puck nodded.

Rod looked away. 'Thanks.'

'Thou hadst need of it,' Puck answered.

Rod squared his shoulders and breathed deeply. 'You had a message for me?'

Puck nodded again. 'Thou art summoned to a meeting of the Coven.'

Rod frowned, shaking his head. 'But I'm not a member.'

Brom O'Berin chuckled like a diesel turning over. 'Nay, thou art of them, for thou art a warlock.'

Rod opened his mouth to answer, thought better of it, and closed his jaws with a snap. He threw up his hands in resignation. 'Okay, have it your own way. I'm a warlock. Just don't expect me to believe it.'

'Well, thou wilt, at least, no longer deny it.' Toby filled Rod's mug with the hot, mulled wine. 'We ha' known thou wert a warlock even before we had set eyes on thee.'

Rod sipped at the wine and looked about him. If he'd thought it was a party last night, his naïveté had been showing. That had just been a *kaffeeklatsch*. This time the kids were really whooping it up.

He turned back to Toby, bellowing to hear his own voice. 'Don't get me wrong; I don't mean to be a cold blanket, but what's the occasion? How come all the celebrating?'

'Why, our Queen lives!' yelled Toby. 'And thou art hero of the night! Thou hast banished the banshee!'

'Hero . . .' Rod echoed, a wry smile twisting his face. He lifted his mug and took a long, long draught.

Suddenly he swung the mug down, spluttering and coughing.

'What ails thee?' Toby asked, concerned. He pounded Rod on the back till the older man wheezed, gasping.

'Leave off,' he said, holding up a hand, 'I'm okay. I just thought of something, that's all?'

'What is thy thought?'

'That banshee ain't real.'

Toby stared. 'What dost thou say?'

Rod clamped a hand on the back of Toby's neck and pulled the boy's ear down to his own level.

'Look,' he yelled, 'the banshee only appears before someone dies, right?'

'Aye,' said Toby, puzzled.

'Before someone *dies*,' Rod repeated, 'not every time someone's just in *danger* of death. And the Queen's still alive!'

Toby pulled back, staring at Rod.

Rod smiled, eyes dancing. 'It's only supposed to show up when death's inevitable.'

He turned, looked out over the great tower room. The witches were dancing on the walls, the ceiling, occasionally the floor, and in mid-air, with a fine disregard for gravity. They were twisting through gyrations that would have given a snake triple lumbago.

Rod looked back at Toby, lifted an eyebrow. 'Doesn't look much like a funeral.'

Toby frowned; then his face split into a grin. 'I think thou hast not seen a Gramarye wake,' he yelled. 'Still, thou art aright; we dance this night for Life, not Death.'

Rod grinned savagely, took another pull from his mug, and wiped his lips with the back of his hand. 'Now, if it's a fake, and it is, the next question is, who put it there?'

Toby's jaw dropped open. He stared.

'Get me Aldis,' Rod shouted.

Toby closed his mouth, gulped, and nodded. He closed his eyes; a moment later, Aldis swooped down and brought her broomstick in for a two-point landing.

'What dost thou wish?' she panted. She was blushing, face lit with excitement and joy. The sight of her gave Rod a sudden pang of mourning for his own lost youth.

He leaned forward. 'See if you can tune in on Durer, Loguire's chief councillor.'

She nodded, closed her eyes. After a few moments, she opened them again, staring at Rod in fear.

'They are much wroth,' she reported, 'that the Queen did not die. But they are more wroth in that they know not who put the banshee on the roof of the castle this night.'

Rod nodded, lips pressed into a tight, thin line. He took a last draught from his mug and rose, turning away toward the stairwell.

Toby reached up, catching his sleeve. 'Where dost thou go?'

'To the battlements,' Rod called back. 'Where else would you look for a banshee?'

The night breeze cut chill through his clothes as he stepped out onto the battlements. The moon, over his shoulder, sent his shadow pacing before him.

The battlements stretched out before him like a great gap-toothed row of incisors.

'Fess,' Rod called softly.

'Here, Rod,' murmured the voice back of his ear.

'Does this banshee seem to be fonder of one stretch of battlements than another?'

'Yes, Rod. During the period in which we have been in Gramarye, the banshee has appeared under the east tower.'

'Always?'

'To judge by an inadequate sample, yes.'

Rod turned to his left, strolling east. 'Well, you go on collecting an adequate sample while I do something about it.'

'Yes, Rod,' said the robot, somehow managing a tone of martyred patience.

Rod looked out over the battlements at the town, nestled below them at the foot of the great hill that served as the foundation for the castle. A long, white road wound up from the town to the drawbridge, with here and there the outpost of a low, rambling inn.

And down there below, in the rotting heart of the town, like some great basalt gravestone, stood the House of Clovis.

A stumbling, a scrabbling behind him. Rod snapped about into a wrestler's crouch, dagger a bite of moonlight in his hand.

Big Tom stumbled out of the winding stairway, with something draped across his arm. He stood, looking about him with wide-white-rimmed eyes, heaving hoarse gusts of air into his lungs.

He turned, saw Rod, and came running, his face flooded with relief. 'Eh, master, thou'rt still whole!'

Rod relaxed and straightened up, sliding the dagger back into its sheath. 'Of course I'm whole! What're *you* doing here, Big Tom?'

The big man stopped, the grin wavering on his face. He looked down at the cold stones, shuffling his feet. ' 'Ell, master, I had heard . . . I . . . well . . .' He looked up; the words came in a rush: 'Tha must not go again' the banshee; but if thou'lt go, thou'lt not go alone.'

Rod studied the big man's face for a long moment, wondering where this deep devotion had come from.

Then he smiled gently. 'Your knees have turned to jelly at the mere thought of the monster, but you still won't let me go alone.'

He clapped Tom on the shoulder, grinning. 'Well, then, come along, Big Tom; and I'm downright glad of your company, I don't mind telling you.'

Tom grinned and looked down at the stones again. It was hard to be sure in the moonlight, but Rod thought there was a faint blush creeping up from the big man's collar.

He turned and set out toward the tower. Tom plodded along by his side. ' 'Ere now, master, thou'lt grow a-cold,' and Tom flung the cloak he had been carrying over his arm around Rod's shoulder.

A warm, friendly gesture, Rod thought as he thanked Big Tom. He was touched that the clumsy ape should be worried about him – but he was also aware that the cloak hampered his knife hand, and was pretty sure Big Tom was aware of it, too.

'Art not afraid, master?'

Rod frowned, considering the question. 'Well, no, not really. After all, the banshee's never been known to hurt anybody. It's just, well, a forecast, you know? Herald of Death and all that.'

'Still, 'tis a marvel thou'rt not afeard. Wilt thou not even walk in the shadows by the wall, master?'

Rod frowned and looked at the shadows along the battlements. 'No, I'll take the centre of the way when I can. I'd always rather walk tall in the sunlight than skulk in the shadows at the side of the road.'

Big Tom was silent a moment, his eyes on the shadows.

'Yet,' he said, 'of necessity, a man must go through the shadows at one time or other, master.'

With a shock, Rod realized Tom had picked up the allegory. Illiterate peasant, *sure*!

He nodded, looking so serious it was almost comic. 'Yes, Big Tom. There's times when he has to choose one side of the road or the other. But for myself, I only stay on the sidelines as long as I have to. I prefer the light.' He grinned. 'Good protection against spirits.'

'Spirits!' Tom snorted. He quickly threw Rod a half-hearted grin.

He turned away, frowning. 'Still, master, I do much marvel that you will take the middle road; for there may a man be attacked from both sides. And, more to the point, he cannot say that he has chosen either the right or the left.'

'No,' Rod agreed, 'but he can say that he has chosen the middle. And as to attack, well, if the road is well-built, the centre is highest; the pavement slopes away to right and left, and the shoulder is soft and may give way beneath you. A man in the middle can see where his enemies are coming from; and it's firm footing. The sides of the road are treacherous. Sure it's an exposed position. That's why not too many have the courage to walk it.'

They walked a moment in silence; then Rod said, 'Did you ever hear of dialectical materialism, Tom?'

'How . . . ?' The big man's head jerked up in surprise, almost shock. He recovered, scowling and shaking his head fervently, and muttering, 'No, no, master, no, never, never!'

*Sure, Big Tom*, Rod thought. Aloud, he said, 'It's a Terran philosophy, Big Tom. Its origins are lost in the Dark Ages, but some men still hold by it.'

'What is Terran?' the big man growled.

'A dream,' Rod sighed, 'and a myth.'

'Are you one man who lives by it, master?'

Rod looked up, startled. 'What? The dream of Terra?'

'No, this dialec – what magic didst thou term it?'

'What, dialectical materialism?' Rod grinned. 'No, but I find some of its concepts very handy, like the idea of a synthesis. Do you know what a synthesis is, Tom?'

'Nay, master.' Tom shook his head, eyes round in wonder.

The wonder, at least, was probably real. The last thing Big Tom could have looked for was Rod to start quoting a totalitarian philosophy.

'It's the middle way,' Rod said. 'The right-hand side of the road is the thesis, and the left-hand side is the antithesis. Combine them, and you get a synthesis.'

'Aye,' Big Tom nodded.

*Pretty quick thinking for a dumb peasant*, Rod noted. He went on, 'The thesis and antithesis are both partly false; so you throw away the false parts, combine the true parts – take the best of both of them – call the result a synthesis, and you've got the truth. See?'

Tom's eyes took on a guarded look. He began to see where Rod was going.

'And the synthesis is the middle of the road. And, being true, it's naturally uncomfortable.'

He looked up; the east tower loomed over them. They stood in its shadow. 'Well, enough philosophizing. Let's get to work.'

'Pray Heaven the banshee come not upon us!' Big Tom moaned.

'Don't worry; it only shows up once a day, in the evening, to predict death within twenty-four hours,' Rod said. 'It's not due again till tomorrow evening.'

There was a sudden scrabbling in the shadows. Big Tom leaped back, a knife suddenly in his hand. 'The banshee!'

Rod's blade was out too, his eyes probing the shadows. They locked with two fiery dots at the base of the tower wall.

Rod stepped out in a crouch, knife flickering back and forth from left hand to right. 'Declare yourself,' he chanted, 'or die.'

A squeal and a skitter, and a huge rat dashed away past him, to lose itself in the shadows near the inner wall.

Big Tom almost collapsed with a sigh. 'Saints preserve us! 'Twas only a rat.'

'Yes.' Rod tried to hide the trembling of his own hands as his knife went back to its sheath. 'There seem to be a lot of rats in the walls of this castle.'

Big Tom straightened again, wary and on his guard.

'But I saw something as that rat ran by me . . .' Rod's voice trailed away as he knelt by the outer wall, running his hands lightly over the stone. 'There!'

'What is it, master?' Big Tom's garlic breath fanned Rod's cheek.

Rod took the big man's hand and set it against his find. Tom drew in a shuddering breath and yanked his hand away.

' 'Tis cold,' his voice quavered, 'cold and square, and – it bit me!'

'Bit you?' Rod frowned and ran his fingers over the metal box. He felt the stab of a mild electric shock and jerked his fingers away. Whoever had wired this gadget must have been the rankest of amateurs. It wasn't even grounded properly.

The box was easy to see once you knew where to look for it. It was white metal, about eight inches on a side, two inches deep, recessed so that its front and top were flush with the stone, halfway between two of the crenellations.

But come to think of it, that faulty grounding might have been intentional, to keep people from tampering.

Rod drew his dagger, glad of the insulation provided by the leather hilt. Carefully, he pried open the front of the box.

He could make out the silvery worm-trails of the printed circuit and the flat, square pillbox of the solid-state components – but the whole layout couldn't have been larger than his thumbnail!

His scalp prickled uneasily. Whoever had built this rig knew a little more about molecular circuitry than the engineers back home.

But why such a big box for such a small unit?

Well, the rest of the box was filled with some beautifully-machined apparatus with which Rod was totally unfamiliar.

He looked at the top of the box; there was a round, transparent circle set in the centre. Rod frowned. He'd never run into anything quite like this before. At a guess, the circuitry was part of a remote-control system, and the machined parts were – what?

'Master, what is it?'

'I don't know,' Rod muttered, 'but I have a sneaking suspicion it's got something to do with the banshee.'

He probed the mechanism with his dagger, trying to find a moving part. He felt sublimely reckless; the gadget could very easily have a destruct circuit capable of blowing this whole section of the battlements halfway back to Sol.

The probing point found something; the machine clicked and began to hum, almost subsonic.

'Away, master!' Big Tom shouted. ' 'Tis accursed!'

But Rod stayed where he was, hand frozen for fear the knife-point would lose whatever contact it had closed.

Smoke billowed out of the transparent circle, shooting ten feet into the air, then falling back. In less than a minute, a small localized cloud had formed.

A second machine clicked, somewhere in front of Rod, and a shaft of light stabbed upward from the outer wall, toward Rod but over his head, shooting into the smoke-cloud. The shaft of light spread into a fan.

Big Tom wailed in terror. 'The banshee! Flee, master, for your life!'

Looking up, Rod saw the banshee towering ten feet above him. It seemed he could almost smell the rotting, tattered shrouds that covered the voluptuous woman's body.

The rabbit mouth opened, showing long, pointed teeth. A hidden loudspeaker hummed into life; the apparition was about to start its wailing.

Rod lifted his dagger a quarter of an inch; the fan of light blacked out, the hiss of the mechanical smoke-pot died.

The wind murmured over the battlements, dispelling the last of the smoke-cloud.

Rod knelt immobile, still staring upward; then, shaking himself, he picked up the front of the box and forced it back into place.

'Master,' whispered Big Tom, 'what was it?'

'A spell,' Rod answered, 'and the banshee it called up was a sham.'

He stood, drumming his fingers on the stone.

He struck his fist against the wall. 'No help for it. Come on, Big Tom, hold my ankles.'

He lay face-downward between the two great granite blocks, his knees above the smoke-pot machine.

'What, master?'

'Hold my ankles,' Rod snapped. 'I've got to take a look at the outside of the wall. And you've got to keep me from falling into the moat.'

Tom didn't answer.

'Come on, come on!' Rod looked back over his shoulder. 'We haven't got all night.'

Big Tom came forward slowly, a huge, hulking shape in the shadow. His great hands clamped on Rod's ankles.

Rod inched forward until his head was clear of the stone.

There, just under his chin, was a small, square box with a short snout: a miniaturized projector, shooting a prerecorded banshee into the cloud of smoke, giving the illusion of three dimensions – a very compact projector and removable screen, all susceptible to remote control.

From where?

Rod craned his neck. All he could see was grey stone.

'Hold tight, Big Tom.' He inched forward, hoping he'd guessed right about the big peasant.

He stopped crawling when he felt the granite lip of the battlements pressing his belt buckle. His upper body jutted free beyond the castle wall, with nothing underneath but air, and, a long way down, the moat.

He looked down.

Mm, yes, that *was* a long way, wasn't it? Now, just what would happen if he'd judged Big Tom wrong? If, contrary to expectation, the big lug let go of Rod's ankles?

Well, if that happened, Fess would send a report back to SCENT headquarters, and they'd send out another agent. No need to worry.

Tom's hoarse, laboured breathing sounded very loud behind him.

*Get it over with quick, boy.* Rod scanned the wall under him.

There it was, just under the projector, a deep, silver-lined cup recessed into the wall – a hyperbolic antenna.

*Why a hyperbolic?* he wondered.

So that the radio impulse that turned the projection machines on could be very, very small, impossible to detect outside the straight line between the transmitting and receiving antennas.

So, if you want to find the transmitting antenna, just sight along the axis of the receiving dish.

And, looking along that line and allowing for parallax, he found himself staring straight at the rotting basalt pile of the House of Clovis.

For a moment, he just stared, dumbfounded. So it hadn't been the councillors after all.

Then he remembered Durer's poison attempt at breakfast, and amended his earlier guess: it hadn't been the councillors *all* the time.

And, come to think of it, that warming-pan trick would have been much easier for a servant to pull than for a councillor.

He was jarred out of his musing rather abruptly; Big Tom's hands were trembling on his ankles.

*Hell, I don't weigh that much*, he thought; but he wriggled backward while he thought.

He thought he heard a sigh of relief as Big Tom hauled him in.

Rod rose and turned. Sweat streamed down Big Tom's face; his complexion looked very much like dirty dishwater, and his lower lip still trembled as he sucked in a noisy deep breath.

Rod looked into the big man's eyes for a long moment, without saying anything.

Then he murmured, 'Thanks.'

Tom held Rod's eyes a moment longer, then turned away.

Rod fell into step beside him.

They were halfway back to the stairwell before Big Tom said, 'And dost thou know who hath sent this enchantment, master?'

Rod nodded. 'The House of Clovis.'

Their boots echoed hollow on the stone.

'Why hast thou not destroyed it?'

Rod shrugged. 'It's a good warning that the Queen's in danger.'

'Then who wilt thou tell of it?'

Rod looked up at the stars. 'My horse,' he said slowly.

'Horse?' Big Tom frowned.

'Yes, my horse. And no one else, until I've figured out just where Tuan Loguire stands – for the Queen or against her.'

'Ah.' Big Tom seemed to think that was explanation enough.

Rod boosted his estimate of Big Tom's status. Apparently the man knew what was going on, more thoroughly than Rod did.

Big Tom was silent till they came to the stairwell.

'Thou wast not a hair's breadth from Death this night, master.'

'Oh, I don't think so.' Rod folded his arms and leaned against the wall. 'That was just a fake banshee; it couldn't have hurt us. And even as it was, I knew the spell that got rid of it.'

'I was not speaking of the banshee, master.'

'I know.' Rod looked straight into Tom's eyes.

Then he turned and started down the stairs.

He'd gone six steps before he realized Big Tom hadn't followed. He looked back over his shoulder. Tom was staring at him, mouth slack with shock.

Then the mouth closed, the face froze. 'Thou didst know thy danger, master?'

'I did.'

Tom nodded, very slowly. Then he looked down to the stairs and came down.

'Master,' he said after the first landing, 'thou'rt either the bravest man or the greatest fool that ever I met.'

'Probably both,' said Rod, keeping his eyes on the torchlit steps.

'Thou shouldst have slain me when first thou guessed.' Tom's voice had an edge.

Rod shook his head, wordless.

'Why not?' Tom barked.

Rod let his head loll back. He sighed. 'Long ago, Tom, and far away – Lord, how far away!'

' 'Tis no time for fairy-tales!'

'This isn't a fairy-tale. It's a legend – who knows? Maybe true. A king named Hideyoshi ruled a land called Japan; and the greatest duke in the land was named Ieyayasu.'

'And the duke wished to be king.'

'I see you know the basic techniques. But Hideyoshi did *not* want to kill Ieyayasu.'

'He was a fool,' Tom growled.

'No, he needed Ieyayasu's support. So he invited Ieyayasu to take a walk in the garden with him, just the two of them, alone.'

Tom stopped, turned to look down at Rod. His eyes glittered in the torchlight. 'And they fought.'

Rod shook his head. 'Hideyoshi said he was getting old and weak, and asked Ieyayasu to carry his sword for him.'

Tom stared.

Then his tongue flicked out over his lips. He swallowed and nodded. 'Aye. What happened?'

'Nothing. They talked a while, and then Ieyayasu gave Hideyoshi his sword again, and they went back to the castle.'

'And?'

'And Ieyayasu was loyal until the old man died.'

Big Tom's eyes were hooded; he could have been carved from wood.

He nodded, mouth tightening. 'A calculated risk.'

'Pretty high-falutin' language for a peasant.'

Tom snarled and turned away. Rod stood a moment, looking after him. Then he smiled and followed.

They were almost back to the guardroom when Tom laid a hand on Rod's shoulder. Rod turned to face him.

'What are you?' Tom growled.

Rod smiled with one side of his mouth. 'You mean who do I work for? Only myself, Big Tom.'

'Nay.' Tom shook his head. 'I'll not believe that. But 'twas not what I asked.'

Rod raised an eyebrow. 'Oh?'

'Oh. I mean what are you, you, yourself, what manner of man?'

Rod frowned. 'Nothing so strange about me.'

'Aye, there is. Thou wilt not kill a peasant out of hand.'

Rod stared. 'Oh?' He pursed his lips. 'That's out of the ordinary?'

'Most surely. And thou'lt fight for a manservant. And trust him. And speak with him, more than commands. What art thou, Rod Gallowglass?'

Rod shook his head and spread his hands in bewilderment. He laughed once, hollow. 'A man. Just a man.'

Tom eyed him for a long moment.

'Thou art,' he said. 'I am answered.'

He turned away to the guardroom door, flung it open.

'Master Gallowglass,' said the page, 'the Queen summons you.'

One of life's greatest and least expensive treasures is false dawn. The world lies waiting for the sun, lit by a glowing sky, chill and fresh, filled with rippling bird song.

Big Tom took one long, deep breath of the morning air, filling his lungs with the innocence he had never known. 'Eh, master!' he called back over his shoulder, 'this is the world for a man!'

Rod answered with a feeble smile as Tom turned away, to ride on ahead of Rod, singing jubilantly and with gusto, though somewhat off-key.

Rod, unfortunately, was in no condition to appreciate the aesthetic qualities of the dawn, having had about three hours of sleep in the last forty-eight hours.

Then, too, there was Catharine.

The interview had been short and sour. She'd received him in her audience chamber, and had kept her eyes on the fire, not once looking at him. Her face had been cold, lips drawn tight against her teeth.

'I fear for my Uncle Loguire,' she had said. 'There are men about him who would rejoice to see his eldest son become the Duke.'

Rod had answered in the same stiff, formal tone. 'If he dies, you lose your strongest friend among the lords.'

'I lose one who is dear to me,' she snapped. 'I care not for friendship among the lords; but I care greatly for my uncle.'

And that, Rod reflected, was probably true – to her credit as a woman, and her detriment as a ruler.

'Do you,' she resumed, 'ride south this day to Loguire's demesne; and do you see that none bring harm to him.'

And that, aside from a very formal leave taking, had been that. Hell hath no stupidity like a woman scorned, Rod thought; she was sending her most competent bodyguard as far away as she could.

'Fess?'

'Yes, Rod?' The horse turned its head to look back at its rider.

'Fess, I am without a doubt the prizest booby ever hatched.'

'You are a great man, Rod, from a line of great men.'

'Oh yeah, I'm *so* great! Here I am, supposed to be turning this kingdom into a constitutional monarchy; and while I'm jauntily wandering southward, the councillors are tearing apart any possibility of a constitution, while the House of Clovis is on the verge of killing off the monarch!

'And here I ride south, with a manservant who would probably gleefully slip a knife between my ribs if his sense of duty got the upper hand over his conscience for half a minute.

'And what have I accomplished? I've established that the place is filled with ghosts, elves, witches, and a lot of other monsters that can't possibly exist; I've given you five or six seizures; and to top it all off, a beautiful woman propositioned me, and I refused! Oh, I'm so great it's unbelievable! If I were just a little bit more efficient, I'd have managed to botch the whole thing by now! Fess, wouldn't I be better off if I just gave up?'

The robot began to sing softly.

'*I am a man of constant sorrow,*
*I've seen trouble all my days. . . .*'

'Oh, shut up.'

# Part Two
# The Witch of Low Estate

Dawn found them in the midst of hayfields, half-mown and dew-laden. Rod looked about him from the top of the rise, looking down on rolling farmland and tidy hedges, with here and there a clump of trees, dark against the rising sun.

'Big Tom!'

Tom turned in the saddle and looked back, then reined in his horse when he saw Rod had halted.

'Breakfast!' Rod called, dismounting. He led Fess off the road to a rock outcrop beneath a thicket of gorse. Tom shrugged and turned his mount.

Rod had the fire laid and kindled by the time Big Tom had hobbled his pony and turned it to graze. The big man stared in amazement as Rod unlimbered a frying pan and coffee-pot, then turned away, shaking his head in wonder, and dried a place to sit on a log further down the slope. He sniffed at the scent of frying ham, sighed, and took out a pack of hard-tack.

Rod looked up, frowning, and saw Big Tom sitting in wet grass with a biscuit and a skin of ale. He scowled and shouted.

'Hey!'

The shout caught Big Tom in mid-swig; he choked, spluttered, and looked up.

'Eh, master?'

'My food not good enough for you?'

Big Tom stared, open-mouthed.

'Come, on, come on!' Rod waved an arm impatiently. 'And bring those biscuits with you; they'll go well fried in bacon-fat.'

Big Tom opened and closed his mouth a few times, then nodded vaguely and stood up.

The water was boiling; Rod pried the lid off the coffeepot and threw in a handful of grounds. He looked up as Big Tom came to the fire, brow furrowed, staring.

Rod's mouth turned down at the corner. 'Well, what're you looking at? Never saw a campfire before?'

'Thou bade me eat with my master!'

Rod scowled. 'Is that some major miracle? Here, give a drag of that ale-skin, will you? That road gets dusty.'

Tom nodded, eyes still fixed on Rod's, and held out the skin. Rod took a swig, looked up, and frowned. 'What's the matter? Never saw a man take a drink? What am I, some alien monster?'

Tom's mouth closed; his eyes turned dark and brooding.

Then he grinned, laughed, and sat down on a rock. 'Nay, master, nay. Thou'rt a rare good man, and that only. Nay, only that!'

Rod frowned. 'Why, what's so rare about me?'

Tom threw two cakes of hard-tack into the frying pan and looked up, grinning. 'In this country, master, a gentleman does not take food with his servant.'

'Oh, that!' Rod waved the objection away. 'It's just you and me out here on the road, Big Tom. I don't have to put up with that nonsense.'

'Aye,' Big Tom chuckled. 'A most wondrous rare man, as I said.'

'And a fool, eh?' Rod served up two slices of bacon on wooden saucers. 'Guess we eat with our knives, Tom. Dig in.'

They ate in silence, Rod scowling at his plate, Tom leaning back and looking out over the countryside.

They were at the head of a small valley, filled now with the morning mist, a trap for small sunbeams. The sun lurked over the hedges, and the mist was golden.

Tom grinned as he chewed and jerked his thumb toward the valley. ''Tis the end of the rainbow, master.'

'Hm?' Rod jerked his head up. He smiled sourly; it was, after all, more of a pot of gold than he'd had any right to expect.

Tom gave a rumbling belch and picked at his teeth with his dagger. 'A golden mist, master, and mayhap golden girls within it.'

Rod swallowed quickly and objected. 'Oh, no! No tomcatting on the side of this trip, Big Tom! We've got to get down to the South and get down there fast!'

'Eh, master!' Tom wailed in shocked protest, 'what harm another hour or four, eh? Besides'—he sat forward and poked Rod in the ribs, grinning— 'I'll wager thou'lt outdo me. What lasses may not a warlock have, mm? . . . Eh, what's the matter?'

Rod wheezed and pounded his chest. 'Just a piece of hard-tack having an argument with my gullet. Tom, for the umpteenth penultimate unprintable time, I am *not* a warlock!'

'Oh, aye, master, to be sure!' Big Tom said with a broad-lipped grin. 'And thou mayst be certain thou'rt as poor a liar as thou art an executioner.'

Rod frowned. 'I haven't killed a man the whole time I've been here!'

'Aye, and this is my meaning.'

'Oh.' Rod turned and looked out over the fields. 'Well, you might as well add lover to that list of things I'm not good at, Tom.'

The big man sat forward, frowning, searching Rod's face. 'In truth, I think he doth mean it!'

'Be sure that I doth.'

Tom sat back, studying his master and tossing his dagger, catching it alternately by the hilt and the point. 'Aye, thou speakest aright of thy knowledge.' He sat forward, looking into Rod's eyes. 'And therefore shall I dare to advise thee.'

Rod grinned and gave him a hollow laugh. 'All right, advise me. Tell me how it's done.'

'Nay.' Tom held up a palm. 'That much I am sure that you knowest. But it is these farm girls against which I must caution thee, master.'

'Oh?'

'Aye. They are—' Tom's face broke into a grin. 'Oh, they are excellent, master, though simple. But –' he frowned again ' – never give them a trace of a hope.'

Rod frowned too. 'Why not?'

' 'Twill be thy undoing. Thou mayst love them well, master, once – but once only. Then must thou leave them, right quickly, and never look back.'

'Why? I'll be turned into a pillar of salt?'

'Nay, thou'lt be turned into a husband. For once given the merest shred of hope, master, these farm girls will stick tighter than leeches, and thou'lt never be rid of them.'

Rod snorted. 'I should have a chance to worry about it! Come on, drink up your coffee and mount up.'

They doused the fire and packed up, and rode down into the red-gold mist.

They had gone perhaps three hundred yards when a long-drawn alto voice hailed them.

Rod looked up, tensed and wary.

Two big peasant girls stood with pitchforks at the base of a haystack in one of the fields, laughing and waving.

Big Tom's eyes locked on them with an almost-audible click. 'Eh, master! Pretty little mopsies, are they not?'

They were pretty, Rod had to admit – though certainly anything but little. They were both full-hipped and high-breasted, wearing loose low-cut blouses and full skirts, their hair tied in kerchiefs. Their skirts were girded up to their knees, to keep them from the dew on the hay.

They beckoned, their laughter a mocking challenge. One of them set her hands on her hips and executed a slow bump-and-grind.

Big Tom sucked his breath in, his eyes fairly bulging. 'Eh, now, master,' he pleaded, 'are we in so much of a hurry as all that?'

Rod sighed, rolling his eyes up, and shook his head. 'Well, I'd hate to see them suffering from neglect, Big Tom. Go ahead.'

Tom kicked his horse with a yelp of joy, leaped the ditch, and galloped full tilt into the field. He was out of the saddle before the horse slowed past a trot, catching a girl in each arm, lifting them off the ground and whirling them about.

Rod shook his head slowly, saluted Big Tom and his playmates, and turned away to find a neighbouring haystack where he could nap in peace.

'Rod,' said the quiet voice behind his ear.

'Yes, Fess?'

'Your conducts disturbs me, Rod. It's not natural for a healthy young male.'

'It's not the first time someone's told me that, Fess. But I'm methodical; I can't keep two girls on my mind at once.'

He found another haystack just over the next hedge. Rod parked in the shadow and unbridled Fess, who began to crop at the hay, to keep up appearances. Rod remounted and jumped from the horse's back to the top of the haystack and wallowed down into the soft, fragrant hay with a blissful sigh. The pungent smell of new-mown hay filled his head, taking him back to his boyhood in the field of his father's manor, during haying time; a *real* Eden, without any soft, nubile problems to run around creating havoc. Just robots . . .

He watched the gilt-edged clouds drifting across the turquoise sky, not realizing when he dozed off.

He came wide awake and stayed very still, wondering what had wakened him. He ran through the catalogue of sensations that were apt to start the alarm clock ringing in his subconscious.

Somebody was near.

His eyes snapped open, every muscle in his body tensed to fight.

He was looking into a very low-cut bodice.

He raised his eyes from the pleasant pastoral view, a task which required no small amount of willpower, and saw two large sea-green eyes looking into his. They were long-lashed, moist, and looked worried.

Their surroundings came into focus: arched eyebrows, a snub nose sprinkled with freckles, a very wide mouth with full, red lips, all set in a roundish face framed in long, flowing red hair.

The full red lips were pouting, the eyes were troubled.

Rod smiled, yawned, and stretched. 'Good morning.'

The pouting lips relaxed into a half-smile. 'Good morning, fine gentleman.'

She was sitting beside him, propped on one hand, looking into his eyes.

'Why do you sleep here alone, sir, when nearby a woman awaits your call?'

It felt as though someone had just poured bitters into Rod's circulatory system; a thrill, and not completely a pleasant one, flooded through him.

He smiled, trying to make it warm. 'I thank you, lass, but I'm not feeling gamesome today.'

She smiled, but there was still a frown between her eyes. 'I thank you for your gentleness, sir; but I scarce can credit your words.'

'Why?' Rod frowned. 'Is it so impossible that a man shouldn't want a frolic?'

The girl gave a forlorn half of a laugh. 'Oh, it might be, milord, but scarce is it likely. Not even with a peasant, and even less with a lord.'

'I'm not a lord.'

'A gentleman, then. That, surely, thou art. And therefore, surely, thou wouldst never lack interest.'

'Oh?' Rod raised an eyebrow. 'Why?'

She smiled, sadly. 'Why, milord, a peasant might fear forced marriage; but a lord, never.'

Rod frowned again and studied the girl's face. He judged her to be a little younger than himself, about twenty-nine or thirty.

And for a peasant girl in this kind of society to be unmarried at thirty . . .

He threw out an arm. 'Come here to me, lass.'

There was hope, for a moment, in the girl's eyes; but it faded quickly, was replaced by resignation. She fell into the hay beside him with a sigh, rolling onto her side to pillow her head on his shoulder.

*Hope*, Rod mused, very conscious of her breasts and hips against the side of his body. *Hope to be tumbled, and thrown away* . . .

He shuddered; and the girl raised her head, concerned. 'Art chilled, milord?'

He turned to her and smiled, a sudden wave of gratitude and tenderness surging up to clog his throat. He clasped her tight against him, closing his eyes to better savour the touch of her body against his own. An aroma filled his head, not rose-oil or lilac, but simply the salt-sweet scent of a woman.

A pain was ebbing away inside him, he realized, faintly surprised, a pain that he had not known was there till it began to leave him.

She clung to him, fists clenched in the cloth of his doublet, face pressed into the angle of his neck and shoulder.

Then, gradually, he began to relax again, his embrace loosening. He lay very still, letting the focus of his mind widen, open him again to the world around him; faint in the distance he heard birdsong, and the gossip of the wind through the hedges and trees. Somewhere near his head, a cricket chirped in the hay.

Her embrace had loosened with his; her arms and head lay leaden on him now.

He kept his eyes closed, the sun beating down on the lids; he lay in crimson light, 'seeing' the world with his ears.

There was a rustle, and her body rose away from his; she had sat up now. She would be looking down at him, hurt aching in her eyes, lower lip trembling, a tear on her cheek.

Pity welled up in him, pity for her and, close behind it, anger at himself; it wasn't her fault that all he wanted just now was peace, not romance.

He opened his eyes, rolling onto his side and frowning up at her.

But there was no hurt in her eyes – only a grave, deep acceptance, and concern.

She raised her fingertip to his cheek, shyly, not quite touching the skin. He caught it, nestling the palm against the line of his jaw, and was amazed at how small her hand was in his own.

He closed his eyes, pressing her hand tighter.

A cow lowed far away; the wind chuckled in the grain.

Her voice was low, and very gentle. 'Milord, use me as you will. I ask no more.'

*I ask no more*. . . . Love, she must have love, if only for a minute, even if desertion came hard on its heels; even if looking back, she must know that it was lust, and not love. Even if it brought only sorrow and pain, she must have love.

He looked into her eyes; they held tears.

He closed his eyes again, and Catharine's face was before him, and Tuan's face next to hers. A part of him stood back, aloof, and contemplated the faces; it remarked on how well they looked together, the beautiful princess and the gallant young knight.

Then his own face came up next to Tuan's, and, *compare*, the aloof part of him murmured, *compare*.

Rod's hand tightened, and he heard the peasant girl give a little cry of startled pain.

He let go his grip, and looked up at her; and Catharine's face swam next to hers.

He looked on the two of them, the one bent on using him, the other bent on being used by him, and anger suddenly burned in a band across his chest, anger at Catharine for her self-righteousness and determination to bend her world to her will; and at the peasant girl for her mute acceptance and deep resignation, for the depth of her warmth and her gentleness. The band of anger across his chest tightened and tightened, anger at himself for the animal in him, as his fingers bit into her shoulders, and he drew her down in the hay. She gasped with the pain, crying out softly till his lips struck hers, crushing and biting and bruising, his fingers clamped on the points of her jaw, forcing her mouth open and his tongue stabbing hard under hers. His hand groped over her body, fingers jabbing deep into the flesh, lower and lower, gnawing and mauling.

Then her nails dug into his back as her whole body knotted in one spasm of pain. Then she went loose, and her chest heaved under him in one great sob.

Half his anger sublimed into nothingness; the other half turned about and lanced into him, piercing something within him that loosed a tide of remorse.

He rolled to the side, taking his weight off her. His lips were suddenly gentle, warm and pleading; his hands were gentle, caressing slowly, soothingly.

She drew in breath, her body tensing again. *Fool*, the detached voice within him sneered, *Fool! You only hurt her the more!*

Ready to turn away from her in shame, he looked up into her eyes . . . and saw the longing burning naked there, craving and demanding, pulling him down into the maelstrom within her. Her lips parted, moist and full and warm, tugging and yielding, pulling him down and down, into blind, light-flooded depths where there was no sight nor hearing, but only touch upon touch.

Rod levered himself up on one elbow and looked down at the girl, lying naked beside him with only his cloak for a rather inadequate coverlet. It clung to her contours, and Rod let his eyes wander over them, drinking in the sight of her, fixing every feature of her body in his mind. It was a picture he did not want to lose.

He caressed her, gently, very tenderly. She smiled, murmured, closing her eyes and letting her head roll to the side.

Then her eyes opened again; she looked at him sidelong, her lips heavy and languid.

'You have emerald eyes,' Rod whispered.

She stretched luxuriously, her smile a little smug, wrapped her arms around his neck, and hauled him down to her, her kisses slow, almost drowsy, and lasting.

Rod looked into her eyes, feeling enormously contented and very much at peace with the world. Hell, the world could go hang!

He raised himself up again, his eyes upon her; then, slowly, he looked away and about them, and the blue of the sky arching overhead . . . and a mound of clothing to each side.

He looked down again; there was nothing in his world now except her, and he found, vaguely surprised, that he rather liked it that way. The peace within him was vast; he felt completely filled, completely satisfied with the world, with life, at one with them and with God – and with her most of all.

He let his hand linger over the cloaked curve of her breast. She closed her eyes, murmuring; then, as his hand stilled, she looked up at him again. Her smile faded to a ghost; concern stole into her eyes.

She started to say something, stopped, and said instead, almost warily, 'Are you well, lord?'

He smiled, his eyes very sober; then he closed them and nodded, slowly.

'Yes. I am very well.'

He bent to kiss her again – slowly, almost carefully – then lifted away. 'Yes, I am well, most strangely well, more than I have ever been.'

The smile lit her face again, briefly; then she turned her eyes away, looking down at her body, then up at him again, her eyes touched with fear.

He clasped her in his arms and rolled onto his back. Her body stiffened a moment, then relaxed; she gave a little cry, half sob and half sigh, and burrowed her head into the hollow of his shoulder and was still.

He looked down at the glory of her hair spread out over his chest. He smiled lazily and let his eyes drift shut.

'Rod.' Fess's voice whispered behind his ear, and the world came flooding in again.

Rod tensed, and clicked his teeth once in acknowledgement.

'Big Tom is dressed again, and coming toward your haystack.'

Rod sat bolt upright, squinted up at the sun; it was almost to the meridian. Time and distance nagged him again.

'Well, back to the world of the living,' he growled, and reached out for his clothes.

'Milord?'

She was smiling regretfully, but her eyes were tight with hurt – a hurt which faded into the deep acceptance and resignation even as he watched.

'The memory of this time will be dear to me, lord,' she whispered, clasping the cloak to her breast, her eyes widening.

It was a forlorn plea for reassurance, a reassurance he could not honestly give, for he would never see her again.

It came to him then that she was expecting refusal of any reassurance, expecting him to lash out at her for her temerity in implying that she had some worth, that she was worthy of thanks.

She knew her plea would bring hurt, yet she pleaded; for a woman lives on love, and this was a woman near thirty in a land where girls married at fifteen. She had already accepted that there was to be no lasting love in her life; she must subsist on the few crumbs she could gather.

His heart went out to her, somewhat impelled by the jab of self-reproach.

So, of course, he told her one of the lies that men tell women only to comfort them, and later realize to be very true.

He kissed her and said, 'This was not Life, lass, it was what living is for.'

And later, when he mounted his horse and turned back to look at her, with Big Tom beside him waving a cheery farewell to his wench, Rod looked into the girl's eyes again and saw the desperation, the touch of panic at his leaving, the silent, frantic plea for a shred of hope.

A shred, Tom had said, would be too much, but Rod would probably never see this girl again. Not even a spark of hope – just a glimmer. Could that do any hurt?

'Tell me your name, lass.'

Only a spark, but it flared in her eyes to a bonfire. 'Gwendylon am I called, lord.'

And when they had rounded a turn in the road and the girls were lost to sight beyond the hill behind them, Tom sighed and said, 'Thou hast done too much, master. Thou shalt never be rid of her now.'

There was this to be said for a roll in the hay: it had sapped enough of Big Tom's vitality so that he wasn't singing any more. Probably still humming, to be sure; but he was riding far enough ahead so Rod couldn't hear him.

Rod rode in silence, unable to rid his mind of flaming hair and emerald eyes. So he cursed at the vision, under his breath; but it seemed to his aloof self that the cursing lacked something – vehemence, perhaps. Certainly sincerity. It was, his aloof self accused, a very half-hearted attempt at malediction.

Rod had to admit it was. He was still feeling very much at one with creation. At the moment, he couldn't have been angry with his executioner . . . And that worried him.

'Fess.'

'Yes, Rod?' The voice seemed a little more inside his head than usual.

'Fess, I don't feel right.'

The robot paused; then, 'How *do* you feel, Rod?'

There was something about the way Fess had said that . . . Rod glanced sharply at the pseudo-horse head. 'Fess, are you laughing at me?'

'Laughing?'

'Yes, laughing. You heard me. Chuckling in your beard.'

'This body is not equipped with a beard.'

'Cut the comedy and answer the question.'

With something like a sigh, the robot said, 'Rod, I must remind you that I am only a machine. I am incapable of emotions . . . I was merely noting discrepancies, Rod.'

'Oh, *were* you!' Rod growled. 'What discrepancies, may I ask?'

'In this instance, the discrepancy between what a man really is and what he wishes to believe of himself.'

Rod's upper lip turned under and pressed against his teeth. 'Just what do I wish to believe?'

'That you are not emotionally dependent upon this peasant woman.'

'Her name is Gwendylon.'

'With Gwendylon. With any woman, for that matter. You wish to believe that you are emotionally independent, that you no longer enjoy what you call "being in love".'

'I enjoy love very much, thank you!'

'That is a very different thing,' the robot murmured, 'than being in love.'

'Damn it, I wasn't talking about *making* love!'

'Neither was I.'

Rod's lips pressed into a thin white line. 'You're talking about emotional intoxication. And if that's what you mean – no, I am not in love. I have no desire to be in love. And if I have any say in the matter, I will never be in love again!'

'Precisely what I said you wished to believe,' mused the robot.

Rod ground his teeth and waited for the surge of anger to pass. 'Now what's the truth about me?'

'That you are in love.'

'Damn it, a man's either in love, or he's not, and he damn well knows which.'

'Agreed; but he may not be willing to admit it.'

'Look,' Rod snapped, 'I've been in love before, and I know what it's like. It's . . . well . . .'

'Go on,' the robot prodded.

'Well, it's like'—Rod lifted his head and looked out at the countryside—'you know the world's there, and you know it's real; but you don't give a damn, 'cause you know for a certainty that you're the centre of the world, the most important thing in it.'

'Have you felt that way recently?' Fess murmured.

'Well . . . yes, damn it.' Rod's mouth twisted.

'With Catharine?'

Rod stared, and glared at the back of the horse's head. 'How the hell would *you* know?' His eyes narrowed.

'Logic, Rod.' The robot's voice had a touch of smugness. 'Only logic. And how did you feel while you were with Gwendylon?'

'Oh . . .' Rod threw his shoulders back, stretching. 'Great, Fess. Better than I ever have. The world's clearer, and the day's younger. I feel so healthy and clearheaded I can't believe it. It's just the opposite to how I feel when I'm in love, but I like it.'

Rod frowned at the back of Fess's head. 'Well?'

The robot plodded on, not answering.

'Cat got your tongue?'

'I am not equipped with a tongue, Rod.'

'Don't change the subject.'

The horse was silent a moment longer; then, 'I was mistaken, Rod. You love, and are loved – but you are not in love.'

Rod frowned down at the roadway. 'Why not, Fess?'

The robot made a sound like a sigh. 'How do the two women differ, Rod?'

'Well . . .' Rod chewed at the inside of his cheek. 'Gwendylon's human. I mean, she's just an ordinary, everyday woman, like I'm an ordinary man.'

'But Catharine is more?'

'Oh, she's the kind of woman I tend to put on a pedestal . . . something to be worshipped, not courted . . .'

'And not loved?' the robot mused. 'Rod, of the two women, which is the better human being?'

'Uh . . . Gwendylon.'

'The prosecution,' said the robot-horse, 'rests.'

The demesne of the Loguires was a great, broad plain between the mountains and the sea. The low, rolling mountains stood at the north and east; beach curved in a wide semi-circle in the south; a sheer, hundred-foot high cliff face towered in the northwest. The ocean battered at its seaward side; a waterfall poured over the other face into the valley. A long, old river twisted over the plain to the sea.

The plain itself was a patchwork of fields, with here and there a cluster of peasant huts – Loguire's people.

Tom and Rod stood at the verge of one of the mountain forests, where the road from the North fell away to the plain.

Rod turned his head slowly, surveying the demesne. 'And where,' he said, 'is the castle?'

'Why, behind the waterfall, master.'

Rod's head jerked around, staring at Tom; then he followed the road with his eyes.

It wound across the plain to the foot of the waterfall; there, where the cliff met the plain, a great gate was carved in the rock, complete with portcullis and a drawbridge over the natural moat formed by an oxbow of the river. The lords of Loguire had honeycombed the cliff for their home.

An exclamation point formed between Rod's eyebrows as they drew together. 'Is that a dike to either side of the drawbridge, Big Tom?'

'Aye, master; and there are said to be charges of gunpowder within it.'

Rod nodded, slowly. 'And the land before the portcullis gate sinks down. So if unwelcome callers come knocking, you blow up the dike, and your front door gets covered with thirty feet of water. Very neat. Then you just sit and wait out the siege. The waterfall gives you plenty of fresh water, so your only worry is food.'

'There are said to be gardens within the keep,' Big Tom supplied helpfully.

Rod shook his head in silent respect. 'So you're completely defended, and stocked for a ten years' siege. This place ever been taken, Tom?'

The big man shook his head. 'Never, master.' He grinned.

'Wonder if the old boy who built this place was maybe a little bit paranoid . . . Don't suppose they'd have room in that place for a couple of weary travellers, do you?'

Big Tom pursed his lips. 'Aye, master, if they were noblemen. The hospitality of the Loguires is famed. But for the likes of me, and even yourself, who are no more than a squire, master, that hospitality lies in the cottages.'

The sun winked. Rod scowled and peered into the sky. 'There's that damn bird again. Doesn't it know we're too big for lunch?' He unlimbered his crossbow and cranked it back to cocked.

'Nay, master.' Big Tom put out a hand. 'You've lost four bolts on it already.'

'I just don't like anything airborne following me, Tom. They're not always what they seem.' Tom's brow furrowed at the cryptic statement. Rod tucked the stock into his shoulder. 'Besides, I've taken one shot a day at it for the last four days; it's getting to be a habit.'

The bow hummed, and the quarrel leaped upward; but the bird sailed up faster. The bolt passed through the place where the bird had been, rose another fifty feet, hit the top of its arc, and began to fall. The bird, fifty feet higher, watched it sink.

Big Tom raised an eyebrow, his mouth quirked up on one side. 'You'll never strike it, master. The fowl knows the meaning of a crossbow.'

'You'd almost think it does.' Rod slung the bow over his shoulder. 'What kind of country is that, with elves under every tree and hawks in the sky shadowing you?'

' 'Tis not a hawk, master,' Big Tom reproved. ' 'Tis an osprey.'

Rod shook his head. 'It started following us the second day out. What would a fish hawk be doing that far inland?'

'Myself, I cannot say. Thou might ask it, though, master.'

'And I wouldn't really be all that surprised if it answered,' Rod mused. 'Well, it isn't doing us any harm, I suppose, and we've got bigger problems at the moment. We came here to get into that castle. Do you sing, Big Tom?'

Tom did a double take. 'Sing, master?'

'Yeah, sing. Or play the bagpipes, or something.'

Tom tugged at his lip, frowning. 'I can make some manner of noise on a shepherd's flute, and the half dead might put the word *music* to it. But what folly is this, master?'

'Fool's folly.' Rod unstrapped a saddlebag and took out a small harp. 'As of now, we're minstrels. Let's hope the cliff-dwellers are a little short on music at the moment.' He pulled an alto recorder out of the saddlebag and gave it to Tom. 'I hope that's enough like your shepherd's flute to do some good.'

'Aye, master, very like it. But—'

'Oh, don't worry, they'll let us in. Folks this far away from the capital tend to be out of touch; they're hungry for news and new songs, and minstrels carry both. Do you know 'Eddystone Light'?'

'Nay, master.'

'Too bad; that's one that always goes over well in a seaport town. Well, no matter, I can teach it to you as we go.'

They set off down the road, singing in accidentals unknown to any human mode or scale. The fish hawk screamed and sheered off.

'Bring ye news from the North?' the sentry had asked eagerly; and Rod, recollecting that minstrels were the closest medieval equivalent to journalists, had replied in the affirmative.

Now he and Tom stood before a gathering of twenty-eight noblemen, their wives and attendants, ranging in age from pretty teenage serving maids to the ninety-year-old Earl of Vallenderie, all with the same eager, hungry glint in their eyes, and Rod without a scrap of news to tell them.

Well, no matter; he'd make it up as he went along. He wouldn't be the first journalist who'd done it.

The crusty old Duke of Loguire sat in a great oaken chair in the midst of the company; he didn't seem to recognize Rod. But Durer did; he stood hunched over Loguire's left shoulder, eyes twisting hate at Rod. But it would have done him no good to expose Rod, and he knew it; Loguire still loved his niece, though he was at odds with her. He would have honoured Rod for saving Catharine's life.

It was Loguire who voiced the question for all his people; and Rod, reflecting that the Duke had very personal reasons for wanting news of the House of Clovis, had replied that as yet, all was quiet in the North. Oh, one heard talk and saw signs of the House; but that was talk, and talk only – so far.

Then he and Tom swung into a foot-stamping rendition of 'Eddystone Light'. The gathering stood in astounded silence a moment; then grins broke out, and hands started clapping the rhythm.

Encouraged, Big Tom picked up both the tempo and the volume; Rod struggled to match him while he scanned the faces of the audience.

The old Duke was trying to look sternly disapproving, and not succeeding too well. A tall young man of about Rod's age stood behind the old man's right shoulder, a grin coming to his lips and a gleam to his eye as he listened to the song, displacing a grimace of discontent, self-pity, and bitterness. The elder son, Rod guessed, with a host of weaknesses Durer could prey upon.

It was easy to pick out Loguire's vassal lords; all were richly dressed, and accompanied by an even more richly-dressed wire scarecrow of a man: the councillors, Durer's boys.

Rod felt strangely certain that anything Durer proposed would have the unanimous approval of all the Southern lords, with only Loguire dissenting.

And Loguire, of course, had one more vote than all the vassal lords put together. Rod remembered Loguire's unsolicited promise to Catharine: 'No harm shall come to the Queen while I live . . .'

'While I live . . .'

The performance was literally a howling success; Rod had managed to keep it on a ribald rather than a political level, walking the thin line between the risqué and the pornographic. The audience had loved it, Rod decided that the tin ear must be a genetic dominant in Gramarye. He'd noticed, too, that the eyes of all the serving girls had been riveted to himself and Big Tom; he was still trying to understand why. It didn't seem to have done Big Tom's ego any harm, though.

But now and again, one of the councillors had asked a question that could not be put off; and when Rod had answered with rumours that the House of Clovis would rise against the Crown, a frantic, acid joy had burned in their eyes.

That, at least, he understood. The important thing about a revolution is that it begin; you can always take control of it later.

That he understood; but now, with the singing done, as he was going to the loft which had been temporarily assigned to Tom and himself, he was still pondering the look on the faces of the serving maids. When they had looked at Tom, he'd been quite sure what it was; he expected to find the loft fully occupied by the time he arrived, since Big Tom had gone on ahead.

But that look couldn't mean the same thing when applied to himself – unless the occupation of minstrel carried a great deal more prestige than he'd thought.

So, all in all, he was even more confused but not too surprised when one of the servant girls intercepted him with a cup of wine.

'Salve for a parched throat, Master Minstrel,' she murmured, her eyes shining as he held the cup out to him.

He looked at her out of the corner of his eye and reluctantly accepted the cup; no call for bad manners, was there?

'And,' she murmured as he drank, 'warmth for your bed, if you will.'

Rod choked and spluttered, lowered the cup, glaring at her; then he looked her up and down quickly. She was full-bodied and high-breasted, with a wide, full-lipped mouth – very like Gwendylon, in some ways . . .

Suddenly suspicious, Rod looked more sharply; but no, this girl's eyes were tilted upward at the outer corners, and her nose was long and straight, not snub. Besides, her hair and eyes were black.

He smiled wryly and drank off the rest of the cup and returned it to her. 'Thank you, lass, right deeply.'

It was indicative, he thought, that she had come to him instead of Big Tom. Tom was certainly the more appealing chunk of man; but Rod was obviously the one who had the status. A bitch like any of them, he thought: she doesn't give a damn for who the man is, just as long as *what* he is is a station higher than hers.

'I thank you,' he said again, 'but I have been long on the road, and am like to swoon from my weariness.' A very pretty speech, he thought; and go ahead, let her think less of my manhood for it. At least she'll leave me alone.

The serving maid lowered her eyes, biting her lip. 'As you will, good master.' And she turned away, leaving Rod staring after her.

Well, that hadn't taken much refusing. Come to think of it, he was a little indignant . . . but had there been just a hint of triumph in her eyes, a shard of rejoicing?

Rod went on his way, wondering if perhaps he hadn't inadvertently stepped into the pages of a Machiavellian textbook.

The door to the loft was closed, as Rod had guessed; a muffled feminine squeal, followed by Tom's bass laugh, further confirmed his guess.

So he shrugged philosophically, settled his harp over his shoulder, and turned back down the long, winding staircase. He could put the time to good use, anyway. The castle had so obviously been built by a paranoid that he was certain there had to be secret passages.

He sauntered down the main corridor, whistling. The granite walls were painted ochre, ornamented with standing suits of armour and here and there a tapestry. Some of the tapestries were huge, reaching from floor to ceiling; Rod noted their locations carefully in his mind. They could very easily conceal the mouths of passageways.

Twelve sub-corridors intersected the main hall at right angles. As he came near the seventh, he noticed that his footsteps seemed to have acquired an echo – a very curious echo, that took two steps for each one of his. He stopped to look at a tapestry; the echo took two more steps and stopped. Looking out of the corner of his eye, Rod caught a glimpse of one of the wizened richly-dressed scarecrows; he thought he recognized Durer, but it was hard to tell by peripheral vision.

He turned away and swaggered on down the hall, humming 'Me and My Shadow'. The echo started again.

Now, Rod was mildly gregarious; he didn't really mind company. But it was a safe bet that he wasn't going to learn very much with Durer on his tail with a salt shaker. Ergo, he had to figure some way to lose his emaciated companion. This would not be easy, since Durer almost surely knew the castle very thoroughly, while Rod knew it not at all.

But the ninth cross-corridor seemed as though it would do nicely for the purpose – it was unlit. Strange, Rod mused; the other halls had all had a torch every several paces. But this was as dark as Carlsbad before the tourists came; it also had a thick carpet of dust, with not a single footprint in evidence. Cobwebs hung thick from the ceiling; trickles of moisture ran down the walls, watering patches of moss.

But the darkness was the main feature. He would leave a nice trail in the dust, but the darkness offered a chance of ducking into a room or side-hall; also, Durer couldn't very well pretend he just happened to be going the same way.

Rod turned into the corridor, sneezing in the cloud of dust he kicked up, and heard a sudden scurrying behind him. A claw grabbed his shoulder; he turned to face the little man, ready to swing.

Yes, it was Durer, glaring at Rod with his usual look of hate and suspicion. 'What seek you in there?' he croaked.

Rod brushed the bony hand off his shoulder and leaned back against the wall. 'Nothing in particular; just looking around. I don't have much of anything to do at the moment, unless you'd like a song?'

'Damn your caterwauling!' Durer snapped. 'And you may leave off your pretence of minstrelsy; I know you for what you are.'

'Oh?' Rod raised an eyebrow. 'How'd you know I'm not really

a minstrel?'

'I heard you sing. Now off to your chamber, if you've no business elsewhere!'

Rod scratched his nose. 'Ah – about that chamber,' he said delicately. 'My companion seems to have found, uh, a better use for it than sleeping. So I'm, ah, sort of locked out, if you follow me.'

'Corruption!' the councillor hissed.

'No, I suspect Big Tom goes about it in a very healthy manner. And since I have no place to stay at the moment, I thought none would mind my wandering about.'

Durer glared at him, a look like a laser beam. Then, very reluctantly, he backed off a pace or two.

'True,' he said. 'There are no secrets here for you to pry out.'

Rod managed to limit his laughter to a mild convulsion in the depths of his belly.

'But did you not know,' the scarecrow continued, 'that this is the haunted quarter?'

Rod's eyebrows shot up. 'You don't say.' He tugged at his lower lip, eyeing Durer judiciously. 'You seem to know the castle pretty well.'

Durer's eyes snapped like a high-voltage arc. 'Any in this castle could tell you that. But I am Durer, councillor to the Duke of Loguire! It is my place to know the castle well – as it is *not* yours!'

But Rod had turned away, looking down the dark hallway. 'You know,' he mused, 'I've never seen a ghost before . . .'

'None have, and lived to tell of it! To enter there is the act of a fool!'

Rod turned, smiling cheerfully. 'Well, I'm qualified. Besides, a meeting with a ghost would make a good ballad.'

The little man stared; then a contemptuous smile twisted into his face. He began to chuckle, sounding strangely like ball bearings rolling over corrugated iron. 'Go then, fool! I should have seen 'twould be no matter whether you went there or not.'

Rod grinned, shrugged, and stepped into the black corridor.

'A moment!' Durer called.

Rod sighed and turned. 'What do you want now?'

'Before you go to your death,' said Durer, his eyes feverishly bright, 'tell me: what are you?'

A chill ran down Rod's back. The little man had seen through his cover.

He leaned against the wall, radiating boredom. 'A minstrel, of course. What else would I be?'

'Nay, fool! Do you think me so blind? You are a spy!'

Rod's hand crept to his dagger-hilt. It was balanced for throwing.

'A spy from the House of Clovis!' Durer howled.

Rod's hand relaxed; he let out a breath that he hadn't known he'd been holding. 'Guess again, little man.'

Durer scowled. 'Not from the House? But then . . . Nay, you are their spy! Even now you will not admit to it!'

A synapse spat in Rod's brain.

He leaned back against the wall, folding his arms, grinning. 'Why, what interest have you in the House of Clovis, good councillor? And why would Clovis wish to know of your doings here?'

'Nay!' Durer hissed, his eyes widening. 'Fool, do you think I would answer such . . . Aie! Curse my old mind, not to have thought it! You are a spy from the Queen!'

Rod stepped away from the wall, loosening the dagger in its sheath. He didn't particularly care if Durer knew Catharine had sent him; but he did want an answer. 'I asked you a question,' he said mildly.

Terror welled up in the little man's eyes. He leaped back against the far wall. 'Hold! At my call a score of soldiers come!'

Rod gave him a look that was somewhere between a sneer and a smile. 'That won't do you much good if you're dead by the time they get here.' He gestured toward the dark corridor. 'Also, I'd probably be gone by the time they arrive.'

The little man stared, horrified, and began to tremble.

But the little bastard had guts, Rod had to give him that. His voice broke like a cicada in autumn, but he kept talking.

'It might be . . . it just might be that it is even as you say, that you are not of Clovis! And if you come from the Queen, why, then, you are welcome among us!'

Rod half-turned his head, giving the little man a measuring, sidewise look.

'I will tell all that you wish to know!' The councillor's hands came up in pathetic eagerness. A strange light came into his eyes. 'Aye, all will I tell you, even to the day that we march on the Queen's capital! Then you may tell her, and she can march south to meet us half-way! Even this will I tell you!'

He leaped forward, hands clawing. 'Only come out from the hallway! If you come from the Queen, I would not have you die!'

Rod's face turned to stone. 'No. You've got something hidden in there, and I've got a strange notion it might be more important than the date set for your rebellion. I think I'll just have a look.' He turned back into the dusty hallway.

Durer ran after him a few steps, almost wailing. 'No, no! You must carry word North! Come away, you fool!'

Rod kept walking.

Behind him, the little man screeched in anger. 'Go, then, to your death! There is no need for you! I will take word to the North myself! Die, like the fool that you are!'

His shrill, hysterical laughter echoed and slapped from the walls, beating into Rod's ears as he strode into the mouldering, lightless depths of the Castle Loguire.

He turned a corner, and the laugh died away. The faint torchlight from the main hall died with it; here the darkness was complete.

Rod walked through it, chewing at the inside of his cheek. Obviously, the little man really expected him to die . . . which was strange, since he had tried to keep Rod from going in. Which meant he'd really wanted Rod to carry word of the rebellion back to Catharine. But why did he want to doublecross the rebels?

Unless it was a triplecross, somehow . . .

Then, too, he obviously had something hidden back in these corridors, and might be afraid Rod would find it and somehow manage to come out alive.

However, he expected Rod to die, which meant automated defences surrounding Durer's Big Secret . . .

Unless, of course . . .

Rod stopped, suddenly realizing he didn't know the way out. He had a hazy recollection of having turned several corners while he'd been pondering; but he couldn't remember which corners, or how many, or which way he'd turned.

He noticed that his voice shook just a trifle when he murmured 'Fess.'

'Yes, Rod,' the calm voice behind his ear answered instantly. It was vastly reassuring.

'Fess, I'm in the haunted part of the castle.'

'Haunted?'

'It has that reputation, yes.'

There was a pause; then the robot said, 'Rod, an analysis of your voice patterns indicates mild fear. Surely you do not believe in ghosts.'

'No, I don't. But I just remembered, Fess – I didn't believe in elves, either. Or banshees. Or—'

'Elves,' Fess replied evenly, 'are a myth.'

'Uh, Fess . . .'

'Yes, Rod?'

'I've seen quite a few elves since we landed.'

'A *fait accompli*,' the robot admitted reluctantly, 'which I am constrained to acknowledge. I have not as yet sufficient data to explain the seeming conflict with known principles.'

'You're as bad as a Catholic,' Rod growled. 'But at least it doesn't give you fits any more?'

'No-o-o.' The robot was thoughtful. 'The initial datum caused an overload; but that datum has since been assimilated.'

'As long as you're sure there's a rational explanation.'

'Precisely.'

'So you're capable of handling the practical matters?'

'Quite capable.'

'Because you're sure you'll be able to fit it into the Laws of Science eventually.'

'Very perceptive, Rod.'

'Sounds like a Jesuit,' Rod growled. 'But the practical matter at hand is that I *am* scared. And for a very good reason. Fess . . .'

'Yes, Rod?'

'If elves can exist on this crazy planet, why not ghosts?'

There was another pause; then Fess admitted, 'There is no evidence that would directly contradict the hypothesis.'

A moan, so deep that Rod could hardly hear it, and so loud that he winced in pain, shook the walls of the hallway.

Rod gasped. 'What was *that*?'

'A complex wave-pattern of low frequency and high amplitude,' Fess answered obligingly.

'Thank you, Dr Slipcam. *What caused it*?'

'There is as yet insufficient data for—'

The moan came again, and a wraith of mist with hollow black eyes and a black circle of mouth swooped straight at Rod's head, starting as a pinpoint far down the hall and towering over him a second later.

Rod screamed and plastered himself against the wall. Fear knotted his belly, fear slackened his limbs, fear jellied his brain and squeezed at his heart.

Another moan sounded, a half-step above the first; Rod jerked his head to his right. Another ghost loomed over him.

A third moan, and Rod's eyes slapped up; a third spectre towered before him.

Three ghosts, towering high about him, ringing him in against the stone wall. Their mouths formed great, lightless O's, cold bony fingers reaching out for him.

Through the moiling panic of his brain fought a single thought: *Fess didn't believe in ghosts.*

'Ghosts!' Rod screamed. 'Ghosts, Fess, ghosts!'

'Ghosts,' droned the robot, 'are immaterial, even if they did exist. They are manifestations of neither energy nor matter, incapable of causing damage to a material being.'

'Tell *them*! Tell *them*!' Rod shrieked.

The hand around his heart tightened. He gasped and coughed. Something was mashing his lungs, a steel band around his chest, tightening, tightening. . . . Fear was a physical thing, a looming presence, armed and hating. Fear could paralyze, fear could kill . . .

'Rod, cover your ears.'

Rod tried to obey the robot's order, and couldn't. 'Fess!' he screamed. 'Fess, I can't *move*!'

A loud, raucous buzz shook his skull, blotting out the moans. It modulated into monotone words: 'C-O-V-E-R Y-O-U-R E-A-R-S.'

And the fear was gone, vanished – or almost gone, at least; reduced to the cold, familiar lump in the pit of the belly. Rod could move again, as easily as he ever had. He put his fingers in his ears. The buzz stopped, and he could hear the ghosts again, their moans dulled and distant through his fingers. The fear rose into his throat again, but it was no longer paralysing.

'Can you hear them, Rod?'

'Yeah, but it's not so bad now. What'd you do, Fess?'

'Nothing, Rod. Their moans have a harmonic frequency in the subsonic range, capable of inducing fear in members of your species.'

'Oh.'

'The fear-inducing tone is a beat frequency produced by the simultaneous emission of subsonic harmonics incorporated in the three moans.'

'So it takes three of them to scare me?'

'Correct, Rod.'

'And they're not really scaring me, just making me feel scared?'

'Again, correct.'

'Well, that's a relief. For a minute there I was afraid I'd all of a sudden turned into a full-blown coward.'

'All men fear, Rod.'

'Yeah, but only a coward lets it stop him.'

'That is a redundant statement, Rod.'

'Oh, the hell with theory! Pardon me while I put it into practice.'

Rod stepped away from the wall, forcing himself to move. He kept walking, right through the ghost in front of him. The moans suddenly ceased; then, with a howl of despair, the ghosts disappeared.

'They're gone,' Rod croaked.

'Of course, Rod. Once you have demonstrated their inability to control you, they begin to fear you.'

'Ye-e-es,' Rod breathed. He set his feet wide apart, jammed his fists on his hips, flung his head back, and grinned. 'Okay, spooks! Any doubts about who's boss?'

He stood, listening to the echoes of his voice die away among the empty corridors. A loud voice could be pretty impressive in here.

A mournful, sepulchral voice answered him out of thin air, moaning. 'Leave us, mortal. Leave us to the peace of our graves. We harm no one here, in our cold, old halls.'

'No one except the people who come in here,' Rod snapped. 'Them you kill, as you would have killed me, through weight of fear alone.'

'Few,' mourned the ghost. 'Very, very few, mortal man. Only madmen, and fools.'

'If you have killed one man here in your halls, you have killed one too many!' Rod rapped back.

'Would you not slay, Man, in defence of your home?'

Rod snorted. 'What right have you to these halls?'

Suddenly the ghost was there, towering over him. 'I once was Horatio, first Duke Loguire!' it thundered in anger. 'I it was built this keep! Have I no right to a poor, cold quarter of its halls?'

Fear lanced Rod's belly; he took a step back, then set his teeth and stepped forward again. 'You got a point there,' he admitted. 'And possession *is* nine-tenths of the law. But how many did you have to kill to gain possession?'

'None.' The ghost sounded very unhappy about it. 'All fled in fear.'

Rod nodded, revising his estimate of the ghost. Apparently Horatio didn't kill if he could help it. Probably delighted when it became necessary, though . . .

'I mean you no harm, Horatio.' He grinned suddenly, sardonically. 'What harm could I do you, even if I wanted to?'

The ghost's head snapped up, empty eyes staring into Rod's. 'You know not, mortal?'

'A ghost,' Fess's voice said hurriedly behind Rod's ear, 'like all supernatural creatures, can be hurt by cold iron or silver, or any medium of good conductivity, though gold is usually regarded as too expensive for such uses.'

The ghost loomed larger over Rod, advancing on him.

Rod stepped back, his dagger at the ready. 'Hold it right there,' he snapped. 'Cold iron, remember?'

'Then, too,' Fess murmured, 'you do know the secret of their power. You could bring in an army with earplugs.'

'Then, too,' said Rod, 'I *do* know the secret of your power. I could bring in an army with earplugs.'

The ghost halted, the corners of its mouth turning down. 'I had thought thou hadst said thou knew not.'

'I do now. One step backward, if you please.'

The ghost reluctantly retreated, groaning, 'What phantom stands at your side to advise you?'

Rod's teeth bared in a grin. 'A black horse, made of cold iron. It's in the castle stables, but it can talk to me from there.'

'A pooka,' Horatio growled, 'a spirit horse, and one who is a traitor to the world of ghosts.'

'No.' Rod shook his head grimly. 'It's not a spirit at all. I said it was made of cold iron, didn't I?'

The ghost shook its head decisively. 'No such thing could exist.'

Rod sighed. 'There are more things in Heaven and Earth, Horatio, than are dreamt of in your philosophy. But that's beside the point. All that matters to you is that I don't mean any harm here. I'm just looking for something. I'll find it and go. Okay?'

'You are master. Why dost thou ask?' the ghost said bitterly.

'Courtesy,' Rod explained. Then a vagrant and vague possibility crossed his mind. 'Oh, by the way, I'm a minstrel. . . .'

The ghost's mouth dropped open; then it surged forward, hands grasping hungrily. 'Music! Oh, sweet strains of melody! But play for us, Man, and we are thine to command!'

'Hold on a second.' Rod held up a hand. 'You built these halls, Horatio Loguire, and therefore do I ask of you the boon that I may walk these halls in peace. Grant me this, and I will play for you.'

'You may walk, you may walk where you will!' the ghost quavered. 'Only play for us, Man!'

Very neat, Rod thought. As good a job of facesaving as he'd ever done. After all, no sense making enemies if you can help it.

He looked up, started, and stared in shock. He was ringed by a solid wall of ghosts, three deep at least, all staring like a starving man in a spaghetti factory.

He swallowed hard and swung his harp around with a silent prayer of thanks that he hadn't been able to leave it in the sleeping-loft.

He touched the strings, and a groan of ecstasy swept through the ghosts like the murmur of distant funeral bells on the midnight wind.

It then occurred to Rod that he was in an excellent bargaining position. 'Uh, Lord Horatio, for *two* songs, will you tell me where the secret passages are?'

'Aye, aye!' the ghost fairly shrieked. 'The castle is thine, my demesne, all that I have! The kingdom, if thou wish it! Only play for us, Man! For ten hundreds of years we have heard not a strain of Man's music! But play, and the whole world is thine!'

His fingers started plucking then, and the ghosts shivered like a schoolgirl getting her first kiss.

He gave them 'Greensleeves', and 'The Drunken Sailor', those being the oldest songs he knew. From there he went on to 'The Ghost's High Noon', and 'The Unfortunate Miss Bailey'. He was about to swing into 'Ghost Riders in the Sky' when it occurred to him that ghosts might not particularly like songs about ghosts. After all, mortals told spook stories for escapism; and by that yardstick, spectres should want songs about humdrum, ordinary, everyday life, something peaceful and comforting, memories of green pastures and babbling brooks, and the lowing herd winding slowly o'er the lea.

So he went through as much of Beethoven's Sixth as he could remember, which was not easy on an Irish harp.

The last strains died away among the hollow halls. The ghosts were silent a moment; then a satiated, regretful sigh passed through them.

Horatio Loguire's great voice spoke quietly at Rod's elbow. 'In truth, a most fair roundelay.' Then, very carefully: 'Let us have another, Man.'

Rod shook his head with a sorrowful smile. 'The hours of the night crowd down upon us, my lord, and I have much that I must do ere daybreak. Another night I shall return and play for you again; but for this night, I must away.'

'Indeed,' Horatio nodded, with another mournful sigh. 'Well, you have dealt fairly with us, Man, and shown us courtesy without constraint to it. And shall we, for hospitality, be beholden to a guest? Nay; but come within, and I will show you doors to the pathways within the walls of this keep, and tell you of their twists and turnings.'

All the ghosts but Horatio disappeared, with the sound of mouse feet running through the autumn leaves. Horatio turned abruptly and fled away before Rod, who dashed after him.

Rod counted his running steps; after fifty, the ghost made a right-angle turn with a fine disregard for inertia and passed through a doorway. Rod made a manful attempt at the inertialess turn, and got away with only a slight skid.

The ghost's voice took on the booming echo of the cavernlike room. 'This was a cavern indeed, ready-made by God, lo, many centuries before I came. Loath to begrudge His gifts, I took it for my great banquet hall.' The room seethed with the voices of a thousand serpent-echoes as the patriarch ghost heaved a vast sigh. 'Boisterous and many were the feastings held within this great hall, Man. Beauteous the maidens and valiant the knights.' His voice lifted, exulting. 'Brilliant with light and music was my banquet hall in that lost day, the tales and sagas older and more vital than the singing of this latter world. Wine flushed the faces of my court, and life beat high through the veins of their temples, filling their ears with its drumming call!

'The call of life . . .' The spirit's voice faded; its echoes died away among the cold cavern stones, till the great hall stood silent in its enduring midnight.

Somewhere a drop of water fell, shattering the silence into a hundred echoes.

'Gone now, O Man,' mourned the ghost. 'Gone and dead, while threescore of the sons of my blood have ruled these marches in my stead, and come home to me here in my halls. Gone, all my bold comrades, all my willing maidens – gone, and dust beneath our feet.'

Rod's shoulders tightened as though a chill wind had touched him between the shoulder blades. He tried to stand a little more lightly in the dust carpet of the old banquet hall.

'And now!' The ghost's voice hardened in sullen anger. 'Now others rule these halls, a race of jackals, hyenas who blaspheme my old comrades by walking in the forms of men.'

Rod's ears pricked up. 'Uh, how's that again, my lord? Somebody's stolen this hall from you?'

'Twisted, stunted men!' grated the wraith. 'A race of base, ignoble cowards – and the lord of them all stands as councillor to a scion of my line, the Lord Duke Loguire!'

'Durer,' Rod breathed.

'Calls he himself by that name,' growled the ghost. 'Then well is he named, for his heart is hard, and his soul is brittle. 'But mark you, Man,' and the ghost turned his cavern eyes on Rod, and the base of Rod's scalp seemed to lift a little away from his skull, for embers burned at the backs of the spectre's eyes, 'mark you well,' it intoned, stretching forth a hand, forefinger spearing at Rod, 'that the hard and brittle steel will break at one strong blow of iron forged. And so may these evil parodies of humankind be broken by a man that you may call a man!'

The ghost's hand dropped. His shoulders sagged, his head bowed forward. 'If,' he mourned, 'if any live in this dark day who may call themselves men in truth . . .'

Rod's eyes broke away from the ghost and wandered slowly about the great chamber. There was only blackness, close and thick. He blinked and shook his head, trying to rid himself of the feeling that the darkness was pressing against his eyeballs.

'My Lord Loguire,' he began, stopped, and said again, 'My Lord Loguire, I may be your lump of iron—I've been called things like that before, anyway. But if I am to break the councillors, I must know as much about them as I can. Therefore tell me: what work do they do within these halls?'

'Witchcraft,' growled the ghost, 'black witchcraft! Though the manner of it I scarce could tell . . .'

'Well, tell me what you can,' Rod prodded. 'Anything you can spare will be gratefully appreciated.'

'Thou speakest like the parish priest a-tithing,' the ghost snorted. 'Naetheless, I will tell thee what I can. Know, then, Man, that these twisted men have builded themselves a great altar here, of a shining metal, not steel, nor silver or gold, nor any metal that I wot of – here in the centre of my hall, where once my courtiers danced!'

'Oh.' Rod pursed his lips. 'Uh, what worship do they make before this altar?'

'What worship?' The ghost's head lifted. 'Why, I would warrant, 'tis a sacrifice of themselves; for they step within that evil artifice, and then are gone; then lo! there they are again, and come forth whole! I can only think they must have given of their life's blood to the dark demon within that shining altar, for they come forth gaunt and shaken. Indeed,' he mused, 'why otherwise would they be shrivelled little men?'

An uneasy prickle began at the base of Rod's skull and worked its way down his neck to spread out across his shoulders. 'I must see this artifice, my lord.' He fumbled at his dagger. 'Let us have some light!'

'Nay!' The shriek tore at Rod's eardrums. The ghost pulsed, shrinking and growing, its outline wavering, like a candle-flame.

'Would you destroy me, Man, and send me screaming to a darker realm than this?'

Rod massaged the back of his neck, trying to loosen the muscles that had cramped themselves together at the ghost's shriek. 'Forgive me, Lord Loguire; I had forgotten. My torch will rest darkened; but you must, then, lead me to this strange altar, that I may see it with my hands.'

'Would you worship there, then?' The hollow eyes deepened ominously.

'No, my lord; but I would know this thing, that I may bring it down in the fullness of time.'

The ghost was silent a moment; then it nodded gravely, and glided ahead. 'Come.'

Rod stumbled forward, hands outstretched, in the ghost's wake, till his palms came up against something hard and cold.

'Beware, Man,' rumbled the ghost, 'for here lie dark powers.'

Hand over hand, Rod felt his way slowly along the metal, glinting softly in the ghost's faint luminescence. Then his right hand fell on nothingness. He groped, found it was a corner, wished the ghost gave off just a little more light, and groped until he had located the outline of a door, or rather a doorway, seven feet high by three wide.

'What lies within, my lord?' he whispered.

'It is a coffin,' the ghost moaned; 'a metal coffin without a lid, standing on end, and you have found its open side.'

Rod wondered what would happen if he stepped into the cubicle; but for some strange reason, he lacked the experimental urge of the true scientist.

He groped across the doorway. A circle pressed into his palm, a circle protruding slightly from the face of the metal block.

Running his fingers over the area to the right of the doorway, he discovered a full array of circles, oblongs, and buttons. The area within their outlines was smoother and less cold than the metal around them – glass, he decided, or plastic. He had found a control panel.

'My Lord Loguire,' he called softly, 'come here to me now, I beg of you, for I must have light.'

The ghost drifted up beside him; and, by the light of its cold radiance, Rod made out a set of meters, a vernier dial, and a set of colour-coded buttons.

The ghost's voice was gentle, almost sympathetic. 'Why do you tremble, Man?'

'It's cold,' Rod snapped. 'Milord Loguire, I'm afraid I have to agree with your opinion of this monstrosity. I don't know what it is, but it ain't pretty.'

The ghost rumbled agreement. 'And that which is evil to look upon must be doubly so in its action.'

'Well, I'm not so sure about that as a basic principle,' Rod demurred, 'but it might apply in this case. Milord, pay no heed to my mumblings in the next small while; I must, ah, recite an incantation against the malice of this, ah, engine.'

He switched to the patois of the galactic deckhand while the ghost scowled in perplexity. 'Fess, you there?'

'Yes, Rod.'

'Have you been listening in?'

'Certainly, Rod.'

'Um. Well, then, uh, this thing's a hunk of metal, rectangular, about, uh, twenty feet long by, say, ten high, and maybe ten wide. Got a little cubicle cut into the front, just about the size of a coffin.'

'Appropriate,' the robot murmured.

'No kibitzing on the job, please. It's white metal with a dull finish, and colder than hell, right now, anyway. Set of controls next to the cubicle – a long strip-meter with a scale and a slider.'

'How is the scale calibrated, Rod?'

'Looks like logarithms, Fess. Arabic numerals. The zero's about three-quarters of the way from left end. Left side of the scale is marked to ten thousand. The right-hand side goes up to, uh, 2,385. Sound like anything you've heard of?'

There was a pause; then the robot answered, 'Filed for analysis. Proceed with the description.'

Rod ground his teeth; apparently the huge gizmo was as much of an unknown to Fess as it was to himself.

'There's a dial with a knob in the middle of it, just to the right of the strip-meter. Reference point at the top, twelve o'clock, negative number to the left, positive to the right. At least, I assume they're numbers. The thing just to the right of the reference point looks something like a French curve, or maybe a paranoid sine wave. Then there's a shape like an upside-down pear. Then there's a pair of circles with a line lying across them. The last one is a question mark lying on its side; then there's infinity in the six o'clock position. Left-hand side is the same way, only all the symbols are marked with a negative sign.'

The robot hummed for a moment; Rod recognized the tune: 'Sempre Libera' from *La Traviata*. Fess was enjoying himself.

'Filed for analysis and reference, Rod. Proceed with description.'

'You don't recognize 'em either, huh?'

'They are totally without precedence in the discipline of mathematics, Rod. But if there is any logic to their derivation, I will decipher them. Proceed.'

'Well, there're seven buttons set flush with the surface, in a row just under the strip-meter, colour-coded. Colours are – uh – hey, it's the spectrum!'

'So I feared,' the robot murmured. 'Use of the spectrum in colour-coding would indicate arbitrary assignation of values. There is no anomaly in the colour sequence?'

'Well, the paint's iridescent . . .'

'Not quite what I meant by anomaly. Well, it is filed. Proceed.'

'Nothing. That's all.'

'All? Only three controls?'

'That's all.'

The robot was silent a moment.

'What do you make of it, Fess?'

'Well . . .' the robot's voice was hesitant. 'The control system appears to be designed for the layman, Rod . . .'

'Why? Because it's so simple?'

'Precisely. Beyond that, there is insufficient data for—'

'Oh, make a guess, damn it! Make a wild guess!'

'Rod, guesswork is not within the capabilities of a cybernetic mechanism, involving as it does an exercise of the intuitive—'

'So extrapolate from available data, already!'

He heard *La Traviata*, as it might have been sung by a wistful audio generator; then Fess said, 'The irregularity of the figure 2,385 would seem to indicate the number of a year, Rod, due to its juxtaposition with the figure ten thousand.'

'Uh, how's that again?'

'The figure ten thousand,' Fess lectured, 'has many probable referents, one of which is the period of recorded human history.'

'Now, wait a minute, Fess. Written history doesn't go back beyond 2000 BC; even I know that.'

'And a miracle it is, Rod, considering your resistance to instruction from your earliest ages.'

'All right, all right! I was a bad little boy who didn't do his homework! I'm sorry! I repent! Just get on with the extrapolation, will ya?'

He heard the burring of serially closing relays that always reminded him of a chuckle; then Fess said, 'Human history prior to the development of written language may be said to have been recorded in the legends and mythology of the vocal tradition, in works such as *The Epic of Gilgamesh*. The period included by such works may be estimated as having begun nearly four thousand years BC. This figure, added to the present date, gives us the figure 9,432, which is a sufficiently close approximation to the figure ten thousand to be included as a referent.'

'Hmm.' Rod gnawed his upper lip. 'Well, when you look at it that way, I suppose 2,385 could be a date. But what does that mean?'

'Why, the inference is obvious, Rod.'

'So I'm a microcephalic idiot. Spell it out.'

The robot hesitated. 'The accuracy of the inference has a very low probability rating. . . .'

'I asked for guesswork, didn't I? Come on, out with it.'

'The artefact, Rod, would by this theory be a vehicle for chronical travel.'

Rod stared at the strip-meter. 'You mean it's a time machine?'

The slider was shoved all the way to the right, resting over the figure 2,385.

'Rod, you must bear in mind that the theory's probability index—'

'A time machine!' Rod's brain whirled. 'Then the little bastards came out of the future!'

'Rod, I have cautioned you before about your tendency to accord an unproved hypothesis the weight of a conviction.'

Rod gave his head a quick shake. 'Oh, don't worry, Fess. It's just a guess, probably wrong. I'm keeping that in mind.'

He turned away from the control panel, eyes glowing. 'A time machine! Whaddaya know!'

He became aware of the faint glow to his left again. Horatio Loguire towered over him, brooding.

'What witchcraft is it, Man?'

Rod frowned, turning back toward the machine. 'Strange, my lord, both dark and strange. I have some knowledge of the various, ah, magics; but this is one with which I have no acquaintance.'

'What then will you do?'

Rod scowled at the floor, looked up with a bleak smile. 'Sleep. And ponder what I have seen.'

'And when will you destroy this plaything of Satan?'

'When I am sure,' murmured Rod, turning back to look at the machine again; 'sure that this is the plague, and not the cure, of this benighted world.'

Loguire's eyebrows drew together as his scowl deepened. He seemed almost to swell, looming taller and wider, dwarfing the man before him. Rod had the insane feeling that an ancient locomotive was roaring down on him.

The voice was distant thunder. 'I charge you, then, with the exorcizing of this demon altar and the rending of its ragtag priests.'

The old boy, Rod decided, had definitely slipped a cog.

The ghost's sword flashed out of its scabbard; involuntarily, Rod fell back into defence stance. Then he straightened, cursing himself; a spectral sword could scarcely hurt him.

The sword floated before him, point downward, a glittering cruciform ghost-light.

'Swear now upon the hilt of this my sword, that you shall not rest until you have purged this land of corruption in the seats of power, that you shall exorcize this dark altar and all its minions, and more: that you shall never till you die desert this Isle of Gramarye in the hour of its peril.'

Awe slacked Rod's jaw; he stared wide-eyed at the sudden power and majesty of the ghost. An alien, formless dread crept into his belly. The hairs at the nape of his neck lifted with a chill of nameless apprehension.

He shrank back. 'My lord, this scarce is necessary. I love the Isle of Gramarye; I would never—'

'Lay your hand upon this hilt and swear!' The words were terse and stern.

Rod fairly cowered, well aware that the oath would bind him to the planet for life. 'My lord, are you asking me to take a loyalty oath? I am insulted that you should doubt my—'

'Swear!' the ghost thundered. 'Swear! Swear!'

'Art there, old mole?' Rod muttered under his breath, but it didn't work; he had never felt less funny.

He stared at the glowing hilt and the stern face beyond it, fascinated. Almost against his will, he took one step forward, then another; he watched his hand as it closed itself around the hilt. His palm felt nothing within it, no pressure of solid metal; but the air within his fist was so cold it paralyzed the knuckles.

'Now swear to me and mine!' Horatio rumbled.

*Oh, well,* Rod thought, *it's only words. Besides, I'm an agnostic, aren't I?*

'I . . . swear,' he said reluctantly, fairly forcing out the words. Then inspiration glimmered in his brain, and he added easily, 'And I further swear that I will not rest until the Queen and all her subjects with one voice shall rule again.'

He took his hand from the sword, rather pleased with himself. That additional clause gave him a clear track to the goal of his mission, whether or not Horatio counted democracy among the perils of Gramarye.

The ghost frowned. 'Strange,' he grumbled, 'a most strange oath. Yet from the heart, I cannot doubt, and binding to you.'

Of course, Rod admitted to himself, the oath still bound him to Gramarye; but he would bridge that gulf when he came to it.

The sword glided back to its scabbard. The ghost turned away, his voice trailing over his shoulder. 'Follow now, and I shall show you to the halls within these halls.'

Rod followed until they came to the wall. The ghost pointed a long, bony finger. 'Grope until you find a stone that yields to your hand.'

Rod reached for the stone the ghost pointed to, and pushed, leaning all his weight against it. The stone groaned and grudgingly gave way, sliding back into the wall. As it fell back, a door ground open with the protest of hinges that were long overdue for an oil break. Cold, dank air fanned Rod's cheek.

'Leave me now,' said the ghost, tall and regal beside him, 'and go to your duty. Yet remember, Man, your oath; and be assured that if ever you should lay it aside, the first Duke Loguire shall ever stand beside your bed until at last you yield to fear.'

'Definitely a comforting thought,' Rod mused. He groped his way down the moss-grown steps, humming 'You'll Never Walk Alone'.

This time, the door to the loft was open, and Tom's deep earthquake snores echoed in the rocky chamber.

Rod paused in the doorway, chewing at his lip. He went back into the hall, pulled a torch from its bracket, and thrust it ahead of him into the room, peering in cautiously, just to be sure there was no one trying to rearouse Tom with a paternity suit in mind.

The wavering light of the torch disclosed the stocky peasant's slumbering form, his cape thrown over his body from the rib cage down. One ursine arm was curled comfortably about the soft, rounded body of a blonde, covered (or uncovered) to the same degree by the cape. Her small, firm breasts were pressed against Tom's side; her head rested on his shoulder, long hair flung in a glorious disarray over her shoulders. One sun-browned arm was flung possessively across the big man's beer-keg chest.

Rod frowned, and stepped over for a closer look. The face was slender, the nose tilted, mouth small, with a smug little smile of content.

It was obviously not the brunette who had accosted Rod in the hallway earlier. He grunted in surprise; so the wench hadn't gone after the servant when she was refused by the master.

Of course, it might be just that she hadn't moved fast enough . . . But no, Big Tom would've been glad to accommodate both.

He replaced the torch, came back to the loft with a nod of grudging admiration at Big Tom, and without bothering to pull off his doublet, dropped into the heap of hay that served for a bed. It brought back fond memories. He yawned, cushioned his head on his forearm, and drifted slowly toward sleep.

'Man Gallowglass!'

The voice boomed in the little room. Rod jerked bolt upright; the girl screamed, and Big Tom swore.

A ghost towered before them, glowing cold in the dark.

Rod came to his feet, flicking a glance at Tom and the girl. She cowered in abject terror against the bear-hide of his chest. Tom's face had already settled into surly (and probably frightened) defiance.

Rod switched his eyes to the ghost, standing tall above him in plate armour, its face incredibly long and thin. The sword at its hip was a rapier; it was not Horatio Loguire.

Rod reminded himself that he was boss, a fact he had almost forgotten. He repaid the hollow gaze with the haughtiest look he could manage. 'What sty were you raised in,' he snapped, 'that you come before a gentleman with such ill ceremony?'

The cavern eyes widened, the ghost's jaw dropping down inside its mouth. It stared at Rod, taken aback.

The mortal pressed his advantage. 'Speak, and with courtesy, or I'll dance on your bones!'

The ghost fairly cringed; Rod had struck pay dirt. Apparently there was some sort of ectoplasmic link between a ghost and its mortal remains. He made a mental note to track down the graves of all relevant ghosts.

'Your pardon, milord,' the ghost stammered. 'I meant no offence; I only—'

Rod cut him off. 'Now that you have disturbed my rest, you may as well speak. What brings you to me?'

'You are summoned—'

Rod interrupted him off again. 'None summon me.'

'Your pardon, lord.' The ghost bowed. 'Milord Loguire requests your presence.'

Rod glared a moment longer, then caught up his harp with a sigh. 'Well, he who deals with spirits must deal at odd hours.' He cocked his head. '*Horatio* Loguire?'

'The same, my lord.'

The servant girl gasped.

Rod winced; he had forgotten his audience. His reputation would be all over the castle by noon.

'Well,' he said, shouldering his harp, 'lead on.'

The ghost bowed once more, then turned toward the wall, stretching out a hand.

'Hold it,' Rod snapped. Better to leave the secret passages secret. 'Go ye to Milord Loguire and tell him I shall come to him presently. You forget that I cannot walk through walls, like yourself.'

The ghost turned, frowning. 'But, my lord . . .'

'Go to Milord Loguire!' Rod stormed.

The ghost shrank away. 'As you will, my lord,' it mumbled hastily, and winked out.

In the sudden darkness, the girl let out her breath in a long, sobbing sigh; and, 'How now, master,' said Big Tom, his voice very calm, with only a trace of wonder, 'do you traffic with spirits now?'

'I do,' said Rod, and flung the door open, wondering where Tom had picked up a word like 'traffic'.

He turned to look at the couple in the light from the doorway, his eyes narrowed and piercing. 'If word of this passes beyond this room, there shall be uneasy beds and midnight guests for the both of you.'

Big Tom's eyes narrowed, but the girl's widened in alarm.

*Good*, thought Rod, *I've threatened her income. Now I can be sure she'll keep quiet.*

He spun on his heel, pulling the door shut behind him. Big Tom would console her, of course, and his master's control over ghosts wouldn't exactly hurt his standing with her.

And, of course, she'd keep her mouth shut.

Which was just as well. For a man who didn't believe in magic, Rod already had altogether too much of a name as a warlock.

He prowled along the hall till he found an empty chamber with access to the hidden tunnel. The granite blocks of·one wall had been carved into a bas-relief of an orange flute being burned at the stake; apparently the Loguires took their adopted Irish name rather seriously. Rod found the one coal in the pile of faggots that was cut a little deeper than the rest, and threw all his weight against it, pushing it to his right. The ancient machinery gave a deep-throated grumble, and a trapdoor pivoted up from the stone flags of the floor.

Rod felt for the steps with his toes, reached up for the great iron ring set in the underside of the trapdoor, and pulled it shut as he went down the stairs.

He emerged from the massive door in the great hall with the dark altar. His phantom guide was there before him, waiting.

The ghost bowed. 'If you would be so good as to follow me, master . . .' It turned away, drifting toward the archway into the corridor.

Rod followed, muttering, 'A little lighter on the sarcasm there.'

They came out into the corridor; and, off to his right, Rod saw the fox-firelight of a cluster of ghosts. They were motionless, their heads bent, looking at something on the floor in the centre of their circle. Rod heard a very mortal, and very terrified, whimper.

Horatio looked up at Rod's approach. He glided apart from the knot of ghosts, his cadaverous face knotted with anger.

'My Lord Loguire!' Rod bowed his most courtly, straightened. 'Why do you summon me?'

The ghost's brow smoothed a little, somewhat mollified. 'Man Gallowglass,' it growled, 'wherefore did you not tell me you had come accompanied into our halls?'

'Accompanied?' Rod's eyebrows lifted. 'Oh, was I, now?'

Loguire's frown deepened again, puzzled. 'In truth, there was one who followed after you, as I found upon my outgoing from the chamber with the strange device.'

'Excelsior,' Rod murmured.

'*Gesundheit*,' said Loguire. 'If we are to have a continual passage of mortals here, I shall have to see to the heating of these halls. But anon: I found your servant, as I have said, directly without the chamber.'

'Servant?' Rod frowned. 'How do you know it was a servant?'

'It was listening at the door. And we may know that it is yours, for when we advanced upon it, it cried your name.'

'Oh.' Rod scratched at the base of his skull, frowning. 'It did, did it?'

'Aye; else would we have slain it. And therefore did I send to you to claim it.'

Loguire stepped aside; the circle of ghosts parted, and Rod stepped up. By the cold light of the ghosts, he saw a huddle of misery trying to push itself into the wall. The face was turned away from him. Long black hair flowed down over the shoulders. It wore a white blouse, full skirt, and black bodice. The last was very well filled.

'My Lord Loguire,' Rod began; his voice cracked; he tried again. 'My Lord Loguire, this is scarcely an "it".' Then, in the gentlest voice he could manage, 'Look at me, wench.'

The girl's head jerked up staring, lips parted. Joy and relief flooded her face. 'My Lord!'

Then her arms were about his neck, so tight he had to fight for breath; and her body was pressed tight against him, head burrowing into his shoulder, her whole frame trembling with sobs. 'My lord, O my lord!'

'My Lord!' Rod echoed, prying at her shoulder to get clearance for his larynx.

He recognized her, of course. It was the servant girl who had propositioned him earlier in the evening.

'There, there, now, lass, it's all right,' he murmured, rubbing her back. The room seemed to reel about him; he picked out a fixed point of light and stared at it.

It turned out to be Horatio Loguire, face contorted by a touch of disgust. 'Take her out from my halls, Man. They are damp enough of their own.'

Rod was just noticing how nicely the peasant girl fitted in his arms. He closed his eyes, savouring the warmth and closeness of her. He nodded. 'Aye, my lord, that I shall. There, there, now, lass, you mustn't cry.' He pulled a handkerchief from his cuff and dabbed at her cheeks with it. 'No more tears, there's a darling, you're raising the humidity, and Horatio's got arthritis, if he can just remember where he put his bones – there, that's right.'

Her head lay against his chest, sniffling. Her eyes closed, her face relaxed; it almost seemed she was asleep. Rod was swept with a sudden wave of tenderness, aided and abetted by a feeling of towering strength contributed by his protective instinct, and silently cursed the adhesive effect of a damsel in distress.

He looked up into the brooding, empty eyes of the Loguire.

'Thou'rt ensnared, Man.'

'Who, me?' Rod scowled and thumped his throat in the carotid region. 'Fire seven times tried this.'

'And found it wanting,' Loguire agreed, 'and seven times tried *that* judgement is. Take her from my halls, Man.'

Rod threw him one last look of defiance and turned to the girl. 'Come lass,' he murmured, 'we must go out from this place now.'

He swung her up into his arms. She stirred, murmured petulantly, and burrowed her head tight into his shoulder again, her arms tight about his neck.

*Babies and women*, Rod thought, exasperated; *they're worse than quicksand.*

'My lord,' he said to Loguire, 'will you lead me? You may understand that I am somewhat turned about . . .'

'Aye,' said the ghost, and turned away down the hall; but not before Rod had glimpsed a faint, phantom smile on the ghost's face . . .

He came out into the torch-lit corridor, where he had met Durer earlier. The little man was gone; apparently he had assumed the worst and gleefully gone his way.

Rod lowered the girl's feet to the floor. She murmured another little inarticulate protest, and pressed her head tighter against him.

Rod tightened his arms about her and brushed his cheek against her hair, drawing out the moment as long as he could.

Then he smiled sadly and lifted his hand to stroke along her jaw, tilting her chin up. The long-lashed eyes were still closed; the full red lips pursed and parted, just a little . . .

Rod steeled himself and said gently, 'You must tell me now, lass. Why did you follow me?'

Her eyes flew open, widened in alarm. Then she bit her lip, bowing her head, and stood away from him, clenching her hands in the cloth of his doublet.

'You must tell me, lass,' he repeated softly. 'Who sent you to spy on me?'

Her head flew up, eyes wide in dismay. She shook her head. 'None, my lord. None, only myself.'

'Oh?' Rod smiled sadly. 'Of your own doing, you followed me into the haunted quarter?'

She looked down again. 'I did not fear the spirits, lord.'

Rod pursed his lips in surprise. If it was so, she had uncommon courage for a serving maid. Her nerve hadn't broken till she actually saw the ghosts – and having experienced their moans himself, Rod could understand her breaking then.

Too, she might have followed him in hopes that he might reconsider his decision to sleep alone. Or maybe she'd thought she could help if he got into trouble. Rod smiled at that last thought. But he had to make sure.

'Still, you have not yet told me: why did you follow me?'

She bit her lip again, her face twisting. Rod waited, quietly.

Grudging every word, she said, 'I – I feared for you, my lord.'

Rod stared; then his mouth twisted into a wry smile. He shook his head, slowly. 'You *feared* for me!'

'Aye!' Her head snapped up, eyes flashing. 'I had no knowing you were a warlock, and . . . a man alone, in those halls . . .'

Her voice trailed off; her eyes dropped again.

Rod heaved a sigh and clasped her to him. She resisted a moment, then yielded.

'Lass, lass!' he murmured. 'What could you have done to help me?'

'I – I have some small way with some spirits, lord.' Her voice was muffled by the cloth of his tunic. 'I had thought . . .'

Rod scowled. Was communication with the spirit world the norm on this kooky planet?

He rubbed her back gently, pressed his cheek against her hair. She could be lying, of course; but that would imply she was an excellent actress, and she seemed a little too ingenuous for that.

He sighed and tightened his arms about her. She murmured sulkily and pushed her hips against him.

Rod closed his eyes and wiped his mind of all but the touch of her body. She felt good, very good. Almost like that farm wench, Gwendylon . . .

His eyes snapped open. He stared into the torch-lit dusk of the hall, picturing the two faces before him, side by side. Dye the hair black, tilt the eyes a little, straighten the nose . . .

She had felt him tense; she looked up at him. 'What is it, my lord?'

The voice was a little higher-pitched, yes; but it had that same quality.

He looked down at her. The complexion was flawless, not a single freckle; but it didn't take that much technology to concoct a make-up base.

He pointed his forefinger between her eyes. 'You,' he said, 'have been deceiving me.' His finger came to rest on the tip of her nose.

There was a flicker of disappointment in her eyes; then she was all innocence. 'Deceiving you, my lord? I – I know not . . .'

Rod flicked his finger; the tip of her nose came off. He smiled grimly, nodding. 'Cornstarch and water. But you were wrong to straighten it; I like it much better with that little tilt at the end.'

He rubbed his fingertip across the corner of her eye; the eye was no longer slanted, and there was a dark smudge on his finger. 'Cornstarch and water, and black paint at the eye-fold. Flour mixed with a little burnt umber on the face, and henna in the hair.'

The corners of her mouth tightened. Her face blushed with the heat of anger under the paint.

He shook his head, brow puckered. 'But why, lass? Your face is so much more beautiful.'

He allowed himself a shot of self-satisfaction as the anger in her face melted into tenderness and longing.

She lowered her eyes. 'I – I could not leave you, lord.'

He closed his eyes, grinding his teeth, and only by main force of will kept himself from squeezing her.

'But . . .' He stopped, and drew a long hissing breath. 'But how did you follow me, lass?'

She looked up, eyes wide in innocence. 'In the guise of an osprey, lord.'

His eyes snapped open with a near-audible click. He stared. 'A witch? You? But . . .'

'You will not despise me for it, lord?' she said anxiously. 'You, who are a warlock?'

His eyes had lost focus. 'Huh? Uh – warlock?'' He shook his head, trying to clear it. 'Uh, I mean . . . No, of course I don't. I mean . . . well, some of my best friends are . . . uh . . .'

'My lord?' She peered into his face. 'Art thou well?'

'Who, me? Of course not! No, wait a minute . . .' He stopped and drew a very, very deep breath. 'Now, look. You're a witch. So. Big deal. I'm far more interested in your beauty than your talents.'

Embers there, in her eyes, ready to flame if he breathed upon them.

He took another deep breath and called his hormones to order. 'Now. Let's get one thing straight.' She brushed up against him, breathing, 'Aye, my lord.'

'No, no! I didn't mean *that*!' He took a step back, hands coming up to hold her off. 'Look. The only reason you followed me here was because you were afraid I'd get into trouble I couldn't handle, right?'

She paused, the glow dying in her eyes under a chill flow of disappointment. She lowered her eyes. 'Aye, my lord.'

The way she said it made him think she was leaving an awful lot to implication; but he hurried on to the next point.

'But now you know I'm a warlock. Right?'

'Aye, my lord.' He could scarcely hear her.

'So you know I don't have to be afraid of anything, right? So there's no reason to follow me any more, right?'

'Nay, my lord!' Her face whipped up to him, glaring; then her chin lifted a little higher, proud and haughty and stubborn. 'Still will I follow you, Rod Gallowglass. There be spells in this world that you wot not of.'

And one of the most galling things about her, he decided, was that she was always so damned *right*. In this crazy, topsy-turvy world, there probably were quite a few 'spells' he couldn't even imagine.

But, on the other hand, there seemed to be a few that she didn't know, either. An amateur witch, most likely, and too old to join the union – she must be almost as old as Rod was. In fact, her 'witchcraft' seemed to consist of cosmetic skill, the ability to go birdie (he hadn't quite figured that one out yet), and a degree of courage that was totally unexpected in a woman.

So she was right, she had good cause to worry about him, he would still be in danger – but so would she.

No. It wouldn't do any good to tell her she couldn't follow him – she would anyway. And he'd come out of it alive, like he always did, but she'd get murdered in a ditch somewhere along the way. Or maybe she'd handicap him enough so they'd both wind up dead.

His head moved from side to side, tightening into a quick shake. He couldn't let her get killed. He had to shake her somehow – and he knew just how.

His mouth quirked into a sour smile. 'It's true, what they say about farm girls: give them a moment of kindness, and you'll never be rid of them. My dear, you have an excellent nuisance rating.'

She gasped, stepped away from him, her face twisting into a grimace of pain, the back of her hand coming up to her lips. Her eyes flooded with tears; she bit on her hand, turned, and fled.

He stared at the floor, listening to her sobs fading, feeling the hollowness grow within him.

*

A fist thundered on the heavy oaken door. Rod struggled up out of the depths of sleep, floundering to sit up in the hay.

Big Tom and his wench lay still, eyes fixed on the door.

Rod grunted and levered himself to his feet. 'Don't worry,' he growled. 'Ghosts don't knock.'

'Ho, minstrel!' a gruff beery voice bellowed. 'Come forth to my master!'

Rod struggled into his doublet and caught up his harp. He swung open the great oak door, shaking his head to clear the traces of his meagre sleep. 'You might at least try to be civil at this hour of the damn morning,' he growled. 'And just who the hell is your master?'

The heavy fist caught him under the ear, sent him sprawling against the wall. He fought down the instant impulse to break the man's neck.

Through a ringing, blurred haze he heard a deep, sadistic chuckle. 'Mind how you speak to your betters, gleeman. 'Tis a good rule for a peasant.'

Rod gathered himself, hands braced against the wall, and sized up his persecutor. It was a common foot soldier in leather and mail, both of which needed cleaning, as did the soldier himself. He might have been a commoner, but he had an uncommon case of BO, and halitosis on top of it, possibly due to the rotting teeth he was exhibiting in a self-satisfied grin.

Rod sighed and straightened, deciding it might be better to play his part; in fact he'd deserved the blow, for having dropped out of character. The jester in medieval society served as an emotional release, not only through entertainment, but also through providing an outlet for aggressions by becoming their object.

'All right,' he said, 'I'm schooled. Let's go.'

The fist caught him beneath the jaw this time. As he rolled with the blow, he heard the gleeful voice growl, 'Thou'rt not schooled enough. To address your betters with *master* is the rule.'

Rod fought the anger down into a cold, calm, calculating rage and lunged, his hands chopping out in three quick blows.

'I've got a better rule for a soldier,' he informed the crumpled heap at his feet. 'First be sure who your betters are. Now take me to your master.'

The master, as it turned out, was Loguire. Rod was ushered into a medium-sized room, high-ceilinged and hung with tapestries. Three tall, narrow windows, through which Rod saw sunlight, dawn-coloured, broken by the shifting prism of the waterfall. The room was filled with its roaring. But the sound was muted; looking closer, Rod saw the windows were double-paned, and three feet deep. Somebody had remembered some of the old technology.

The walls were hung with tapestries; there was a heavy carpet underfoot. A great oval table took up the centre of the chamber. At its head sat Loguire; at his right, his eldest son. Durer sat at his left. The other places were taken up by eight men who had a familiar look. Rod's eyes widened as he recognized them: the Duke de' Medici, the Earl of Romanov, the Duke Bourbon, and the Prince Habsburg, and their councillors.

After Loguire, they were the four most powerful of the Great Lords. And if these five were gathered together, might not the other seven be close by?

All were at breakfast, but none of them really seemed to realize they were eating. Take Anselm, there, Loguire's son – he ate like a machine, glaring at his plate, face set like a sculpture of cold fury.

His father sat with head bowed, hands pressed tight to the table before him.

At a guess, Rod decided, there had been a bit of a quarrel here, between father and son, and Loguire had won – but only by ordering his son to shut up.

And Rod had been called in to heal the breach. Oy! The things people expect of performers!

Durer's face was lit with a subterranean glow of vindictive joy; the other councillors had milder versions of the same look. Whatever had happened here had gone the way Durer wanted; in fact, he'd probably instigated it. The man was the perfect catalyst, Rod decided: he never got involved in the reactions he caused.

Loguire looked up at his son, mute appeal in the old, red-rimmed eyes. But Anselm gave him not so much as a glance, and Loguire's face firmed into flint.

Turning, the old man saw Rod. 'Minstrel!' he barked. 'Why stand you there idle? Give us merriment!'

Durer's head snapped around, his eyes locked on Rod. Alarm chased shock across his face, to be followed by distilled, murderous hate.

Rod smiled cheerfully, bowed, and touched his forelock in salute. Inwardly, he wondered what song could possibly burn away the tensions in this room. He strongly suspected the custom was to clear the air by beating the minstrel for failing to fulfil his assignment.

He began to play 'Matty Groves', figuring his only chance lay in giving them something more gruesome than anything that could possibly have just taken place.

He held off on the words for a few minutes, though, to give him time to study the faces of the four lords. Their looks ranged from ruminative speculation to outright (though veiled) contempt, the last apparently directed at the old Duke. It would seem that Loguire had no virulent supporters here; the balance of opinion seemed to rest with his son.

'Minstrel!'

Rod looked up; it was Anselm who had spoken.

The young man's face seemed to have soured so much it had curdled. 'Have you a song for a lad made a fool by a woman, yet doubly a fool, still, to love her?'

'Ha' done!' Loguire snapped; but before Anselm could reply, Rod said, 'Many, my lord, of a man still loving a woman who scorned him; and in all of them, the lady comes back to him.'

'Comes back!' Anselm spat. 'Aye, she'd take him back – to hang him in shame at her castle gate!'

The old Duke drew himself to his feet, roaring, 'Enough of your slander!'

'Slander!' Anselm's chair crashed over as he rose to meet his father. 'And is it slander to say she has spit on the proud name of Loguire, aye, and not once but twice, and will do so again?

'Nay!' He slammed his fist on the board, turning to rake the lords with his glare. 'This vile wench shall learn that she dare not trample the honour of her peers! We must tear her from the seat of power and break her beneath us for ever and aye!'

Loguire's face reddened, his throat swelled with a rebuke; but before he could speak it, Rod murmured, 'Nay, my lord, not so harsh. Not a defeat, but a discipline.'

He was caught in a crossfire of laser-beam glares from Anselm and Durer; but Loguire boomed 'Aye!' with a giant's joy and relief. 'He speaks out of place, but his speaking is true! Our young Queen is headstrong; but so is a filly before it is bridled. She must learn her authority is not absolute, that there are checks upon her power; but she is the sovereign, and must not be torn down!'

Anselm made a gurgling sound, his face swollen red and his eyes starting forth from their sockets, choking with rage; then he managed to speak, fairly stuttering in his wrath.

'Nay, now! Now I say nay! A woman for a sovereign? 'Tis a mockery! And a whoring, arrogant bitch of a—'

'Be still!' Loguire thundered, and even the four great lords shrank away from the savage power of his voice.

As for Anselm, he fairly cowered, staring appalled at the white-bearded giant before him, who almost seemed to swell and tower high as they watched.

Then, slowly, and with greater dignity than Rod had ever seen in a man, the true regal dignity that only comes unaware, Loguire resumed his seat, never taking his eyes from his son. 'Retire to your chambers,' he said in a cold, still voice. 'We shall speak no more of this till the conclave at sunset.'

Anselm somehow managed to summon the strength to lift his chin again, a gesture that somehow seemed pompous and ridiculous, and turned on his heel. As he stalked to the door, his eyes fell on Rod. Rage and humiliation boiled up in him, and he swung up his arm to favour the minstrel with a back-handed slap.

'Nay!' barked Loguire, and Anselm froze.

'This man,' said the Duke, speaking in centimetres, 'has spoken truth. I will not have him maltreated.'

Anselm locked glares with his father; then his look faltered, and dropped. He turned away; the door slammed behind him.

'Minstrel,' rumbled Loguire, 'play!'

Rod let his fingers ramble through 'The Old Man of Tor Tappan' while he reflected.

So there would be a council of war tonight, eh? And the main issue would apparently be constitutional monarchy versus warlordism, though only he and Durer might know it. Well, he knew which side he was on.

He looked again at the straight-backed old Duke, eating token bits of food, lips pressed tight under his flowing white beard, brow locked in a slight scowl, only the slightest hint of his grief showing in the deep, shadowed eyes.

Yes, Rod knew which side he was on.

They met in the great hall, large enough to act as a hangar for a good-sized spaceship, if the Gramarians had known what a spaceship was.

The stone floor was inlaid with Loguire's coat of arms. Great silver sconces supported torches every yard or so along the walls. The ceiling was concave and gilded, with an immense silver chandelier suspended from its centre. There were no windows; but that made little difference, since night had fallen.

Loguire sat in a great carved chair at one end of the hall, bunting of his family's colours draped on the wall behind him. His chair was raised on a four foot dais, so that the standing lords must look up at him.

There were a good many of them, not only the twelve greats, but with them a host of counts, barons, and knights, their vassals.

And at each one's elbow stood, or rather hunched, a thin-faced, bony little man, with scant light hair lying close against his scalp.

Rod surveyed the hall; his lips pursed into a soundless whistle. He hadn't realized the councillors were so numerous. There were at least fifty, maybe seventy.

And there might be more outside his field of view. At the moment, he had literal tunnel-vision, and one-eyed at that. The torches that illuminated the hall sat in sconces that were held to the wall with three rough bolts.

But one of the sconces behind Loguire's throne was missing a bolt, and the stone behind it was bored through for an inch, then hollowed out to the depth and width of a man's head. The head, at the moment, was Rod's, where he stood in the clammy darkness of a narrow passage behind the wall.

His peephole afforded him an excellent view of the back of Loguire's head, and some nice over-the-shoulder shots of anyone addressing him.

His right hand rested on a lever; if he pushed it down – if it wasn't rusted tight – the stone before him *should* swing wide to make a handy door. From the looks on the faces of the lords confronting the Duke, it might be very handy.

The man immediately in front of the Duke was Anselm. Bourbon and de' Medici stood at either side of the young man. Durer, of course, stood at Loguire's left hand.

Loguire rose heavily. 'We are met,' he rumbled. 'Here in this room is gathered all the noble blood of Gramarye, the true power of the land.' He scanned the faces before him slowly, looking each of his brother Great Lords directly in the eye.

'We are met,' he said again, 'to decide on a fitting rebuke for Catharine the Queen.'

The Duke of Bourbon stirred, unfolding his arms and setting his feet a little further apart. He was a great black bear of a man, with shaggy brows and a heap of beard on his chest.

His fists clenched, his mouth tightened. There was something furtive, sheepish, in his stance.

He glared at Loguire. 'Nay, good Uncle, you have the wrong of it. We are met to say how we may pull her down, she who would trample upon the honour and the power of our noble Houses.'

Loguire stiffened, his eyes widening in outrage. 'Nay!' he choked, 'there is not cause enough . . .'

'Cause!' Bourbon straightened, his black beard jumping with his jaw. 'She hath taxed our lands more heavily than ever in the traditions of our lore, and wasted the substance upon the filth and dirt of peasants; she sends her judge amongst us every month to hear complaints from all the manor; and now she will appoint her priests within our lands – and we have no cause? She robs us of our rightful rule within our own demesnes, and then upon this all insults us to our faces by hearing the petitions of besotted beggars ere she will bend her ear to ours!'

De' Medici had bent to listen to the slight man at his elbow; now he straightened, smiling faintly, and murmured, 'And was it custom, ever, for a monarch to receive petitions from his peasants within his own Great Hall?'

'Never!' thundered Bourbon. 'But now our gentle monarch will place the rabble thus before us! And these, my *reverend* Duke, be but the greatest of her enormities, and the atrocities she hath wreaked upon the custom of the land. And this while she is but a child! What will she do, my lord, when she is grown!'

He paused for breath, then shook his head and growled, 'Nay, good coz! We must needs pull her down!'

'Aye,' murmured de' Medici, and 'Aye,' declared the other lords, and 'Aye' rolled through the hall and swelled, till the word came full, clamouring from every throat, again and yet again.

'Aye!' and 'Aye!' and 'Aye!'

'Now I say *nay*!' Loguire roared above them all.

The hall fell still. Loguire drew himself up to his full height and breadth, looking more a king than duke.

His voice was only a little calmer, falling like the toll of a battle tocsin. 'She is the sovereign. Capricious, aye, and arbitrary, hot and headstrong, aye. But these are faults of youth, of a child who must be taught that there are limits to her power. We must now show her those limits that she has exceeded. That may we do, and nothing more. Our cause does not admit of further action.'

'A woman cannot rule wisely,' murmured de' Medici's councillor, and de' Medici took it up: 'My good and gentle cousin, God did not make Woman wise in ruling.'

Bourbon took his cue. 'Aye, good Uncle. Why will she give us not a king? Let her marry, if she doth wish this land well-governed.'

Rod wondered if Bourbon was a disappointed suitor. There was something vaguely lecherous about him, and nothing at all romantic.

'The rule is hers by right!' Loguire rumbled. 'Hers is the blood Plantagenet, the Crown of this land since its birth! What, good nephew, have you so easily forgotten the oath you swore in fealty to that good name?'

'Dynasties grow corrupt,' muttered Bourbon's councillor, eyes gleaming.

'Aye!' Bourbon bellowed. 'The blood Plantagenet has thinned and soured, *good* my lord!'

*Ah, so!* Rod thought. *He's not an uncle any more . . .*

'Weakened sore, my lord!' Bourbon ranted. 'Weakened till it can no longer sire a man, but only a woman, slip of a girl, with a woman's moods and whims, to reign! The bloodline of Plantagenet is worn and spent; we must have new blood now for our kings!'

'The blood of Bourbon?' Loguire lifted an eyebrow, his smile contemptuous.

Bourbon's face swelled red, eyes bulging. He had begun to splutter when de' Medici's voice interposed itself smoothly.

'Nay, good cousin, not the blood of Bourbon. What throneblood should we have but the noblest in all the South?'

Loguire stared, the blood draining out of his face in shock and horror. 'I will not!' he hissed.

'Nay, my lord, and this we knew.' de' Medici went oily on. 'Yet must we have good blood, and a man of courage and decision, a man of youth who knows what must be done and will not hesitate to do it.'

His voice rose. 'What king should we have but Anselm, Loguire's son?'

Loguire's head jerked as though he had been slapped. He stared, his face paling to a waxen texture, taking on a greyish hue.

He reached behind him with a palsied hand, groping for his chair, and age draped heavy on his shoulders.

He lowered himself to the edge of the seat, leaning heavily on the arm. His vacant eyes sought out his son, then turned slowly from side to side.

'Villains!' he whispered. 'Bloody, bawdy villains! And thus you steal my son . . .'

Anselm's chin was lifted in defiance, but guilt and fear had hollowed his eyes. 'Nay, my lord, I was with them from the first.'

Loguire's empty eyes sought him out again. 'But thou, even thou . . .'

His voice strengthened. 'But it is, thou more than any. Above all, it is thou!'

Durer now stepped forward, away from Loguire, to take his place by Anselm's side, his smile split into a grin of triumph.

Loguire's eyes gradually focused on him. Their eyes met, and held.

A slight rustle passed through the hall as all the councillors craned for a better view.

'Nay,' Loguire whispered. 'it was *thou* . . .'

He straightened slowly. Then, deliberately and slowly, he looked each Great Lord in the eyes once more. His eyes turned back to Durer.

'You are all of one mind.' His voice had gained strength; but it was the strength of bitterness and contempt. 'The debate has been before this, has it not? For you are all agreed; each man among you has quarrelled with his conscience and won over it.'

His voice hardened even more. 'What wasp has flown among you, to sting your souls to such accord?'

Durer's eyes snapped fire. His mouth broke open for retort; but Loguire cut him off.

'Thou! Thou from the star! Thou camest to me five years ago, and I, aged fool, thought "Well and good"; and as thy bastard, cringing servants crept one by one into our households, still I rejoiced – poor, aged, doddering fool!'

He lifted his eyes to seek out Anselm's. 'Anselm, who once I called my son, awake and hear! Beware the man who tastes thy meat, for he it is who best may poison it.'

Rod suddenly realized how the meeting would end. The councillors couldn't risk leaving Loguire alive; the old man was still strong and vital, still indomitable. He just might be able to sway the lords to loyalty again. The chance was slight, but definite, and Durer couldn't afford it.

Anselm straightened his shoulders, his face set with rebellion. He clapped a hand to Durer's shoulder, not noticing that the little man's teeth grated as his jaws clamped shut.

'This man I trust,' he stated in what might have been intended to be ringing tones. 'He was with me from the first, and I welcome his wisdom – as I will welcome yours, if you are with us.'

Loguire's eyes narrowed. 'Nay,' he spat. 'Away with you, false child, and your tongue of treachery! I had sooner die than join you.'

'You shall have your preference,' Durer snapped. 'Name the manner of your dying.'

Loguire glared, then threw himself to his full height in one lurching motion.

Anselm stared, then reddened. 'Be – be still, Durer! He is – is a fool, aye, and a traitor to the land. But he is my father, and none shall touch him!'

Durer's eyebrows shot up. 'You would harbour snakes within your bed, my lord? Naetheless, it is the wish of all the nobles, not yours alone, that must be done.'

He raised his voice, shouting, 'What say you, lords? Shall this man die?'

There was a moment's pause. Rod rested his hand on the door-lever; he had to get Loguire out of there. He could open the door and pull Loguire into the passage before anybody realized what was happening . . .

But could he close it before they came running? Probably not; there were just too many too close. And Durer, at least, would react very quickly.

If only the hinges and springs were in decent shape! But he had a notion they hadn't been too well maintained in the last few centuries.

A chorus of reluctant 'Ayes' rolled through the great hall.

Durer turned to Loguire, bowing his head politely. 'The verdict, my lord, is death.'

He drew his poniard and started forward.

And the light went out.

Rod stood a moment in the total blackness, stunned. How . . .?

Then he threw his weight on the lever. He jerked out his dagger as the stone slab groaned open. Act now, understand later.

The grating of the stone door broke the instant of shocked silence. Pandemonium struck as every voice in the hall started shouting – some in anger, some in distress, some calling for a porter to bring a torch.

The noise would be a good cover. Rod lunged out of the passage, groping blindly till he slammed into somebody's rib cage. The Somebody roared and lashed out at him. Rod ducked on general principles, felt the blow skim his hair. He flicked the button on the handle of his dagger and identified Somebody as the Duke Loguire in the flicker of light that stabbed up from the hilt.

A kindling-wood, twisting body struck into Rod with a howl of rage. Rod gasped and stumbled as steel bit into his shoulder. Apparently Durer had seen the flicker of light, too.

The dagger wrenched itself out of Rod's shoulder; he felt the warm welling flow out of the blood, and rolled away.

But the scarecrow was on him again. Rod groped, and by great good luck caught the man's knife-wrist.

But the little man was unbelievably strong. He forced Rod's arm down, down, and Rod felt the dagger's point prick his throat.

He tried to force his other hand up to help push the needle-point away. His shoulder screamed pain, but the hand wouldn't budge.

The dagger pricked a fraction of an inch deeper. Rod felt blood rise on his throat, and fear clawed its way up from his guts.

Total, numbing, paralysing fear – and Rod heard a booming moan.

Durer gasped; the poniard clattered to the floor, and the weight rose off Rod's body.

The whole hall rang with a triple, very low moan, counterpointed with shrieks of terror.

Three huge white forms towered high in the blackness. At the tops were skeletal faces, their mouths rounded into O's: Horatio and two other erstwhile Lords Loguire, having the time of their afterlives.

Rod forced a shout out of his terror. 'Fess! Sixty cycles!'

His head clamoured with the raucous buzzing, and the fear evaporated. His light flicked again, found Loguire. Rod sprang, struck him in the midriff. The breath went out of the old lord in a *whoof!* and he doubled over Rod's shoulder – the good one, fortunately.

Rod turned and ran, stumbling, hoping he was headed in the right direction.

Behind him, Durer was shrieking, 'Clap your hands to your ears, fools! Fools! Fools!'

Rod blundered about in the dark, Loguire's weight dragging heavier on his shoulder. He couldn't find the door! And now he heard staccato steps in short, quick bursts – Durer, trying to find Rod by blind chance. And now that he had his earplugs in, Durer would once again be a formidable enemy. Also, Rod couldn't fight with one shoulder shot and the other under Loguire.

Cold air fanned his cheek, and a dim white form brushed past him. 'Follow!' boomed Horatio Loguire.

Rod followed.

He ran after Horatio, his good arm out like a brokenfield runner. It didn't help; his wounded shoulder slammed against the stone of the doorway and spun him around with a wrench of pain. He gasped, almost dropping Loguire, and stumbled back against the wall of the narrow passage.

He leaned against the wall, breathing hoarsely.

'Quickly, Man!' boomed Horatio. 'The slab! You must close it!'

Rod nodded, gasping, and groped for the lever, hoping Loguire would stay balanced on his shoulder. His hand found rusty metal. He hauled upward; the door grated shut.

He stood hunched over, just breathing.

After a small eternity, Loguire began to struggle. Rod called up the energy to lower him to the floor. Then, still panting, he looked up at Horatio.

'Many thanks,' he wheezed, 'for this timely rescue.'

Horatio waved away the thanks, coming dangerously close to a smile. 'Why, Man, how could you fulfil your oath to me dead?'

'Oh, I dunno.' Rod sagged against the wall. 'You seem to manage all right. I'd love to know how you pulled the fuse on those torches.'

'Pulled . . . the fuse?' Horatio frowned.

'You know, the trick with the lights.'

The ghost's frown deepened. 'Was that not your doing?'

Rod stared. Then he raised a hand, palm out. 'Now, wait a minute. Wait a minute. Now. You thought I did it . . . and I thought you did it.'

'Aye.'

'But, you didn't do it?'

'Nay.'

'And I didn't do it.'

'It would seem not.'

'Then –' Rod gulped '– who . . .?'

'Who is this?' Loguire rumbled at Rod's elbow.

A beam of light stabbed through the peephole.

Horatio gave one moan of fear, and winked out.

Rod put his eye to the peephole. The torches were lit again. Durer was on the dais, stabbing the air about him with his dagger and screaming, 'Where? Where?'

Rod lifted his head away from the peephole and smiled up at Loguire thinly. 'I don't think we ought to stay to find out, my lord. Shall we go?'

He turned to go; but Loguire's fingers dug into his shoulder. Rod gasped. 'Please, milord – would you mind – the other shoulder, please . . . .'

'What man was that?' Loguire growled.

'Man?' Rod looked about him. 'What man?'

'Why, he who stood before us in white!'

'Oh.' Rod scanned the old man's face. Apparently Loguire was still in shock, not quite yet ready to face reality, such as it was. 'Uh, just a relative, milord.'

'Your relative? Here?'

'No, milord. Yours.' He turned away, groping down the passage. After a moment, Loguire followed.

The light from the peephole fell off after a few yards. Rod groped his way, cursing; it would be pitch dark when they turned the corner to go down the narrow steps.

He turned the corner, fumbling out his dagger – and saw a ball of fox-fire before him. He stared, an eerie tingling nesting at the base of his neck; then, as his eyes adjusted to the dim glow, he made out a face and a body (it was impossible to see them as a unit, since each was worthy of independent study), one arm extended, with the fox-fire sitting on her palm. Her face was tense with worry.

'Gwendylon,' he stated.

Her face flooded with relief and joy, but only for a moment; then the light of mischief was in her eyes.

She bobbed in a mock curtsy. 'My lord.'

'My Aunt Nanny!' he growled. 'What the hell are you doing here?'

Her eyes widened in offended innocence. 'I followed you, lord.'

'No, no, no!' Rod squeezed his eyes shut. 'That's not in the script. You were supposed to hate me now. You were supposed to quit following me.'

'Never, lord.' Her voice was very low.

He looked up to see if she was joking. No luck. Tom's line about farm girls ran through his mind.

'What,' he said, nodding at the ball of fox-fire, 'have you got there?'

'This?' She glanced at the ball of light. 'Only a little spell my mother taught me. 'Twill light us through this maze, lord.'

'Light,' Rod agreed. 'And may I ask how you killed the torches in the great hall?'

She started to answer, then frowned. ''Tis not quickly said, lord. Have we time?'

Rod studied her face with his lips pursed. 'But it was you who did it?'

'Aye, lord.'

'Just another little spell that . . .'

'My mother taught me, yes.' She nodded brightly.

'Oka-a-a-y!' He shrugged. 'Why not? Let's go, babe.'

He started groping his way down the narrow stairs, wincing as his shoulder brushed the wall.

'My lord!' Gwendylon gasped, her hand darting out to touch his shoulder. 'You're hurt!'

He half-turned toward her, lurching against the wall, still groping for the stone; but the full, firm mound that his hand found was anything but granite.

He jerked his hand away. She stared at him a moment, surprised; then her lids drooped, she smiled lazily, and caught up his hand, pulling it toward her. 'Milord, you need not—'

'Yegad!' He pulled his hand away, shrinking back against the wall. She swayed toward him, lips parting.

'My dear lady . . .!'

'I ha' ne'er claimed that title,' she murmured, her voice warm, rich, and husky. Her body pressed softly against him.

'Woman, please!' Rod made a valiant attempt to push his way into the stone. 'I can't imagine a less aesthetic atmosphere.'

'Neither time nor place matter to me lord, when you are near,' she breathed into his ear, and nibbled.

*And I thought I had some lines*, Rod told himself. 'Look,' he said, wriggling, 'we don't have time, we don't have room . . .' He gasped and shivered as she caught just exactly the right spot. 'Look, baby, just get us out of here, and I'm yours to command!'

She caught her breath and stood just far enough back to look up at him. 'Truly, lord?'

'Well, uh . . .' Rod backpedalled furiously. 'For twenty-four hours, anyway.'

'That will do,' she murmured smugly, with a similar quality in her smile.

He glowered down at her for a moment; then, 'Take those canary feathers out of your mouth,' he growled, 'and get us out of here!'

'Aye, lord!' She turned in a swirl of skirts and ran lightly down the mossy steps.

He watched her run for a moment, a gleam coming into his eye.

He caught up to her in three bounds and swung her around to face him.

She looked up in surprise, then turned on the sultry look again. 'My lord, we must not delay . . .'

'This won't take long,' he answered, and pulled her hard against him. Her lips were moist and warm, and parted . . .

She gave a happy little sigh and pushed him away. 'Well! And what was that for?'

'Promissory note.' He grinned.

She giggled, then spun away, tugging him down the hall. 'We

must hurry!'

He freed his arm and watched her run.

A deep, warm chuckle sounded behind him.

Rod threw Loguire a look of disgust. 'Dirty old man,' he growled, and ran after Gwen.

The slimy stones of the passage slid by on either side, scarcely three inches from each shoulder. Up a flight of steps, turn, up another flight, the stones greasy and slippery with dripping water, seepage from the lake overhead. Patches of pale moss grew like sores on the walls. Old spiderwebs festooned the low ceiling.

At the top of the twelfth staircase, Rod heard water chuckling somewhere in the distance.

'The inlet to the lake,' Gwendylon informed him. 'We shall come out along its border.' She glanced back over her shoulder. 'Your shoulder, Lord Rod?'

'Oh, it'll wait,' he growled.

'Doth it yet bleed?'

'No; the doublet seems to have stanched it. Be a hell of a cleaning bill though.'

'Hmm.' She turned away, hurrying. ' 'Twill hold till we come to the riverbank, then. Hurry, lords; we must be away ere they think to search in the stables.'

Rod frowned. 'Why? Are we coming out in the stableyard?'

'Nay, by the river; but when they look in the stables, they shall see that your black and the Duke's dun stallion have fled.'

'You don't say!' He cleared his throat and spoke a little louder than necessary. 'And where would my horse be?'

'By the riverbank, Rod,' Fess's voice murmured, 'with Big Tom and two real nags.'

Gwendylon had started to answer, but Rod cut her off. 'Yes, yes, they're by the riverbank, I know.'

Gwen looked faintly surprised.

'But how,' Rod went on, 'did Big Tom know we'd be needing horses?'

She frowned at him a moment, then turned away.

' 'Twas at my urging, lord. 'Twas but a thought, and could do little harm. I had a seeming they might be needed.'

'A seeming,' Rod echoed. Was she clairvoyant, too?

'Aye, lord, a seeming.' She slowed suddenly. 'Walk wary, lords.' She stepped carefully over something lying in the passage.

Rod stopped and stared at it.

It was a miniature human skeleton, perhaps eighteen inches long; but the proportions were those of an adult, not a baby. It was green with mould.

He looked up at Gwendylon. 'This has not been here so very long,' he said. 'What is it?'

'One of the Wee Folk, lord.' Her mouth hardened. 'There ha' been evil spells in this keep of late.'

Rod looked up, surprised at the tone of her voice, ignoring Loguire's startled exclamation.

Her face was flint, set in a mould of bitterness. 'Poor wee fellow,' she murmured. 'And we dare not stop to give him burial.' She spun about and hurried on.

Rod stepped carefully over the tiny skeleton and followed.

'What manner of spell?' he asked as he caught up to her.

' 'Twas a sort of . . . singing . . . in the air, lord, though not for the ear, but the mind. If you or I tried to move against it, 'twould but stop us; like a wall. But it slew the Wee Folk.'

Rod frowned. 'A *singing*, you say?'

'Aye, lord. Yet not of the ear, as I told you.'

A force field! But that was impossible. Ask any physicist, he'd tell you . . .

'How long ago?'

'It was cast five years agone, milord. It lasted no more than a month, for its master took no note of my stopping it, nor did he cast it again.'

Rod stopped so fast Loguire stumbled into him. He stared at the gentle, very feminine form hurrying down the passage before him. Then he closed his mouth, swallowed, and followed.

A force field! And five years ago, that was when Durer had shown up . . .

Rod thought again of the dial on the supposed time machine. Then he stared at Gwen's long, red hair, swinging with her steps.

And she had stopped it? A machine out of the future, and *she* had stopped it?

He looked at his farm girl with new respect.

'Uh, Gwen, dear . . .'

'Aye, my lord?' She looked back at him, with a look of pleased surprise and a faint blush.

He frowned. *What . . .?* Oh. He'd called her 'Gwen'. Also 'dear'.

'Aye, my lord, exorcized it. But the Wee Folk would not come here more, and I too thought it wise.'

*Yes*, Rod mused, *very wise*. Durer & Co. would not have taken kindly to diminutive spies, and could probably have devised some very unpleasant preventatives. He fastened his eyes on Gwendylon's retreating back, watching her absently; she was just full of surprises, this one . . .

'We come near, lords!'

Rod jerked his head up and saw a point of dim light ahead. The ball of light in Gwen's hand flickered out.

A moment later, they stepped through the weathered, weed-grown mouth of the tunnel into the moonlit night. The river flowed by a few dozen yards away, bordered with willow and cypress. The breeze was chill after the dampness of the tunnel. Loguire shivered.

'Master!' came a soft, low cry, and Big Tom stepped out of the riverbank shadows, leading three horses.

Rod grabbed Gwendylon's hand and ran for the horses . . . and was brought up sharp by a most unfeminine jerk on his arm — fortunately, the good one.

'Nay, my lord,' she said firmly. 'First we must see to your arm.'

'Which one,' Rod grumped, swivelling his good shoulder; it had developed a sudden ache. 'Look, we don't have time . . .'

'It will slow us in our ride soon or late,' she said sternly. 'Better to tend it now, when it will take but a moment.'

Rod sighed and capitulated. He watched her run to the riverbank with a connoisseur's interest and wondered what the strange, pleasant feeling inside him was.

'She hath the right of it,' growled Loguire, swinging Rod about to face him. 'Clamp your teeth.'

He unbuttoned Rod's doublet. Rod's nascent protest was cut off by a gasp of agony as Loguire snapped the doublet open, tearing the scab off in the process.

'Let it bleed freely a moment,' Loguire growled, jerking the doublet off the injured shoulder.

Then Gwendylon came up with a handful of some sort of herb and a small wineskin — *trust Big Tom to have one on him*, Rod thought — and perhaps five minutes later, Rod swung her onto Fess's saddle and leaped up behind her. He dug his heels into Fess's sides. Gwendylon started at the muted clang, and, as Fess sprang out into a gallop, she twisted about to frown, puzzled, at Rod.

'That's why I call him Old Ironsides,' Rod explained. 'Just relax and lean back against me. It's going to be a long ride.'

'But, my lord, I have no need to—'

'There're only three horses, Gwen. Somebody has to ride double. Don't worry, Fess won't even notice the difference.'

'But my lord, I—'

'Hush. My Lord Loguire!' he called back over his shoulder. 'Lead us, my lord; you know this land best.'

Loguire nodded mutely and spurred the big bay; it speeded a little, and passed Rod. Rod followed him, listening to the drum of hooves from Tom's mount behind him.

'Believe me, my lord, there is no need for—'

'Time enough to talk later,' Rod growled. 'We're leaving a trail as clear as Polaris. We've got to get far enough away fast enough so it won't matter if they follow us.'

Gwendylon sighed. 'Look behind you, my lord.'

Rod turned, and saw a crowd of at least a hundred elves lined along their trail with miniature brooms, sweeping away every trace of their passing – even straightening the grass the horses' hooves had flattened.

Rod squeezed his eyes shut. 'No. Oh, no. Why me, Lord? Why me?'

He turned back to Gwendylon. 'Gwen, did you call out these . . . Gwen!'

The saddle was empty. She was gone.

'Gwen!' he shouted, and sawed back on the reins.

'Really, Rod,' protested the murmur in his mastoid, 'I must ask that you attempt to control—'

'*Gwendylon!*' Rod yelled.

A cry like the mew of a seagull drifted down from the sky.

Rod looked up.

The osprey. The same one. He was willing to swear to it. Anyway, he was willing to swear.

The bird plummeted low and circled Rod's head, mewing urgently.

How the hell could she make a fish hawk sound so feminine?

The osprey shot away in front of him, skimming low over the ground after Loguire's horse.

Then it wheeled back, circled his head again, then lit out on the straightway again.

'Yeah, yeah,' Rod growled, 'I get the message. I should quit holding up the party. Fess, follow that bird! Fess? Fess!'

The horse stood stiff-legged, head swinging between the fetlocks.

Oh, well, it had been a strain on Rod's neurology, too. He slapped at the reset button.

They rode the moon down, slowing to a trot after the first half-hour. Loguire was slumped in his saddle, almost too exhausted to stay on his horse, by the time the air freshened with dawn.

Rod, frankly, wasn't in much better shape. He reined in beside the Duke. 'There're haystacks in that field over there, my lord. We must pause to rest. It will be dawn soon, and we dare not travel by day.'

Loguire lifted his head, blinking. 'Aye. Aye, most certain.' He reined in his horse. Rod and Tom followed suit.

They broke through the hedge at the roadside and trotted for the nearest haystack. Rod dismounted and caught Loguire as he all but fell from his saddle. Big Tom unsaddled the horses and turned them out to the field with a slap on the rump as Rod half-led, half carried the old nobleman to the top of the haystack.

He lowered Loguire into the hay, stepped back, and murmured, 'Fess.'

'Yes, Rod.'

'Get those nags far away from here, someplace where it's not too likely they'll be noticed, will you? And bring them back at sundown.'

'I will, Rod.'

Rod stood a moment, listening to the fading drum of hooves.

He looked down at Loguire; the old man was out cold: the strain, and the long night ride, to say nothing of how long it had been since he'd slept.

Rod pulled hay over the sleeping lord to hide him. Looking for Big Tom, he saw shins and feet disappearing into the side of the haystack. The saddles and bridles had already disappeared into the hay.

The feet were likewise removed from sight; then there was a protracted rustling, and Tom's ruddy face popped out of his burrow-hole. 'Thou must take tha'self from sight quickly, master. 'Twill be sunrise ere long, and the peasants mustn't see us.'

'They won't come near this stack?'

'Nay. This field is far from the keep, so 'twill be some days yet ere they take in this hay.'

Rod nodded. He threw up his hands and jumped, sliding down the side of the stack. He turned to see Tom's burrow fast closing. He grinned. 'Good night, Big Tom.'

'Good morn, master,' answered the muffled voice within.

Rod chuckled, shaking his head, as he went to the nearest other haystack. He climbed to the top, mashed the hay down into a bowl, and stretched out with a blissful sigh.

There was a soft mew, and the osprey dropped down beside him into the hay. It fell onto its side, its form fluxed and stretched, and Gwendylon was lying beside him.

She smiled mischievously and began to untie the strings of her bodice. 'Twenty-four hours, my lord. Sunrise to sunrise. You ha' said you would obey my commands for so long.'

'But – but – but . . .' Rod stared and swallowed as the bodice fell open and was thrown away. The blouse began to inch upward.

He swallowed again and stammered, 'Bu-but somebody's got to keep watch!'

'Never fear,' she murmured. The blouse went flying. 'My friends shall do that.'

'Your friends?' In a detached sort of way, Rod noted that in this culture the concept of the brassière was not yet developed.

Gwendylon was, though.

'Aye, the Wee Folk.' Skirt and slippers joined the discard pile with one smooth, sinuous motion.

The setting sun turned the straw blood-gold as Rod's head poked up out of the hay.

He looked around, sniffed the cool, fresh evening breeze, and expelled a sigh of great satisfaction.

He felt immensely well.

He thrust the covering of hay aside with one sweep of his arm and reflected that it had been a busy day, as his eyes travelled slowly and lovingly over Gwen's curves.

He leaned forward and touched his lips to hers for a long, deep kiss. He felt her come awake beneath him.

He drew back; her eyes opened halfway. Her lips curved in a slow, sultry smile.

She stretched, slow and feline. Rod was surprised to feel his pulse quicken. His opinion of himself went up a notch.

His opinion of her was altogether too high already. With a twinge of alarm, Rod realized he was regretting that he was a travelling man. He also realized something was gnawing at the base of his conscience. She looked into his eyes and sobered. 'What saddens you, lord?'

'Don't you ever worry about being used, Gwen?'

She smiled lazily. 'Do you, lord?'

'Well, no . . .' Rod frowned at his palms. 'But that's different. I mean, I'm a man.'

'I would never ha' guessed,' she murmured, biting his ear lobe in the process.

He grinned and twisted, trying to retaliate; but she wasn't done with his ear yet.

'Men are fools,' she murmured between bites. 'You are forever saying what is not instead of what is. Be done with the night, and live in the evening while you are in it.'

She eyed him then through heavy lids with a somewhat proprietary joy, looking him up and down slowly.

*Oh, well*, Rod thought, *so much for my one attempt to be honourable* . . . 'Kamere!' After all, there was only one way to wipe that smug smile off her face.

Big Tom chose just that moment to call, 'Master! The sun has set, and we must away.'

Rod let go of Gwen with a disgusted growl. 'That boy has definitely the greatest sense of timing . . .' He started pulling on his hose. 'Up and away, my dear!'

'Must we, lord?' she said, pouting.

'We must,' he answered. 'Duty calls – or at least Big Tom. Onward for the glory of France! or something like that . . .'

Two nights of pushing the pace, alternating canter and walk, brought them back to the capital.

As they came to the bridge over the river that curved around the town, Rod was surprised to see two foot soldiers armed with pikes, torches flaring by their sides in the darkness of the seventh hour of night.

'I shall clear the way,' Tom muttered, and spurred his horse ahead of Rod and Loguire. 'Stand aside,' he called to the guards, 'for my masters wish to enter.'

The pikes clashed as they crossed, barring the bridge. 'Who are your masters?' retorted the one of them. 'Be they rebels? Or Queen's men?'

'Rebels?' Tom frowned. 'What ha' passed in the Queen's Town while we ha' been to the South?'

'The South?' The guard's eyes narrowed. ' 'Tis the lords of the South that rebel.'

'Aye, aye!' Big Tom waved the objection away impatiently. 'We ha' been there on the Queen's affairs – spies, i' truth. We bear word that the lords of the South rise in revolt, and the name of the day that they march; but how has this news come here afore us?'

'What is this badinage?' snapped Loguire, riding up with Rod at his side. 'Stand aside, sirrahs, that a man of noble blood may enter!'

The guards' heads swivelled to stare up at Loguire; then both pikes jumped forward, their points scarce an inch from his chest. 'Dismount and stand, Milord Duke of Loguire!' The first guard's voice was firm, but deferential. 'We must hold you in arrest, on command of her Majesty the Queen.'

And the other guard bawled, 'Captain! Captain of the Guard!'

Loguire stared in disbelief. Rod nudged his way past the lord and glared at the guard. 'Name the crime for which the Queen holds Milord Loguire in arrest!'

The guard's eyes flicked from Loguire's face to Rod's, and back; then, dubiously, he answered, 'Most high treason to the body and person of her Majesty the Queen.'

Loguire's jaw sagged. Then his lips pressed thin and his brows beetled down, hiding his eyes in caves of shadow. His face seemed bloody in the torchlight.

'I am most sternly loyal to her Majesty the Queen!' he exploded. 'Be done with your impertinence and stand aside!'

The sentry swallowed and stood his ground. 'It is said Loguire leads the rebels, milord.'

'Soldier.' Rod spoke quietly, but with the tone of an old field sergeant.

The sentry's eyes jumped to him, but the pike didn't waver.

'You know me,' and Rod's voice held the veiled threat of non-com authority.

It had more effect than all Loguire's lofty phrases. The soldier licked his lips and agreed, 'Aye, master.'

'Who am I?'

'You are Master Gallowglass, late of the Queen's Guard.'

'*Still* of the Queen's Guard,' Rod corrected, still softly. 'Sent to the South a week agone, to guard Milord Loguire.'

Loguire's head jerked up; his eyes blazed at Rod.

'We ha' known that you were gone,' the soldier mumbled.

'And now you know why.' Rod kept his voice under careful control, managing to imply that the Queen's Own Wrath would fall on the guard's miserable head if he disobeyed. 'My Lord Loguire cries sanctuary from his kinswoman and suzerain, her Majesty the Queen. She would be wroth to hear him detained. Let us pass.'

The guard took a firmer hold on his pike, gulped, and thrust out his jaw stubbornly. 'The order ha' gone forth that Milord Loguire be held in arrest in the Queen's dungeon, good master. More than that I know not.'

'Dungeon!' Loguire thundered, beet-red. 'Am I a tuppenny footpad, to be crooked from a hedgerow to a dungeon cell? Is it thus that the Queen would acknowledge her vassal? Nay, nay! The blood Plantagenet hath not ebbed so low! Knave, I'll hale thy lying tongue from thy head!'

His hand went to his dagger, and the soldier cowered back; but Rod's hand stayed the nobleman's.

'Calm yourself, milord,' he murmured. ' 'Tis Durer hath sent this word here before us. The Queen could not know of your loyalty.'

Loguire checked his temper with vast effort, subsiding into a sort of gurgling fury. Rod leaned over and whispered to Tom.

'Tom, can you find someplace to hide the old man where he'll be safe?'

'Aye, master,' Tom frowned down at him. 'With his son. But why . . . ?'

'At the House of Clovis?'

'Aye, master. 'Twould take all the Queen's men, and great bombards, to hale them forth from the House.'

'I would have said a good strong wind would've done it,' Rod muttered, 'but I guess it's the best we can do. So . . .'

'Speak so that all may hear!' shouted a new voice.

'That had a familiar ring,' Rod muttered, looking up.

Sir Maris strode forth between the two vastly relieved guardsmen. 'Well done, Rod Gallowglass! Thou hast brought a most pernicious rebel to the safekeeping of our stronghold!'

Loguire's narrowed eyes stabbed hate at Rod.

'Do not speak among yourselves,' Sir Maris went on; 'I forbid it. And hearken well to my orders, for there are twelve good crossbowmen with their quarrels aimed at your hearts.'

Loguire sat back in his saddle, tall and proud, his face composed in the granite of fatalism.

'Twelve?' Rod gave Sir Maris a one-sided mocking smile. 'Only twelve quarrels, to kill the Loguire? Good Sir Maris, I must think you grow rash in your old age.'

The granite mask cracked; Loguire darted a puzzled glance at Rod.

Rod dismounted and stepped out toward the bridge, away from the horses. He shook his head woefully. 'Sir Maris, Sir Maris! My good Sir Maris, to think that—'

Suddenly he whirled, with a high, piercing cry, slapping at the horses' chests. 'Turn and ride!' he shrieked. 'Ride!'

Sir Maris and his men stood frozen with surprise as the horses reared, wheeled about, and sprang away. An instant later, twelve crossbow bolts bit the ground where they had been.

One archer had been a little quicker than his fellows; his bolt struck Fess's metal hindquarters with a clang and ricocheted off into the river.

There was an instant's shocked silence; then the whisper ran through the ranks, swelling with fear: 'Witch horse! Witch horse!'

'Cloud the trail, Fess,' Rod murmured, and the great black horse reared, pawing the air and screaming combat; then it wheeled away and was gone, lost in the night, hoofbeats drumming away.

Rod smiled grimly, sure that Fess's trail would cross and recross Tom and Loguire's till an Italian spaghetti cook wouldn't be able to unsnarl it.

He peered up into the sky. He couldn't see beyond the circle of torchlight, but he thought he heard a faint mewing.

He smiled, again, a little more sincerely this time. *Let Catharine try to imprison. Let her try.*

Then his smile settled and soured as he turned to face Sir Maris.

The old knight was struggling manfully to look angry; but the fear in his eyes blared as loud as a TV commercial. His voice quavered. 'Rod Gallowglass, you have abetted the escape of a rebel.'

Rod stood mute, eyes glittering.

Sir Maris swallowed hard and went on. 'For high treason to the body and person of her Majesty Queen of all Gramarye, Rod Gallowglass, in arrest I must hold thee.'

Rod inclined his head politely. 'You may try.'

The soldiers muttered fearfully and drew back. None wished to match arms with the warlock.

Sir Maris' eyes widened in alarm; then he spun and grabbed one of his soldiers by the arm. 'You there! Soldier! Soldier!' he hissed. 'Run ahead and bear word to the Queen. Say what transpires here.'

The soldier bolted, overwhelmingly glad to lose out on the action.

Sir Maris turned back to Rod. 'Thou must now come to judgement before the Queen, Master Gallowglass.'

*Oho!* thought Rod. *I'm a master now, am I?*

'Wilt thou go to her freely?' said Sir Maris apprehensively. 'Or must I compel thee?'

Rod fought to keep his shoulders from shaking with laughter at the dread in the old knight's voice. His reputation had decided advantages.

'I will come freely, Sir Maris,' he said, stepping forward. 'Shall we go?'

Sir Maris' eyes fairly glowed with gratitude.

Abruptly, he sobered. 'I would not be in thy place for a castle and dukedom, Rod Gallowglass. Thou must needs now stand alone before our Queen's tongue.'

'Well, yes,' Rod agreed. 'But then, I've got a few things to say to her too, now haven't I? Let us go then, Sir Maris.'

Unfortunately, the march to the castle gave Rod time to mull over Catharine's latest churlish tricks; so by the time they came to the door to her chambers, Rod's jaw was clenched and shivering with rage.

And, equally unfortunately, there was a reception committee, consisting of two sentries, the soldier who had been sent ahead as messenger, and two pikes pointed right at Rod's midriff.

The procession halted. 'And what,' said Rod, with icy control, 'is *this* supposed to mean?'

The messenger stammered an answer. 'Th-the Queen forbids that the w-warlock be brought before her unch-chained.'

'Oh.' Rod pursed his lips for a moment, then gave the messenger a polite lift of the eyebrow. 'I am to be chained?'

The messenger nodded, on the verge of panic.

The pikes crashed as Rod knocked them away to each side. He grabbed the messenger by the scruff of the neck and threw him into the pack of Guardsmen as they surged forward. Then he lashed out with a kick that wrenched the crude metal hinges from their bolts.

The door crashed down, and he strode in over it, stepping hard.

Catharine, the Mayor of the Queen's Town, and Brom O'Berin shot to their feet from their chairs around a map-laden table.

Brom sprang to bar Rod's path. 'What devil possesses you, Rod Gallowglass, that you—'

But Rod was already past him and still moving.

He swung to a stop before the table, glaring across at her, his eyes chips of dry ice.

Catharine stepped back, one hand coming to her throat, disconcerted and afraid.

Brom leaped to the tabletop, thundering, 'What means this unseemly intrusion, Rod Gallowglass? Get thee hence, till the Queen shall summon thee!'

'I would prefer not to come before her Majesty in chains—' His words were cold and clipped. 'And I will not allow that a nobleman of the highest rank be clapped in a common, noisome dungeon with rats and thieves.'

'*Thou* wilt not allow!' Catharine gasped, outraged; and, 'Who art thou to allow or not allow?' roared Brom. 'Thou hast not even gentle blood!'

'Then I must think that blood is opposed to action,' Rod snapped.

He flung the table out of his way and advanced on the Queen. 'I had thought you noble.' The word was a sneer. 'But now I see that you will turn against your very family, even to one near as nigh you as a father! Certes, if you would fight any of your nobles, you must needs fight a kinsman; but your very uncle? Fie, woman! Were he the foulest murderer, you had ought to receive him with courtesy and the honour due his station. Your finest chamber you should appoint his cell; 'tis but your duty to blood!'

He backed her up against the fireplace, glowering deep into her eyes. 'Nay, were he but a murderer, no doubt you would receive him with all honour! But no, he has committed the heinous crime of objecting to your high-handed, arbitrary laws, and the further calumny of maintaining his honour against your calculated insults. He will insist on being accorded the respect due a man during the reign of a vindictive, childish, churlish chit of a girl who hath the title of a Queen but none of the graces, and for this he must needs be damned!'

'Fie, sirrah,' she quavered, waxen pale, 'that you would speak so to a lady!'

'Lady!' he snorted.

'A lady born!' It was a forlorn, desperate cry. 'Will you, too, desert me? Will you speak with the tongue of Clovis?'

'I may speak like a peasant, but you act like one! And now I see why all desert you; for you would whip to scorn Loguire, who alone of all your lords is loyal!'

'Loyal!' she gasped. 'He, who leads the rebels?'

'*Anselm* Loguire leads the rebels! For keeping faith with you, the old Duke is now deposed in favour of his son!'

He smiled bitterly as the horror and guilt dawned in her, then turned his back upon her and stepped away, giving her time to realize the breadth of her betrayal. He heard a long-drawn, shuddering breath behind him; Brom rushed past him to aid his Queen. He heard a chair creak as Brom made her sit.

Looking up, he saw the Lord Mayor staring past him wide-eyed. Rod cleared his throat; the burgher's eyes shifted to him. Rod jerked his head toward the door. The Mayor glanced back at the Queen, hesitating. Rod toyed with the hilt of his dagger. The Mayor saw, blanched, and fled.

Rod turned back to the stricken girl.

Brom, at her elbow, threw Rod a glance of withering hatred and growled, 'Ha' done! Have you not cut deep enough?'

'Not yet.' Rod's lips thinned. He stepped up to the Queen again, his voice cold. 'This good nobleman, the Duke Loguire, your own uncle, out of love for you stood against the whole of your nobility, *even his own son!*' His voice crackled. Her eyes jerked up to him, filling with dread. 'And it is your doing, by your high-handed lawmaking and utter lack of diplomacy, that Anselm turned against his father. He had two sons, and you have robbed him of both!'

She shook her head, faster and faster, lips shaping silent denials.

'Yet still he is loyal!' Rod murmured. 'Still he is loyal, though they would have slain him for it – and damn near did!'

She stared in horror.

Rod tapped his shoulder. 'This took the dagger that would have pierced his heart. And even at that, 'twas only by a miracle, and the help of one of the witches whom you scarce acknowledge, that I managed to bring him out alive!'

Brom's head snapped up, searching Rod's face for something. Rod frowned, and went on.

'But bring him out I did, at peril of my life, and brought him safely back. And what do I find? He is to be held a prisoner! And not even as befits a royal prisoner! No, not to be treated with due courtesy and deference, but as a common cutpurse, in a lightless, damp, dank dungeon!'

He paused for effect, rather proud of the last bit of alliteration.

But he had overdone it a bit; she rallied. Her chin came up, and she sniffled back some tears. 'Before my laws, sirrah, all are equal!'

'Yes,' Rod agreed, 'but that should mean you treat a peasant like a lord, not that you treat a lord like a peasant!'

He leaned over her, his face an inch from hers. 'Tell me, Queen: why is it that Catharine must treat all with contempt?'

It was a lie; she didn't treat all with contempt, just the noblemen; but anguish and sudden self-doubt showed in her eyes.

Still she tilted her chin a fraction of an inch higher, and declaimed, 'I am the Queen, and all must bow to my power!'

'Oh, they bow, they bow! Until you slap them in the face; then they slap back!'

He turned away, glowering at the hearth. 'And I can't say I blame them, when you deprive them of liberty.'

Catharine stared. 'Liberty? What talk is this, sirrah? I seek to give the serfs greater liberty!'

'Aye, so you seek.' Rod smiled sourly. 'But how do you go about giving it? You gather all ever more tightly unto you. You deprive them today, that you may give them more later!'

He slammed his fist onto the arm of her chair. 'But later will never come, don't you see that? There is too much ill in the land, there will always be another evil to fight, and the Queen's word must be law unquestioned to command the army against the evil.'

He drew his hand back slowly, eyes burning. 'And so it will never come, the day that you set them free; in your land, none will have liberty, save the Queen.'

He locked his hands behind his back and paced the room. 'There is only just so much of it to go around, you know – this liberty. If one man is to have more, another must needs have less; for if one is to command, another must obey.'

He held his hand before her, slowly tightening it into a fist. 'So little by little, you steal it away, till your slightest whim is obeyed. You will have complete freedom, to do whatever you wish, but you alone will be free. There will be none of this liberty left over for your people. All, all, will be gathered unto Catharine.'

His hand loosened and clasped her throat lightly. She stared and swallowed, pressing against the back of the chair.

'But a man cannot live without at least a little liberty,' he said softly. 'They must have it, or die.' His hand tightened slowly. 'They will rise up against you, made one by their common enemy – you. And then will squeeze their liberties out of you again, slowly, slowly.'

Catharine tore at his hand, fighting for breath. Brom leaped to free her. But Rod loosed her first.

'They will hang you from your castle gates,' he murmured, 'and the nobles will rule in your stead; your work will all be undone. And of this you may be certain, for thus was it ever with tyrants.'

Her head jerked up, hurt deep in her eyes. She gasped for breath to speak, shaking her head in ever harder denial.

'No, not I,' she finally rasped. 'Not that, no! Never a tyrant!'

'Always a tyrant,' Rod corrected gently, 'from your birth. Always a tyrant to those about you, though you never knew it till now.'

He turned away, hands locked behind his back. 'But now you know, and know also that you have none to blame but yourself for rebellion. You pushed them and pushed them, harder and harder, your nobles – for the good of your people, you said.'

He looked back over his shoulder. 'But was it not also to see which among them would dare say you nay? To see which among them were men?'

Contempt curdled her face. 'Men!' The word was obscenity. 'There are no men in Gramarye any more, only boys, content to be a woman's playpretties!'

He smiled, one-sided. 'Oh, there be men still. Men in the South, and men in the House of Clovis – or one, at least, there. Men, my Queen, but gentle men, loving their Queen, and loath to strike at her.'

Her lids lowered, the contempt playing over her lips in a smile. 'It is as I have said: there are no men in Gramarye more.'

'They are men,' Rod answered, very quietly, 'and they march north to prove it.'

She stared.

Then slowly sat back. 'Well, then, they march north, and I shall meet them on Breden Plain. Yet still there is none among them I would call man. Beasts, every one.'

'Oh, you shall meet them.' Rod gave her a syrupy, mocking smile. 'And what shall you use for an army? And who will command it?'

'I will command,' she replied haughtily, 'I and Brom. And there be five hundred of the Queen's Guard, and seven hundred of the Queen's Army, and threescore knights at my manors.'

'Sixty knights!' Rod's lips tightened, pulling down at the corners. 'Not even enough to give the Southern knights entertainment for one full charge! Sixty knights out of how many hundreds in your kingdom? And all the rest arrayed there against you! And twelve hundred footmen against the rebels' thousands!'

Her hands seized the arms of the chair in a spasm, to hide their trembling; fear drained her face of its colour. 'We shall win, for the honour of Plantagenet or Gramarye, or die nobly.'

'I have yet,' Rod said tightly, 'to see a noble death in battle. They're all just a little on the messy side.'

'Be still!' she snapped, then closed her eyes and bowed her head, knuckles whitening on the chair arms.

She rose, proud and calm again, and Rod couldn't help a brief, admiring thought for her spunk.

She sat at the table, drew up parchment and quill, scribbled a moment, then folded the parchment and held it out to Rod. 'Bear this to my Uncle Loguire,' she said. ' 'Tis a command that he appear here before me, and a warrant of safe-conduct; for I bethink me that I shall need all loyal to me by my side ere greatly long.'

Rod took the parchment and crumpled it slowly in his fist.

He flung it into the fire without taking his eyes from Catharine. 'You shall write a letter to the Duke, and I shall bear it,' he said in an antarctic voice; 'but in it you shall beg of him the courtesy of an audience.'

Her back stiffened and her chin came up. Rod warmed his voice hastily, smiling. 'Come, come, my Queen! You already have all the liberty; can you not expend a little in courtesy?'

His eyes darkened, the smile faded. 'Or will you be swept by the sin of pride, and allow your liberty to become licence?'

He stepped a little closer, towering over her. 'Will your people pay the price of your pride, my Queen? Or will you?'

She glared back at him a moment, but something inside her was clamouring for attention. She dropped her eyes and sat quiet a moment, then turned to the table again and wrote.

She folded the letter, sealed it, and held it out to him. He took it, bowed a little too deeply, with a click of the heels, and turned for the door.

He caught a quick scurry of movement along the baseboard out of the corner of his eye. He turned, saw a mouse duck under the tapestry, where it stayed very still.

Rod's jaw tightened. He crossed the room in two strides, lifted the tapestry.

The mouse looked up at him, its eyes very wide, very green, and very intelligent.

'I do not appreciate eavesdroppers,' Rod said coldly.

The mouse flinched, but stared back defiantly.

Rod frowned at a sudden thought. Then his stern look melted. He picked the mouse up, gently, held it level with his eyes, with a tender look that did a very nice job of negating any image of dignity he might have built up.

He shook his head slowly. 'You didn't really think I'd need help in here, did you?'

The mouse lowered its eyes, whiskers twitching a little.

'Certes,' murmured Catharine, 'methinks the man is possessed.'

'Your Majesty,' Brom said with a musing tone and a gleam in his eye, 'may speak more truth than she knows.'

The drawbridge echoed hollowly under Rod's striding feet. He ran lightly down the slope, away from the castle, and slipped into a copse of spruce.

'Fess,' he called softly.

'Here, Rod.' The great black steel horse came through the trees.

Rod smiled, slapped the metal side affectionately.

'How the hell'd you know I'd come here?'

'Quite simple, Rod. An analysis of your behaviour patterns, coupled with the fact that this grove is the closest to—'

'Skip it,' Rod growled. 'Big Tom took Loguire to the House of Clovis?'

'Affirmative, Rod.'

Rod nodded. 'Under the circumstances, it's probably the safest place for the Duke. What a comedown for a nobleman.'

He swung into the saddle, then fumbled in his doublet and brought out the little mouse. It looked up at him apprehensively.

'Well,' he sighed, 'it doesn't seem to make any difference what I tell you to do; you're going to go right ahead and do whatever you want anyway.'

The mouse lowered its eyes, trying to look guilty and ashamed; but its whiskers quivered with delight.

It rubbed its cheek against the skin of his palm.

'Affection will get you nowhere,' Rod growled. 'Now, listen. You go to the House of Clovis; that's where I'm bound. That's an order.'

The mouse looked up at him with wide, innocent eyes.

'And it's one order I can be sure you'll obey,' Rod went on, 'since it's what you were going to do anyway. But, look!' A note of anxiety crept into his voice. 'Be careful, will ya?'

He brought his hand forward and kissed the mouse's nose, very gently.

The mouse leaped, wriggled with delight, dancing gleeful on his hand; as it danced, it reared up, its front paws stretching and broadening into wings. Its tail fanned out; feathers sprouted on its body; its nose blurred and became a beak, and a wren was dancing on Rod's hand.

Rod caught his breath. 'Uh . . . yeah,' he said after a while. 'That's just a little hard to take the first time I watch it happen. But don't worry, I'll get used to it.'

The bird hopped from his hand, flew once around his head, hovered in front of him, then sprang arrowing into the sky.

Rod looked after the wren, murmured, 'Do you think she'll do what I tell her this time, Fess?'

'She will.' There was a strange quality to the robot's voice.

Rod looked sidewise at the great black head. 'Thought robots couldn't laugh.'

'A misconception,' Fess replied.

'Git.' Rod knocked his heels against the steel sides. Fess leaped into his long, steel canter.

'What else could I do?' Rod growled.

'With that lady,' Fess answered, 'nothing. But have no regrets, Rod. It's excellent policy. Many kings have used it.'

'Yes,' Rod mused. 'And after all, being obeyed is the important thing, isn't it?'

Fess galloped silently into the moonlit courtyard on rubber-padded hooves and stopped abruptly. Rod's chest slammed against the horse's neck.

'Whuff!' He slammed back into the saddle. 'Ohhhh! My tailbone! Look, Fess, warn me before you pull a stunt like that, will ya? Inertia may be just a nuisance to you, but it hits me right where I live.'

'Where is that, Rod?'

'Never mind,' Rod growled, dismounting. 'Suffice to say that I just learned why the cavalry used split saddles.'

He crossed the courtyard, glancing at the moon as he went. It was low in the sky; dawn was not far off.

He pounded on the door. There was a rustle of movement inside, then the door opened. The gnarled, bent figure of the Mocker stood before him.

'Aye, milord?' he said with a snaggle-toothed grin.

Wouldn't do to let him know that Rod knew he was the power behind the throne. Rod stepped in through the door, scarcely noticing the little man's presence. 'Take me to the Lord Loguire, fellow.'

'Certes, milord.' The Mocker scurried around Rod and opened the inner door. Rod passed through it, pulling off his gauntlets . . . and stepped into the middle of a semicircle of beggars and thieves, standing three deep and armed with truncheons and knives.

They grinned, their eyes hungry; here and there one licked his lips.

Their faces were dirty and scarred, mutilated, and festering with sores; their clothes were threadbare, patched, torn; but their knives were remarkably well kept.

Rod tucked his gloves into his belt, hands stiffening into karate swords, and turned to the Mocker. That worthy was now flanked by five or six prime samples of the lees of society.

'I come here in friendship.' Rod's face was immobile.

'Do ye, now?' The Mocker grinned, exposing bleeding gums, and cackled. Suddenly his eyes gleamed with hate. 'Declare yourself, lordling!'

Rod frowned. 'Declare myself how?'

'For the noblemen, for the Queen, or for the House of Clovis!'

'Be done with your blathering!' Rod snapped. 'I have small stomach for nonsense, and I'm beginning to feel very full. Take me to Loguire, *now*!'

'Oh, aye, that we shall. Yes, milord, at once, milord, straight-away.' He rubbed his hands, chortling with glee. Then his glance darted over Rod's shoulder, and he nodded.

Rod started to turn, but something exploded on the back of his head. Stars reeled about him, then blackness.

Slowly, Rod became aware of pink light, pain, and a thousand discordant bass fiddles tuning up inside his head.

Slower yet, he became aware of something cold and slimy against his cheek. The pink light, he realized, was sunlight filtered through closed eyelids.

The pain pulled itself in and concentrated in his head. He winced, then by heroic measures managed to open his eyes, and winced again.

Everything was blurred, out of focus, sunlight and blobs of colour.

The slime under his cheek was moss, and the coldness beneath it was stone.

He shoved hard with his hands; the slimy surface swung away, left him reeling, leaning on his hands heavily, stomach churning.

He shook his head, flinched at the pain, and blinked several times. His lids rasped over gummy eyeballs, but slowly his vision cleared. He forced his eyes to focus on . . . the face of Tuan Loguire.

Tuan sat with his back against black, old stone. There were huge iron staples in the stone, and the chains that hung from them ran to manacles on Tuan's wrists and ankles. He sat in a heap of dirty, mouldering straw, in the watery light of a weak sunbeam.

Tuan smiled with irony as heavy as the rusty chains on his body, and lifted a hand in greeting, chain jangling with the movement. 'Welcome.'

Rod turned his eyes away, looking about him. The old Duke sat against the next wall, chained beside his son. 'Cold welcome, Rod Gallowglass,' the old lord mumbled, face heavy and brooding. 'It is scant safety your serving-man has brought me to.'

Treachery! Rod should have known better than to trust Tom. 'Big Tom, you . . !'

'Here, master.'

Rod looked, turning; Big Tom sat against the far wall, chained like the rest of them.

Tom smiled sadly, bent a reproachful, bloodhound-eyed look on his master. 'I had thought you would free us, master. Yet here art thou, chained one amongst us.'

Rod scowled, looked down at his wrist. A rusty, thick iron band circled it. It had mates on his ankle and other wrist.

He looked up at Tom, smiled, and raised his hand, giving the chain a shake. 'Ever hear tell that stone walls don't make a prison?'

'Who spoke those words was a fool,' said Tom bitterly, from the shadows.

Rod lifted his eyes to the small, barred window set high in the wall. It was the only light in the room, a chamber perhaps ten feet wide by fifteen long, with a ten foot high ceiling, all moss-grown, rotting stone, floored with mouldering straw.

The only decoration was a skeleton, held together by mummified ligament, chained to the wall like themselves.

Rod eyed the silent partner warily. 'Not such great housekeepers, are they? They could at least have lugged the bones into the nether room.'

He turned to the window again. 'Fess,' he mumbled, low enough so the others couldn't make out the words. 'Fess, where are you?'

'In the most filthy, broken-down stable I've ever seen,' the robot answered, 'along with five of the sorriest nags outside of a glue factory. I think we're supposed to be the cavalry of the House of Clovis, Rod.'

Rod chuckled softly. 'Any mice with large green eyes running around, Fess?'

'No, Rod, but there is a wren perched on my head.'

Rod grinned. 'Ask her if she has any power over cold iron.'

'How am I to speak with her, Rod?'

'Broadcast on human thought-wave frequency of course! She's a telepath, you idiot savant!'

'Rod, I strongly resent the derogatory connotations of references to my abilities in areas in which I am not programmed to—'

'All right, all right, I'm sorry, I repent! You're a genius, a prodigy, an Einstein, an Urth! Just ask her, will you?'

There was a pause; then Rod heard a faint series of chirpings in the background.

'What's the chirping, Fess?'

'Gwendylon, Rod. She reacted significantly to the novel experience of telepathy with a horse.'

'You mean she almost fell off her perch. But did she say anything?'

'Of course, Rod. She says that now she is certain you're a warlock.'

Rod groaned and rolled his eyes up to the ceiling. 'Look, get her back to business, will you? Can she get us out of these chains and cut the bars on our window?'

There was another pause; then Fess answered, 'She says she has no power over cold iron, Rod, nor has any witch or elf that she knows. She suggests a blacksmith, but fears it is impractical.'

'Genesis, Exodus, Leviticus . . . Well, tell her I'm glad she hasn't lost her sense of humour. And ask her how the hell she's going to get us out of here!'

'She says there is no need for hard language, Rod.'

'You didn't have to transmit me literally, you bumblebrain!'

'And she thinks that the Prince of the Elves may be able to free you. She thinks he will come, but he is some short distance away, so it may be a while.'

'I thought she said elves couldn't handle cold iron!'

There was another pause; then Fess said, 'She says that the Prince of the Elves is not quite an elf, Rod, being but half of the Old Blood.'

'Only half . . . Wait a minute!' Rod scowled. 'You mean he's a half-breed between elf and mortal?'

'Precisely, Rod.'

Rod tried to imagine how an eighteen-inch elf and a six-foot mortal could have a child; his brain reeled.

'She departs now, Rod, to summon him, and will return as quickly as she may, but will be a while. She bids you be of stout heart.'

'If my heart were any stouter, it'd be positively obese! Give her my . . . No, just tell her I thank her, Fess.'

He seemed to hear a faint sigh behind his ear, and the robot said, with a touch of resignation, 'I'll tell her, Rod.'

'Thanks, Fess. Stay lively.'

Rod turned back to his prison. The Loguires were both plastered against the wall, looking at him strangely.

'He speaks to thin air,' murmured Tuan. 'Certes, the man is possessed!'

'Seems to me I've heard that before,' Rod mused, 'and the air in here is anything but thin.'

'Still,' muttered Loguire, ' 'tis the act of one crazed!'

Big Tom rumbled a laugh. 'Not so, my lords. This man speaks with spirits.'

Rod smiled bleakly. 'How come so cheerful all of a sudden, Big Tom?'

The big man stretched, chains clashing. 'I had thought for a moment they had beaten you, master. Now I know 'twas fool thinking.'

'Don't be so sure, Tom. Cold iron is a tough spell to break.'

'Nay, master.' Tom's eyelids drooped lazily. 'Thou'lt find a way to it, I warrant.'

He clasped his hands over his belly, leaned his head back against the wall.

Rod smiled as Tom began snoring. He looked at the Loguires and jerked his head toward Tom. 'There's confidence for you. While I work things out, he takes a nap.'

'Let us hope 'tis a faith warranted,' said Tuan. He eyed Rod dubiously.

'Let's,' Rod echoed grimly.

He nodded at the Duke. 'Been renewing acquaintance?'

Loguire smiled. 'I rejoice to see my son again, though I had lief it were more open welcome.'

Tuan frowned at his hands. 'It is sad news he hath brought me, Rod Gallowglass, most sad and sorrowful.' He looked at Rod, bright anger in his face. 'I had known my brother hateful and ambitious, but I had not thought he would sink into treason.'

'Oh, don't be too hard on the poor boy.' Rod leaned back against the wall, closing his eyes wearily. 'Durer's got him spellbound. And if his magic came so close on the father, how could it fail on the son?'

'Aye,' Tuan agreed darkly. 'Myself had fallen like prey to the Mocker.'

'Oh?' Rod opened one eye. 'You've realized that, have you?'

'Oh, aye! A most excellent villain is that! He will bow him most humbly before you, while his henchman is slitting your purse – and thus hath he served me!'

Rod pursed his lips. 'He's the one who gave you the idea for organizing the beggars?'

'Aye.' Tuan nodded heavily. 'I had first thought only to provide them relief from hunger and chill; but his word in my ear made me think of an army, for defence of the Queen. And I had seen and heard in the South that which led me to think such an army might well be needed.'

The old Duke made a choking sound.

'Pardon, my father,' said Tuan, bowing his head, 'but I knew even thou couldst not check them forever. But I had not thought' —and his voice hardened—' 'twould be treason from Anselm.'

Rod twisted, feeling decidedly uncomfortable. 'Well, as I said, you shouldn't blame him too much. After all, he did try to keep Durer from killing your father.'

He stretched his legs and crossed them. 'So when the Mocker learned that the South was up in arms, he decided it was time to assert his rightful authority and overthrow the Queen. Right?'

'Aye.' Tuan's lips tightened as though he had his first taste of straight vermouth. 'When I spoke against, saying that 'twas our time to defend the Queen, he called me traitor, and –' he frowned, words coming very hard '– one of the beggars would ha' slain me. But the Mocker would not hear of it; no, he threw me here without food or fire.'

He looked up at Rod, frowning. 'Which is most truly strange, Rod Gallowglass. Would not you ha' thought he would ha' killed me himself?'

'No.' Rod closed his eyes, shaking his head. 'He needs somebody to be figurehead king after they've pulled down Catharine.'

'Nay, not a king,' Tuan said, brooding. 'He cries that we shall ne'er have a king more, but only a sort of chieftain, raised by acclaim of the people.'

'"A sort of chieftain".' Rod scowled. 'What name does he call this chieftain by?'

'Dictator.' Tuan chewed at the inside of his cheek. 'A most strange title. There shall be no nobles or king, only the dictator. In all truth, most strange.'

Rod's mouth tightened with sourness. 'Not so strange as all that. But you don't mean to say the beggars think they can take the castle?'

'Nay, but it is known that the South is in arms, and Catharine was never one to be waiting till the battle was brought to her.'

'Oh.' Rod chewed that one over. 'You mean the Mocker's pretty sure she'll march south to meet them?'

'Most assuredly. And the Mocker will march south behind her.'

Rod nodded. 'So when the armies join battle, the beggars will attack the royal forces from the rear.'

'Ever their way,' rumbled Loguire.

Tuan nodded agreement. 'And caught between two forces, her armies will last scarce half an hour.'

'And what does the Mocker propose to do about the councillors and noblemen after the battle's over? Durer means to make your brother king.'

'So it would seem,' Tuan agreed, 'but the Mocker hath an answer to that, and to all the noblemen.'

'Oh?' Rod raised an eyebrow.

'Aye. 'Tis a tube of metal fitted into a crossbow stock, nothing more; but it throws a ball of lead which can pierce the stoutest armour.'

'And he means to put one of these into the hands of every man in the army?'

'Oh, nay.' Tuan frowned. 'He hath but the five of them, one for himself, one for each of his three lieutenants, and one for his fourth lieutenant.' Tuan jerked his head toward Tom's recumbent mountain form. 'But that one hath lately fallen into disfavour. He assures us the five tubes shall answer for the full force of noblemen and councillors.'

But Rod was staring at Tom. 'Big Tom?' He gulped. 'A lieutenant?'

'Aye.' Tuan frowned. 'Did you not know he was of Clovis?'

Tom opened one hound's eye and looked back at Rod.

Rod looked away, cleared his throat, and pursed his lips. 'Well, ah, that does explain a few things.'

He switched his eyes back to Tom. 'So you're part of the Inner Circle?'

Big Tom smiled sourly and held up one timber forearm. The chain clashed and rattled. 'Was,' he said.

'He stood against them,' rumbled Loguire, 'stood against his fellows and this – how do you name him? The Mocker? – stood against the Mocker and his three jackals when they commanded I be prisoned with my son. "Nay," quoth your man Tom, "I must needs take him back to my master, where he will be aid to your plans." "The plans are changed," quoth they, and would not hear of enlarging me; and then your man Tom, here, fought cheek by jowl at my side, and accounted for a most goodly number of them.' This last was said in a tone of surprised respect.

Tom grinned, and Rod saw with a shock that one tooth was missing from the big man's smile. 'Thou art a braw brawler tha'self,' Tom chuckled. 'I ha' not thought gentlemen could fight so well without armour or sword.'

Rod peered into the shadows at Tom's end of the room and saw that the big man's eye was swollen and purple; also, there was a slash with a new scab across one lumpy cheek.

He sat back, smiling on one side of his face. 'How many heads did you bash in, Big Tom?'

'Scarce a round score,' Tom replied with disgust. 'I had but this one stalwart gentleman to guard my back, and there were too many of us.'

Rod grinned, wondering if Loguire knew just how deeply he had been complimented.

He stretched, yawned. 'Well, that pretty well brings us up to date. Anybody got a poker deck?'

The two Loguires frowned, puzzled; but a flicker of recognition passed in Big Tom's eyes.

Rod smiled sourly at the big peasant, and Tom's face turned wooden. He stared back at Rod.

'Oh, come on now, Tom!' Rod snapped. 'Your secret's official knowledge now. No more point to playing games, is there?'

Tom glowered at him; then slowly, his face livened again, to a brooding, meditative look.

He leaned back against the wall, half closing his eyes. 'Aye, tha hast the right of it, as when hast thou not?'

With a sinking feeling, Rod began to realize that Big Tom saw him as more than just an employer, or a piece in the game.

'My lot is cast with thee now,' said Tom, 'whether I would have it or no; so wherefore should I dissemble?'

'Dissemble?' Rod cocked an eyebrow at his serving-man. 'Pretty high-falutin' vocabulary for a simple peasant, Big Tom.'

Tom waved a hand impatiently. 'Be done with your games! I am unmasked; do me the courtesy to take off your own.'

Rod froze.

Then, slowly, he smiled. 'You're quicker than the average ursine, Big Tom. How long have you known?'

The Loguires stared, totally lost.

Big Tom gave a short bark of laughter. 'Why, master, since first you used judo on me!'

'Ah.' Rod's eyebrows lifted. 'From the first, then? So that's why you wangled the batman job.'

Tom smiled lazily.

'Under orders?'

Tom nodded.

Rod lowered his eyes, studying the chain on his wrist.

'What are you, master?'

'A warlock.' Rod winced inside; but it was the best answer under the circumstances.

Big Tom spat. 'Games, master, games! 'Twas yourself said to be done with 'em! You are not of the councillors, else you would not ha' stolen the Lord Loguire away from them; and you are not of the House, or I would ha' known you of old. What are you, then?'

'A warlock,' Rod repeated. 'A new player in the game, Big Tom, and one who stands squarely behind the Queen. X, the unknown factor in the councillors' and Clovis' equations, here by pure happenstance and coincidence.'

'Warruh!' Big Tom spat again. 'I ha' small faith in happenstance, master. I ha' known that you back the Queen; may I ask who stands behind you?'

'Strange manner of talk,' growled Loguire, angering, 'for a footman to his lord.'

Rod smiled bleakly. 'A most strange footman, my lord.'

'Aye, and a most strange lord,' Tom snarled. 'Who backs you, Rod Gallowglass?'

Rod studied the big man, then shrugged. The word would mean nothing to the Loguires, and Tom was on his side now anyway.

'SCENT,' he answered.

Tom stared; then, almost whispering, he said, 'I ha' thought the last of them were dead.' He swallowed, bit his lip. 'Eh, but tha'rt alive. Tha might be a ghost; but nay, tha'rt alive, or the witch would scarce be so fond of thee. I ha' heard ye were dispersed, after ye won; but nay, I ought to ha' known. 'Twas secret, and secret from all, mayhap; but thou lived.'

'Won?' Rod frowned.

And was answered by a frown of even deeper perplexity from Tom.

Then the big man's face cleared. He grinned, rocking back against the wall, and roared with laughter.

The Loguires stared from him to Rod, who spread his hands, shaking his head. They looked back at Tom, wiping his eyes and eking the remains of his laugh into chuckles. 'Eh, eh, now I see it, aye, now, and fool that I was not to see it before. What age art thou, master?'

'Age?' Rod scowled. 'Thirty-two. Why?'

'Nay, nay!' Tom shook his head impatiently. 'What age art thou *from*?'

Rod's mouth formed a round, silent O as the light dawned. 'It *was* a time machine!'

Big Tom's face froze as he realized the implications of Rod's answer.

'And,' Rod pressed, 'there's another one hidden in this building, isn't there?'

'Enough!' Big Tom snapped, and his eyes were very cold. 'You know too much already, Rod Gallowglass.'

Fear gathered in Rod's belly and crawled up his spine as he saw chill, amoral murder come into the man's eyes.

'Big Tom.' He cleared his throat, spoke in a swift, driving monotone. 'Big Tom, your own kind have turned against you now. You owe them no allegiance; and the wrongs they said they'd fix, I can fix, too. Go back to them, and they'll kill you. I won't, you know that.'

The annihilation ebbed from Tom's eyes, the huge body relaxed.

'Nay,' Tom growled, 'thou hast right again, though not in the way tha knowest. They ha' but bottled me up for now, till the great deeds are done; but they will hale me forth again, for I am too costly a man to discard so lightly. But tha'rt right they will slay me – in a year, two years, or five, when my office is done. And I do wish to live.'

Rod raised an eyebrow sceptically. 'They don't doubt your loyalty?'

Big Tom chuckled deeply. 'They ha' no need to, master. I disagree only on means, not on goals. But I disagree, and for that, soon or late, they will slay me.'

'Rod,' said a quiet voice that only he could hear.

Rod held up a hand. 'Hold it! Late news on the Rialto!'

'Rod, the Prince of the Elves has arrived. He is leading a squad of elves toward your cell.' There was a touch of laughter to the robot's voice.

'All right, what's so funny?' Rod muttered.

'You have a surprise in store, Rod.'

Two gnarled, bent, white-bearded figures scurried up to the window. Rod frowned.

'Fess, those are gnomes, not elves.'

'Gnomes? Oh, yes, metal-working elves. Purely semantics, Rod. They are still incapable of dealing with iron.'

The gnomes pulled out a hammer and cold chisel with a faint bronze sheen, then stepped back and handed them to a larger, darker figure that blocked out the sunlight.

The Loguires, chained under the window, craned their necks backward to try to see as the first blow sounded.

Big Tom frowned. 'There be something that pricks at my memory about that form at the window. Ah, for light, to see his face!'

Rod frowned. 'What's so great about his face? Probably pretty ugly.'

Tom gave a toothy grin. ' 'Twould be excellent fine to tell my children, good master, if I should live long enough to sire them. No mortal has yet looked upon the faces of the royalty of the Elves, though they are said to be aged past believing. They are . . . uh . . . ah . . . mmmmmm!'

Tom's head lolled forward; he began to snore.

Two other snores answered him. Turning, Rod saw the Loguires, chins on their chests, sleeping blissfully.

Rod stared.

A metal bar dropped from the window and bounced on the floor. The ends were sheered through.

Rod whistled. This Prince of the Elves might be old, but he certainly wasn't languishing – not if he could still cut through inch-thick iron with nothing but a cold chisel and a mallet.

The third bar fell down. There was a scrabbling sound, and the squat, broad form shot through the window and leaped to the floor.

Rod stared, squeezed his eyes shut, and shook his head. Then he looked again, and understood why Tom and the Loguires had suddenly dozed off.

He swallowed, fought for composure, and smiled. 'Well met, Brom O'Berin.'

'At your service.' The little man bowed, smiling maliciously. 'I owe you a rap on the head, Master Gallowglass, for the way that you spoke to the Queen: a rap on the head, or great thanks, I know not which.'

He turned to the window and called softly in a strange, fluid tongue. The cold chisel arced through the air and fell to his feet. He reached up and caught the hammer as it dropped.

'Now, then.' He dropped to his knees and pressed Rod's forearm flat against the floor. 'Stir not, or thou'lt have a gouge out of thy wristbone.' He set the chisel against the first link of chain and tapped lightly with the hammer. The link fell off, sheared through. Brom grunted and moved to Rod's other side.

'Thou'lt wear bracelets when I've done,' he grumbled, 'but no chains. The manacles must wait till we're at the castle smithy.'

'Uh . . . that's pretty hard bronze you've got there,' Rod ventured, watching the chisel slide through the iron.

'Most hard,' Brom agreed, attacking the ankle chains. 'An old recipe, known long in my family.'

'Uh . . . in your family?'

'Aye.' Brom looked up. 'There were elves in lost Greece, too, Rod Gallowglass. Didst thou not know?'

Rod didst not; but he didn't figure this was the time to mention it.

He stood up, free of the chains at least, and watched Brom cutting the others loose. The Prince of the Elves bit explained a lot about Brom: his size and bulk, for one thing.

'Never knew you were royalty, Brom.'

'Hm?' Brom looked back over his shoulder. 'I would have thought thou'd have guessed it. Why else am I named as I am?'

He turned back to his work. Rod frowned. Name? What did that have to do with anything? Brom? O'Berin? He couldn't see the connection.

'There, the last,' said Brom, cutting through Big Tom's foot shackle. 'Do thou now lend me aid of thine shoulder, Master Gallowglass.'

He jumped back out through the window. Rod got a shoulder in Tom's midriff and, staggering, somehow manhandled him over to the window as a rope flew through.

Rod tied it under Tom's arms, threw the loose end out, and called 'Heave!'

He heard Brom grunt, and marvelled again at the little man's muscles as Big Tom moved jerkily up the wall, still snoring happily.

What with the beer belly and the muscles, and the minimal size of the window, Big Tom was a tight fit.

'Why don't you just wake him and let him shove himself out?' Rod grunted as he shoved at Tom's ample rear.

'I have no wish for my office to be known among mortals,' came Brom's muffled reply.

The window now framed only Tom's sizeable posterior and sequoia shanks. Rod eyed the former, weighing the merits of a well-placed kick, and decided against it.

'So, why'd you let me stay awake?' he grunted as he pushed.

'One amongst you must needs aid me with the others,' answered Brom, but Rod had a notion that wasn't quite the whole story.

He left off the questions, however, until his cellmates were deposited on the ground outside the window. Tuan's shoulders had proved even more of an obstacle than Tom's belly; they had to back him up, feed his hands through in front of his head, while Rod wondered fleetingly about brachiator ancestry.

Then Brom hauled Rod out, muttering something about the fish being undersized these days. Rod snarled a return compliment as he gained his feet, then bowed double, putting his head on Brom's level.

'And what's that for?' Brom growled.

'For belting,' Rod answered. 'You owe me a rap on the head, remember?'

The dwarf chuckled, clapped him on the shoulder. 'Nay, lad; you did only that which I should ha' done myself years ago; but I had never the heart. But come now, we must away.'

Brom caught up Tuan's midsection. The gnomes took his shoulders and feet, and bore him away toward the ruined fountain in the centre of the courtyard.

More gnomes materialized out of the stonework and tucked their shoulders under Big Tom.

Rod shook his head wonderingly, and stooped to sling Loguire over a shoulder.

Brom fumbled with a stone at the fountain's base and pulled it away to disclose the dark mouth of a small tunnel three feet in diameter.

Rod tapped Brom on the shoulder. 'Wouldn't this be a little easier if we woke them first?'

Brom stared, scandalized; then his face darkened. 'We go to Elfland, Master Gallowglass! And no mortal may journey there and remember it!'

'I have.'

'Well, truth,' Brom admitted, turning back to the Tuan problem, 'but then thou'rt not so mortal as some. Thou'rt a warlock.' He disappeared into the burrow.

Rod started to reply, then thought better of it. He contented himself with a few grunted remarks about discrimination and a report to the Human Rights Commission as he lugged Loguire into the tunnel.

Two gnomes started to swing the stone back into place, but Rod stopped them with an upraised hand.

'Fess,' he murmured, looking at the stable, 'we're on our way. Get out of that hole and meet me at the castle.'

There was a moment's silence; then a crash and the sound of splintering wood came from the stables. The door crashed open, and the great black horse came trotting out into the morning sunlight, head held high, mane streaming.

Heads popped out of slit-windows in the inn as a bleary-eyed hostler came stumbling out of the stable in Fess's wake, screaming for the horse to stop.

'Come on, get moving!' Rod growled, but instead, Fess stopped and looked back over his shoulder at the hostler.

The youth came running up, shouting, one hand outstretched to grab Fess's bridle.

A great, blue electric spark crackled from Fess's hide to the youth's hand.

The hostler screamed and fell backward, nursing his hand and moaning as he rolled on the cobbles. Fess was off in a swirl and a clatter of hooves.

'Show-off,' Rod growled as the horse disappeared.

'Not at all, Rod,' came the horse's quiet answer. 'Merely providing an instructive object lesson – at low amperage, it shook him up but didn't hurt him – and enhancing your reputation as a warlock.'

Rod shook his head slowly. 'As if it needed enhancing!'

'Why, Master Gallowglass,' one of the gnomes chuckled in a voice strongly reminiscent of a rusty can opener, 'wouldst thou have us believe thou'rt *not* a warlock?'

'Yes! Uh, that is, I uh . . .' Rod glanced back at the tunnel. 'Warlock? Of course I'm a warlock! Till we get through Elfland, anyway. Shall we go, boys?'


Not so very much later, they sat around the fire in the Queen's council chamber. Catharine had apologized profusely to Loguire, pointedly ignoring Tuan the while; and the amenities over, reverted to type.

Tuan sat to the left of the fireplace, eyes fixed in brooding on the flames.

Catharine sat in the angle of the room, as far from Tuan as possible, with a heavy oak table and Brom O'Berin carefully interposed between.

'. . . and that is full standing in the South, my Queen,' said Loguire, gnarled hands twisting as he wound up his report, which had abounded in nuances of intrigue that Rod couldn't follow at all. 'I am no longer duke; and the rebel lords march already.'

Catharine stirred. 'Thou shalt be Duke Loguire again,' she stated coldly, 'when we have beaten these traitors!'

Loguire smiled sadly. 'They shall not be easily beaten, Catharine.'

'"Your Majesty"!' she snapped.

'"Catharine"!' Rod barked.

She glared at him.

He glared back.

Catharine turned haughtily away. 'What am I, Brom?'

'"Your Majesty",' Brom answered with the ghost of a smile. 'But to your uncle, and to his son, your cousin, you must needs be Catharine.'

Rod fought down a smile as Catharine sank back in her chair, staring aghast at Brom.

She composed herself, and gave Brom the best *et tu Brute?* look in her repertoire. 'I had thought you were for me, Brom O'Berin.'

'Why, so I am,' Brom smiled, 'and so is this gyrfalcon, here'—he jerked a thumb toward Rod—'if you would but see it.'

Catharine favoured Rod with a cold glance. 'A gyrfalcon, aye.' Her voice hardened. 'And what of the popinjay?'

Tuan's head shot up as though he'd been slapped. He stared at her, appalled, eyes wide with hurt.

Then his mouth tightened, and a crease appeared between his eyebrows.

*Some day*, Rod thought, *she will push him just a little too far, and that may be the luckiest day of her life – if she lives through it.*

'I am for you,' Tuan breathed. 'Even now, Catharine my Queen.'

She smiled, smug and contemptuous. 'Aye, I had known you would be.'

*Oh, bitch!* Rod thought, his fist tightening. *Bitch!*

Catharine noticed the silent motions of his lips.

She smiled archly. 'What words do you mumble there, sirrah?'

'Oh, ah, just running through a breath-exercise my old voice-and-diction coach taught me.' Rod leaned back against the wall, folding his arms. 'But about the rebels, Queenie dear, just what do you propose to do about them?'

'We shall march south,' she snapped, 'and meet them on Breden Plain!'

'Nay!' Loguire bolted from his chair. 'Their force is ten to our one, if not more!'

Catharine glared at her uncle, the corners of her mouth curled into tight little hooks. 'We shall not stay to be found like a rat in a crevice!'

'Then,' said Rod, 'you will lose.'

She looked down her nose at him (no mean trick, when she was seated and he was standing). 'There is naught of dishonour in that, Master Gallowglass.'

Rod struck his forehead and rolled his eyes up.

'What else ought I do?' she sneered. 'Prepare for a siege?'

'Well, now that you mention it,' said Rod, 'yes.'

'There is this, too,' Tuan put in, his voice flat. 'Who shall guard your back 'gainst the House of Clovis?'

Her lip curled. 'Beggars!'

'Beggars and cut-throats,' Rod reminded her. 'With very sharp knives.'

'Shall the Queen fear a beggar?' she snapped. 'Nay! They are dust at my feet!'

'That which crawls in the dust at your feet is a snake,' Brom rumbled, 'and its fangs are sharpened, and poisonous.'

She caught her lip between her teeth and lowered her eyes, uncertain; then she lifted her chin again, and glared at Tuan.

'So you have armed them against me, and beaten them into an army, ruled and ordered and forged them into a dagger for my back! Most bravely well done, King of Vagabonds!'

Rod's head snapped up. He stared. He turned his head slowly toward Tuan, a strange light in his eyes.

'I will march,' said Catharine. 'Will you march at my side, my Lord Loguire?'

The old lord bent his head slowly in affirmation. 'You play the fool, Catharine, and will die; but I will die with you.'

Her composure wavered for a moment; her eyes moistened.

She turned briskly to Brom. 'And you, Brom O'Berin?'

The dwarf spread his hands. 'Your father's watch-dog, milady, and yours.'

She smiled fondly.

Then her eyes snapped hard as she looked at Tuan. 'Speak, Tuan Loguire.'

The youth raised his eyes, very slowly, to the fires. 'It is strange,' he murmured, 'at but twenty-two years of age, to look back over so very short a time, and see so much folly.'

Rod heard a choked gasp from Catharine.

Tuan slapped his thigh. 'Well, then, 'tis done; and if I have lived in folly, I might as well die in it.'

He turned, his eyes gentle, brooding. 'I shall die with you, Catharine.'

Her face was ashen. 'Folly . . .' she whispered.

'He knows not what wisdom he speaks,' Brom growled. He looked over Tuan's shoulder at Rod.

'What say you to folly, Rod Gallowglass?'

Rod's eyes slowly focused on Brom's. '"Wise fool, brave fool",' he murmured.

Brom frowned. 'How say you?'

'I say that we may yet live through this!' Rod grinned, eyes kindling. 'Ho, King of the Vagabonds!' He slapped Tuan's shoulder. 'If the Mocker and his henchmen were gone, could you sway the beggars to fight for the Queen?'

Tuan's face came alive again. 'Aye, assuredly, were they gone!'

Rod's lips pulled back in a savage grin. 'They shall be.'

The moon was riding high when Rod, Tuan, and Tom darted from the shadow of the tottering wall to the shadow of the ruined fountain in the courtyard of the House of Clovis.

'Thou wouldst make most excellent burglars, thou,' growled Big Tom. 'I might ha' heard thee a league or three away.'

It hadn't been easy to persuade Tom to come along. Of course, Rod had started on the wrong tack; he'd assumed Tom's loyalties to the proletarian idea had died when he was clapped into irons. He'd clapped Tom on the back, saying, 'How'd you like a chance to get back at your friends?'

Tom had scowled. 'Get back at 'em?'

'Yeah. They booted you out, didn't they? Threw you in the calaboose, didn't they? After your blood now, ain't they?'

Tom chuckled, 'Nay, master, not by half! Eh, no! They'd ha' freed me when the trouble was done!'

'Oh.' Rod scowled. 'I see. Trained men are hard to come by.'

Tom's face darkened. 'Thou seest too quick for my liking.'

'Well, be that as it may . . .' Rod slung an arm around the big man's shoulder, almost dislocating his arm in the process. 'Uh, in that case . . . what did they lock you up for?'

Tom shrugged. 'Disagreement.'

'Ways and means, eh?'

'Aye. They held for attacking Queen and nobles both at one time, though 'twould mean dividing of forces.'

'Sounds risky. What did you want to do?'

'Why, to bring down the noblemen and their councillors first, under guise of loyalty to the throne. Then we might slowly woo all the land to the House of Clovis, and, secured by the people, pull down the Queen and Brom O'Berin with two blows of a knife.'

Rod swallowed and tried to remember that the man was on his side now. 'Very neat.' He slapped Tom on the back. 'Spoken like a good little Bolshevik. How much does that way of doing things mean to you, Tom?'

Big Tom gave him a long, calculating look. 'What price were you minded of, master?'

Rod grinned. 'Shall we throw your four colleagues in the cell they'd reserved for you?'

' 'Twould be pleasant,' said Tom slowly. 'What comes after, master?'

'Why, then,' said Rod, 'the House of Clovis fights on the Queen's side, against the nobles. That gives you a better chance of beating the councillors and nobles; afterward, you can follow through with your own plan.'

Tom nodded, slowly. 'But will the beggars fight for the Queen?'

'That, we leave to Tuan Loguire.'

Tom's face stretched into a huge grin. He threw back his head and roared, slapping Rod on the back.

Rod picked himself up off the floor, hearing Big Tom gasp between spasms of laughter, 'Eh, I should ha' thought of it, master! Aye, that boy will charm them! You know not the powers of that silver tongue, master. The lad could make a leopard believe it had no spots!'

Rod held his peace, trying to remember if he'd seen a leopard on Gramarye, while he tried to rub the sore spot between his shoulders.

'Thou'll twist thine arm loose that way.' Tom grinned. He turned Rod around and began to massage his back. 'Thou knowest, master, if together we bring down the councillors, 'twill be thy head, alongside Brom's and the Queen's, that I'll next be a-chasing.'

Rod closed his eyes, savouring the massage. 'It oughta be a great fight. A little further to the left, Big Tom.'

So now they stood in the shadows of the fountain with Tuan between them, planning assault on the mouldering heap of stone that stood across a moon-filled expanse of courtyard.

Rod counted his pulse beats, wondering if his heart had really slowed that much, until Tom whispered, 'No alarm. They ha' not seen us, good masters. Ready thyselves, now.'

Tom gathered himself, looking like a diesel semi that had decided to turn cat-burglar.

'Now!' he growled, and ran.

They charged lightly, quietly, through the seeming glare of the moonlight to the welcoming shadow of the walls, then flattened themselves against the stone, hearts thudding, breath held as they strained their ears for some sound of alarm.

After a small eternity of three minutes, Big Tom loosed his breath in a great, gusty sigh.

'Eh, then, lads!' he hissed. 'Come along, now.'

They crept around the corner of the great dank stone pile. Big Tom splayed his fingers out wide, set his elbow at the corner of the wall, and marked the spot where his second finger ended. He put his other elbow against the mark.

'Big Tom!' Rod called in an agonized whisper, 'we don't have time for—'

'Hsst!' Tuan's fingers clamped on Rod's shoulder. 'Silence, I pray thee! He measures in cubits!'

Rod shut up, feeling rather foolish.

Tom made a few more measurements, which apparently resulted in his finding what he was looking for. He pulled a pry from the pouch at his belt and began to lever at the base of a three-foot block.

Rod stared, uncomprehending. It would take all night and most of the next day to dig the block out. What was Tom trying to do?

Tom gave a last pry, and caught the sheet of stone as it fell outward. It was perhaps an inch thick.

He laid the slab on the ground and looked up at his companions. His grin flashed chill in the moonlight. 'I had thought I might have need of a bolthole one day,' he whispered. 'Gently now, lads.'

He ducked head and arms through the hole, kicked off with his feet, and slithered through.

Rod swallowed hard and followed Tom. Tuan came through at his heels.

'All in?' Tom whispered as Tuan's feet stood hard to the floor, and the moonlight was cut off as Tom fitted the stone plug back into place.

'Light,' he whispered. Rod cupped his hand over the hilt of his dagger and turned it on, letting a ray of light escape between two fingers. It was enough to see Big Tom grope up a worm-eaten panel from the floor and fit it back into place in the bolthole.

Tom straightened, grinning. 'Now let them wonder at our coming. To work, masters.'

He turned away. Rod followed, looking quickly about him.

They were in a large stone room that had once been panelled. The panels were crumbled and fallen away for the most part. The room held only cobwebs, rusty iron utensils, and long trestle tables, spongy now with rot.

' 'Twas a kitchen, once,' Tom murmured. 'They cook at the hearth in the common room, now. None ha' used this place for threescore years or more.'

Rod shuddered. 'What's a good kid like you doing in a place like this, Tom?'

Big Tom snorted.

'No, I mean it,' said Rod urgently. 'You can judge a god, an ideal, by the people who worship it, Tom.'

'Be still!' Tom snapped.

'It's true, though, isn't it? The councillors are all rotten, we know that. And the Mocker and his buddies are lice. You're the only good man in the bunch. Why don't you—'

'Be still!' Tom snarled, swinging about so suddenly that Rod blundered into him. Rod felt the huge, hamlike hand grabbing a fistful of his doublet, right at the throat, and smelled the beery, garlic reek of Tom's breath as the man thrust his face close to Rod's.

'And what of the Queen?' Tom hissed. 'What says she for her gods, eh?'

He let Rod go, with a shove that threw him back against the wall, and turned away.

Rod collected himself and followed, but not before he had caught a glimpse of Tuan's eyes, narrowed and chill with hate, in the beam of the torch.

'We approach a corner,' Tom muttered. 'Dampen the light.'

The torch winked out; a few moments later, Rod felt the stone wall fall away under his left hand. He turned, and saw a faint glow at the end of the blackened, short hallway ahead.

Big Tom stopped. ' 'Tis a corner again, and a sentry beyond. Walk wary, lads.'

He moved away again, stepping very carefully. Rod followed, feeling Tuan's breath hot on the back of his neck.

As they neared the corner, they heard a rhythm of faint snores to their right, from the new hallway.

Big Tom flattened himself against the wall with a wolfish grin. Rod followed suit . . . and drew away with a gasp and a convulsive shudder.

Tom scowled at him, motioning for silence.

Rod looked at the wall and saw a thick blob of greyish-white stuff fastened to the wall. It had brushed the back of his neck, and he could say with authority that the texture was flaccid, the touch cold and moist.

He looked at the obscene glop and shuddered again.

' 'Tis but witch-moss, Rod Gallowglass,' Tuan whispered in his ear.

Rod frowned. 'Witch-moss?'

Tuan stared, incredulous. 'Thou'rt a warlock, and knowest not witch-moss?'

Rod was saved from an answer by the cessation of the snores from around the corner.

The trio caught their collective breath and flattened themselves against the wall, Rod carefully avoiding the witch-moss. Tom glared at his sidekicks.

The moment of silence stretched out as thin as the content of a congressman's speech.

'Hold!' shouted a voice from around the corner.

Their muscles snapped tight in a spasm.

'Where do you go at this hour?' the sentry's voice snarled.

Dread clambered its way up Rod's spine.

A quaking, nasal voice answered the sentry. 'Nay, I do but seek the jakes!'

The three men let their breath out in a long, silent sigh.

'*Sir*, when yer speak to a soldier!'

'Sir,' the whining voice echoed, surly.

'What was your reason for walking past curfew?' the sentry threatened in ominous tones.

'I do but seek the jakes, *sir*,' the nasal voice whined.

The sentry chuckled, mollified. 'And the jakes are near to the women's hall? Nay, I think not! Back to your pallet scum! Your doxie's not for you this night!'

'But I—'

'Nay!' the guard snapped. 'You do know the rule, fellow. Do you ask of the Mocker first.' The voice became almost confidential. ' 'Tain't so much as all that, chum. Like as not he'll give yer the paper says yer can do't, an' set yer a fit place an' time. He's free 'nough about it.'

The nasal one hawked and spat.

'Come on, now,' the guard growled. 'Yer've but to ask of him.'

'Aye,' sneered the nasal voice, 'and ask again every night that I'm wishin' to see her! Hell, 'twas the one thing in this world that came cheap!'

The guard's voice hardened again. 'The Mocker's word is the law in this House, and my club'll remind you of it, if my word's not enough!'

There was a pause, then an angry, despairing snarl, and feet padded away.

There was silence again; after a while, the guard began to snore again.

Rod glanced at Tuan. The boy's face was dead white, lips pressed so tight the colour'd gone out of them.

'I take it you didn't know anything about this?' Rod whispered.

'Nay,' Tuan whispered back. 'Once they'd set me by, they wasted no time. A guard at each hall, a writ ere two may share a bed – this is worse than the lords of the South!'

Tom's head jerked up. 'Nay!' he snarled. ' 'Tis but inconvenience. The gains to be got from it are well worth the price.'

For his part, Rod agreed with Tuan. Police state, control over every facet of the people's lives – yes, the Mocker's Marxism was showing.

'What gains are worth *that* price?' Tuan snorted, raising his whisper a trifle.

'Why,' growled Big Tom, at minimum bullfrog volume, 'more food for all, more and better clothing, none poor and none starving.'

'And all thanks to planned parenthood,' Rod murmured, with an apprehensive glance at the corner.

'And how may this come?' asked Tuan, hiking his voice another notch and ignoring Rod's frantic signals. 'From a writ of consent for a lovemaking? I cannot see how!'

Tom's lip twisted in scorn, and the bullfrog croaked louder. 'Nay, you cannot! But the Mocker can!'

Tuan stared; then his jaw tightened, and his hand slipped to his dagger. 'Do you place yourself and your kind above a nobleman, churl?'

'Uh, gentlemen,' Rod whispered.

Big Tom tensed, grinning; his eyes danced mockery.

'Blood will tell,' he said, full voice.

Tuan's dagger leaped out as he sprang.

Tom lugged out his minor sword.

Rod threw out his hands, stiff-arming both of them at the collarbone. 'Gentlemen, *gentlemen*! I realize you both feel very strongly about the issues at hand; but it is my bounden duty to remind you that a sentry fully capable of bringing the wrath of the House down on our heads is dozing, and not too heavily either, just around the corner!'

'This is not to be borne, Rod Gallowglass!'

'Aye,' chuckled Big Tom, 'the truth was ever hard to bear.'

Tuan lunged, trying to stab at Tom over Rod's head. Rod shoved back on the boy's collarbone and ducked as the knife arced past his head.

Tom chuckled softly. 'There is a nobleman for you! A fool could see the reach is too great! Ever will he overreach himself, when he knows he must fail.'

Rod eyed Tom sideways. 'You're slipping, Big Tom. That was almost a compliment.'

'Nay!' Tom hissed, his eyes fire. 'To attempt the impossible is the act of a fool! The nobles are fools, and the roads to their utopias are paved with the bones of the peasants!'

Tuan spat. 'And what else are they—'

'Be still!' Rod gave them both a shake. 'Could I possibly persuade you to overlook your obvious differences in favour of the common good for a moment?'

Tom straightened to his full height and looked down his nose at Tuan. '*Little* man,' he crooned.

Rod let go of Tuan and swung on Big Tom, grabbing the big man's collar with both hands. Tom grinned and brought up a hamlike fist. 'Aye, *master?*'

'What's the utopia right now, Big Tom?' Rod breathed.

Tom's grin faded to a frown. 'Why, that the people of Gramarye should rule their land for themselves.'

'Right!' Rod let go of Tom's collar, patting the man's cheek. 'Bright boy! You get the silver star this week! And what do you have to do first?'

'Kill the councillors and noblemen!' Tom grinned.

'*Very* good! A gold star for the boy! You'll make valedictorian yet, Big Tom! Now, if you *really* want to be a good boy, tell teacher what you have to do before that!'

Tom sobered. 'Jail the Mocker.'

'A-plus! And what comes before that?'

Big Tom knit his brown, confused. 'What?'

'*Be quiet!*' Rod roared in his face, in a stage whisper. He spun on Tuan. 'Now! What do we do about that sentry?' And to himself, he mumbled, 'Sheesh! I should maybe have brought a political convention in here!'

Tuan's chin jutted out stubbornly. 'Ere we go further, this fellow must acknowledge me lord!'

Tom took a breath for a fresh blast.

'Down, boy!' Rod said hurriedly. 'High blood pressure's bad for you! Is Tuan Loguire a nobleman born, Tom?'

'Aye,' Tom grudged, 'but that does not—'

'Is Loguire one of the greatest of the noble houses?'

'It is, but—'

'And your mother and father were peasants?'

'Yes, but that's not to say that—'

'And you have absolutely no wish to have been born a nobleman!'

'Never!' Tom hissed, eyes glowing. 'May I be hanged from the highest gallows in Gramarye if ever I had wished that!'

'And you wouldn't want to be a nobleman if you could!'

'Master!' Big Tom pleaded, wounded to the core. 'Hast so little regard for me that thou couldst think such of me?'

'No, I trust you, Big Tom,' said Rod, patting his shoulder, 'but Tuan has to be shown.' He turned to the young nobleman. 'You satisfied? He knows his place, doesn't he?'

'Aye.' Tuan smiled like a fond father. 'Fool I was to doubt him.'

Understanding came into Tom's eyes as his mouth dropped open. His heavy hand closed on Rod's neck. 'Why, thou lump of. . . !'

Rod reached up and squeezed Tom's elbow just at the funny bone. Tom let go, eyes starting from their sockets, mouth sagging in a cry of agony that he dared not voice.

'Now,' said Rod briskly, 'how do we get rid of that sentry?'

'Oh, thou scum!' Tom breathed. 'Thou slimy patch of river-moss, thou mongrel son-of-a-democrat, thou!'

'Precisely,' Rod agreed.

'Nay, but tell me,' Tuan breathed in Rod's ear, eyes glowing. 'What didst thou do to him? Thou didst but touch him and—'

'Uh . . . warlock trick,' said Rod, falling back on the easiest, though most distasteful, excuse. He caught the back of Tuan's neck and jerked the youth's head down into the huddle with himself and Big Tom. 'Now, how do we knock out that sentry?'

'There is but one way,' murmured Tuan. 'Wake him and fight him.'

'And let him give the alarm?' Tom stared, horrified. 'Nay, nay! Come catpaw behind him, and give him a blow o' the head!'

'That,' said Tuan grimly, 'lacks honour!'

Tom spat.

'Big Tom's plan is okay,' said Rod, 'except what happens if he wakes while we're sneaking up? And there's a very good chance of it; that lecherous beggar proved it for us!'

Tom shrugged. 'Then a quick rush, and a hope. If we die, then we die.'

'And the Queen dies with us,' Rod growled. 'No good.'

Tom pulled out his short sword and balanced it on a finger. 'I'll strike him in the throat with this blade at full fifty paces.'

Tuan stared, appalled. 'A man of your own men, sirrah!'

'One for the good of the cause.' Tom shrugged. 'What of it?'

Tuan's eyes froze. 'That is worse than a stab in the back! We must needs give him lief to defend himself.'

'Oh, aye!' Tom snorted. 'Lief to defend himself, and to raise the whole House with his cries! Lief to—'

Rod clapped a hand over each mouth, glad that he hadn't brought three men with him. He hissed at Big Tom, 'Be patient, will you? He's new to commando work!'

Tom sobered.

Tuan straightened, eyes icy.

Rod put his mouth next to Tom's ear and whispered, 'Look, if you hadn't known he was an aristocrat, how would you have judged him?'

'A brave man, and a strong fighter,' Tom admitted, 'though foolish and young, with too many ideals.'

Rod shook a finger at him. 'Prejudice, Big Tom! Discrimination! I thought you believed in equality!'

'Well said,' Tom growled reluctantly; 'I'll bear him. But one more of his pious mouthings and . . .'

'If we get this job done fast, he won't have a chance to. Now I've got an idea.'

'Then why didst thou ask us?' growled Tom.

' 'Cause I didn't get my idea till you two started haggling. What we need is a compromise solution, right? Tuan won't stand for a knife in the back, or a knife while the guy's sleeping, or for killing a loyal retainer who might make good cannon fodder tomorrow. Right?'

'Aye,' Tuan agreed.

'And Big Tom won't stand for him giving the alarm – and neither will I, for that matter: we're all good fighters, but just the three of us against the whole Houseful of cut-throats is straining the bonds of fantasy just a little bit far. So, Tom! If that sentry should come running around this corner all of a sudden, will you clobber him lightly?'

'Aye!' Tom grinned.

'*Lightly*, I said. Does that satisfy honour, Tuan?'

'Aye, since he faces us.'

'Good! Now, if we could just get him to chase a mouse around this corner, we'd be all set.'

'Aye,' Tuan agreed, 'but where's the mouse that would so nicely oblige us?'

'The master could make one,' Tom growled.

'Make one?' Rod stared. 'Sure if I had a machine shop and a . . .'

'Nay, nay!' Tuan grinned. 'I know not those spells; but thou hast the witch-moss, and thou'rt a warlock! What more dost thou need?'

'Huh?' Rod swallowed. 'Witches make things out of that stuff?'

'Aye, aye! Dost thou not know? Living things, small things – like mice!'

The missing piece in the puzzle of Gramarye clicked into place in Rod's mind. 'Uh, say, how do they work that trick?'

'Why, they have but to look at a lump of the stuff, and it becomes what they wish it!'

Rod nodded slowly. 'Very neat, ve-ry neat. The only hitch in the plan is, that's not my style of witch-craft.'

Tuan sagged. 'Thou craftest not witch-moss? Then how are we to . . . ? Still, 'tis most strange that thou shouldst not know of it.'

'Not so,' Tom dissented. 'A very poor briefing bureau . . .'

'Oh, shut up!' Rod growled. 'There are other ways to get a mouse.' He cupped his hands around his mouth and called softly, 'Gwen! Oh, Gwe-en!'

A spider dropped down on a thread right in front of his nose.

Rod jumped. 'Ye cats! Don't *do* that, girl!'

'Vermin!' Tom hissed, and swung his hand back for a swat.

Rod poked him in the solar plexus. 'Careful, there! Squash a spider, and you get bad luck, you know – namely, me!'

He cupped the spider in his hand and caressed it very gently with a finger. 'Well, at least you didn't choose a black widow. Prettiest spider I ever saw, come to think of it.'

The spider danced on his hand.

'Listen, sweetheart, I need a mouse to bring me that sentry. Can you handle it?'

The spider shape blurred, fluxed, and grew into a mouse.

It jumped from his hand and dashed for the corner.

'Oh, no you don't!' Rod sprang, cupped a hand over it, then very carefully picked it up. 'Sorry, sweetheart, you might get stepped on – and if anything like that happened to you, I'd be totally crushed.'

He kissed its nose, and heard Tom gagging behind him. The mouse wriggled in ecstasy.

'No,' said Rod, running a fingertip over its back and pinching the tail, 'you've got to make me one instead, out of that blob of witch-moss. Think you can handle it, pet?'

The mouse nodded, turned, and stared at the witch-moss.

Slowly, the blob pulled itself in, extruded a tendril into a tail, grew whiskers at the top end, changed colour to brown, and a mouse crept down off the wall.

Tom gulped and crossed himself.

Rod frowned. 'Thought you were an atheist.'

'Not at times like this, master.'

The witch-moss mouse scurried around the corner.

Big Tom lifted his dagger, holding it by the tip, the heavy, weighted handle raised like a club.

The snores around the corner stopped with a grunt.

'Gahhh! Nibble on me, will ya, y' crawlin' ferleigh?'

The sentry's stool clattered over. He stamped twice, missed both times; then the waiting men heard running footsteps approaching.

Tom tensed himself.

The mouse streaked around the corner.

The sentry came right behind it, cursing. His feet slipped on the turn. He looked up, saw Tom, and had just time enough to begin to look horrified before Tom's knife-hilt caught him at the base of the skull with a very solid thunk.

Rod let out a sigh of relief. 'At last!'

The sentry folded nicely into Tuan's waiting arms. The young nobleman looked at Rod, grinning.

'Who fights by the side of a warlock,' he said, 'wins.'

'Still, it was a pretty ratty trick,' said Rod sheepishly.

Tom winced and pulled a length of black thread from his pouch.

'Nay, that will not hold him,' Tuan protested.

Tom's only answer was a grin.

'Fishline?' Rod lifted an eyebrow.

'Better,' said Big Tom, kneeling, beginning to wrap up the sentry. 'Braided synthetic spider silk.'

'And we owe it all to you,' said Rod, petting the mouse in his hand.

It wriggled its nose, then dived between the buttons on his doublet.

Rod stifled a giggle, cupped a hand over the lump on his belly. 'Hey, watch it! That tickles!'

Tom had the sentry nicely cocooned, with a rag jammed in his mouth and held in place by a few twists of thread.

'Where shall we hide him?' Tuan whispered.

'There's nary a place close to hand,' Tom muttered, tongue between his teeth as he tied a Gordian knot.

'Hey!' Rod clapped a cupped hand over a lump moving south of his belt buckle. 'Cut that out!'

'There's a torch-sconce on this wall,' said Tuan, pointing.

'The very thing,' Tom growled. He heaved the inert sentry up, hooked one of the spider-thread loops over the sconce.

Rod shook his head. 'Suppose someone comes by this way? We can't have him hanging around like that.'

He reached in his doublet and hauled the mouse away from its exploratory tour of his thorax. 'Listen, baby, you know what a dimensional warp is?'

The mouse rolled its eyes up and twitched its whiskers. Then it shook its head firmly.

'How about a uh, time-pocket?'

The mouse nodded eagerly; then the little rodent face twisted up in concentration . . . and the sentry disappeared.

Tuan goggled, mouth gaping open.

Big Tom pursed his lips, then said briskly, 'Ah . . . yes! Well, let's get on with it, then.'

Rod grinned, put the mouse on the floor, turned it around, gave it a pat on the backside.

'Get lost, you bewitching beast. But stay close; I might need you.'

The mouse scampered off with a last squeak over her shoulder.

'The Mocker will be sleeping in what was Tuan's chamber, I doubt not,' Tom muttered, 'and his lieutenants, we may hope, will not be far off.'

'May not one of them be wakeful?' whispered Tuan. 'Or might one be set Master of the Watch?'

Tom turned slowly, eyeing Tuan with a strange look on his face. He raised an eyebrow at Rod. 'A good man,' he admitted, 'and a good guess.' Then, 'Follow,' and he turned away.

They were able to bypass the only other sentry between themselves and the common room.

The room itself, cavernous and slipshod as ever, was lit only by the smoky glow from the great fireplace, and a few smouldering torches. It was enough, however, to make out the great stone staircase that curved its way up the far wall with a grace that belied its worn treads and broken balustrade.

A gallery jutted out into the hall at the top of the stair. The doors opening off it gave onto private rooms.

A broad-shouldered, hatchet-faced man sat sprawled and snoring in a huge chair by the side of the vast fireplace. A sentry stood guard at the foot of the great staircase, blinking and yawning. Two more guards slouched at either side of the door in the centre of the balcony.

'Here's a pretty mess,' said Big Tom, ducking back into the hallway. 'There's one more of them than there are of us, and they be so far between that two must surely take alarm as we disable two others.'

'To say nothing of that wasteland of lighted floor that we have to cross to get to any of them,' Rod added.

'We might creep up through the tables and stools,' Tuan suggested, 'and he at the foot of the stairs must surely nod himself asleep ere long.'

'That takes care of the two on the ground floor,' Rod agreed, 'but how about the pair on the balcony?'

'To that,' said Tuan, 'I have some small skill at the shepherd's bow.'

He drew out a patch of leather with two rawhide thongs wrapped about it.

'How didst thou learn the craft of that?' Tom growled as Tuan unwound the strings. ' 'Tis a peasant's weapon, not a lordling's toy.'

There was a touch of contempt in the glance Tuan threw Tom. 'A knight must be schooled in all weapons, Big Tom.'

Rod frowned. 'I didn't know that was part of the standard code.'

'It is not,' Tuan admitted. 'But 'tis my father's chivalry, and mine, as you shall see. Both yon knaves shall measure their length on cold stone ere they could know what has struck them.'

'I don't doubt it,' Rod agreed grimly. 'Okay, let's go. I'll take the one by the fireplace.'

'Thou'lt not,' Big Tom corrected him. 'Thou'lt take him by the stairway.'

'Oh? Any particular reason?'

'Aye.' Tom grinned wolfishly. 'He in the great chair is the lieutenant that Tuan foresaw – and one among those who ha' jailed me. 'Tis my meat, master.'

Rod looked at Tom's eyes and felt an eerie chill wind blow up along his spine.

'All right, butcher,' he muttered. 'Just remember, the lady's not for carving, yet.'

'"Let each man pile his dead according to his own taste and fashion",' Tom quoted. 'Go tend your corpses, master, and leave me to mine.'

They dropped to their bellies and crawled, each to his own opponent.

To Rod, it was an eternity of table-legs and stool feet, with plenty of dropped food scraps between, and the constant fear that one of the others might reach his station first and get bored.

There was a loud, echoing clunk.

Rod froze. One of the others had missed his footing.

There was a moment's silence; then a voice called, 'What was that?' Then, 'Eh, you there! Egbert! Rouse yourself, sot, and have a mind for the stairs you're guarding!'

'Eh? Wot? Wozzat?' muttered a bleary, nearer voice; and, 'What fashes ye?' grumbled a deeper, petulant voice from the fireplace. 'Must ye wake me for trifles?'

There was a pause; then the first voice said, with a note of obsequiousness, ' 'Twas a noise, Captain, a sort of a knock 'mongst the tables.'

'A knock, he says!' growled the captain. 'A rat, mayhap, after the leavings, nowt more! Do ye wake me for that? Do it more, an' thou'lt hear a loud knock indeed, a blow on thy hollow head.' Then the voice grumbled to itself, 'A knock, i'faith! A damned knock!'

Then there was silence again, then a muted clang as one of the sentries shifted his weight uneasily.

Rod let out a sigh of relief, slow and silent.

He waited for the sentry to start snoring again.

Then he wormed his way forward again, till at last he lay quiet under the table nearest the stairway.

It seemed he lay there for a very long time.

There was a piercing whistle from the fireplace, and a clatter as Big Tom overturned a stool in his charge.

Rod sprang for his man.

Out of the corner of his eye, he saw Tuan leap upright, his sling a blurred arc; then Rod crashed into the sentry, fist slamming at the midriff, left hand squeezing the throat.

The man folded. Rod chopped at the base of the skull lightly, just under the iron cap, and the sentry went limp.

He looked up just in time to see a sentry on the balcony sag to the floor. The other lay writhing on the stones, hands clasped at his throat.

Rod was up the stairs in five leaps. He landed a haymaker on the man's jaw. The man's eyes closed as he went under.

His larynx was pushed out of line. It was not a pretty sight. But at that, he'd been lucky. If it had been a direct blow, his trachea would have been crushed.

His companion hadn't been so lucky. The pebble had crushed his forehead. Blood welled over his face and puddled to the floor.

'Forgive me, man,' whispered Tuan, as he contemplated his handiwork. Rod had never seen the boy's face so grim.

'Fortunes of war, Tuan,' he whispered.

'Aye,' Tuan agreed, 'and had he been my peer, I could dismiss it at that. But a man of my blood is intended to protect the peasants, not slay them.'

Rod looked at the boy's brooding face and decided it was men like the Loguires who had given aristocracy what little justification it had had.

Tom had glanced once and turned away to bind the remaining man, his face thunderous.

There had been only the one casualty; the captain and stair-guard lay securely trussed with Tom's black thread.

Tom came up, glowering at Tuan. ' 'Twas well done,' he growled. 'You took two of them out, and were able to spare the one; tha'rt a braw fighter. And for the other, do not mourn him: thou couldst scarce take the time for better aim.'

Tuan's face was blank in confusion. He couldn't rightly object to Tom's manner; yet it was disquieting to have a peasant offer him fatherly advice, and forgiveness.

Rod gave him a way out of it. 'You used to sleep there?' He jerked a thumb over his shoulder at the door the sentries had guarded.

He broke through Tuan's abstraction; the youth turned, looked, and nodded.

'Well, that's where the Mocker'll be, then.' Rod looked up at Tom. 'That captain downstairs was one of the Mocker's cadre?'

'Aye.'

'That leaves two lieutenants, then. How's chances for one of them being in each of these rooms next to the Mocker's?' As Tom pulled at his lower lip and nodded, Rod went on: 'One for each of us, then. You boys take the lieutenants. I'll take the Mocker.'

He turned to the door. Big Tom's meaty hand fell on his shoulder.

'How now?' growled the big peasant. 'How is the Mocker your meat, not mine?'

Rod grinned. 'I'm the middleman, remember? Besides, what belt do you hold?'

'Brown,' Tom admitted.

'And the Mocker?'

'Black,' Tom answered reluctantly. 'Fifth dan.'

Rod nodded. 'I'm black, eighth dan. You take the lieutenant.'

Tuan frowned. 'What is this talk of belts?'

'Just a jurisdictional dispute; don't worry about it.' Rod turned to the centre door.

Big Tom caught his arm again. 'Master,' and this time he sounded like he meant it. 'When this is done, thou must teach me.'

'Yeah, sure, anything. I'll get you a college degree, just let's get this over with, shall we?'

'I thank thee.' Tom grinned. 'But I've a doctorate already.'

Rod did a double take, then stared at him. 'In what?'

'Theology.'

Rod nodded. 'That figures. Say, you haven't come up with any new atheist theories, have you?'

'Master!' Tom protested, wounded. 'How can one prove or disprove the existence of a non-material being by material data? 'Tis an innate contradiction of—'

'Gentlemen,' said Tuan sarcastically, 'I greatly dislike to interrupt so learned a discourse, but the Mocker awaits, and may shortly awake.'

'Huh? Oh! Oh, yes!' Rod turned to the door. 'See you in a few minutes, Big Tom.'

'Aye, we must have further converse.' Tom grinned and turned away to the right-hand door.

Rod eased his own door open, hands stiffened.

The door creaked. It groaned. It shrieked. It lodged formal protest.

Rod threw himself forward, having just time to realize that the Mocker had left his hinges carefully unoiled as a primitive but very effective burglar alarm, before the Mocker screamed 'Bloody Murder!' and jumped from his bed, hands chopping.

Rod blocked an overhand blow and thrust for the solar plexus. His hand was skilfully rerouted, the Mocker's scream for help dinning in his ears.

Rod had just time to appreciate the humour of a black belt calling for help before he saw the kick smashing at his groin.

He leaped back, and the Mocker leaped after him. This time, the kick landed.

Rod rolled on the floor, curled around his agony.

He saw the foot aimed at his jaw and managed to turn his head aside just enough; the foot glanced off the side of his head.

He saw a shower of red asterisks, glowing against black, and shook his head frantically, trying to clear it.

Through the ringing in his ears, he heard another scream, suddenly cut off, then a thud; then Big Tom was bellowing, 'Thy sling, Tuan! There'll be guards to answer that scream!'

Then the big man was bending over him, face close. 'How bad art thou hurt, master?'

Rod had never known stale beer and onions could smell so good.

'I'm all right,' he gasped. 'The blow landed a little off-centre, thank heaven!'

'Canst thou stand?'

'In a minute. Gwen may be in for a temporary disappointment, though. How'd you do it, Big Tom?'

'Caught his foot on the upswing,' Tom grinned, 'and threw him high. Then I got in an uppercut ere he landed.'

Rod stared. 'A what?'

'An uppercut. A haymaker.'

Rod rolled over, got his knees under him, shook his head in amazement. '"Uppercut takes out Black Belt." Call the newspapers.'

There was a cry outside, choked off suddenly.

Rod's head snapped up, listening. Then he stumbled to his feet, hands still pressed to his groin, and all but fell out of the door, ignoring Big Tom's solicitous protests.

Three more bodies lay on the stone floor of the common room.

Tuan stood at the balcony rail, sling stretched tight between his hands, jaw clamped shut, bleak dismay in his eyes.

'First the one came,' he said in a monotone, 'then the other, then the third. The first two I dispatched ere they could cry; but on the third, I was tardy.' Tuan turned back to the hall. After a moment, he said, slow and hard, 'I do not like this killing.'

Then his vision cleared.

'Huh.' Rod nodded, gasping, as a brief spasm of nausea made him clutch at the railing. 'No man worthy to be called a man does like it, Tuan. Don't let it worry you. It's war.'

'Oh, I ha' slain before.' Tuan's lips pressed thin. 'But to slay men who three days agone drank my health . . . !'

Rod nodded, closing his eyes. 'I know. But if you have any hope of being a king, Tuan, or even a good Duke, you've got to learn not to let it bother you.'

He looked up at the boy. 'Besides, remember – they'd have killed you if they could.'

Tom came out on the balcony, carrying the trussed-up Mocker in his arms, like a baby.

He looked briefly at the common room; his face hardened. 'More killing?'

He turned away, laying the Mocker carefully on the floor next to the prone bodies of his lieutenants, and sighed. '*Ay de mi!* But 'tis the times, and the fashion.'

He bent to the work of binding up one of the lieutenants, a tall, emaciated skeleton of a man with a scar where he should have had an ear, a souvenir of royal justice.

Rod looked, and nodded; the Mocker had chosen his confederates well. They had cause for hating the monarch.

Rod slowly straightened, wincing at the pain.

Tuan glanced at him. 'Thou ought to seat thyself and take rest, Rod Gallowglass.'

Rod pulled in a sharp, quick breath and shook his head. 'It's just pain. Hadn't we better cart these three down to the dungeon?'

A gleam sparked in Tuan's eye. 'Nay. Bind them and keep them here; I have uses for them.'

Rod frowned. 'What do you mean, *uses*?'

Big Tom held up a hand. 'Do not ask, master. If Tuan has need of them, let him have them. This lad knows his craft; I ha' ne'er seen, and but rarely heard, of any man who could so sway the mob.'

He turned and leaped down the stairs, checked for heartbeats in the fallen men, bound up the one that still lived, and dragged them all under the balcony. Then he caught up the third lieutenant from the hearth, slung him over a shoulder.

'Tom!' Tuan called, and the big man looked up.

'Bring that horn that hangs o'er the mantel, and the drum beside it!' Tuan called.

Tom nodded and took down the battered, curled hunting horn from its nail and plucked one of the rude drums – nothing more than an empty cask with hide stretched over each end – from its place on the mantel.

Rod frowned, perplexed. 'What do you want the drum and bugle for?'

Tuan grinned. 'Canst play at the horn?'

'Well, I wouldn't exactly qualify for first chair in the Philharmonic, but . . .'

'Thou'lt do,' said Tuan, eyes dancing.

Big Tom bounded back up the stairs with the Mocker's lieutenant over one shoulder and the trumpet and drum over the other.

He dropped the instruments and laid the bound man by his companions.

He straightened, fists on hips, grinning. 'Halloa, my masters! What would you have us do with 'em, lordling?'

'Do thou take the drum,' said Tuan, 'and when I give the word, hang these four from the balcony rail, but not by their necks. 'Tis far more to our credit we've taken them living.'

Rod cocked an eyebrow. 'Not that old wheeze about being powerful enough to be merciful?'

He didn't hear the answer, because Tom started pounding the drum. The tenor throbbing filled the room.

Rod caught up the horn.

Tuan grinned, jumped up on the rail, stood with feet wide apart and arms folded. 'Summon them, Master Gallowglass,' he shouted.

Rod set the mouthpiece to his lips and blew 'Reveille'.

It sounded rather weird on a hunting horn, but it had its effect. Before he was halfway through with the second chorus, the hall had filled with beggars, muggers, lame, one-armed, thieves and cutpurses and murderers.

Their muttering, surf and wind before a storm, filled the hall as an undercurrent to the drum and horn. They were fresh-woken, bleary-eyed and fuzzy-brained, hurling a thousand incredulous questions at one another, shaken and cowed to see Tuan, whom they had jailed, standing tall and proud in the hall he'd been exiled from.

He should fear them; he should have feared to return; and if he had come back, it should have been as a thief in the night, skulking and secret.

Yet here he stood, free in their eyes, summoning them to him with bugle and drum – and where was the Mocker?

They were shaken, and more than a little afraid. Men who had never been taught how to think now faced the unthinkable.

Rod ended with a flourish, and flipped the trumpet away from his lips, whirling it in a flashing circle to land belldown at his hip.

Big Tom gave the drum a last final boom.

Tuan held his hand out to Tom and began clicking his fingers very softly.

The drum spoke again, throbbing, insistent, but very soft.

Rod looked up at Tuan, who was grinning, arms akimbo, a royal elf come into his kingdom. He looked down at the audience, shaken and fearful, staring, mouths agape, at the lordly, commanding figure above them.

Rod had to admit it was a great way to open a speech.

Tuan flung up his arms, and the hall stilled, except for the low-pitched throb of Tom's drum.

'You cast me out!' Tuan shouted.

The mob shrank back on itself, muttering, fearful.

'Cast out, thrown to exile!' Tuan called. 'You had turned your eyes from me, turned away from me, thought never to look upon me!'

The muttering grew, began to take a surly, desperate quality.

'Was I not banished?' Tuan called, then, 'Be still!' he snapped.

And, miraculously, the room stilled.

He levelled an accusing forefinger at the crowd and growled, 'Was I not banished?'

This time there were a few muttered 'Ayes'.

'Was I not?'

The mutter of 'Ayes' grew.

'Was I not?'

'Aye!' rolled across the heads of the crowd.

'Did you not call me traitor?'

'Aye,' the crowd growled again.

'Yet here I stand,' Tuan cried, 'strong and free, and master again of the House of Clovis!'

Nobody disputed it.

'And where are the real traitors, who would ha' seen you all torn to bits in hopeless battle? The traitors, who ha' turned this House to a jail in my absence? Where are they now, to dispute my mastership?'

He rested his hands on his hips while the crowd took up the question in its own ranks, and Tom quickly lashed ten feet of thread to the Mocker's bonds, lashing the other end to a railing-pillar. As the mutters of 'Where?' and 'The Mocker!' began to grow, he served the three lieutenants likewise.

Tuan let the mutters swell and grow; then, just as they hit their peak, he gave Tom the signal.

Tom and Rod threw the bound men over, where they hung two on each side of Tuan. The Mocker had regained consciousness; he began writhing and kicking at the end of his rope.

A shocked silence filled the hall.

Tuan grinned and folded his arms.

The crowd roared, like one huge, savage beast, and pressed forward. The front ranks began to jump at the dangling feet. Obscene epithets, cursing the Mocker and his men, blasted from the packed floor.

'Behold!' Tuan shouted, throwing up his arms, and the crowd fell silent. 'Behold them, the traitors who once you called masters! Beyond them, the traitors, thieves who took from you all the liberty I had gained for you!'

Big Tom was grinning, eyes glowing and fixed on the young lord, swaying to the rhythm of the boy's words.

For, truly, the lad seemed twelve feet tall now.

'Were you not born without masters?' Tuan shouted.

'Aye!' the crowd roared at him.

'You were born to freedom!' Tuan bellowed. 'The freedom of outlawry and poverty, aye, but born free!'

Then, 'Were you not born wild?' he fairly shrieked; and:

'Aye!' the crowd shrieked in response, 'Aye, aye! Aye!'

'Did I steal your freedom from you?'

'Nay, nay!'

A twisted hunchback with a patch over his eye shouted, 'Nay, Tuan! You gave us more!'

The crowd clamoured.

Tuan crossed his arms again, grinning, letting the acclamation run its course.

When it had just passed its peak, he threw up his arms again, and shouted. 'Did I tell you?'

Silence fell.

'Did I tell you that you must have my permission for a night's loving?'

'Nay!' they roared back, both sexes united for a change.

'And never I will!'

They cheered.

Tuan grinned, and bowed his head in thanks, almost shyly.

'And yet!' Tuan's voice dropped down low, surly, angry. He hunched forward, one fist clenched, shaking it at the audience. 'When I came back to your halls this dark eventide, what did I find?' His voice rose, building. 'You had let these base knaves steal away all I had given you!'

The crowd roared.

Tuan flicked his left hand: Tom struck the drum with a boom that cut the crowd short.

'Nay, more!' Tuan cried. His forefinger jabbed out at the crowd, his eyes seeking hot individual faces. His voice was cold, now, and measured. 'I found that in your base cowardice you had let them steal from you even that liberty you were born with!'

The crowd murmured, frightened, unsure. The front ranks shrank back.

'Even your birthright you had let them steal from you!'

The murmuring was a wave of fright at the contempt in the silver tongue.

'You would let them take from you even bed freedom!'

He flicked his hand; the drum boomed.

'And you call yourselves men!' Tuan laughed, harsh and contemptuous.

The murmuring wave came back at him now, with sullen, protesting voices. 'We are men!' someone cried, and the crowd took it up, 'We are men! We are men! We are men!'

'Aye!' shrieked the eye-patched hunchback. 'But give us these dangling knaves who ha' robbed us, Tuan, and we shall prove we are men! We shall rend them, shall flay them! We shall leave not an ounce of flesh to cling to their bones! We shall crack even their bones and hale out the marrow!'

The crowd howled in blood-lust.

Tuan straightened and folded his arms, smiling grimly. The crowd saw him; their roar subsided to a growl, with an undertone of guilt, then broke up into sullen lumps of murmurs, and stilled.

'Is this manhood?' said Tuan, almost quietly. 'Nay!' His arm snapped out, pointing, accusing. 'I ha' seen packs of dogs could do better!'

The muttering ran through the crowd, growing angrier, louder and louder.

'Careful, there!' Rod called to Tuan. 'You'll have them tearing us apart next!'

'No fear,' said Tuan, without taking his eyes from the crowd. 'Yet let it work a while.'

The muttering rose sharply. Here and there a man shouted, angry shouts, fists waved at Tuan where he stood on the balcony rail.

Tuan flung up his arms again, shouting, 'But I say you are men!'

The crowd quieted, staring.

'There are others who slander you; but I call you men!' Then, looking from face to face: 'And who will gainsay me?'

For a moment, they were quiet; then someone called, 'None, Tuan!' and another answered, 'None!'

'None!' called the several, and 'None!' called the many, till 'None!' roared the crowd.

'Will you prove you are men?' Tuan shouted.

'Aye!' they cried, crowding closer with blood-thirst.

Tuan's hands shot out waist-high, palms down, fingers spread. The crowd stilled.

His voice was hushed, chanting. 'You were born to filth and the scabs of disease!'

'Aye,' they muttered.

'You were born to the sweat of your joints, and the ache of your back in hard labour!'

'Aye!'

'You were born to the slack, empty belly and the want of a home!'

'Aye!'

'Who filled your bellies? Who gave you a roof for your head in this very house?'

'You did!'

'Who gave you a fortress?'

'You did!'

'Who?'

'You!'

'Tell me the name!'

'Tuan Loguire!' they shrieked.

'Aye!' Tuan's hands went out again; he stood crouched, eyes afire.

'This was the misery I took from you. But who gave it to you at birth? Who is it has beaten you down, century upon century, from father to son, age upon age to the time of your remotest grandfathers?'

The crowd muttered, uncertain.

'The peasants?'

'Nay,' the crowd answered.

'Was it the soldiers?'

'Aye!' they shouted, come to life again.

'And who rules the soldiers?'

'The nobles!'

Rod winced at the hate they packed into the word.

'Aye! 'Twas the nobles!' Tuan shouted, thrusting upward with his fist, and the crowd howled.

He let pandemonium reign for a few moments, then threw up his arms again.

Then his hands dropped down to belt-level again; he fell into the crouch.

'Who!' he demanded, and the drum throbbed behind him. 'Who! Who alone of all the high-born took your part? Who gave you food when you cried for it, heard your petitions? Who sent judges among you, to give you justice instead of a nobleman's whim?'

His fist thrust upward with his whole body behind it. 'The Queen!'

'The Queen!' they echoed him.

'She shut her ears to the noblemen, that she might hear your cries!'

'Aye!'

'She hath shed tears for you!'

'Aye!'

'Yet,' cried the hunchback, 'she cast you out, our Tuan Loguire!'

Tuan smiled sourly. 'Did she? Or did she send me among you!' He threw up his arms, and they roared like an avalanche.

'It is the Queen who has given you your birthright again!'

'Aye!'

'Are you men?' Tuan shouted.

'We are!'

'Will you fight?'

'We will fight! We will fight!'

'Will you fight the noblemen?'

'Aye!'

'Will you fight for your Queen?'

'Aye!'

'Will you fight the noblemen for Catharine your Queen?'

'Aye! Ayeayeaye*aye!*'

Then the noise of the crowd covered all. The people leaped and shouted; men caught women and swung them about.

'Have you weapons?' Tuan shouted.

'Aye!' A thousand daggers leaped upward, gleaming.

'Catch up your packs, fill them with journeybread! Burst out of this house, through the south gate of the city! The Queen will give you food, give you tents! So run you all to the South, south along the great highway to Breden Plain, there to wait for the noblemen!

'Go do it!' he shouted. 'Go now! For the Queen!'

'*For the Queen!*'

Tuan flipped his hand; the drum boomed loud and fast. 'Hunting call!' Tuan snapped in an aside to Rod.

Rod flourished the trumpet to his lips and began the quick, bubbling notes.

'Go!' Tuan roared.

The people broke, to their rooms, to the armoury. In ten minutes time they had caught up packs, staffs, and knives.

'It is done!' Tuan leaped down off the rail to the balcony floor. 'They'll ha' run down to Breden Plain in two days!' He grinned, slapping Big Tom's shoulders. 'We ha' done it, Tom!'

Tom roared his laughter and threw his arms about Tuan in a bear-hug.

'Whew!' Tuan gasped as Tom dropped him. He turned to Rod. 'Do you, friend Gallowglass, tell the Queen, and see that the word of it goes out to her soldiers. Tell her to send meat, tents, and ale, and right quickly. And do you hurl these lackeys'—his thumb jerked at the Mocker and his lieutenants—'deep into the Queen's dungeon. Farewell!' And he was bounding and leaping down the stairs.

'Hey, wait a minute!' Rod shouted, running to the rail. 'Where do you think you're going?'

'To Breden Plain!' Tuan shouted, stopping to look back up. 'I must guard my people, or they'll strip the countryside worse than any plague of locusts could do, and kill themselves off in a fight o'er the spoils. Do you tell Catharine of my'—he paused; a shadow crossed his face—'loyalty.'

Then he was gone, leading the mob that boiled out the great front doors of the house, running before them in a wild, madcap dance.

Rod and Tom exchanged one glance, then turned and ran for the stairs to the roof.

They watched from the rooftop as the chanting mob poured out the south gate. Somehow, by means of the chant, Tuan had got them moving in good order, almost marching.

'Do you think he needs any help?' Rod murmured.

Tom threw back his head and guffawed. 'Him, master? Nay, nay! Rather, help those who come up against him, with that army at his back!'

'But only one man, Tom! To lead two thousand misfits!'

'Canst doubt it, master, when thou hast seen his power? Or didst thou not see?'

'Oh, I saw.' Rod nodded, light-headed. 'There's more witchcraft in this land than I thought, Big Tom. Yes, I saw.'

'Waken the Queen, and beg of her that she join us here in her audience chamber!' Brom snapped at a hastily-wakened lady-in-waiting. 'Go!'

He slammed the door and turned to the fireplace, where Rod sat with a bleary-eyed Toby, rudely awakened after only an hour of sleep; the nightly party in the Witches' Tower had run a little late tonight. He held a steaming mug in his hand and a throb in his head.

'Assuredly,' he muttered thickly, 'we wish to aid the Queen in any manner we may; but what aid would we be in a battle?'

'Leave that to me.' Rod smiled. 'I'll find something for you to do. You just get the Queen's Witches down to Breden Plain by . . . uh . . .'

'Three days hence.' Brom smiled. 'We march at dawn, and will be three days in our journey.'

Toby nodded, hazily. 'We shall be there, my masters. And now, with your leave . . .'

He started to rise, gasped, and sank back in his chair, hand pressed to his head.

'Easy there, boy!' Rod grasped an elbow, steadying him. 'First hangover?'

'Oh, nay!' Toby looked up, blinking watery eyes. ' 'Tis but the first time I've been wakeful when the drunk turned to the hangover. If you'll pardon me, masters . . .'

The air slammed at their eardrums as it rushed in to fill the space where Toby had been.

'Uh . . . yes,' Rod said. He shook his head and eyed Brom. 'Teleportative, too?'

Brom frowned. 'Tele-what?'

'Uh . . .' Rod closed his eyes a moment, cursing the slip of the tongue. 'I take it he's just gone back to bed.'

'Aye.'

'He can disappear from here and reappear there?'

'Quick as thought, aye.'

Rod nodded. 'That's what I thought. Well, it oughta come in handy.'

'What wilt thou have them do, Rod Gallowglass?'

'Oh, I dunno.' Rod waved his mug airily. 'Conjure up feathers inside the Southern knights' armour, maybe. Or something like that, good for a joke. They'll just die laughing.'

'Thou knowest not what thou'lt be having them do, yet thou wouldst bring them?'

'Yeah, I'm beginning to think a little witchcraft can come in handy at times.'

'Aye.' Brom smiled covertly. 'She hath saved your life twice over, hath she not?'

Rod swung about. 'She? Who? She who, huh? What're you talking about?'

'Why, Gwendylon!' Brom's smile absorbed mischief.

'Oh, yes! Uh . . . you know of her?' Rod raised a cautious eyebrow; then he smiled, relaxing. 'No, of course you'd know of her. I forget; she's on pretty good terms with the elves.'

'Aye, I know of her.' Brom's eyebrows pinched together. 'Nay, but tell me,' he said, almost anxiously, 'didst thou love her?'

'Love her?' Rod stared. 'What the hell business is that of yours?'

Brom waved a hand impatiently. ' 'Tis of concern to me; let it pass at that. Dost thou love her?'

'I won't let it pass at that!' Rod drew himself up with a look of offended honour.

'I am Prince of the Elves!' Brom snapped. 'Might I not have concern for the most powerful witch in all Gramarye?'

Rod stared, appalled. 'The most . . . *what?*'

Brom smiled sourly. 'Thou didst not know? Aye, Rod Gallowglass. 'Tis a most puissant wench thou hast grappled with. Therefore, do you tell me: dost thou love her?'

'Well, uh, I, uh . . . I don't know!' Rod sat, cradling his head in his hands. 'I mean, uh, this is all so sudden, I, uh . . .'

'Nay, nay!' Brom growled impatiently. 'Surely thou must know if thou lovest!'

'Well, I mean, uh . . . well, no, I don't know! I mean, that's a subject that it's a little hard to be objective about, isn't it?'

'Thou dost not know?' Thunderclouds gathered in Brom's face.

'No, damn it, I don't!'

'Why, thou fool of a puking babe, thou mock of a man! Dost thou not know thine own heart?'

'Well, uh, there's the aortic ventricle, and, uh . . .'

'Then how am I to know if thou lovest her?' Brom thundered.

'How the hell should *I* know?' Rod shouted. 'Ask my horse!'

A quivering page thrust his head in, then came quivering into the room. 'My lords, her Majesty the Queen!'

Brom and Rod swung about, bowed.

Catharine entered in a dressing gown of the royal purple, her loosened hair a pale, disordered cloud around her head. She looked very tired, and scarcely wakened.

'Well, milords,' she snapped, seating herself by the fire, 'what great news is it makes you waken me at so slight an hour?'

Rod inclined his head toward the page. The boy paled, bowed, and left.

'The House of Clovis is up, into arms, and away,' Rod informed her.

She stared, lips parting.

'They have boiled out of the south gate, and this very night run south toward Breden Plain.'

Catharine's eyes closed; she sank back in her chair with a sigh. 'May Heaven be praised!'

'And Tuan Loguire,' Rod murmured.

Her eyes opened, staring. 'Aye. And Tuan Loguire,' she said reluctantly.

Rod turned away, running his hand over the mantel. 'They must be sent food and drink, so that they will not strip the countryside as they pass. And a courier must ride ahead to tell soldiers to let them pass.'

'Aye,' she said grudgingly, 'surely.'

Her eyes wandered to the fire. 'And yet it is strange, that they who have ever raised their voices in clamour against me, now should fight for me,' she murmured.

Rod looked at her, his smile tight and ironic.

'Tuan . . .' she murmured.

Brom cleared his throat and stumped forward, hands locked behind his back. 'And this very night,' he growled, 'have I spoken with the King of the Elves; all his legions are ours.'

She was her old self again, smiling sourly. 'Legions of elves, Brom O'Berin?'

'Oh, don't underestimate them.' Rod rubbed the back of his head, remembering a clout on the skull and a prisoned werewolf. 'And to top it off, we've got your own personal coven of witches—'

'And the most powerful witch in all Gramarye,' Brom interjected.

'Uh, yes, and her,' Rod agreed, with a shish-kebab glance at Brom. 'All ready and eager to serve the only ruler in history who has protected witches.'

Catharine's eyes had slowly widened as she listened; now her eyes took on a distant look, and wandered to the fire. 'We will win,' she murmured. 'We will win!'

'Well, uh, with all due respect to your Majesty, uh, it might be a trifle more correct to say we stand an even chance.'

Breden Plain was a delta, open to the south but closed on the north by the meeting of two rivers. A dense thicket of trees ran along each river, bordering the field. The field itself was tall grass and lavender.

Not that they could see much of it, Rod thought as he squatted by a campfire. A thick, chill mist covered the field; at least Rod, who had seen something of civilized smog, would have called it a mist; but Tuan, chafing his hands across the fire from Rod, shook his head and muttered, 'A most dense and unclement fog, Master Gallowglass! 'Twill weigh heavily on the spirit of the troops!'

Rod cocked an eyebrow at him and listened to the sounds of revelry drifting over the field from the beggars' pickets. The witches were at it, too; the usual party had started at noon today, out of respect for the weather.

His shoulders shrugged with a snort of laughter. 'Well, don't let it worry you, Tuan. The precog – uh, witches, say it'll be a beautiful, sunny day, tomorrow.'

'And St George be praised, we will not have to fight until then!' Tuan drew his cloak about him shivering.

The latest word from Brom's miniature spies – whom Rod had immediately dubbed the Hobgoblin Associated Reconnaissance Korps – was that the Southern troops were just half a day away. Catharine had arrived with Brom and her army the preceding evening, and the beggars had been resting a full day already. They were, in fact, so primed and ready that Tuan was having a little trouble holding them in check; they were all for marching south and attacking the noblemen on the run.

'Still,' said Rod, tugging at his lip, 'I don't see why we should wait for morning to do the fighting. We could ambush them tonight, when they're drawing up their troops.'

'Attack at night!' Tuan gasped, horrified.

Rod shrugged. 'Sure, why not? They'll be tired from a day's march, and won't know where we are. We'd stand a much better chance of winning.'

'Aye, and you would stand a better chance of killing a man if you kicked at his head while he was down!'

Rod sighed and forbore saying that he had once done exactly that, when the man was one of five excellently trained, seasoned killers who'd ambushed him. As a matter of fact, he'd fought dirtier than that with a lot less justification; but this didn't seem quite the time for telling it.

He did say, 'I thought the point in fighting was to win.'

'Aye,' Tuan agreed, staring out into the fog toward the south end of the meadow, 'but not by such foul means. Who would be loyal to a Queen who maintained her power thus?'

And that, Rod admitted, was the kernel of it. Prestige was everything on this world; and honour was the cornerstone of prestige.

'Well,' he sighed, 'you're the doctor.'

Tuan frowned at him. 'Doctor? I have no skill in healing.'

'No, but you're an excellent practical psychologist. So I'll follow your lead when it comes to handling people.'

Tuan smiled sadly, shaking his head. 'Friend Rod, I have no skill at ruling.'

Rod allowed himself a sceptical look. 'Well, maybe not, but you're one hell of a leader.'

'Ho!' a voice bellowed.

Rod turned and grinned at the huge shape that loomed in the fog. 'Everyone happy over there?'

Big Tom shouldered his way out of the mist, grinning. 'Most happy, master. They've ne'er in their lives drunk such wine, or so much of it.'

'Hmmm.' Rod tugged at his lip. 'Better roll the wine away in a little while. We don't want them drunk so soon before battle.'

But, 'Nay,' Tuan corrected, almost automatically, Rod noticed. 'Let them drink their fill; 'twill put them abed sooner. Then rouse them early in the morning and give each a tankard or two – then they'll fight like the very demons.'

Well, Rod had to allow that was true. They weren't asking precision from the beggars, just wanted them to get out and beat up the enemy.

The night was pricked with the pinholes of watch-fires, softened by the lifting mist.

More dots of light sprang up to the south, where the noblemen and councillors were bringing up their army.

In the northern meadow, there was bawdy laughter and shouting, and the din of music, where the beggars were in the last stages of gleeful compliance with the order to get drunk as fast as possible.

On the hillside across the river there was a stern, disapproving silence, and the gentle glow of lamps within silken tents, where Catharine and her army of regulars went sober to bed.

But in the largest tent, Catharine's, things were anything but quiet.

'Nay, nay, and again I say nay!' she cried, angrily pacing the floor.

She swung about, clapping her hands sharply. 'I shall have no more of your arguments! Have done, have done; for I *will* ride tomorrow at the head of my armies! I shall brook no further objection!'

Rod and Brom exchanged glances.

Tuan's face was beetroot-red with anger, frustration, and worry.

'Begone,' snapped Catharine, and turned her back.

Reluctantly, the three men bowed, and filed out of the tent.

'What she will, she will,' Brom growled. 'We three must guard her, then, and leave the plan of the battle to Sir Maris.'

'That's one sure road to defeat,' Rod growled. 'His way of running a battle is as outdated as the phalanx.'

Brom sighed and rubbed his eyes. 'But as I have said, I will die by her. Yet mayhap we shall live, for I have a slight plan.'

He stumped away into the darkness before they could question him, from which Rod inferred that his 'plan' was limited to buoying up Rod's and Tuan's spirits by insinuating that there was yet hope.

'We shall die in her defence,' Tuan whispered, drawn and pale. 'Yet when we are gone, she will die too, and for that I am loath.' He spread his hands helplessly. 'But what can I do?'

'Well. . .' Rod pursed his lips, and looked back over his shoulder at the lighted tent. 'I know one way to make sure she won't ride tomorrow . . .'

'Tell it, then!' Tuan's face lit with frantic eagerness.

'Make sure she won't be able to sit down in the morning.'

Tuan stared. A slow flush crept into his face, then drained away, leaving him pale and trembling. 'What . . . dost . . . thou mean?' His voice was choked and threatening. He lifted a clenched, trembling fist.

Rod looked at him, frowned. 'Why, spank her. Smack her so hard she'll have to stand till next Sunday. How else would you do it?'

Tuan's fist slowly dropped; the colour came back to his face in a blush. 'Oh,' he said, and turned away. 'I' truth,' he said, ' 'Twould be well done.'

'It's that, or let her die.'

Tuan nodded, life coming back to him. He turned to the Queen's tent, paused a minute, then squared his shoulders. 'That shall I do, then. Pardon me, friend Gallowglass, for my anger; for a moment I had thought you meant . . . something else.'

He took a deep breath and stepped off briskly toward the tent.

He paused at the entrance, nodded at the guards, squared his shoulders again, and marched in.

Rod smiled, amused. 'And I thought I had a dirty mind!'

He chuckled, shaking his head, and turned toward the witches' campfires, reflecting that Tuan's years in the House of Clovis had taught him a lot about life.

Gwendylon materialized out of the darkness (literally). She smiled shyly. 'What amuses my lord?'

Rod grinned, caught her by the waist, and swung her up for a kiss, a warm kiss, and lasting.

'My lord!' she said, blushing prettily, patting her hair back into place.

The night breeze wafted a sudden slapping sound to them,

accompanied by squeals and cries.

The guards at the tent jerked bolt upright, then swung toward the tent. One put up a hand to swing aside the cloth of the doorway; but the second caught the hand and cried, 'Does your Majesty require aid?'

'Stay out!' squealed an agonized voice. 'On pain of your life, do not enter!'

The sentries exchanged puzzled looks, then shrugged and turned back to their posts, albeit with some nervous looks over their shoulders.

The squeals became muffled, then turned into sobs. The slapping sounds ceased.

Then all was still.

Rod looked down at Gwen. 'What are you grinning about?'

She looked up at him out of the corner of her eyes. 'I ha' told you, my lord, that I can hear all thoughts but yours.'

'Oh?'

'Aye. And there are most goodly thoughts in that tent at this moment.'

The lights in the tent went out.

Gwendylon giggled and turned away. 'Come, my lord. 'Twould be most improper to listen further. Come. Thou must be early abed this night.'


'Waken, Rod Gallowglass!'

Something jarred his shoulder.

Rod growled and levered his eyes open. 'What the hell do you think—'

He stopped as he saw the look on Brom's face.

'Aye,' Brom growled. 'Now robe thyself and come with me.'

'I don't sleep naked on battle nights,' Rod growled, and rose very carefully, so as not to disturb Gwendylon.

His face softened for a moment as he looked down at her. He touched his lips to her cheek. She stirred, murmured in her sleep, and smiled.

Then he rose, his face hardening.

Brom was already striding away through the chill predawn mist, beckoning curtly.

'All right, what's happened?' Rod growled as he caught up with Brom.

'Nay, be still!' Brom snapped, and was silent till they had climbed the hillside far above the tents.

Then he swung on Rod and snapped, 'Now tell me! Dost thou love her?'

Rod's face emptied.

Then he said, softly, 'You woke me just to ask that?'

'It is of some importance to me,' Brom snapped. 'Dost thou love her!'

Rod folded his arms, leaning back on one hip. 'Just what the hell business is it of yours? What right have you to know my soul?'

Brom looked away, his face working; and when he spoke, the words seemed almost dragged out of him.

'She is my daughter, Rod Gallowglass.'

He glanced up at Rod's stunned face, and a sardonic gleam came into his eye. 'Aye. Thou scarce can credit it, canst thou?'

He turned away, looking out over the valley. His voice softened with memory and musing.

'She was naught but a servant-wench in the King's halls, Rod Gallowglass – yet I loved her. She was small, scarce half the height of another woman, yet still a head taller than I. And mortal, much too mortal.

'And she was beautiful, ah, so beautiful! And, strange though it may seem, highly desired by the men of the court. And yet' — Brom's voice took on a tone of wonder and awe — 'yet she loved me. She alone, of all women living, elf or mortal, saw me not as dwarf, elf or Prince — but only as a man.

'And desired me . . .

'And loved me . . .'

He broke off, shaking his head in wonder.

He sighed. 'I loved her, Rod Gallowglass, I loved her only, and begat a child within her.'

His face darkened. He locked his hands behind his back and scowled at the ground. 'When she proved by child, and her time grew apace, and she would soon be so swollen that all would know, and would shame her with cruel jests, though we were wed, I sent her away to the wild wood, to my people. And there, midwived by elves and leprechauns, she birthed a beautiful, laughing, part-elven child.'

His eyes misted over. He lifted his head, staring through Rod. 'She died. When her daughter was aged of two years, she died of a chill. And we buried her there, 'neath a tree in the forest. And yearly I come there . . .'

His eyes focused on Rod again. 'But I had, still, the child.'

He turned away, restless. 'Yet what should I do? Raise her near me, and have her know her father for a gnarled thing, and the butt of bad jests? Raise her to shame of me?

'She was raised in the woods, therefore, knowing her mother's grave and the elves, but never her father.'

Rod started to protest, but Brom waved him silent. 'Be still! 'Twas better so!'

He turned slowly, murder in his eyes. 'As 'tis still. And if ever she learns of it from thee, Rod Gallowglass, I'll hale out thy tongue by its roots, and lop off thy ears.'

Stone-faced, Rod studied him, and found nothing to say.

'And therefore, now tell me!' Brom slammed his fists against his hips and lifted his chin. 'For know this: half-mortal am I, and may therefore be slain; and it may be that this day I shall die.'

His voice lowered. 'So tell me, tell a poor, anxious father, an thou wilt: dost thou love my child?'

'Yes,' Rod said, low. Then, 'So it was no accident that I met her on my ride south?'

Brom smiled, sourly. 'Nay, of course not. Couldst thou ever have thought that it was?'

The east was reddening, embarrassed with dawn, and the mist lifting as Rod rode into the beggars' camp to waken them.

But Tuan was there before him, going from pallet to pallet, shaking the beggars awake. A soldier was with him, placing a mug of hot mulled wine by each pallet.

Tuan looked up, saw Rod, and came up to him with arms outstretched and a grin a yard wide.

He clapped Rod on the shoulder, gripped his hand in a crushing shake. There was a deep, almost intoxicated quiet content in his eyes.

'My thanks, friend Rod,' he said simply. 'Dost thou wish my life? Thou mayst have it! Such is the debt that I owe.'

Rod smiled slyly. 'So you made doubly sure, did you? Well, all the better.'

Tuan seemed to have things well in hand in the beggars' camp, so Rod turned Fess's steps toward the witches' lines.

All was in good order there; the baskets with ropes and harnesses stood ready; and the morning brew was passing from hand to hand. It was a potent beverage, something like concentrated tea with a touch of brandy, and served much the same purpose: a stimulant, to bring the witch powers to their peak.

Elves were underfoot everywhere about the camp, distributing good luck tokens and preventive-magic charms to all who would take them. Witches or no witches, the little folk argued, it never hurt to be sure. The charms could do no harm, and they might . . .

There was nothing for Rod to do there, either, so he rode in search of Gwendylon.

He found her seated in the midst of a knot of witches, old ones, as Gramarye witches went; they must have been into their twenties.

Gwendylon seemed to be explaining something to them with great earnestness, marking diagrams in the dust with a pointed stick. They were hanging on her words as though every syllable might mean life or death.

It didn't look like a good time to interrupt.

Rod turned and rode through a maze of scurrying forms, cooking smells, clamour of voices and discordant bugle calls, out past the pickets into Breden Plain.

The first rays of sunlight slanted through the meadow now, burning away the last tatters of mist. The long grass was moist and chill with the dew, the sky clear and blue.

And the glitter of spear-points flashed from the south verge of the field. Sun gleamed off burnished armour. The wind blew him the metallic din, the horse-cries, and the mutter of a war-camp awaking. The councillors, too, were awake early.

Hooves approaching; Rod turned to see a page pelting across the meadows toward him.

'How now, my lad?' Rod called, grinning and waving for appearances.

'Thou must come to the Queen, Master Gallowglass,' the page gasped, out of breath, as he clutched at Rod's stirrup. 'My Lord O'Berin and the Lords Loguire are there already before you. 'Tis a council of war!'

The council of war was quickly over, no more than a summary of existent plans, and a brief prayer, plus the news that Catharine wouldn't ride after all. Rod had noticed that Catharine had stood through the meeting.

Then they were up and away, each to his station: Sir Maris to the centre, old Duke Loguire to the right flank, and Rod to the left flank. Brom would stay high on the hillside with Catharine and Gwendylon, to direct the whole battle, an innovation Rod had recommended, and which Brom had accepted without reservation:

the little man was a mighty fighter, but his legs weren't long enough to hold his seat in a joust.

Tom, offered the option of fighting with the beggars or staying by Rod, had chosen the latter option, probably because he wanted to be in the thick of the battle.

Tuan, of course, would stay with his beggars.

As Tuan swung into the saddle, Catharine stopped him with a hand on his knee. Rod saw her tie a veil of silk about Tuan's upper arm.

Then her hands lifted to him, pleading. Tuan caught them and pressed them to his mouth, bowed to kiss her lips, then wheeled his horse away, rode perhaps ten yards forward, then wheeled again.

They stood frozen a moment, the young Queen and the white knight. Then Tuan reared his horse, pivoted, and galloped after his ragtag-and-patchwork troops.

Rod smiled covertly.

'The time to feel smug is not yet, Rod,' Fess reminded him.

Rod made a face. 'Who do you think you are, Pinocchio's Cricket?'

He turned back for one last look at Gwendylon, standing near the Queen's tent; then he rode for the left flank.

He was the only horseman who rode without armour.

It was full, fourteenth-century plate armour, on both sides of the field; but the Southern armour was massed together in a solid, glaring wall, while Catharine's knights were spaced out, twenty yards apart, over the length of the enemy line.

*Yes, there are a few holes*, Rod thought. And the single line of foot soldiers behind the Queen's knights didn't compare too favourably with the packed masses that backed the rebel lords. No, it was not a sight to inspire confidence.

But the beggars weren't in sight. Nor, for that matter, were the witches. Or the elves.

The rebels were in for some very unpleasant surprises.

At the southern end of the field, a bugle called.

The rebel knights couched their lances.

The Queen's knights followed suit.

There was a long, straining, pause; then the horses plunged forward.

Horses' hooves muttered and rose to the roar of an avalanche as the two metal lines fell toward each other.

And as they fell, the North's line drew in upon itself till the knights rode shoulder to shoulder in the centre.

A cheer went up from the rebel line as they saw easy victory coming; it would be easy for the rebel flanks to sweep around the Northern line and trap the Queen's forces.

The Queen's knights met the centre of the rebel line with a grinding crash. Knights were unhorsed and blood spurted, but the centre of the line held.

And with a victorious roar the rebels swung about to outflank the North . . .

The yell broke into wild screams as the ground fell away beneath their mounts.

Knights and horses floundered in a six-foot trench.

The elves had done a good night's work.

The footmen came running up to their masters' rescue; but now the beggars broke howling from the trees at the sides of the field, with knife and sword and bludgeon, and fell on the footmen with extreme good will.

Still, they were vastly outnumbered.

But now the aerial arm got into the action. Teams of four levitating, fuzz-cheeked warlocks supported a swinging basket beneath them; and in each basket was a telekinetic witch. The warlocks fired arrows into the scrimmage at random, their hands freed by the leather harness at their waists; and pebbles flew out of the baskets, guided by the witches, to strike with more than enough impact to stun. Arrows speared up at them out of the Southern ranks; but the witches deflected them, and sometimes even managed to turn them back on their owners.

The simple, orderly battle deteriorated into hand-to-hand chaos.

But the Southern knights were still overly busy. The Code dictated that only a knight could fight another knight – a foot soldier could be killed just for trying it, and Heaven help him if he tried and won!

So Catharine's knights worked their way outward from the centre along the rebel lines, a large percentage of them dying on the way. But the percentage of rebels was greater, for Catharine, like her father before her, had seen fit to give her knights a little extra in the way of training.

Toby, the young warlock, suddenly appeared in the air just above Rod. 'Master Gallowglass! The Duke Loguire is sorely pressed; you must come to him!'

He disappeared as abruptly as he had come. It might not have been the greatest form of military communication, but it was better than the rebels had.

Rod dispatched his current preoccupation with a parry and a thrust between breastplate and helmet and backed Fess out of the mêlée.

He ran around the lines to the other end of the line, where a spindly, armoured-clad form with a glowing sword had just finished cutting its way through the troops to Loguire. One of the councillors was trying to save the day by eliminating the leadership. The sword had a strange, radiant quality. Rod didn't know what it was, but it was something mighty potent disguised as a sword.

Rod sailed into the ruckus, bulldozing his way through grappling pairs of beggars and soldiers, slipping in blood and loose heads.

Loguire saw the blow coming and threw up his shield to ward it off. The councillor's sword sheared through it silently, but missed Loguire. The old Duke yelled in pain as the heat was conducted through shield and armour to his skin and momentarily dropped his guard.

The councillor swung the sword up for the final blow.

Fess slammed full tilt into the councillor's horse. The animal went down and the councillor went flying with a scream of terror, sword flinging wide from his grasp.

Soldiers scurried back to be clear when the magic sword fell.

Rod, without the slightest tremor of conscience, wheeled about and trampled the councillor under Fess's iron hooves. The man gave a bubbling scream, choked off; and the scream rang on in Rod's mind.

Now his conscience began to clamour; but he locked it away till the battle was done.

He whirled about toward the sword, hearing the soldiers gasp 'Witchcraft!'

'No, just magic,' Rod shouted as he swung down, caught the sword, and remounted. 'That's not so strange, is it?'

He threw the sword to Loguire hilt-first; the old nobleman caught it and saluted him, and Rod broke out of the lines again.

The battle clamoured about him, steel on steel and bone and gristle, no quarter asked. The locked armies lay in the middle of the field like some great, pulsing, obscene amoeba.

Overhead the esper-witches turned and wheeled home, no longer able to tell friend from foe.

Rod charged back and forth through the battle-lines – Fess ploughing his way easily through mere mortal flesh – guarding the three generals and as many knights as he could, directing the clearing of the wounded when he could, adding the weight of his arm to break deadlocks.

The beggars seemed to have the soldiers hopelessly outclassed; this was their kind of fighting. Many of them were killed, but seldom without having first accounted for six or more of the enemy, with wooden staves, rusty swords, keen knives, and total disrespect for age and/or rank.

Rod thought of Karl Marx and winced.

Big Tom had long since gotten lost in the battle. Rod hoped he was all right.

Then at the back of the rebel line, Big Tom rose up roaring 'To me! To me!'

A thousand beggars rallied to him and began to chop their way through the Southern ranks.

The idea spread; beggar groups sprang up all along the line, and began to press the amoeba of war in on itself.

Big Tom was hewing his way through to a very definite goal.

Rod frowned and stood up in his stirrups, trying to plot Big Tom's course.

There, in the centre of the battle, twenty frantic scarecrows laboured furiously to construct some sort of machine: a spidery tripod topped by a wasp-waisted contraption with alien curves. It was the councillors, with their last hope.

Rod rapped with his heels, and Fess leaped – but the robot had responded a touch slow. With a sense of dread, Rod realized that the strain of battle was beginning to tell on Fess.

The horse bounded over the heads of the army and ploughed to the force of councillors, just as Tom broke through from the other side, with only a fraction of his beggar troops.

A long, lurking moment of silence filled the little circle as the councillors saw their executioners.

Then the councillors howled, drawing back into a tight circle about the machine, the ferocity of despair in their eyes, their glowing swords leaping out.

Tom's boys circled out around the councillors and closed in.

The councillors' swords were deadly; but they had to hit to be effective, and the beggars were good at hitting and getting clear.

A lot of beggars dropped, cut in half; but a lot more lived. They outnumbered the councillors four to one. They whittled away at the ranks.

The councillors screamed, chopping, and died.

In the centre of the circle, Rod could make out one lonely figure still working frantically at the machine – Durer.

Then, suddenly, there were only five councillors left.

Durer spun away from the machine with a shriek of despair and lugged something out of his wallet-pouch.

A laser-pistol.

Rod dropped down to Fess's far side, the bulk of the horse between him and the councillors, knowing that only a head shot could hurt the robot, and snapped open a hidden panel in his horse's side. In it was his last-ditch defence: the latest-issue DDT laser pistol.

He fumbled the weapon out, hearing the screams of the beggars as their legs were sheared off at the knee, and shot around under Fess's neck.

His shot creased Durer's leg. The scarecrow-man clasped his knee and fell, howling.

Tom bellowed.

The beggars stepped in. Oaken staves whirled, knocking the remaining councillors off their feet.

The staves rose high, poised a moment, and fell with a sickening, moist crunch.

Big Tom bellowed victorious laughter and scooped up a fallen councillor's sword.

Durer rolled back up to one knee and fired.

The red pencil of light caught Tom in the shoulder. He roared, spinning, and fell.

Half-crawling, half-leaping, Durer went for him, struggling to get a clear shot.

Rod snapped a shot at him, and missed.

Durer howled and dived behind a fallen body.

Rod slammed his heels into Fess. 'Quick! Before he can recover to shoot!'

The horse leaped; the laser beam caught it in the belly – a hollow steel belly, no harm.

But the robot's legs stiffened, its head lolled forward, even while it was in the air.

Rod sprang free as Fess landed, crumpled, rolled.

Rod rolled too, came up to see Durer, risen to one knee, level the pistol at him.

Tom's huge body smashed into him.

Durer caromed away, pistol flying wide from his hand.

The same had happened to Rod's. He cast about him, frantically searching.

Tom rolled, came to his feet, lurched after Durer, catching up a fallen councillor's sword . . . and tripped over a body.

Quick as an eel, Durer was up, catching Tom's fallen sword, chopping down . . .

Rod dived.

His shoulder caught Durer in the belly, whipped the little man around; the sword landed harmlessly in the earth.

Durer leaned on the sword, kept his feet, and swung the sword up, turning to Rod.

Rod rolled to his knees, saw the sword coming . . .

Tom bellowed, slammed into Rod, striking him out of the sword's path.

The glowing sword fell, shearing off Tom's shoulder and a third of his rib cage.

Rod screamed as he rolled to his feet and swung around. His arm locked around Durer's throat, his knee came up into the small of the back. Something snapped.

Durer screamed and went limp, screaming still, the sword falling from his fingers.

Rod threw him down.

Still screaming, the scarecrow groped for the sword.

Rod dropped to his knee and chopped down.

The calloused edge of his hand smashed larynx and vertebrae.

Durer gurgled, convulsed, and lay still.

Rod stood, gasping, and turned, to see Tom's shoulder pumping blood in great gouts, the big man's face contorted in a silent grimace.

Rod was down again, groping frantically in the welter of blood and spare bodies.

He came up with the laser pistol and swung back to Tom.

The remaining beggars lurched forward, too slow; before they could reach him, Rod pulled the trigger and, holding it down, sliced off another half-inch along Tom's wound. Tom screamed.

Then they were on Rod, mauling and clubbing.

'Nay!' Tom rasped, a sickening parody of his former bellow. 'Fools, let him be! Do y'not see! He stopped the blood!'

He sank back as the grasping hands hesitated, then loosened. Rod limped back to him, bruised on face and body, rubbing the worst of them – his scarcely-healed shoulder.

He sank to one knee by the gasping hulk of a man, face still wrenched with pain. The stink of cauterized flesh filled his head.

Tom forced his eyes open a fraction and tried to grin. ' 'Twas . . . well meant . . . master. Two minutes ago, it . . . might ha' saved me.'

Rod jerked off his cloak, balled it up, thrust it under Tom's head. 'Lie back and rest,' he growled through a tight throat. 'You're a healthy hunk, you'll make it. You haven't lost all that much blood.'

'Nay,' Tom panted, 'too much . . . lost. And the . . . body's shock . . .'

His face twisted with a spasm of pain. Rod turned away to Fess, slapped the reset switch and fumbled in one of the horse's hidden pockets for an ampoule.

He limped back to Tom, slapped the ampoule against the burned flesh.

Tom relaxed with a huge sigh as the anaesthetic took hold. 'My thanks, master,' he murmured weakly. 'That hast given me, at least, painless death.'

'Don't talk that way.' Rod's face was frozen. 'There's many a roll in the hay for you yet.'

'Nay, master.' Tom shook his head, closing his eyes. 'My time is nigh.'

'You're not going to die. You'll leave me in your debt if you do. I won't have it.'

'A pox on what thou wilt or wilt not!' Tom spat, with a touch of life again. 'I am not thine to command or deny now, lordling. He who now hath me in thrall is far more puissant than thou, and will one day command thee also.'

He sagged back on the pillow, heaving gasps of air.

Rod knelt silent by his side.

Tom's remaining hand groped over his belly to catch Rod's forearm. 'Aye, thou'rt now in my debt, though 'twas not of my choice.'

'Not your choice?' Rod scowled. 'What are you talking about? You saved my life!'

'Aye, and thereby lost my own. But I would never ha' done so with a clear head.'

'Clear head?'

'Aye. In battle, one sees and one does whatever comes first to mind. 'Twas thee, or living my life longer to serve the House of Clovis; and in the heat of the battle I chose thee, in my folly!'

He was silent a moment, breathing hoarsely; then his hands tightened again. 'Yet while I die, thou wilt live in my debt!

And what thou canst not pay to me, thou must pay to my people.'

Rod tried to draw his hand back. 'No!'

'Aye!' Tom's eyes flew wide, glaring, angry. ' 'Tis the payment I demand! Thy life for mine, thy life spent here on Gramarye, to work for the good of my people!'

'I'm not my own master . . .'

'Nay, thou art.' Tom sank back, weary. 'Thou art, and if thou knowest it not, thou'rt true fool.'

'The price is too high, Tom. My death in battle, yes, gladly. But living here, all my days, I cannot. I too serve a dream . . .'

' 'Twas my choice, also,' Tom sighed, 'the dream or the man. Nay, then, choose what thou wilt.'

'I'm under a geas . . .'

'Then my geas also is on thee, freeing thee from the other. Thou must serve me and mine now . . .'

The dying face darkened. 'I had thought I knew what was best for them . . . but now, as all darkens about me . . .'

He heaved up suddenly, body wracked with a spasm, coughing blood. Rod threw his arms about the big man, holding him up.

The spasm passed. Tom clutched weakly at Rod's arm, gasping. 'Nay, then . . . thy mind is . . . clearer . . . thou must decide . . .'

'Be still,' Rod pleaded, trying to lower him again. 'Don't waste what little life is left—'

'Nay!' Tom clutched at him. 'Let me speak! Espers . . . Tribunal . . . they'll make it . . . work . . . We . . . fight them . . . here . . . in the . . .'

'Be still,' Rod pleaded. 'Save your breath, I know what you're saying.'

Tom craned his neck to look up at him. 'You . . .'

Rod nodded. 'Yes. You told me the last little bit I needed, just now. Now lie down.'

Tom sagged in his arms. Rod lowered him gently, letting his head rest in the blood-soaked cape.

Tom lay panting. 'Tell me . . . I must know . . . if you know . . .'

'Yes, I know,' Rod murmured. 'The DDT will win out. You can only fight it back here. And you fight each other as well.'

'Aye.' Tom nodded, a barely perceptible movement. 'Thou . . . must decide . . . now . . . and . . . master . . .'

He mumbled, too soft to hear, and laboured for another breath, eyes opening, anxious.

Rod bent forward, putting his ear to Tom's lips.

'Don't die for . . . a dream . . .'

Rod frowned. 'I don't understand.'

He waited, then said, 'What do you mean, Tom?'

There was no answer.

Rod straightened slowly, looking down at the vacant eyes, the loose mouth.

He touched the base of the throat, the jugular.

He let his fingertips rest there long minutes, then slowly reached up to close the man's eyes.

He stood, slowly, and turned away, his eyes not seeing.

Then, slowly, his eyes focused. He looked around at the staring, pathetic beggars, their eyes fixed on the huge body.

A slight, slender shape stepped hesitantly into the ring. 'M-master Gallowglass?'

Rod turned, saw, and stepped forward as the beggars began to move in, to kneel by Tom's body.

Rod moved away from them, head hanging heavily.

He raised his eyes. 'What is it, Toby?'

'Milord . . .' Toby's face was strangely tragic in its confusion as he looked at the group of beggars, disturbed without knowing why. 'Milord, they . . . They cry for quarter, milord. Shall we give it them?'

'Quarter? Oh, yes. They want to surrender.' Rod nodded, closing his eyes.

He turned and looked at the group of beggars. 'Oh, I don't know. What does Brom say?''

'My lord O'Berin says, aye, grant it them, but the Queen says nay. The Lords Loguire are with Brom.'

'And still the Queen says nay.' Rod nodded, bitterness tightening his mouth. 'And they want me to break the deadlock, is that it?'

'Aye, milord.'

The circle of beggars parted a little. Rod saw Tom's waxen, still face.

He turned back to Toby. 'Hell, yes. Give 'em quarter.'

The sun had sunk behind the hills, leaving the sky a pale rose, darkening to the east.

The twelve Great Lords stood, bound in chains, before Catharine.

Near her sat Loguire and Tuan, Brom and Sir Maris.

Rod stood a little distance away, leaning back against Fess, arms folded, chin sunk on his breast.

The old Duke Loguire's head was also bowed, deep misery in his eyes, for his son Anselm stood a pace in advance of the rest of the lords, directly before the Queen.

Catharine held her head high, eyes shining with triumph and pride, face flushed with the joy of her power.

Rod looked at her and felt a twist of disgust in his belly; her arrogance had returned with her victory.

At a sign from Brom O'Berin, two heralds blew a flourish. The trumpets whirled away from their lips, and a third herald stepped forward, loosening a scroll.

'Be it known to all by these presents, that on this day the miscreant vassal, Anselm, son of Loguire, did rise in most vicious rebellion against Catharine, Queen of Gramarye, and is threfore liable to the judgement of the Crown, even unto death, for the crime of high treason!'

He rolled the scroll and slapped it to his side. 'Who speaks in defence of Anselm, chief of the rebels?'

There was a silence.

Then old Loguire rose.

He bowed gravely to Catharine. She returned his courtesy with a glare, astonished and angry.

'Naught can be said in defence of a rebel,' Loguire rumbled. 'Yet for a man who, in the haste of hot blood, rises to avenge what he may consider to be insults to his father and house, much may be said; for, though his actions were rash and, aye, even treacherous, still he was moved by honour, and filial piety. Moreover, having seen the outcome of rash action, and being under the tutelage of his duke and his father, might well again realize his true loyalties and duties to his sovereign.'

Catharine smiled; her voice was syrup and honey. 'You would then, milord, have me enlarge this man, upon whose head must be laid the deaths of some several thousand, once again to your protection and discipline; to you who have, as this day has proved, failed once already in these duties?'

Loguire winced.

'Nay, good milord!' she snapped, face paling, lips drawing thin. 'Thou hast fostered rebels against me before, and now seek to do it again!'

Loguire's face hardened.

Tuan half-bolted from his chair, flushed with anger.

She turned to him with a haughty, imperious look. 'Has milord of the beggars aught to say?'

Tuan fought for calm, grinding his teeth. He straightened and bowed gravely. 'My Queen, father and son have this day battled valiantly for you. Will you not, therefore, grant us the life of our son and our brother?'

Catharine's face paled further, eyes narrowing.

'I thank my father and brother,' said Anselm, in a clear, level voice.

'Be still!' Catharine fairly shrieked, turning on him. 'Treacherous, villainous, thrice-hated dog!'

Rage came into the Loguires' eyes; still they held themselves silent.

Catharine sat back in her chair, gasping, clasping the arms tight, that her hands might not tremble. 'Thou wilt speak when I ask thee, traitor,' she snapped. 'Till then, hold thy peace!'

'I will not hold my peace! Thou canst not hurt me more; I will have my say! Thou, vile Queen, hast determined I shall die, and nothing will sway thee! Why, then, slay me!' he shouted. 'The penalty for treason is death! I had known as much before I rebelled; slay me and be done with it!'

Catharine sat back, relaxing a trifle. 'He is sentenced by his own mouth,' she said. 'It is the law of the land a rebel shall die.'

'The law of the land is the Queen,' rumbled Brom. 'If she says a traitor shall live he shall live.'

She spun to him, staring in horror. 'Wilt thou, too, betray me? Will not one of my generals stand beside me this day?'

'Oh, be done with it!' Rod stormed, looming up over the throne. 'No, not one of your generals will support you now, and it seems to me that might give you some slight hint you're in the wrong. But oh, no, not the Queen! Why hold a trial? You've already decided he'll die!' He turned away and spat. 'Come on, get this farce of a trial over with,' he growled.

'Thou too?' she gasped. 'Wilt thou also defend a traitor, one who hath caused death to three thousand . . .'

'*You* have caused the death of three thousand,' Rod bellowed. 'A noble man of low birth lies dead in that field, his right side torn away, the birds pecking at him, and why? To defend a wilful child who sits on a throne, not worth the life of a beggar! A child who is so poor a queen she gave birth to rebellion!'

Catharine cowered back in her throne, trembling. 'Be still!' she gasped. 'Was it I who rebelled?'

'Who was it gave the nobles cause to rebel by too-hasty reforms and too-lofty manner? Cause, Catharine, cause! There is no rebellion without it; and who but the Queen has given it?'

'Be still, oh be still!' The back of her hand to her mouth, as though she would scream. 'You may not speak so to a Queen!'

Rod looked down at the cowering Queen. His face twisted with disgust.

He turned away. 'Ah, I'm sick to the belly! Let them live; there has been too much death this day already. Let them live. They'll be loyal, without their councillors to needle them. Let them live, let them all live. They're schooled now, even if you're not.'

'This cannot be true!' Catharine gasped.

'It is not!' Tuan stepped forward, his hand going to his sword. 'The Queen gave cause, aye, but she did not make the rebellion.'

Catharine's eyes leaped up to him with a look of radiant gratitude.

'Speak truth,' Tuan went on, 'and you may chastise her. But when you charge her with that which she hath not done—' he shook his head slowly '—I cannot let you speak.'

Rod ached to spit in his face.

Instead, he turned again to Catharine, who sat straight again, regaining her haughty look.

'Do not forget,' he said, 'that a queen who cannot control her own whims is a weak queen.'

She paled again, and 'Walk wary!' Tuan snapped.

Rage surged up in Rod, higher and higher as he stood rigid against it, till it broke some bond within him and drained away, leaving an icy calm and a great clarity, a clarity in which he saw what he must do and why . . . and what the consequences to himself must needs be.

Catharine was almost smiling now, smug and haughty again, seeing Rod hesitate at Tuan's threat.

'Hast more to say, sirrah?' she demanded, lifting her chin.

'Yes,' Rod said between his teeth. 'What kind of queen is it who betrays her own people?'

His hand whipped out and slapped her.

She screamed, falling back in the chair, and Tuan was on him, fist swinging square into Rod's face.

Rod ducked under the blow and grappled Tuan to him, shouting 'Fess!'

Tuan's fists slammed into his belly, trip-hammer blows; but Rod held on, seeing the other generals rushing up.

But Fess got there first.

Rod tried to forget what a nice, clean young kid Tuan was and drove his knee into Tuan's groin.

He let go and leaped to the saddle as Tuan fell, doubled with pain, rattling in his throat.

Fess spun and leaped over the heads of the ·approaching Guardsmen.

He landed and stretched into a gallop. Rod heard Catharine screaming Tuan's name and grinned savagely.

Then his grin stretched into a silent scream as pain exploded in his wounded shoulder.

Turning, he saw the nock of a crossbow bolt sticking out of his shoulder.

And, beyond the bouncing shoulder, in the midst of the circle of Guardsmen around the throne, Catharine bending over Tuan, who knelt, still curled around his pain, with a Guardsman's crossbow dropping from his hand.

They came back to a hill overlooking the field as dusk gathered, having run a long circle through wood and field and waded a mile of stream to hide their trail.

Rod slumped out of the saddle as Fess came to the edge of a grove. He limped to a large tree and sat, leaning back against the trunk, hidden from eyes in the field below by the gathering gloom.

He looked down over the glowing fires on the field, listening to the faint sounds of the victory merry-making.

He sighed and turned to the problem at hand, or more accurately, at shoulder. He opened his doublet and probed the shoulder gently, wincing with the pain that he felt even through the anaesthetic he'd applied on the run.

The barbed bolt-head seemed buried just in front of collarbone and joint; by some miracle, it had missed both bone and artery.

There was a faint puff of air, like a miniature shockwave, and he looked up to see Gwendylon bending toward him, tears welling from her eyes. 'My lord, my lord! Art badly hurt?'

Rod smiled and reached up to pull her head down to his. He held her against him for a good, long time.

'Nay, then,' she said, blushing as she drew away, 'I warrant thou'rt not so sorely wounded as I had feared.'

'Ah, lass, lass!' Rod leaned back, cradling her in his arm. 'I was lonely, on that ride.'

'I'd ha' come to you sooner, lord,' she said apologetically, 'but I must needs have waited till you'd come to rest.

'Now to that shoulder.' She took on a brisk, almost businesslike air. ' 'Twill hurt some, my lord.'

Rod ground his teeth as she stripped the blood-soaked tunic off his shoulder. 'Bandages in the saddlebag,' he gritted as she finished.

She turned to Fess, brought out the small metal box, frowned. 'What is this red cross here, my lord?'

'Just a symbol,' Rod wheezed. 'Means it's a, uh, healing kit.'

She knelt by his side again, very still.

Rod frowned, wondering what she was doing.

Then pain lanced him again, and he felt the bolt-head receding, withdrawing slowly along the channel it had cut on its way in, and, seemingly, all of its own accord.

Through a pain-blurred haze, a random thought burrowed: these witches were the answer to the surgeon's prayer.

The bolt-head eased itself past his skin, then suddenly whirled spinning through the air to smash itself against a stone.

'Thus,' she hissed, 'may I serve all who would harm thee, my lord.'

Rod shivered as he realized the extent of the power he'd been dallying with.

She reached for the bandages.

'No, no!' Rod touched her arm with his good hand. 'The powder in the silver envelope first. It'll stop the bleeding.'

'I would rather use compress of herbs,' she said dubiously. 'But as thou wilt have it, my lord.'

Rod shuddered as the sulpha bit into him.

Then the pain numbed, and she was winding the bandage.

'It seems you're always bandaging that shoulder,' Rod muttered.

'Aye, my lord. I would that thou wert more chary of it.'

Someone coughed, somewhat delicately, nearby.

Rod looked up and saw a squat silhouette lurking in the shadows.

Rod's mouth tightened. 'Well, if it isn't the Atrophied Ajax himself!'

Gwendylon laid a reproving finger gently on his lips.

Rod gave a short nod, irritated at himself; the fingers lifted away.

He beckoned with his good arm. 'Well, come on and join the

party, Brom. But be careful; the fruits of victory are sour tonight.'

Brom came forward, hands locked behind him, head bowed, and sat on a nearby root.

Rod frowned. There was something sheepish, almost furtive, in the dwarf's manner. 'What's eating you?' he growled.

Brom sighed and rested his hands on his knees. 'Thou hast caused me much heartache this day, Rod Gallowglass.'

Rod smiled, one-sided. 'Sounds more like a bellyache. I take it you weren't too pleased at the way things went?'

'Oh, nay, I was most enormously pleased! And yet –' Brom rested his chin on his clenched hands, looking sheepish again – 'I confess that at first I was somewhat wroth with thee.'

'You don't say!'

'Aye; but that was before I realized your plan.'

'Oh?' Rod raised one eyebrow. 'But you did figure out what I was up to?'

'Nay. I grow old, Rod Gallowglass . . .'

Rod snorted.

'My thanks.' Brom inclined his head. 'But 'tis truth; I grow old, and must needs be shown.'

'And what were you shown?'

'Oh, 'twas a most touching scene!' Brom smiled with a touch of sarcasm. 'At first Catharine could but cry, "My love, thou'rt hurt!" and call for doctors and herbs, till Tuan managed to rise, saying his hurt was but slight; and then she fell to weeping on his shoulder, the while crying him her lord and protector and the guard of her honour, and would not be comforted till he'd swore he would wed her!' Brom's smile softened, 'Aye, 'twas most tender to look upon.'

Rod nodded wearily, closing his eyes. 'When's the wedding?'

'As soon as they shall be thrice called in a church. Catharine would have had it right then, but Tuan cried no, that she was Queen and the flower of womanhood, and must be wed as befitted her estate.'

'A promising beginning.'

'Oh, 'twas more promising still! For Tuan then turned to the twelve lords and, quoth he, "And how shall we deal with these?" And Catharine cried, "Oh, as thou wilt, my lord, as thou wilt! But be done with them right quickly, and come away!"'

'Very auspicious,' Rod agreed. 'What did he do with them?'

'Struck off their chains, and bade them once more take up the care of their demesnes. But he required of them each a hostage, of twelve years old or less, of their blood and body and legitimate household, to dwell in the Queen's castle.'

Rod frowned, nodded. 'Should work. He gets a deterrent, and a chance to raise a new generation very loyal to the throne.' He leaned back against the rough bark, feeling totally drained. 'Glad it worked.'

'Aye.' Brom's eye glowed 'This land shall stand ever in thy debt, Rod Gallowglass. Thou hast saved our Crown, and banished the ghost of a long and full bloody civil war; and, moreover, thou hast given us a King.'

'And a Public Enemy No. 1,' Rod said bitterly.

A shadow darkened Brom's face.

Rod lifted an eye to him. 'You must admit that I'm slightly *persona non grata*.'

'Aye,' Brom growled, 'yet ever wilt thou find sanctuary in the land of the elves.'

Rod smiled weakly. 'Thanks, Brom.'

'Yet tell me!' Brom hunched forward, frowning. 'How is it thou hast come? When all looked bleak in our land, and hope had been exiled, then did you come, falling from the skies like an answer to prayer – you, who had no stake in our countryside, no manor to defend. Our cares were not yours, yet you made them so.'

He thrust his head forward, eyes burning. 'Why hast thou saved us?'

Rod's smile soured. 'For the Dream.'

Brom frowned. 'How. . . ?'

Rod looked up at the stars. He hesitated a moment, then said, 'Fess, record this.'

He turned to Brom, then to Gwendylon, lifting his good arm to point to the sky.

'Look up there. See those stars? Each one has worlds circling about it, worlds like this one, where lovers meet and men feud, and kings topple.

'But most of them are united under one rule, one government – the Decentralized Democratic Tribunal. And the voice that commands is that of the people themselves.'

'Nay!' Brom boomed. 'How can that be?'

'Because each man's voice can be heard, his opinion adding weight to those of his fellows. That's the key, communications. You can't have that kind of government here because your communications are lousy, which is strange, because you've got the potential for the best system, if you'd just use it.'

He folded his arms and leaned back. 'But they've got bad trouble up there. They're growing, you see. Every day, at least one new world joins the Tribunal. At that rate, they'll have reached the limit of their communications. After that, they'll start running downhill to dictatorship.'

'But how is this thy concern?' Brom growled.

'I work for them. I'm the salesman. I'm the boy who goes out and get new planets ready for membership . . . if they want it, which they always do, *once they're ready!*'

'And what is this readiness?' Brom smiled, fighting for tolerance.

'Communications, as I told you, but even more than that, learning. Education.'

He sighed. 'The education, we've got beaten. Took a long while, but it's beaten. Communications, though, that's another matter.

' 'Cause there's one other ingredient to freedom: a frontier. It prevents a stratified society – never mind what that is, my Lord O'Berin, King of the Elves – and a stratified society is another road to totalitarianism.

'So the Tribunal's got to keep growing. But if it grows much more, slowing communications will be its death. And I, very personally, don't want that. Because the Dream has a name, you see – Freedom. That's my Dream. And that's why Gramarye means so much to me.'

Brom scowled. 'I do not comprehend.'

Rod turned to him, smiling. 'The witches. Their power to hear thoughts. That's the communications system we need.'

He watched understanding, and a certain dread, dawn in Brom's face, then turned away.

'We need them,' he said, 'we need lots of them. Up till now, their numbers have been growing slowly. But, under Catharine's protection, they'll grow faster; and from their winning in today's battle, they'll begin to be respected, and before too long, every parent will be hoping for a witch to be born in the family. Then their numbers will soar.'

Brom scowled. 'But how is it this world alone, of all the ones you speak of, hath witches?'

'Because the men who brought life to the land, your ancestors, who dropped from the skies, selected only those persons who had at least a trace of witch power in them, to come here. They didn't know they had it, it was too little, and hidden too deeply, to be seen; but as the generations rolled and they married one another again and again, that little bit grew and grew, until at last a witch was born.'

'And when was that?' Brom smiled tolerantly.

'When the elves appeared. Also the banshees, werewolves, and other supernatural fauna. Because there's a strange substance on this planet, called witch-moss, that shapes itself to the forms a witch thinks of. If the witch thinks of an elf, the moss turns into an elf.'

Brom paled. 'Dost thou say . . .'

'Don't feel bad about it, Brom,' Rod said quickly. 'All men were once just pulsing blobs floating in the sea; it's just that in your remote ancestor's case, the process was speeded up a trifle, through the witches. And it was your first ancestor, not you; my guess is that the critter formed out of the moss is such a perfect copy, it can breed true – and even cross-breed with mortal men.'

He leaned back and sighed. 'Be proud, Brom. You and your people are the only ones who can claim to be real native citizens.'

Brom was silent a long moment; then he growled, 'Aye, then, this is our land. And what wouldst thou do with it, warlock from the skies?'

'Do?' Rod cocked an eye. 'Only what you yourself are trying to do, Brom, through the reforms you've suggested to Catharine. Equality before the law, isn't that your aim?'

'It is, aye.'

'Well, it's mine, too. And my job is to show you the least bloody road to it, which job I have just finished.'

He scowled, suddenly brooding.

Brom studied him. Gwendylon touched his head, stroking the hair, worried.

Rod looked up at her and tried to smile.

He turned to Brom. 'That's why I fought for Catharine, you see: because she protects the witches, and because she's a reformer; and so is Tuan, thank Heaven.

'And that's why the councillors and the Mocker fought against her.'

Brom scowled. 'I am old, Rod Gallowglass. Show me.'

Rod looked up at the stars again. 'Someday the Tribunal will govern all the stars you can see, and a lot more that you can't. And almost all the people who live on those worlds will be witches, because they'll have the blood of Gramarye flowing in their veins.

'How's that for a laurel wreath, Brom? "Father to a Galaxy . . ."'

'But some people won't be witches. And because they're not, they'll hate the witches, and their government, more violently than you can imagine. That kind is called a fanatic.

'And they'll go for any system of government, any, as long as it isn't democracy. And they'll fight democracy with every breath in their bodies.'

'If it is to be as you say,' growled Brom, 'these men will lose; for how could they fight so many worlds?'

'They can't,' Rod answered, 'unless they kill it before it's born.'

'But how shall they do that? For to kill the witch in the womb, they must come to the womb, here to Gramarye, and try to . . . why . . . to slay . . .'

Brom stared, horrified.

'Catharine,' Rod finished for him, nodding sourly. 'Right, Brom. The councillors and the leader cadre of the House of Clovis are somebody's great-great-fifty-times-great-grandchildren.'

'But how could that be?' Brom gasped. 'What man can visit his ancestors?'

'They can. They've got a thing called a time machine. There's one of them hidden somewhere in the House of Clovis, and another in the haunted tunnels of the Castle Loguire.

'So guard those four men in your dungeon very carefully, Brom. They might have a few surprises in store.'

'Be assured that I will!'

'And the councillors are all dead.' Rod leaned back, eyes closing. 'Which nicely wraps up the report. Send it home, Fess. Oh, and corroborative material: a description of the time machine, and descriptions of the witches' main tricks – you know, telekinesis, levitation, telepor—'

'I do know, Rod,' the robot's voice reminded him.

'Umph. Some self-effacing retainer *you* are. Well, send it home.'

The warp transmitter deep within Fess's basketball brain spat a two-second squeal at the stars.

All was silent a moment; then Gwendylon said, hesitantly, 'My lord?'

Rod lifted an eyelid and smiled. 'You shouldn't call me that. But I like it.'

She smiled, shyly. 'My lord, you ha' finished your work here . . .'

Rod's face darkened.

He turned away, glowering down at the earth.

'Where will you go now, Rod Warlock?' Brom murmured.

'Oh, cut it out!' Rod snapped.

He turned away again, sullen. 'I'm not a warlock,' he growled. 'I'm an agent from a very advanced technology, and as such have a bag of tricks like you wouldn't believe, but they're all cold iron and its breed. I haven't a witch trick to my name, and I certainly don't have the tiniest shred of witch power.'

He lifted his eyes to the stars again. 'I'm not a warlock, not the slightest bit, not so much as the meanest of your peasants. I don't belong here.'

He felt a tearing in him as he said it.

'I chose this life,' Rod growled. 'I take orders, yes, but I do it voluntarily.'

'A point,' Brom admitted, 'but a weak one. By choice or not by choice, thou'rt still enslaved.'

'Yes,' Rod admitted. 'But some must give up their freedom, so that their children may have it.'

But it didn't even sound convincing to him.

Brom gusted a sigh and slapped his thighs, standing. He gazed at Rod, his eyes weary and old.

'If thou must go, thou must go; a geas is a thing no man can deny. Go on to the stars, Rod Gallowglass, but be mindful: if ever thou seekest a haven, 'tis here.'

He turned and strode away, down the hillside.

Gwendylon sat quietly beside him, clasping his hand.

'Tell me,' she said after a little while, 'is it only one dream that takes you away from me?'

'Yes. Oh, yes.' Rod's hand tightened on hers. 'You sort of blotted out any other dreams.'

She turned, smiling tremulously, tears glittering on her lashes. 'Then may not I accompany you to the stars, good my lord?'

Rod clamped down on her hand, throat tightening. 'I wish that you could; but you'd wither and die there, like an uprooted flower. You belong here, where they need you. I belong there. It's as simple as that.'

'No.' She shook her head sadly. 'You go not for belonging, but for a geas. But, good my lord'—she turned, tears flowing now—'is not my geas as strong as your dream?'

'Look,' he said tightly, 'try to understand. A man has to have a dream. That's the difference between animals and man, a dream.

And a man who's lost his dream is something less than a man, and worthy of no woman. How could I dare claim you if I wasn't a man?

'A man has to prove his worth to himself, before he can claim a woman, and the dream is the proof. As long as he's working for it, he's got a right to her, because he's worth something. I could stay here and be very, very happy with you. But in my depths I'd know I didn't deserve you. Because I'd be a drone, a male with no purpose. How could I father children if I knew their mother was more valuable to the world than I am?'

'Then it wouldst be thou who wouldst wither and die?' she murmured.

Rod nodded.

'But the geas, my lord, if not mine alone, is not Big Tom's geas added to it, and the old Duke Loguire's enough to balance the geas of the stars?'

Rod sat rigid.

'They bade you watch over their people,' she murmured. 'And what would become of them, lord, if these fiends from tomorrow come again? As surely they will, if they hate as deep as thou sayest.'

Rod nodded, very slowly.

'And what of the Dream then, my lord?' she murmured.

Rod sat rock-still for a moment.

'Fess,' he said quietly.

'Yes, Rod?'

'Fess, send them my resignation.'

'Your *what*?'

'My resignation!' Rod snapped. 'And hurry it up!'

'But Rod, your duty . . . the honour of your house . . .'

'Oh, stuff it! The councillors might be back, Fess, even if we smash the time machines. They did it once, they can do it again. Send it!'

Fess obediently beeped at the stars.

Then, slowly, Rod's head lolled forward.

'My lord?' Gwendylon gasped.

Rod raised a hand weakly. 'I'm all right. I've done the right thing, and the one that'll make me happiest. For the first time in my life, I'm working on my own.

'And that's it. I've cut myself off. They're not backing me anymore – the house, the clan, Big Brother watching over me . . .'

'Thou hast a house here, lord,' she murmured.

'I know, I know. And in a little while this'll pass, and I'll be happier than I ever have been. But now . . .'

He looked up at her, smiled weakly. 'I'll be all right.'

'Rod,' Fess murmured.

He lifted his head. 'Yes, Fess?'

'They have replied, Rod.'

Rod tensed. 'Read it.'

'*Report accepted. Request send co-ordinates for verifying expedition.*'

Rod nodded, mouth twisting back with bitterness. 'Send 'em. Go on.'

'*Request you reconsider resignation. Accept permanent assignment planet Gramarye guard against further infiltration-subversion.*'

Rod straightened, staring. 'What?'

'They would like to make your chosen position official, Rod,' the robot replied.

'What is it, my lord?'

'They want me to stay on,' Rod answered mechanically.

He turned to her, life replacing the stunned look. 'They want me to stay on!'

'Stay on where, my lord?' she asked, catching the first traces of his enthusiasm.

'Stay on here!' he bellowed, jumping to his feet and flinging his arm wide to include the whole planet. 'Here on Gramarye! As an agent! Gwen, I'm free! And I'm home!'

He dropped to his knees, spinning to face her, hands biting into her shoulders.

'I love you!' he bellowed. 'Marry me!'

'At once and forever, my lord!' she cried, clasping his face in her hands, and the tears poured.

He grabbed for her, but she held him off with a palm over his lips. 'Nay, my lord. Only a warlock may kiss a witch.'

'All right, I'm a warlock, I'm a warlock! Just kiss me, will you?'

She did.

He locked his hands in the small of her back, grinning.

'Hey,' he said, 'is it true, what they say about farm girls?'

'Aye, my lord.' She lowered her eyes and began unbuttoning his doublet. 'You'll never be rid of me now.'

# King
# Kobold Revived

# To my readers

This isn't a new book.
But it isn't an old book, either.
Let me tell you how it happened. . . .

Back in 1970, when *King Kobold* was first published, I waited with bated breath to see what the critics thought of it – and was rather disheartened to find they weren't exactly overwhelmingly enthusiastic. That's when I decided I shouldn't pay too much attention to the critics.

Unfortunately, I couldn't ignore Lester del Rey. I had always admired his perspicacity and penetrating insight (i.e., he always agreed with my opinion about new books. Please understand that, at the time, I had never met him.). When *del Rey* said, 'It isn't a bad book, if you don't expect too much of the evening spent with it,' I knew I was in trouble. Worse, letters began arriving – and they agreed with del Rey! And though del Rey had been gentle and charitable, the fans felt no such need for restraint.

So, when the good people at Ace indicated an interest in reissuing *King Kobold*, I said, 'Not until I rewrite it!'

Please remember, I'd had twelve years to mull over the flaws of the original, and figure out how to fix them. There were some changes that I knew I definitely wanted to make, and quite a few others that I was thinking about.

So the book you hold in your hand is not the product of a publisher who tried to jazz things up to hype sales; it's the result of a mulish writer who refused to go through having fans call him nasty names again. If you bought the original *King Kobold* fourteen years ago and misplaced your copy – sorry, this ain't quite the same book you read back then. And, if you never *did* read *King Kobold* (an offence I will overlook only if you were too young to read), this ain't the plot you've been hearing about. Better, I hope, but not the same. If your favourite scenes are missing – well, sorry. Or, worse yet, your favourite character – well, I'm even sorrier; but I just don't think he really worked (not 'she' – she was a total nonentity, and I don't see how anybody could miss her – except maybe 'him'). All in all, I'm pretty satisfied with this revised version; it's still essentially the same story, but I think it's much more solid, and a much better read (all right, so I haven't cut out *all* the lousy jokes). Besides, if you *really* liked it better the other way – well, there's always the original edition. You'll have to search a little to find a copy, but if you'd rather read it, you can.

Thank you all, for pestering your bookstores for *King Kobold*, and bringing it out of hiding again. Here it is, the same story – what happened to Rod and Gwen when they'd only been married a few years, and only had one baby warlock to contend with I hope you enjoy it. I did.

Christopher Stasheff
Montclair State College
October 4, 1983

# Prologue

*Sorrowful it was, and great cause for Mourning, that so young a King should die, and that in his Bed; yet Death doth come to all, yea, the High and the lowly alike, and' tis not by our choosing, but by God's. Thus it was that King Richard was taken from us in the fourteenth year of his Reign, though he had not yet seen forty-five summers; and great lamentation passed through the land. Yet must Life endure, and the motion of it never doth cease, so that we laid him to rest with his ancestors, and turned our faces toward our new Sovereign, his daughter Catharine, first Queen of that name to Reign, though it had been scarcely twenty years since her birth.*

*'Then the Lords of this land of Gramarye sat them down in Council, and rose up to advise the young Queen of her actions, and at their head stood the Duke Loguire, time-honoured and revered, foremost of the Lords of this Land, and Uncle to the Queen. Yet she would not hearken to him, nor to any of her Lords, but set her face toward the doing of things as she saw them, and would not heed Council. And what she wished done, she set in the hands of the Dwarf Brom O'Berin, who had come to the Court as her father's Jester, but King Richard had raised him to Chancellor; and Queen Catharine ennobled him. This did affront all the Peers of the Land, that she should set a Dwarf in their midst, and he baseborn, for she would trust none among them.*

*Then did Loguire send his younger son Tuan, who long had courted Catharine ere her Father died, to beg of her that she plight him her Troth, and come with him to the Altar to become his Wife. And she called this foul treason, that he should seek the Crown under guise of her Hand, and banished him from the land, and set him adrift in a coracle, that the East wind might take him to the Wild Lands, to dwell among Monsters and Beastmen, though all of his crime was the love of her. Then was his father full wroth, and all the Lords with him; but Loguire held his hand, and so, perforce, must they all; but Tuan his son swam back to the shore, and stole within the Land again, by night, and would not be exiled.*

*Then did Catharine the Queen meet with her great Lords all, in her great Hall in Runnymede, and did say unto them, 'Lo, it seemeth thou dost take boys from the plough, who know neither Letters nor Holiness, and doth set them above thy people as priests, that they may more certainly do thy bidding; and know that such practice doth offend the Lord God, and affronteth thy Queen; wherefore, henceforth, I shall appoint thee full measure of Priests, and send them unto thee; and I will not brook nay-saying.' Then were the Lords wroth indeed, but Loguire held up his hand, and they checked. And it came to pass as the Queen had said, that the souls of her people were governed by monks that she sent out from Runnymede, though they did oftimes confirm the priests the Lords had set over their Parishes; yet some among them had grown slack and, aye, even sinful; and these the Queen's monks removed, and set others of their number up in their steads.*

*Then did the Queen summon all her Lords unto her again, and did say unto them, 'Lo, I have seen the Justice that is done on thine estates, both by thyselves and by the Judges thou dost appoint; and I have seen that the manner of Justice thou dost deliver is not all of one piece; for Habsburg in the East will hew off a man's hand for the theft of a loaf of bread, while Loguire in the South will only outlaw a man for a Murder; and I have seen that my people grow restive therefore, and are like to forsake the ways of Law in their confusion. Therefore wilt thou no longer deliver thyselves of Justice, nor set others to judge thy folk for thee; but all shall be judged by men that I shall send among thee, from my Court in Runnymede.' Then all the Lords waxed wroth indeed, and would have haled her down from her Throne; but the Duke Loguire withheld them, and turned his face away from the Queen, and withdrew to his Estates, and so did they all; but some among them began to plot Treason, and Loguire's eldest son Anselm made one of them.*

*Then, of a night, thunder did roll and fill all the World, though the skies were clear, and the Moon bright and full, and folk looked up and wondered, and did see a star fall from the Heavens, and they turned away marvelling, and praying that it might prove an Omen, heralding the healing of their Land of Gramarye, as indeed it did; for the Star fell to land, and from it stepped the High Warlock, Rod Gallowglass, tall among the sons of men, high of brow, noble of mien, with a heart of golden courage and thews of steel, merciful to all, but stern in justice, with a mind like sunlight caught in crystal, that clearly understood all the actions of all men, and his face was comely above all others.*

*He came unto the Queen, but she knew him not, and thought him only one among her soldiers; yet there was poison in the air about her, and he knew it, and did banish it; and thereupon she knew him. And she sent him to the South, to guard her Uncle, for she knew that Treason brewed, and not only toward herself. And the Warlock did as she bade him, and took with him, for a servant, the giant Tom. And they came unto Loguire secretly, under the guise of Minstrels, yet they had not been heard to sing. And there were ghosts within Loguire's castle, and the High Warlock did befriend them.*

*Then did Loguire summon all the Lords of the Realm, and they came to him at his castle in the South, that he might counsel them to withhold their power yet awhile; but being met, they brewed their Treason 'gainst him.*

And there were witches in the land, and warlocks too; and word did go from mouth to mouth, the Rumour that speaks more loudly than the heralds, that the Queen had welcomed to her keep all witchfolk who did wish her protection, and there they held wild Revels through the night, for many were the Good Folk who had sought to burn them; and folk began to murmur that the Queen herself had something of witchcraft in her.

And the High Warlock did befriend the witches, even Gwendylon, most powerful among them, and she was young, and comely, and he spoke to her of Love.

And Lord Tuan came by night unto the town of Runnymede, that he might be near unto the Queen, though she despised him, and he came unto the beggars, and sought Sanctuary amongst them; and he taught them Governance, and they made him King among them. Yet the one among them whom Lord Tuan most trusted, he who held the purse and was called 'the Mocker', bethought himself of Lord Tuan's mock crown.

Then, when all the Lords were met at Loguire's demesne in the South, and Anselm with them, they did stand against Loguire's face and refute his leadership, raising up young Anselm to the Dukedom in his father's stead; and one Durer, erstwhile Loguire's councillor, drew blade against him. Then did the High Warlock by High Magic snuff out all the lamps and torches, so that Loguire's hall lay all in darkness, for his Hall lay underground, and had no windows. And the High Warlock conjured up the ghosts that dwelt within that keep, and they did pass amongst the folk within that hall, and all were sore afeared, aye, even those great Lords that there were met; and the Warlock stole the Duke Loguire away, and brought him secretly unto the Queen at Runnymede.

Then did the Lords summon up their armies, and all did march against the Queen. But the High Warlock spake unto the Elves that dwelt within that land, and they did swear to fight beside him, and the Witches also. And the High Warlock called up young Tuan Loguire, and he marched forth with all his beggars; and thus they came to Breden Plain: a Queen, a Warlock, and a dwarf, with an army made of witches, elves, and beggars.

Then, under the Sun, the Lords charged out in bold array, but their horses sank into the Earth, for elves had mined it; and they hurled their spears and arrows 'gainst the Queen, but witches turned their shafts, and they fell back amongst the Armies of the Lords, and there did grievous harm. Then did Lord Tuan lead his beggars forth, and his father beside him, to finish what the witches had begun, and all the Field fell into mêlée. And the giant Tom rose up amidst that churning mass, and hewed *a path unto the Lords and all their Councillors, and the beggars followed, and did beat down all those men-at-arms and Councillors, and made prisoners of the Lords; but the giant Tom did, in that carnage, perish, and the Warlock mourned him, and the beggars also.*

*Then would the Queen have slain the Lords, or chained them into Servitude, but the Warlock spoke against it, and the Queen gazed upon his lowering brow, and knew fear. But Tuan Loguire stood beside her, and faced against the Warlock, and cried that all should be as the Queen had said; but the Warlock felled him with a most foul blow, and struck the Queen in remonstrance, and rode away upon his charmed steed, that no mortal mount could near; yet Lord Tuan in his agony shot forth a bolt that struck the Warlock as he fled.*

*Then did Queen Catharine cry Lord Tuan as the Staff of her strength and the Guard of her honour, and spoke to him of love, and gave him the Lords to do with as he wished. Then did Lord Tuan free them, but with their heirs as hostages, and he took their armies for the Crown. And he did take Queen Catharine unto the altar, and became our King thereby, and reigned with Catharine the Queen.*

*But the Warlock sought out the witch Gwendylon and she did draw Lord Tuan's bolt from out him, and enchanted the wound so that it did no harm; and the Warlock spoke to her of love, and brought her to the altar.*

*And the Lords went back to their demesnes, and there ruled Justly, for the King's Eye was upon them, and all was peaceful in the land of Gramarye, and contentment returned unto its folk.*

*So matters stood for two years and more, and men began to trust their Lords once more, and to look kindly upon their fellows again.*

*Then the night wind blew wailing and keening from the southern shore, and the sounds of War . . .'*

> *Chillde's Chronicles of the*
> *Reign of Tuan and Catharine*

*According to the records, the planet was colonized by a crackpot group who dressed up in armour and held tournaments for fun; they called themselves the 'Romantic Émigrés'. This kind of group acted as a selective mechanism, attracting people with latent psi powers. Put them all together on one planet and let them inbreed for a few centuries, and you get espers – which is what they've got here. Only a small percentage of the population, of course, but I have grounds for believing the rest are latents. They think they're normal, though, and call the espers 'witches' if they're female, and 'warlocks' if they're male.*

*What's worse, there's a native fungus that reacts to projective telepaths; the locals call it 'witch moss', because if the right kind of*

'witch' thinks hard at it, it turns into whatever she's thinking about.
So the ones who don't know they're witches sit around telling fairy tales
to their children, and, first thing you know, the landscape is filled with
elves and ghosts and werewolves – I'll show you my bites sometime.

In this agent's humble opinion, the place is a communications gold
mine and the answer to the prayers of our noble Decentralized Democratic
Tribunal. A democracy can't survive if its territory gets too big for the
speed of its communications system, and the last projection I heard was
that the DDT would hit critical size in about a hundred and fifty years. If
I can turn this planet into a democracy, it'll have just what the DDT needs
– instantaneous communication over any distance. All the guesswork I've
read about telepathy says it'll be instantaneous, regardless of distance,
and what I've seen on this planet bears that out.

But if the planet is vital to the success of democracy, it is equally vital
for totalitarians and anarchists to keep it away from the democrats –
and they're trying to do just that. The totalitarians are represented by
a proletarian organization called the House of Clovis, which is trying
to organize all the beggars and petty criminals, and doing a pretty good
job of it, too. The anarchists are working on the noblemen; each of the
twelve Great Lords has a councillor who is, I'm pretty sure, one of the
anarchists.

Where have they come from? Well, they might just have sneaked in
from off-planet – but I've found at least one gizmo that can't be anything
but a time machine, and I've got good reason to believe there're more.

What upsets me about the place is the uncertainty factor. Given the
local genetic make-up, and the telepathically sensitive fungus, virtually
anything could happen – which means that, if I wait long enough, it
probably will. . . .

Excerpt from Report on Beta Cassiopeiae Gamma (local name
'Gramarye'), by Rodney d'Armand, Agent for Society for Conversion
of Extraterrestrial Nascent Totalitarianisms

The heavy clinging fog lay dense, nearly opaque, over the heaving sea. The rolling, endless crash of breakers against the headlands at the harbour's mouth came muted and distant.

High above, circling unseen, a bird called plaintive sentry cries.

The dragon shouldered out of the swirling mist, its beaked, arrogant head held high.

Four more like it loomed out of the fog at its back.

Round, bright-painted shields hung on their sides.

Oars speared out from the shields, lifting in unison and falling feathered to the waves.

The dragon's single wing was tightly furled around the crossbar lashed to the tall, single mast that thrust upward out of its back.

Squat, hulking, helmeted shapes prowled silently about the mast.

The dragon had an eagle's beak, and a tall, ribbed fin for a crest. Two long, straight horns probed out from its forehead.

The surf moaned on the shore as the dragon led its mates past the headland.

The child screamed, howling for his mother, thrashing himself into a tangle with the thick fur blanket.

Then the oil lamp was there, just a rag in a dish, but warm and safe, throwing its yellow glow upward on the mother's weary, gentle face.

She gathered the quivering, sobbing little body into her arms, murmuring, 'There now, love, there. Mama's here. She won't let him hurt you.'

She held the child tightly, rubbing his back until the sobbing ceased. 'There now, Arthur, there. What was it, darling?'

The child sniffled and lifted his head from her shoulder. 'Bogeyman, Mama. Chasing me, and – he had a great big knife!'

Ethel's mouth firmed. She hugged the child and glared at the lamp-flame. 'The bogeymen are far across the sea, darling. They can't come here.'

'But Carl says . . .'

'I know, I know. Carl's mama tells him the bogeyman will get him if he's bad. But that's just a silly story, darling, to frighten silly children. You're not silly, are you?'

Arthur was silent a while; then he murmured into the folds of his mother's gown, 'Uh . . . no, Mama . . .'

'Of course you're not.' She patted his back, laid him down in the bed, and tucked the fur robe under his chin. 'That's my brave boy. We both know the bogeyman can't hurt us, don't we?'

'Yes, Mama,' the child said uncertainly.

'Sleep sweetly, darling,' the mother said, and closed the door softly behind her.

The oil lamp set the shadows dancing softly on the walls. The child lay awake awhile, watching the slow ballet of light and dark.

He sighed, rolled over on his side. His eyes were closing as they strayed to the window.

A huge misshapen face peered in, the eyes small and gleaming, the nose a glob of flesh, the mouth a gash framing great square, yellowed teeth. Shaggy brown hair splayed out from a gleaming, winged helmet.

He grinned at the child, pig eyes dancing.

'Mama! Mamamamamamamama! *Bogeyman*!'

The bogeyman snarled and broke through the stout wooden wall with three blows of a great ironbound club.

The child screamed and ran, yanking and straining at the heavy bedroom door.

The bogeyman clambered through the broken wall.

The door was flung wide; the mother stared in horror, clutching her child to her and screaming for her husband. She wheeled about and fled.

The bogeyman gave a deep, liquid chuckle, and followed.

In another cottage, a bogeyman seized a child by the ankles and swung his head against the wall. He lifted his huge club to fend off the father's sword, then whirled the club into the father's belly, swung it up to strike the father's temple. Bone splintered; blood flowed.

The mother backed away, screaming, as the beastman caught up the father's fallen sword. He turned to the mother, knocked her aside with a careless, backhand swipe of the club, and stove in the family strong-chest with one blow.

In the first cottage, the oil lamp, knocked aside in the beastman's passage, licked at the oil spilled on walls and floor.

Other cottages were already ablaze.

Women and children ran screaming, with chuckling beastmen loping after them.

The men of the village caught up harpoons and axes, rallying to defend their wives and children.

The beastmen shattered their heads with ironbound cudgels,

clove chests with great razor-edged battle axes, and passed on, leaving dismembered bodies behind them.

Then drumming hooves and a troop of cavalry burst into the village; the fires had alerted the local baron. He sat now at the head of a score of horsemen drawn up in the beastmen's path.

'Fix lances!' he roared. 'Charge!'

The beastmen chuckled.

Lances snapped down, heels kicked horsehide; the cavalry charged . . . and faltered, stumbled, halted, soldiers and horses alike staring at the beastmen for long, silent minutes.

Each beastman flicked his glance from one soldier to another, on to a third, then back to the first, holding each one's eyes for a fraction of a second.

Jaws gaped, eyes glazed all along the cavalry line. Lances slipped from nerveless fingers.

Slowly, the horses stepped forward, stumbled, and stepped again, their riders immobile, shoulders sagging, arms dangling.

The beastmen's little pig eyes glittered. Their grins widened, heads nodded in eager encouragement.

Step-stumble-step, the horses moved forward.

The beastmen shrieked victory as their clubs swung, caving in the horses' heads. Axes swung high and fell, biting deep into the riders. Blood fountained as men fell. Heads flew, bones crunched under great splay feet, as the beastmen, chuckling, waded through the butchered cavalry to break in the door of the village storehouse.

The Count of Baicci, vassal to the Duke of Loguire, lay headless in the dirt, his blood pumping out to mingle with that of his cavalry before the thirsty soil claimed it.

And the women and children of the village, huddled together on the slopes above, stared slack-jawed at their burning houses, while the dragon ships, wallowing low in the waves with the weight of their booty, swung out past the bar.

And, as the long ships passed the headland, the wind blew the villagers an echo of bellowing laughter.

The word was brought to King Tuan Loguire at his capital in Runnymede; and the King waxed wroth.

The Queen waxed into a fury.

'Nay, then!' she stormed. 'These devil's spawn, they lay waste a village with fire and sword, slay the men and dishonour the women, and bear off the children for bondsmen, belike – and what wilt thou do, thou? Assuredly, thou wilt not revenge!'

She was barely out of her teens, and the King was scarce older; but he sat straight as a staff, his face grave and calm.

'What is the count of the dead?' he demanded.

'All the men of the village, Majesty,' answered the messenger, grief and horror just beneath the skin of his face. 'A hundred and fifty. Fourteen of the women, and six babes. And twenty good horsemen, and the Count of Baicci.'

The Queen stared, horrified. 'A hundred and fifty,' she murmured, 'a hundred and fifty.'

Then, louder, 'A hundred and fifty widowed in this one night! And babes, six babes slain!'

'God have mercy on their souls.' The King bowed his head.

'Aye, pray, man, pray!' the Queen snapped. 'Whilst thy people lie broke and bleeding, thou dost pray!' She whirled on the messenger. 'And rapine?'

'None,' said the messenger, bowing his head. 'Praise the Lord, none.'

'None,' the Queen repeated, almost mechanically.

'*None*?' She spun on her husband. 'What insult is this, that they scorn our women!'

'They feared the coming of more soldiers, mayhap . . .' the messenger muttered.

The Queen gave him all the scorn she could jam into one quick glance. 'And 'twere so, they would be lesser men than our breed; and ours are, Heaven knows, slight enough.'

The messenger stiffened. The King's face turned wooden.

He leaned back slowly, gaze fixed on the messenger. 'Tell me, good fellow – how was it a whole troop of cavalry could not withstand these pirates?'

The Queen's lip curled. 'How *else* could it chance?'

The King sat immobile, waiting for the messenger's answer.

'Sorcery, Majesty.' The messenger's voice quavered. 'Black, foul sorcery. The horsemen rode doomed, for their foes cast the Evil Eye upon them.'

Silence held the room. Even the Queen was speechless, for, on this remote planet, superstition had a disquieting tendency to become fact.

The King was the first to speak. He stirred in his throne, turned to the Lord Privy Councillor.

This meant he had to look down; for, though Brom O'Berin's shoulders were as broad as the King's, he stood scarcely two feet high.

'Brom,' said the King, 'send forth five companies of the King's Foot, one to each of the great lords whose holdings border the sea.'

'But one company to each!' the Queen fairly exploded. 'Art thou so easily done, *good* mine husband? Canst thou spare but thus much of thy force?'

The King rose and turned to Sir Maris the Seneschal. 'Sir Maris, do you bring forth three companies of the King's Guard. The fourth shall bide here, for the guarding of Her Majesty Queen Catharine. Let the three companies assemble in the courtyard below within the hour, provisioned for long and hard riding.'

'My liege, I will,' said Sir Maris, bowing.

'And see that mine armour is readied.'

'Armour!' the Queen gasped. 'Nay, nay, O mine husband. What wouldst thou do?'

'Why, what I must.' The King turned to her, catching her hands between his own. 'I am King, and my people are threatened. I must ride to the wreck of this village and seek out the trail of these beastmen. Then must I build ships and follow them, if I may, to their homeland.'

'Oh, nay, good my lord!' Catharine cried, clinging to him. 'Have we not men-at-arms enough in our armies but you also must ride forth to die? Oh, my lord, nay! What would I do if thou shouldst be – if thou shouldst take hurt?'

The King held her close for one moment, then held her away, tilted her chin, and kissed her lips gently. 'Thou art Queen,' he said softly. 'The brunt of this sorrow must thou bear; such is the office of Queens. Here in the place of power must thou bide, to care for our people while I ride. Thou must hazard thine husband for the good of thy people, as I must hazard my life – for such is the office of Kings.'

He held her close for a long, timeless while, then kissed her lingeringly. He straightened, her hands clasped between his, then turned to go.

An embarrassed cough stopped him.

He turned, frowning. 'Art still in this place, Brom? I had thought . . .'

'My liege,' the dwarf interrupted, 'what thou shalt command, I shall do – but wilt thou command nothing more?'

The King's face darkened.

Brom's voice was tight with determination. 'If there is the Evil Eye in this, Majesty, 'tis matter for witches.'

The King turned away, glowering, his lips pressed thin.

'Thou hast the right of it, Brom,' he admitted grudgingly. 'Well enough, then, we must. Send to the witches in the North Tower, Brom, directing them to summon'—his face twisted with dislike—'the High Warlock.'


The High Warlock was currently leaning his back against a tree trunk with his fundament firmly founded on *terra firma*, watching the sunrise with one eye and his wife with the other. Both were eminently worth watching.

The sun was splendour itself as it rose orange-gold out of the oiled green of the pine-tops into a rose-and-blue sky; but his flame-headed wife was all that was grace and loveliness, singing lightly as she sank her hands into the tub of dishwater beside the cooking-fire in the dry warmth of their cave home.

It wasn't just the domesticity that made her lovely, of course. Her long, loose red hair seemed to float about her, framing a round face with large, sea-green, long-lashed eyes, a snub nose, a wide mouth with full, tempting lips. Her figure was spectacular under the white peasant blouse and tight bodice and long, full, bright-coloured skirt.

Of course, her figure was, at the moment, more a matter of inference than observation; but the Warlock had a good memory.

The memory was a little too good; his wife's beauty occasionally reminded him of his own – well, shall we say, plainness?

No, we should say ugliness – or, rather, homeliness; for there was something attractive about his face. He had the appeal that is common to overstuffed armchairs, old fireplaces, and potbellied stoves. Hounds and small children loved him on sight.

And by this quality he had won her (it would be, perhaps, more accurate to say that she had won him, after an extended battle with his inferiority complex); for if a beautiful woman is betrayed often enough, she will begin to value trustworthiness, warmth, and affection more than romance.

At least, she will if she is the kind of woman to whom love is the goal, and romance just the luxury; such a woman was Gwen.

Such a woman will eventually be capable of loving a man with a good heart, even though his face be a bargain assortment of inclined planes, hollows, and knobs in Expressionist juxtaposition; and such a man was Rod Gallowglass.

He had a receding hairline; a flat, sloping forehead; prominent bushy eyebrows; deep eye-sockets with a matched set of grey eyes; a blade of a nose; high, flat cheekbones; and a wide, thin-lipped mouth. The mouth kept a precarious perch on top of a square, jutting chin.

Nevertheless, she loved him, which fact was to Rod a miracle, a flagrant violation of all known laws of nature.

Not that he was about to object, of course.

He slid down onto the base of his spine, let his eyelids droop, and let the peace of the summer morning seep into him, lulling him into a doze.

Something struck his belly, knocking the wind out of him and jolting him wide awake. He jerked upright, knife in hand.

'Da-dee!' cooed the baby, looking enormously pleased with himself.

Rod stared at the kid. Little Magnus was holding tight to the bars of his playpen; he hadn't quite learned to stand by himself yet.

Rod managed a feeble grin and levered the corner of the oak playpen off his belly. 'Very good, Magnus!' He patted the baby's head. 'Good boy, good boy!'

The baby grinned, fairly hopping with delight.

The playpen rose six inches from the ground.

Rod made a frantic grab and forced it back down, hands on the lid.

Ordinarily, playpens do not have lids. But this playpen did; otherwise, the baby might have floated out.

'Yes, yes, that's a wonderful baby! Smart little fella, there! *Very* good baby – *Gwen!*'

'What dost thou wish, my lord?' Gwen came up to the mouth of the cave, drying her hands on her apron.

Then she saw the playpen.

'Oh, *Magnus!*' she mourned in that tone of hurt disappointment only mothers can master.

'No, no!' Rod said quickly. 'He's good boy, Gwen – isn't he? I've just been telling him what a good boy he is. *Good* boy, *good* baby!'

The baby stared, tiny brow wrinkling in utter confusion.

His mother had much the same look.

But her eyes widened as she realized the only way the playpen could've moved out of the cave while her back was turned. 'Oh, Rod!'

'Yeah.' Rod grinned with more than a touch of pride. 'Precocious, isn't he?'

'But – but, my lord!' Gwen shook her head, looking dazed. 'Only witches can move things other than themselves. Warlocks cannot!'

Rod pried open the playpen and took his son in his arms. 'Well, he couldn't have done it by levi – uh, flying, could he?'

'Nay, he hath not strength enough to lift the playpen along with him – that he would have to do by his own bone and sinew. But warlocks cannot . . .'

'Well, this one can.' He grinned down at the baby and chucked it under the chin. 'How about that? I've fathered a genius!'

The baby cooed and bounced out of Rod's arms.

'Whup! Come back here!' Rod jumped and snagged a fat little ankle before the baby could float off in the morning breeze.

'Oh, Magnus!' Gwen was on them in a rush, cradling the baby in her arms. 'Oh, my bold babe! Thou shalt most surely be a most puissant warlock when thou art grown!'

The baby smiled back at her. He wasn't quite sure what he'd done that was right, but he wasn't going to argue.

Rod beamed with fatherly pride as he hefted the oaken playpen back into the cave. He was amazed at his son; that playpen was *heavy*!

He got a hank of rope and started tying the pen down. 'That kid!' he said, shaking his head. 'Scarcely a year old – he can't even walk yet, and . . . Gwen, what's the age when they start levitating?'

'Levi— Oh, you mean flying, my lord!' Gwen came back into the cave, the baby straddling one hip. 'Thirteen years, or thereabouts, my lord, is the age for young warlocks to fly.'

'And this kid started at nine months.' Rod's chest swelled a trifle – his head, too. 'What age do little witches start making their broomsticks fly?'

'Eleven, my lord, or mayhap twelve.'

'Well, he's a little ahead of schedule for that, too – except that warlocks aren't supposed to make broomsticks fly at all. What a kid!' He didn't mention that Magnus was obviously a major mutation.

He patted the baby's head. The child wrapped a chubby hand around his father's finger.

Rod turned shining eyes to Gwen. 'He'll make a great agent when he's grown.'

'My lord!' Gwen's brow knit in concern. 'Thou wilt not take him from Gramarye?'

'Perish the thought!' Rod took Magnus and tossed him up in the air. 'He'll have his work cut out for him right here.'

Magnus squealed with delight and floated on up toward the roof.

Rod executed a high jump that would have done credit to a pole-vaulter and snagged his errant son. 'Besides, he may not even want to join SCENT – who knows?'

Rod was an agent of the Society for the Conversion of Extra-terrestrial Nascent Totalitarianisms, the subversive wing of the multi-planet Decentralized Democratic Tribunal, the first and only human interstellar government in history not to be based on Terra. The Senate met by electronic communications; the Executive resided on a starship which was usually to be found between planets. Nonetheless, it was the most efficient democratic government yet established.

SCENT was the organization responsible for bringing the Lost Colonies of earlier Terrestrial empires back into the fold. Rod was on permanent assignment to Gramarye, a planet that had been colonized by mystics, romantics, and escapists. The culture was medieval, the people superstitious – and a small percentage of the population had 'witch-powers'.

Consequently, the DDT in general, and SCENT in particular, were immensely interested in Gramarye; for the 'witches' and 'warlocks' were espers. Some had one set of psi powers and some had another – but all were telepaths to some degree. And, since the efficiency (and, consequently, the viability) of a democracy varies directly with the speed of its communications, and since telepathic communication was instantaneous, the DDT treasured its only colony of espers very highly.

So Rod had been assigned to guard the planet, and to carefully nudge its political system onto the road that would eventually lead to democracy and full membership in the DDT.

'Hey, Fess,' Rod called.

The great black horse grazing in the meadow outside the cave lifted its head to look at its master. Its voice sounded through a small earphone buried in Rod's mastoid bone.

'Yes, Rod?'

Rod snorted. 'What're you cropping grass for? Who ever heard of a robot burning hydrocarbons?'

'One must keep up appearances, Rod,' Fess reproved him.

'Next thing I know, you'll be keeping up with the Joneses! Listen, bolt-head – it's an occasion! The kid pulled his first telekinesis stunt today!'

'Telekinesis? I had thought that was a sex-linked female trait, Rod.'

'Well, all of a sudden it ain't.' He put the baby in the playpen and clamped the cover down before Magnus had a chance to drift out. 'How about that, Fess? This kid's gonna be a champion!'

'It will be my great pleasure to serve him,' the robot murmured, 'as I have served his forebears for five hundred years, since the days of the first d'Armand, who founded . . .'

'Uh, skip the family history, Fess.'

'But, Rod, it is a vital portion of the child's heritage; he should . . .'

'Well, save it until he learns to talk, then.'

'As you wish.' The mechanical voice somehow managed a sigh. 'In that case, it is my duty to inform you that you will shortly be receiving company, Rod.'

Rod stilled, cocking an eyebrow at his horse. 'What do you see?'

'Nothing, Rod; but I detect the sounds characteristic of bipedal locomotion of a small being conveying itself through long grass.'

'Oh.' Rod relaxed. 'An elf coming through the meadow. Well, they're always welcome.'

An eighteen-inch body burst out of the grass at the cave-mouth.

Rod grinned. 'Welcome, merry wanderer of the night.'

'Puck!' Gwen squealed. She turned to their guest. 'Assuredly, thou art most . . .'

She stopped, seeing the look on the elf's face.

Rod had sobered too. 'What's right, Puck?'

'Naught,' said the elf grimly. 'Rod Gallowglass, thou must needs come, and right quickly, to the King!'

'Oh, I must, must I? What's so urgent all of a sudden? What's all the panic about?'

'Beastmen!' The elf gasped for breath. 'They have raided the seacoast at the Duchy of Loguire!'

The Royal Guard rode south, with the King at their head.

A lone rider sat his grazing horse at the side of the road, playing a pipe with a low and mournful sound.

Tuan frowned, and said to the knight beside him, 'What ails yon fellow? Is he so bemused by his own music that he doth not see armed horsemen approaching?'

'And can he not see thy crown?' the knight responded, dutifully putting into words what his sovereign was thinking. 'I shall waken him, Majesty.' He kicked his horse's sides and cantered ahead.

'Ho, fellow! Dost thou not see His Majesty approacheth?'

The rider looked up. 'Why, so he does! Say, isn't that a handy coincidence? I was just thinking about him.'

The knight stared, then backed his horse away. 'Thou'rt the High Warlock!'

'"High"?' Rod frowned. 'Not a word of truth in it. Totally sober, good knight – haven't even *thought* about intoxicants since last Friday!'

The knight frowned, irritation overcoming awe. 'Eh, thou'rt as unmannerly as a churl! Know that the King hath created thee High Warlock!'

' 'Tis even so,' the King confirmed, drawing rein beside them. Then, rather unwillingly, 'Well met, Lord High Warlock – for this poor Isle of Gramarye doth lie in need of thine art, and thy wisdom.'

Rod inclined his head. 'I am ever obedient to my adoptive homeland's call. But why do I get a high title out of it? I'd come just as quickly without it.'

' 'Tis thy due, is it not?' Tuan's lips pressed thin. 'And it describes thy place aptly. Folk fight better when they know from whom to take orders, and to whom to give them.'

'An understatement,' Rod admitted. 'You've gotta have a clear flow chart if you want to get anything done. Very true, Your Majesty; I should've known better than to question you.'

Tuan's eyebrows lifted. 'Pleasantly said; I would not have expected it of you.'

'Oh, you should have.' Rod grinned. 'I always give respect where it's due.'

'And withhold it where 'tis not?' Tuan frowned. 'Am I, then, so rarely worthy of respect?'

Rod's grin widened. 'Only when you try to use authority you don't have – which doesn't happen very often, now that you're a king. And, of course, when you back someone who's in the wrong.'

Tuan's frown darkened. 'When have I done such?'

'Just before you got my knee in your groin. But I must admit that the Queen isn't trying to play God anymore.'

Tuan flushed, turning away from Rod.

'And, of course, you were trying to be her champion, and laying down the law.' Rod ignored the danger signals. 'Which you had no right to do – at the time. Still don't, really.'

'Have I not?' Tuan snapped, whirling to face Rod. 'I am now King!'

'Which means that you're supposed to be foremost among your peers. It doesn't make you a superior breed – and doesn't give you the right to make laws if your barons are against them.'

'You cannot truly believe that I would do so.'

'Well, no, not you,' Rod admitted. 'Catharine, however . . .'

'Rarely is the Queen not swayed by my counsel,' Tuan grated. 'What we do, we do in concert.'

'Then you both agree on marching south to fight the beastmen?'

Tuan managed to stay with the change of topic. 'We have discussed it; and, aye, we are agreed. I do not say we take joy in the prospect.'

'Well, say it,' Rod invited. 'Or are you really going to tell me you don't like being out in the field again?'

Tuan stared, taken aback. Then he grinned sheepishly. 'In truth, my heart doth lift as I gaze upon open fields and feel harness on my back. I will own, 'tis good to be out from chambers and councils.'

Rod nodded. 'That's what I expected; you're a born general. Still can't understand how you manage to be a good king, too.'

Tuan shrugged impatiently. ' 'Tis like to the order of battle, save that the "troops" one doth command are reeves and bailiffs.'

'But it does require a totally different library of knowledge.'

'That, Catharine hath,' Tuan said very honestly. 'I need only to steady her judgement, and issue her commands in such wise that they shall not arouse rebellion.'

Which was true, Rod reflected; half of the offence Catharine gave was due to the way she said things, rather than what she said. 'Well, you've just earned my respect again.'

Tuan frowned. 'For what? For kingship?'

'No, for candour. But now the burden of monarchy moves back into your field of knowledge, Majesty. What do you propose to do about these raiders?'

'Go to where they have been, expecting that they will strike again, and not far from where they struck first,' Tuan answered. 'When the bee findeth a flower filled with nectar, doth he not return to that place to find other flowers nearby?'

'Yes, and usually with more bees. I notice you brought a few stingers of your own.'

Tuan glanced back at the army behind him. 'The beastmen should be hard put to best these stout hearts.'

'From the report I had, it's not their hearts that're in danger.' Rod turned Fess, falling in alongside Tuan. The King kicked his heels into his horse's ribs, and the column began to move south again. Tuan nodded. 'Thou dost speak of the Evil Eye.'

'I doth,' Rod agreed. 'How much faith do you put in that part of the report?'

Tuan shrugged. ' 'Tis wisest to believe it true, and guard against it as best we may.' He pinned Rod with a stare. 'What charm is there against it?'

Rod shrugged. 'Beats me; I've never run into it before. Haven't the slightest idea how it works. For all I know, they might just be so ugly that you freeze in horror when you look at 'em.'

Tuan shook his head firmly. 'Nay. If the report is true, 'tis magic, not simple fear.'

'Well, "disgust" was more of what I had in mind. And, of course, the report itself might not be too accurate. Who'd it come from, anyway?'

'Mothers and grand-folk who were fleeing as they saw. And three of the footmen still live, though with grievous wounds; they have not spoken much, but what little they have said confirms the report, that 'twas the Eye that froze them.'

'Not exactly ideal spying conditions, in either case,' Rod mused, 'and not enough information to work up anything to counter it. Still, it does seem that they have to look you in the eye to freeze you; so pass the word to look at their hands, their hats, their teeth – anything but their eyes.'

'Well, 'tis better than naught,' Tuan sighed. 'But I would thou couldst find a better remedy, Lord Warlock. A soldier is hard put to avoid his enemy's eyes, in the mêlée.'

'Well, it's the best I can do, for the moment,' Rod grumped. 'I'll try to get some firsthand experience if they attack again. Then maybe I . . .'

'Nay.' Tuan drew up sharply and looked Rod in the eye. 'Thou must learn this to thy sorrow, Lord Gallowglass, as I have had to: thou must needs stand apart, with me, on high ground, to aid in the directing of the battle.'

With a sinking heart, Rod knew Tuan was right; an army did fight better when it had overall direction. 'Your Majesty is of course always right. I'll stay out of it as long as you do.'

Tuan eyed him sceptically. 'Do not think that will aid thee. I have gained in patience.'

He wasn't doing so badly in perceptiveness, either; three years ago, he would've missed the sarcasm. 'All of this assumes, however, that we have time to pick our ground before the fighting starts.'

'Ah.' Tuan turned back to the south and began riding again. 'That is thy part.'

'Oh?' Rod eyed him warily. 'Am I supposed to magically transport this whole army to the ground you choose?'

'Nay. Thou'rt to secure us warning that raiders come, far enough in advance that we may ride to the place they will attack, and be there before them.'

'Oh.' Rod's lips held the shape of the letter after it was gone. 'That's all I've got to do, huh? Mind telling me how? Am I supposed to set sentries pacing a mile offshore?'

'Aye, if thou canst derive a spell that will prevent them from sinking.'

'Oh, nothing easier! It's called "rowboats".' Rod frowned. 'Hold on, now. That almost sounds sensible.'

'Aye, it doth.' Tuan turned to him. 'A line of sentries in small craft just beyond the horizon, to watch for a mast. But how will they sound the alarm?'

'They could row.'

'The beastmen will row more quickly; there do be more of them, and they will be aided by wind. Would they not overtake thy sentry and slay him?'

'True.' Rod frowned. 'Well, how about if the sentry was a warlock? Then he could telep—uh, conjure himself ashore, and leave them an empty rowboat.'

'A likely thought.' Tuan nodded. 'But thy warlocks hear thoughts. Could not he raise the alarm more quickly if there were another of the witch-folk ashore, listening for his thoughts?'

'True. That would be quicker, and . . . *wait* a minute!' Rod struck his forehead with the heel of his hand. 'What's the matter with me? Sorry, Your Majesty; I'm slow today. Why bother putting the warlock in the boat? Why not just have him stay ashore and listen for approaching beastman thoughts?'

'Nay, certes!' Tuan squeezed his eyes shut. 'Did I truly need a High Warlock to tell me this? Where are my wits?'

There was a good chance he'd left them back at the royal castle in Runnymede, but Rod didn't think it was politic to say so. Besides, Tuan could've replied that Rod's brains currently had long red hair and a figure worth killing for.

Then the King opened his eyes, with doubt in them. 'Yet art thou certain they do think?'

'That is a distinct possibility. Maybe if I go to the western coast and shout, "*Cogito, ergo sum*", they'll all disappear.'

'Is that a mighty spell?'

'No, just wishful thinking; I'm putting Descartes before the horse.' There was a short, nasty buzzing in Rod's ear; Fess didn't think much of his sense of humour. 'Seriously, though, Your Majesty, that shouldn't be a problem. Anything alive and moving under its own power has *some* sort of neurological activity. I've got one young witch who can read an earthworm's thoughts, and they don't even *have* any.'

'But can they hear thoughts far enough away to give us time to set our battle line where they mean to land?'

'Don't worry about that one, either. I had another young lady listen to the thoughts of one of the dino—uh, "terrible lizard" giants over on the mainland, once. She wasn't herself again for three days . . .'

'Then thou hast thy sentry-force made.'

Rod frowned. 'Yeah, but I just had another nasty thought. How come none of the witches ever heard beastman thoughts before?'

That stopped Tuan, too. He frowned and thought it over for a few seconds. Then he looked up with a bright smile. 'Mayhap because they were not there?'

Rod sat still for a moment. Then he sighed and shrugged. 'Why not? On Gramarye, anyway.' There was a local variety of fungus that was very sensitive. Not that its feelings could be hurt or anything; but if a projective telepath thought at it hard enough, it would turn into whatever the projective was thinking about. Yes, it was very possible that the beastmen hadn't been there before. All it would take was an old granny, one who didn't know her own strength, telling horror stories to amuse the children . . .

He didn't think he wanted to meet that granny. 'Say, uh, Your Majesty . . . what happens when our sentries *do* find them?'

'Why, then we ride against them with steel and fire,' Tuan said grimly.

'Yes, but – Gramarye is a moderately big island. What if they strike someplace where our army isn't?'

'As they have indeed done.' Tuan nodded. 'Well, I have commanded each of the seacoast lords to muster a force of worthy size, and keep it ever ready. E'en so, the best of barons' forces can only hold them till my armies come; if it can do more, I have more than beastmen to worry me.'

It was a good point; a baron who could defeat a party of raiders was bound to think of taking on the royal army. 'But it could take a while for your army to get there – say, a few days.'

'Indeed.' Tuan turned to him, frowning. 'Canst thou not discover a spell to move mine army to the battlefield ere the beastmen come to it, High Warlock?'

' 'Fraid that's beyond even my powers.' Rod had a brief, dizzying vision of Tuan's knights and men-at-arms clustered onto huge antigravity plates, skimming over the countryside; but he manfully thrust it from him, remembering that technology comes in whole chunks, not just bits and pieces. If he taught them how to make antigrav plates, they'd figure out very quickly how to make automatic cannon and television chains – and how much chance would democracy have in a land whose king had the technology for totalitarianism, and whose people still thought loyalty was the supreme virtue? Right – about as much as a camel in a glacier. 'But you don't need magic to do it – just a complete force of horsemen.'

'Why, how is that?' Tuan looked worried; to him, 'horseman' meant 'knight'.

'Well, I know it sounds like heresy – but you don't have to have just the captains mounted. Common soldiers can learn to ride too.'

Tuan stared, scandalized.

'Not on full-scale war-horses, of course,' Rod said quickly. 'The rankers can ride ponies. They can go just as fast as the destriers on the long haul, where they keep it down to a canter, if they don't wear much armour. And you can keep the whole force right there, in Runnymede, since it's pretty close to being the centre of the island. Then, when my witch-sentries send word, you can just yell, "Horse and hattock! Ho, and away!" and they can be mounted up and gone in ten minutes. Then, if you keep alternating canter and trot and give each soldier a spare mount, they can be anywhere within Gramarye in two days.'

'And the beastmen could land within one.' Tuan scowled, chewing at his lip. 'E'en so, the idea has merit. A thousand men would suffice; certes these beastmen will not bring more. Then I could keep five such forces, placed so that any one of them could be at the seacoast in either of two provinces in less than a day.' He turned a beaming smile on Rod. 'I' truth, 'twill succeed! And if the footmen must ride, what of it? When they come to the field, they can dismount and fight as they always have!'

And, Rod realized with a sinking heart, the King would have discovered an excellent means of enforcing his will on the barons, whether they liked him or not. But what else could he do? Let bogeymen gobble up the taxpayers? 'I think it'll work, Your Majesty.'

'But a name! It must have a name!' Tuan's eyes glowed with excitement. 'They will fight better, these soldiers, if their force doth bear a name that may ring down the ages!'

Tuan was good at that – these little bits of nonsense that ultimately made a great deal of difference: honour, chivalry, things like that. Men fought harder for these intangibles tthan for cold cash, frequently. If Tuan said his men would fight harder if their regiment had a famous name, Rod wasn't going to argue. 'How about the Flying Legion?'

'Will this truly be an army, my lord?' Gwen stood beside him on the hillside, looking out over the little valley that had sprouted tents and horses.

'Only the vanguard,' Rod assured her. 'Tuan's still got his standing army of five thousand – and most of them are standing because they don't know how to ride. Here we're gathering a thousand good riders from all over the island, ones who already have some experience in war. Tuan's going to recruit another five thousand pedestrians for the main force, though.'

Far below, a lieutenant shouted, and his squadron leaped into a gallop, charging down on another hapless unit with wicker swords.

Gwen watched and shuddered. 'They are not terribly deft, my lord.'

'I said they were experienced, not talented.' Rod turned away and strolled along the flank of the hill, holding her hand. 'Give 'em a little training and practice, though, and you'll never see a better troop of cavalry – I hope. Who's this?' He stopped, scowling at a brown-robed figure with a neat round bald spot who sat cross-legged about fifty yards ahead of them, a huge book open in his lap. He had an inkhorn in his left hand, and a quill in his right.

'A good friar, it would seem,' Gwen answered. 'Why art thou concerned, mine husband?'

'Because I don't remember ordering any.' Rod strode up to the monk. 'Good morning, Father.'

'Good morning to thee, goodman.' The priest turned a sunny, beaming countenance up to Rod. Then his jaw dropped and he scrambled to his feet. 'Why, 'tis the High Warlock!'

'Careful, there; don't spill your ink.' Rod reached out a hand to steady the inkhorn. 'It's nice to be recognized, but I'm not worth jumping up for – not unless you're in uniform, anyway.'

'Nay; I know thee for one of the greatest men ever to walk the soil of Gramarye.' Everything about the monk was round – his stomach, his face, his eyes. 'Who else could have rescued Catharine the Queen from the peasant mob who sought her life and the band of barons who sought her throne?'

'Well, her husband did a pretty good job; he was in on that, too, if you remember. In fact, that battle had a lot to do with his *becoming* her husband.'

'Yet, not so much as thyself,' the monk chirped.

Rod cleared his throat; the friar was coming unpleasantly close to the truth. Time for a change of subject. 'What're you doing here, Father?'

'Oh!' The monk looked down at his book. 'Only amusing an idle moment, Lord Warlock. A wise man will ever be doing; so, when there is naught else afoot, I fill the time with the writing of a chronicle of the events that occur whiles I live.'

'A Chronicle? Hey! History in the making!' Rod couldn't resist. 'Am I in it?'

'Indeed, Lord Warlock! What Historie of Gramarye could be complete without full accounting of thee?'

'I had rather account for him at home,' Gwen said dourly, coming up beside Rod. 'Yet I do not think thou didst quite catch mine husband's meaning, good Father.'

'Yeah? Oh! Yeah!' Rod looked up, and cleared his throat. 'That's right, Father. When I said, 'What're you doing here?' I meant, here with the *army*, not just at this particular moment. What's your business?'

'Why, the saving of souls,' answered the priest in round-eyed innocence. 'Our good Abbot hath appointed me chaplain to the King's Foot – but His Majesty did say to me that he had a surfeit of chaplains, and sent me to thee.'

'Oh, he did, did he?' Rod could see Tuan doing it, too. The young King loved all his subjects, but the average medieval monk tended to be continually exhorting, which could try even Tuan's patience. 'I can see I'll have to have a word with His Majesty. Well, at least he sent me an amateur historian.'

'Milord!' A squire came galloping up and reined in near Rod. 'Lord O'Berin's greetings, milord. He doth send to tell thee the folk from Loguire have come!'

'Oh, really!' Rod grabbed the priest's hand and gave it a quick shake, quill-pen and all. 'Well, it was a real pleasure to meet you, Father, but I've gotta run now . . . Uh, what was your name again?'

'Brother Chillde, I am called. But do not stay to speak with a foolish friar, Lord Warlock, when matters of state await thee.'

'Well, military matters, really. Gwen, come listen.' He caught her hand as he turned away, pacing down the hill. 'These're a few of the survivors from the beastman attack.'

'Ah! I will listen, and gladly.' A frown puckered Gwen's brow. 'I misdoubt me that there may have been something of magic about these beastmen.'

'If there is, and they mention it, you'll find it.' As they paced over the valley floor, Rod remembered his son. 'Where's Magnus?'

Gwen's eyes flashed, and her chin came up. 'Rather, ask why I have come here.'

'I did wonder, but not too much – I was just glad to have you. Why? What did Brom do?'

'He came to our home and told me that I could no longer sit idly by, playing at housewifery. As though 'twere play!'

Rod winced, remembering how the dust flew at home – he couldn't even be a *little* messy anymore – and the rotten (for her) mood Gwen was in by the end of each day. 'Well, he can say that – he's got a troop of elves to keep his quarters tidy. But he is right, dear – we need your talents in the field just now. The cave'll have to gather dust.'

Gwen shuddered. 'Well, mayhap; 'tis after all folks' lives we speak of, and we will not be home for some time, I think. Magnus, however, cannot wait; I must needs spend at least the half of my waking time with him, unless 'tis a day of battle.'

'Yeah, I know.' Rod winced at a twinge of conscience. 'But where *is* the boy?'

'Brom found a half-dozen elfin beldams to watch over him. I took him to their grotto, and I could see they knew something of children, so I left him with them.'

'Not altogether willingly, I gather.'

'Oh, I will never feel easy with my babe out of my sight!' Gwen cried. 'Yet it must be, and I know I am foolish to worry.'

'Yes, you probably are.' Rod squeezed her hand. 'I'm sure any nursemaids Brom finds for you will be very capable.' Gwen couldn't know just *how* sure – Brom had made Rod swear never to tell her that Brom was her father. He felt a little shy about it, being a dwarf. But he did care for Magnus like one of his own – which the child was, of course. No, any baby-sitter Brom picked would be extremely reliable. 'Even if they are elves.'

'*Especially* if they are elves.' Gwen skewered him with a glance.

'Who else could keep thy son bound, Warlock?'

'Only another warlock, or witch.' Rod grinned into her glare. 'Witch.'

'Well, that is true.' Her gaze softened. 'Though the most of them are too young; and the ones who are aged enough are sour old spinsters and hermits, living midst the wild mountains. No, I do trust Brom's elves.'

'After all, who else would he get?' Rod spread his hands. 'He *is* the King of the Elves, after all.'

'Aye.' Gwen smiled, amused. 'If Their Majesties only knew their Privy Councillor's true nature – and office!'

'They'd kick him out of the household and try to sign a treaty with him. No, I think the current setup's much more efficient.'

'Aye, with Brom ever at Tuan's elbow.'

'And Magnus with the elves, and you with me.' Rod sighed. 'My son, the changeling! Besides, you can keep checking on him, can't you?'

'Oh, I do at all odd moments, I assure you!' Gwen stopped and stood stock-still, her eyes losing focus. Then she relaxed and began walking again, with a nod. 'Aye, he is well.'

'Helps to be a mind reader, doesn't it?' Rod grinned. 'Which is, of course, one of the reasons why I like having you along on this trip.' He stopped at Brom's tent, nodded to the sentries, and lifted the tent flap. 'After you, dear.'

Inside, two servants stood near a long table, holding trays laden with food. A handful of peasants sat at the board, chewing huge mouthfuls and washing them down with ale. A dusty man sat at one end of the table, eating with equal gusto but in smaller bites – a knight out of armour, to judge by his clothes. At the other end of the table sat a man less than three feet high, with shoulders almost as wide as he was tall, arms and legs thicker with muscle than Rod's, and a huge head with shaggy black hair and beard. His head snapped up as Rod entered; then he leaped down and strode over to the witch-pair, booming, 'Well, 'tis time thou hast come! Here these good folk are near to surfeited with food and ale – and I sent for thee as soon as they did arrive.'

'Well, we're never easy to find.' Rod stepped over to the table. 'Who is this gentleman?'

'Sir Reginald De La Place, vassal to the Duke Loguire,' Brom explained. 'He it is hath brought these peasants to us. Sir Reginald, this titled lout is Rod Gallowglass, Lord High Warlock.'

'Lord Warlock!' The knight jumped to his feet. 'I am honoured!'

'Glad to hear it,' Rod said, inclining his head. 'My wife, the Lady Gwendylon.'

The knight bowed, and Gwen beamed.

'And these poor folk be victims.' Brom clapped the nearest peasant on the shoulder. 'But a week agone, they had houses. What hast thou now, goodman?'

The peasant gulped his current mouthful. 'Eh, we ha' cottages again, milord – or the half of us do, then. 'Tis not so long, to build a wall of wattle.'

'And daub,' Brom amplified. 'I ha' seen our folk at work, Lord Warlock. They build a house in but a day. Yet there were a score of cottages in their village.'

Rod noticed the apprehensive way the peasants were eyeing him. 'It's all just a rumour, folks. I'm not really a warlock – just a bad scholar who's learned a few tricks.'

If anything, their apprehension deepened.

'Well, I tried,' Rod sighed. 'Tell me, goodman – what did these beastmen look like?'

'Ah, terrible things they was, milord! Tall as houses, and horned like the moon!'

'And hairy,' the woman across from him added. 'All over covered with hair, they was.'

'But not on their faces,' another woman chimed in. 'Beardless, they was.'

'And they rode on a dragon,' the man said firmly. 'A dragon it was – and it swam away with 'em on its back!'

'Nay, 'tweren't a beast!' the first woman scoffed. 'What would ye know about it? Ye was half dead with a cracked skull when they sailed away!' She turned to Rod. 'We were blessed, milord. Seven of our menfolk dead, but he wasn't one of 'em.'

'All of 'em hurted, though,' the woman next to her muttered, 'and six bairns killed.'

Rod's face darkened. 'What were the dragons he was talking about, then?'

'Ships, milord! Only their ship! But the front of it was carved into a dragon's head, and the stern was carved into a tail!'

'Dragon ships? Were they long and narrow?'

'The very thing!' the woman chortled. 'Hast seen 'em, then, milord?'

'Only in a history book – and those raiders did have beards. And not much body hair . . .'

'And horns, milord?'

'Helmets,' Rod explained, 'helmets with horns on 'em. At least, that's what people *thought* they wore – but they didn't really. Not in battle.'

'Can't be the same ones, then,' the man said firmly.

'No,' Rod agreed, 'I don't think the originals could have sailed this far from their home ports. They were mighty sailors, but they did need water.'

'Then, why would these beastmen be dressed like to them, my lord?' Gwen wondered.

'Because somebody's been telling 'em stories. Speaking of which, do grannies tell folk tales about horned raiders in dragon ships?'

The peasants shook their heads, wide-eyed.

'Well, it was a chance,' Rod sighed. 'But if the grannies haven't been telling tales, who has?'

'Didn't look like just a ship in the moonlight, with them devils yellin' and swingin' their clubs,' the big peasant muttered, fingering his bandage gently.

'Of course not,' Rod agreed. 'That's why they carved it that way – to scare the . . .' His eyes lost focus. 'Wait a minute! Of course! That's why whoever told 'em about dragon ships and horned helmets . . . did tell 'em! To help them scare poor people like you! After all, if it worked for the Vikings . . .'

'What are "vikings," milord?' one of the women asked timidly.

'The horned raiders I was telling you about.'

'Could they freeze people with a look?'

Rod shook his head. 'No, of course not – though I suppose they wanted to. You mean these gorillas *could*?'

'Froze us near to stone,' the man growled. 'One of 'em looked me in the eye, and all of a sudden, *his* eyes seemed to pierce right through to the back of me head. I tried to move, but I couldn't.'

'Ye was scared,' the second woman scoffed, 'frighted stiff, like a babe with a snake.'

The man's face reddened. 'Was ye there on the green with us, woman? Did ye look into their eyes? Oh, aye, those glittering eyes frighted me – but I've been frighted in battle afore, when our young Lord Anselm fought the Queen . . . and . . . um . . .' He eyed Brom furtively.

'And his younger brother, who is now our King,' Brom growled. 'None will fault thee for that, goodman. What choice hadst thou? When thy lord summons thee to fight, thou must needs fight. Yet, in that battle, did fear freeze thee?'

'Nay, good my lord!' The peasant shook his head. 'I swung my pike the harder for it. Yet when that grisly monster's eyes pierced my brain, I sought to strike in wild anger – but mine arm would not answer! I strained, I tugged at it with all my will, but it would not . . .' He broke off with a shudder. 'Lord in Heaven save me! May I never live through such a moment again! To not be able to budge, yet see that huge club swinging down at me . . .' He squeezed his eyes shut and turned away, shaking his head.

'Softly, now.' Rod clapped him on the shoulder. 'You did bravely, goodman. You did all that a man could do.'

' 'Twas the Evil Eye,' the man muttered. ' 'Twas witchcraft.'

Rod turned to Gwen with a questioning gaze.

'There are tales of it,' she answered slowly, 'of witches and warlocks who could freeze folk with a glance. Yet I never have met one with such a power.'

'And you know most of the witches in Gramarye.' Rod turned back to the peasant, nodding. 'So our enemy is something new, in more ways than one. But if it had not been for yourself, goodman, we would not have known that. My deepest thanks.'

'At your lordship's service.' The big peasant recovered a bit, and managed to smile up at Rod. ' 'Twas . . . 'twas real, then?'

'Is the lump on your head real?' Rod retorted. 'Then, the club that made it certainly was, and so was the beastman who swung it. As to the Evil Eye – well, when a battle-tried veteran freezes, it couldn't very well be anything else.' *Not on this world, anyway*, he thought.

'Thank ye, milord.' The peasant smiled up at him.

'Don't worry. I would've frozen too.' Rod clapped him on the shoulder again, and turned to Gwen. 'Know any counterspells?'

Her lips parted to answer as she spread her hands – and suddenly there was a baby in them, kicking and crowing, 'Mama! Found you, Mama! Found you!'

Gwen stared, startled. Then a delighted grin curved her lips, and she hugged the child close to her. 'Hast thou indeed, thou naughty babe! Come, didst thou seek thy mother through thy mind only?'

'Huh!' The baby nodded, very pleased with himself.

'A telepathic tracker?' Rod was staring too. 'My son's a headhunter?'

' 'Tis a head I'll be having, though not his,' Brom growled. 'Whose charge was this bairn? Hobgoblin!'

Something small popped through the door and scurried over to Brom. 'Pardon, King of Shadows!' It was a miniature man about a foot and a half tall, heavy in the shoulders and deep in the voice.

'The elf-wives' powers have waned; the babe lost interest in their games, and their spells could not hold him.'

'Then, they must con new charms, and hold him by delight alone,' Brom growled. 'Though 'tis true, I know of nothing that could hold this bairn when he doth not wish it.'

'Naughty babe!' Gwen reproved Magnus. He gurgled happily in reply.

'At least, when he had 'scaped I found him in the half of a minute,' the elf pointed out.

' 'Tis true, and any who would wish to harm him would fare ill against thee,' Brom admitted. 'Yet bid them hold him better, Robin.'

'Naughty child!' Gwen scolded. 'Though glad I am to see thee, yet must thou know thy mother hath a task which must be done. I cannot be with thee now, my sweet, much though I wish to. Come, hie thee back to thy nurse, and bide until I call thee.'

'Uh-uh!' The baby scowled, and shook his head.

'Magnus,' Gwen began, in a tone that implied a nuclear bomb (or, at least, a tactical warhead) was about to explode.

But Brom interrupted. 'Nay then, manikin! Hast never heard of bogeymen?'

The child stared down at him in blue-eyed wonder.

'Never?' Brom rumbled. 'Ah, woefully dost thou neglect this child's education if he ha' not yet heard of childhood's horror!'

'Well, that's kinda the point,' Rod answered, nettled. 'I see absolutely no point in scaring kids half to death and giving them dread of perfectly ordinary things. If I tell him to be good, he's got to do it simply because he believes in me.'

'Pray he doth; if this bairn ceased to believe in me, I might cease to be!' Brom growled. 'Yet what robbery is this, to take from him one of childhood's most delicious thrills – the dread of the horrible monster that he knows, at heart's bottom, doth not truly live? The bogeymen, child, are huge, shambling things, all covered with hair, with tiny glowing eyes, and long, sharply pointed teeth!'

Magnus cuddled back against Gwen with a delighted squeal.

' 'Tis true!' Brom held up a forefinger. 'Vile things are they, that do seek to harm both children and parents! And thy mother and father must needs sally forth against them, to drive them from this land for good and all – yet they cannot go if they are not sure that thou art safe.'

Magnus stared at Brom wide-eyed, beginning to understand.

'So hie thee back to thy nurses!' Brom clapped his hands.

'Hie thee hence, and bide with them till thy mother doth summon thee! Bide thee with thy nurses in safety, that thy mother and father may chase the bogeymen from this land!'

Magnus looked up at Gwen out of the corner of his eyes. 'Baby come too?'

'I fear not,' Gwen said firmly, holding him up under the arms so that she could look directly into his eyes. 'Thou must needs do as thine Uncle Brom . . .'

Rod was the only one who noticed the shadow pass over Brom's face.

'. . . as thine Uncle Brom doth say, and flit back to Elfland, to thy nurses, there to bide whiles thy father and I do chase these monsters. Yet I'll summon thee whene'er I may, to play awhile. Now, wilt thou go?'

The baby glowered at her, then nodded reluctantly.

'Good babe!' Gwen kissed him. 'Now, hie thee hence!'

Magnus looked up at Rod. He reached out to squeeze a chubby hand – then found himself holding empty air. Magnus had disappeared.

'Bairns do understand more than we think,' Brom rumbled, 'if we are but open with them.' He frowned at the peasants. 'And what dost thou gape at, village fools? Hast never seen a babe afore?'

The men gave a start and glanced at Rod guiltily; but the women sighed, and one of them said to Gwen, 'Now, bless thee, lady! Praise Heaven mine were only common babes!'

'Certes, they tried thee as sorely as ever mine try me,' Gwen answered, amused. 'I have, after all, some powers to use in dealing with him. Yet bless thee for thy wishes, goodwife.'

One of the guardsmen stepped into the tent. 'Milords, His Majesty doth ask that thou attend upon him.'

Brom looked up, frowning. 'What coil's this?'

'Word hath flown from witch to witch, milord. A dragon ship doth sail toward Bourbon.'

Half an hour later, while the main army was still striking its tents and packing up, the Flying Legion cantered up out of the valley and struck off toward the east. Rod rode at their head, with Toby the teenage warlock beside him. 'I didn't have time for the full report, Toby. Who spotted the beastmen?'

'Matilda, milord. She and Marion, her sister, flew to the east to dwell within a cottage on a cliff-top that Lord Habsburg built for them – all as His Majesty commanded.'

Rod nodded. 'And they take turns just sitting and listening for strange thoughts, right?'

Toby nodded. 'Even as His Majesty did command – an hour listening, then an hour doing other things, then an hour listening again.' He glanced at Rod out of the corner of his eye. ' 'Twas thou who didst bid His Majesty so instruct us, was it not?'

Rod frowned and shook his head. 'What would I know about hearing thoughts, Toby? It was Gwen's idea. So, who heard the beastman-thoughts – the one who was on duty, or both of them?'

'The one who was "off-duty", Lord Warlock. She slept, and waked screaming.'

'The one who slept?' Rod stared. Then he nodded slowly. 'Well, I suppose it makes sense. Maybe her telepathic sensitivity gets a boost when she's asleep.'

'We do seem to have dreams that are not our own,' Toby admitted.

'Really! Hm! Wish I'd known that – might've come in handy.'

'Cannot Gwendylon hear thy thoughts when she doth sleep?' Toby asked carefully.

Rod shook his head. 'Neither asleep nor awake. I seem to be telepathically invisible.' His tone was carefully neutral, hiding his feelings nicely. He tried not to think about it; it made him feel inferior to Gwen. 'What did Matilda dream?'

'She dreamt that she pulled an oar aboard a dragon ship, and heard the chieftains speaking of old gods which they used to worship, and a new god which they worship now. Yet all of it was without words, and the new god seemed somehow monstrous, though there was no picture of it.'

'Well, that's not surprising. Haven't you ever had that flash of thought, the whole concept suddenly clear, before you get around to putting it into words?'

Toby frowned. 'I have indeed, though I had not thought of it. And the thought Matilda heard lasted no longer than such a flash.'

'Really?' Rob pricked up his mental ears. 'Odd, that. Was there a strong emotion under it?'

Toby nodded. 'Very strong; a surge of fear and dread. The beastman's soul, for a second, did clamour toward the sky and the old gods. Then he realized what he did, and the thought ended. Yet it was enough to waken Matilda, and waken her screaming.'

'Small wonder; *I'd* wake up halfway out of the room. But it tells us a lot.'

'Aye. It tells us beastmen draw near the eastern coast.'

'Well, a bit more than that. It tells us the beastmen have a religion. So far, we didn't even have any reason to think they had souls.'

'I had not thought of that,' Toby admitted.

'It also tells us that they've just had a conversion, and at least one of the converts wasn't exactly wholehearted about it. Wonder who the new god is? And what kinds of methods his missionaries use . . .' Rod was remembering Constantine's baptism and a new shirt, or death. 'But more importantly, it tells us the beastmen's thoughts can be heard when there are very strong emotions behind them – and gives us some reason to think they may be able to hide their thoughts deliberately.'

Toby frowned. 'Why, how is that?'

'Because you said the thought ended just after the beastman realized what he was doing. That means either that he deliberately hid his thoughts somehow, or that his thoughts can only be read when he's at an emotional peak.'

'Why, that is so!' Toby looked up at Rod wide-eyed.

Rod squirmed; he hated hero worship, especially when it was directed at him. It made a man feel so responsible . . . 'Of the two, I'd guess they can hide their thoughts. There must've been *some* sort of strong emotion in them when they sacked the Loguire coast, but no witches heard them.'

'But would not a one of them have let slip a thought in the heat of battle?'

Rod nodded. 'You'd think so, wouldn't you? So maybe it's the other way around; maybe their thoughts can only be read when they're pushing them out. That surge of thought Matilda picked up sounds like a prayer – and a prayer is deliberately aimed away from yourself; you're *trying* to reach someone else with that kind of thought.'

'Then, let us be glad there is one strong believer amongst them.'

'Yes, and that the old gods happened to be out of sight at the moment and needed a strong push behind a prayer if it was going to reach them.'

'But how could a god be *in* sight?' Toby looked puzzled. 'They are naught but dreams.'

'Point well taken,' Rod admitted, 'but the beastmen might not know that yet. Especially if they've got an idol. . . . Hm! Now you've got me wondering. . . .'

'About what, Lord Warlock?'

'About their new god. I wonder just how new he is? What he wants his worshippers to do?'

Toby's eyes suddenly lost focus. 'Lord Warlock . . . word from Marion . . . the dragon ship hath shown no sign of turning in toward shore. It sails on past Bourbon. . . .' He frowned a second in concentration, probably his equivalent of 'Acknowledged; that's a copy', then turned back to Rod. 'The beastmen sail on, northward.'

'Then, we'll head north too. Sergeant!' Rod called back over his shoulder. 'Turn left at the next crossroad!' He turned back to Toby. 'Send word to His Majesty.'

'Aye, Lord Warlock.' Toby's eyes lost focus again. Rod watched him in silence for a few minutes, till the young warlock's eyes cleared again. He turned to Rod with a half smile. 'His Majesty turns the main army northward. He is quite pleased with his new way of sending messages betwixt the parts of an army.'

'I should think he would be. Any medieval commander would've given his right arm for an advantage like that. You know, Toby, when this is all over I'll bet His Majesty tries to set up a permanent witch-and-warlock network – only for royal messages, of course.'

Toby frowned. 'That is not wholly a happy thought, Lord Warlock.'

'No, neither for you, nor for the general population. Though you must admit it would guarantee you full employment.'

'Fuller than I wish, I doubt not.'

'Well, that's a point. It is nice to be able to keep the work-day down to eight hours – and it's even nicer to have some choice as to whether or not you're going to take the job in the first place. No, it's okay for an emergency, but we definitely shouldn't encourage this kind of thing during peacetime.'

'Save for thy messages, of course,' Toby said with his tongue in his cheek.

'Well, of course. But that's a different case, isn't it? I mean, I'm almost a member of the tribe.'

'By marriage,' Toby agreed. 'Aye, when all's said and done, thou *art* a warlock.'

Rod opened his mouth to deny it, thought what would happen if he did, and closed his mouth again.

The sun was only a red glow behind Rod's right shoulder as he rode down the winding road toward the Romanov beach. 'No faster than a trot, Sergeant! Let these folk by! We're here to defend them, not trample them!'

Peasants thronged the road, with huge packs on their backs and handcarts behind them, hauling their few household goods. Rod swore. 'They'd take their whole cottages if they could! Well, at least they're not stampeding. Here's the real evidence of the good you've done, Toby.'

'How so, Lord Warlock?' Toby reined his horse over to let the peasants pass by.

'Because they've got time to evacuate, thanks to the Magic Early Warning system. They even had time to pack up before they started fleeing!'

The Flying Legion swerved over to the side of the road, single file, following Rod's and Toby's example. The peasants, seeing them coming, struggled to compress their ranks and leave room for them.

'God save the High Warlock and his legion!' a voice yelled, and the whole flowing crowd joined in a ragged cheer. The soldiers grinned and sat a little straighter in the saddle.

'Always nice to be appreciated,' Rod observed. Toby smiled, amused.

A hand caught Rod's shin. He looked down into a wrinkled, yellow-eyed face rough with beard stubble. 'Drive them away, Lord Warlock! Why can ye not keep 'em from comin'?'

'Off wi' ye, now!' The man behind him gave the old whiner a shove. 'Here's men goin' t' mortal danger, and you'd ask 'em to hurry!' Rod smiled his thanks, and the younger man grinned back. 'Save your worship!' He hurried on.

'There will ever be such, will there not?' Toby said quietly.

Rod nodded. '"Save us, save us! And please arrange hotel accommodations while you're doing it!" But there'll always be the ones behind them too, who tell 'em to shut up and let us get on about our business.'

They struggled on through the crowd. The peasants streamed by, and they came out onto the beach while the sky still glowed with dusk. A hundred nervous men looked up at the sound of hoofbeats, and raised a frantic cheer. Rod grinned and waved, muttering under his breath, 'Gallop, Fess. Make it look good. Pick out their officer and stop on a penny next to him.'

The black steel horse leapt into a gallop and thundered around in a curve, pulling up beside a cloaked horseman in plate armour. 'Hail, Sir Knight! I am Rod Gallowglass, Lord High Warlock, and these men are His Majesty's Flying Legion.'

'Thou art well come indeed!' cried the knight. 'Now, praised be King Tuan for your coming!' Which was pretty good, considering that only three years ago this man must've been riding behind his lord, Duke Romanov, against the royal army, such as it had been. 'I am Sir Styenkov.'

'We're just reinforcements,' Rod assured. 'I don't want to upset your battle plan; we'll just fall in beside you. What'd you planned?'

'What could I, with only an hundred?' The knight spread his hands helplessly. ' 'Tis all that Their Majesties allow us to keep under arms – God save them, 'tis generous to allow even that! But what can they do? Draw up in a line, and wait.'

'I suppose so. But I've got two hundred more behind me. And yours are veterans, aren't they?'

Styenkov nodded. 'All fought in the rebellion, aye. They are not like to break and flee.'

'Then draw 'em back up the beach as far as you can, and let 'em wait. There's only one dragon ship; at least, the witches haven't said anything about there being more than one.' He frowned at the thought. 'Hm. I've been careless. Toby!'

'Aye, Lord Warlock.'

'Has anyone done a flyby on the raiders? Actually flown over them, to see how many there are?'

Toby's eyes lost focus for a minute; then they cleared, and he shook his head. 'Nay, milord. None ha' thought to do so.'

'Then do it, okay?'

'Aye, milord!' Toby sprang up into the air like a javelin trying for a new record, and disappeared into the low-hanging clouds. Sir Styenkov stared after him, open-mouthed. Rod turned to follow his gaze. 'Hm. Yeah, that could be a problem, couldn't it?'

'Only for the beastmen! What fabulous force hast thou assembled, Lord Warlock?'

'Oh, you mean Toby? No, he's the only one with me; the rest are normal. Picked veterans, every one of 'em, but normal.' Rod wondered how true that could be of any native of Gramarye. 'No, I was talking about the clouds.'

'Oh.' For the first time, Styenkov seemed to notice the overcast. 'Aye, those clouds look sullen. Well, I've fought in rain aforetimes.'

'Me too, and it was a thoroughly nasty business. Still, we can't exactly send out an emissary and ask the beastmen to come back on a clear day, can we? But we might manage a different kind of surprise for them, if you pull your men way back, Sir Styenkov, and mine hide behind those rocks, over there'—he gestured toward an outcrop over to his left—'and behind that shrubbery. He pointed to a line of trees on the right, that grew down almost to the water's edge.

Sir Styenkov's eyes lighted. 'Then the beastmen will charge up to hack at my men, and yours may close upon them, like to the jaws of a vice!'

'Before they get to your men,' Rod added. 'Though, of course, when they see this beach with good cover at each side, they might smell a trap and decide to go look for easier game.'

'I would not object to that . . .'

A gust of wind fanned Rod's cheek, and Tony said, 'There is only the one of them, Lord Warlock.'

Sir Styenkov nearly swallowed his beard.

'He has to fly out there because he doesn't know where he's going,' Rod explained. 'But when he wants to come back he knows where it is, so he can teleport. It's faster that way.' He turned to Toby. 'How many men?'

'An hundred on deck. There may be more below – but I think not; their ship is small.'

'It would have been an even fight without us,' Rod observed. 'Still, maybe my men can make things move a little faster, save a few lives, things like that.'

'Touching that.' Sir Styenkov scratched his nose. 'Shall we take prisoners?'

'Huh?' Rod reflected that Sir Styenkov's mood had certainly improved. 'Take prisoners? Of course!'

Sir Styenkov nodded. 'I had thought so. Thou dost need information, and wish to set them talking, dost thou not?'

'Well, that too,' Rod agreed. 'But mostly, I want to find out if they *can* talk. How far off shore were they, Toby?'

'Mayhap half a mile, milord.'

'That sounds like time to get into position.' Rod strode off toward his troops, bawling, 'Places, everyone!'

As he came up to the Flying Legion, he noticed the locals pulling back up the beach. Good; Sir Styenkov wasn't *too* overconfident. 'Sir Lionel! Sir Hampden!'

'Aye, milord,' his lieutenants answered in chorus.

'Sir Lionel, take your hundred over to that outcrop of rocks and hide them. Sir Hampden, take yours over to that line of trees. Charge out to fall upon the enemy when you hear the pipes.'

'Aye, milord!' And the two lieutenants turned away, bawling orders to their sergeants. The sergeants started bellowing before the lieutenants had quite finished, and the beach filled with yells and the tramp of troops. In five minutes, it was clear. Rod turned, grinning, to wave to Sir Styenkov; then he turned and loped across the beach to the rock outcrop.

The beach lay empty, waiting. Tiny drops began to fall, scarcely more than a mist. Sir Styenkov's soldiers shifted nervously, muttering to one another. Rod heard a few whispers here and there among his own troops. 'Hear any thoughts, Toby?'

'Nay, Lord Warlock.' Toby's eyes were unfocused, watching the landscape of the mind rather than the world around him. 'Whoever sent that one prayer, prays no longer.'

'Then, there's no way of telling how close they are. Can't be long now, though.'

In the distance, thunder rumbled.

Then it came, gliding out of the mist with muted splashing – a tall, gaunt serpent, mouth wide in a snarl, wicked horns probing from its forehead. Shadowy figures moved on its back.

Rod held his breath.

The dragon drove up onto the beach, slowing to a stop with the grinding of sand against wood. Beastmen began to drop off its back – squat, hulking, helmeted shapes, with round shields covering their torsos and heavy, double-bladed axes in their hands.

Rod squinted, trying to make out details through the rain, but it was no use. He could scarcely see more than a silhouette.

'Let me fight, Lord Warlock,' Toby hissed in his ear.

Rod whirled, pressing a finger to his lips and shaking his head with a furious scowl. Confound the kid, did he want to give away the whole ambush? Rod could've sworn his lieutenants could've heard that whisper a hundred yards away in the tree line. He wished Toby *could* read his mind – but he had to settle for a glare and a head-shake. The lad's juvenile male hormones were getting the better of him, urging him on to glory and an early funeral. Which was his own business – but Rod's business was making sure Toby'd still be alive afterwards for his main assignment. Which would be more than dangerous enough.

The young man stepped back, smouldering.

Rod turned back to the beach just as the beastmen saw Styenkov's soldiers. Whatever they yelled to each other was lost in a rumble of thunder, but they quickly scuttled into place, pulling themselves into a rough semblance of a line. Then they began to move forward slowly.

One or two of Styenkov's soldiers began to march toward the beastmen. He shouted them back into line. Good man. The rest of his men brandished their pikes, waiting for the enemy.

The beastmen were halfway up the beach now. Rod could hear a low rumble as they called to one another. They were beginning to realize something was wrong; their tone was one of alarm, and their advance was grinding down to a halt. What was tipping Rod's hand? He darted a glance at Styenkov's soldiers, then looked again. Here and there, a man had straightened up a little, pike drooping – and stood frozen at a completely improbable angle. Rod realized they were the ones who had forgotten the standing order and had looked the enemy square in the eye. Now they were temporary statues, frozen by the Evil Eye.

So it really worked! It *wasn't* imagination!

But the rest of Styenkov's men were watching the enemy's hands, or feet – and were still very much a menace. The beastmen slowed and stopped – apparently they didn't have too much taste for an even fight. They hunched in on themselves, heads hunkered down; they seemed to be waiting. For what?

The beastmen began to make bellowing noises in deep rumbling bass voices. Rod suddenly realized that they were calling out in unison. He strained, trying to pick intelligible phonemes out of booming voices. It was getting easier, because they were getting their timing better; it was almost one unified shout now. Rod listened, then shook his head; there was no way of saying what it meant in their own language. To him, though, it sounded like: 'Cobalt! Cobalt! Cobalt!'

. . . Which was ridiculous; at their level of technology, they couldn't even have the concept of bombs, let alone atomic fission.

Thunder rocked the land, and the beach lit up with an explosion of lightning. Then there was only gloom again, darker for having had the sudden light. Rod peered through the murk – and stared. Sir Styenkov's men stood frozen in their buskins!

A ragged cheer rumbled up from the beastmen, and they waddled forward, making a grating sound. With a shock, Rod realized they were laughing.

But they were moving so slowly! Why? Didn't they want to reach their intended victims?

Then Sir Styenkov's whole line lurched forward. Then they lurched again, and again – and, step-stumbling-step, they marched toward their butchers!

Something bumped into Rod's shoulder. He whirled – just in time to catch Toby. The young warlock's body was rigid, and his eyes had lost focus. Had he been tuned in on a soldier's mind when the Evil Eye froze him?

Then Rod saw one of Styenkov's soldiers slow and stop. His head lifted slowly; then he shivered, looked about him wildly, realized what had happened, set his pike on an enemy, and started marching again with grim purpose. Further down the line, another soldier began to waken, too.

Rod stared down at Toby. The young idiot had found a way to get into the fight after all!

Thunder broke over them, and lightning stabbed the land again.

The soldiers froze solid again, and Toby's whole body whip-lashed in a single massive convulsion; then he went limp, eyes closed.

Rod stared, appalled. Then he touched the carotid artery in the boy's throat and felt the pulse. Reassured, he lowered the young warlock. 'Fess!'

'Here, Rod.' The great black horse loomed up out of the darkness.

'Just stand over him and protect him.'

'But, Rod . . .'

'No "buts"!' Rod turned, sprinting away toward the battle-line, whipping out his sword. 'Flying Legion! Charge!'

Fess sighed, and stepped carefully over Toby's still form, so that the young warlock lay directly beneath his black steel body.

Rod caught up with Styenkov's line just as they began stumbling toward the beastmen again. He looked from one to another frantically; their eyes were glazed, unseeing.

The beastmen began to waddle forward again, making the chugging, grating noise that passed for laughter with them. Rod whirled about, staring at them, just as they broke into a lumbering run. Rod glanced back at the stumbling soldiers, then ahead; the enemy were only huge, hulking shadows against the grey of stormclouds, great shadows looming closer.

Lightning flashed, and the beastmen roared a cheer. And Rod froze solid, but only with shock – because, for the first time, he had a really good look at a beastman.

And he recognized it.

Neanderthal.

There was no mistaking the sloping forehead, the brow ridges, the chinless jaw, the lump at the base of the skull . . . He had an overwhelming desire to look one in the mouth and check its dentition.

Then a chill hand clutched his belly. What could Neanderthals be doing on Gramarye?

Attacking, obviously. He noticed two war clubs swinging up, then starting to swing down toward him. He leaped aside just as the first whistled past him, then threw himself into a lunge, sword arrowing toward the other clubman. Its round shield swung up; the beastman caught Rod's point neatly. For a moment, Rod stared directly into the little piggy eyes over the top of the shield – little piggy eyes that seemed to grow, and glow, with a bright, flaming bead at their centres that probed into his brain, leaving a trail of cold fire that didn't burn, but froze. It fascinated; it held all his attention, numbing his brain, stopping all thought. Dimly, off to the side, he noticed the huge war club swinging up for another blow; but that didn't matter. All that really mattered was that bright burning bead at the centre of the eyes . . .

A furious scream rang in his ears, blotting out the sounds of battle, a scream such as a Valkyrie might make if she were actually allowed to attack; and a sudden warmth seemed to wrap around his mind, pushing away the bright, burning bead, away and away until it was only a pair of eyes again . . . the eyes of a warrior beastman whose huge war club was windmilling down to crush Rod's head.

He leaped back, yanking his sword free from the shield, and the club whistled past harmlessly. Behind the round shield, the beastman snarled and swung his club up again. Rod advanced and feinted high, at the face. The shield snapped up to cover, and Rod riposted and slashed downward. The sword-tip whipped across the creature's thighs, tracing a line of bright red. It shrieked, clutching at its legs, and collapsed rolling on the ground. Rod didn't stay to watch; he turned to glance at the battle-line – and saw a war axe swinging straight at his sinuses, with a broad gloating grin behind it (yes, the dentition *was* right). Rod leaped to the side and chopped down, lopping off the axe-head.

High above him, the Valkyrie screamed again – now he recognized it; he'd heard it just last week, when Gwen had caught Magnus teleporting the cookie jar over to the playpen. Confound it, didn't the woman know he couldn't fight as well if he was worrying about her safety?

On the other hand, she was staying far above the battle – not really in any immediate danger, especially since the beastmen were limited to clubs and axes; not an arrow among the lot of 'em. He swung about, chopping at another Neanderthal. Snarling, four of them turned on him. Beyond them, he saw with shock, half the soldiers lay dead on the beach, their blood pouring into the sand. Fury boiled up in him, and he bellowed even as he gave ground, sword whirling furiously in feints and thrusts, keeping his attackers back just barely out of club-range. Beyond them, he saw frozen soldiers coming to life again; and a ragged shout of rage went up as they saw their dead companions. The nearest beastman looked back over his shoulder, his swing going wide. Rod thrust in under his shield, and he screamed, doubling over. His companions gave ugly barks, and pressed in. Behind them, two soldiers came running up, blades swinging high. Rod darted back out of the way and braced himself at the sickening thud of steel into meat. Their targets dropped, and the remaining beastman whirled on his two attackers in desperation. Rod shouted 'Havoc!' and darted in. Startled, the beastman whirled back to face Rod – and doubled over Rod's steel. Rod yanked back just before a pike slammed down to end the warrior's agony. Its owner gave a bloodlust-bellow of victory, and turned back to the battle-line. Rod followed, fighting down sickness. No time for it now; he had to remind the soldiers. 'Their eyes! Don't look at their eyes!'

So, of course, half of the soldiers immediately confronted the enemy stare-to-stare, and froze in their tracks.

The Valkyrie screamed again, and the soldiers jolted awake. Their pikes lifted just in time to block war axes . . .

And lightning seared, thunder exploding around it.

As the afterimages ebbed, Rod saw the soldiers standing frozen again. High above him, a sudden wail trailed away.

'Gwen!' Rod bellowed. He stared into the sky, frantically probing the darkness – and saw the darker shadow hurtling downward. He spun, scrambling back up the beach, then whipped about, staring up at the swooping silhouette, running backwards, tracking it as it grew larger and larger . . .

Then it cracked into him, rock, bone, and sinew. Pain shot through his head, and the sky filled with stars. A myriad of tiny stabs scored his back and sides, and a chorus of cracking sounds, like a forest falling, filled his ears. His diaphragm had caved in; he fought for breath in near-panic. Finally air seeped in; he sucked it thankfully, the more so because it was filled with the perfume he'd given Gwen last Christmas. He looked down at the unguided missile that had flattened him, and at a noble bush that had given its life for the cause. He felt gratitude toward the shrub; Gwen was delicate, but she was no lightweight, especially when she was coming down at twenty miles an hour.

He struggled upward, lifting his wife clear of the bush and laying her carefully out just under the next shrub down the line. As far as he could tell, she was perfectly all right; no breaks or wounds. She'd have a hell of a bruise tomorrow, of course . . . And she was unconscious; but he was pretty sure that had happened before she fell.

Rain suddenly drenched him. He remembered the last lightning- flash, and turned to look down the beach. Through the downpour he could just barely make out frozen forms toppling, and a dozen or so that fought back. Another lightning-flash showed them clearly laying furiously about them with their pikes; and they kept fighting, even as the lightning faded. A few, then, had heeded him and were watching their enemies' hands and weapons instead of their eyes. Too late to do them much good, though – they were outnumbered three to one.

Rod struggled back to his feet, ungallantly heaving Gwen up over his shoulder in a fireman's carry, and stumbled blindly back over the scrubline in a shaky trot. 'Fess! Talk me in!'

'Turn toward the sea, Rod,' the robot's voice murmured through the earphone set in Rod's mastoid process. 'Approach fifty feet . . . turn right now . . . another twenty feet . . . Stop.'

Rod dug his heels in, just barely managing to counter Gwen's momentum. He put out a hand and felt the synthetic horsehair in front of him. 'Good thing they built your eyes sensitive to infrared,' he growled.

He threw Gwen over the saddlebow, then dropped to one knee, reaching under the robot horse to lift Toby's head in the crook of his elbow. He slapped the boy's cheeks lightly, quickly. 'Come on, lad, wake up! You've done your bit, contrary to orders; now it's time to get out of here.'

'What . . . Where . . .' Toby's eyelids fluttered. Then he looked up at Rod, squinting against a painful headache. 'Lord Warlock! What . . .'

'You tried to get into the battle by proxy, and got knocked out in person,' Rod explained. 'Gwen tried the same thing and got the same result. Now *we've* got to get out of here, before our few remaining soldiers get wiped out. Come on, lad – up in the air. Let's go!'

Toby stared up at him painfully. Slowly, he nodded. He squeezed his eyes shut, his face screwing up in concentration; then, suddenly, he was gone. Air boomed in to fill the space where he'd been.

Rod leaped up and swung into the saddle, bracing his wife's still form with one hand as he bellowed, 'Retreat! Retreat!'

The dozen soldiers left standing leaped backward, then began to yield ground a step at a time. The beastmen roared and followed, but the Gramarye pikes whirled harder than ever with the power of desperation, keeping the Neanderthals at a distance. There were too many beastmen ganging up on each soldier, though; given time, they'd wipe out the Gramarye force.

Rod didn't intend to give them that time. 'All right, Iron Horse – *now*!'

Fess reared back, pawing the air with a whinnying scream. The beastmen's heads snapped up in alarm. Then the great black horse leaped into a gallop, charging down at them. At the last second, he wheeled aside, swerving to run all along their line. The beastmen leaped back in fright, and the soldiers turned and ran. Fess cleared the battle-line; the beastmen saw their fleeing foes, shouted, and lumbered after them.

Fess whirled with another scream and raced back along the Neanderthal line. The beastmen shouted and leaped back – except for one who decided to play hero and turned to face the galloping horse, club raised.

Rod hunkered down and muttered, 'Just a little off-centre – with English.'

Fess slammed into the Neanderthal, and he caromed off the horse's chest with a howl. He landed twenty feet away, and was silent. His companions stood poised, wavering.

On the saddlebow, Gwen stirred, lifting her head with a pained frown. She took one look and grasped the situation.

The beastmen growled to one another, softly at first, but gaining volume and anger. They began to waddle back up the beach, their low, ugly rumble filling the air.

Gwen's eyes narrowed, and the beastmen's clubs exploded into flame.

They howled, hurling their clubs after the Gramarye soldiers, turned, and ran.

Gwen glared after them. Then her head began to tremble, and she collapsed again.

'Retreat!' Rod snapped. Fess pivoted and raced back up the beach after the soldiers.

They came to rest high in the rocks atop the cliff, behind the long, sloping beach. 'You did well,' Rod assured the soldiers. 'No one could have done better.'

One of the men spread his hands helplessly. 'How can we fight an enemy who can freeze us in our tracks, milord?'

Rod dismounted and lifted Gwen down tenderly. 'I think my wife's given us the basic idea. I'll work it out with her when she

comes to.' He knelt, lowering Gwen to the ground behind two
boulders, cradling her head and shoulders against his chest. He
winced at a sudden pain in his arm and remembered a club hitting
him there. He remembered a few other blows, too, now that he
thought about it. With the adrenalin of battle beginning to wear
off, the bruises were beginning to hurt. With surprise, he noticed
a bright crimson streak across his chest – one of the axe-blows
had come closer than he'd realized. When he understood just
how close, he began to get the shakes. He clamped down on them
sternly; there'd be time for that later. 'What're they doing, men?'

'They begin to feel brave again, milord.' One of the soldiers was
lying among the seaward rocks, peering out between two boulders.
'They are stepping away from their dragon.'

'Any sign of the villagers?'

'None, milord. All fled in time.'

Rod nodded. 'Well, it's a shame about the village, but they can
rebuild it.'

' 'Tis not destroyed yet, milord.'

'Yet,' Rod echoed. 'There's a wineskin in my saddlebag, boys.
Pass it around.'

A soldier leaped and wrenched the wineskin out. He squirted a
long streak into his mouth, then passed it to his comrade.

'Toby!' Rod yelled. Nothing happened.

Gwen stirred in Rod's arms, squinting against a raging headache, looked up, saw Rod, and relaxed, nestling against his chest,
closing her eyes. 'I am safe.'

'Praise Heaven,' Rod breathed.

'What doth hap, my lord?'

'We lost, darling. You came up with a good idea, but they
outnumbered you.'

She shook her head, then winced at the pain it brought. 'Nay,
my lord. 'Twas the lightning.'

'Lightning?' Even through his exhaustion, Rod felt something
inside him sit up and take notice. 'Well . . .'

'Milord,' the sentry called, 'fire blossoms in the village.'

Rod nodded with a grimace. 'Whole place'll be one big torch
in a few minutes. The beastmen won't find much to pick there,
though. Peasants don't own much – and what they do have they
can carry.'

'There is the granary, milord,' one of the locals pointed out,
'and the smokehouse.'

Rod shrugged. 'So they'll have a picnic on the way home. Don't worry, lad – the King and Queen will send you food for the winter. Grain they could've had for the asking.' He looked down at Gwen. 'Can you find Toby, darling?'

Gwen nodded and closed her eyes, then winced. Rod felt a stab of guilt – but he needed the young warlock.

Air slammed outward with a soft explosion, and Toby stood before him. 'Milord Warlock?'

One of the soldiers stared, then turned away, muttering and crossing himself.

Rod pretended not to notice. 'Feel up to some action again?'

'Assuredly, an thou dost wish it, milord.' Toby's knees were shaking with exhaustion.

'I do,' Rod said. 'I hate to ask it of you, but we've got to salvage something out of this. When they ship out, can you follow them?'

Toby stared off into space for a moment, then nodded. 'There are clouds. They will not see me.'

'You don't have to go all the way,' Rod pointed out. 'Just see 'em on their way, then call for one of your mates. He can teleport out to you, and you can disappear. Just get them started.'

Toby nodded slowly. 'Wise, milord. We will.'

'The flames slacken, milord.'

'Yes. Thank heaven for the rain.' But Rod looked up, frowning; the sentry's voice had changed. A different soldier lay among the rocks, his arm in a fresh, gleaming sling.

Rod stared. 'Hey – who gave you that?'

The sentry looked up, surprised, then nodded toward another soldier who sat, teeth gritted against pain, while a chubby figure in a brown robe wrapped linen around a long gash in his arm.

'Father Chillde,' Rod said slowly.

The monk looked up, then smiled sadly. 'I fear I have come too late, Milord Gallowglass. At least I may be of some service now.'

'We appreciate it, of course – but the chaplain doesn't *have* to come into battle.'

The sad smile stayed. 'There are two ways of thinking of that, milord.'

Nice to know they had a dedicated one – and his mere presence was definitely a comfort to the soldiers. Him, and the wine.

'They move back toward their ships,' the sentry reported.

'There will be much work for me when they have gone,' the priest said sadly.

Rod shook his head. 'I don't think so, Father. From what I saw during battle, they didn't leave any wounded.'

The priest's mouth pressed thin. ' 'Tis to be lamented. But there will be other work, more's the pity.'

Rod turned toward him, frowning. 'What . . . ? Oh. Yeah – the Last Rites.' He turned back toward the beach. 'But it won't just be our dead down there, Father. How about the beastmen? Think they have souls?'

'Why – I had not thought of it,' the priest said, surprised. 'But is there reason to think they would not?'

One of the soldiers growled a reply.

The monk shook his head. 'Nay, goodman. I ha' known Christian men to do worse – much worse.'

'*I* would, could I but get one of them alone,' another soldier snarled.

'There – do you see?' The priest spread his hands. 'Still, souls or none, I misdoubt me an they be Christian.'

'They called upon their false god at the battle's beginning, did they not?'

'Was that the burden of their chant?' another soldier wondered. '"Go Bald", was it not?'

'Something of the sort,' the first growled.

Rod frowned; he'd heard 'Cobalt', himself. Well, each interpreted it according to words he knew. What did it really mean, though? He shrugged; it could be some sort of heathen god, at that.

'They have boarded their ship,' the sentry called. 'They are launching . . . they turn . . .'

'May I build a fire now?' Father Chillde asked.

Rod shrugged. 'Please do, Father – if you can find shelter for it and anything dry enough to burn.' He turned to the young warlock. 'Sure you feel up to it, Toby?'

The esper nodded, coming to his feet. He was looking a little better, having rested. 'I will start them, at least. When I've learned the trick of following a ship without being seen, I'll call another of our band and teach it to him.'

Rod nodded. 'See you soon, then, Toby.'

'Thou shalt, Lord Warlock.' Toby sprang into the air. The soldiers stared after him, gasping, as he soared up and up, then arrowed away over the waves. A few crossed themselves, muttering quick prayers.

'There is no need for that,' Father Chillde said sharply. 'He is naught but a man, like to yourselves, though somewhat younger and with a rare gift. But he is not proof 'gainst arrows or spears; if you would pray, beseech God for his safety.'

Rod stared at the chubby priest, surprised. Then he nodded his head in slow approval.

'He has gone through the clouds,' the sentry reported.

Rod nodded. 'Wise, once he's figured out which way they're headed. He'll probably drop down for a quick peek now and then, just to check on them.'

'They have crossed the bar,' the sentry reported. 'They stand out to sea.'

Rod sighed and came to his feet, cradling Gwen in his arms. 'It's over, men. Let's go.'

Below them, on the beach, the village smouldered.

'Nay, my lord. 'Twas the lightning, I am certain of it!' Gwen spoke calmly, but her chin was a little more prominent than usual.

'Lightning!' Queen Catharine cried. She threw her hands in the air. 'Why not the thunder, then? Or the wind, or the rain? Lightning, i' sooth!'

'Nay, Majesty – hear her out.' Tuan touched her arm gently, restraining – but Rod noticed he'd become awfully formal all of a sudden.

'"Majesty", indeed!' Catharine stormed, turning on him. 'What wouldst thou, mine husband? To blame it on the lightning! Nay, 'twas these beastmen only – themselves, and no more! They are vile sorcerers, and the spawn of Hell!'

'You may have a point there,' Rod admitted. 'We're not really disagreeing, you see – we're just getting into the *how* of their sorcering.'

'Why, by peering into thine eye,' Catharine shrieked, whirling back on him. 'Lightning, forsooth! Was it at *lightning* that thy soldiers stared?'

'Nay, certes,' Gwen said wearily. ' 'Tis true, when they stared at the beastmen's eyes, then could the beastmen cast their spell. And 'tis a foul spell!' She shuddered. 'I had some taste of it when I sought to lift it. 'Tis a vile thing that doth fascinate with ugliness!'

'"Fascinate" is the term,' Rod agreed. 'They focused all the soldier's attention on one single point – the beastmen's pupils. Then . . .'

'Then they could spare no attention for fighting?' Tuan nodded heavily. 'Vile, indeed, that will not even allow a soldier the chance of defence.'

Catharine rounded on Gwen. 'Hast thou never encountered a

spell like to this before?'

'There are tales of it,' Gwen said slowly, 'of the Evil Eye. I, though, have never found it in life.'

'I have,' Rod said slowly, 'though it was a milder version.'

Tuan frowned. 'When?'

'In prefligh — uh, in apprenticeship,' Rod hedged, 'when I was being trained in the, uh' — he took a deep breath and gave up on honesty — 'in the wizardry I use. This particular form of magic was called 'hypnotism', but it looked a lot like this Evil Eye. It came to the same thing in the long run; it's just that they had to do it much more slowly.'

'Aye, therein is it most phenomenal.' Tuan frowned. 'How can they fascinate so quickly?'

'Therein I have some experience,' Gwen said slowly. ' 'Tis a matter of throwing one's thoughts into another's mind.'

Fess's voice murmured in Rod's ear, 'Your wife is describing projective telepathy, Rod.'

'Scientific terminology is wonderful,' Rod growled. 'It lets sceptics believe in magic. In fact, it transforms them into instant authorities.'

Catharine turned on him, glowering. 'Of whom dost thou speak, sirrah?'

*Not you*, Rod thought, remembering the rumours that the Queen had a touch of 'witch-power' herself. Aloud, he said, '*To* whom is more the point – and the problem is that the beastmen do it to whomever they want. I think we've got a pretty good idea of *how* they do it now – but how do we fight back?'

'Why, as we did.' Gwen looked up in surprise.

Rod frowned down at her. ' "We"?' He felt a chill trickle down his back.

'Toby and I,' Gwen explained. 'What we did was even as thou didst say, mine husband – we cast our thoughts into the soldiers' minds and made them see what the glowing point at which they stared was in truth – naught but a pair of tiny eyes. We made them see again the face around the eyes, and the body 'neath the face.'

'Yeah,' Rod said with a curt nod. 'Then they stepped up the strength of their Evil Eye and knocked you both out.'

But Gwen shook her head. 'Not "they", milord. 'Twas the lightning.'

Catharine threw up her hands in despair and whirled away.

'Lightning or not, they *did* knock you out,' Rod growled, 'and you'll pardon me, but I didn't like the look of it.'

Gwen spread her hands. 'What wouldst thou, my lord? There were but Toby and myself – and we acted at the same moment, but not in concert.'

'Huh?' Rod's scowl deepened. '"Not in concert"? What did you want – a drum-and-bugle corps?'

'Nay, my lord.' Gwen visibly fought for patience. 'We could not join our powers – and there were too many soldiers for poor two of us. We did attempt to cast our thoughts into all their minds – but we did it side by side, not by blending both our powers into one.'

'I take it you think it's possible to merge your power,' Rod said softly.

'Mayhap.' Gwen frowned, gaze drifting to the window. 'When two who can hear thoughts do touch, there is ever some greater sense of contact – threat, I should say; for I've never known two who have risked reaching out through touch to thoughts.'

The door shot open, and Brom O'Berin stumped in, followed by two men-at-arms, each with a shoulder under one of Toby's arms. The young warlock limped between them, panting, 'Nay! I . . . I can bear mine own . . .'

'Thou canst scarcely bear thine head upon thy shoulders, now,' Brom growled. 'Indeed, an thou wert a crab tree, thou couldst not bear an apple. There,' he said to the two men-at-arms, nodding toward a chair. They lowered the young warlock carefully, and he sagged back, mouth gaping open, eyes closed, panting in huge hoarse gasps.

'What ails him?' Gwen cried.

'Naught but exhaustion.' Brom's mouth held tight. 'Were his news not vital, I would have sent him to his bed.'

'Young idiot! I *told* him to call for a relief!' Rod strode over to the teenager and caught up a wrist, feeling for the pulse. 'Didn't you bring any wine?'

Brom turned to the doorway and snapped his fingers. A page scurried in, wide-eyed and apprehensive, bearing a tray with a flagon and a flask. Brom caught them up, poured the mug half-full, and held it to Toby's lips. 'A sip only, my lad, then a draught. Attempt it, there's a good fellow.'

Toby sipped, and promptly coughed. Rod thumped him on the back till the boy nodded weakly, then sipped again. It stayed down, so he took a big swallow.

'Feel a little better now?' Rod asked.

Toby nodded and sighed.

'Don't fall asleep on us,' Rod said quickly. 'What did you see?'

'Only the dragon ship, and miles and miles of water,' Toby sighed. 'I sickened at the sight. I swear I'll never drink the stuff again!' And he took a long pull on the wine.

'Steady there, now,' Rod cautioned. 'So they sailed a lot. Which way did they go?'

'West,' Toby said firmly, 'west and south. I called for Giles, and set him to the following, whiles I appeared upon my bed and slept till he did call to say he'd sighted land. Then I appeared beside him and sent him home. He was sorely tired, seest thou, whilst I was fresh.'

From the grey cast of the youth's face, Rod doubted that. 'There was also a little matter of possible danger if you'd reached their homeland.'

'Well, that too,' Toby admitted. 'In any case, the journey's end was mine affair. The danger was not great; the sky was lightening but not yet dawning, and clouds still hung low and heavy.'

'E'en so, I had hoped thou wouldst not take too great a chance,' Gwen said. 'What had the beastmen come home to?'

'A bend of land in the coastline,' Toby explained, 'low land, with high sky-reaching cliffs behind it a mile or two from shore.'

Rod nodded. 'How big was the low land?'

'Mayhap some five miles wide.'

'He describes an alluvial plain,' Fess's voice murmured in Rod's ear.

'You're a better observer than I knew,' Rod told the youth. 'What was on the plain?'

'A village.' Toby looked up at him. 'Huts of daub and wattle, at a guess – round and with thatched roofs. Around and about their fields they did lie, with greening crops.'

'Farmers?' Rod frowned, puzzled. 'Not the kind of people you'd expect to go pillaging. Any idea how many huts there were?'

Toby shook his head. 'More than I could count at ease, Lord Warlock. 'Twas as far across as any village I ha' seen in Gramarye.'

'Village,' Rod repeated. 'Not a town?'

Toby pursed his lips. 'Well . . . mayhap a *small* town . . . Still, the houses were set far apart.'

'Maybe a thousand households, then. How'd they react when they saw the dragon ship come back?'

'They did not,' said Toby.

'What?' Rod gawked. 'They didn't react? Not at all?'

'Nay – they did not see it. 'Twas not yet dawn, as I've said, and the dragon ship did not come to the village. Nay, it sailed instead to southward, and found a narrow river-mouth just where the cliffs came down to join the water. Then the beastmen unshipped oars and furled their sail and rowed their ship upstream, until they slipped into a crack within the cliff-wall from which their river issued.'

'A crack.' Rod kept his face expressionless.

Toby nodded. ' 'Twas a crack thou couldst have marched thy Flying Legion through, milord; but in that vast wall of rock 'twas nonetheless a crack.'

'So they sailed into a river-pass.' Rod frowned, trying to make sense of it. 'What happened then?'

'Naught to speak of. When they slipped into the cliff-face, I dropped down to the cliff-top, where I lay and watched. Anon, I saw them slip out on a footpath, without their shields or helmets, and naught of weapons save the knives at their belts. They trudged across the plain, back to the village. I did not follow, for I feared sighting by an early-riser.'

Rod nodded. 'Wise. After all, we found out everything we really needed to know.' He frowned. 'Maybe more.'

'What then?' Brom demanded.

Toby spread his hands. 'Naught. The work was done . . . and I commenced to feel as weary as though I'd not had a night of sleep.'

'Not surprising, with the psychic blast you pulled yesterday,' Rod reminded him. 'And teleporting takes some energy out of a man too, I'll bet.'

'I think that it doth,' Toby agreed, 'though I'd not noticed it aforetime.'

'Well, you're not as young as you used to be. What are you now, nineteen?'

'Twenty,' Toby answered, irritated.

'That's right, it's a huge difference. But that does mean your body's stopped growing, and you no longer have that frantic, adolescent energy-surplus. Besides, what's the furthest you've ever teleported before?'

'On thine affairs, some ten or twenty miles.'

'Well, this time, you jumped . . . oh, let's see now . . .' Rod stared off into space. 'All night in a sailing ship . . . let's assume the wind was behind it . . . say, ten miles an hour. Maybe ten hours, factored by Finagle's Variable Constant . . .' He looked back at Toby. 'You jumped a hundred miles or more. Twice. No wonder you're tired.'

Toby answered with a snore.

'Take him up,' Brom instructed the men-at-arms, 'and bear him gently to his bed. He hath done great service for our land this morn.'

One of the soldiers bent to gather up Toby's legs, but the other stopped him with a hand on his shoulder. 'Nay. Only lift the chair.' The first soldier looked up, nodded approvingly, and picked up the chair legs as his companion lifted the back. Rod instantly memorized the second one's face, marking him as one who might have potential.

The door closed behind them, and Brom turned on Rod. 'What makest thou of this, Lord Warlock?'

'Confusion,' Rod answered promptly. 'For openers, I want him to draw a map when he wakes up. Beyond that?' He shrugged. 'We do have a tidy little mystery, don't we?'

'Aye,' Brom agreed. 'Why would they come so silently back to their lair?'

'Mayhap 'twas not all returned from this sally,' Tuan offered, 'and they feared the censure of the slain ones' kin.'

'Possible, I suppose.' Rod frowned. 'But it doesn't seem very likely. I mean, I suppose there really are some hard-hearted cultures who take that attitude – you know, 'Return with your shield, or on it', and all that. But their mission wasn't exactly a total flop, you know. Their ship did come back stuffed. They took everything that wasn't nailed down before they burned the stuff that was.'

'E'en so, they did have dead,' said Brom, 'and if they'd gained recruits by promising great bounty with little danger, they would now have reason to fear the wrath of the kin of the slain ones.'

'Ah, I see you know the ways of recruiting-sergeants,' Rod said brightly. 'But they'd have to face that anger anyway as soon as the rest of the villagers found out they were back. I mean, sooner or later, somebody was bound to notice they were there. So why sneak in?'

Catharine looked up slowly, her face lighting. 'They stole back like thieves in the night, did they not?'

Rod frowned and nodded. 'Yeah. How does that . . .' Then his eyes widened. 'Of course! Your Majesty has it!'

'What?' Brom looked from one to the other, frowning.

'Aye, she hath!' Gwen jumped up. 'The whole of this expedition was done in secret!'

'Aye!' Tuan's eyes fired. 'Indeed, that hath the ring of truth!'

'Hypothesis does not account for all available data,' Fess said flatly behind Rod's ear.

'But it's got the right feel,' Rod objected. 'Now, just how they managed to hide the little fact that they were gone for thirty-six hours, I don't know; but I could think of a few ways, myself.'

Gwen looked up, alarmed.

'That means, Your Majesty,' Rod said, hastily turning to the King, 'that we're not being attacked by a hostile nation.'

'Nay, only thieves who come in ships.' Tuan frowned. 'Is there not a word for such as they?'

'Yeah; they call 'em "pirates".' Rod wasn't surprised that the people of Gramarye had forgotten the term; their culture was restricted to one huge island and had been isolated for centuries.

Tuan frowned thoughtfully, gazing off into space. 'How doth one fight a seaborne bandit?'

'By knowing something about the sea.' Rod turned to Brom. 'Is there anybody in Gramarye who does?'

Brom frowned. 'We have some fisherfolk in villages along the coast.'

'Then, get 'em,' Rod called back over his shoulder as he headed for the door. 'Get me a fisherman who knows something about the winds and the coastlines.'

'An thou wishest it, we shall. But where dost thou go, Lord Warlock?'

'To find out what's current,' Rod called back.

'But there's got to be a current here somewhere!'

'They are not visible on standard reflected-light photographs, Rod,' Fess explained, 'and when we arrived on Gramarye we had no reason to take infrared stills.'

Rod's starship was buried under ten feet of clay in a meadow a few hours ride from Runnymede. He had persuaded the elves to dig a tunnel to it so he could visit it whenever he wanted.

Now, for instance. He was enjoying the rare luxury of Terran Scotch while he pored over a set of still pictures on the chart-table screen. 'I don't see anything, Fess.'

'Isn't that what you expected, Rod?'

Fess's robot brain, a globe the size of a basketball, hung in a niche in the curving wall. Rod had temporarily taken it out of the steel horse body and plugged it in to act as the ship's automatic control section. Not that he was going anywhere; he just needed Fess to operate the ship's auxiliary equipment, such as the graphic survey file. And, of course, the autobar.

'Well, yes, now that you mention it.' Rod scowled at the aerial picture of the Gramarye coastline, the mainland coastline opposite, and the open sea in between. Fess had taken the pictures during their orbital approach to the planet two years earlier. Now they were stored as rearrangements within the electrical charges of giant molecules within the crystal lattice of the on-board computer memory. 'I hadn't expected to find anything except plants and animals – but I hadn't said so. Better watch out, Metal Mind – you're getting close to intuitive hunches.'

'Merely integrating large numbers of nonverbal signs, Rod,' the robot assured him.

'I should be so good at integrating.' Rod stabbed a finger at a bump on the mainland coastline. 'Expand that one for me, will you?'

The glowing plate in the tabletop stayed the same size, of course, but the picture within its borders grew, expanding out of sight at the edges, so that the bump became larger and larger, filling the whole screen.

Rod drew an imaginary line with his finger. 'Quite a demarcation here – this arc that goes across the bump. Divides the vegetation rather neatly, don't you think?'

'I do not think, Rod; I simply process data.'

'One of these days, you'll have to explain the difference to me. What's this stuff in the upper left? Looks like the tops of a lot of ferns.'

'It may well be so, Rod. The majority of the planet is in its Carboniferous Era, and giant ferns are the dominant plant form.'

'There's a strip of beach alongside them. What's that lying on it?'

'A primitive amphibian, Rod.'

'Kind of fits in with the whole ambience,' Rod said, nodding. 'Wonder what's under the Carboniferous flora?'

'Carboniferous fauna, I would presume.'

'You certainly would. No bogeymen?'

'Human habitation usually occurs in cleared spaces, Rod.'

'You never know; they might have something to hide. But if you're going to talk about a cleared space, here's the rest of the bump.' Rod frowned, peering closely. 'Looks like there might be some small trees there.'

Fess was silent for a few seconds, then said slowly, 'I agree, Rod. Those do appear to be trees. Stunted, but trees nonetheless.'

'Odd-looking for a fern, isn't it? Where did trees come from, Fess?'

'There can only be one source, Rod – the Terra-formed island of Gramarye.'

'Well, let's be fair – maybe some of the seed got scattered during the Terra-forming.'

'Quite possible, Rod – but it is the mechanism of scattering that is of importance. There must be some sort of communication between this mainland area and Gramarye.'

'Such as the ocean current I'm looking for? Well, well!' Rod peered closer, delighted. 'Let's see – besides the trees, it's just a featureless light green. Can you check what makes that colour, Fess?'

The picture stayed the same size on the screen, but the robot analysed the pattern of electrical charges that was the recorded image. 'It is grass, Rod.'

Rod nodded. 'Again, that couldn't come from a Carboniferous fern-patch. But it's such a clean break between the ferns and the grassland! What could make such a clear demarcation, Fess?'

'Exactly what you are no doubt thinking of, Rod – a line of cliffs, the cliffs Toby mentioned.'

'I *was* kind of thinking along that line, now that you mention it.' Rod looked down at the picture. 'So we could be looking at the beastmen's lair. It does match Toby's description – except for one little thing.'

'I see no anomaly, Rod.'

'Right. It's not what *is* there – it's what isn't. No village.'

Fess was silent for a moment. Then he said, 'I see your point. There is no sign of human – or subhuman – habitation.'

'No dragon ships drawn up on the beach, anyway.'

'There is only one logical conclusion, Rod.'

'Yeah.' Rod leaned back and took a sip of Scotch. 'I know what *I* think it is – but let's hear what you've got in mind first.'

'Surely, Rod. We recorded these pictures two years ago during our first approach to this planet. Apparently the beastmen were not here then. Therefore, they arrived within the last two years.'

'That's kinda what I was thinking, too . . . Say!' Rod leaned forward again. 'That reminds me. I've been meaning to tell you about something I noticed during the battle.'

'Some historical inaccuracies in the beastmen's Viking equipage, Rod?'

'Well, an anachronism, anyway. Fess, those beastmen are Neanderthals.'

The little ship was very quiet for a few seconds.

Then Fess said, 'That is impossible, Rod.'

Rod answered with a wicked grin. 'Why? Just because the last Neanderthal died off at least fifty thousand years before the Norse began to go a-viking?'

'That was rather the general trend of my thoughts, yes.'

'But why should that bother you?' Rod spread his hands. 'We found a time machine hidden away in the back hallways of Castle Loguire, didn't we?'

'Yes, but we disabled it shortly after we defeated Anselm Loguire.'

'Sure – but how did it get there in the first place?'

'Why . . . a time-traveller must have been sent back to build it.'

'Quick figuring, Reasoning Robot.' Rod pointed a finger at the nearest vision pickup. 'And if they could do it once, they could do it again.'

'Why . . . that is certainly logical . . .'

'Sure is. "Sensible" is another matter. But that time machine didn't exactly look as though it had been improvised, you know?'

'Surely you are not implying that they are mass-produced.'

'Well, not *mass*-produced, really – but I did have in mind a small factory somewhen. Two or three a year, maybe.'

A faint shudder vibrated the little ship. 'Rod – do you have any idea how illogical such an event could make human existence?'

Rod looked up in alarm. 'Hey, now! Don't go having any seizures on me!'

'I am not that completely disoriented by the concept, Rod. I may have the robotic equivalent of epilepsy, but it requires an extremely illogical occurrence to trigger a seizure. A time machine factory may be illogical in its effects, but not in its sheer existence.'

That wasn't quite the way Fess had reacted to his first discovery of a time machine, but Rod let it pass. 'Well, I did have some notion of just how ridiculous widespread time machines could make things, yes. Something like having Neanderthals dressed up in Viking gear, showing up on a planet that's decided to freeze its culture in the Middle Ages. That what you had in mind, Fess?'

'That was a beginning, yes,' the robot said weakly. 'But are you certain they were Neanderthals, Rod?'

'Well, as sure as I can be.' Rod frowned. 'I mean, conditions were a little rushed, you know? I didn't get a chance to ask one of them if he'd be good enough to take off his helmet so I could measure his skull, if that's what you mean.'

'No, but several beastmen did meet with fatal accidents during the battle. Perhaps we should send a scribe with a tape measure.'

'Brother Chillde will do; might as well put him to *some* use. But he'll just confirm what I'm telling you, Fess: heavy jaw, no chin, brow ridges, sloping forehead – and I mean *really* sloping; obviously no prefrontal lobes.'

'An occipital lump, Rod?'

Rod scowled. 'Well now, *that* I can't really say. I mean, after all, that's down at the base of the skull where the helmet would hide it. Check that on one of the, ah, specimens, would you?'

'I shall leave written directions to that effect, Rod – in your name, of course. So, then, you are positing someone removing a tribe of Neanderthals from approximately 50,000 BC Terra, and transporting them here?'

'Where else could they dig up Neanderthals?'

'The theory of parallel evolution . . .'

'Parallel lines don't converge. Still, you never know; we'll leave the possibility open.'

'But for the time being, we will assume they were taken from Terra. And whoever brought them here outfitted them with Viking ships, armour, and weaponry. Presumably this unidentified party also taught them navigation. But why would they have attacked you?'

Rod shrugged. 'Presumably because the unidentified party told them to – but we'll leave that one open for the moment.'

'As we must also leave open the question of the unidentified party's identity.'

'Well, that doesn't have to be *too* open.' Rod frowned. 'I mean, whoever it is has got to have a time machine – and we already know two organizations so equipped who're involved in Gramarye.'

'The futurian anarchists, and the futurian totalitarians. Yes.'

'Right. And, with two candidates like that available, I don't see any need to posit a third.'

'Which of the two would you favour in this case?'

'Oh, I'd say the anarchists probably masterminded it,' Rod reflected. 'It strikes me as being their style.'

'In what way?'

Rod shrugged. 'Why Viking gear? Presumably for the same reason the Vikings used it – to strike terror into the hearts of their victims. And striking terror like that serves the general purpose of making chaos out of whatever social order is available. Besides, they like to get somebody to front for them – the "power behind the throne", and all that.'

'Or behind the pirates, in this case. Still, your point is well taken, Rod. The totalitarians do tend toward more personal involvement. Also, they prefer careful, hidden preparation resulting in a revolution, not continual harassing that slowly disintegrates local authority. Yes, the anarchists are the logical perpetrators.'

'And if that's logical, it's probably also wrong.' Rod leaned forward over the chart screen again. 'Which reminds me – there's a complete difference in vegetation, depending on which side of the cliffs you're on.'

'Totally different, Rod. Grasses exclusively.'

'What, not even a fungus among us?'

'Well, there are a few mosses and lichens.'

'How come nothing more?'

'The vegetation would seem to indicate a small area in which the temperature is far below that of the surrounding forest. I conjecture that a cold breeze blows off the sea at that point, chilling the area around the bay. The cliff-wall prevents it from reaching the interior.'

Rod looked up. 'Hey! Would that indicate a cold current?'

'In all probability, Rod.' The robot's voice sounded a little patronizing.

'That's the current that would go past Gramarye.'

'It would seem so,' Fess answered.

Rod smiled sourly and tossed his shot glass into the recycler. 'Well, enough loafing.' He stood up, strode over to the wall, and began to loosen the clamps that held Fess's basketball brain. 'What happens after that cold current hits the shoreline, Fess?'

'It would probably be warmed by contact with the tropical mainland just south of the cliffs, Rod. Then it would be forced out to sea by the mass of the continent.'

Rod nodded. 'From the mainland's position and contour, that means the current would be sent northeast – back toward Gramarye.'

'Quite possibly, Rod – but you should not hypothesize without sufficient data.'

'All right.' Rod tucked the silver basketball under his arm. 'Anything you say, Fess. Besides, it's time for lunch.'

'You know robots do not eat, Rod.'

'That's funny, I thought you might be in the mood for a few bytes. . . .'

The sentry at the door to the solar stepped in and announced, 'The Lord High Warlock, Majesties.'

Rod pushed past him and stopped, taking in the tall, saturnine man with the lantern jaw who stood facing Catharine and Tuan.

His face was tanned and leathery. He wore a short brocaded coat, fur-trimmed, over doublet and hose, and clenched a round hat in his hands.

Then Rod remembered his manners and turned to bow. 'Your Majesties! I've been doing a little research.'

'I trust our new source will aid it, Lord Warlock.' Catharine nodded toward the stranger. 'May I present Master Hugh Meridian, captain of a merchant ship.'

'Merchant ship?' Rod turned to the seaman, startled. 'I didn't know we had any.'

'I' truth, we do, milord.' The shipmaster gave him a frosty bow. ' 'Tis quicker, and less costly, to ship goods along the coastline than to haul them over the highways.'

'Of course; it would be. I should've thought of it. But how did you learn that we needed seafaring advice, Master Meridian?'

'We sent word quickly to the fisherfolk at Loguire's estates, and those in Romanov. Each claimed they did know there were currents sweeping past the shore, farther out than they generally sailed,' Tuan answered. 'Yet all claimed further that they knew naught more.'

'Of course; they couldn't know where the currents went.' Rod frowned. 'They never go out farther than they can come back, all in one day. But they did know about you, Captain?'

The captain nodded. 'Ever and anon, the lords hire out their fisherfolk to be my crews, milord. They know of me, aye.'

'And you know where the currents go.' Rod started to look for a chair, then remembered it was bad form to sit in Their Majesties' presence. Brom could; but Brom was special. 'At least you know where they go, around the Isle of Gramarye.'

'I do, milord – though it might be better to say I know where the currents do *not* go.'

'Really? There're currents all around the island?'

'Not quite; the western coast is bare of them.'

'Odd.' Rod frowned. 'Can you show me on a map?'

'Map?' Captain Meridian looked lost for a second; then he fumbled a small book out of his belt-pouch. 'Aye, I can show where I ha' writ about it in my rudder; yet is't not easier to hear it?'

'No, no! I want you to *show* me, on . . .' Rod let his voice trail off, remembering that medieval people didn't have maps as he knew them; the idea of graphing out the outlines of a coast was foreign to them. Maps had had to wait for the Renaissance, with its concept of continuous, uniform space. Rod turned to the door, stuck his head out, and advised the sentry, 'Parchment and pen, soldier – and quickly.' He turned back into the room. 'We'll have one in a minute, Majesties. Master Meridian, imagine yourself being a bird, flying over the Isle of Gramarye, looking down on its coasts.'

Meridian smiled. ' 'Tis a pleasant enough conceit, Milord Warlock – but I cannot see that it serves any purpose.'

'Ah, but it does!' Rod held up a forefinger. 'I'll draw you a picture of the coasts as the bird would see them.'

The door opened, and a round-eyed page popped in with parchment, pen, and ink.

'Thank you, lad!' Rod seized the tools and marched to the solar's table. He rolled out the parchment and began sketching. 'This is the western coast, Captain Meridian.' He drew a long jagged curving line, then pointed back toward its top. 'There's the Duchy of Savoy, and here's Habsburg.' He turned the bottom of the line into a point, and began to draw a lateral line, full of jags and gouges. Captain Meridian followed his hand, frowning, trying to relate this ink-scrawl to the realities of rocks, tides, currents, and distant hills seen through the mist. Finally, his face lit and his finger stabbed down at the southernmost curve. 'Yonder is Cape Souci! Many's the time I've had to shorten sail to keep the southwesterly gale from rolling my ship over as we rounded that headland!'

'Southwesterly?' Rod looked up. 'Does the current come past there?'

Captain Meridian nodded eagerly. 'Aye, aye! 'Tis that very place. Westerly of that, milord, I know naught of the current; indeed, I know naught at all, for never have I had any occasion to sail there. But north of that, there is no current; the whole westerly shore hath naught but tides and local stirrings.'

Rod nodded. 'That's where the current comes to Gramarye, then. This is the southern shore, Master Meridian.' He drew a long curve; then his pen wandered north. Meridian watched spellbound as the outline of the island took shape before him.

' 'Tis witchcraft,' he sighed when Rod was done, and pointed at the map. 'Yonder is the Bay of Roland, and hither lies the coast of Romanov. This is the mouth of the River Fleuve, and yon peninsula is Tristesse Point.' He looked up at Rod. 'Thou art indeed the Lord High Warlock! By what magic canst thou tell the shape of this coastline so well?'

'Oh, I know some people who do a lot of flying,' Rod shrugged. 'Anything I've missed?'

'Not of the coast itself.' Meridian turned back to the map and pointed. 'But you must draw the Grand Skerry here, midway down the west coast – and Geburn Rock here' —his finger jabbed at the map just off the coast of Romanov—'and . . . but, another time.' He waved the thought away. 'There are a host of such things that are not on your map, but that any seafarer would need to know of.'

'Such as currents?' Rod dipped the pen in the ink and handed it to him, feather first. 'Would you show me where they lie, Master Meridian?'

The captain's eyes widened. Slowly, he took the pen and began to sketch. Rod watched flowing, sweeping lines grow from the pen-point, coming from Heaven knew where at Cape Souci, flowing along the southern coast, sweeping around the eastern coast and the Baronetcy of Ruddigore, around the Duchy of Bourbon and along the northern coast, past Romanov, past Habsburg – and out into the unknown again.

Meridian set the pen back into the inkwell with a sigh. 'Better I cannot do, Lord Warlock.' He looked up at Rod. 'I know no more.'

'Well, I might happen to be able to add something there.' Rod took up the pen. 'One of our young warlocks just made a quick, overnight trip into the west, you see.' He began to sketch a concave curve in the lower left-hand corner of the parchment. 'He saw something like this . . .' The curve hooked into a right angle with an upstanding bump. Rod sketched a dotted line across the base of the bump, then reached up to begin sketching where Captain Meridian had left off with the current. 'He was following that last party of raiders home, and from what he said, I'd guess they sailed along this route – which means the northern current flows down the southwest, like this . . .' His pen strokes swept down to the mainland, then turned sharply to flow around the bump. 'You know, of course, Master Meridian, that Gramarye is only an island, and that there's a mainland over to the west, a continent.'

Captain Meridian nodded. 'We had known o' that, Lord Warlock – yet only that, and naught more. Too, that much came only from tales that grandfathers told grandsons.'

'Well, our young warlock checked on it, and it's there, right enough.' Rod's pen strokes flowed around the bump. 'We think this semipeninsula is what the beastmen call "home". It's a safe bet that the current flows past there.' He didn't feel any need to tell the captain just how safe the bet was. 'Then it flows on southward, hugging the shoreline, till it's warmed by this outward bulge of the continent, which also forces it back out to sea, toward the northeast – and, of course, it just keeps going in the same line. . . .' His pen sketched strokes upward and to the right until they joined up with Captain Meridian's line at Cape Souci. 'And there's where it comes back into your ken.' He straightened up, dropping the quill back into the inkwell. 'And there you have it, Master Meridian. Between the two of us, we've filled in a map of the current.'

A discreetly modest, electronic cough sounded in Rod's ear.

'Of course, we had a bit of help gaining the basic information,' Rod added. 'Does it all make sense?'

The shipmaster nodded, eyes glowing. 'Indeed it doth, milord.' He turned to Tuan and Catharine. 'Behold, Thy Majesties!' He traced the current with a forefinger. 'The beastmen bring their dragon ships out into the eastward current, here. It carries them across, first to Loguire, so; then, out into the current, around the eastern coast, and away to the west again, o'er the roof of Gramarye, and so back to their home again.' His finger completed the circuit, arriving back at the bump on the mainland's coastline.

Tuan drew in a long, hissing breath. 'Aye, Master Meridian. So. We understand.'

The door opened, and the sentry stepped in. 'Majesties – Gwendylon, Lady Gallowglass.'

Gwen stepped in, and dropped a quick curtsy.

'Well met, my dear.' Catharine rose from her chair and stepped toward Gwen, one hand outstretched. 'Well met, in good time. These silly men are like to make mine head to spin with their nonsensical talk of currents and capes.'

Gwen rose, catching Catharine's hand with a smile of shared amusement.

Rod did a double take. Then he straightened up, watching the ladies out of the corner of his eye. Catharine and Gwen had never exactly been on close terms, especially since Catharine had seemed quite interested in Rod before he brought Tuan back into her life. He didn't think Gwen knew about that – but then, you never can tell with a telepath. All in all, this warm greeting worried him. 'What have you two been planning?'

'Planning? Why, naught!' Catharine was all offended innocence. 'E'en so, we have found some space to discuss the errors of thy ways, Lord Warlock – and thou, my noble husband.'

Tuan looked even more wary than Rod. 'Indeed, sweet lady. And in what ways am I lacking?'

'Thou dost always speak of ways to go about beating other males with thy clubs, and cleaving them with thy swords. We, though, have seen 'tis of greater import to ward thy soldiers from thy foemen's clubs and axes!'

'A point well taken,' Tuan admitted, 'if thou couldst also thus ward their wives and babes, and the lands and stock that give them sustenance.'

'I hate to admit it,' Rod agreed, 'but knocking a man out with your club *is* a very effective way of making sure he doesn't knock you.'

'Ah, but in this instance, my lord, thou must needs make thy soldier able to strike such a blow,' Gwen reminded. 'For that, thou must needs ward him from the beastmen's Evil Eye.'

Rod exchanged a sheepish glance with Tuan. 'They've got us, Your Majesty. We've been so busy thinking about launching the counterattack that we haven't put much time into the psychic defences.'

'Be easy of heart, lords,' Catharine assured them, 'for we have.'

'Indeed,' Gwen chirped. 'The means is ready to hand, as Toby and I did manifest when the beastmen fought our soldiers.'

Tuan frowned. 'I fear that I mistook. Didst thou give warding?'

'Oh, they surely did!' Rod assured him. 'We probably wouldn't even have saved the handful of men who did survive that battle if Gwen and Toby hadn't, ah, broken the spell of the Evil Eye.'

'I mind me that thou didst say thou hadst, for short spaces, dispelled the charm.' Tuan rubbed his chin. 'Yet 'twas only for brief minutes.'

'Indeed, their thoughts were too heavy for us,' Gwen admitted. 'Yet be mindful, my liege, that there were but two of us, and that we acted each alone.'

'You're trying to say they simply overpowered you,' Rod interpreted. 'But what's to stop them from doing it again?'

'Why, more witches!' Gwen's face bloomed into a rosy smile.

Catharine tucked Gwen's arm into her own, nodding. 'Indeed, Lord Warlock! Thy wife doth think that, if witches do join hands, they may then be able to act in concert. Thus, if we may have a score of witches altogether, they might among them counter the Evil Eye of one dragon-full of beastmen.'

'Just twenty of you, against a hundred of them?' Rod felt his backbone chill. 'You'll pardon me, but I don't like the odds.'

'Nor do we,' Gwen said earnestly. 'It would indeed be well if we could have more witches.'

The chill along the backbone turned colder. 'Somehow, I don't like the sound of this.'

'Nor I,' Tuan agreed. 'What dost thou plan, my wife?'

'A royal summons.' Catharine's chin tilted up. 'There are witches, husband, who do hide about the hinterlands, on farms and in small villages, seeking to disguise their powers for fear their friends and kin may turn away from them. These have not come unto the Royal Coven through fear of us, or reluctance to leave their folk.'

'You're going recruiting,' Rod said in a hollow tone.

'An thou dost call it so. I will!' Catharine tossed her head. 'Bethink thee – would a summons from a mere herald bring a frightened lass to court? Nay. Yet the presence of her Queen would command her loyalty.' She glared at Tuan, daring him to contradict her.

'And where do you fit into this?' Rod levelled a doubtful gaze on his wife.

'Lady Gallowglass shall rest here, to train the Royal Witches in the breaking of the Evil Eye, whilst I do wander round and 'bout the countryside, summoning shy witches to the court.' Catharine patted Gwen's arm protectively, glaring at Rod.

Rod opened his mouth to argue (he couldn't resist it, even if there wasn't much to argue about; Catharine was just asking for it too plainly), but the door slammed open and a pale-faced guard stepped in and bowed. 'Majesties!'

Catharine whirled, transferring her glare to the page. 'What means this unseemly outburst, sirrah?'

'Word hath come through the witches, Majesties! Beastmen have landed at the mouth of the River Fleuve!'

'Call out the army!' Rod snapped to Tuan. He headed for the door. 'I'll get the Flying Legion out – or what's left of 'em!'

'Nay, milord!' the page cried. 'They have landed under flag of truce!'

'What!' Rod spun around, staring.

The sentry nodded. 'Aye, milord. There are but a handful of them, and they have surrendered themselves to the knights of My Lord of Bourbon. Even now, they ride toward Runnymede, guarding well their beastmen –' he hesitated, then turned a questioning glance to the king – 'guests?'

'They are if they indeed landed under a flag of truce.' Tuan rose. 'Send word to guard them well, for I doubt not there are many of our goodfolk who would gladly slay them. Lord Warlock, come!' And he strode toward the door.

'Where dost thou go?' Catharine demanded.

Tuan turned back at the door. 'I ride to meet them, sweeting, for we must converse with them as soon as we may. An hour lost could mean ten lives.'

He marched through the portal, and Rod hurried to catch up with him. He shut the door on Catharine and Gwen with a feeling of relief.

*Then did the High Warlock ride east to meet the beastmen who had come so strangely under a Flag of Truce, and His Majesty the King rode with him; for, though they were few in number, the beastmen were huge and fierce of mien, like unto Demons in their visages, who moved over the face of the Earth like ravening lions. They were tusked like boars, with their heads beneath their shoulders, and bore huge spiked clubs, stained with old blood; and ever and anon did they seek someone to slay. So, when they had come nigh the beastmen, His Majesty the King bade the High Warlock guard them closely with his magic, lest they forget their Truce or it proved to be vile Treachery. And the High Warlock wove a spell about them, standing tall beneath the sun, towering over the beastmen; and his eyes flashed like diamonds in dawnlight, and the aspect of his visage struck Terror into their hearts, so that they stood mute. Then he wove a Spell about them, a cage unseen, a Wall of Octroi, through which they might speak, but never strike. Then spake he unto the King, saying, 'Lo, these monsters are now circumscribed, and naught can harm ye the whiles ye speak unto them.' Then spake King Tuan, 'What manner of men are ye, and wherefore have ye come unto this land of Gramarye?' Then one among them did stand forth and say, in accents barbarous, that he was the highest Lord of their wild savage Realm, but the other Lords had risen up against their King and overthrown him, wherefore this small band had come beseeching King Tuan's mercy. Then was King Tuan's heart moved to Pity, and he spake and said, 'Poor noble hearts! For I perceive that these treacherous villains who have laid waste my Kingdom have wasted ye likewise!' And he brought them back with him to Gramarye; yet the High Warlock kept woven tight his net unseen about them. . . .*

*Chillde's Chronicles of the*
*Reign of Tuan and Catharine*

'Your name is *what?*' Rod stared, unbelieving.

'Yorick.' The beastman spread his hands. 'Whatsamatter? Ain'cha never heard the name before?'

'Well, yes, but never in real life – and as to fiction, you don't exactly look English.' He glanced back over his shoulder at the soldiers who stood behind him with levelled pikes, then looked up at their companions who stood in a ring around the Neanderthals, pike-points centred on the beastmen. Rod considered telling them to lower their weapons, but decided it would be a little premature.

'A word from you, and they'd drop those spears like magic,' the beastman pointed out.

'Yeah, I know.' Rod grinned. 'Ain't it great?'

'On your side, maybe.' Yorick rubbed a hand over his eyes. 'I keep getting the feeling I've been through this all before.'

'Nay, dost thou truly?'Tuan said, frowning. 'I too have such a sense.'

The Neanderthal shook his head. 'Really weird. Like I've lived through this already. Except . . .' He turned to Rod. 'You ought to be about a foot taller, with piercing eyes and a wide, noble brow.'

Rod stiffened. 'What do you mean, *ought to*?'

The Neanderthal held up a palm. 'No offence. But you ought to have a haughty mien, too – whatever that is.'

'Indeed,' Tuan agreed. 'And thou shouldst be hunch-backed, with fangs protruding from the corners of thy jaws, and a look of murdering idiocy in thine eye.'

Yorick reared, startled. Then his face darkened and his eyebrows pulled down to hide his eyes (he had a lot of eyebrow). He stepped forward, opening his mouth – and Rod jumped in quickly. 'You, ah, both have this same, ah, sense of, ah, *déjà vu*?'

'Nice phrase.' Yorick nodded in approval. 'I knew there was a word for it.'

Now it was Rod's turn to stare. Then he said, 'Uh – you've heard *déjà vu* before?'

'Know I have, know I have.' Yorick bobbed his head, grinning. 'Just couldn't place it, that's all.'

The handful of beastmen behind him growled and muttered to each other, throwing quick, wary glances at Rod and Tuan.

'How about you?' Rod turned to Tuan. '*Déjà vu*. Ever heard it before?'

'Never in my life,' Tuan said firmly. 'Doth that signify?'

' 'Course it does.' Yorick grinned. 'It means I'm not a native. But you knew that, didn't you, High Warlock? I mean, it's pretty plain that I didn't evolve here.'

'Yeah, but I sorta thought you'd all been kidnapped.' Rod frowned. 'But one of you was in on the kidnapping, weren't you?'

Yorick winced. 'Please! I prefer to think of it as helping place refugees.'

'Oh, really! I thought that kind of placement usually involved finding a willing host!'

'So, who was to host?' Yorick shrugged. 'The land was just lying there, perfectly good; nobody was using it. All we had to do was kick out a few dinosaurs and move in.'

'You never thought we folk over here on Gramarye might have something to say about it, huh?'

'Why? I mean, you were over here, and we were over there, and there was all this ocean between us. You weren't even supposed to know we were there!'

'Lord Warlock,' Tuan interrupted, 'this news is of great interest, but somewhat confusing.'

'Yes, it is getting a little complicated,' Rod agreed. He turned back to Yorick. 'What do you say we begin at the beginning?'

'Fine.' Yorick shrugged. 'Where's that?'

'Let's take it from your own personal point of view. Where does *your* story begin?'

'Well, this lady picked me up by the feet, whacked me on the fanny, and said, "It's a boy!" And this man who was standing near . . .'

'No, no!' Rod took a deep breath. 'That's a little *too* far back. How about we start with your learning English. How'd you manage that?'

Yorick shrugged. 'Somebody taught me. How else?'

'Dazzling insight,' Rod growled. 'Why didn't I think of that? Could we be a little more specific about your teacher? For one thing, the way you talk tells me he wasn't from a medieval culture.'

Yorick frowned. 'How'd you guess? I mean, I know they didn't exactly send me to prep school, but . . .'

'Oh, really! I would've thought they'd have enrolled you in Groton first thing!'

Yorick shook his head firmly. 'Couldn't pass the entrance exam. We Neanderthals don't handle symbols too well. No prefrontal lobes, you know.'

Rod stared.

Yorick frowned back at him, puzzled. Then his face cleared into a sickly grin. 'Oh. I know. I'll bet you're wondering, if I can't handle symbols, how come I can talk. Right?'

'Something of the sort did cross my mind. Of course, I do notice that your mates have something of a language of their own.'

'Their *very* own; you won't find any other Neanderthal tribe that uses it.'

'I wasn't really planning to look.'

Yorick ignored the interruption. 'These refugees come from so many different nations that we had to work out a lingua franca. It's richer than any of the parent languages, of course – but it's still got a very limited vocabulary. No Neanderthal language gets very far past "Me hungry. That food – go kill."'

'This, I can believe. So how were you able to learn English?'

'Same way a parrot does,' Yorick explained. 'I memorize all the cues and the responses that follow them. For example, if you say, "Hello", that's my cue to say "Hello" back; and if you say, "How are you?" that's my cue to say, "Fine. How're you?" without even thinking about it.'

'That's not exactly exclusive to Neanderthals,' Rod pointed out. 'But the talking you've been doing here is a little more complicated.'

'Yeah, well, that comes from mental cues.' Yorick tapped his own skull. 'The concept nudges me from inside, see, and that's like a cue, and the words to express that concept jump out of memory in response to that cue.'

'But that's pretty much what happens when we talk, too.'

'Yeah, but you know what the words *mean* when you say 'em. Me, I'm just reciting. I don't really understand what I'm saying.'

'Well, I know a lot of people who . . .'

'But they could, if they'd stop and think about it.'

'You don't know these people,' Rod said with an astringent smile. 'But I get your point. Believing it is another matter. You're trying to tell me that you don't understand the words you're saying to me right now – even if you stop to think about each word separately.'

Yorick nodded. 'Now you're beginning to understand. Most of them are just noises. I have to take it on faith that it means what I want it to mean.'

'Sounds pretty risky.'

'Oh, not too much – I can understand the gist of it. But most of it's just stimulus-response, like a seeing-eye parrot saying "Walk" when he sees a green light.'

'This is a pretty complicated explanation you've just been feeding me,' Rod pointed out.

'Yeah, but it's all memorized, like playing back a recording.' Yorick spread his hands. 'I don't really follow it myself.'

'But your native language . . .'

'Is a few thousand sound effects. Not even very musical, though – musical scales are basically prefrontal, too. Manipulating pitches is like manipulating numbers. I love *hearing* music, though. To me, even "Mary Had a Little Lamb" is a miracle.'

Tuan butted in, frowning. 'Doth he say that he is a blinking idiot?'

'Hey, no, now!' Yorick held up a hand, shaking his head indignantly. 'Don't sell us short. We're smart, you know – same size brain as you've got. We just can't talk about it, that's all – or add and subtract it either, for that matter. We can only communicate concrete things – you know – food, water, stone, fire, sex – things you can see and touch. It's just abstractions that we can't talk about; they require symbols. But the intelligence is there. We're the ones who learned how to use fire – and how to chip flint into weapons. Not very good tools, maybe – but we made the big breakthrough.'

Rod nodded. 'Yeah, Tuan, don't underestimate that. We think we're smart because we invented the nuclea – uh . . .,' Rod remembered that he wasn't supposed to let the Gramaryans know about advanced technology. It might disrupt their entire culture. He opted for their version of the weapon that endangered civilization. 'The crossbow. But taming fire was just as hard to figure out.'

'Good man.' Yorick nodded approvingly. 'You *sapiens* have been able to build such a complicated civilization because you had a good foundation under you before you even existed; you inherited it when you evolved. But *we're* the ones who built the basement.'

'Neanderthals had the intelligence,' Rod explained. 'They just couldn't manipulate symbols – and there's just so far you can go without 'em.'

Yorick nodded. 'Analytical reasoning just isn't our strong suit. We're great on hunches, though – and we've got great memories.'

'You'd have to, to remember all these standard responses that you don't understand.'

Yorick nodded. 'I can remember damn near anything that ever happened to me.'

'How about who taught you English?'

'Oh, sure! That's . . .' Then Yorick gelled, staring. After a minute, he tried the sickly grin again. 'I, uh, didn't want to get to that, uh, quite so soon.'

'Yes, but we did.' Rod smiled sweetly. 'Who did teach you?'

'Same guy who gave me my name,' Yorick said hopefully.

'So he had a little education – and definitely wasn't from a medieval culture.'

Yorick frowned. 'How'd you make so much out of just one fact?'

'I manipulated a symbol. What's his name?'

'The Eagle,' Yorick sighed. 'We call him that 'cause he looks like one.'

'What? He's got feathers?' Rod had a sudden vision of an avian alien, directing a secondhand conquest of a Terran planet.

'No, no! He's human, all right. He might deny it – but he is. Just got a nose like a beak, always looks a little angry, doesn't have much hair – *you* know. He taught us how to farm.'

'Yeah.' Rod frowned. 'Neanderthals never got beyond a hunting-and-gathering culture, did you?'

'Not on our own, no. But this particular bunch of Neanderthals never would've got together on their own anyway. The Eagle gathered us up, one at a time, from all over Europe and Asia.'

Rod frowned. 'Odd way to do it. Why didn't he just take a tribe that was already together?'

'Because he didn't want a tribe, milord. He wanted to save a bunch of innocent victims.'

'Victims?' Rod frowned. 'Who was picking on you?'

'Everybody.' Yorick spread his arms. 'The Flatfaces, for openers – like you, only bigger. They chipped flint into tools, same as we do – only they're a lot better at it.'

'The Cro-Magnons,' Rod said slowly. 'Are your people the last Neanderthals?'

'Oh, nowhere near! That was our problem, in fact – all those other Neanderthals. They'd've rather kill us than look at us.'

Suddenly, Rod could place Yorick – he was paranoid. 'I thought it worked the other way around.'

'What – that we'd as soon kill them as look at them?'

'No – that you'd kill them *when* you looked at them.'

Yorick looked uncomfortable. 'Well, yes, the Evil-Eye thing – that was the problem. I mean, you *try* to cover it up as best you can; you *try* to hide it – but sooner or later somebody's gonna haul off and try and whack you with a club.'

'Oh, come on! It wasn't inevitable, was it?'

'Haven't lived with Neanderthals, have you?'

'Oh.' Rod cocked his head. 'Not very civilized, were you?'

'We lived like cavemen,' Yorick confirmed.

'Oh. Right.' Rod glanced away, embarrassed. 'Sorry – I forgot.'

'Great.' Yorick grinned. 'That's a compliment.'

'I suppose it is,' Rod said slowly. 'But how come your quarrels had to turn violent?'

Yorick shrugged. 'What can I tell you? No lawyers. Whatever the reason, we do tend to clobber – and you can't help yourself then; you *have* to freeze him in his tracks.'

'Purely in self-defence, of course.'

'Oh yeah, purely! Most of us had sense enough not to hit back at someone who was frozen – and the ones who didn't, couldn't; it takes some real concentration to keep a man frozen. There just ain't anything left over to hit with.'

'Well, maybe.' Rod had his doubts. 'But why would he want to kill you, when you hadn't hurt him?'

'That made it worse,' Yorick sighed. 'I mean, if I put the freeze on you, you're gonna feel bad enough . . .'

The clanking and rustling behind Rod told him that his soldiers had come to the ready. Beside him Tuan murmured, ' 'Ware, beastman!'

Yorick ploughed on, unmindful of them. 'But if I *don't* clobber you, you're gonna read it as contempt, and hate me worse. Still, it wasn't the person who got frozen who was the problem – it was the spectators.'

'What'd you do – sell tickets?'

Yorick's mouth tightened with exasperation. 'You know how hard it is to be alone in these small tribes?'

'Yeah . . . I suppose that would be a problem.'

'Problem, hell! It was murder! Who wants you around if you can do *that* to them? And there's one way to make sure you won't be around. No, we'd have to get out of the village on our own first. Usually had a lot of help. . . .'

'It's a wonder any of you survived.' Then something clicked in Rod's mind. 'But you would, wouldn't you? If anyone got too close, you could freeze him.'

'Long enough to get away, yes. But what do you do when you've got away?'

'Survive.' Rod stared off into the sky, imagining what it would be like. 'Kind of lonely . . .'

Yorick snorted. 'Never tried to make it on your own in a wilderness, have you? Loneliness is the least of it. A rabbit a day keeps starvation away – but a sabretooth has the same notion about you. Not to mention dire wolves or cave bears.'

Rod nodded thoughtfully. 'I can see why you'd want to form a new tribe.'

'With what?' Yorick scoffed. 'We weren't exactly overpopulated, you know. It was a long way between tribes – and not very many Evil-Eye espers in any one of 'em. You might have one in a hundred square miles – and do you know how long a hundred miles is, on foot in rough country?'

'About two weeks.' But Rod was really thinking about Yorick's choice of word – he'd said 'esper', not 'witch' or 'monster.' 'This is where your "Eagle" came in?'

Yorick nodded. 'Just in time, too. Picked us up one by one and brought us to this nice little mountain valley he'd picked out. Nice 'n' high up, plenty of rain, nice 'n' cool all year 'round . . .'

'*Very* cool in winter – I should think.'

'You should, 'cause it wasn't. Pretty far south, I suppose – 'cause it never got more than brisk. 'Course, there wasn't enough game for the whole four thousand of us.'

'Four thousand? A hundred miles or more apart? What'd he do – spend a lifetime finding you all?'

Yorick started to answer, then caught himself and said very carefully, 'He knew how to travel fast.'

'*Very* fast, I should think – at least a mile a minute.' Rod had a vision of a ground-effect car trying to climb a forty-five-degree slope. 'And how did he get you up to that mountain valley? Wings?'

'Something like that,' Yorick confessed. 'And it wasn't all that big a valley. He taught us how to use bows and arrows, and we had a whee of a time hunting – but the Eagle knew that could only last just so long, so he got us busy on planting. And, just about the time game was getting scarce, our first maize crop was getting ready to harvest.'

'*Maize*?' Rod gawked. 'Where the hell'd he get that?'

'Oh, it wasn't what you think of as maize,' Yorick said quickly. 'Little bitty ears, only about four inches long.'

'In 50,000 BC maize was just a thick-headed kind of grass,' Rod grated, 'like some parties I could mention. And it only grew in the New World. Neanderthals only grew in the Old.'

'Who says?' Yorick snorted. 'Just because we weren't obliging enough to go around leaving fossils doesn't mean we weren't there.'

'It doesn't mean you were, either,' Rod said, tight-lipped, 'and you've got a very neat way of not answering the question you're asked.'

'Yeah, don't I?' Yorick grinned. 'It takes practice, let me tell you.'

'Do,' Rod invited. 'Tell me more about this "Eagle" of yours. Just where did he come from, anyway?'

'Heaven sent him in answer to our prayers,' Yorick said piously. 'Only we didn't just call him 'Eagle' anymore – we called him the 'Maize King'. That way, we could stay cooped up in our little mountain valley and not bother anybody.'

'A laudable ideal. What happened?'

'A bunch of Flatfaces bumped into us,' Yorick sighed. 'Pure idiot chance. They came up to the mountains to find straight fir trees for shafts, and blundered into our valley. And, being Flatfaces, they couldn't leave without trying a little looting and pillaging.'

'Neanderthals never do, of course.'

Yorick shook his head. 'Why bother? But they just had to try it – and most of 'em escaped, too. Which was worse – because they came back with a whole horde behind 'em.'

Rod was still thinking about the 'most'. 'You're not going to try to tell me your people were *peaceful*?'

'Were,' Yorick agreed. 'Definitely "were". I mean, with five hundred screaming Flatfaces charging down on us, even the most pacifistic suddenly saw a lot of advantages in self-defence. And the Eagle had taught us how to use bows, but the Flatfaces hadn't figured out how to make them yet; so we mostly survived.'

Again, 'most'. 'But the Eagle decided he hadn't hidden you well enough?'

'Right.' Yorick bobbed his head. 'Decided we couldn't be safe anywhere on Earth, in fact – so he brought us here. Or to Anderland, anyway.' He jerked his head toward the west. 'Over that way.'

'The mainland,' Rod translated. 'Just – brought you.'

'Right.'

'*How!?*'

'I dunno.' The Neanderthal shrugged. 'He just took us to this great big square thing and marched us through, and . . . here we were!' He grinned. 'Just like that!'

'Just like that.' It was strange, Rod reflected, how Yorick's IQ could change when he wanted it to. From the sound of it, the Neanderthals had walked through a time machine. Dread gnawed at Rod's belly – was this Eagle one of the futurian totalitarians who had staged the rebellion two years ago? Or one of the futurian anarchists, who had tried to stage a *coup d'état*?

Or somebody else from the future, trying to horn in on Gramarye?

Why not? If there were two time-travelling organizations, why not a third? Or a fourth? Or a fifth? Just how many time machines were hidden away on this planet, anyway? Could Gramarye be *that* important?

But it could be, he admitted silently to himself. He'd learned from a renegade Futurian that Gramarye would eventually become a democracy, and would supply the telepaths that were vital to the survival of an interstellar democracy. That meant that the futurian anarchists and totalitarians were doomed to failure – unless they could subvert Gramarye into dictatorship, or anarchy. The planet was a nexus, a pivotal element in the history of humanity – and if it was the pivot, Rod was its bearing.

The Eagle was obviously a futurian – but from which side? Rod certainly wasn't going to find out from Yorick. He could try, of course – but the Neanderthal was likely to turn into a clam. Rod decided not to press the point – let Yorick finish talking; just sit back and listen. That way, Rod would at least learn everything the Neanderthal *was* willing to say. First get the basic information; then dig for the details. Rod forced a grin and said, 'At least you were safe from Flatfaces . . . I mean, Cro-Magnons.'

'We sure were. In fact, things were really hunky-dory, for a while. We chased out the dinosaurs, except for the ones who couldn't run fast enough . . .'

'How'd you handle them?'

'With a knife and fork. Not bad, with enough seasoning. Especially if you grind 'em up and sprinkle it on top of some cornbread, with some cheese sauce.'

'I, uh, think we can, uh, delay that tangent.' Rod swallowed hard against a queasy stomach. 'But I'm sure the regimental cook would love to hear your recipes.' There was a gagging sound from the soldiers behind him, and Tuan swallowed heavily. Rod changed the subject. 'After you took care of the wildlife, I assume you cleared the underbrush?'

'And the overbrush; made great little houses. Then we put in a crop and practised fishing while we watched it grow.'

'Catch anything?'

'Just coelacanths, but they're not half bad with a little —'

'How about the farming?' Rod said quickly.

'Couldn't be better. Grew real fast, too, and real big; nice soil you've got here.'

'A regular Garden of Eden,' Rod said drily. 'Who was the snake?'

'A bright-eyed boy, eager to make good.'

Rod had been getting bored, but he suddenly gained interest. 'A boy?'

'Well, okay, so he was about forty. And the brightness in his eye was pure greed – but you couldn't call him grown-up, really. Still couldn't tell the difference between reality and fantasy. He decided he was a magician and a priest all rolled into one, and went around telling everybody they should worship the Elder God.'

Rod frowned. 'Who is the "Elder God"?'

'"What" would be more like it. Nobody's ever seen it, mind you
. . .'

'That's the way it is with most gods.'

'Really? From all the stories I hear, it's just the other way around.
But this shaman drew pictures of him for us; it was a huge bloated
grotesque thing, with snakes for hair and little fires for eyes. Called
him the Kobold.' Yorick shuddered. 'Gives me the creeps, just to
think about it.'

'Not the type to inspire confidence,' Rod agreed. 'And he was
hoping to win converts with this thing?'

Yorick nodded. 'Didn't get 'em, though – at least, until his buddy
Atylem got lost at sea.'

'His buddy got lost. This made people think his god was true?'

'No, it was because Atylem came back.'

'Oh – the Slain and Risen One.'

'Not really. Atylem had been out fishing, see, and he hadn't
come back. But finally he did, two weeks later – and he said he'd
found a whole new land five days across the water. And it was just
chock-full of Flatfaces!'

'Oh.' Rod lifted his head slowly, eyes losing focus. 'So. Your
people decided the Eagle was wrong, eh?'

'You're quick, milord.'

'And that meant the Kobold was right.'

Yorick nodded. 'Doesn't really make sense, does it?'

Rod shrugged. 'That's the way people think. I mean, we're
talking about public opinion, not logic.'

'Sure.' Yorick spread his hands. 'Put yourself in their place. Why
would the Eagle bring you so close to your old enemies if he were
really powerful and wise?'

'But they were all the way across the water,' Rod said reasonably,
'a day's journey.'

'That's what we all said.' Yorick nodded toward his friends. 'We
were Eagle's leadership cadre, you see. I was his right-hand man –
and Gachol over there was his left-hand.'

'And the rest were the fingers?'

'You got it. Anyway, we all said the Flatfaces couldn't bother us
much – not with all that water to cross. But one day we looked up,
and there was a Flatface floating in the sky.'

Rod stiffened, galvanized. Toby, on his spy mission! But hadn't
Yorick left something out? A little matter of a raid?

But the Neanderthal ploughed on. 'Well! The fat was in the fire, I
can tell you! That shaman – Mughorck was his name – he was out

and about the village before the Flatface was out of the sky, shouting about how Eagle had betrayed us and now the Flatfaces were gonna come over like a ton of devilfish and knock us all into the gizzard!'

'Didn't anybody argue with him?'

'A few of us did try to point out that one Flatface does not an army make – nor a navy, for that matter. But, I mean, this Flatface was *flying*! Everybody was panicking. Some of them were so scared, they actually started digging themselves holes to crawl into! I mean, they were talking magic, and they were talking sorcery – and Eagle had made a big point of telling them that he *wasn't* magical, and he *wasn't* a sorcerer. Not that anybody believed him, of course, but . . .'

'But it laid the egg of doubt,' Rod inferred. 'I should be so lucky!'

The apeman frowned. 'How's that again?'

'Uh, nothing,' Rod said hastily. 'I take it the people began to believe him, at just the wrongest time?'

'Right. After all, there was Mughorck the shaman, running around telling people that he *was* magical, and *was* a sorcerer – and that his god, the Kobold, could make them strong enough to defeat the Flatfaces, and, well . . . people don't think too clearly when they're scared stiff. First thing you knew, everybody was yelling and shouting that the shaman was right, and the Kobold had to be a true god, after all.'

'Didn't you begin to get the feeling that the climate was turning unhealthy?'

'Just about then, yeah. We – ' Yorick jerked his head toward his companions '– began to feel the wind shifting. So we headed up to the High Cave, to tell the Eagle to fly.'

'I hope he listened to you.'

'Listened! He was ahead of us – as usual. He had our knapsacks all packed. While we were slinging our packs onto our backs, he slapped our bows into our hands. Then he told us to disappear into the jungle and build a raft.'

'Raft?' Rod frowned.

Yorick nodded. 'We had some really thick trees, with really thick bark, and they floated really well. He told us not to worry about where we were going – just to paddle it out into the ocean and hang on. Oh, and he told us to bring plenty of food and lots of drinking water, 'cause we might be on that raft for a long time.'

'Without a sail or oars, it must've been.' Rod noted silently that the Eagle, whether or not he was a wizard, obviously knew the odd bit about science – which he should have, if he'd been running a time machine. It seemed that he knew about the Beastland-Gramarye current. 'Did he tell you where you'd land?'

'Yeah – the Land of the Flatfaces. But he told us not to worry about it, because *these* Flatfaces were *good* people, like him.' He clapped his hand over his mouth, eyes wide.

The slip, Rod decided, had been a little too obvious. 'Didn't you want me to know he was good?'

'Uh . . . yeah.' Yorick took his hand away, bobbing his head eagerly, grinning. 'Yeah, sure. That he was good, that's all.'

'Thought so. I mean, you couldn't've been worried about letting me know he was a Flatface – that's been pretty obvious all along.'

'Oh.' Yorick's face fell. 'You guys *are* good at manipulating symbols, aren't you?'

But how could a Neanderthal realize that words were symbols? His education was showing again. 'So you built your raft and paddled out into the ocean – and the current brought you here.'

'Yeah.' Yorick eyed the wall of spearpoints that hedged him in. 'And I don't mind telling you that, for a while there, we thought maybe the Eagle had been wrong about you.'

Rod shrugged. 'Can you blame them? Some of these men are locals; and your boys hit a village not far from here a few days ago. They turned it into toothpicks and meatloaf – and some of my soldiers had relatives there.'

'They *what*?' Yorick stared at him in stark horror. Then he whirled to his own men, pouring out a furious cascade of gutturals and barks. His companions' heads came up; they stared in horror. Then their faces darkened with anger. They answered Yorick in growls of rage. He turned back to Rod. 'I don't mean to sound callous, milord – but are you sure about this?'

Rod nodded, fighting to keep his face expressionless. Yorick and his men were either actually surprised and shocked by the news – or very good actors. 'They hit a village up north, too. I was there; I saw it. Most of the villagers got away, but they carved up my soldiers like hams at a family reunion.'

Yorick's face worked for a moment; then he turned his head and spat. 'That skinny catbait Mughorck! He's got to be behind it somehow!'

'Didst thou, then, know nothing of this?' Tuan demanded.

Yorick shook his head. 'No one in the village did.'

'There were five score of men at least aboard that longship,' Tuan said. 'Many in your village must have known of it.'

'If they did, they did a real good job of keeping the secret,' Yorick growled. Then he pursed his lips. ' 'Course, nobody really would've noticed, with that epidemic going on.'

'Epidemic?' Rod perked up his ears. 'What kind?'

'Oh, nothing really serious, you understand – but enough so that people had to take to their beds for a week or two with chills and fever. You'll understand we were a little preoccupied.'

'I'll understand they were goldbricking,' Rod snapped. 'This fever didn't happen to affect only single men, did it?'

Yorick gazed off into space. 'Now that you mention . . .'

'Simple, but effective,' Rod said to Tuan. 'If anybody came knocking and didn't get any answer, they'd figure the guy was sleeping, or too sick to want to be bothered.' He turned back to Yorick. 'Nobody thought to stop in to check and see if they wanted anything, I suppose?'

Yorick shrugged. 'Thought, yes – but you don't go into somebody's house without being invited. We left food at the door every night, though – and it was always gone the next morning.'

'I'll bet it was – and your shaman's friends had extra rations.'

'You've got a point.' Yorick's face was darkening. 'But we never thought to check on the sick ones – we trusted each other. You don't know how great it is, when you've been alone all your life, to suddenly have a whole bunch of people like yourself. And we wouldn't stop in just to say hello when we were pretty sure the person was feeling rotten; nobody wanted to catch it.'

Rod nodded grimly. 'Simple. Despicable, but simple.' He turned back to Tuan. 'So we got hit with private enterprise – a bunch of buckoes out for their own good, without regard to how much harm it might do their neighbours.'

'So that louse Mughorck was sending out secret commando raids to get you Flatfaces angry,' Yorick growled. 'No wonder you sent a spy.'

'Wouldn't you?' Rod countered. His eyes narrowed. 'Come to think of it, maybe you have.'

'Who, us?' Yorick stared, appalled. 'Make sense, milord! This is like walking in on a hibernating cave bear and kicking him awake! Do you think we'd take a chance like this if we had any choice?'

'Yes,' Rod said slowly. 'I don't think you're short on courage. But you wouldn't be dumb enough to come walking in without a disguise, either – especially since at least one of you speaks good Terran English.'

Beside him, Tuan nodded heavily. 'I think they are what they seem, Lord Warlock – good men who flee an evil one.'

'I'm afraid I'd have to say so too,' Rod sighed. 'But speaking of good men – what happened to the Eagle?'

Yorick shrugged. 'All he said was that he was going to hide.'

'And take his gadgets with him, I hope,' Rod said grimly. 'The enemy has entirely too many time machines already.'

'"Enemy"?' Tuan turned to him, frowning. 'There is naught here but an upstart hungry for power, Lord Gallowglass.'

'Yeah, one who thinks Gramarye looks like a delicious dessert! If that's not "the enemy", what is?'

'The futurian totalitarians,' Fess murmured through the earphone implanted in Rod's mastoid, right behind his ear, 'and the futurian anarchists.'

'But you know my devious mind,' Rod went on, ostensibly to Tuan. 'I always have to wonder if there's a villain behind the villain.'

Tuan smiled, almost fondly. 'If this suspicion will aid thee to guard us as thou hast in the past, why, mayst thou ever see a bear behind each bush!'

'Well, not a bear – but I usually do see trouble bruin.'

'Optimists have more fun, milord,' Yorick reminded him.

'Yeah, because pessimists have made things safe for 'em. And how do we make things safe when we never know where the enemy's gonna strike next?'

Yorick shrugged. 'Mughorck can only field a thousand men. Just put five hundred soldiers every place they might hit.'

'*Every* place?' Rod asked with a sardonic smile. 'We've got three thousand miles of coastline, and we'd need those five hundred soldiers at *least* every ten miles. Besides, five hundred wouldn't do it – not when the enemy can freeze 'em in their tracks. We'd need at least a couple of thousand at each station.'

Yorick shrugged. 'So, what's the problem?'

Rod felt anger rise, then remembered that Neanderthals couldn't manipulate symbols – including simple multiplication. 'That'd be about six hundred thousand men, and we've . . .'

Yorick stopped him with a raised palm. 'Uh . . . I have a little trouble with anything more than twenty. If it goes past my fingers and toes . . .'

'Just take my word for it; it's a lot more men than we have available. Medieval technology doesn't exactly encourage massive populations.'

'Oh.' Yorick seemed crestfallen. Then he brightened. 'But you could post sentries.'

'Sure – and we did. But there's still the problem of getting the army to where the raiders are in time to meet them.'

'It can't be all *that* hard!'

Rod took a deep breath. 'Look – we have to move at least as many men as your whole village.'

'What for – to fight just a lousy thousand?'

'I don't think you realize just how much of an advantage that Evil Eye gives your men,' Rod said sourly.

'Not all that much. I mean, one man can only freeze one other man. Maybe two, if he pushes it – but not very well.'

Rod stared at him for a moment.

Then he said, 'One boatload of your men held a small army of ours totally frozen.'

'*What*!?'

Rod nodded. 'That'd be about, uh, two hands of my men for every one of yours.'

Yorick stared at his outspread fingers and shook his head. 'Can't be. No way. At all.'

Rod gazed at him, then shrugged his shoulders. 'Apparently, somebody found a way to do it.' He remembered what Gwen had said about the lightning.

'Then figure out a way to *undo* it,' Yorick said promptly. 'You Flatfaces are good at that kind of thing. We can show you how the Freeze – what'd you call it, the Evil Eye? – we can show you how it works.'

'That might help . . .'

'Sure it will! You gotta be able to figure out something from that!'

'Oh, I do, do I? How come?'

'Because,' Yorick said, grinning, 'you can manipulate symbols.'

Rod opened his mouth to answer – but he couldn't really think of anything, so he closed it again. That's what set him apart from ordinary men. He just smiled weakly and said, 'Manipulating symbols doesn't *always* produce miracles, Yorick.'

'I'll take a chance on it. You just tell us what we can do, and we'll do it.'

'Might they not be of some value with our force?' Tuan inquired.

Rod turned to him, frowning. 'Fighting side by side with our soldiers? They'd get chopped up in the first battle by our own men.'

'Not if we were to employ them to slip ahead of our main force to reconnoitre the enemy's forces. Let us train them in the use of longbow, crossbow, and lance, and send them ahead to wreak havoc ere we arrive.'

Rod shook his head. 'The nearest knight would charge them in a second. They're not exactly inconspicuous, you know.' Suddenly his eyes widened; he grinned. 'Oh!'

'Oh?' Tuan said warily.

'Yeah. If they stand out too much to do any good here – then we should use them someplace where they won't!'

Tuan's face slowly cleared into a beatific smile. 'Aye, certes! Train them well, and send them back to Beastland. Then they can attack this Mughorck's men unbeknownst!'

'Well, not quite. Just because they all look alike to us doesn't mean they look alike to one another. But they *could* hide out in the bush and recruit some others from among the disaffected, and . . .'

'Aye! Build up a small army!'

'Well, I wasn't thinking on that scale . . .'

'Couldn't manage an army.' Yorick shook his head. 'Fifty men, though, I might be able to get – but that's fifty, tops.' He glanced back at his colleagues, then up at Rod. 'That's all our hands together – right?'

'Right.' Rod fought down a grin. 'But put 'em in the right place, at the right time . . .'

'Aye, fifty men who know the lay of the land.' Tuan's eyes kindled. ' 'Twould be well done indeed, Master Beastman.'

'"Yorick" is good enough,' the Neanderthal said with a careless wave of his hand. 'Fifty, I think I could get. Yeah. We could hide out in the jungle on the other side of the cliffs from the village. No more than fifty, though. Most of the men have wives and children. That makes a man cautious.'

Rod nodded toward the other Neanderthals. 'How about your guys?'

Yorick shook his head. 'All bachelors. We wondered why the Eagle didn't choose any of the married men for his cadre – and I don't mind telling you, some of the ladies were pretty upset about it.'

'Don't worry – it was nothing compared to how they would've squawked the first time their husbands had to work late.' Rod thought of Gwen with a gush of gratitude. 'So they thought the Eagle was a misogynist?'

'No; he turned handsprings any time anyone married. And if one of the Inner Circle got spliced, he was even happier. Kicked 'em into the Outer Circle, of course – but he always said the guy was being promoted, to husbandry.'

'Odd way to look at it.' Rod mulled it over. 'Maybe accurate, though . . .'

'It *is* a job, all by itself,' Yorick agreed. 'But the lack of dependents sure came in handy when we had to leave town in a hurry.'

'Think the Eagle had that in mind all along?'

'I'm sure of it – now. So, we'll get bachelors for this guerrilla force, for you – but what do you want us to do with them?'

'Thou must needs assault them from their rear, whilst we storm in from the ocean,' Tuan answered. 'Then, mayhap, we can bring thine Eagle from his eyrie.'

'Or wherever he's hiding.' Yorick nodded. 'Sounds like a great idea.'

'Then, it's a deal.' Rod held out a hand – carefully, it must be admitted.

Yorick frowned at Rod's hand for a moment. Then he grinned. 'Oh, yeah! Now I remember!' He grabbed Rod's hand in both of his and pumped it enthusiastically. 'Allies, huh?'

'Allies,' Rod confirmed. 'By the way, ally . . .'

'Anything, milord,' Yorick said expansively.

'Viking gear.'

'Huh?'

'Viking gear,' Rod said again. He was glad to see the phrase had meant absolutely nothing to the Neanderthal. 'Your shaman's raiders came decked out in Viking gear – you know, horned helmets, round shields . . .'

'Yeah, yeah, I know what Vikings were,' Yorick said in annoyance. 'Dragon ships too?'

Rod nodded. 'Any idea why?'

'Well, nothing very deep – but I'll bet it scared hell out of the locals.'

Rod stared at him for a second.

'Makes sense, if you're trying to adapt terrorism to a medieval culture,' Yorick explained.

'Too much sense,' Rod agreed. 'Come on, let's get back to Runnymede – we've got to start a military academy for you.'

The train headed northward with a squad of spearmen leading; then Rod and Tuan; then the Neanderthals, *à la carte* – or à la wagon, anyway, commandeered from the nearest farmer (the Neanderthals had never even thought of riding horses; eating, maybe . . .); and well-surrounded by spearmen and archers. The soldiers and the beastmen eyed each other warily through the whole trip.

'I hope your wife doesn't mind surprise guests,' Rod cautioned Tuan.

'I am certain she will be as hospitable as she ever is,' Tuan replied.

'That's what I was afraid of . . .'

'Come, Lord Warlock! Certes, thou'lt not deny my gentle wife's goodness!'

'Or your good wife's gentleness,' Rod echoed. 'We'll just have to hope these cavemen know what a bed and a chair are.'

'I doubt not we'll have to teach them the uses of many articles within our castle,' Tuan sighed, 'save, perhaps, their captain Yorick. He doth seem to have acquired a great deal of knowledge ere this.'

'Oh, yeah! He's a regular wise guy! But I'm not so much worried about *what* he's learned, as who he learned it from.'

Tuan glanced at him keenly. 'Dost thou speak of the Eagle?'

'I dost,' Rod confirmed. 'What'd you get out of our little cross-examination?'

'I was cross that we had so little opportunity to examine. The fellow hath a deliberate knack for turning any question to the answer he doth wish to give.'

'Nicely put,' Rod said judiciously. It was also unusually perceptive, for Tuan. 'But I think I did figure out a few items he didn't mean to tell us. What did you hear between his bursts?'

Tuan shrugged. 'I did learn that the Eagle is a wizard.'

'Yeah, that was pretty obvious – only I'd say he was *my* kind of wizard. He does his magic by science, not by, uh, talent.'

Tuan frowned, concerned. 'How much of this "science" hath he taught to Yorick?'

'None. He couldn't have; it depends on mathematics. The basic concepts, maybe – but that's not enough to really do anything with. He has taught Yorick some history, though, or the big lug wouldn't've known what the Vikings were. Which makes me nervous – what *else* did the Eagle teach Yorick, and the rest of his people, for that matter?'

Tuan waved away the issue. 'I shall not concern myself with such matters, Lord Warlock. These beastmen, after all, cannot have sufficient intelligence to trouble us – not these five alone – when they cannot truly learn our language.'

'I . . . wouldn't . . . quite . . . say . . . that . . .' Rod took a deep breath. 'I will admit that not being able to encode and analyse does limit their ability to solve problems. But they've got as much grey matter between their ears as you and I do.'

Tuan turned to him, frowning. 'Canst thou truly believe that they may be as intelligent as thyself or myself?'

'I truly can – though I have to admit, it's probably a very strange sort of intelligence.' He glanced back over his shoulder at the group of Neanderthals. The spearmen surrounding them happened to lean toward the outside at that moment, affording Rod a glimpse of Yorick's face. He turned back to the front. '*Very* strange.'

Gwen snuggled up to him afterward and murmured, 'Thou hast not been away so long as *that*, my lord.'

'So now I need a reason?' Rod gave her an arch look.

'No more than thou ever hast,' she purred, burrowing her head into the hollow between his shoulder and his jaw.

Suddenly Rod stiffened. 'Whazzat?'

'Hm?' Gwen lifted her head, listening for a moment. Then she smiled up at him. ' 'Twas naught but a tree branch creaking without, my lord.'

'Oh.' Rod relaxed. 'Thought it was the baby. . . . You *sure* he's snug in his crib?'

'Who may say, with an infant warlock?' Gwen sighed. 'He may in truth be here – yet he might as easily be a thousand miles distant.' She was still for a moment, as though she were listening again; then she relaxed with a smile. 'Nay, I hear his dream. He is in his crib indeed, my lord.'

'And he won't float out, with that lid on it.' Rod smiled. 'Who would ever have thought I'd have a lighter-than-air son?'

'Dost thou disclaim thine own relative?'

Rod rolled over. '*That* comment, my dear, deserves . . .' He jerked bolt-upright. 'Feel that?'

'Nay,' she said petulantly, 'though I wish to.'

'No, no! Not *that*! I meant that puff of wind.'

'Of wind?' Gwen frowned. 'Aye, there was . . .' Then her eyes widened. 'Oh.'

'Yeah.' Rod swung his legs over the side of the bed and pulled on his robe. 'There's a warlock within.' He raised his voice, calling, 'Name yourself!'

For answer, there was a knock on the front of the cave.

'Of all the asinine hours of the night to have company calling,' Rod grumbled as he stamped down the narrow flight of stairs to the big main room.

A figure stood silhouetted against the night sky in the cave mouth, knocking.

'Wait a minute.' Rod frowned. 'We don't have a door. What're you knocking on?'

I know not,' the shadow answered, 'yet 'tis wood, and 'tis near.'

'It's a trunk,' Rod growled. 'Toby?'

'Aye, Lord Warlock. How didst thou know of mine arrival?'

'When you teleported in you displaced a lot of air. I felt the breeze.' Rod came up to the young warlock with a scowl.

'What's so important that I have to be called out at this time of night? I just got back! Have our, ah, "guests" escaped?'

'Nay, Lord Warlock. They are snug in their dunge . . . ah, guest room. Still, His Majesty summons thee.'

'What's the matter? Did the cook leave the garlic out of the soup again? I keep telling him this isn't vampire country!'

'Nay,' Toby said, his face solemn. ' 'Tis the Queen. She is distraught.'

The guard saw Rod coming, and stepped through the door ahead of him. Rod stamped to a halt, chafing at the bit. He could hear the sentry murmuring; then the door swung open. Rod stepped through – and almost slammed into Tuan. The young King held him off with a palm, then lifted a finger to his lips. He nodded his head toward the interior of the room. Rod looked and saw Catharine seated in a chair by the hearth, firelight flickering on her face. Her eyes reflected the flames, but they were cold, in a face of granite. As he watched she bent forward, took a stick from the hearth and broke it. 'Swine, dog, and offal!' She spat. 'All the land knows the Queen for a half-witch, and this motley half-monk hath bile to say . . .' She hurled the broken stick into the fire, and the flames filled her eyes as she swore, 'May he choke on the cup of his own gall and die!'

Rod murmured to Tuan, 'What's got her so upset?'

'She rode out about the countryside, with heralds before her and guardsmen after, to summon all who might have any smallest touch of witch-power within them to come to the Royal Coven at Runnymede.'

Rod shrugged. 'So she was recruiting. Why does that have her ready to eat sand and blow glass?'

Catharine looked up. 'Who speaks?'

' 'Tis the Lord Warlock, my love.' Tuan stepped toward her. 'I bethought me he'd find thy news of interest.'

'Indeed he should! Come hither, Lord Warlock! Thou wilt rejoice exceedingly in the news I have to tell, I doubt not!'

Rod could almost feel his skin wither under her sarcasm. He stepped forward with a scowl. 'If it has anything to do with witches, I'm all ears. I take it your people didn't exactly give you a warm reception?'

'I would have thought 'twas the dead of winter!' Catharine snapped. 'My heralds told me that, ere my coach came in view, they felt 'twas only the royal arms on their tabards saved them from stoning.'

'Not exactly encouraging – but not exactly new, either. Still, I had been hoping for a change in public attitude toward our espers . . . uh, witches.'

'So had I also, and so it might have happed – had there not been a voice raised against them.'

'Whose?' Rod's voice held incipient murder.

'A holy man.' Catharine made the words an obscenity.

Rod's mouth slowly opened, then snapped shut. He straightened, a touch of disgust in his face. 'I should have known.'

' 'Tis a renegade friar,' said the Queen, toying with her ring, 'or seems to be. I ha' spoke with Milord Abbot, and he disclaims all knowledge of the recreant.'

'A self-appointed Jonah.' Rod smiled, with acid. 'Lives in a cave in the hills on berries and bee-stings, calling himself a holy hermit and a prophet, and sanctifying his flesh by never sullying it with the touch of water.'

'He doth preach against me,' said Catharine, her hand tightening on the glass, 'and therefore against the King also. For I gather the witches to me here in our castle, and therefore am I unworthy of my royal blood, and mine husband of his crown, though he be anointed sovereign of Gramarye; for mine own slight witchcraft, saith this preacher, is the work of the devil.'

Progress, Rod noted silently. Two years ago, she wouldn't have admitted to her own telepathic powers, rudimentary though they were.

'And therefore,' said the Queen, 'are we agents of Satan, Tuan and I, and unfit to rule. And certes, all witches in our land must die.' She released her wineglass, striking the table with her fist.

Catharine let her head drop into her hands, massaging the temples with her fingertips. 'Thus is all our work, thine, mine, and Tuan's, our work of two years and more, brought low in a fortnight; and this not by armies, nor knights, but by one unclean, self-ordained preacher, whose words spread through the land faster than ever a herald might ride. It would seem there is no need of battles to unseat a King; rumour alone is enough.'

'I think,' Rod said slowly, 'that this is one little virus that had better be quarantined and eliminated, but fast.'

'Fear not that,' Tuan growled. 'Sir Maris hath even now dispatched men throughout the kingdom to listen for word of this monster. When we find him he will be in our dungeons ere the sun sets.'

The words sent a cold chill down Rod's spine. Sure, when *he* said it, it sounded okay – but when it came from the King, it had the full iron ring of censorship in its worst form. For the best of reasons, of course – but it was still censorship.

That was about when he began to realize that the real danger here was Gramarye's reaction to attack, not the raids themselves.

'I'm not so sure it'd do much good to lock up just one man,' he said slowly.

'"Just one"?' Catharine looked up, her eyes wild. 'What dost thou say?'

'There could be several.' Rod chose his words carefully. 'When you have beastmen attacking from the outside, and you suddenly discover enemies inside . . .'

'Aye, I should have thought!' Tuan's fist clenched. 'They would be in league, would they not?'

'We call them "fifth columnists", where I come from.' Rod stared at the flames. 'And now that you mention it, Tuan, the thought occurs to me . . .'

'The enemy behind the enemy again?' Tuan breathed.

Rod nodded. 'Why couldn't it be the same villain behind both enemies?'

'Of what dost thou speak?' Catharine demanded.

'The beastmen's king be o'erthrown, sweet chuck.' Tuan stepped up behind her, clasping her shoulder. 'Their king, whom they call the Eagle. He hath been ousted by one whom they name Mughorck the shaman. Mughorck is his name; and by 'shaman', they mean some mixture of priest, physician, and wizard.'

'A priest again!' Catharine glared up at her husband. 'Methinks there is too much of the religious in this.'

'They can be very powerful tools,' Rod said slowly.

'They can indeed. Yet, who wields these tools?'

'Nice question. And we may need the answer FESSter than we can get it.'

Behind his ear, Fess's voice murmured, 'Data cannot yet support an accurate inference.'

Well, Rod had to admit the truth of it; there wasn't any real evidence of collusion. On the way back north, he'd pretty much decided that the shaman was probably backed by the futurian totalitarians. Might even be one himself; never ignore the wonders of plastic surgery. What he'd effected was, essentially, a palace revolt with popular support, bearing an uncomfortable resemblance to the October Revolution in Russia in 1917, back on old Terra.

But that was quite another breed from the witch-hunt the Gramaryan preachers were mounting, which wasn't the kind of movement that lent itself well to any really effective central control. A single voice could start it, but it tended to get out of hand very quickly. A central power could direct its broad course but couldn't determine the details. It was an anarchist's technique, destroying the bonds of mutual trust that bound people together into a society – and it could lay the groundwork for a warlord.

Of course, if a warlord took over a whole nation, the distinction between warlord and dictator became rather blurry; but the anarchist's technique was to keep several warlords fighting, and increase their numbers as much as possible.

'Dost thou truly believe,' Tuan asked, 'that both are prongs of one single attack?'

Rod shook his head. 'Can't be sure; they could just as easily be two independent efforts, each trying to take advantage of the other. But for all practical purposes, we're fighting two separate enemies, and have to split our forces.'

'Then,' said Tuan with decision, 'the wisest course is to carry the fight to one enemy, and maintain a guard against the other.' He looked down at Catharine. 'We must double the size of our army, at least, my love; for some must stay here to guard whilst some go overseas to the beastmen's domain.'

'Thou dost speak of war, mine husband – of war full and bloody.'

Tuan nodded gravely.

Catharine squeezed her eyes shut. 'I had feared it would come to this pass. Eh, but I have seen men in battle ere now – and the sight did not please me.'

That, Rod decided, was another huge improvement.

Catharine looked up at Tuan again. 'Is there no other way?'

He shook his head heavily. 'There cannot be, sweet chuck. Therefore must we gather soldiers – and shipwrights.'

Tuan, Rod guessed, was about to invent a navy.

*

All Rod had said was, 'Take me to the beastmen.' He hadn't asked for a tour of the dungeons.

On second thought, maybe he had.

The sentry who guided him turned him over to a fat warder with a bunch of huge keys at his belt. Then the soldier turned to go. Rod reached out and caught his arm. 'Hold on. The beastmen're supposed to be our guests, not our captives. What're they doing down here?'

The sentry's face hardened. 'I know not, Lord Warlock. 'Tis as Sir Maris commanded.' Rod frowned; that didn't sound like the old knight. 'Fetch me Sir Maris forthwith – uh, that is, give him my compliments and tell him I request his presence down here.' Then he turned to follow the warder while the sentry clattered off angrily.

Rod lost track of his whereabouts very quickly; the dungeon was a virtual maze. Probably intentionally . . .

Finally the warder stopped, jammed a one-pound key into a porthole lock in a door that was scarcely wider than he was. He turned it with both hands, and the key grated through a year or two's worth of rust. Then the warder kicked the door open, revealing a twenty-foot-square chamber with a twelve-foot ceiling and five glowering beastmen who leaped to their feet, hands reaching for daggers that weren't there any more. Then the flickering light of the warder's torch showed them who their visitor was, and they relaxed – or at least Yorick did, and the others followed suit.

Rod took a breath to start talking, then had to shove his face back into the hall for a second one. Braced against aroma, he stepped through the doorway, looking around him, his nose wrinkling. 'What in the name of Heaven do you call *this*?'

'A dungeon,' Yorick said brightly. 'I thought that's where we were.'

'This is an insult!'

Yorick nodded slowly. 'Yeah . . . I'd say that was a good guess . . .'

Rod spun about, glaring at the warder. 'These men are supposed to be our guests!'

'Men?' the warder snorted. Then he squelched his feelings under an occupational deadpan. 'I but do as I am bid, Lord Warlock.'

'And what's *this*?' Rod reached out a foot to nudge a wooden bowl next to Yorick's foot.

'Gruel,' Yorick answered.

Rod felt his gorge rise. 'What's in it?'

'They didn't bother telling us,' Yorick said. 'But let me guess – an assortment of grains from the bottom of the bin. *You* know – the ones that fell out of the bag and spilled on the floor . . .'

'I hope you didn't eat any of it!'

'Not really.' Yorick looked around. 'To tell you the truth, it's not what's *in* it that bothers me. It's how *old* it is.'

Rod scowled. 'I thought that was a trick of the light.'

'No.' Yorick jerked his head up at a window set high in the wall – barred, of course. 'We took it over into the sunshine while there still was some. It really is green. Made great bait, though.'

'Bait?' Rod looked up with foreboding.

'Yeah. We've been holding a rat-killing contest.' Yorick shrugged. 'Not much else to do with the time.' He jerked his head toward a pile of foot-long corpses. 'So far, Kr“oligh's ahead, seven to four.'

Against his better judgement, Rod was about to ask who had the four when the warder announced, 'Comes Sir Maris.'

The old knight stepped through the door, his head covered with the cowl of his black robe; but the front was open, showing chain mail and a broadsword. 'Well met, Lord Warlock.'

*That's debatable*, Rod thought; but he had always respected and liked the old knight, so he only said, 'As are you, Sir Maris.' He took a deep breath to hold down the anger that threatened to spill over now that it had a logical target. 'Why are these men housed within a prison?'

Sir Maris blinked, surprised at the question. 'Why – His Majesty bade me house them according to their rank and station!'

Rod let out a huge, gusty breath. 'But, Sir Maris – they are not criminals! And they are not animals, either.'

'Assuredly they cannot be much more!'

'They can – *vastly* more!' Rod's anger drowned under the need to make the old knight understand. 'It's the soul that matters, Sir Maris – not intelligence. Though they've enough of that, Lord knows. And their souls are every bit as human as ours. Just as immortal too, I expect.' Rod didn't mention that there were two ways of interpreting that statement. 'Their appearance may differ from ours, and they may wear only the skins of beasts; but they are free, valiant warriors – yeomen, if you will. And, within their own land and nation, the least of *these* is the equal of a knight.'

Sir Maris's eyes widened, appalled; but Yorick had a complacent smile. 'A little thick, maybe, milord – but gratifying. Yes, gratifying. We *are* refugees, though.'

Rod clasped Sir Maris's shoulder. 'It'll take a while to understand, I know. For the time being, take my word for it: the King would be appalled if he knew where they were. Take them up to a tower chamber where they may climb up to the roof for air.'

'To walk the *battlements*, my Lord Warlock?' Sir Maris cried in outrage. 'Why, they might signal the enemy!'

Rod closed his eyes. 'The enemy has never come closer than the coast, Sir Maris – hundreds of miles away. And these men are *not* the enemy – they've *fled* from the enemy!' He glanced back at the Neanderthals. 'And, come to that – please give them back their knives.'

'Arms!?' the old knight gasped. 'Lord Warlock – hast thou thought what they might *do* with them?'

'Kill rats,' Rod snapped. 'Which reminds me – give them rations fit for a fighting man. Bread, Sir Maris – and meat!'

The old knight sighed, capitulating. 'It shall be as thou hast —'

'Dada!' Rod's shoulder suddenly sagged under twenty pounds of baby. He reached up in a panic to catch Magnus's arm, then remembered that, for Magnus at least, falling was scarcely a danger. He let out a sigh of relief, feeling his knees turn to jelly. 'Don't *do* that to me, son!'

'Da'y, s'ory! Tell s'ory!'

'A story? Uh – not just now, son.' Rod lifted the baby from his shoulder and slung him in front of his stomach. 'I'm a little busy.'

The beastmen stared, then began muttering apprehensively to one another.

'Uh – they're saying that baby's gotta be a witch,' Yorick advised gently.

'Huh?' Rod looked up, startled. 'No, a warlock. That's the male term, you know.'

Yorick stared at him for a beat, then nodded deliberately. 'Right.' He turned and said something to the other Neanderthals. They looked up, their faces printed with fear of the supernatural. Yorick turned back to Rod. 'They're not what I'd call "reassured" milord.'

So, it started that early, Rod noted. He shrugged. 'They'll get used to it. It's endemic around here.' He looked directly into Yorick's eyes. 'After all, we're not exactly used to your instant freeze, either, are we? I mean, fair is fair.'

'Well, yeah, but the Evil Eye isn't witch-power, it's . . .' Yorick held up a finger, and ran out of words. He stared at Rod for a second, then nodded his head. 'Right.' He turned back to the beastmen to try to explain it.

'No, no time for a story.' Rod bounced Magnus against his belt. 'Go ask Mommy.'

'Mommy *gone*.' The baby glowered.

Rod froze.

Then he said, very quietly, 'Oh.' And, 'Is she?'

Magnus nodded. 'Mommy gone *away*!'

'Really!' Rod took a deep breath. 'And who's taking care of you while she's gone?'

'Elf.' The baby looked up, grinning. 'Elf slow.'

Rod stared at him. Then he nodded slowly. 'But elf catch up with Baby.'

The child's smile faded.

'Baby naughty to run away from elf,' Rod pursued, punching the moral of the story.

Magnus hunkered down with a truculent look.

'Baby *stay* with the nice elf,' Rod advised, 'or Daddy spank.' Rod tried not to look too severe.

Magnus sighed, took a deep breath, and squeezed his eyes shut.

'No, no! Don't go back quite yet!' Rod squeezed the kid a little tighter.

Magnus opened his eyes in surprise.

'Let's get back to Mommy for a second,' Rod said casually. 'Where . . . did Mommy . . . *go*?'

'Dunno.' The baby shook his head, wide-eyed. 'Mommy say . . .'

'There thou art, thou naughty babe!' A miniature whirlwind burst through the door and up to Rod, where it screeched to a halt and resolved itself into the form of an eighteen-inch-high elf with a broad mischievous face and a Robin Hood costume. At the moment, he looked definitely chagrined. 'Lord Warlock, my deepest apologies! He did escape me!'

'Yes, and I've scolded him for it.' Rod kept a stern eye on Magnus. The baby tried to look truculent again, but began to look a little tearful instead. 'I think he'll stay with you this time, Puck,' Rod went on, smiling. The baby saw, and tried a tentative smile himself. Rod tousled his hair, and he beamed. Rod eyed the elf sideways. 'Did Gwen tell you where she was going?'

'Aye, Lord Warlock. When the Queen did return from her progress of the province, she did summon thy wife to tell her what ill luck she had had in seeking out witches to swell the ranks of the Royal Coven – and spoke unto her the why of it, too.'

'The hedge priest.' Rod nodded grimly. 'I've heard about him. I take it she wasn't happy?'

'Indeed she was not. But thy wife was never one to think of revenge.'

Remembering some of the things Rod had seen Gwen do, he shuddered. 'Lucky for him.'

'It is indeed. Yet she did not think of what he had done; she thought only of other ways to gain more witches for the Royal Coven.'

'Oh?' Rod felt dread creeping up over the back of his skull. '*What* ways?'

'Why – she did believe the surest way now would be to seek out the ancient witches and warlocks who have hidden away in the forests and mountains, for they care not what the people think or say.'

The dread gained territory. 'Yeah, but – I thought they were supposed to be sour and bitter, as likely to hex you as help you.'

'They are indeed,' Puck acknowledged. 'E'en so, if aught can bring them to give aid, 'twould be thy sweet Gwendylon's cajoling.'

'Yeah, provided they don't hex her first.' Rod whirled to plop Magnus into Puck's arms. Puck stared at the baby in surprise, but held him easily – even though Magnus was at least as big as he.

'Where'd she go?' Rod snapped. 'Which witch?'

'Why, the most notorious,' Puck answered, surprised, 'the one whose name all folk do know, who comes first to mind when mothers tell their babies witch tales . . .'

'The champion horror-hag, eh?' Sweat sprang out on Rod's brow. 'What's her name? Quick!'

'Agatha, they call her – Angry Aggie. She doth dwell high up in the Crag Mountains in a cave, noisome, dark, and dank.'

'Take care of the kid!' Rod whirled toward the door.

Air boomed out and Toby was there, right in front of him. 'Lord Warlock!'

The beastmen shrank back, muttering fearfully to one another. Yorick spoke soothingly to them – or it would've been soothingly if his voice hadn't shaken.

'Not *now*, Toby!' Rod tried to step around him.

But the young warlock leaped in front of him again. 'The beastmen, Lord Warlock! Their dragon ships approach the coast! And three approach where formerly there was but one!'

'Tell 'em to wait!' Rod snapped, and he leaped out the door.

Being a robot, Fess could gallop much faster than a real horse when he wanted to; and right now Rod wanted every ounce of speed the black horse could give him. Fess had been reluctant to go faster than twenty miles per hour until Rod had had an oversized knight's helmet outfitted with webbing, making it an acceptable crash helmet; but he still wouldn't ride with the visor down.

'But don't you dare try to get me to wear the rest of the armour!'

'I would not dream of it, Rod.' Which was true; being a machine, Fess did not dream. In fact, he didn't even sleep. But he did do random correlations during his off hours, which served the same function. 'However, I would appreciate it if you would strap yourself on.'

'Whoever heard of a saddle with a seat belt?' Rod griped; but he fastened it anyway. 'You shouldn't have to stop that fast, though. I mean, what do you have radar for?'

'Precisely.' Fess stepped up the pace to sixty miles per hour. 'But I must caution you, Rod, that such breakneck speed on a horse will not diminish your reputation as a warlock.'

'We'll worry about public relations later. Right now, we've got to get to Gwen before she runs into something fatal!'

'You have a singular lack of confidence in your wife, Rod.'

What? Rod's double take was so violent, he almost knocked himself off the saddle. 'I'd trust her with my life, Fess!'

'Yes, but not with hers. Do you really think she would have gone on this mission alone if she thought there were any real danger?'

'Of course I do! She's not a coward!'

'No, but she has a baby and a husband who need her. She would no longer be willing to risk her life quite so recklessly.'

'Oh.' Rod frowned. 'Well – maybe you've got a point.' Then his sense of urgency returned. 'But she could be underestimating them, Fess! I mean, that sour old witch has been up in those hills for probably forty years, at least! Who knows what kind of deviltry she's figured out by now?'

'Probably Gwendylon does. Your wife *is* a telepath, Rod.'

'So's Agatha. And what Gwen can read, maybe Agatha can block! Come *on*, Fess! We've got to *get* there!'

Fess gave the static hiss that was a robot's sigh, and stepped up the pace. Drowsy summer fields and tidy thatched cottages flew by.

'She's up *there*?' Rod stared up at an almost sheer wall of rock towering into the sky above him, so close that it seemed to snare laggard clouds.

'So said the peasant we asked, Rod. And I think he was too terrified by our speed to have prevaricated.'

Rod shrugged. 'No reason for him to lie, anyway. How do we get up there, Fess?'

'That will not be so difficult.' The robot eyed the uneven surfaces of the cliff face. 'Remember, Rod – lean into the climb.' He set hoof on the beginning of a path Rod hadn't even noticed before.

'If that peasant is watching, he's going to go under for good now,' Rod sighed. 'Who ever saw a horse climbing a mountain before?'

'Everything considered,' Fess said thoughtfully as he picked his way along a ledge a little narrower than his body, 'I believe it would have been faster to have replaced my brain-case into the spaceship and flown here.'

'Maybe, but it would've been a lot harder to explain to the peasantry – *and* the lords, for that matter.' Rod eyed the sheer drop below, and felt his stomach sink. 'Fess, I don't suppose this body was built with a few antigravity plates in it?'

'Of course it was, Rod. Maxima designers consider all eventualities.' Fess was a little conceited about the planetoid where he'd been manufactured.

'Well, it's a relief to know that, if we fall, we won't hit too hard. But why don't we just float up to the cave?'

'I thought you were concerned about our passage's effect on observers.'

'A point,' Rod sighed. 'Onward and upward, Rust Rider. *Excelsior!*'

Ahead and to their left, a cave-mouth yawned – but it was only six feet high. Rod eyed it and pronounced, 'Not quite high enough for both of us.'

'I agree. Please dismount with caution, Rod – and be careful to stay against the rock wall.'

'Oh, don't worry – I won't stray.' Rod slid down between Fess and the cliff-face, trying to turn himself into a pancake. Then he eased past the great black horse and sidled along the ledge toward the black emptiness of the cave-mouth. He edged up to it, telling himself that a real witch couldn't possibly look like the ones in the fairy tales; but all the cradle epics came flooding back into his mind as he oozed toward the dank darkness of the witch's lair. The fact that Angry Aggie was mentioned by name in the Gramarye versions of most of those stories, in a feature, popular, but not entirely sympathetic role, did not exactly help to calm him. A comparison of the relative weights of logic and childhood conditioning in determining the mature human's emotional reactions makes a fascinating study in theory; but firsthand observation of the practical aspects can be a trifle uncomfortable.

A wild cackle split the air. Rod froze; the cackle faded, slackened, and turned into sobbing. Rod frowned and edged closer to the cave . . . Gwen's voice! He could hear her murmuring, soothing. Rod felt his body relax; in fact, he almost went limp. He hadn't realized he'd been *that* worried. But if Gwen was doing the comforting, well . . . she couldn't be in *too* much danger. Could she?

Not at the moment, at least. He straightened and took a firm step forward to stride into the cave – but the testy crackle of the old woman's voice froze him in his tracks.

'Aye, I know, they are not *all* villains. They could not be, could they? Yet I would never guess it from my own life!'

Gwen, Rod decided, was amazing. She couldn't have been here more than half an hour ahead of him, and already she had the old witch opened up and talking.

Gwen murmured an answer, but Rod couldn't make it out. He frowned, edging closer to the cave – just in time to hear old Agatha say, 'Rejoice, lass, that thou dost live in the new day which has dawned upon us – when the Queen protects those with witch-power, and a witch may find a warlock to wed her.'

'In that, I know I am fortunate, reverend dame,' Gwen answered.

Rod blushed. He actually blushed. This was going too far. He was eavesdropping for certain now. He straightened his shoulders and stepped into the cave. 'Ahem!' It was very dim. He could scarcely make out anything – except two female figures seated in front of a fire. The older one's head snapped up as she heard him. Her face was lit by the firelight below, which made it look unearthly enough; but even by itself, it was a hideous, bony face.

For a second, she stared at him. Then the face split into a gargoyle grin, with a huge cackle. 'Eh, what have we here? Can we not even speak of men without their intruding upon us?'

Gwen looked up, startled. Then her face lit with delighted surprise. 'My lord!' She leaped to her feet and came toward him.

The old woman's face twisted into a sneer. She jerked her head toward Rod. 'Is it thine?'

'It is.' Gwen caught Rod's hands; her body swayed toward him for a moment, then away. Rod understood; public display of affection can be offensive, especially to those who don't have any. But her eyes said she was flattered and very glad of his support.

Her lips, however, said only, 'Why dost thou come, husband?'

'Just a little worried, dear. Though I see it was foolish of me.'

'Not so foolish as thou might have thought,' the witch grated. 'Yet thou art lately come, to be of aid.' She frowned in thought. 'Nay, but mayhap thou'rt timely come also; for, an thou hadst been with her when first she had appeared in my cave-mouth, I doubt not I would have sent thee both packing.'

Rod started to add, 'If you could,' then thought better of it. 'Uh. Yeah. Sorry to intrude.'

'Think naught of it,' Agatha said acidly, 'no other man has.' She transferred her gaze to Gwen. 'Thou'rt most excellent fortunate, to be sure.'

Gwen lowered her eyes, blushing.

'Yet, I doubt thou knowest the true extent of thy fortune.' The witch turned back to the fireplace, jammed a paddle into a huge cauldron, and stirred. 'There was no tall young wizard for me, but a horde of ploughboys from mountain villages, who came by ones and by fives to me for a moment's pleasure, then came threescore all together, with their mothers and sisters and wives and their stern village clergy, to flog me and rack me and pierce me with hot needles, crying, "Vile witch, confess!" till I could contain it no longer, till my hatred broke loose upon them, smiting them low and hurling them from out my cave!'

She broke off, gasping and shuddering. Alarmed, Gwen clasped Agatha's hands in her own, and paled as their chill crept up to her spine. She had heard the tale of how, long years ago, the witch Agatha had flung the folk of five villages out of her cave, how many had broken their heads or their backs on the slopes below. No witch in Gramarye, in all the history of that eldritch island, had been possessed of such power. Most witches could lift only two, or perhaps three, at a time. And as for hurling them about with enough force to send them clear of a cave – why, that was flatly impossible.

Wasn't it?

Therefore, if a witch had indeed performed such a feat, why, obviously she must have had a familiar, a helping spirit. These usually took the form of animals; but Agatha had kept no pets. Therefore – why, there still had to be a familiar, but it must have been invisible.

' 'Twas then,' panted the witch, 'that I came to this cavern, where the ledge without was so narrow that only one man could enter at once, and so that in my wrath I might never injure more than a few. But those few . . .'

The scrawny shoulders slackened, the back bowed; the old witch slumped against the rough table. 'Those few, aie! Those few . . .'

'They sought to burn thee,' Gwen whispered, tears in her eyes, 'and 'twas done in anger, anger withheld overlong, longer than any man might have contained it! They debased thee, they tortured thee!'

'Will that bring back dead men?' Agatha darted a whetted glance at Gwen.

Gwen stared at the ravaged face, fascinated. 'Agatha . . .' She bit her lip, then rushed on. 'Dost thou wish to make amends for the lives thou hast taken?'

'Thou dost speak nonsense!' The witch spat. 'A life is beyond price; thou canst not make amends for the taking of it!'

'True,' Rod said thoughtfully, 'but there is restitution.'

The whetted glance sliced into him, freezing almost as effectively as the Evil Eye.

Then, though, the gaze lightened as the witch slowly grinned. 'Ah, then!' She threw her head back and cackled. It was a long laugh, and when it faded Agatha wiped her eyes, nodding. 'Eh! I had pondered the why of thy coming; for none come to old Agatha lest they have a wish, a yearning that may not be answered by any other. And this is thine, is it not? That the folk of the land be in danger; they stand in need of old Agatha's power! And they have sent thee to beg me the use of it!'

Her gaunt body shook with another spasm of cackling. She wheezed into a crooning calm, wiping her nose with a long bony finger. 'Eh, eh! Child! Am I, a beldam of threescore years and more, to be cozened by the veriest, most innocent child? Eh!' And she was off again.

Rod frowned; this was getting out of hand. 'I wouldn't exactly call it "cozening".'

The witch's laughter chopped off. 'Wouldst thou not?' she spat. 'But thou wilt ask aid of me, aye! And wilt seek to give me no recompense, nay!' She transferred her gaze to Gwen. 'And thou wilt do as he bids thee, wilt thou not?'

'Nay!' Gwen cried, affronted. 'I have come of my own, to beg of thee . . .'

'Of thine own!' The witch glared. 'Hast thou no stripes to thy back, no scars to thy breasts where their torturers have burned thee? Hast thou not known the pain of their envy and hate, that thou shouldst come, unforced, uncajoled, to beg help for them?'

'I have.' Gwen felt a strange calm descend over her. 'Twice I was scourged, and thrice tortured, four times bound to a stake for the burning; and I must needs thank the Wee Folk, my good guardians, that I live now to speak to thee. Aye, I ha' known the knotted whip of their fear; though never so deeply as thou. Yet . . .'

The old witch nodded, wondering. 'Yet, you pity them.'

'Aye.' Gwen lowered her eyes, clasping her hands tight in her lap. 'Indeed, I do pity them.' Her eyes leaped up to lock with Agatha's. 'For their fear is the barbed thong that lashes us, their fear of the great dark that stands behind such powers as ours, the dark of unknown, and the unguessable fate that we bring them. 'Tis they who must grope for life and for good in midnightmare, they who never ha' known the sound of love-thoughts, the joy of a moonlit flight. Ought we not, then, to pity them?'

Agatha nodded slowly. Her old eyes filmed over, staring off into a life now distant in time. 'So I had thought once, in my girlhood . . .'

'Pity them, then,' said Gwen, sawing hard at the reins of her eagerness. 'Pity them, and—'

'And forgive them?' Agatha snapped back to the present, shaking her head slowly, a bitter smile on her gash of a mouth. 'In my heart, I might forgive them. The stripes and the blows, the burning needles, the chains and the flaming splinters under my nails – aye, even this might I forgive them . . .'

Her eyes glazed, gazing back down the years. 'But the abuse of my body, my fair, slender girl's body and my ripe-blossomed woman's body, all the long years, my most tender flesh and the most intimate part of my heart, the tearing and rending of that heart, again and again, to feed them, their craving, insensible hunger . . . no!' Her voice was low and guttural, gurgling acid, a black-diamond drill. 'No, nay! That, I may never forgive them! Their greed and their lust, their slavering hunger! Forever and ever they came, to come in and take me, and hurl me away; to come for my trembling flesh – then spurn me away, crying, "Whore!" Again and again, by one and by five, knowing I would not, could not, turn them away; and therefore they came and they came . . . Nay! That, I may never forgive them!'

Gwen's heart broke open and flowed; and it must have shown in her face, for Agatha transfixed her with a shimmering glare. 'Pity them if you must,' she grated, 'but never have pity for me!'

She held Gwen's eyes for a moment, then turned back to the cauldron, taking up her paddle again. 'You will tell me that this was no fault of theirs,' she muttered, 'any more than it was of mine, that their hunger forced them to me as truly as mine constrained me to welcome them.'

Her head lifted slowly, the eyes narrowing. 'Or didst thou not know? Galen, the wizard of the Dark Tower. He it was who should have answered my hunger with his own. The greatest witch and the greatest warlock of the kingdom together, is it not fitting? But he alone of all men would never come to me, the swine! Oh, he will tell you he hath too much righteousness to father a child into a Hell-world like this; yet the truth of it is, he fears the blame of that child he might father. Coward! Churl! Swine!'

She dug at the caldron, spitting and cursing. 'Hell-spawned, thrice misbegotten, bastard mockery of a man! Him –' she finished in a harsh whisper ' – I hate most of all!'

The bony, gnarled old hands clutched the paddle so tight it seemed the wood must break.

Then she was clutching the slimy wooden paddle to her sunken dried breast. Her shoulders shook with dry sobs. 'My child,' she murmured. 'O my fair, unborn, sweet child!'

The sobs diminished and stilled. Then, slowly, the witch's eyes came up again. 'Or didst thou not know?' She smiled harshly, an eldritch gleam in her rheumy yellowed eye. 'He it is who doth guard my portal, who doth protect me – my unborn child, Harold, my son, my familiar! So he was, and so he will ever be now – a soul come to me out of a tomorrow that once might have been.'

Gwen stared, thunderstruck. 'Thy familiar. .?'

'Aye.' The old witch's nod was tight with irony. 'My familiar and my son, my child who, because he once might have been, and should have been, bides with me now, though he never shall be born, shall never have flesh grown out of my own to cover his soul with. Harold, most powerful of wizards, son of old Galen and Agatha, of a union unrealized; for the Galen and Agatha who sired and bore him ha' died in us long ago, and lie buried in the rack and mire of our youth.'

She turned back to the cauldron, stirring slowly. 'When first he came to me, long years ago, I could not understand.'

Frankly, Rod couldn't either – although he was beginning to suspect hallucinations. He wondered if prolonged loneliness could have that effect in a grown person – developing an imaginary companion.

But if Agatha really believed in this 'familiar', maybe the hallucination could focus her powers so completely that it would dredge up every last ounce of her potential. That could account for the extraordinary strength of her psi powers . . .

Agatha lifted her head, gazing off into space.

'It seemed, lo, full strange to me, most wondrous strange; but I was lonely, and grateful. But now–' her breath wheezed like a dying organ ' – now I know, now I understand.' She nodded bitterly. ''Twas an unborn soul that had no other home, and never would have.'

Her head hung low, her whole body slumped with her grief.

After a long, long while, she lifted her head and sought out Gwen's eyes. 'You have a son, have you not?'

There was a trace of tenderness in Agatha's smile at Gwen's nod.

But the smile hardened, then faded; and the old witch shook her head. 'The poor child,' she muttered.

'Poor child!' Gwen struggled to hide outrage. 'In the name of Heaven, old Agatha, why?'

Agatha gave her a contemptuous glance over her shoulder. 'Thou hast lived through witch-childhood, and thou hast need to ask?'

'No,' Gwen whispered, shaking her head; then, louder, 'No! A new day has dawned, Agatha, a day of change! My son shall claim his rightful place in this kingdom, shall guard the people and have respect from them, as is his due!'

'Think thou so?' The old witch smiled bitterly.

'Aye, I believe it! The night has past now, Agatha, fear and ignorance have gone in this day of change. And never again shall the folk of the village pursue them in anger and fear and red hatred!'

The old witch smiled sourly and jerked her head toward the cave-mouth. 'Hear thou that?'

Rod saw Gwen turn toward the cave-mouth, frowning. He cocked his ear and caught a low, distant rumble. He realized it had been there for some time, coming closer.

The heck with the cover. 'Fess! What's that noise?'

' 'Tis these amiable villager folk of thine,' said old Agatha with a sardonic smile, 'the folk of twelve villages, gathered together behind a preacher corrupted by zeal, come to roust old Agatha from her cave and burn her to ashes, for once and for all.'

'Analysis confirmed,' Fess's voice said behind Rod's ear.

Rod leaped to the cave-mouth, grabbed a rocky projection, and leaned out to look down.

Halfway up the slope, a churning mass filled the stone ledges.

Rod whirled back to face the women. 'She's right – it's a peasant mob. They're carrying scythes and mattocks.'

A sudden gust blew the mob's cry more loudly to them.

'Hear!' Agatha snorted, nodding toward the cave-mouth. Her mouth twisted with bitterness at the corners. 'Hear them clamouring for my blood! Aye, when an unwashed, foaming madman drives them to it!'

She looked down at the swarming mob climbing ledge by ledge toward them. Steel winked in the sun.

Gwen felt the clammy touch of fear; but fear of what, she did not know. 'Thou speakest almost as though thou hadst known this beforehand . . .'

'Oh, to be certain, I did.' The old witch smiled. 'Has it not come often upon me before? It was bound to be coming again. The time alone I did not know; but what matter is that?'

The ledges narrowed as the horde surged higher. Gwen could make out individual faces now. 'They come close, Agatha. What must we do against them?'

'Do?' The old witch raised shaggy eyebrows in surprise. 'Why, nothing, child. I have too much of their blood on my hands already. I am tired, old, and sick of my life; why then should I fight them? Let them come here and burn me. This time, at least, I will not be guilty of the blood of those I have saved.'

Agatha turned away from the cave-mouth, gathering her shawl about her narrow old shoulders. 'Let them come here and rend me; let them set up a stake here and burn me. Even though it come in the midst of great torture, death shall be sweet.'

Rod stared, appalled. 'You've got to be joking!'

'Must I, then?' Agatha transfixed him with a glare. 'Thou shalt behold the truth of it!' She hobbled over to a scarred chair and sat down. 'Here I rest, and here I stay, come what will, and come who will. Let them pierce me, let them burn me! I shall not again be guilty of shedding human blood!'

'But we *need* you!' Rod cried. 'A coven of witches scarcely out of childhood needs you! The whole land of Gramarye needs you!'

'Wherefore – the saving of lives? And to save their lives, I must needs end these?' She nodded toward the roaring at the cave-mouth. 'I think not, Lord Warlock. The very sound of it echoes with evil. Who saves lives by taking lives must needs be doing devil's work.'

'All right, so don't kill them!' Rod cried, exasperated. 'Just send them away.'

'And how shall we do that, pray? They are already halfway up the mountain. How am I to throw them down without slaying them?'

'Then, do not slay them.' Gwen dropped to her knees beside Agatha's chair. 'Let them come – but do not let them touch thee.'

Rod's eyes glowed. 'Of course! Fess's outside on the ledge! He can keep them out!'

'Surely he is not!' Gwen looked up, horrified. 'There must be an hundred of them, at the least! They will pick him up and throw him bodily off the cliff!'

Rod's stomach sank as he realized she was right. Not that it would hurt Fess, of course – he remembered that antigravity plate in the robot's belly. But it wouldn't keep the peasants out, either.

'What is this "Fess" thou dost speak of?' Agatha demanded.

'My, uh, horse,' Rod explained. 'Not exactly . . . a horse. I mean, he looks like a horse, and he sounds like a horse, but . . .'

'If it doth appear to be an horse, and doth sound like to an horse, then it must needs be an horse,' Agatha said with asperity, 'and I would not have it die. Bring it hither, within the cave. If it doth not impede them, they will not slay it.'

Loose rock clattered, and hooves echoed on stones as Fess walked into the cave. Behind Rod's ear his voice murmured, 'Simple discretion, Rod.'

'He's got very good hearing,' Rod explained.

'And doth understand readily too, I wot,' Agatha said, giving Fess a jaundiced glance. Then her eye glittered and she looked up, fairly beaming. 'Well-a-day! We are quite cosy, are we not? And wilt thou, then, accompany me to my grave?'

Gwen froze. Then her shoulders straightened, and her chin lifted. 'If we must, we will.' She turned to Rod. 'Shall we not, husband?'

Rod stared at her for a second. Even in the crisis, he couldn't help noticing that he had been demoted from 'my lord' to 'husband'. Then his mouth twisted. 'Not if I can help it.' He stepped over to the black horse and fumbled in a saddlebag. 'Fess and I have a few gimmicks here . . .' He pulled out a small compact cylinder. 'We'll just put up a curtain of fire halfway back in the cave, between us and them. Oughta scare 'em outa their buskins. . . .'

'It will not hold them long!' Agatha began to tremble. 'Yet, I see thou dost mean it. Fool! Idiot! Thou wilt but madden them further! They will break through thy flames; they will tear thee, they will rend thee!'

'I think not.' Gwen turned to face the cave-mouth. 'I will respect thy wishes and not hurl them from the ledge; yet, I can fill the air with a rain of small stones. I doubt me not an that will affright them.'

'An thou dost affright them, they will flee! And in their flight, they will knock one another from the ledge, a thousand feet and more down to their deaths!' Agatha cried, agonized. 'Nay, lass! Do not seek to guard me! Fly! Thou'rt young, and a-love! Thou hast a bairn and a husband! Thou hast many years left to thee, and they will be sweet, though many bands like to this come against thee!'

Gwen glanced longingly at her broomstick, then looked up at Rod. He met her gaze with a sombre face.

'Fly, fly!' Agatha's face twisted with contempt. 'Thou canst not aid a sour old woman in the midst of her death throes, lass! Thy death here with me would serve me not at all! Indeed, it would deepen the guilt that my soul is steeped in!'

Rod dropped to one knee behind a large boulder and levelled his laser at the cave-mouth. Gwen nodded and stepped behind a rocky pillar. Pebbles began to stir on the floor of the cave.

'Nay!' Agatha screeched. 'Thou must needs be away from this place, and right quickly!' Turning, she seized a broomstick and slammed it into Gwen's hands; her feet lifted off the floor. Rod felt something pick him up and throw him toward Gwen. He shouted in anger and tried to swerve aside, but he landed on the broomstick anyway. It pushed up underneath him, then hurtled the two of them toward the cave-mouth – and slammed into an invisible wall that gave under them, slowed them, stopped them, then tossed them back toward old Agatha. They jarred into each other and tumbled to the floor.

'Will you make up your *mind*!' Rod clambered to his feet, rubbing his bruises. 'Do you want us out, or don't . . .' His voice trailed off as he saw the look on the old witch's face. She stared past his shoulder toward the cave-mouth. Frowning, he turned to follow her gaze.

The air at the cave-mouth shimmered.

The old witch's face darkened with anger. 'Harold! Begone! Withdraw from the cave-mouth, and quickly; this lass must be away!'

The shimmering intensified like a heat haze.

A huge boulder just outside the cave-mouth stirred.

'Nay, Harold!' Agatha screeched. 'Thou shalt not! There ha' been too much bloodshed already!'

The boulder lifted slowly, clear of the ledge.

'Harold!' Agatha screamed, and fell silent.

For, instead of dropping down onto the toiling peasants below, the boulder lifted out and away, rising swiftly into the sky.

It was twenty feet away from the cave when a swarm of arrows spat out from the cliff above, struck the boulder, and rebounded, falling away into the valley below.

The old witch stood frozen a long moment, staring at the heat haze and the boulder arcing away into the forest.

'Harold,' she whispered, 'arrows . . .'

She shook her head, coming back to herself. 'Thou must not leave now.'

'He ha' saved our lives,' said Gwen, round-eyed.

'Aye, that he hath; there be archers above us, awaiting the flight of a witch. Mayhap they thought I would fly; but I never have, I ha' always stayed here and fought them. It would seem they know thou'rt with me. A yard from that ledge now, and thou wouldst most truly resemble two hedgehogs.'

Agatha turned away, dragging Gwen with her toward the back of the cave. 'Thou, at least, must not die here! We shall brew witchcraft, thou and I, for a storm of magic such as hath never been witnessed in this land! Harold!' she called over her shoulder to the heat haze. 'Guard the door!'

Rod started to follow, then clenched his fists, feeling useless.

Agatha hauled a small iron pot from the shelf and gasped as its weight plunged against her hands. She heaved, thrusting with her whole body to throw it up onto a small tripod that stood on the rough table. 'I grow old,' she growled as she hooked the pot onto the tripod, 'old and weak. Long years it ha' been since I last stewed men's fates in this.'

'Men's fates . . .?' Gwen was at her elbow. 'What dost thou, Agatha?'

'Why, a small cooking, child.' The old witch grinned. 'Did I not say we would brew great magic here?'

She turned away and began pulling stone jars from the shelf. 'Kindle me a fire, child. We shall live, lass, for we must; this land hath not yet given us dismissal.'

A spark fell from Gwen's flint and steel into the tinder. Gwen breathed on the resulting coal till small flames danced in the kindling. As she fed it larger and larger wood scraps, she ventured, 'Thou art strangely joyous for a witch who ha' been deprived of that which she wanted, old Agatha.'

The old witch cackled and rubbed her thin, bony hands. 'It is the joy of a craftsman, child, that doth his work well, and sees a great task before him, a greater task than ever his trade yet ha' brought him. I shall live, and more joyous and hearty than ever before; for there is great need of old Agatha, and great deeds a-doing. The undoing of this war thou hast told me of will be old Agatha's greatest work.'

She took a measure from the shelf and began ladling powders from the various jars into the pot, then took a small paddle and began stirring the brew.

Gwen flinched at the stench that arose from the heating-pot. 'What is this hideous porridge, Agatha? I have never known a witch to use such a manner of bringing magic, save in child's tales.'

Agatha paused in her stirring to fasten a pensive eye on Gwen. 'Thou art yet young, child, and know only half-truths of witchery.'

She turned back to stirring the pot. 'It is true that our powers be of the mind, and only of the mind. Yet true it also is that thou hast never used but a small part of thy power, child. Thou knowest not the breadth and the width of it, the colour and the warp and the woof of it. There be deep, unseen parts of thy soul thou hast never uncovered; and this deep power thou canst not call up at will. It lies too far buried, beyond thy call. Thou must needs trick it into coming out, direct it by ruse and gin, not by will.' She peered into the smoking, bubbling pot. 'And this thou must do with a bubbling brew compounded of things which stand for the powers thou doth wish to evoke from thy heart of hearts and the breadth of thy brain. Hummingbird's feathers, for strength, speed, and flight; bees, for their stings; poppyseed, for the dulling of wits; lampblack, for the stealth and silence of night; woodbine, to bind it to the stone of the cliffs; hearth-ash, for the wish to return to the home.'

She lifted the paddle; the mess flowed slowly down from it into the pot. 'Not quite thick enow,' the old witch muttered, and went back to stirring. 'Put the jars back on the shelves, child; a tidy kitchen makes a good brew.'

Gwen picked up a few jars, but as she did she glanced toward the cave-mouth. The clamour was much louder. 'Old Agatha, they come!'

The first of the villagers stormed into the cave, brandishing a scythe.

'Their clamour shall but help the brew's flavour,' said the old witch with a delightedly wicked grin. She bent over the pot, and crooned.

The peasant slammed into the invisible haze barrier, and rebounded, knocking over the next two behind him. The fourth and fifth stumbled over their fallen comrades, adding nicely to the pile. The stack heaved as the ones on the bottom tried to struggle to their feet. The top layers shrieked, leaped up, and fled smack-dab into the arms of their lately-come reinforcements. The resulting frantic struggle was somewhat energetic, and the ledge was only wide enough for one man at a time; the peasants seesawed back and forth, teetering perilously close to the edge, flailing their arms for balance and squalling in terror.

' 'Tis a blessing the ledge is so narrow, they cannot come against me more than one at a time.' Agatha wrapped a rag around the handle of the pot and hefted it off the hook, strands of muscle straining along her arms. 'Quickly, child,' she grated, 'the tripod! My son Harold is summat more than a man, but he cannot hold them long, not so many! Quickly! Quickly! We must prepare to be aiding him!'

She hobbled into the entryway. Gwen caught up the tripod and ran after her.

As she set down the tripod and Agatha hooked the pot on it again, two sticks of wood thudded against the ledge, sticking two feet up above the stone.

'Scaling ladders!' gasped Agatha. 'This was well planned, in truth! Quickly, child! Fetch the bellows!'

Gwen ran for the bellows, wishing she knew what old Agatha was planning.

As she returned – handing the bellows to Agatha where she crouched over the pot in the middle of the entryway – a tall, bearded figure appeared at the top of the ladder, clambering onto the ledge. The man levelled his dark, polished staff at the cave-mouth. The staff gave a muted clank as he set its butt against the stone.

'An iron core!' Agatha pointed the bellows over the pot at the preacher and began pumping them furiously. 'That staff must not touch my son!'

But the forward end of the staff had already touched the heat haze. A spark exploded at the top of the staff. Skolax howled victory and swung his staff to beckon his forces. The peasants shouted and surged into the cave.

'Bastard!' Agatha screamed. 'Vile Hell-fiends! Murrain upon thee! Thou hast slain my son!'

She glared furiously, pumping the bellows like a maniac. The steam from the pot shot forward toward the mob.

They stopped dead. A deathly pallor came over their faces. Little red dots began appearing on their skins. They screamed, whirling about and flailing at their comrades, swatting at something unseen that darted and stung them.

For a moment, the crowd milled and boiled in two conflicting streams at the cave-mouth; then the back ranks screamed and gave way as the phantom stings struck them too, and the mob fled back along the ledge, away from the cave.

Only the preacher remained, struggling against the flock of phantom bees, his face swelling red with ghost-stings.

The old witch threw back her head and cackled shrill and long, still pumping the bellows. 'We have them, child! We have them now!' Then she bent grimly over the pot, pumping harder, and spat, 'Now shall they pay for his death! Now shall my Eumenides hie them home!'

With a titanic effort, Skolax threw himself forward, his staff whirling up over the witch's head. Gwen leaped forward to shield her; but the staff jumped backward, jerking the preacher off his feet and throwing him hard on the stone floor. Agatha's triumphant cry cut through his agonized bellow: 'He lives! My son Harold lives!'

But the preacher lifted his staff as though it were a huge and heavy weight, his face swelling with ghost-stings and rage. 'Hearken to me! Hearken to Skolax! Tear them! Rend them! They cannot stand against us! Break them – *now*!' And he lurched toward his victims with a roar.

Rod leaped forward, grabbing the staff, yanking it out of the preacher's hands with a violent heave. But the whole crowd surged in after him, screaming and shouting. Fingers clawed at the witches; scythes swung . . .

Then light, blinding light, a sunburst, a nova – silent light, everywhere.

And silence, deep and sudden, and falling, falling, through blackness, total and unrelieved, all about them, and cold that drilled to their bones . . .


# 2


And something struck his heels, throwing him back. Something hard, heels, hips, and shoulders, and he tucked his chin in from reflex.

And fire burned in the blackness.

A campfire, only it burned in a small iron cage, black bars slanting up to a point.

Rod's eyes fastened on that cage for the simple reassurance of solid geometry in a world suddenly crazy. It was a tetrahedron, a fire burning inside a tetrahedron.

But what the hell was it doing here?

And for that matter, where was 'here'?

Rephrase the question; because, obviously, the fire and cage belonged here. So . . .

What was Rod doing here?

Back to Question Number Two: Where was 'here'?

Rod started noticing details. The floor was stone, square black basalt blocks, and the fire burned in a shallow circular well, surrounded by the basalt. The walls were distant, hard to see in the dim light from the fire; they seemed to be hung with velvet, some dark deep colour, not black. Rod squinted – it looked to be a rich maroon.

The hell with the curtains. Gwen . . .

A sudden, numbing fear pervaded Rod. He was scarcely able to turn his head, was afraid to look, for fear she might not be there. Slowly, he forced his gaze around the darkened chamber, slowly . . .

A great black form lay about ten feet from him: Fess.

Rod knelt and felt for broken bones, taking things in easy stages. Satisfied that he didn't have to be measured in fractions, he clambered carefully to his feet and went over to the horse.

Fess was lying very still, which wasn't like him; but he was also very stiff, each joint locked, which was like him when he had had a seizure. Rod didn't blame him; being confronted with that journey, he could do with a seizure himself – or at least a mild jolt; bourbon, for instance. . . .

He groped under the saddlehorn and found the reset switch.

The black horse relaxed, then slowly stirred, and the great head lifted. The eyes opened, large, brown, and bleary. Not for the first time, Rod wondered if they could really be, as the eye-specs claimed, plastic.

Fess turned his head slowly, looking as puzzled as a horse-hair-over-metal face can, then turned slowly back to Rod.

'Di-dye . . . chhhab a . . . zeizure, RRRRRodd?'

'A seizure? Of course not! You just decided you needed a lube job, so you dropped into the nearest grease station.' Rod tactfully refrained from mentioning just how Fess had 'dropped in'.

'I . . . fffai-led you innn . . . duhhh . . . momenduv . . .'

Rod winced at the touch of self-contempt that coated the vodered words and interrupted. 'You did all you could; and since you've saved my life five or six times before, I'm not going to gripe over the few times you've failed.' He patted Fess between the ears.

The robot hung his head for a moment, then surged to his feet, hooves clashing on the stone. His nostrils spread; and Rod had a strange notion his radar was operating, too.

'We arrre inna gread chall,' the robot murmured; at least when he had seizures, he made quick recoveries. 'It is stone, hung with maroon velvet curtains; a fire burns in the centre in a recessed well. It is surrounded by a metal, latticework tetrahedron. The metal is an alloy of iron containing nickel and tungsten in the following percentages . . .'

'Never mind,' Rod said hastily. 'I get the general idea.' He frowned suddenly, turning away, brooding. 'I also get the idea that maybe my wife isn't dead; if she was, her body would have been there. So they've kidnapped her?'

'I regret . . .'

'"That the data is insufficient for . . ."' Rod recited with him. 'Yeah, yeah. Okay. So how do we find her?'

'I regret. . . .'

'Skip it. I've got to find her.' He struck his forehead with his fist. 'Where is she?'

'In the next room,' boomed a deep, resonant voice. 'She is unharmed and quite well, I assure thee. Agatha is there also.'

A tall old man with long white hair streaming down over his shoulders and a long white beard down his chest, in a long, dark-blue monk's robe with the hood thrown back, stood by the fire. His robe was sprinkled with silver zodiac signs; his arms were folded, hands thrust up the wide, flaring sleeves. His eyes were surrounded by a network of fine wrinkles under white tufts of eyebrows; but the eyes themselves were clear and warm, gentle. He stood tall and square-shouldered near the fire, looking deep into Rod's eyes as though he were searching for something.

'Whoever you are,' Rod said slowly, 'I thank you for getting me out of a jam and, incidentally, for saving my life. Apparently I also owe you my wife's life, and for that I thank you even more deeply.'

The old man smiled thinly. 'You owe me nothing, Master Gallowglass. None owe me aught.'

'And,' Rod said slowly, 'you owe nothing to anyone. Hm?'

The wizard's head nodded, almost imperceptibly.

Rod chewed at the inside of his cheek and said, 'You're Galen. And this is the Dark Tower.'

Again the old man nodded.

Rod nodded too, chewing again. 'How come you saved me? I thought you ignored the outside world.'

Galen shrugged. 'I had an idle moment.'

'So,' said Rod judiciously, 'you save two witches, my horse, and my humble self, just to kill time.'

'Thou art quick to comprehend,' said Galen, hiding a smile deep in his beard. 'I had no pressing researches at the moment.'

'Rod,' Fess's voice murmured, 'an analysis of vocal patterns indicates he is not telling the whole truth.'

'For this I need a computer?' Rod muttered dryly.

Galen tilted his head closer, with a slight frown. 'Didst thou speak?'

'Oh, uh – just an idle comment about the physical aspects of thought.'

'Indeed.' The old wizard's head lifted. 'Dost thou, then, concern thyself with such problems?'

Rod started to answer, then remembered that he was talking to a wizard who had locked himself away for forty years and had gained power continually throughout that time – and it wasn't because he'd been fermenting. 'Well, nothing terribly deep, I'm afraid – just the practical side of it.'

'All knowledge is of value,' the wizard said, eyes glittering. 'What bit of knowledge hast thou gained?'

'Well . . . I've just been getting some firsthand experience in the importance of the prefrontal lobes.' Rod tapped his forehead. 'The front of the brain. I've just had a demonstration that it acts as a sort of tunnel.'

'Tunnel?' Galen's brows knit. 'How is that?'

Rod remembered that the original Galen had written the first definitive anatomy text back at the dawn of the Terran Renaissance. Had to be coincidence – didn't it? 'There seems to be a sort of wall between concept and words. The presence of the concept can trigger a group of sounds – but that's like someone tapping on one side of a wall and someone on the other side taking the tapping as a signal to, oh, let's say . . . play a trumpet.'

Galen nodded. 'That would not express the thought.'

'No, just let you know it was there. So this front part of the brain' – Rod tapped his forehead again – 'sort of makes a hole in that wall and lets the thought emerge as words.'

Galen slowly nodded. 'A fascinating conjecture. Yet, how could one verify its accuracy?'

Rod shrugged. 'By being inside the mind of someone who doesn't have prefrontal lobes, I suppose.'

Galen lost his smile, and his eyes lost focus. 'Indeed we could – an we could find such a person.'

Rod couldn't help a harsh bark of laughter. 'We've got 'em, Master Wizard – more than we want. Much more! The peasants call 'em "beastmen", and they're raiding our shores.' He remembered the alarm, and guilt gnawed at him. 'Raiding 'em right now, come to think of it.'

'Truly?' The old wizard actually seemed excited. 'Ah, then! When I finish my current tests I will have to let my mind drift into one of theirs!'

'Don't rush 'em,' Rod advised. 'But please do rush *me*! I'm needed at the home front to help fight your test group – and I'd kinda like to take my wife back with me.'

'As truly thou shouldst.' Galen smiled. 'Indeed, there is another here whom thou must also conduct away from this Dark Tower.'

'Agatha? Yeah, I want her too – but not for the same reasons. Would you happen to know where they are?'

'Come,' said Galen, turning away, 'thy wife is without the chamber.'

Rod stared after him a moment, surprised at the old man's abruptness; then he shrugged and followed, and Fess followed Rod.

The wizard seemed almost to glide to the end of the cavernous room. They passed through the maroon hangings into a much smaller room – the ceiling was only fifteen feet high. The walls were hung with velvet drapes, cobalt blue this time, and one huge tapestry. The floor boasted an Oriental carpet, with a great black carved wood chair at each corner. Roman couches, upholstered in burgundy plush, stood between the chairs. A large round black wood table stood in the centre of the room before a fair-sized fireplace. Six huge calf-bound volumes lay open on the table.

Rod didn't notice the splendour, though; at least, not the splendour of the furnishings. The splendour of his wife was something else again.

Her flame-red hair didn't go badly with the cobalt-blue drapes, though. She stood at the table, bent over one of the books.

She looked up as they came in. Her face lit up like the aurora. 'My lord!' she cried, and she was in his arms, almost knocking him over, wriggling and very much alive, lips glued to his.

An eternity later – half a minute, maybe? – anyway, much too soon, a harsh voice grated, 'Spare me, child! Pity on a poor old hag who never was one tenth as fortunate as thou!'

Gwen broke free and spun about. 'Forgive me, Agatha,' she pleaded, pressing back against her husband and locking his arms around her waist. 'I had not thought . . .'

'Aye, thou hadst not,' said the old witch with a grimace that bore some slight resemblance to a smile, 'but such is the way of youth, and must be excused.'

'Bitter crone!' Galen scowled down at her from the dignity of his full height. 'Wouldst deny these twain their rightful joy for no reason but that it is joy thou never knew? Hath the milk of love so curdled in thy breast that thou canst no longer bear . . .'

'Rightful!' the witch spat in a blaze of fury. 'Thou darest speak of "rightful", thou who hast withheld from me . . .'

'I ha' heard thy caterwauls afore,' said Galen, his face turning to flint. 'Scrape not mine ears again with thy cant; for I will tell thee now, as I ha' told thee long agone, that I am no just due of thine. A man is not a chattel, to be given and taken like a worn, base coin. I am mine own man to me alone; I never was allotted to a woman, and least of all to thee!'

'Yet in truth thou wast!' Agatha howled. 'Thou wert accorded me before thy birth or mine and, aye, afore the world were formed in God's own mind. As sure as night was given day, wert thou allotted me; for thou art, as I am, witch-blood, and of an age together with me! Thy hates, thy joys, are mine . . .'

'Save one!' the wizard grated.

'Save none! Thine every lust, desire, and sin are each and all alike to mine, though hidden deep within thy heart!'

Galen's head snapped up and back.

Agatha's eyes lit with glee. She stalked forward, pressing her newfound advantage. 'Aye, thy true self, Galen, that thou secretest veiled within thy deepest heart, is like to me! The lust and body weakness that ever I made public thou hast in private, mate to mine! Thus thou hast hid for threescore years thy secret shame! Thou hast not honesty enow to own to these, thy covered, covert sins of coveting! Thou art too much a coward . . .'

'Coward?' Galen almost seemed to settle back, relaxing, smiling sourly. 'Nay, this is a cant that I ha' heard afore. Thou wanest, Agatha. In a younger age, thou wouldst not so soon have slipped back upon old argument.'

'Nor do I now,' the witch said, 'for now I call thee coward of a new and most unmanly fear! Thou who cry heedlessness of all the world without the walls of thy Dark Tower; thou, who scornest all the people, fearest their opinion! Thou wouldst have them think thee saint!'

Galen's face tightened, eyes widening in a glare.

'A saint!' Agatha chortled, jabbing a finger at him. 'The Saint of Hot and Heaving Blood! A saint, who hast as much of human failing as ever I did have, and great guilt! Greater! Aye, greater, for in thy false conceit thou hast robbed me of mine own true place with thee! For thou art mine by right, old Galen; 'twas thou whom God ordained to be my husband, long before thy mother caught thy father's eye! By rights, thou shouldst be mine; but thou hast held thyself away from me in cowardice and pompousness!'

Galen watched her a moment with shadowed eyes; then his shoulders squared, and he took a breath. 'I receive only the curse that I have earned.'

Agatha stared for a moment, lips parting. 'Thou wilt admit to it!'

Then, after a moment she fixed him with a sour smile. 'Nay. He means only that he hath saved mine life six times and more; and thus it is his fault that I do live to curse him.'

She lifted her head proudly, her eyes glazing. 'And in this thou mayst know that he is a weakling; for he cannot help himself but save us witches. It is within his nature, he who claims to care naught for any living witch or ploughman. Yet he is our guardian and our saviour, all us witches; for, if one of us should die when he might have prevented it, his clamouring conscience would batter down the weakness of a will that sought to silence it, and wake him in the night with haunted dreams. Oh, he can stand aloof and watch the peasant and the noble die, for they would gladly burn him; but a witch, who has not hurt him, and would render him naught but kindness – had he the courage or the manhood to be asking it – these he cannot help but see as part and parcel like him; and therefore must he save us, as he ha' done a hundred times and more.'

She turned away. 'Thou mayst credit him with virtue and compassion if thou wishest; but I know better.'

' 'Tis even as she saith,' said the old man proudly. 'I love none, and none love me. I owe to none; I stand alone.'

Old Agatha gave a hoot of laughter.

'Uh . . . yes,' said Rod. The fight seemed to have reached a lull, and Rod was very eager to be gone before it refuelled.

And since Galen's brow was darkening again, it behoved Rod to make haste.

'Yes, well, uh, thanks for the timely rescue, Galen,' he said. 'But now, if you'll excuse us, we really gotta be getting back to Runnymede, uh – don't we, Gwen?'

He paused suddenly, frowning at the old wizard. 'I don't, uh, suppose you'd consider coming back with us?'

Agatha's head lifted slowly, fire kindling in her eye.

'I thank thee for thy kindness in offering of hospitality,' said the old wizard in a voice rigid with irony. 'Yet greatly to my sorrow, I fear that I cannot accept.'

'Oh, to thy sorrow, to be sure!' spat Agatha. 'Indeed, thou art the sorriest man that e'er I knew, for thou hast brought me sorrow deep as sin!'

She spun toward Rod and Gwen. 'And yet, fear not; thy folk shall not go all unaided! There lives, at least, still one old witch of power threescore-years-and-ten in learning, who will not desert her countrymen in this time of need! There lives still one, aye, be assured; though this old gelding –' she jerked her head toward Galen—'will idly stand and watch thy folk enslaved, a power strong as his will guard thy land!' She stretched out her hand. 'Come take me with thee, get us gone, for my stomach crawls within me at his presence! He thinks of naught but himself.'

'And thou dost not?' Galen grated, glaring at the old witch. 'Is this aught but a sop to thy thwarted wish for mothering of a child thou never hadst?'

Agatha flinched almost visibly and turned, hot words on her tongue; but Galen raised an imperious hand and intoned:

'Get thee hence, to Runnymede!'

White light flared, burning, blinding.

When the afterimages faded, Rod could see, as well as feel, Gwen in his arms, which feeling had been very reassuring while the sun went nova.

He could dimly make out Agatha too, leaning shaken against a wall, a grey granite wall.

And a high timbered ceiling, and a knot of young witches and warlocks gathered around them, staring, eyes and mouths round.

Their voices exploded in clamouring questions.

*Yep, home*, Rod decided. It was obviously the Witches' Tower in the King's Castle at Runnymede.

He wondered what would happen if Galen ever got mad enough to tell someone to go to Hell.

One young warlock's face thrust closer as he dropped to one knee.

'Lord Warlock! Where hast thou been?'

'Galen's Dark Tower,' Rod croaked, and was rewarded with a huge communal gasp. He looked around at eyes gone round as wafers. 'And as to how we got here – well, he sent us home.'

The teenagers exchanged glances. 'We can wish ourselves from place to place,' said one of the warlocks, 'but none of us can do it to another.'

'Yeah, well, Galen's a little older than you, and he's learned a few more tricks.' Privately, Rod wondered – that did amount to a new kind of psi power, didn't it? Well, he was prepared for constant surprises. 'Your name's Alvin, isn't it?'

'Thus am I called, Lord Warlock.'

Rod rubbed a hand over his eyes. 'I seem to remember, before I lit out to find Gwen, something about the beastmen attacking?'

'Aye, milord. Their three long ships were only the vanguard. Behind them, their fleet did darken the waters.'

'Fleet?' Rod snapped completely out of his grogginess. 'How many of them were there?'

'An army,' a girl answered from behind Alvin. 'Thou couldst not call it less.'

Rod staggered to his feet, looking around. He saw the great black horse standing stiff-legged, head hanging low. Rod stumbled over to him and slid a hand under the head. It lifted, turning to look at him. Rod frowned. 'No seizure, huh?'

'Indeed I did not,' the robot's voice said in his ear only, 'since I had experienced it once, and knew it to be possible. It thus did not cause great enough anxiety to trigger a seizure.'

'So,' Rod said carefully, 'you were awake during the whole thing.'

The horsehead lifted higher. 'I was. I . . . recorded it . . . all. . . . I must play it back . . . very slowly . . . later . . . later. . . .'

'Just offhand, what would you say . . . happened? Just at a guess.'

'A preliminary analysis would indicate that we passed through another dimension.' Fess's body shuddered. 'At least, I hope that is what I will decide happened.'

'Yeah.' Rod swallowed. 'Uh. Well . . . decide it later, okay?' He set his foot in the stirrup and swung up onto the saddle. 'We've got to get to the coast. Where'd you say they landed, Alvin?'

'At the mouth of the River Fleuve, milord. We wait as reserve, yet have heard no call.'

Rod took a more thorough look at the handful left in the room and realized there wasn't a one over fourteen. Small wonder they hadn't been called. If they had been, things would have been *really* desperate. Rod nodded. 'The Fleuve isn't too far. I might still get in on the action.' He leaned down from his saddle to plant a quick kiss on Gwen. 'Keep the home fires burning, dear. Come help pick up the pieces when you've got your strength back.' He swung back upright and kicked his heels against Fess's sides. The black horse started trotting toward the doorway, protesting, 'Rod, the lintels are too low.'

'So I'll duck. Upward and onward, Steel Steed! Ho, and away!'

'You forgot the "horse and hattock",' Fess reminded him.

Fess swept down the road to the south in the easy, tireless, rocking-chair gait possible only to electric horses. Rod sat back in the saddle and enjoyed the ride.

'Of course,' he was saying, 'it's possible this revivalist is just what he seemed to be, nothing more – just a neurotic, unordained religious nut. But somehow I find myself able to doubt it.'

'Coincidence is possible,' Fess agreed, 'though scarcely probable.'

'Especially since his activities are weakening the war effort very nicely – nicely for the beastmen, that is. And why else would he start operating at just this particular time? He must have begun preaching a week or two before Catharine began recruiting; otherwise we would have had at least a *few* volunteers.'

'We may assume, then, that there is some correlation between the two phenomena – the war and the preacher,' Fess opined.

'Correlation, Hell! He's working for 'em, Fess! How else could you explain it?'

'I do not have an alternate theory prepared,' the robot admitted. 'Nonetheless, the probability of direct collusion is extremely low.'

'Oh, come off it!'

'Examine the data, Rod. The Neanderthals and the preacher are separated by approximately a hundred miles of ocean. Moreover, there is no physiological resemblance apparent from the reports we have received.'

'A point,' Rod admitted. 'Still, I say . . .'

'Pardon the interruption,' Fess said suddenly, 'but . . . you are aware that I am using radar . . .'

'I should hope so, when we're going sixty miles an hour!'

'Two flying objects have just passed overhead.'

Rod's stomach sank. 'Just a couple of birds, right?'

'I'm afraid not, Rod.'

Rod darted a glance at the sky. There they were, already dwindling in the distance – two broomsticks, with women attached. 'They didn't!'

'I fear they did, Rod. I estimate their equivalent ground speed in excess of one hundred miles per hour. And, of course, they can fly in a direct, straight line.'

'They're gonna get to the battlefield before us!' Rod glared after the ladies, then heaved a sigh and relaxed. 'Well . . . I suppose I should be glad they'll be there in time to help out . . . Gwen will have enough sense to keep them both up in the sky, won't she?'

'I trust not, since she will need to be able to concentrate all her powers in fighting the Evil Eye.'

'Yeah . . . I'd forgotten about that. Well!' Rod sighed and sat back. 'That's a relief!'

'I should think it would cause greater anxiety, Rod.' Fess actually sounded puzzled.

'No – because she'll probably settle down wherever the Royal Witchforce is stationed – and Tuan'll have 'em very well guarded.' Rod grinned. 'She'll be safe in spite of herself. But just in case . . . step up the pace, will you?'

*Then did the Foemen fall upon us in endless waves. Their long ships were myriad, a plague of Dragons clawing up out of the ocean onto the beach, vomiting forth beastmen in their thousands. Tall, they were, and fanged, with their heads beneath their shoulders, and Murder in their eyes. Our doughty soldiers blanched and fell back; but the King exhorted them, and they held their places. Then did the High Warlock rise up before them, and Thunder smote the air, and Lightning blasted the ground about him. In a voice like unto a trumpet, he swore unto the soldiers that his Witches would ward the Evil Eye away from them; therefore he bade them march forth to meet and best the foemen, for the sakes of their Wives and Daughters and Sweethearts. Courage flowed from him to the heart of every soldier, and they began their march.*

*But the beastmen then had formed their line, and the lightning glittered from their shields and helms. They roared with bestial Lust and set forth against King Tuan's army.*

*With a shout, the soldiers charged; yet each beastman caught the eyes of two among them, or mayhap three, then half a dozen, and froze them where they stood. Then did the beastmen laugh – a hideous, grating Noise – and 'gan to stride forward to make Slaughter.*

*But the High Warlock cried out to his Witchfolk there on the hill from whence they watched the battle, and they joined hands in prayer, speeding forth the greatest of their Powers, grappling with the beastmen's darkling Strength, and freeing the minds of all the soldiers from its Spell. The army then cried out in anger, striding forth with pikes upraised; but Thunder crashed, and Lightning smote the land, leaping up into the beastmen's eyes, to freeze the soldiers there again within their tracks; and on their hill, the Witchfolk lay in a swoon, like unto Death – for the power of the demon Kobold had seared their minds.*

*And the beastmen grunted laughter and swung huge war axes, laying low the soldiers of the King.*

*The High Warlock cried out then in his Rage, and did ride down upon them on his steed of Night, laying about him with a sword of Fire, hewing through the beastmen's line; while his wife and an ancient Hag of the Hills did hear his cry, and sped unto the battle. There they joined hands, and bent their heads in prayer, and did betwixt them what all the King's Witchfolk together had done – grappled with the Kobold's power, and lifted its spell from off our soldiers' minds. Yet too many amongst them had fallen already; they could defend themselves but little more.*

*Then did the High Warlock again charge the beastmen's line, chanting high his ancient War Song, and the soldiers heard it and took heart. They gave ground then, step by step, and laid waste such beastmen as were foolhardy enough to come nigh them; thus King Tuan brought them away from that cursed beach whereon so many of their Comrades did lie slain; thus he brought them up into the hills – battered, bruised, yet an army still – and bade them rest themselves and bind their wounds, assuring them their Time would come again.*

*And the High Warlock turned unto his wife upon the Hill, to consider how they might yet confound the beastmen; and they left the monsters to number their dead, and dig themselves deep Holes to hide in.*

> *Chillde's Chronicles of the Reign of Tuan and Catharine*

Fess trotted up to the crest of the hill, and Rod stared down at the most miserable collection of teenage warlocks and witches he'd ever seen. They lay or sat on the ground, heads hanging, huddling inside blankets. Brother Chillde wove his way among them, handing out steaming mugs. Rod wondered what was in them – and wondered even more if the Lord Abbot knew that Brother Chillde was actually helping witchfolk. The little monk seemed, to say the least, unorthodox.

Then Rod realized that one of the blanketed ones was his wife.

'Gwen!' He leaped off Fess's back, darting down to kneel by her side. 'Are you . . . did you . . .' He gave up on words and gathered her into his arms, pressing her against his chest. 'You *feel* okay . . .'

'I am well enough, my lord,' she said wearily; but she didn't try to pull away. 'Thou shouldst have greater care for these poor children – and for poor old Agatha.'

'Have care for thyself, if thou must,' spat the old crone. 'I am nearly restored to full energy.' But she seemed just as droopy as the kids.

'What happened?' Rod grated.

Gwen pushed a little away from him, shaking her head. 'I scarce do know. When we came, Toby and all his witchlings and warlocks lay senseless on the ground, and our soldiers stood like statues on the beach. The beastmen passed among them, making merry slaughter. Therefore did Agatha and I join hands to pool our power against the beastmen's Evil Eye – and, oh, my lord!' She shuddered. 'It was as though we heaved our shoulders up under a blackened cloud that lay upon us like unto some great, soft . . .' She groped for words. ' 'Twas like the belly of a gross fat man, pushing down upon us – dark and stifling. Seemly it could soak up all the force that we could throw unto it; yet we heaved up under, Agatha and I; we did lift it off our soldiers' minds so that they could, at least, defend themselves – though scarcely more; they were sorely outnumbered. Then lightning rent the sky, and that huge, dark bank fell down upon us, smothering.' She shook her head, eyes closed. ' 'Tis all that I remember.'

'Yet 'twas enow.'

Rod looked up; Brother Chillde stood near them, his eyes glowing. 'Thy wife, milord, and her venerable crone held off the beastmen's power long enow.'

'Long enough for what?'

'For King Tuan to retreat back up this slope with the remnant of his soldiers, far enough so that the beastmen durst not follow. Nay, they stayed below, and began to dig their graves.'

'Theirs or ours?' Rod grated. He surged to his feet, giving Gwen's hand a last squeeze, and strode to the brow of the hill.

A hundred feet below, the river-mouth swept into a long, gentle curve – a bow; and the beastmen were stringing that bow. They were digging, but not graves – a rampart, a fortress-line. Already, it was almost complete. Rod looked down and swore; they'd have a hell of a time trying to dig the beastmen out of *that*!

Then he saw what lay on the near side of the rampart – a jumbled row of bloody bodies, in the royal colours.

Rod swore again. Then he spat out, 'They had to be planning it. They just had to. Somebody had to have put the idea into Gwen's mind – the idea to go see old Agatha; somebody had to have told that nutty preacher to attack Agatha's cave right then. *Right* then, so I'd be pulled away and couldn't be here! Damn!'

'Do not berate thyself so severely, Lord Warlock,' Tuan said wearily behind him. ' 'Twas not thy absence that defeated us.'

'Oh?' Rod glared up at him. 'Then what was it?'

Tuan sighed. 'The power of their Kobold, like as not!'

'Not!' Rod whirled away to glare down at the beach. 'Definitely "not"! That Kobold of theirs can't be anything but a wooden idol, Tuan! It's superstition, sheer superstition!'

'Have it as thou wilt.' Tuan shrugged his shoulders. 'It was the beastmen's Evil Eye, then. We did not think its power would be so great, yet it blasted our witches' minds and froze our soldiers in their tracks. Then the beastmen slew them at their leisure.'

' 'Twas the lightning,' Agatha grated in a hollow voice.

Tuan turned toward her, frowning. 'What goodly beldam is this, Lord Warlock? Our debt to her is great, yet I wot me not of her name.'

'That's just 'cause you haven't been introduced. She's, uh, well . . . she's kinda famous, in her way.'

Agatha grimaced, squinting against a throbbing headache. 'Temporize not, Lord Warlock. Be direct, e'en though it may seem evil. Majesty, I am called "Angry Agatha".' And she inclined her head in an attempt at a bow.

Tuan stared, and Rod suddenly realized that the King was young enough to have heard some nasty nursery tales himself. But Tuan was never short on courage; he forced a smile, took a deep breath, squared his shoulders, and stepped up to the old lady. 'I must needs thank thee, revered dame, for without thee, my men and I had been naught but butcher's meat.'

Agatha peered up at him through narrowed eyes; then slowly she smiled. 'Mine head doth split with agony, and I ache in every limb; yet would I do this service again for so handsome a thanking.' The smile faded. 'Aye, or even without it; for I think that I have saved some lives this day, and my heart is glad within me.'

Tuan stood, gazing down at her for a moment.

Then he cleared his throat and turned to Rod. 'What manner of hill-hag is this, Lord Warlock? I had thought the ancients 'mong the witches were all sour and bitter and hated all of humankind.'

'Not this one, it turns out,' Rod said slowly. 'She just hated the way people treated her . . .'

'Oh, still thy prattle!' Agatha snapped. 'I do hate all men, and all women, too, Majesty – unless I'm near them.'

Tuan turned back to her, nodding slowly with glowing eyes. 'Now, God save thee! For hypocrisy such as thine would confound the very Devil! Praise Heaven thou wert here!'

'And curse me that I wasn't!' Rod snapped, turning to glower down at the entrenched beastmen.

'Again thou hast said it!' Tuan cried, exasperated. 'What ails thee, Lord Warlock? Why dost thou say that thou wert absent, when thou wert here in truth, and fought as bravely as any – aye, and more!'

Rod froze.

Then he whirled about. '*What*!'

'Thou wast here, indeed.' Tuan clamped his jaw shut. 'Thou wert here, and the beastmen could not freeze thee.'

'I' truth, they could not!' Brother Chillde cried, his face radiant. 'Thou didst sweep across their line, Lord Warlock, like unto a very tempest, laying about thee with thy sword of flame. Five at a time thou didst grapple with, and conquer! Their whole line thou didst confound and craze! And 'twas thou who didst give heart unto our soldiers, and didst prevent their retreat from becoming a rout.'

'But . . . that's impossible! I . . .'

' 'Tis even as he doth say, my lord.' Gwen's voice was low, but it carried. 'From this hilltop did I see thee far below; and 'twas thou who didst lead, even as this good friar saith.'

Rod stared at her, appalled. If *she* didn't know him, who did?

Then he turned away, striding down the back of the hill.

'Hold, Lord Warlock! What dost thou seek?' Tuan hurried to keep pace with him.

'An on-the-spot witness,' Rod grated. 'Even Gwen could be mistaken from a distance.'

He skidded to a stop beside a knot of soldiers who huddled under the protection of a rocky overhang. 'You there, soldier!'

The soldier lifted his tousled blond head, holding a scrap of cloth to a long rent in his arm.

Rod stared, amazed. Then he dropped to one knee, yanking the cloth off the wound. The soldier yelled, galvanized. Rod glanced up and felt his heart sink; surely that face belonged to a boy, not a man! He turned back to the wound, inspecting it. Then he looked up at Tuan. 'Some brandywine.'

' 'Tis here,' the young soldier grated.

Rod looked down and saw a bottle. He poured a little on the cut and the soldier gasped, long and with a rattle, his eyes nearly bulging out of his head. Rod tore open his doublet and tore a strip of cloth from his singlet. He held the wound closed and began to wrap the bandage around it. 'There's a lot of blood, but it's really just a flesh wound. We'll have to put some stitches in it later.' He looked up at the young ranker. 'Know who I am?'

'Aye,' the young man gasped. 'Thou'rt the Lord High Warlock.'

Rod nodded. 'Ever seen me before?'

'Why, certes! Thou didst stand beside me in the mêlée! Thou wert then no farther from me than thou art now!'

Rod stared up at him. Then he said, 'Are you *sure*? I mean, *absolutely* sure?'

'Nay, be sure that I am! Had it not been for the sight of thee, I'd ha' turned and fled!' Then his eyes widened and he glanced quickly at his companions, flushing; but they only nodded sombre agreement.

'Take heart.' Tuan slapped his shoulder. 'Any would have fled such a battle, an they could have.'

The young soldier looked up, finally realized the King himself stood near, and almost fainted.

Rod grasped his shoulder. 'You saw me, though. You really did see me.'

'Truly, my lord.' The young man's eyes were wide. 'I' truth, I did.' He lowered his eyes, frowning. 'And yet – 'tis strange.'

'Strange?' Rod frowned. 'Why?'

The young soldier bit his lip; then the words spilled out. 'Thou didst seem taller in the battle – by a head or more! I could have sworn thou didst tower above all soldiers there! And thou didst seem to glow. . . .'

Rod held his eyes for a moment longer.

Then he went back to wrapping the bandage. 'Yeah, well, you know how it is during a battle. Everything seems bigger than it really is – especially a man on a horse.'

'Truth,' the young soldier admitted. 'Thou wast astride.'

'Right.' Rod nodded. 'Big roan horse.'

'Nay, milord.' The young soldier frowned. 'Thy mount was black as jet.'

*

'Calm down, Rod,' Fess's voice murmured, 'you are beside yourself.'

'I am?' Rod looked around in a panic.

'It was a figure of speech,' the robot assured him. 'Lower your anxiety level – you are quite definitely a singular personality.'

'I'd like to be sure of that.' Rod frowned down at the soldiers around him. He was walking through the camp, surveying what was left of Tuan's army. Whether he'd been there during the battle or not, the mere sight of him was putting heart back into them. Personally, he felt sheepish, even guilty; but . . .

'Your presence is good for morale, Rod,' Fess murmured.

'I suppose,' Rod muttered. Privately, he wondered if he wasn't 'showing himself' to reassure himself that he was indeed himself. 'I mean, the phenomenon is totally impossible, Fess. You do understand that, don't you?'

Soldiers stared up at him in awe. Rod ground his teeth; he knew the rumour would fly through the camp that the Lord Warlock had been talking to his 'familiar'.

'Certainly, Rod. Attribute it to mass hysteria. During the battle, they needed the reassurance that the Lord High Warlock stood by them, to oppose the beastmen's magic. Then one soldier, in the heat of the fight, mistook some other knight for yourself, and doubtless cried out, "Behold the High Warlock!" And all his fellows, in the gloom of a lightning-lit battle, also imagined that they saw you.'

Rod nodded, a little reassured. 'Just a case of mistaken identity.'

'Lord Warlock?'

'Um?' Rod turned, looked down at a grizzled old sergeant who sat in the mud. 'What's the matter, ancient?'

'My boys hunger, Lord Warlock.' The ancient gestured to a dozen men in their young twenties, who huddled near him. 'Will there be food?'

Rod stared down at him.

After a moment, he said, 'Yeah. It'll just take a little while. Rough terrain, and wagons – you know.'

The ancient's face relaxed. 'Aye, milord.'

As Rod turned away, he heard a soldier say, 'Surely he will not.' The man beside him shrugged. 'A king is a king. What knows he of a common man-at-arms? What matters it to him if we are slain and frozen?'

'To King Tuan, it matters greatly,' the other said indignantly. 'Dost not recall that he was King of Beggars ere he was King of Gramarye?'

'Still . . . he is a lord's son . . .' But the other seemed to doubt his own prejudice. 'How could a lordling care for the fate of common men!'

'Assuredly thou'lt not believe he wastes his soldiers' lives?'

'And wherefore should I not?'

'Because he is a most excellent general, if for no reason other!' the first cried, exasperated. 'He'll not send us to our deaths unheeding; he is too good a soldier! For how shall he win a battle if he has too small an army?'

His mate looked thoughtful.

'He'll husband us as charily as any merchant spends his gold.' The first soldier leaned back against a hillock. 'Nay, he'll not send us 'gainst the foe if he doth not believe that most of us will live, and triumph.'

The other soldier smiled. 'Mayhap thou hast the truth of it – for what is a general that hath no army?'

Rod didn't wait for the answer; he wandered on, amazed by Tuan's men. They weren't particularly worried about the Evil Eye. Dinner, yes; being sent against the beastmen with the odds against them, yes; but, magic? No. Not if Tuan waited till he had the proper counterspell. 'Put the average Terran in here,' he muttered, 'put him against an Evil Eye that really works, and he'd run so fast you wouldn't see his tracks. But the way these guys take it, you'd think it was nothing but a new kind of crossbow.'

'It is little more, to them,' Fess's voice murmured behind his ear. He stood atop the cliff, far above, watching Rod walk through the camp. 'They have grown up with magic, Rod – as did their fathers, and their grandfathers, and their ancestors – for twenty-five generations. The phenomena do not frighten them – only the possibility that the enemy's magic might prove stronger.'

'True.' Rod pursed his lips, nodding. Looking up, he saw Brother Chillde winding a bandage around an older soldier's head. The man winced, but bore the pain philosophically. Rod noticed several other scars; no doubt the man was used to the process. Rod stepped up to the monk. 'You're all over the field, good friar.'

Brother Chillde smiled up at him. 'I do what I may, Lord Warlock.' His smile didn't have quite the same glow it had had earlier.

'And a blessing it is for the men – but you're only human, Brother. You need some rest yourself.'

The monk shrugged, irritated. 'These poor souls do need mine aid far more, milord. 'Twill be time enough for rest when the wounded rest as easily as they may.' He sighed and straightened, eyeing the bandaged head. 'I've eased the passing of those who had no hope, what little I could. 'Tis time to think of the living.' He looked up at Rod. 'And to do what we can to ensure that they remain alive.'

'Yes,' Rod said slowly, 'the King and I were thinking along the same lines.'

'Indeed!' Brother Chillde perked up visibly. 'I am certain thou dost ever do so – yet what manner of aiding dost thou have a-mind?'

The idea crystallized. 'Witches – more of 'em. We managed to talk one of the older witches into joining us this time.'

'Aye.' Brother Chillde looked up at the hilltop. 'And I did see that she and thy wife, alone, did hold off the beastmen's Evil Eye the whiles our soldiers did retreat. Indeed, I wrote it in my book whilst yet the battle raged.'

Rod was sure he had – in fact, that's why he'd told the monk. He seemed to be the only medieval equivalent to a journalist available, there being no minstrels handy.

Brother Chillde turned back to Rod. 'Thy wife must needs be exceeding powerful.'

Rod nodded. 'Makes for an interesting marriage.'

Brother Chillde smiled, amused, and the old soldier chuckled. Then the monk raised an eyebrow. 'And this venerable witch who did accompany her – she, too, must have powers extraordinary.'

'She does,' Rod said slowly. 'Her name's "Angry Agatha".'

The old soldier's head snapped up. He stared; and two or three other soldiers nearby looked up too, then darted quick glances at each other. Fear shadowed their faces.

'She decided it's more fun to help people than to hurt them,' Rod explained. 'In fact, she's decided to stay with us.'

Every soldier within hearing range began to grin.

' 'Tis wondrous!' Brother Chillde fairly glowed. 'And dost thou seek more such ancient ones?'

Rod nodded. 'A few more, hopefully. Every witch counts, Brother.'

'Indeed it doth! Godspeed thine efforts!' the monk cried. And as Rod turned away, Brother Chillde began to bandage another damaged soldier, chattering, 'Dost'a hear? The High Warlock doth seek to bring the ancient wizards and the hill-hags to aid us in our plight!'

Rod smiled to himself; just the effect he'd wanted! By evening, every soldier in the army would know that they were fighting fire with blazing enthusiasm – and that the witches were going out for reinforcements.

He stopped, struck by another thought. Turning, he looked back up the hillside. Tuan stood, silhouetted against a thundercloud, arms akimbo, surveying the devastation below him.

*You shouldn't lie to your army. That'd just result in blasted morale – and, after a while, they'd refuse to fight, because they couldn't be sure what they'd be getting into, that you wouldn't be deliberately throwing their lives away.*

Rod started back up the hill. He'd promised the rank and file more witch-power; he'd better convince Tuan.

Tuan's head lifted as Rod came up to the brow of the hill; he came out of his brown study. 'An evil day, Rod Gallowglass. A most evil day.'

'Very.' Rod noticed the use of his name, not his title; the young King was really disturbed. He stepped up beside Tuan and gazed sombrely down at the valley with him. 'Nonetheless, it could have been worse.'

Tuan just stared at him for a moment. Then, understanding, relaxed his face; he closed his eyes and nodded. 'I' truth, it could have. Had it not been for thy rallying of the troops . . . and thy wife, and Angry Agatha . . . i' truth, all the witches . . .'

'And warlocks,' Rod reminded. 'Don't forget the warlocks.'

Tuan frowned. 'I trust I will not.'

'Good. Then you won't mind seeking out some more of them.'

'Nay, I surely will not,' Tuan said slowly. 'Yet where wilt thou discover them?'

Rod sighed and shook his head. 'The ladies had the right idea, Tuan. We should've gone out recruiting.'

Tuan's mouth twisted. 'What young witch or warlock will join us now, with this crazed preacher raising the whole of the land against them?'

'Not too many,' Rod admitted. 'That's why I've realized Gwen had the right idea.'

Tuan's frown deepened in puzzlement. 'Of what dost thou speak?'

'The old ones, my liege – starting with Galen.'

For the first time since Rod had known him, he saw fear at the back of Tuan's eyes. 'Rod Gallowglass – dost thou know whereof thou dost speak?'

'Yeah – a grown wizard.' Rod frowned. 'What's so bad about that? Don't we *want* a little more mystical muscle on our side?'

'Aye – if he's on our side i' truth!'

'He will not be,' croaked Agatha from a boulder twenty feet away. 'He doth care for naught but himself.'

'Maybe.' Rod shrugged, irritated. 'But we've got to try, don't we?'

'My lord,' Gwen said softly, 'I ha' told thee aforetime, 'tis the lightning that lends them their strength – and not even old Galen can fight 'gainst a thunderbolt.'

Rod turned slowly toward her, a strange glint coming into his eye. 'That's right, you did mention that, didn't you?'

Gwen nodded. 'We did free our soldiers from the Evil Eye – but the lightning flared, and the witches lay unconscious. 'Twas then the soldiers froze, and the beastmen mowed them like hay in summer.'

'Lightning,' Rod mused.

He turned away, slamming his fist into his palm. 'That's the key, isn't it? The lightning. But how? Why? The answer's there somewhere, if only I could find it and FESSten to it.'

'Here, Rod,' his mentor murmured.

'Why would the Evil Eye be stronger right after a lightning flash?' Rod seemed to ask of no one in particular.

The robot hesitated a half-second, then answered. 'Directly prior to a lightning flash, the resistance of the path the bolt will follow lowers tremendously, due to ionization, thus forming a sort of conductor between the lithosphere and the ionosphere.'

Rod frowned. 'So?'

Tuan frowned, too. 'What dost thou, Lord Warlock?'

'Just talking to myself,' Rod said quickly. 'A dialogue with my alter ego, you might say.'

Fess disregarded the interruption. 'The ionosphere is also capable of functioning as a conductor, though the current passed would have to be controlled with great precision.'

Rod's lips formed a silent O.

Gwen sat back with a sigh. She had long ago acquired the wifely virtue of patience with her husband's eccentricities. He would've been patient with hers as well, if he could find any (he didn't think of esper powers as eccentric).

Fess ploughed on. 'The ionosphere is thus capable of functioning as a conductor between any two points on earth – though it would tend toward broadcast; to avoid loss of power some means of beaming would need to be developed. There are several possibilities for such limiting. Signals may thus travel via the ionosphere rather than by the more primitive method of . . .'

'Power, too,' Rod muttered. 'Not just signals. Power.'

Gwen looked up, startled and suddenly fearful.

'Precisely, Rod,' the robot agreed, 'though I doubt that more than a few watts would prove feasible.'

Rod shrugged. 'I suspect psi powers work in milliwatts anyway.'

Tuan frowned. 'Milling what?'

'That's right. You wouldn't need much for a psionic blast.'

Tuan eyed him warily. 'Rod Gallowglass . . .'

'All that would be needed,' said Fess, 'is a means of conducting the power to ground level.'

'Which is conveniently provided by the ionization of the air just before the lightning bolt, yes! But how do you feed the current *into* the ionosphere?'

Tuan glanced at Gwen; they both looked apprehensive.

Old Agatha grated, 'What incantation's this?'

'That,' said Fess virtuously, 'is *their* problem, not ours.'

Rod snorted. 'I thought you were supposed to be logical!'

Tuan's head came up in indignation. 'Lord Warlock, be mindful to whom you speak!'

'Huh?' Rod looked up. 'Oh, not you, Your Majesty. I was, uh . . . talking to my, uh, familiar.'

Tuan's jaw made a valiant attempt to fraternize with his toes. Rod could, at that moment, have read a gigantic increase in his reputation as a warlock in the diameters of Tuan's eyes.

'So.' Rod touched his pursed lips to his steepled fingertips. 'Somebody overseas lends the beastmen a huge surge of psionic power – in electrical form, of course; we're assuming psionics are basically electromagnetic. The beastmen channel the power into their own projective telepathy, throw it into the soldier's minds – somehow, eye contact seems to be necessary there . . .'

'Probably a means of focusing power. Unsophisticated minds would probably need such a mental crutch, Rod,' Fess conjectured.

'And from the soldiers' minds, it flows into the witches', immediately knocking out anyone who's tuned in! Only temporarily, thank Heaven.'

'An adequate statement of the situation, Rod.'

'The only question now is: who's on the other end of the cable?'

'Although there is insufficient evidence,' mused the robot, 'that which is available would seem to indicate more beastmen as donors.'

'Maybe, maybe.' Rod frowned. 'But somehow this just doesn't seem like straight ESP . . . Oh, well, let it pass for the moment.

The big question is not where it comes from, but how we fight it.'

Tuan shrugged. 'Thou hast said it, Lord Warlock – that we must seek out every witch and wizard who can be persuaded to join us.'

'We tried that, remember?' But Rod smiled, a light kindling in his eyes. 'Now that we've got some idea about how the Evil Eye gains so much power so suddenly, we should be able to make better use of the available witch-power.'

The phrase caught Tuan's military attention. A very thoughtful look came over his face. 'Certes . . .' He began to smile himself. 'We must attack.'

'What!?'

'Aye, aye!' Tuan grinned. 'Be not concerned, Lord Warlock – I have not gone brain-sick. Yet, consider – till now, it has not been our choice whether to attack or not. Our enemy came in ships; we could only stand and wait the whiles they chose both time and place. Now, though, the place is fixed – by their earthworks.' He nodded contemptuously toward the riverbank below. 'We do not now seek a single long ship in the midst of a watery desert – we have a camp of a thousand men laid out before us! We can attack when we will!'

'Yeah, and get chopped to pieces!'

'I think not.' Tuan grinned with suppressed glee. 'Not if we fight only when the sky is clear.'

A slow smile spread over Rod's face.

Tuan nodded. 'We will make fray whilst the sun shines.'

'You must admit that the idea has merit, Rod,' Fess said thoughtfully. 'Why not attempt it full-scale, immediately?'

'Well, for one thing, those earthworks *are* a major barrier.' Rod sat astride the great black robot-horse on top of the cliffs in the moonlight. 'And for another, well . . . we're *pretty* sure it'll work, Fess, but . . .'

'You do not wish to endanger your whole army. Sensible, I must admit. Still, logic indicates that . . .'

'Yes, but Finagle's Law indicates caution,' Rod interrupted. 'If we made a full-scale frontal attack by day, we'd *probably* win – but we'd lose an awful lot of men. We *might* be defeated – and Tuan only bets on a sure thing, if he has a choice.'

'I gather he is not the only one who favours caution. Allow me to congratulate you, Rod, on another step towards maturity.'

'Great thanks,' Rod growled. 'A few more compliments like that, and I can hold a funeral for my self-image. How old do I have to be before you'll count me grown-up – an even hundred?'

'Maturity is mental and emotional, Rod, not chronological. Still, would it seem more pleasant if I were to tell you that you are still young at heart?'

'Well, when you put it *that* way . . .'

'Then, I will,' the robot murmured. 'And to do you justice, Rod, you have never been a reckless commander.'

'Well . . . thanks.' Rod was considerably mollified. 'Anyway, that's why we're just gonna try a raid first. We'll hit 'em under a clear sky where they're weak.'

A dark shadow moved up beside them, about even with Rod's stirrup. 'The moon will set in an hour's time, Rod Gallowglass.'

'Thanks, Your Elfin Majesty.' Rod looked down at Brom. 'Any particular point in the earthworks that's weaker than the others?'

'Nay. Yet should we spring up the riverbanks to attack them, then would they fall back amazed and confused, and elves might hap upon them and trip them in flight.'

Rod grinned. 'While our men relieve their camp of everything portable, eh? Not such a bad idea.'

'I shall be amused,' Brom rumbled.

'*You* shall? *They'll* just die laughing.'

The moon set, and Tuan gave the signal. A picked band of soldiers (all former foresters) clambered into the small boats Rod had hurriedly requisitioned from the local fishermen and rowed toward the beastmen's camp with feathered oars.

But the advance party was already at work.

The sky was clear, the stars drifted across the hours; but there was no moon this night. The Neanderthal camp lay deep in gloom.

There are superstitions holding that the dark of the moon is a time conducive to magical, and not always pleasant, events. They are justified.

Watchfires dotted the plain locked within the semicircle of cliffs. Groups of beastmen huddled around the fires while sentries paced the shore. In the centre of the camp, a large long hut announced the location of the chiefs.

The beastmen were to remember this night for a long time, wishing they could forget. Looking back, they would decide the defeat itself wasn't all that bad; after all, they fought manfully and well, and lost with honour.

It was the prelude to the battle that would prove embarrassing . . .

While one of the small groups gathered around one of the fires were companionably swopping gripes as soldiers always have, a diminutive shadow crept unseen between two of them, crawled to the fire, and threw something in. Then it retreated, fast.

The beastmen went on grumbling for a few minutes; then one stopped abruptly and sniffed. 'Dosta scent summat strange?' he growled.

The beastman next to him sniffed – and gagged – gripping his belly.

The smell reached the rest of the group very quickly, and quite generously. They scrambled for anywhere, as long as it was away, gagging and retching.

Closer to the centre of the camp, a dark spherical object hurtled through the air to land and break open in the centre of another group of beastmen. With an angry humming sound, tiny black flecks filled the air. The beastmen leaped up and ran howling and swatting about them with more motivation than effect. Little red dots appeared on their skins.

At another group, a series of short, violent explosions from the fire sent the beastmen jumping back in alarm.

At still another fire, a beastman raised his mug to his lips, tilted his head back, and noticed that no beer flowed into his mouth. He scowled and peered into the mug.

He dropped it with an oath as it landed on his toe, and jumped back with notable speed, holding one foot and hopping on the other as a small human figure scampered out of the mug with a high-pitched, mocking laugh.

The elf howled in high glee and scampered on through the camp.

Another beastman swung after him, mouthing horrible oaths as his huge club drove down.

A small hand swung out of the shadows and clipped through his belt with a very sharp knife.

The loincloth, loosened, wobbled a little.

In another two bounds, it had decidedly slipped.

The elf scampered on through the camp, chuckling, and a whole squad of beastmen fell in after him, bellowing, clubs slamming the ground where the elf had just been.

A small figure darted between them and the fugitive, strewing something from a pouch at its side.

The Neanderthals lunged forward, stepped down hard, and jumped high, screaming and frantically jerking leprechaun shoe-tacks out of their soles.

The fleeing elf, looking over his shoulder to laugh, ran smack into the ankles of a tall, well-muscled Neanderthal – a captain who growled, swinging his club up for the death-blow.

A leprechaun popped up near his foot and slammed him a wicked one on the third toe.

The captain howled, letting go of his club (which swung on up into the air, turning end over end) as he grabbed his hurt foot, hopping about.

He hopped up, and the club fell down and the twain met with a very solid and satisfying thunk.

As he went down, the fleeing elf – Puck – scampered away chortling.

He skipped into a tent, shouting, 'Help! Help! Spies, traitors, spies!'

Three beastmen dashed in from the nearest campfire, clubs upraised and suspicions lowered, as the tent's occupants swung at Puck and missed him. Outside, a score of elves with small hatchets cut through the tent ropes.

The poles swayed and collapsed as the tent fabric enfolded its occupants tenderly. The beastmen howled and struck at the fabric, and connected with one another.

Chuckling, Puck slipped out from under the edge of the tent. Within twenty feet, he had another horde of beastmen howling after him.

But the beastmen went sprawling, as their feet shot out from under them, flailing their arms in a losing attempt at keeping their balances – which isn't easy when you're running on marbles. They scrambled back to their feet somehow, still on precarious balance, whirling about, flailing their arms, and in a moment it was a free-for-all.

Meanwhile, the captain slowly sat up, holding his ringing head in his hands.

An elf leaned over the top of the tent and shook something down on him.

He scrambled up howling, slapping at the specks crawling over his body – red ants can be awfully annoying – executed a beautiful double-quick goose step to the nearest branch of the river and plunged in over his head.

Down below, a water sprite coaxed a snapping turtle, and the snapper's jaws slammed into the captain's already swollen third toe.

He climbed out of the water more mud than man, and stood up bellowing.

He flung up his arms, shouting, and opened his mouth wide for the hugest bellow he could manage, and with a *splock*, one large tomato, appropriately over-ripe, slammed into his mouth.

Not that it made any difference, really; his orders weren't having too much effect anyway, since his men were busily clubbing at one another and shouting something about demons . . .

Then the marines landed.

The rowboats shot in to grate on the pebbles, and black-cloaked soldiers, their faces darkened with ashes, leaped out of the boats, silent in the din. Only their sword-blades gleamed. For a few minutes. Then they were red.

An hour later, Rod stood on the hilltop, gazing down. Below him, moaning and wailing rose from the beastmen's camp. The monk sat beside him, his face solemn. 'I know they are the foe, Lord Gallowglass – but I do not find these groans of pain to be cause for rejoicing.'

'Our soldiers think otherwise.' Rod nodded back toward the camp and the sounds of low-keyed rejoicing. 'I wouldn't say they're exactly jubilant – but a score of dead beastmen has done wonders for morale.'

Brother Chillde looked up. 'They could not use their Evil Eye, could they?'

Rod shook his head. 'By the time our men landed, they didn't even know where the enemy was, much less his eyes. We charged in; each soldier stabbed two beastmen; and we ran out.' He spread his hands. 'That's it. Twenty dead Neanderthals – and their camp's in chaos. We still couldn't storm in there and take that camp, mind you – not behind those earthworks, not with a full army. And you may be very sure they won't come out unless it's raining. But we've proved they're vulnerable.' He nodded toward the camp again. 'That's what they're celebrating back there. They know they can win.'

'And the beastmen know they can be beaten.' Brother Chillde nodded. ' 'Tis a vast transformation, Lord Warlock.'

'Yes.' Rod glowered down at the camp. 'Nasty. But vast.'

'Okay.' Rod propped his feet up on a camp stool and took a gulp from a flagon of ale. Then he wiped his mouth and looked up at Gwen and Agatha. 'I'm braced. Tell me how you think it worked.'

They sat inside a large tent next to Tuan's, the nucleus of a village that grew every hour around the King's Army.

'We've got them bottled up for the moment,' Rod went on, 'though it's just a bluff. Our raids are keeping them scared to come out because of our "magic" – but as soon as they realize we can't fight the Evil Eye past the first thunderclap, they'll come boiling out like hailstones.'

The tassels fringing the tent doorway stirred. Rod noted it absently; a breeze would be welcome – it was going to be a hot, muggy day.

'We must needs have more witches,' Gwen said firmly.

Rod stared at her, appalled. 'Don't tell me you're going to go recruiting among the hill-hags again! Uh – present company excepted, of course.'

'Certes.' Agatha glared. The standing cup at her elbow rocked gently. Rod glanced at it, frowning; surely the breeze wasn't *that* strong. In fact, he couldn't even feel it . . .

Then his gaze snapped back to Agatha's face. 'Must *what*?'

'Persuade that foul ancient, Galen, to join his force here with ours,' Agatha snapped. 'Dost thou not hearken? For, an thou dost not, why do I speak?'

'To come up with any idea that crosses your mind, no matter how asinine.' Rod gave her his most charming smile. 'It's called "brainstorming".'

'Indeed, a storm must ha' struck thy brain, if thou canst not see the truth of what I say!'

The bowl of fruit on the table rocked. He frowned at it, tensing. Maybe a small earthquake coming . . .?

He pulled his thoughts together and turned back to Agatha. 'I'll admit we really need Galen. But how're you going to persuade him to join us?'

'There must needs be a way.' Gwen frowned, pursing her lips.

An apple shot out of the bowl into the air. Rod rocked back in his chair, almost overturning it. 'Hey!' Then he slammed the chair forward, sitting upright, frowning at Gwen, hurt. 'Come on, dear! We're talking serious business!'

But Gwen was staring at the apple hanging in the air; an orange jumped up to join it. 'My lord, I did not . . .'

'Oh.' Rod turned an exasperated glare on Agatha. 'I might have known. This's all just a joke to you, isn't it?'

Her head pulled back, offended. 'What dost thou mean to say, Lord Warlock?'

A pear shot out of the bowl to join the apple and the orange. They began to revolve, up and around, in an intricate pattern.

Rod glanced up at them, his mouth tightening, then back to Agatha. 'All right, all right! So we know you can juggle – the hard way, no hands! Now get your mind back to the problem, okay?'

'I?' Agatha glanced at the spinning fruits, then back to Rod. 'Surely thou dost not believe 'tis *my* doing!'

Rod just stared at her.

Then he said carefully, 'But Gwen said *she* wasn't doing it – and she wouldn't lie, would she?'

Agatha turned her head away, disgusted, and ended looking at Gwen. 'How canst thou bear to live with one so slow to see?'

'Hey, now!' Rod frowned. 'Can we keep the insults down to a minimum, here? What am I supposed to be seeing?'

'That if I have not done it, and she hath not done it, then there must needs be another who *doth* do it,' Agatha explained.

'Another?' Rod stared up at the fruit, his eyes widening as he understood. He felt his hackles trying to rise. 'You mean . . .'

'My son.' Agatha nodded. 'Mine unborn son.' She waved a hand toward the spinning fruits. 'He must needs fill the idle hour. Dost'a not know that young folk have not great patience? Yet is he good-hearted withal, and will not wreak any true troubles. Dismiss him from thy mind and care. We spake, just now, of the wizard Galen . . .'

'Uh . . . yeah.' Rod turned back to the two ladies, trying very hard to ignore the fruit bobbing above him. 'Galen. Right. Well, as I see it, he's a true isolate, a real, bona fide, dyed-in-the-haircloth hermit. Personally, I can't think of a single thing that could persuade him to join us.'

'I fear thou mayest have the truth of it,' Gwen sighed. 'Certes, I would not say that he is amenable.'

Air popped and a baby was sitting in her lap, clapping his hands. 'Momma, Momma! Pa'y cake! Pa'y cake!'

Gwen stiffened, startled. Then a delighted smile spread over her face. 'My bonny babe!' Her arms closed around Magnus and squeezed.

Rod threw up his hands and turned away. 'Why bother trying? Forget the work! C'mere, son – let's play catch.'

The baby chortled with glee and bounced out of Gwen's lap, sailing over to Rod. He caught the boy and tossed him back to Gwen.

'Nay, husband.' She caught Magnus and lowered him to the ground, suddenly becoming prim. ' 'Tis even as thou sayest – we have matters of great moment in train here. Back to thine elf-nurse, child.'

Magnus thrust out his lip in a pout. 'Wanna stay!'

Rod bent a stern glance on his son. 'Can you be quiet?'

The baby nodded gleefully.

Gwen gave an exasperated sigh and turned away. 'Husband, thou wilt have him believing he can obtain aught he doth wish!'

'But just one bit of noise, mind you!' Rod levelled a forefinger at the baby. 'You get in the way just one little bit, and home you go!'

The baby positively glowed. He bobbed his head like a bouncing ball.

'Okay – go play.' Rod leaned back in his chair again. 'Now. Assuming Galen can't be persuaded – what do we do?'

Agatha shrugged. 'Nay, if he will not be persuaded, I can not see that we can do aught.'

'Just the words of encouragement I needed,' Rod growled. 'Let's try another tack. Other veterans. Any other magical hermits hiding out in the forests?'

'Magnus, thou didst promise,' Gwen warned.

Agatha frowned, looking up at the tent roof. 'Mayhap old Elida . . . She is bitter but, I think, hath a good heart withal. And old Anselm . . .' She dropped her eyes to Rod, shaking her head. 'Nay, in him 'tis not bitterness alone that doth work, but fear also. There is, perhaps, old Elida, Lord Warlock – but I think . . .'

'Magnus,' Gwen warned.

Rod glanced over at his son, frowning. The baby ignored Gwen and went on happily with what he had been doing – juggling. But it was a very odd sort of juggling; he was tossing the balls about five feet in front of him, and they were bouncing back like boomerangs.

Rod turned to Gwen. 'What's he doing?'

'Fire and fury!' Agatha exploded. 'Wilt thou not leave the bairn to his play? He doth not intrude; he maketh no coil, nor doth he cry out! He doth but play at toss-and-catch with my son Harold, and is quiet withal! He maketh no bother; leave the poor child be!'

Rod swung about, staring at her. 'He's doing *what*?'

'Playing toss-and-catch,' Agatha frowned. 'There's naught so strange in that.'

'But,' Gwen said in a tiny voice, 'his playmate cannot be seen.'

'Not by us,' Rod said slowly. 'But, apparently, Magnus sees him very well indeed.'

Agatha's brows knitted. 'What dost thou mean?'

'How else would he know where to throw the ball?' Rod turned to Agatha, his eyes narrowing. 'Can *you* see your son Harold?'

'Nay, I cannot. Yet what else would return the apples to the child?'

'I was kinda wonderin' about that.' Rod's gaze returned to his son. 'But I thought you said Harold was an unborn spirit.'

'Summat of the sort, aye.'

'Then, how can Magnus see him?' Gwen lifted her head, her eyes widening.

'I did not say he had not been born,' Agatha hedged. She stared at the bouncing fruit, her gaze sharpening. 'Yet I ha' ne'er been able to see my son aforetimes.'

'Then, how come Magnus can?' Rod frowned.

'Why, 'tis plainly seen! Thy son is clearly gifted with more magical powers than am I myself!'

Rod locked gazes with Gwen. Agatha was the most powerful old witch in Gramarye.

He turned back to Agatha. 'Okay, so Magnus is one heck of a telepath. But he can't see a body if there's none there to see.'

'My son ha' told me that he did have a body aforetime,' Agatha said slowly. ' 'Twould seem that he doth send outward from himself his memory of his body's appearance.'

'A projective telepath,' Rod said slowly. 'Not a very strong one, maybe, but a projective. Also apparently a telekinetic. But I thought that was a sex-linked trait. . . .'

Agatha shrugged. 'Who can tell what the spirit may do when it's far from its body?'

'Yes – his body,' Rod said softly, eyes locked on the point where the fruit bounced back toward Magnus. 'Just where *is* this body he remembers?'

Agatha sighed and leaned back in her chair, closing her eyes and resting her head against the high back. 'Thou dost trouble me, Lord Warlock; for I cannot understand these matters that Harold doth speak of.'

'Well, maybe Gwen can.' Rod turned to his wife. 'Dear?'

But Gwen shook her head. 'Nay, my lord. I cannot hear Harold's thoughts.'

Rod just stared at her.

Then he gave himself a shake and sat up straighter. 'Odd.' He turned back to Agatha. 'Any idea why you should be able to hear him, when Gwen can't?'

'Why, because I am his mother.' Agatha smiled sourly.

Rod gazed at her, wondering if there was something he didn't know. Finally, he decided to take the chance. 'I didn't know you'd ever borne children.'

'Nay, I have not – though I did yearn for them.'

Rod gazed at her while his thoughts raced, trying to figure out how she could be barren and still bear a son. He began to build an hypothesis. 'So,' he said carefully, 'how did you come by Harold?'

'I did not.' Her eyes flashed. 'He came to me. 'Tis even as he doth say – he is my son, and old Galen's.'

'But, Galen . . .'

'Aye, I know.' Agatha's lips tightened in bitterness. 'He is the son that Galen and I *ought* to have had, but did not, for reason that we ne'er have come close enough to even touch.'

'Well, I hate to say this – but . . . uh . . .' Rod scratched behind his ear, looking at the floor. He forced his eyes up to meet Agatha's. 'It's, uh, very difficult to conceive a baby if, uh, you never come within five feet of one another.'

'Is't truly!' Agatha said with withering scorn. 'Yet, e'en so, my son Harold doth say that Galen did meet me, court me, and wed me – and that, in time, I did bear him a son, which is Harold.'

'But that's impossible.'

'The depth of thy perception doth amaze me,' Agatha said drily. 'Yet Harold is here, and this is his tale. Nay, further – he doth say that Galen and I reared him, and were ever together, and much a-love.' Her gaze drifted, eyes misting, and he could scarcely hear her murmur: 'Even as I was used to dream, in the days of my youth . . .'

Rod held his silence. Behind him, Gwen watched, her eyes huge.

Eventually, Agatha's attention drifted back to them. She reared her head up to glare at Rod indignantly. 'Canst thou truly say there is no sense to that? If his body has not been made as it should have been, canst thou be amazed to find his spirit here, uncloaked in flesh?'

'Well, yes, now that you mention it.' Rod leaned back in his chair. 'Because, if his body was never made – where did his spirit come from?'

'There I can thresh no sense from it,' Agatha admitted. 'Harold doth say that, when grown, he did go for a soldier. He fought, and bled, and came away, and this not once, but a score of times – and rose in rank to captain. Then, in his final battle, he did take a grievous wound, and could only creep away to shelter in a nearby cave. There he lay him down and fell into a swoon – and lies there yet, in a slumber like to death. His body lies like a waxen effigy – and his spirit did drift loose from it. Yet could it not begin that last adventure, to strive and toil its way to Heaven . . .' She shuddered, squeezing her eyes shut. 'And how he could be eager for such a quest is more than I can tell. Yet indeed he was –' she looked back up at Rod, frowning '– yet could he not; for though his body lay in a sleep like unto death, yet 'twas *not* death – nno, not quite. Nor could the spirit wake that body neither.'

'A coma.' Rod nodded. 'But let it alone long enough, and the body'll die from sheer starvation.'

Agatha shrugged impatiently. 'He's too impatient. Nay, he would not wait; his spirit did spring out into the void, and wandered aeons in a place of chaos – until it found me here.' She shook her head in confusion. 'I do not understand how aught of that may be.'

'A void . . .' Rod nodded his head slowly.

Agatha's head lifted. 'The phrase holds meaning for thee?'

'It kind of reminds me of something I heard of in a poem – "the wind that blows between the worlds". I always did picture it as a realm of chaos . . .'

Agatha nodded judiciously. 'That hath the ring of rightness to it. . . .'

'That means he came from another universe.'

Agatha's head snapped up, her nostrils flaring. 'Another universe? What tale of cock-and-bull is this, Lord Warlock? There is only this world of ours, with sun and moons and stars. *That* is the universe. How could there be another?'

But Rod shook his head. '"How" is beyond my knowledge – but the, uh, "wise men" of my, uh, homeland, seem to pretty much agree that there *could* be other universes. Anyway, they can't prove there aren't. In fact, they say there may be an infinity of other universes – and if there are, then there must also be universes that are almost exactly like ours, even to the point of having – well – another Agatha, and another Galen. Exactly like yourselves. But their lives took – well, a different course.'

'Indeed they did.' Agatha's eyes glowed.

'But, if Harold's spirit went looking for help – why didn't it find the Agatha in that other universe?'

'Because she lay dead.' Agatha's gaze bored into Rod's eyes. 'She had died untimely, of a fever. So had her husband. Therefore did Harold seek out through the void, and was filled with joy when he did find me – though at first he was afeard that I might be a ghost.'

Rod nodded slowly. 'It makes sense. He was looking for help, and he recognized a thought-pattern that he'd known in his childhood. Of course he'd home in on you. . . Y'know that almost makes it all hang together.'

'I' truth, it doth.' Agatha began to smile. 'I ne'er could comprehend this brew of thoughts that Harold tossed to me; yet what thou sayest doth find a place for each part of it, and fits it all together, like to the pieces of a puzzle.' She began to nod. 'Aye. I will believe it. Thou hast, at last, after a score of years, made sense of this for me.' Suddenly, she frowned. 'Yet his soul is here, not bound for Heaven, for reason that his body lies in sleeping death. How could it thus endure, after twenty years?'

Rod shook his head. 'Hasn't been twenty years – not in the universe he came from. Time could move more slowly there than it does here. Also, the universes are probably curved – so, *where* on that curve he entered our universe could determine what time, what year, it was. More to the point, he could reenter his own universe just a few minutes after his body went into its coma.'

But Agatha had bowed her head, eyes closed, and was waving in surrender. 'Nay, Lord Warlock! Hold, I prithee! I cannot ken thine explanations! 'Twill satisfy me, that thou dost.'

'Well, I can't be *sure*,' Rod hedged. 'Not about the why of it, at least. But I can see how it fits in with my hypothesis.'

'What manner of spell is that?'

'Only a weak one, till it's proved. Then it becomes a theory, which is much more powerful indeed. But for Harold, the important point is that he needs to either kill his body, so he can try for Heaven – or cure it and get his spirit back into it.'

'Cure it!' Agatha's glare could have turned a blue whale into a minnow. 'Heal him or do naught! I would miss him sorely when his spirit's gone to its rightful place and time – but, I will own, it must be done. Still, I'd rather know that he's alive!'

'Well, I wasn't really considering the alternative.' Rod gazed off into space, his lips pursed.

Agatha saw the look in his eyes and gave him a leery glance. 'I mistrust thee, Lord Warlock, when thou dost look so fey.'

'Oh, I'm just thinking of Harold's welfare. Uh, after the battle – a while after, when I was there and you'd recovered a bit – didn't I see you helping the wounded? You know, by holding their wounds shut and telling them to think hard and believe they were well?'

'Indeed she did.' Gwen smiled. 'Though 'tis somewhat more than that, husband. Thou must needs think at the wound thyself, the whiles the wounded one doth strive to believe himself well; for the separate bits of meat and fat must be welded back together – which thou canst do by making them move amongst one another with thy mind.'

'*You* can, maybe.' Inwardly, Rod shuddered. All he needed was for his wife to come up with one more major power – all corollaries of telekinesis, of course; but the number of her variations on the theme was stupefying.

He turned back to Agatha. 'Uh – did you think up this kind of healing yourself?'

'Aye. I am the only one, as far as I can tell – save thy wife, now that I've taught her.' Agatha frowned, brooding. 'I came to the knowing of it in despair, after I'd thrown aside a lad who sought to hurt me . . .'

Rod had to cut off that kind of train of thought; the last thing he wanted was for Agatha to remember her hurts. 'So. You can help someone "think" themselves well – telekinesis on the cellular level.'

Agatha shook her head, irritated. 'I cannot tell thy meaning, with these weird terms of thine – "tele-kine"? What is that – a cow that ranges far?'

'Not quite, though I intend to milk it for all it's worth.' Rod grinned. 'Y'know, when we were at Galen's place, he told me a little about his current line of research.'

Agatha snorted and turned away. '"Researches"? Aye – he will ever seek to dignify his idle waste of hours by profound words.'

'Maybe, but I think there might be something to it. He was trying to figure out how the brain itself, that lumpy blob of protoplasm, can create this magic thing called "thought".'

'Aye, I mind me an he mentioned some such nonsense,' Agatha grated. 'What of it?'

'Oh, nothing, really.' Rod stood up, hooking his thumbs in his belt. 'I was just thinking, maybe we oughta go pay him another visit.'

The dark tower loomed before them, then suddenly tilted alarmingly to the side. Rod swallowed hard and held on for dear life; it was the first time he'd ever ridden pillion on a broomstick. 'Uh, dear – would you try to swoop a little less sharply? I'm, uh, still trying to get used to this . . .'

'Oh! Certes, my lord!' Gwen looked back over her shoulder, instantly contrite. 'Be sure, I did not wish to afright thee.'

'Well, I wouldn't exactly say I was *frightened* . . .'

'Wouldst thou not?' Gwen looked back at him again, wide-eyed in surprise.

'Watch where you're going!' Rod yelped.

Gwen turned her eyes back to the front as her broomstick drifted sideways to avoid a treetop. 'Milord,' she chided, 'I knew it was there.'

'I'm glad somebody did,' Rod sighed. 'I'm beginning to think I should've gone horseback after all – even though it would've been slower.'

'Courage, now.' Gwen's voice oozed sympathy. 'We must circle this Dark Tower.'

Rod took a deep breath and squeezed the shaft.

The broomstick began to swing around the tower, following Agatha's swoop ahead of them. Rod's stomach lurched once before he forgot it, staring in amazement at the Tower. They were sixty feet up, but it soared above them, a hundred feet high and thirty wide, the top corrugated in battlements. Altogether, it was an awesome mass of funeral basalt. Here and there, arrow-slits pierced the stones – windows three feet high, but only one foot wide.

'I wouldn't like to see his candle bill,' Rod grunted. 'How do you get *in*?'

The whole bottom half of the Dark Tower reared unbroken and impregnable, pierced by not so much as a single loophole.

'There *has* to be a door.'

'Wherefore?' Gwen countered. 'Thou dost forget that warlocks do fly.'

'Oh.' Rod frowned. 'Yeah, I did kinda forget that, didn't I? Still, I don't see how he gets in; those loopholes are mighty skinny.'

'Yonder.' Gwen nodded toward the top of the Tower, and her broomstick reared up.

Rod gasped and clung for dear life. 'He *would* have to have a heliport!'

Agatha circled down over the battlements and brought her broomstick to a stop in the centre of the roof. She hopped off nimbly; Gwen followed suit. Rod disentangled himself from the broom straws and planted his feet wide apart on the roof, grabbing the nearest merlon to steady himself while he waited for the floor to stop tilting.

'Surely, 'twas not so horrible as that.' Gwen tried to hide a smile of amusement.

'I'll get used to it,' Rod growled. Privately, he planned not to have the chance to. 'Now.' He took a deep breath, screwed up his courage, and stepped forward. The stones seemed to tilt only slightly, so he squared his shoulders, took a deep breath, and took another step. 'Okay. Where's the door?'

'Yonder.' Agatha pointed.

Right next to a merlon and its crenel, a trapdoor was set flush with the roof. Rod stepped over to it – carefully – and frowned down, scanning the rough planks. 'I don't see a doorknob.'

'Why would there be one?' Agatha said beside him. 'Who would come up here, other than the ancient cockerel himself? And when he doth, I doubt not he doth ope' this panel from below.'

'And just leaves it open? What does he do about rain?'

Agatha shook her head. 'I misdoubt me an he would come up during foul weather.'

'True,' Rod said judiciously. 'He probably only comes up to stargaze – so why bother, when there aren't any stars?'

He drew his dagger and dropped to one knee. 'Gotta be careful about this – it's good steel, but it *could* break.' He jabbed the tip into the wood and heaved up. The trap rose an inch; he kicked his toe against it to hold it, pulled the dagger out, and dropped it, then caught the wood with his fingertips and heaved again – with a whine of pain; the manoeuvre certainly didn't do his manicure any good. But he hauled it up enough to get his boot-toe under, then caught it with his fingers properly and swung it open. 'Whew! So much for basic breaking-and-entering!'

'Well done!' Agatha said, mildly surprised.

'Not exactly what I'd call a major effort.' Rod dusted off his hands.

'Nor needful,' the old witch reminded him. 'Either thy wife or myself could ha' made it rise of its own.'

'Oh.' Rod began to realize that, with very little persuasion, he could learn to hate this old biddy. In an attempt to be tactful, he changed the subject. 'Y'know, in a culture where so many people can fly, you'd think he'd've thought to use a lock.'

At his side, Gwen shook her head. 'Few of the witchfolk would even dare to come here, my lord. Such is his reputation.'

That definitely was not the kind of line to inspire confidence in a hopeful burglar. Rod took a deep breath, stiffened his muscles to contain a certain fluttering in the pit of his stomach, and stared down the stairs. 'Yes. Well – I suppose we really should have knocked . . .' But his head was already below the level of the roof.

The stairs turned sharply and became very dark. Rod halted; Agatha bumped into his back. 'Mmmmf! Wilt thou not give warning when thou'rt about to halt thy progress, Lord Warlock?'

'I'll try to remember next time. Darling, would you mind? It's a little dark down here.'

'Aye, my lord.' A ball of luminescence glowed to life on Gwen's palm. She brushed past him – definitely too quickly for his liking – and took up the lead, her will-o'-the-wisp lighting the stairway.

At the bottom, dark fabric barred their way – curtains overlapping to close out draughts. They pushed through and found themselves in a circular chamber lit by two arrow-slits. Gwen extinguished her fox fire, which darkened the chamber; outside, the sky was overcast, and only grey light alleviated the gloom. But it was enough to show them the circular worktable that ran all the way around the circumference of the room, and the tall shelf-cases that lined the walls behind the tables. The shelves were crammed with jars and boxes exuding a mixture of scents ranging from spicy to sour; and the tables were crowded with alembics, crucibles, mortars with pestles, and beakers.

Agatha wrinkled her nose in distaste. 'Alchemy!'

Rod nodded in slow approval. 'Looks as though the old geezer has a little more intellectual integrity than I gave him credit for.'

'Thou canst not mean thou dost condone the Black Arts!' Agatha cried.

'No, and neither does Galen, apparently. He's not satisfied with knowing that something works – he wants to know why, too.'

'Is't not enough to say that devils do it?'

Rod's mouth tightened in disgust. 'That's avoiding the question, not answering it.'

Glass tinkled behind him. He spun about.

A jar floated above an alembic, pouring a thin stream of greenish liquid into it. As Rod watched, the cover sank back onto the jar and tightened in a half-turn as the jar righted itself, then drifted back up onto a shelf.

'Harold!' Agatha warned. 'Let be; these stuffs are not thine.'

'Uh, let's not be too hasty.' Rod watched a box float off another shelf. Its top lifted, and a stream of silvery powder sifted into the alembic. 'Let the kid experiment. The urge to learn should never be stifled.'

' 'Tis thou who shouldst be stifled!' Agatha glowered at Rod. 'No doubt Harold's meddling doth serve some plan of thine.'

'Could be, could be.' Rod watched an alcohol lamp glow to life under the alembic. 'Knocking probably wouldn't have done much good anyway, really. Galen strikes me as the type to be so absorbed in his research that . . .'

'My lord.' Gwen hooked fingers around his forearm. 'I mislike the fashion in which that brew doth bubble.'

'Nothing to be worried about, I'm sure.' But Ron glanced nervously at some test tubes on another table, which had begun to dance, pouring another greenish liquid back and forth from one to another. They finally settled down, but . . .

'That vial, too, doth bubble,' Agatha growled. 'Ho, son of mine! What dost thou?'

Behind them, glass clinked again. They whirled about to see a retort sliding its nose into a glass coil. Flame ignited under the retort, and water began to drip from a hole in a bucket suspended over the bench, spattering on the glass coil.

'My lord,' Gwen said nervously, 'that brew doth bubble most marvellously now. Art thou certain that Harold doth know his own deeds?'

Rod was sure Harold knew what he was doing, all right. In fact, he was even sure that Harold was a lot more sophisticated, and a lot more devious, than Rod had given him credit for. And suspense was an integral part of the manoeuvre, pushing it close to the line. . . .

But not this close! He leaped toward the alembic. Gases being produced in the presence of open flame bothered him.

'*What dost thou?*'

The words boomed through the chamber, and Galen towered in the doorway, blue robe, white beard, and red face. He took in the situation at a glance, then darted to the alembic to dampen the fire, dashed to seize the test tube and throw it into a tub of water, then leaped to douse the lamp under the retort.

'Thou dost move most spryly,' Agatha crooned, 'for a dotard.'

The wizard turned to glare at her, leaning against the table, trembling. His voice shook with anger. 'Vile crone! Art so envious of my labours that thou must needs seek to destroy my Tower?'

'Assuredly, 'twas naught so desperate as that,' Gwen protested.

Galen turned a red glower on her. 'Nay, she hath not so much knowledge as that – though her mischief could have laid this room waste, and the years of glassblowing and investigating that it doth contain!' His eyes narrowed as they returned to Agatha. 'I do see that ne'er should I ha' given thee succour – for now thou'lt spare me not one moment's peace!'

Agatha started a retort of her own, but Rod got in ahead of her. 'Uh, well – not really.'

The wizard's glare swivelled toward him. 'Thou dost know little of this haggard beldam, Lord Warlock, an thou dost think she could endure to leave one in peace.'

Agatha took a breath, but Rod was faster again. 'Well, y'see – it wasn't really her idea to come back here.'

'Indeed?' The question fumed sarcasm. ' 'Twas thy good wife's, I doubt me not.'

'Wrong again,' Rod said brightly. 'It was mine. And Agatha had nothing to do with tinkering with your lab.'

Galen was silent for a pace. Then his eyes narrowed. 'I' truth, I should ha' seen that she doth lack even so much knowledge as to play so learned a vandal. Was it thou didst seek explosion, Lord Warlock? Why, then?'

' 'Cause I didn't think you'd pay any attention to a knock on the door,' Rod explained, 'except maybe to say, "Go away".'

Galen nodded slowly. 'So, thou didst court disaster to bring me out from my researches long enough to bandy words with thee.'

'That's the right motive,' Rod agreed, 'but the wrong culprit. Actually, not one single one of us laid a finger on your glassware.'

Galen glanced quickly at the two witches. 'Thou'lt not have me believe they took such risks, doing such finely detailed work, with only their minds?'

'Not that they couldn't have,' Rod hastened to point out. 'I've seen my wife make grains of wheat dance.' He smiled fondly, remembering the look on Magnus's face when Gwen did it. 'And Agatha's admitted she's healed wounds by making the tiniest tissues flow back together – but this time neither of them did.'

'Assuredly, not *thou* . . .'

' 'Twas thy son,' Agatha grated.

The laboratory was silent as the old wizard stared into her eyes, the colour draining from his face.

Then it flooded back, and he erupted. 'What vile falsehood is this? What deception dost thou seek to work now, thou hag with no principle to thy name of repute? How dost thou seek to work on my heart with so blatant a lie? Depraved, evil witch! Thou hast no joy in life but the wreaking of others' misery! Fool I was, to ever look on thy face, greater fool to e'er seek to aid thee! Get thee gone, get thee hence!' His trembling arm reared up to cast a curse that would blast her. '*Get thee to* . . .'

'It's the truth,' Rod snapped.

Galen stared at him for the space of a heartbeat.

It was long enough to get a word in. 'He's the son of another Galen, and another Agatha, in another world just like this one. You know there are other universes, don't you?'

Galen's arm hung aloft, forgotten; excitement kindled in his eyes. 'I had suspected it, aye – the whiles my body did lie like to wood, and my spirit lay open to every slightest impress. Distantly did I perceive it, dimly through chaos, a curving presence that . . . But nay, what nonsense is this! Dost thou seek to tell me that, in one such other universe, I do live again?'

'"Again" might be stretching it,' Rod hedged, 'especially since your opposite number is dead now. But that a Galen, just like you, actually did live, yes – except he seems to have made a different choice when he was a youth.'

Galen said nothing, but his gaze strayed to Agatha.

She returned it, her face like flint.

'For there was an Agatha in that other universe, too,' Rod said softly, 'and they met, and married, and she bore a son.'

Galen still watched Agatha, his expression blank.

'They named the son Harold,' Rod went on, 'and he grew to be a fine young warlock – but more "war" than "lock". Apparently, he enlisted, and fought in quite a few battles. He survived, but his parents passed away – probably from sheer worry, with a son in the infantry . . .'

Galen snapped out of his trance. 'Do not seek to cozen me, Master Warlock! How could they have died, when this Agatha and I . . .' His voice dwindled and his gaze drifted as he slid toward the new thought.

'Time is no ranker, Master Wizard; he's under no compulsion to march at the same pace in each place he invests. But more importantly, events can differ in different universes – or Harold would never have been born. And if the Galen and Agatha of his universe could marry, they could also die – from accident, or disease, or perhaps even one of those battles that their son survived. I'm sure he'd be willing to tell you, if you asked him.'

Galen glanced quickly about the chamber, and seemed to solidify inside his own skin.

'Try,' Rod breathed. 'Gwen can't hear him, nor can any of the other witches – save Agatha. But if you're the analogue of his father, you should be able to . . .'

'Nay!' Galen boomed. 'Am I become so credulous as to hearken to the tales of a stripling of thirty?'

'Thirty-two,' Rod corrected.

'A child, scarcely more! I credit not a word of this tale of thine!'

'Ah, but we haven't come to the evidence yet.' Rod grinned. 'Because, you see, Harold didn't survive one of those battles.'

Galen's face neutralized again.

'He was wounded, and badly,' Rod pressed. 'He barely managed to crawl into a cave and collapse there – and his spirit drifted loose. But his body didn't. No, it lay in a lasting, deathlike sleep; so his spirit had no living body to inhabit, but also had not been freed by death and couldn't soar to seek Heaven. But that spirit was a warlock, so it didn't have to just haunt the cave where its body lay. No, it went adventuring – out into the realm of chaos, seeking out that curving presence you spoke of, searching for its parents' spirits, seeking aid . . .'

'And found them,' Galen finished in a harsh whisper.

Rod nodded. 'One, at least – and now he's found the other.'

Galen's glances darted around the chamber again; he shuddered, shrinking more tightly into his robes. Slowly then, his frosty glare returned to Rod. 'Thou hadst no need to speak of this to me, Lord Warlock. 'Twill yield thee no profit.'

'Well, I did think Harold deserved a chance to at least try to meet you – as you became in this universe. Just in case.'

Galen held his glare, refusing the bait.

'We have the beastmen bottled up, for the time being,' Rod explained, 'but they're likely to come charging out any minute, trying to freeze our soldiers with their Evil Eye. Our young warlocks and witches will try to counter it with their own power, feeding it through our soldiers. They wouldn't stand a chance against the beastmen's power by themselves – but they'll have my wife and Agatha to support them.'

'Aye, and we're like to have our minds blasted for our pains,' Agatha ground out, 'for some monster that we wot not of doth send them greater power with each thunderbolt. Though we might stand against them and win, if thou wert beside us.'

'And wherefore should I be?' Galen's voice was flat with contempt. 'Wherefore should I aid the peasant folk who racked and tortured me in my youth? Wherefore ought I aid their children and grandchildren who, ever and anon all these long years, have marched against me, seeking to tear down my Dark Tower and burn me at the stake? Nay, thou softhearted fool! Go to thy death for the sake of those that hate thee, an thou wishes – but look not for me to accompany thee!'

'Nay, I do not!' Agatha's eyes glittered with contempt. 'Yet, there's one who's man enough to do so, to bear up with me under that fell onslaught.'

Galen stared at her, frozen.

'Harold's a dutiful son,' Rod murmured. 'I thought you might like the chance to get acquainted with him.' He left the logical consequence unsaid. Could a spirit be destroyed? He hoped he wouldn't find out.

'I credit not one single syllable!' Galen hissed. ' 'Tis but a scheme to cozen me into placing all at risk for them who like me not!' He turned back to Rod. 'Thou dost amaze me, Lord Warlock; for even here, in my hermitage, I had heard thy repute and I had thought thee lord of greater intellect than this. Canst thou author no stronger scheme to gain mine aid, no subtle, devious chain of ruses?'

'Why bother?' Rod answered with the ghost of a smile. 'The truth is always more persuasive.'

Galen's face darkened with anger. His arm lifted, forefinger upraised, to focus his powers for teleporting them away. Then, suddenly, his head snapped about, eyes wide in shock for a moment before they squeezed shut in denial.

Agatha winced too, but she grinned. 'Ah, then! That shout did pierce even thy strong shield!'

The wizard turned his glare to her. 'I know not what trickery thou hast garnered to thus stimulate another's mind . . .'

'Oh, aye, 'tis trickery indeed! Oh, I have studied for years to fashion the feel and texture of another's mind, and all for this moment!' Agatha turned her head and spat. 'Lord Warlock, let us depart; for I sicken of striving to speak sense unto one who doth seek to deafen his own ears!'

'Aye, get thee hence,' Galen intoned, 'for thy scheme hath failed! Get thee hence, and come not hither again!'

'Oh, all right!' Rod shuddered at the thought of another broomstick ride. 'I was kinda hoping to catch the express . . .'

'Thou wilt come to joy in it, husband,' Gwen assured him, pushing past, 'if thou canst but have faith in me.'

'Faith?' Rod bleated, wounded. 'I trust you implicitly!'

'Then thou'lt assuredly not fear, for 'tis my power that doth bear thee up.' Gwen flashed him an insouciant smile.

'All right, all right!' Rod held his hands up in surrender. 'You win – I'll get used to it. After you, beldam.'

Agatha hesitated a moment longer, trying to pierce Galen's impenetrable stare with her whetted glance, but turned away in disgust. 'Aye, let him remain here in dry rot, sin that he doth wish it!' She stormed past Rod, through the curtains, and up the stair.

Rod glanced back just before dropping the curtain, to gaze at Galen, standing frozen in the middle of his laboratory, staring off into space, alone, imprisoned within his own invisible wall.

Rod clung to the broomstick for dear life, telling himself sternly that he was *not* scared, that staring at the grey clouds over Gwen's shoulder, hoping desperately for sight of Tuan's tent, was just the result of boredom. But it didn't work; his stomach didn't unclench, and the only object ahead was Agatha, bobbing on her broomstick.

Then, suddenly, there was a dot in the sky two points off Agatha's starboard bow. Rod stared, forgetting to be afraid. 'Gwen – do you see what I see?'

'Aye, my lord. It doth wear a human aspect.'

It did indeed. As the dot loomed closer, it grew into a teenage boy in doublet and hose, waving his cap frantically.

'Human,' Rod agreed. 'In fact, I think it's Leonatus. Isn't he a little young to be out teleporting alone?'

'He is sixteen now,' Gwen reminded. 'Their ages do not stand still for us, my lord.'

'They don't stand for much of anything, now that you mention it – and I suppose he is old enough to be a messenger. See how close you can come, Gwen; I think he wants to talk.'

Gwen swooped around the youth in a tight hairpin turn, considerably faster than Rod's stomach did. 'Hail, Leonatus!' she cried – which was lucky, because Rod was swallowing heavily at the moment. 'How dost thou?'

'Anxiously, fair Gwendylon,' the teenager answered. 'Storm-clouds lower o'er the bank of the Fleuve, and the beastmen form their battle-line!'

'I knew there was something in the air!' Rod cried. *Ozone, probably*. 'Go tell your comrades to hold the fort, Leonatus! We'll be there post haste!' Especially since the post was currently air mail.

'Aye, my lord!' But the youth looked puzzled. 'What is a "fort"?'

'A strong place,' Rod answered, 'and the idea is to catch your enemy between it and a rock.'

'An thou dost say it, Lord Warlock.' Leonatus looked confused, but he said manfully, 'I shall bear word to them,' and disappeared with a small thunderclap.

Rod muttered, 'Fess, we're coming in at full speed. Meet me at the cliff-top.'

'I am tethered, Rod,' the robot's voice reminded him.

Rod shrugged. 'So stretch it tight. When you're at the end of your tether, snap it and join me.'

They dropped down to land at the witches' tent, just as the first few drops of rain fell.

'How fare the young folk?' Agatha cried.

'Scared as hell,' Rod called back. 'Will they ever be glad to see you!' He jumped off the broomstick and caught up his wife for a brief but very deep kiss.

'My lord!' She blushed prettily. 'I had scarcely expected . . .'

'Just needed a little reminder of what I've got to come home to.' Rod gave her a quick squeeze. 'Good luck, darling.' Then he whirled and pounded away through the drizzle.

He halted at the edge of the cliff-top by the river, staring down. He was just in time to see the first wave of beastmen spill over their earthworks and lope away up the river valley, shields high and battle-axes swinging. Rod frowned, looking around for the Gramarye army. Where was it?

There, just barely visible through the drizzle, was a dark, churning mass, moving away upstream.

'Fess!'

'Here, Rod.'

Rod whirled – and saw the great black horsehead just two feet behind him. He jumped back, startled – then remembered the sheer drop behind him and skittered forward to slam foot into stirrup and swing up onto the robot-horse's back. 'How'd *you* get here so fast?'

'I do have radar.' Fess's tone was mild reproof. 'Shall we go, Rod? You are needed upstream.'

'Of course!' And, as the great black horse sprang into a canter, 'What's going on?'

'Good tactics.' The robot's tone was one of respect, even admiration. He cantered down the slope, murmuring, 'Perhaps Tuan should explain it to you himself.'

Rod scarcely had time to protest before they had caught up with the army. Everything was roaring confusion – the clanging clash of steel, the tramping squelch of boots in ground that had already begun to turn to mud, the bawling of sergeants' orders, and the whinnies of the knights' horses. Rod looked all about him everywhere, but saw no sign of panic. Sure, here and there the younger faces were filled with dread and the older ones were locked in grim determination and the army as a whole was moving steadily away from the beastmen – but it was definitely a retreat, and not a rout.

'Why?' Rod snapped.

'Tuan has ordered it,' Fess answered, 'and wisely, in my opinion.'

'Take me to him!'

They found the King at the rear, for once, since that was the part of the army closest to the enemy. 'They fall back on the left flank!' he bawled. 'Bid Sir Maris speed them; for stragglers will surely become corpses!'

The courier nodded and darted away through the rain.

'Hail, sovereign lord!' Rod called.

Tuan looked up, and his face lit with relief. 'Lord Warlock! Praise Heaven thou'rt come!'

'Serves you right for inviting me. Why the retreat, Tuan?'

'Assuredly thou dost jest, Lord Warlock! Dost thou not feel the rain upon thee? We cannot stand against them when lightning may strike!'

'But if we don't,' Rod pointed out, 'they'll just keep marching as long as it rains.'

Tuan nodded. 'The thought had occurred to me.'

'Uh – this could be a good way to lose a kingdom. . . .'

'Of this, too, I am mindful. Therefore, we *shall* turn and stand – but not until they are certain we're routed.'

Rod lifted his head slowly, eyes widening. Then he grinned. 'I should've known better than to question your judgement on tactics! But will they really believe we'd just flat-out run, when we've been fighting back for so long?'

'They'll expect some show of resistance, surely,' Tuan agreed. 'Therefore wilt thou and the Flying Legion ride out against them.' He nodded toward the right flank. 'They await thee, Lord Warlock.'

His commandos raised a cheer when they saw him, and he raised them with quick orders. A minute later, half of them faded into the grass and scrub growth that lined the riverbank. The other half, the ones with the hip-boots, imitated Moses and drifted into the bulrushes.

Rod stayed with the landlubbers, easing silently back along the bankside till they reached a place where the beach widened, walled with a semicircle of trees, the spaces between them filled with brush. Ten minutes later, the first scouts from the beastman advance guard came up even with them. Rod waited until they were right in the middle of the semicircle, then whistled a good imitation of a whippoorwill. But the cry was a strange one to the beastmen, and something rang fowl. One Neanderthal looked up, startled, his mouth opening to cry the alarm – when a dozen Gramarye commandos hit him and his mates.

The rangers surrounded the beastmen completely, so Rod didn't see what happened; all he knew was that it lasted about thirty seconds, then his men faded back into the trees, leaving three corpses in the centre of the glade, pumping their blood into the pale sand.

Rod stared, shaken and unnerved. Beside him, his sergeant grinned. ' 'Twas well done, Lord Warlock.'

'I'll take your word for it,' Rod muttered. 'What'd these boys do in peacetime – work in a slaughterhouse?'

The sergeant shrugged. 'Any farm lad must know how to slit the throat of a swine, and these ogres are little more.'

Rod had to bite back a sudden impulse to explain the conflict as the beastmen saw it. 'They're the enemy,' he agreed unhappily, 'and this is war. They've already pretty well proved that they'll kill us if we don't kill them first.' Privately, he wondered how many of them really wanted to.

Later. Right now, it was time to play monster. 'Tell the men to spread out along the back-trail, sergeant.'

The sergeant turned away to mutter a few words, but that was the only effect Rod saw or heard. He sat his saddle securely anyway, knowing his men had spread out toward the beastmen. He sat securely, and waited.

After about five minutes, the vanguard came up. Their leader saw the corpses in the centre of the glade and held out an arm to stop his men. While they stared, shocked, Rod called like a gull, and fifty commandos slid from the brush, swords slashing throats before the beastmen even realized they'd been attacked.

As the first Neanderthals fell, the others turned with a roar, axes whirling down. Rod's men leaped back, but a couple weren't quick enough. He let the anger fuel him as he commanded Fess, 'Go!' The great black steel horse leaped out into the battle as Rod shouted, 'Havoc!' The beastmen's eyes all riveted on this new threat, so they didn't notice the shadows that slid out of the rushes behind them in answer to Rod's cry. Beastmen began dropping at the rear as Rod and his men began their deadly gavotte, skipping back out of reach of the beastmen's axes as they tried to catch Gramarye glances, but Rod's men held to their hard-learned tactic – staring at the enemy's weapons, not at his pupils. Here and there a soldier accidentally looked at the reddened eyes of the foe, and slowed. It even happened to Rod – being on horseback, he attracted eyes. One Neanderthal managed to catch him squarely, and suddenly he was ploughing through molasses, panic touching him as he felt two rival impulses battling in his brain, and realized neither of them was his own.

Then a spreading warmth coursed through his head and down his spine, a familiar touch, and he could almost scent Gwen's perfume as his shield-arm leaped up to give the axe a slight push that deflected it to just barely miss, while his sword stabbed down over the beastman's shield. He felt it sink in, jar against bone, and yanked back on it furiously, turning to the next forman, trying hard to ignore the falling body.

Then lightning strobe-lit the beach, and thunder broke upon their heads. Rod blocked axe-blows frantically, realizing that almost half his force was frozen. Axes swung and the Gramarye soldiers fell, while their opponents turned to help their fellows gang up on soldiers. Darting frantic glances from one to another, most of the soldiers slipped and chanced to look a Neanderthal in the eye – and froze.

Rod bellowed in anger and fear and chopped down at a beastman. He dodged aside, revealing a grinning face that stared up at Rod, catching his gaze full in the eyes.

It was as though Rod's riposte had slammed into a wall. Frantically, he pushed at the sword, but it wouldn't move, and an axe was swinging up at him. Only a spare tendril lingered in his mind, probing weakly at a dark wall that seemed to have settled there . . .

Then a blazing shield tore into the dark mass, shredding it to tatters – and Rod's arms answered his summons. He whipped aside as the axe swung past, then bobbed back to stab downward. His men tore into the beastmen like wildcats, out-numbered but determined to bring down ten times their number by sheer ferocity. But more beastmen were welling up behind the vanguard, more and more; and, in a stab of fear, Rod saw a long, slender dragon ship shouldering up out of the drizzle behind the masses of enemy.

But a roaring bellow shook the beach, and the beastmen looked up in sudden terror at five thousand Gramarye soldiers pouring down along the riverbank.

Rod bit back a shout of triumph; all his men kept silence and channelled the surge of energy into a series of quick stabs. Beastmen dropped before them, then came out of their trances enough to turn and defend themselves; but it was frantic and scrambling now, for the soldiers outnumbered them.

Stabbing and blocking fiercely, Rod became dimly aware of a rhythmic rumble coming from the enemy.

'Rod,' Fess's voice ground out like a slowing recording, 'the strain increases . . . I may fail you . . .'

'Hold on while you can!' Rod shouted, and mentally prepared himself to leap down and use Fess as a back-shield.

The rumbling grew louder, became coherent; the enemy army chanted, as with one voice, 'Kobold! Kobold! Kobold!'

And it almost seemed that their god heard them; the whole riverbank was suddenly transfixed by a shimmering glare, and thunder wrapped them inside a cannon shot.

As the glare dimmed, soldiers slowed. A beastman caught Rod's gaze and he felt himself pushing his arms with agonizing slowness again.

Then the white-hot shield burned through the dark mass again, and his arms leaped free. The whole Gramarye army erupted in a shout of joy and fought with new, savage vigour. A bellow of anger answered them, but it was tinged with despair; and the beastmen seemed to shrink together, forming a wall against the Gramarye spears. But the island wolves harried at that wall, chipping and digging, loosing the blood that it held dammed; and the night was a bedlam of screaming and the crashing of steel.

Suddenly, Rod realized that they were gaining ground. But how could they be, when the enemy had their backs to the water? Looking up, he saw beastmen scrambling single-file back aboard the dragon ships.

'They flee!' he cried, exultant. 'The enemy runs! Harrow them!'

His men responded with a crazed scream, and fought like madmen. They couldn't really do much more than scratch and chip; the beastmen's wall was solid, and became all the more so as it shrank in on itself as one boat glided away and another replaced it. But finally, the last few turned and ran to scramble up the sides of the boat. Soldiers leaped to chase them, but Rod, Tuan, and Sir Maris checked them with whiplash commands that echoed through every knight to every sergeant; and, looking up, the soldiers saw the beastmen already aboard poised to throw down everything from axes to rocks upon them. Seeing the soldiers checked, they did throw them, with crazed howls; and shields came up, bouncing the missiles away harmlessly. But as they did, the dragon ship slid out into the current, swooped around in a slow, graceful curve, and drifted away downstream.

Tuan stabbed a bloody sword up at the sky with a victorious scream. Looking up, the astonished army realized they had won. Then a forest of lances and swords speared up with a screaming howl of triumph.

Before the echoes had faded, Rod had turned Fess's head downstream again. 'You made it through, Old Iron!'

'I did, Rod.' The electronic voice was still a little slowed. 'They could only come at me from the front in this battle.'

Rod nodded. 'A huge advantage. Now head for the witches' tent, full speed!'

The sentries outside the tent recognized him and struck their breastplates in salute. Rod leaped off his horse and darted in.

Guttering candles showed young witches and warlocks sprawled crazily all over the floor, unconscious. In the centre, Agatha slumped against one tent-post, her head in her hands, and Gwen huddled against the other, moaning and rubbing the front and sides of her head.

Fear stabbed. Rod leaped to her, gathered her into his arms. 'Darling! Are you . . .'

She blinked up at him, managed a smile. 'I live, my lord, and will be well again – though presently mine head doth split . . .'

'Praise all saints!' Rod clasped her head to his breast, then finally let the shambles about him sink in. He turned back to Gwen, more slowly this time. 'He showed up, huh?'

'Aye, my lord.' She squinted against the pain. 'When the second bolt of lightning struck, all the younglings were knocked senseless. Agatha and I strove to bear up under the brunt of that fell power, and I could feel Harold's force aiding her. But we all feared a third bolt, knowing we could not withstand it . . .'

'And Galen was mentally eavesdropping, and knew you probably couldn't hold out against it.' Rod nodded. 'But he didn't dare take the chance that his "son" might be burned out in the process, even though that son wasn't born of his body.'

'Do not depend on his aid again,' came a croak from across the tent, and the pile of cloth and bones that was Agatha stirred. 'Beware, Warlock, he doth know that thou wilt now seek to use him by placing Harold at risk.'

'Of course.' Glints danced in Rod's eyes. 'But he'll come, anyway.'

\*

Tuan had left squadrons on both banks, chafing with anger at not being able to take part in the battle; but now, as they saw the dragon ships sailing down toward them, they yelled with joy and whipped out their swords.

The beastmen took one look and kept on sailing.

Frustrated, the young knights in charge gave certain orders; and a few minutes later, flaming arrows leaped up to arc over and thud into decks and sails. The archers amused themselves for a few minutes by watching beastmen scurry about the decks in a panic, dousing flames. But as soon as they were all out, the next squad down the river filled the air with fire-arrows, and the fun began all over again. So, even though Tuan sent a squad of revived witchfolk to fly alongside the fleet, keeping carefully out of arrow-range, they weren't needed. Still, they stood by, watchful and ready, as the dragon ships sailed down the Fleuve and out to sea.

On the horizon, the dragon ships paused, as though considering another try. But a line of archers assembled on the sea-cliffs with telekinetic witches behind them, and the resulting fire-arrows managed to speed all the way out to the horizon before they fell to rekindle charred ships.

The dragon ships gave up, turned their noses homeward, and disappeared.

In the midst of the cheering and drinking, Rod shouldered through to Tuan. He grabbed the King by his royal neck and shouted in his ear to make himself heard. 'You know it's not really over yet, don't you?'

'I know,' the young King replied with dignity, 'but I know further that this night is for celebration. Fill a glass and rejoice with us, Lord Warlock. Tomorrow we shall again study war.'

He was up and functioning the next morning, though not happily. He sat in a chair in his tent, grey daylight filtering through the fabric all around him. The sky was still overcast, and so was Tuan. He pressed a cold towel against his forehead, squinting. 'Now, Lord Warlock. I will hear the talk that I know I must heed: that our war is not done.'

Brom O'Berin stepped close to the King's chair, peering up into his face. 'I misdoubt me an thou shouldst speak of war when thine head is yet so filled with wine its skin is stretched as taut as a drumhead.'

Tuan answered with a weak and rueful smile. ' 'Twill do no harm,

Lord Councillor; for I misdoubt me an we shall speak of aught which I know not already.'

'Which is,' Rod said carefully, 'that if we don't follow them, they'll be back.'

Tuan nodded, then winced, closing his eyes. 'Aye, Lord Warlock. Next spring, as soon as thunderstorms may start, we shall see them here upon our shores again – aye, I know it.'

Brom frowned. 'Yet hast thou thought that they'll have reasoned out a way to conquer all the power our witches can brew up?'

Tuan grimaced. 'Nay, I had not. It strengthens my resolve. We must needs bring the war home to them; we must follow them across the sea, and strike.'

'And the time to strike is now,' Brom rumbled.

Tuan nodded and looked up at Rod. 'Yet how shall we bring our army there, Lord Warlock? Canst thou transport so many men and horses with a spell?'

Rod smiled, amused. 'I don't think even Galen could send that many, my liege. But we have discovered that Gramarye has a thriving merchant fleet who would no doubt be delighted to lend their services to helping wiping out a potential pirates' nest.'

Tuan nodded slowly. 'I do believe 'twould gain their heartfelt cooperation, an thou wert to word it so.'

'It's just a matter of figuring out their area of self-interest. We've also got an amazing number of fishing boats, and their owners will probably be very quick to agree we should forestall any poaching on their fishing-grounds, before it starts.'

The King nodded – again very slowly. 'Then thou dost think we may have transport enow.'

'Probably. And what we lack, I think shipwrights can turn out with around-the-clock shifts by the time we've gathered all the provisions we'll need. No, transportation's not the problem.'

'Indeed?' The King smiled weakly. 'What is, then?'

'Fighting the beastmen on their home ground when they're battling for their lives – and for their wives' and children's lives, too.'

Tuan stared at him for a moment. When he spoke his voice was a ghostly whisper. 'Aye, 'twill be a bloody business. And few of those who sail shall be wafted home.'

'If we make it a fight to the death,' Rod agreed.

'What else can it be?' Brom demanded, scowling.

'A *coup d'état*.' Rod grinned. 'According to Yorick and our other beastman-guests, this invasion is the result of a junta managing to seize power in Beastland.'

Tuan shrugged, irritated. 'What aid is that, if these people have adhered to their new leader?' But as soon as he'd said it, his gaze turned thoughtful.

Rod nodded. 'After a defeat like this, they're not going to be very happy with the leadership of that shaman, Mughorck, and his Kobold-god. And from what Yorick said, I kinda got the feeling that they never really were screamingly enthusiastic about him anyway – they were just bamboozled into putting him into power in the panic of the moment. If we can make it clear right from the beginning that we're fighting Mughorck, and not the beastmen as a whole – then maybe they'll be willing to surrender.'

Tuan nodded slowly. 'Thou dost speak eminent good sense, Lord Warlock. But how wilt thou convey to them this intention?'

'That,' Rod said, 'is for Yorick to figure out.'

'Nothing to it, m'lord.' Yorick waved the problem away with one outsized ham-hand. 'Oldest thing in the book – a nice little whispering-campaign.'

'Whispering-campaigns are *that* old?' Rod had a dizzying vision of 50,000 years of slander. 'But how'll you get it started?'

Yorick glanced at his fellows, then shrugged as he turned back to Rod. 'No help for it – we'll have to go in ahead of you and do it ourselves.' When Rod stared, appalled, Yorick grinned. 'What were you thinking of – leaflets?'

'I was really thinking we might be able to do something with telepathy,' Rod sighed, 'but none of our projectives know the language. Yorick's right – he and his men have got to get the word started somehow. The question is – can we trust them?'

'Trust a man of the foe?' Catharine cried. 'Nay, Lord Warlock, I would hope you would not!'

'But he's really on our side,' Rod argued, 'because he's fighting the same enemy – the shaman, Mughorck.'

They sat in a small chamber – only forty feet square – of the royal castle in Runnymede. The Oriental carpet, tapestries on the walls, gleaming walnut furniture, graceful hourglass-shaped chairs, and silver wine goblets belied any urgency. But even though the fireplace was cold, the talk was heated.

'He doth say Mughorck is his enemy,' Catharine said scornfully. 'Yet, might he not be an agent of just that fell monster?'

Rod spread his hands. 'Why? For what purpose could Mughorck send an agent who couldn't possibly be mistaken for a Gramarye native? Not to mention his handful of cronies who don't even speak our language.'

'Why, for this very purpose, lad,' Brom O'Berin grunted, 'that we might send them in to strengthen our attack, whereupon they could turn their coats, warn their fellows, and have a hedge of spears for our soldiers to confront when they land.'

'Okay,' Rod snorted, disgusted. 'Farfetched, but possible, I'll grant you. Still, it just doesn't *feel* right.'

Catharine smiled wickedly. 'I had thought 'twas only ladies who would decide great matters by such feelings.'

'All right, so you've got a point now and then,' Rod growled. 'But you know what I mean, Your Majesty – there's some element of this whole situation that just doesn't fit with the hypothesis that Yorick's an enemy.'

Catharine opened her mouth to refute him, but Brom spoke first. 'I take thy meaning – and I'll tell thee the element.'

Catharine turned to him in amazement, and Tuan looked up, suddenly interested again.

' 'Tis this,' Brom explained, 'that he doth speak our language. Could he have learned it from Mughorck?'

'Possibly, if Mughorck's an agent of the Eagle's enemies,' Rod said slowly. 'If the Eagle taught Yorick English, there's no reason why Mughorck couldn't have, too.'

'Still, I take thy meaning.' Tuan sat up straighter. 'We know that Yorick doth hold the Eagle to be some manner of wizard; if we say that Mughorck is too, then we have pitted wizard 'gainst wizard. Would not then their combat be with one another? Why should we think they care so greatly about us that they would combine against us?'

'Or that Mughorck would oust Eagle only to be able to use the beastmen 'gainst us,' Brom rumbled. 'Why could we be of such great moment to Mughorck?'

'Because,' Fess's voice said behind Rod's ear, 'Gramarye has more functioning telepaths than all the rest of the Terran Sphere together; and the interstellar communication they can provide will in all probability be the single greatest factor in determining who shall rule the Terran peoples.'

And because the Eagle and Mughorck were probably both time-travelling agents from future power-blocs who knew how the current struggle was going to come out and were trying to change it here,

Rod added mentally. Aloud, he just said sourly, 'It's nice to know this chamber has such thick walls that we don't have to worry about eavesdroppers.'

'Wherefore?' Tuan frowned. 'Is there reason to question the loyalty of any of our folk?'

'Uhhhhhh . . . no.' Rod had to improvise quickly, and surprisingly hit upon truth. 'It's just that I brought Yorick along, in case we decided we wanted to talk to him. He's in the antechamber.'

Catharine looked up, horrified, and stepped quickly behind Tuan's chair. The King, however, looked interested. 'Then, by all means, let's bring him in! Can we think of no questions to ask that might determine the truth or falsehood of this beastman's words?'

Brom stomped over to the door, yanked it open, and rumbled a command. As he swaggered back Rod offered, 'Just this. From Toby's report, the beastmen's village is very thoroughly settled and the fields around it are loaded with corn, very neatly cultivated. That settlement's not brand-new, Tuan. If the Eagle had come here with conquest in mind, would he have taken a couple of years out to build up a colony?'

The young King nodded. 'A point well-taken.' He turned as the beastman ambled in, and Catharine took a step back. 'Welcome, captain of exiles!'

'The same to you, I'm sure.' Yorick grinned and touched his forelock.

Brom scowled ferociously, so Rod figured he'd better butt in. 'Uh, we've just been talking, Yorick, about why Mughorck tried to assassinate the Eagle.'

'Oh, because Mughorck wanted to conquer you guys,' Yorick said, surprised. 'He couldn't even get it started with the Eagle in the way, preaching understanding and tolerance.'

The room was awfully quiet while Tuan, Brom, Catharine, and Rod exchanged frantic glances.

'I said something?' Yorick inquired.

'Only what we'd all just been saying.' Rod scratched behind his ear. 'Always unnerving, finding out you guessed right.' He looked up at Yorick. 'Why'd Mughorck want to conquer us?'

'Power-base,' Yorick explained. 'Your planet's going to be the hottest item in the coming power-struggle. Your descendants will come out on the side of democracy, so the Decentralized Democratic Tribunal will win. The only chance the losers will have is to come back in time and try to take over Gramarye. When Mughorck took

over we realized he must've been working for one of the future losers
. . . What's the matter, milord?'

Rod had been making frantic shushing motions. Tuan turned a
gimlet eye on him. 'Indeed, Lord Warlock.' His voice was smooth as
velvet. 'Why wouldst thou not wish him to speak of such things?'

'For that they are highly confusing, for one.' Catharine knit her
brows, but the look she bent on Rod was baleful. 'Still, mine
husband's point's well taken. For whom dost *thou* labour, Lord
Warlock?'

'For my wife and child, before anyone else,' Rod sighed, 'but
since I want freedom and justice for them, and you two are their
best chance for that condition – why, I work for you.'

'Or in accord with us,' Tuan amended. 'But hast thou other
affiliations, Lord Warlock?'

'Well, there is a certain collaborative effort that . . .'

'. . . that doth give him information vital to the continuance of
Your Majesties' reign.' Brom glanced up at them guiltily. 'I ha'
known of it almost since he came among us.'

Some of the tension began to ease out of Tuan, but Catharine
looked more indignant than ever. 'Even thou, my trusted Brom!
Wherefore didst thou not tell this to me?'

'For reason that thou hadst no need to know it,' Brom said simply,
'and because I felt it to be Lord Gallowglass's secret. If he thought
thou shouldst know it, he would tell thee – for, mistake not, his
first loyalty is here.'

Catharine seemed a bit mollified, and Tuan was actually smiling
– but with a glittering eye. 'We must speak more of this anon, Lord
Warlock.'

But not just now. Rod breathed a shuddering sigh and cast a quick
look of gratitude toward Brom. The dwarf nodded imperceptibly.

'Our cause of worry is before us.' Tuan turned back to Yorick.
'It would seem, Master Yorick, that thou dost know more than thou
shouldst.'

Yorick stared. 'You mean some of this was classified?'

Rod gave him a laser glare, but Tuan just said, 'Where didst thou
learn of events yet to come?'

'Oh, from the Eagle.' Yorick smiled, relieved. 'He's been there.'

The room was very still for a moment.

Then Tuan said carefully, 'Dost thou say this Eagle hath gone
bodily to the future?'

Yorick nodded.

'Who's he work for?' Rod rapped out.

'Himself.' Yorick spread his hands. 'Makes a nice profit out of it, too.'

Rod relaxed. Political fanatics would fight to the death, but businessmen would always see reason – provided you showed them that they could make a better profit doing things your way.

But Tuan shook his head. 'Thou wouldst have us believe the Eagle brought all thy people here and taught them to farm enough to support themselves. Where's the profit in that?'

'Well,' Yorick hedged, 'he does undertake the occasional humanitarian project . . .'

'Also, for certain assignments you boys probably make unbeatable agents,' Rod said drily.

Yorick had the grace to blush.

'Or is it,' rumbled Brom, 'that he doth fight the future-folk who backed Mughorck? Would thy people not be a part of that fight?'

Yorick became very still. Then he eyed Rod and jerked his head toward Brom. 'Where'd you get him?'

'You don't want to know,' Rod said quickly. 'But we do. How were you Neanderthals a weapon in the big fight?'

Yorick sighed and gave in. 'Okay. It's a little more complicated than what I said before. The bad guys gathered us together to use us as a tool to establish a very early dictatorship that wouldn't quit. You'll understand, milord, that we're a bit of a paranoid culture.'

'Can't imagine why,' Rod said drily.

'What is this "paranoid"?' Tuan frowned. 'And what matters it to government?'

'It means you feel as though everyone's picking on you,' Yorick explained, 'so you tend to pick on them first, to make sure they can't get you. Governments like that are very good at repression.'

Catharine blanched, and Tuan turned to Rod. 'Is there truth in what he doth say?'

'Too much,' Rod said with a woeful smile, 'and anyone with witch-power tends to be repressed. Now you know why I'm on your side, my liege.'

'Indeed I do.' Tuan turned back to face Yorick. 'And I find myself much less concerned about thine other associations.'

But Rod was watching Catharine closely out of the corner of his eye. Was she realizing that she'd been on the road to becoming a tyrant when she'd reigned alone? Mostly over-compensating for insecurity, of course – but by the time she'd gained enough experience to be sure of herself, she'd have had too many people who hated her; she'd have had to stay a tyrant.

But Tuan was talking to Yorick again. 'Why doth thine Eagle fight these autocrats?'

'Bad for trade,' Yorick said promptly. 'Dictatorships tend to establish very arbitrary rules about who can do business with whom, and their rules result in either very high tariffs or exorbitant graft. But a government that emphasizes freedom pretty much has to let business be free, too.'

'Pretty much.' Rod underscored the qualifier.

Yorick shrugged. 'Freedom's an unstable condition, my lord. There'll always be men trying to destroy it by establishing their own dictatorships. Businessmen are human too.'

Rod felt that the issue deserved a bit more debate, but the little matter of the invasion was getting lost in the shuffle. 'We were kind of thinking about that whispering-campaign you mentioned. Mind explaining how you could work it without getting caught? And don't try to tell me you guys all look alike to each other.'

'Wouldn't think of it.' Yorick waved away the suggestion. 'By this time, see, I'm pretty sure there'll be a lot of people who're fed up with Mughorck. In fact, I even expect a few refugees from his version of justice. If you can smuggle me back to the mainland, into the jungle south of the village, I think I can make contact with quite a few of 'em. Some of them will have friends who'll be glad to forget any chance meetings they might have out in the forest gathering fruit, and the rumour you want circulated can get passed into the village when the friend comes back.'

Tuan nodded. 'It should march. But couldst thou not have done this better an thou hadst remained in thine own country?'

Yorick shook his head. 'Mughorck's gorillas were hot on my trail. By now, he should have other problems on his hands; he won't have forgotten about me and my men, but we won't be high-priority any more. Besides, there might even be enough refugees in the forest so that he's not willing to risk any of his few really loyal squads on a clean-out mission; the odds might be too great that they wouldn't come back.'

The King nodded slowly. 'I hope, for thy sake, that thou hast it aright.'

'Then, too,' Yorick said, 'there's the little matter that, if I'd stayed, there'd have been no message to pass. Frankly, I needed allies.'

'Thou hast them, an thou'rt a true man,' Tuan said firmly.

Catherine, however, looked much less certain.

Yorick noted it. 'Of course I'm true. After all, if I betrayed you and you caught me, I expect you'd think of a gallows that I'd be the perfect decoration for.'

'Nay, i' truth,' Tuan protested, 'I'd have to build one anew especially for thee, to maintain harmony of style.'

'I'm flattered.' Yorick grinned. 'I'll tell you straightaway, though, I don't deserve to be hanged in a golden chain. Silver, maybe . . .'

'Wherefore? Dost thou fear leprechauns?'

Tuan and Yorick, Rod decided, were getting along entirely too well. 'There's the little matter of the rumour he's supposed to circulate,' he reminded Tuan.

Yorick shrugged. 'That you and your army have really come just to oust Mughorck, isn't it? Not to wipe out the local citizenry?'

'Thou hast it aright.'

'But you do understand,' Yorick pointed out, 'that they'll have to fight until they know Mughorck's been taken, don't you? I mean, if they switched to your side and he won, it could be very embarrassing for them – not to mention their wives and children.'

'Assuredly,' Tuan agreed. 'Nay, I hope only that, when they know Mughorck is ta'en, they'll not hesitate to lay down their arms.'

'I have a notion that most of them will be too busy cheering to think about objecting.'

' 'Tis well. Now . . .' Tuan leaned forward, eyes glittering. 'How can we be sure of taking Mughorck?'

'An we wish a quick ending to this battle,' Brom explained, 'we cannot fight through the whole mass of beastmen to reach him.'

'Ah – now we come back to my original plan.' Yorick grinned. 'I was waiting for you guys to get around to talking invasion. Because if you do, you see, and if you sneak me into the jungles a week or two ahead, I'm sure my boys and I can find enough dissenters to weld into an attack force. Then, when your army attacks from the front, I can bring my gorillas . . .'

'You mean guerrillas.'

'That, too. Anyway, I can bring 'em over the cliffs and down to the High Cave.'

'"The High Cave"?' Tuan frowned. 'What is that?'

'Just the highest cave in the cliff-wall. When we first arrived we all camped out in caves, and Eagle took the highest one so he could see the whole picture of what was going on. When the rank and file moved out into huts, he stayed there – so Mughorck will have to have moved in there, to use the symbol of possession to reinforce his power.'

'Well reasoned,' Brom rumbled, 'but how if thou'rt mistaken?'

Yorick shrugged. 'Then we keep looking till we find him. We shouldn't have too much trouble; I very much doubt that he'd be at the front line.'

Tuan's smile soured with contempt.

'He's the actual power,' Yorick went on, 'but the clincher'll be the Kobold. When we take the idol, that should really tell the troops that the war's lost.'

'And you expect it'll be in the High Cave too,' Rod amplified.

'Not a doubt of it,' Yorick confirmed. 'You haven't seen this thing, milord. You sure as hell wouldn't want it in your living room.'

'Somehow I don't doubt that one bit.'

'Nor I,' Tuan agreed. He glanced at his wife and his two ministers. 'Are we agreed, then?'

Reluctantly, they nodded.

'Then, 'tis done.' Tuan clapped his hands. 'I will give orders straightaway, Master Yorick, for a merchantman to bear thee and thy fellows to the jungles south of thy village. Then, when all's in readiness, a warlock will come to tell thee the day and hour of our invasion.'

'Great!' Yorick grinned with relief: then, suddenly, he frowned. 'But wait a minute. How'll your warlock find us?'

'Just stare at a fire and try to blank your mind every evening for a few hours,' Rod explained, 'and think something abstract – the sound of one hand clapping, or some such, over and over again. The warlock'll home in on your mind.'

Yorick looked up, startled. 'You mean your telepaths can read *our* minds?'

'Sort of,' Rod admitted. 'At least, they can tell you're there, and where you are.'

Yorick smiled, relieved. 'Well. No wonder you knew where the raiders were going to land next.'

'After the first strike, yes.' Rod smiled. 'Of course, we can't understand your language.'

'Thanks for the tip.' Yorick raised a forefinger. 'I'll make sure I don't think in English.'

Rod wasn't sure he could, but he didn't say so.

Yorick turned back to the King and Queen. 'If you don't mind,

I'll toddle along now, Your Majesties.' He bowed. 'I'd like to go tell my men it's time to move out.'

'Do, then,' Tuan said regally, 'and inform thy men that they may trust in us as deeply as we may trust in them.'

Yorick paused at the door and looked back, raising one eyebrow. 'You sure about that?'

Tuan nodded firmly.

Yorick grinned again. 'I think you just said more than you knew. Godspeed, Majesties.' He bowed again and opened the door; the sentry ushered him out.

Catharine was the first to heave a huge sigh of relief. 'Well! 'Tis done.' She eyed her husband. 'How shall we know if the greatest part of his bargain's fulfilled, ere thy battle?'

'Well, I wasn't quite candid with him,' Rod admitted. He stepped over to the wall and lifted the edge of a tapestry. 'What do you think, dear? Can we trust him?'

Gwen nodded as she stepped out into the room. 'Aye, my lord. There was not even the smallest hint of duplicity in his thoughts.'

'He was thinking in English,' Rod explained to the startled King and Queen. 'He had to; he was talking to us.'

Tuan's face broke into a broad grin. 'So that was thy meaning when thou didst speak of "eavesdroppers"!'

'Well, not entirely. But I did kind of have Gwen in mind.'

'Yet may he not have been thinking in his own tongue, beneath the thoughts he spoke to us?' Catharine demanded.

Gwen cast an approving glance at her. Rod read it and agreed; though Catharine tended to flare into anger if you mentioned her own psi powers to her, she was obviously progressing well in their use, to have come across the idea of submerged thoughts.

'Mayhap, Majesty,' Gwen agreed. 'Yet, beneath those thoughts in his own tongue there are the root-thoughts that give rise to words, but which themselves are without words. They are naked flashes of idea, as yet unclothed. Even there, as deeply as I could read him, there was no hint of treachery.'

'But just to be sure, we'll have Toby check out his camp right before the invasion,' Rod explained. 'He's learned enough to be able to dig beneath the camouflage of surface thoughts, if there is any.'

The door opened, and the sentry stepped in to announce, 'Sir Maris doth request audience, Majesties.'

'Aye, indeed!' Tuan turned to face the door, delighted. 'Mayhap he doth bring word from our sentries who have kept watch to be certain the beastmen do not turn back, to attempt one last surprise. Assuredly, present him!'

The sentry stepped aside, and the seneschal limped into the chamber, leaning heavily on his staff, but with a grin that stretched from ear to ear.

'Welcome, good Sir Maris!' Tuan cried. 'What news?'

' 'Twas even as thou hadst thought, Majesty.' Sir Maris paused in front of Tuan for a sketchy bow, then straightened up, and his grin turned wolfish. 'Three ships did curve and seek to sail into the mouth of a smaller river that runs athwart the Fleuve.'

'They were repulsed?' Glints danced in Tuan's eyes.

'Aye, my liege! Our archers filled their ships with fire, the whiles our soldiers slung a weighty chain across the river. When they ground against it and found they could sail no further, they sought to come ashore; but our men-at-arms presented them a hedge of pikes. Nay, they turned and fled.' He turned to Rod. 'Our thanks, Lord Warlock, for thy good aid in this endeavour!'

Rod started, staring, and Gwen caught his arm and her breath; but Sir Maris whirled back to the King, fairly crowing, 'He did seem to be everywhere, first on this bank, then on that, amongst the archers, then amongst the pikemen, everywhere urging them on to feats of greater valour. Nay, they'll not believe that they can lost now.'

Gwen looked up, but Rod stood frozen.

'Yet, withal,' said the old knight, frowning, 'why hadst thou assigned command to me? If the High Warlock were there to lead, he should have had command as well!'

'But,' said Tuan, turning to Rod, 'thou wast ever here in Runnymede, with ourselves, the whiles this raid was foiled!'

'I noticed,' Rod croaked.

'My lord, not all things that hap here are impossible,' Gwen sighed.

'Oh, yes, they are. Take you, for example – that someone as wonderful as you could even exist is highly improbable. But that you could not only exist but also fall in love with someone like me – well, that's flatly impossible.'

Gwen gave him a radiant smile. 'Thou wilt ever undervalue thyself, Rod Gallowglass, and overvalue me – and thus hath made a cold world turn warm for me.'

That look in her eyes he couldn't resist; it pulled him down, and down, into a long, deep kiss that tried to pull him deeper. But eventually Rod remembered that he was on the deck of a ship, and that the crew were no doubt watching. He was tempted to consign them all to the Inferno, but he remembered his responsibilities and pulled out of the kiss with a regretful sigh. 'We haven't been doing enough of that lately.'

'I am well aware of that, my lord.' Gwen fixed him with a glittering eye.

'And I thought the Neanderthals had an "Evil Eye"!' Rod breathed, and turned to hook her hand firmly around his elbow as he strolled down the deck. 'For now, however, let's enjoy the seabreeze and the salt air. After all, this is the closest thing to a pleasure cruise we're ever apt to get.'

'As thou dost say, my lord,' she said demurely.

'Just so you don't mistake my doppelgänger for me,' Rod amended.

Gwen shook her head firmly. 'That could not hap at any distance less than an hundred feet.'

'Well, I hope not – but quite a few people seem to have been making the error.'

'Ah, but how well do they know thee?' Gwen crooned. 'If they've seen thee at all before, it has been only briefly and from a distance.'

'Yeah, but there're some who . . . well, there's one!' Rod stopped next to a brown-robed form that sat cross-legged on the deck, leaning against the rail with a half-filled inkhorn in his left hand, writing in a careful round hand in a book of huge vellum sheets. 'Hail, Brother Chillde!'

The monk looked up, startled. Then a smile of delight spread over his face. 'Well met, Lord Warlock! I had hoped to espy thee here!'

Rod shrugged. 'Where else would I be? It's the King's flagship. But how do you come to be here, Brother Chillde?'

'I am chaplain,' the monk said simply. 'And I wish to be near to the King and his councillors as may be, an I am able; for I strive to record what doth occur during this war as well as I may.'

'So your chronicle's coming well? How far back have you managed to dig?'

'Why, I began four years agone, when the old King died, and have writ down all I've seen or heard that has occured during, first, the reign of Catharine, then during the reign of both our goodly King and Queen.' He beamed up at them. 'Yet, in this present crisis I have been fortunate to be in the thick of it, almost from the first. My journal shall be precise, so that folk yet unborn, and many hundreds of years hence, may know how nobly our folk of this present age did acquit themselves.'

'A noble goal.' Rod smiled, though without, perhaps, as much respect as the project deserved. 'Be sure what you write is accurate, though, won't you?'

'Never fear. I've asked several folk for their accounts of each event, and thus believe I've found somewhat of the truth. Yet, for the greater part, I've writ only what I've seen myself.'

Rod nodded with approval. 'Can't do better than primary source material. May your endeavour prosper, Brother Chillde.'

'I thank thee, lord.'

And Rod and Gwen strolled on down the deck as the monk bent over his journal again. When they were safely out of earshot, Rod murmured to Gwen, 'Of course, eyewitness accounts aren't necessarily what really happened. People's memories are always coloured by what they want to believe.'

'I can well credit it.' Gwen glanced back at the monk. 'And he's so young and filled with the ideals of youth! I doubt me not an Catharine and Tuan seem to him impossibly regal and imposing – and the beastmen immensely vile, and . . .'

'Mama!'

Gwen recoiled in surprise, then blossomed into a radiant smile as she realized she was suddenly holding an armful of baby. 'Magnus, my bonny boy! Hast thou, then, come to wish thy parents well on this their venture?'

Her eyes darkened as the baby nodded, and Rod guessed she was thinking that Mama and Papa might not come home to Baby. She needed a distraction. 'What's he got there – a ball?'

The spheroid was dull and grey, about four inches in diameter – and its surface suddenly rippled. Rod stared.

Gwen saw his look of disgust and said quickly, 'Be not concerned, my lord. 'Tis naught but witch moss with which, I doubt me not, he hath been toying.'

'Oh.' Rod knew the substance well; it was a variety of fungus that had the peculiar property of responding to the thoughts of projective telepaths. Rod had a strong suspicion that it had contributed to the development of elves, werewolves, and other supernatural creatures around the Gramarye landscape. 'When did he begin to play with . . .'

He broke off, because the ball was changing in the child's hand – and Magnus was staring at it in surprise. It stretched itself up, flattening and dwindling toward the bottom, where it divided in half lengthwise for half its height, and two pieces broke loose at the sides. The top formed itself into a smaller ball, and dents and lines began to define the form.

'What doth he make?' Gwen whispered.

'I'm afraid to guess.' But Rod knew, with a sickening certainty, what he was going to see.

And he was right – for the lump finished its transformation and swung up a wicked-looking war axe, opening a gash of a mouth to reveal canines that would have done credit to a sabre-toothed tiger. Its piggy eyes reddened with insane blood-lust, and it began to shamble up Magnus's arm.

The child shrieked and hurled it as far away from him as he could. It landed on the deck, caving in one side; but that side bulged out into its former form as it pulled itself to its feet and shambled off down the deck, looking for something to ravish.

Magnus ploughed his head into Gwen's bosom, wailing in terror. 'There, love – 'tis gone,' she assured him, 'or will be in a moment . . .' And she glared at the diminutive monster, eyes narrowing. It took one step, and its leg turned into mush.

'It's a beastman,' Rod whispered, 'a vicious parody of a Neanderthal.'

Another step, and the model beastman turned into a ball again.

'But the kid didn't see any of the battles!' Rod protested. 'How could he . . .'

'My lord,' Gwen grated, 'it will not hold its shape unless I force it. Another mind fights me for the forming of it.'

'Then, get rid of it – fast! You never know, it might find another one like it, and breed true!'

'Done,' Gwen snapped.

The witch moss turned into a ball so smooth that it gleamed, then shot off the deck and far, far away, heading for the horizon.

Gwen turned her attention back to Magnus. 'There, there, child! 'Twas no fault of thine; 'twas some mean and heartless person who crafted thy ball thus, to afright a babe!' She looked up at Rod with murder in her eyes. 'Who would ha' done such a thing?'

'I don't know, but I'll find out.' Rod was feeling in a mayhem mood himself. He glanced quickly about the decks, even up into the rigging, trying to find anyone gazing at them – but there were only two sailors in sight, and neither was even looking in their direction.

But Brother Chillde still scribbled in his book.

Rod stared. No. It couldn't be.

But . . .

He stepped over to Brother Chillde again, lightly, almost on tiptoe, and craned his neck to peer over the monk's shoulder at the words he was writing.

. . . *Huge they were*, the manuscript read, *with arms that hung down to their knees, and fangs that sank below their chins. Their eyes were maddened bits of red, more suited to a swine than a man, in a head like unto a ball, but too small for so great a body. Their sole weapon was a huge and murderous axe, and with it they quested always, seeking for living things to slay.*

'Thou knowest not what thou dost ask,' Puck cried. 'Ever was I made for battle, Rod Gallowglass! Hast thou any comprehension of the opportunities for mischief that occur when men do war?'

'Very much,' Rod answered grimly. 'Look, I know it's a hardship to stay out of the fighting – but you've got to think of the good of the whole of Gramarye, not just of your own excitement.'

'Who says I must?' the elf demanded with a truculent scowl.

'I,' answered Brom O'Berin; and Puck took one look at his sovereign's face and shrank back.

'Well, then, so I must,' he sighed. 'But wherefore must it be I? Are there no other elves who can execute so simple a task?'

'None,' Rod said with absolute certainty. 'It only seems simple to you. I can think of a few other elves who *might* be able to bring it off – but you're the only one I'm sure of.'

Puck visibly swelled with self-importance.

'You're the only one,' Rod pressed on, 'who has the imagination, and the gift of gab, to pull this off.'

'Thou wilt do it,' Brom commanded sternly, 'else thou wilt answer to me, hobgoblin, when the battle's ended.'

'Ah, then, I shall,' Puck sighed – but preened himself, too. 'E'en so, Warlock – I ken not why the monk will need one to detail to him what doth occur when he hath two eyes to see with.'

'Yes, well, that's the first thing you'll have to arrange, isn't it? Some way of making his eyes unusable for the duration of the battle. Nothing permanent,' Rod added hastily, seeing the gleam in Puck's eye.

'Well-a-day,' the elf sighed, 'so be it. We shall benight him only for an hour or two. But what purpose doth that serve, when I am but to tell to him what doth occur?'

'But you're not,' Rod contradicted. 'You're supposed to tell him what *isn't* happening.'

'What word is this?' Puck stared. 'Do I hear aright? I am to say,

"Nay, be of good cheer! It doth not rain, nor doth the moon shine! The soldiers do not shake the beastmen's hands in friendship, nor do they lose a foot of land!' What foolery is this?'

'Not quite what I had in mind, that's for sure.' Rod fought a smile. 'Don't be so negative, Puck. Think of it like this: "Our brave, heroic line doth advance, and the murderous mass of craven beastmen stumble toward them with mayhem in their eyes! They catch our soldiers' gazes, and our goodmen freeze, terror-stricken by the Evil Eye! But the witch-folk wrench them free, and the High Warlock doth rise up, a gleaming paragon on a giant steed of jet, to call them onward! Inspired by his valour, our soldier-men take heart; they shout with anger and do charge the foe!"'

Puck gave him a jaundiced eye. 'Thou'rt not slow to trumpet thine own virtues, art thou?'

'Well, not when it's warranted,' Rod said, abashed. 'And in this case, it's downright vital. Brother Chillde won't believe anything less of me, Puck – and, whatever other effect you achieve, you've got to make him believe what you tell him, totally.'

Air boomed outward, and Toby stood before them. 'Lord Warlock, thou'rt wanted on the poop deck.'

'From the poop deck?' Rod raised an eyebrow in surprised sarcasm. 'All that way? Gee, Toby, I hope you didn't tire yourself out.'

The young warlock reddened. 'I know thou dost enjoin us, Lord Warlock, to not appear and disappear, or fly, when simple walking will be nearly as fast . . .'

'Darn right I do. Totally aside from what it does to your fitness and your character, there's the little matter of its effects on the non-psi majority.'

'I did forget,' Toby sighed. 'When great events are in train, such matters seem of slight import.'

'That's why you need to make normal conduct a habit. But what great event's in train now?'

'*I* am!' the young warlock cried in exasperation. 'I have but now returned from bearing word of our arrival to Master Yorick and his band! Wilt thou not come attend to me?'

'Oh!' Rod bolted off his stool, feeling like a pompous idiot. 'What an ass I am!'

Puck perked up and opened his mouth.

'Just a figure of speech,' Rod said quickly. 'But accurate. Here I am, catechizing you about details, when you've just finished a hazardous mission! My deepest apologies, Toby – and I'm glad to see you're back intact. And, of course, you can't report to me here – you've got to say it the first time where the King can hear it.'

'No offence, milord,' Toby said with a grin. He stepped over to the door and held it open. 'And, since *thou* canst not transport thyself from place to place, I'll company thee on foot.'

'I, too,' Brom growled. 'I must hear what progress this grinning ape hath made.'

The door slammed behind them, leaving Puck alone to mutter imprecations to himself.

'Welcome, Lord Warlock,' Tuan said quietly, as the door closed behind them, 'and thou, too, Lord Brom.' His eyes glittered. 'Now! May we hear this warlock's tale?'

Toby looked around at the glowing eyes, all fixed upon him, and succumbed to sudden embarrassment. 'Where . . . what shall I tell?'

'Everything that happened,' Rod suggested, 'starting from the beginning.'

Toby heaved a sigh. 'Well, then! I listened for the beastmen's thoughts, and felt a mind belabouring with emptiness. This did resemble the "sound of one hand clapping" that the High Warlock had told me of, so I drifted toward where it seemed the loudest, and looked down. I was far past the beastmen's village, and the feelings of their thoughts had thinned; but now I felt the thrust of several minds, mayhap threescore. Yet all I saw were treetops.'

Rod nodded. 'They hid well. What then?'

'I listened close, till the un-clapping mind had begun to think of other matters – yet, even there, no inkling-thought of treachery did come. Therefore did I drift down into a treetop and clambered down into their midst, the less to afright them.'

Tuan smiled thinly. 'That might somewhat lessen their startlement, I wot – yet not abundantly. What said they when they beheld thee?'

'Oh, the first beastman that laid eyes upon me shrieked and whirled up a war club, and I readied myself to disappear; but I also held up open hands, and he stayed his blow, then nodded toward his left. I went thither, and he followed me, though with ne'er a bit of trust in's eyes. And thus came I unto Master Yorick.'

'Where?' Rod pounced on it.

Toby looked up, surprised. 'He sat beside a nearly smokeless fire with several others, only one among many, till he looked up and saw me. Then he stood, and grinned, and came up to me, hand upheld in salute.'

Tuan had caught Rod's point. 'Ah, then. He sat among his men as an equal, with neither state nor honour.'

'None that I could see. I' truth, there were as many women as men around that fire – yet they did defer to him, that much was plain.'

'How many were there?' the King demanded.

'A score of men, at least; and he assured me others stood sentry-guard, the whiles a squadron patrolled the jungle's edge, nigh to the village, to aid those who sought to escape. His force, he said, has strength of twoscore and more.'

'How many women and children are there?' Catharine sounded anxious.

'A dozen that I could see, of women; each had two babes, or three.'

'Thriving little family group.' Rod smiled. 'If we didn't clean out Mughorck, Yorick'd have his own village going.'

'Aye, and betimes the two villages would battle.' Tuan smiled with irony. 'Mayhap we ought to keep our men at home and let our foemen slay one another.'

'Thou canst not mean to say it!' Catharine flared.

'Nor do I,' Tuan sighed, 'for Yorick and his folk are allies now; and if Mughorck did battle him, Mughorck would surely win, since that he hath thousands. Nay, we must needs strike whiles yet we have a force to aid us. What did he say of the rumour he had hoped he'd seed?'

'He said that in these few weeks time it hath increased amazingly.' Toby grinned. 'Indeed, saith Master Yorick, "'Tis ready to be reaped and sheaved, and gathered into barns."'

'The seed, then, fell on fertile ground,' Brom rumbled.

Toby nodded. 'Thus saith Yorick: "There are some hundreds of widows now where there were none two months agone – and what hath their blood bought? Why, naught – save the fear of vengeance." Aye, milord, these folk were more than ready to believe that vengeance would be aimed only at the Kobold and his priest Mughorck.'

'What of the High Cave?' Brom rumbled. 'Hath he sign that the ones we seek do lair therein?'

'They do.' Toby nodded. 'Those lately come agree with those who 'scaped two months agone – the Eagle's High Cave now holds the Kobold and his priests.'

'The Eagle – aye. What of him?' Tuan frowned.

'He dwells near them, but not with them,' Toby answered, returning his frown. 'Ever and anon doth Yorick go to speak with him, but he dwells not with his folk.'

'Afraid?' Rod demanded.

'Not of Yorick's band. Yet he seems to think Mughorck might come in search of him, and doth not wish his loyalists to be caught in a net that might be laid for him.'

'I think the Neanderthals aren't the only ones who're paranoid,' Rod noted with a lift of the eyebrow toward Tuan. 'Well, Your Majesty, it sounds as though our partisans are in good shape, and definitely ready to pitch in on our side.'

'I would so conjecture.' But Tuan still watched Toby. 'Art thou certain there was no hint of treachery in his manner, nor in his thoughts?'

The young warlock shook his head firmly. 'Nay, my liege – and I did probe. There might be summat hid in the fastnesses of his heart . . . but if there is, 'tis beyond my comprehension.'

'Mayhap there is,' Tuan said frowning, 'but when there's no sign, we would be fools to turn away their aid.'

'Still,' Rod pointed out, 'we could try to be ready for a last-minute change of heart.'

'We must be so, indeed,' Tuan agreed. 'Let us count the beastmen loyal only when the battle's won.'

'Which will not be easy.' Rod stood, frowning down. 'We'll be on the beastmen's home territory this time. They won't need lightning to bring them their extra power; they'll have it right there at hand.'

'Indeed, 'twill be a most fell battle,' Tuan agreed. 'Art thou certain of this ancient wizard's aid?'

Rod started to answer, then hesitated.

'So I feared,' Tuan said grimly.

Rod nodded unhappily. 'But if he jumped in to save his "son" once, he's *almost* certain to do it again.'

'Well, one can but pick the strongest ground and do one's best,' Tuan sighed. 'For, after all, no outcome's certain in battle, commerce, love, or life. Godspeed ye, my commanders – and may we all meet again, when tomorrow's sun hath dawned.'

The Neanderthal village breathed uneasily in its slumber, bathed by the moon. The sentries on cliff-top and in small boats were bone-weary but not at all sleepy, for Mughorck had filled them with fear of the wild-eyed, ferocious Flatfaces who were so powerful as to be able to throw off the effects of the Evil Eye. What other powers did they have? How soon would they descend upon the hapless people, filled with vengeful blood-lust?

But, countering these tales, was the rumour that filtered throughout the village now – that the Flatfaces' anger was blunted; that Yorick had pleaded with them and brought them to see that this madness of raiding and invasion was only Mughorck's doing, and that when the Flatfaces came they would be satisfied with only Mughorck, and his lieutenants. And, of course, the Kobold . . .

The sentries shuddered. What race of wizards was this, who could dare to strive against a god?

Thus their thoughts ran through the hours while the moon slowly drifted down toward the horizon, then slipped below it – and the land lay shadowed, its darkness lightened only by the stars. The sentries, weary to begin with, began to grow sleepy. The night was almost past; the Flatfaces had not come. For a few more hours, they were safe . . .

Then they started, staring. What were those dark shapes that scuttled over the water toward the beach, so many as to seem like a field of darkened stars? In disbelief, the sentries squeezed their eyes shut, shook their heads – but when they looked again the squat, dark shapes still drove toward the beach. Surely these could not be the Flatfaces, flooding in so silently . . .

But the dark shapes ploughed up the beach, grinding to a halt, and scores of smaller shadows dropped off their sides. Nightmare though it seemed, this was no dream! The sentries clapped horns and conch shells to their lips, and blew the alarm!

Neanderthals tumbled out of their huts, pulling on helmets, hefting war axes, groggy but waking fast, calling to one another in alarm.

The Gramarye soldiers formed their line and marched toward the village.

The High Warlock rode back and forth behind the lines, cautioning, 'No shouting yet! Remember, silence! The more noise they make, the more eerie we'll seem.'

But the beastmen pulled a ragged line together and stumbled toward the Gramarye soldiers with querulous, ragged war cries.

'Now!' Rod bellowed, and the soldiers charged with a hundred-throated ear-splitting shriek.

The lines crashed together, and the long pikes did their murder. Axes chopped through their shafts, but the beastmen died. Then, here and there, a beastman began to catch a soldier's eyes, and the Gramarye line slowed as its members began to freeze.

In the flagship's cabin, the witches and warlocks sat in a circle, hands joined, staring at the ceiling.

The Gramarye line gained speed again as the numbing darkness lifted from the soldiers' minds.

Frantically, the beastmen reached for the power of the Kobold.

A second wave of Gramarye soldiers charged up the beach, and new pikes poked through the line. The first wave retreated, minds dizzy from the Evil Eye.

'We are come, Lord Warlock,' Tuan called, as he reined in his steed next to Fess. 'Do as thou must; Sir Maris and I will care for our men.'

'All thanks, my liege!' Rod called back. He ducked down, lying flat on Fess's back. 'Now, Steel Steed! Head for the low scrub!'

The robot-horse leaped into a gallop, heading for the brush and low trees at the edge of the beach. 'Rod, this subterfuge is scarcely needed! My thoughts were not even growing fuzzy yet!'

'For once, I'm not worried about you having a seizure in the middle of a battle.'

'Then, why this retreat?' Fess slowed and halted behind a screen of brush.

'Just wait. Trust me.' Rod parted the bushes and peeked out toward the beach. The battle was raging nicely, he noticed. But that wasn't his prime concern. He scanned the beach – more especially, the brush. It was very dark, so of course he couldn't be sure. The Gramarye soldiers had lighted torches to see their enemy by, and the light spilled over, dimly illuminating the edges of the beach; he thought he could just barely make out some dim, amorphous mass, bulging very slowly, and growing larger – but he couldn't be sure.

The second wave of soldiers had carried the charge almost into the Neanderthal camp before sheer reflex had made individual beastmen begin seeking out the eyes of single opponents. Power flowed into the beastmen; their eyes burned more brightly. The Gramarye line slowed to a grinding halt.

In the flagship's cabin, Agatha and Gwen squeezed the hands of the witches to each side of them and shut their eyes, bowing their heads.

Pikes, spears, and swords began to move again, slowly, gathering force to block the beastmen's swings.

The beastmen chopped hysterically in the desperation born of superstitious fear – but wildly, too, dropping their guards. The pikes drove in, and blood flowed out.

\*

Coming down the gangplank, Brother Chillde tripped, stumbled, and fell, sprawling on the sand with a howl of dismay.

Puck chuckled, tossed aside the stick he'd jabbed between the monk's feet, and scurried to his side, moving his hands in arcane, symbolic gestures, and chanting under his breath,

> 'Chronicler, whose zeal doth blind thee
> To the truth t'which sight should bind thee,
> Be thou bound in falsehood's prison!
> For an hour, lose thy vision!'

'What . . . what doth hap?' Brother Chillde cried, pushing himself up out of the sand. He glanced about him, then squeezed his eyes shut, shook his head, and opened them again. 'What! Is the night become so dark? Is there no light at all?' Then his face twisted into a mask of terror as the truth hit him. 'I am blinded! Heaven forgive me – my sight is lost!'

'Here, now, fellow,' Puck growled in a deep and throaty voice as he strode up to Brother Chillde, 'what ails thee? Eh, thou'rt o' the cloth!'

'Oh, kind sir!' Brother Chillde flailed about him, caught Puck's shoulder, and grasped it. 'Have pity on me, for I'm struck blind!'

'What sins are these,' Puck rumbled, 'that must needs meet such desperate punishment?'

'I cannot say.' Brother Chillde bowed his head. 'Pride, mayhap – that I should dare to scribble down all that did hap within this war . . .' His head snapped up, sightless eyes staring. 'The battle! Oh, stranger, take pity! I have laboured all these months to record in writing each separate event of this war! I cannot miss the knowledge of the final battle! Pray, have mercy! Stay, and speak what thou dost see! Tell me the course of the day!'

'I should be gone,' Puck growled, 'to aid in tending other wounded.'

'Hast thou hurt, then?' Brother Chillde was suddenly all solicitousness, groping about him. 'Nay, let me find it! I shall bandage . . .'

'Spare thy trouble,' Puck said quickly, 'for the flow already hath been staunched. Yet I'll own I have no occupation now . . .'

'Then, stay,' Brother Chillde implored, 'and speak to me of all that thou mayst see.'

'Well, I will, then,' Puck sighed. 'Attend thou, then, and hear, for thus it doth occur.'

'May Heaven bless thee!' Brother Chillde cried.

Puck took a deep breath, recalling the main thrust of Rod's prompting. 'The beastmen and our brave soldiers are drawn up in lines that do oppose. They grapple, they struggle; battle axes flail; pikes hover and descend. The clank of arms doth fill the air, and soldiers' groans and horses' neighs – eh, but that thou canst hear of thine own.'

'Aye, but now I ken the meaning of the sounds!' Brother Chillde clutched Puck's shoulder again. 'But the High Warlock! What of the High Warlock?'

'Why, there he rides,' Puck cried, pointing at empty air. 'He doth rise up on's huge black horse, a figure strong and manly, with a face that doth shine like unto the sun!' He grinned, delighted with his own cleverness. 'Nay, his arms are corded cables, his shoulders a bulwark! He fairly gleams within the starlight, and his piercing eye doth daunt all who do behold him! Now rides he against the centre of the line; now doth it bend and break! Now do his soldiers rush to widen the breach that he hath made!'

In the scrub brush, Rod eyed the heaving lump of jelly apprehensively. He'd watched smaller lumps of fungus ooze over to merge with it; the whole mass had grown amazingly. Now it was bulging very strangely, stretching upward, higher and higher, coalescing into a giant double lump. It thrust out a pseudopod that began to take on the shape of a horsehead, and the top narrowed from front to back and broadened from side to side. A piece split off on each side to assume the shapes of arms; a lump on top modelled itself into a head.

'I can scarcely believe it,' Rod hissed.

'Nor I.' Fess's voice wavered. 'I know of the fungus locally termed witch moss, and its link to projective telepaths – but I never suspected anything on this scale.'

Neither had Rod – for he was staring at himself. Himself the way he'd always wanted to be, too – seven feet tall, powerful as Hercules, handsome as Apollo! It was his face; but with all the crags and roughness gone, it was a face that could have dazzled a thousand Helens.

'*Terre et ciel!*' the figure roared, hauling out a sword the size of a small girder, and charged off into the battle on a ten-foot war-horse.

'Brother Chillde,' Rod sighed, 'is one hell of a projective!'

'He is indeed,' Fess agreed. 'Do you truly believe he does not know it?'

'Thoroughly.' Rod nodded. 'Can you really see the Abbot letting him out into the world if he knew what Brother Chillde was?' He turned Fess's head away. 'Enough of the sideshow. He'll keep the beastmen busy – and anybody who's looking for me will see me.'

'Such as Yorick?' Fess murmured.

'Or the Eagle. Or our own soldiers, come to that – "my" presence there will sure lend them courage – especially when I look like that!' He sort of hoped Gwen didn't get a close look at his doppelgänger; she might never be satisfied with reality again. 'Now we can get on with the real work of the night – and be completely unsuspected, too. To the cliff-face, Fess – let's go.'

The robot-horse trotted through the starlight, probing the brush with infrared to see the path. 'Is this truly necessary, Rod? Surely Yorick has an adequate force.'

'Maybe,' Rod said with a harsh smile, 'but I'd like to give him a little backup, just in case.'

'You do not truly trust him, do you?'

Rod shrugged. 'How can you really trust anybody who's always so cheerful?'

On the beach, Brother Chillde cried, 'Why dost thou pause? Tell me!'

But Puck stared, stupefied, at the giant shining Rod Gallowglass who galloped into the fray.

'The High Warlock!' Brother Chillde chattered, 'The High Warlock! Tell me, what doth he?'

'Why . . . he doth well,' Puck said. 'He doth very well indeed.'

'Then he doth lead the soldiers on to victory?'

'Nay . . . now, hold!' Puck frowned. 'The soldiers do begin to slow!'

' 'Tis the Evil Eye!' Brother Chillde groaned, 'and that fell power that doth bolster it!'

It did seem to be. The soldiers ground to a virtual halt. The beastmen stared a moment in disbelief, then shouted (more with relief than with blood-lust) and started chopping.

In the witches' cabin, the young folk grimaced in pain, shoulders hunching under the strain as a huge, black amoeba strove to fold itself over their minds.

Rod and Fess galloped up the series of rock ledges that led to the High Cave, and found Brom waiting.

Rod reined in, frowning up at the dwarf where he stood on a projection of rock a little above Rod's head.

'Didn't expect to find *you* here, Brom. I'm glad of it, though.'

'Someone must see thou dost not play the fool in statecraft in the hot blood of this hour,' the dwarf growled. 'I fail to see why thou wilt not trust these beastmen allies by themselves; but, if thou must needs fight alongside of them 'gainst the Kobold and, mayhap, against *them*, when the Kobold is beaten, I will fight by thy side.'

'I'm grateful,' Rod said, frowning. 'But what's this business about beating the Kobold? It's only a wooden idol, isn't it?'

'So I had thought, till I came here,' Brom growled. 'But great and fell magic doth lurk on this hillside, magic more than mortal. Mughorck is too slight a man for the depths of this foul power, or I mistake him quite. I feel it deep within me, and—'

There was a yell up ahead of them within the cave, then the clash of steel and a chaos of howling.

'It's started,' Rod snapped. 'Let's go.'

Fess leaped into a gallop as Brom hurtled through the air to land on the horse's rump. Rod whipped out his sword.

They rode into a mammoth cave more than a hundred feet deep and perhaps seventy wide, coated with glinting limestone, columned with joined stalactites and stalagmites, and filled with a dim eldritch light.

Three Neanderthals lay on the floor, their throats pumping blood.

All about the cave, locked pairs of Neanderthals struggled.

But Rod saw none of this. His eyes, and Brom's, went straight to the dais at the far end of the cave.

There, on a sort of rock throne, sat a huge-headed, pot-bellied thing with an ape's face, concave forehead, and bulging cranium. Its limbs were shrivelled; its belly was swollen, as though with famine. It was hairless and naked except for a fringe of whiskers around its jowls. Its eyes were fevered, bright, manic; it drooled.

Two slender cables ran from its bald pate to a black box on the floor beside it.

The spittle dribbled from its chinless mouth into its scanty beard.

Behind it towered three metal panels, keys and switches, flashes of jewelled light, and a black gaping doorway.

At its feet, Yorick and a short skinny Neanderthal strained, locked in combat.

Its eyes flicked to Rod's.

Icicles stabbed into Rod's brain.

The monstrosity's eyes flicked to Brom's, then back to Rod's.

Brom moved slowly, like a rusted machine, and the Kobold's eyes flicked back to him. Brom moved again, even more slowly.

The Kobold's jaw tightened; a wrinkle appeared between its eyes.

Brom froze.

In the witches' cabin, the air seemed to thicken next to Agatha, like a heat haze. It began to glow.

A young witch slumped unconscious to the ground. A fourteen-year-old warlock followed her into a blackout, then a fifteen-year-old. A few moments later, a seventeen-year-old witch joined them, then a young warlock in his twenties.

One by one, the young psis dropped, to sprawl unconscious.

Agatha and Gwen caught each other's free hands, bowing their heads, every muscle in their bodies rigid, hands clasped so tightly that the knuckles whitened.

Then Gwen began to sway, only a centimetre or so at first, then wider and wider till suddenly her whole body went limp and she fell.

Agatha dropped Gwen's hands, clenched her fists; her face tightened into a granite mask and a trickle of blood ran down from the corner of her mouth.

Above her, the heat haze brightened from red to yellow. Then the yellow grew brighter and brighter.

A blast shook the tent, a hollow booming, and Galen knelt there before Agatha. He clutched her fists, and his shoulders heaved up, hunching under some huge, unseen weight. He bowed his head, eyes squeezing shut, his whole face screwing up in agony.

The heat haze's yellow dimmed, became orange.

On the beach, the soldiers began to move again, slowly at first, then faster and faster, stepping aside from axe-blows, returning pike-stabs.

The beastmen howled in fear and fought in panic.

But the High Cave lay silent, like some fantastic Hall of Horrors in a wax museum. An occasional whine or grunt escaped the Neanderthals frozen body-to-body in combat, straining each against the other – Kobold's men to Eagle's partisans, Mughorck locked with Yorick.

Rod and Brom stood frozen, the Kobold's glittering, malevolent eyes fixed on them, holding its frozen prey in a living death.

There was agony in Rod's eyes. A drop of sweat ran down from his hairline.

Silence stretched out in the glimmering, ghostly elf-light.

On the beach, the soldiers slowly ground to stasis again, their muscles locking to stone.

The Neanderthals roared and swung their axes like scythes, mowing through the Gramarye ranks, their victory song soaring high.

In the cabin, Galen bent low, the black weight pressing down, squeezing, kneading at his brain. The other soul was still there with him, fighting valiantly, heaving with him against the dark cloud.

And the High Cave lay silent.

A crowing laugh split the air, and a wriggling infant appeared on Rod's shoulders, straddling his neck, chubby hands clenched in his hair, drumming his collarbone with small heels. 'Horsey! Gi'y'up! Da'y, gi'y'up!'

The Kobold's gaze focused on the baby boy.

Magnus looked up, startled, and stared at the creature for a moment, then darted a glance at his frozen father. Terror started to show around the edges of the boy's expression; but hot, indignant anger darkened his face faster. He clutched his father's temples and glared back at the monster.

Rod shuddered, his neck whiplashing as the dark mantle wrenched free of his mind.

He tore his eyes from the Kobold's, saw Mughorck and Yorick locked straining in the embrace of hatred.

Rod leaped forward, ducking and dodging through the paired immobile Neanderthals, and sprang. His stiffened hand lashed out in a chop at the back of Mughorck's neck. The skinny tyrant stiffened, mouth gaping open, and slumped in Yorick's arms.

Yorick dropped the contorted body and lunged at the black box, slapping a switch.

Slowly, the Kobold's eyes dulled.

Galen's body snapped upward and back.

His hands still held Agatha's.

For a moment, minds blended completely, point for point, id, ego, and conscience, both souls thrown wide open as the burden they had strained against disappeared – open and vulnerable to the core. For one lasting, soul-searing moment, they knelt, staring deeply into each other's eyes.

Then the moment passed. Galen scrambled to his feet, still staring at Agatha, but his eyes mirrored panic.

She gazed up at him, lips slowly curving, gently parting, eyelids drooping.

He stared, appalled. Then thunder cracked, and he was gone.

She gazed at the space he'd filled with a lazy, confident smile.

Then a shout of joy and triumph exploded through her mind. Her gaze darted upward to behold the heat haze one last time before it vanished.

On the beach, the Gramarye soldiers jerked convulsively and came completely to life, saw the carnage around them, the mangled remains of friends, brothers, and leaders, and screamed bloody slaughter.

But a howl pierced the air, freezing even the soldiers. They stared as a beastman in the front line threw down his axe and shield and sank to his knees, wailing and gibbering to his mates. They began to moan, rocking from side to side. Then, with a crash like an armoury falling, axes and shields cascaded down, piling up in waist-high windrows.

Then the beastmen sank to their knees, hands upraised, open, and empty.

Some of the soldiers snarled and hefted their pikes; but Tuan barked an order, and knights echoed it; then sergeants roared it. Reluctantly, the soldiers lowered their weapons.

'What hath happed?' Sir Maris demanded.

'I can only think 'tis some event within their minds,' Tuan answered in a low voice, 'mayhap to do with that fell weight being lifted from ours.'

'But why have they not fought to the death?'

'For that, haply we may thank Master Yorick's rumour-mongering.' Tuan squared his shoulders. 'Yet, when we bade him spread that word, we did effectively make compact with him, and with all his nation. Bid the men gather up the weapons, Sir Maris – but be certain they do not touch a hair of any beastman's head!' He turned his horse away.

'Why, so I shall,' the old knight growled reluctantly. 'But whither goest thou, my liege?'

'To the High Cave,' Tuan said grimly, 'for I misdoubt me as to what occurreth there.'

Fess's hooves lifted, slamming down at the back of a Neanderthal's head. The beastman slumped.

Rod caught two beastmen by the neck, yanked them apart, and smashed their heads back together. He turned away, letting them drop, and saw a pair of rocks flying through the air to brain two beastmen. 'Tag!' cried Magnus; and, as the Neanderthals fell, he gurgled, 'Fun game!'

Rod repressed a shudder, and turned just in time to see Brom heave at a beastman's ankles. The Neanderthal fell like a poleaxed steer, and Brom sapped him with the hilt of his knife.

But beastmen came in mismatched pairs here, and Brom had guessed wrongly. The other half roared and lunged at him.

The dwarf grabbed an arm and pulled sharply. The beastman doubled over, his head slamming against the rock floor.

'Nice work,' Rod called approvingly. 'That's why I've been knocking out both halves of each couple. We can winnow out the friends from the foes later.'

Yorick finished trussing up Mughorck like a pot roast, and turned to join the battle; but just as he did, Fess nailed the last beastman. 'Aw-w-w! I always miss the fun!'

Rod looked around the huge cave and saw that there was nothing left standing except himself, Brom, Fess, Yorick, and Magnus. Though Magnus wasn't really standing, actually; he was floating over an unconscious beastman, lisping, 'S'eepy?'

'Hey, we did it!' Yorick strode around Mughorck's inert form with his hand outstretched – but he kept on rounding, circling further and further toward the mouth of the cave as he came toward Rod. Rod suddenly realized Yorick was pulling Rod's gaze away from the back of the cave. He spun around just in time to see the black doorway behind the monster glow to life, a seven-by-three-foot rectangle. Its light showed him a short twisted man. From the neck down, he looked like a caricature of Richard III – an amazingly scrawny body with a hunched back, shrivelled arm, shortened leg – and so slender as to seem almost frail.

But the head!

He was arresting, commanding. Ice-blue eyes glared back at Rod from beneath bushy white eyebrows. Above them lifted a high, broad forehead, surmounted by a mane of white hair. The face was crags and angles, with a blade of a nose. It was a hatchet face, a hawk face . . .

An eagle's face.

Rod stared, electrified, as the figure began to dim, to fade. Just as it became transparent, the mouth hooked upward in a sardonic smile, and the figure raised one hand in salute.

Then it was gone, and the 'doorway' darkened.

'Impressive, isn't he?' Yorick murmured behind him.

Rod turned slowly, blinking. 'Yes, really. Quite.' He stared at Yorick for a moment longer, then turned back to the 'doorway'.

'Time machine?'

'Of course.'

Rod turned back. 'Who is he? And don't just tell me the Eagle. That's pretty obvious.'

'We call him "Doc Angus", back at the time lab,' Yorick offered. 'You wouldn't have heard of him, though. We're very careful about that. Publicly, he's got a bunch of minor patents to his credit; but the big things he kept secret. They just had too much potential for harm.'

'Such as – a time machine?'

Yorick nodded. 'He's the inventor.'

'Then'—Rod groped for words—'the anarchists . . . the totalitarians . . .'

'They stole the design.' Yorick shook his head ruefully. 'And we thought we had such a good security setup, too! Rather ingenious how they did it, really . . .' Then he saw the look on Rod's face, and stopped. 'Well, another time, maybe. But it is worth saying that Doc Angus got mad at them – real mad.'

'So he decided to fight them anywhere he could?'

Yorick nodded. 'A hundred thousand BC., a million BC, one million AD – you name it.'

'That would take a sizable organization, of course.'

'Sure – so he built one up and found ways to make it finance itself.'

'And if he's fighting the futurian anarchists *and* the futurian totalitarians,' Rod said slowly, 'that puts him on *our* side.'

Yorick nodded.

Rod shook his head, amazed. 'Now, *that's* what I call carrying a grudge!'

'A gripe,' Yorick chuckled. 'That's the name of the organization, actually – GRIPE, and it stands for "Guardians of the Rights of Individuals, Patentholders Especially".'

Rod frowned. Then understanding came, and the frown turned to a sour smile. 'I thought you said he didn't patent the time machine.'

'That just made him madder. It was his design, and they should have respected his rights. But the bums don't even pay him royalties! So he gathered us together to protect patent rights up and down the time line, especially his – and democracy guards individual rights better than any other form of government, including patent rights; so . . .'

'So he backs us. But how does that tie in with several thousand psionic Neanderthals cavorting around our planet?'

Yorick tugged at an earlobe, embarrassed. 'Well, it wasn't supposed to work out quite this way . . .'

'How about telling me how it *was* supposed to work?' Rod's voice was dangerously soft.

'Well, it all began with the totalitarians . . .'

Rod frowned. 'How?'

'By tectogenetics.' Yorick hooked a thumb over his shoulder at the Kobold. 'You may have noticed they're pretty good at it. The future has worked up some dandy genetic engineering gadgets.'

Rod nodded, still frowning. 'All right, I'll buy it. So, what did they engineer?'

'Evil-Eye Neanderthals.' Yorick grinned. 'They cooked up a strain of mutant projective telepaths and planted 'em all over Terra. Figured they'd breed true and become dominant in whatever society they were in – take over completely, in fact. It would've made things a lot easier for the futurians if they'd been able to prevent democracy's ever getting started at all.'

Rod shuddered. 'It sure would have.' He had a quick mental vision of humanity evolving and progressing down through the long road of history, always shackled to the will of one group of tyrants after another. 'I take it they're genetically a different race from the other Neanderthals.'

Yorick nodded. 'Can't interbreed to produce fertile offspring. So they'd stay a minority and they wouldn't dare loosen the reins, for fear of being wiped out by the non-psis.'

Rod began to realize that humanity had had a close call. 'But you caught them at it.'

Yorick nodded. 'Caught 'em, and managed to persuade all the little groups of projectives to band together. The totalitarians made the mistake of just letting nature take its course; they left 'em unsupervised.'

'Which you didn't, of course.'

'Well, we thought we were keeping a close watch.' Yorick seemed embarrassed. 'But the totalitarians dropped some storm troopers on us one night, killed most of the GRIPE force and chased away the rest, then set up a time machine and herded all the Neanderthals to Gramarye.'

Rod's eyes widened. 'Now it begins to make sense. What'd they expect the beastmen to do, take over right away?'

'I'm sure they did. Leastways, by the time we managed to find 'em again they were running around in horned helmets and talking about going a-viking – and I don't think they dreamed that up on their own.'

'So you hit the totalitarian force with everything you had and stole your Neanderthals back. But why couldn't you have taken them someplace else?'

'Have pity on the poor people, milord! Would you want them to spend their whole existences being balls in a cosmic game of ping-pong? No, we figured it was better to let them stay and try to keep them under protection. We mounted a strong guard – but we forgot about infiltration.'

'Mughorck.' Rod's mouth twisted. 'Then he isn't really a Neanderthal?'

'Oh, he's the genuine article, all right – just as much as I am!'

Rod stared at Yorick. Then, slowly, he nodded. 'I see. They "adopted" him in infancy and raised him to be an agent.'

Yorick nodded. 'A farsighted plan, but it paid off. When the fat hit the fire we couldn't do anything about it. It was either kill the people we'd been trying to civilize, or run – so we ran.' For a moment, he looked miserable. 'Sorry we slipped up.'

Rod sighed. 'Not much we can do about it now, I suppose.'

'No, not really,' Yorick answered. ' 'Fraid you're stuck with 'em.'

It was the perfect moment for Tuan to come charging into the cave.

He took one look at the Kobold and sawed back on the reins, freezing – just for a moment, of course; the monster was shut down. But it was a sight to give anyone pause.

Behind him, sandals and hooves clattered and Brother Chillde jerked to a halt to stare, paralysed, at the monster. 'My liege . . . what . . .'

Tuan turned to him, frowning, then caught a glimpse of what was behind the monk. He looked again, and stared. 'Lord Warlock!'

Rod turned, frowning. 'Yes?'

'But how didst thou . . .' Tuan turned back to him, and whites showed all around his eyes. 'But thou wert even now . . .' He jerked around to stare past Brother Chillde again.

Rod followed his gaze, and saw . . .

Himself.

A giant self, astride a behemoth of a horse; a handsome self, with the form of a Greek statue.

Brother Chillde stared at the double, then whipped around to stare at Rod, then back to the double, back to Rod – and the double began to shrink, the horse began to dwindle; the doppelgänger's face became more homely, its features more irregular, its muscles less fantastic – and Rod found himself staring at an exact duplicate of himself.

Brother Chillde's gaze still swivelled back and forth from one to the other like a metronome. 'But what . . . how . . .'

'By thyself,' Brom rumbled behind him. 'It is thou who hath made this co-walker, friar, though thou didst not know it.'

Brother Chillde sighed as his eyes rolled up and his knees buckled. He collapsed in a dead faint.

'He'll get over it,' Rod assured the company.

'Thy double will not,' Brom snorted as he watched the co-walker blur, sag, and melt into a huge heap of fungus.

A sponge rubber club hit Rod in the back of the neck, and a little voice demanded fretfully, 'Gi'y'up!'

Rod grinned, reached up, and plucked his son off his shoulders.

Magnus's eyes went round and wide; foreboding entered his face. 'Naw'y baby?'

'No, good baby. By accident, maybe, but good baby, anyway.' He tickled Magnus's tummy, and the baby chuckled and squirmed. 'But Daddy's busy just now, and I've got a job for you.'

Magnus bobbed his head. 'Baby help!'

'Right.' Rod pointed to the heap of witch moss. 'Get rid of that for me, will you?'

The baby frowned at the pile, then screwed his face up in intense concentration. The fungus began to twitch, to heave; it separated into fifty or sixty fragments, each of which stretched up, developed arms and legs, helmets, shields, and armour – and an army of toy knights stood waiting at attention.

'Pretty!' Magnus chirped, and drifted up out of Rod's arms. 'March!'

He drifted toward the doorway, calling commands that were frequently incomprehensible as his new model army marched before him out the cave-mouth and down the ramp.

A broomstick swooped in the entrance just before Magnus left it, and an arm reached out and pulled him firmly against a hip. 'And where wouldst thou go, my bonny babe?'

'Mommy!' Magnus cried in delight and threw his arms around her neck.

Another broomstick wobbled in beside Gwen's. Agatha cast a brief smiling glance at the pair, then came in for a landing.

'Hail, reverend dame!' Tuan called. 'Are all thy witches well?'

'All,' Agatha agreed, hobbling forward. 'But then, I'm certain the High Warlock could ha' told ye as much.'

Tuan cast a questioning glance at Rod, who nodded. 'I didn't really *know*, you understand – but when the mental fog lifted for the third time, I was pretty sure.' He turned to Agatha. 'And how's your son?'

'Vanished,' Agatha retorted, 'and with joy; for when that unholy weight lifted from our minds, Galen's thoughts blended fully with mine and, from their combination, Harold was able to lift what he required. He's homeward sped, to wake his body.'

Rod eyed her narrowly. 'You don't exactly seem heart-broken.'

'I am not.' Her eye glinted. 'I've knowledge of the old stiff stick now; I've seen deeply into him, and know what he holds hid.'

Rod frowned, puzzled. 'And that's enough to make you happy?'

'Aye; for now I'll invade his Tower truly.'

'But he'll throw you out again!'

'I think not.' Agatha's smile widened into a grin. 'I think that he will not.'

Rod stared at her for a long moment; then he shrugged. 'You must know something I don't know.'

'Aye.' Gwen met Agatha's eyes with a smile that held back laughter. 'I think she doth.'

'Godspeed ye, then.' Tuan inclined his head towards Agatha. 'And the thanks of a kingdom go with thee. If thou wilt come to Runnymede in some weeks time, we'll honour thee as thou shouldst be.'

'I thank thee, Majesty,' Agatha rejoined, 'but I hope to be too deeply occupied for such a jaunt.'

Tuan's eyebrows shot up in surprise, but Agatha only dropped a curtsy, albeit a stiff one, and snapped her fingers. Her broomstick shot up beside her; she leaped astride it and floated up into the air.

'Milords, uncover!' Tuan snapped – entirely unnecessary, since no male present was wearing a hat. But they all dutifully pressed their hands over their hearts in respect as they watched the veteran witch sail out the cave-mouth and up into the night.

Rod turned to Gwen with concern. 'That's a long way to go, all the way back to the mainland – and after all the drain of the battle, too! Is she going to be all right?'

'Fear not, my lord,' Gwen said, with a secretive smile. 'I believe she shall fare excellently.'

Rod frowned at her, wondering if he was missing something.

Then he sighed and turned away. 'Oh, well, back to the aftermath. What do you think we should do with Brother Chillde, my liege?'

Tuan shrugged. 'Tend him when he doth wake; what else is there to do? But why was he so taken at the sight of thy double?' He shuddered. 'And, come to that, who did craft it?'

'He did,' Rod answered. 'He's a very powerful projective telepath, but he doesn't know it – and he watched the battles very intensely, trying to remember everything that happened. But he wasn't trained as an observer, so he kept getting what he really *did* see confused with what he *wanted* to see – and what he wanted to see most was the High Warlock performing feats of valour.' Rod had the grace to blush. 'I'm afraid he's come down with a bad case of hero-worship.'

'I comprehend,' Tuan said drily.

'Well, not completely. For this final battle, I'm afraid we used the poor young fellow. I persuaded Puck to make Brother Chillde temporarily blind and to describe the High Warlock the way Brother Chillde wanted to see him – bigger than life, impossibly perfect. The poor friar was sucked in totally, and unknowingly created a witch-moss High Warlock who helped the troops keep up their courage, and had everybody thinking I was down here so my visit to the High Cave could be a complete surprise. Not that it did much good,' he answered, with a glance at the Kobold.

'Aye – the monster.' Tuan followed his gaze. 'We must make disposition of it, must we not?'

The whole company turned to stare at the false god.

'What is this fell creature?' Tuan breathed.

'A Kobold,' Rod growled, face twisting with disgust and nausea. 'Does it need any other name?'

'For you and me, yes,' Yorick growled. 'What do you think it was, Lord Warlock? A chimpanzee?'

'Its parents were.' Rod turned away. 'I can't see much in the way of surgical scars, so I'm pretty sure they were; but the normal strain might be quite a few generations back. It's obviously been genetically restructured; that's the only way you could get a monster like that.' He turned back to the Kobold. 'Of course, I suppose you could say it's a tectogenetic masterpiece.

They doctored the chromosomes to make the poor beast into a converter – feed current into it, DC, I suppose, and out comes psionic energy.' He dropped his gaze to the black box, then looked a question at Yorick.

The Neanderthal nodded, nudging the black box with his foot. 'Atomic-power pack. Wish I could figure out how to shut this thing off permanently.'

'You mean it's liable to go on again?'

'Not unless somebody flips the switch.' Yorick eyed the monster warily. 'Still, it would be an almighty comfort if that were impossible.' He cocked his head on one side and closed one eye, squinting, looking the Kobold up and down. 'I suppose it *is* a triumph of genetic engineering, if you look at it the right way. That bulging cerebrum can handle one hell of a lot of power. And no forebrain, did you notice that? Lobotomy in the womb. It can't do anything on its own. No initiative.'

'Just a living gadget,' said Rod grimly.

'Which may be just as well,' Yorick pointed out. 'We might conjecture about what it would do if it had a mind of its own . . .'

Rod shuddered, but growled, 'It couldn't do much. Not with those atrophied limbs. All it can do is just sit there.' He swallowed hard and turned away, looking slightly green. 'That forehead . . . how can you just sit there and look at it?'

'Oh, it's a fascinating study, from a scientific viewpoint,' Yorick answered, 'a real triumph, a great philosophic statement of mind over matter, an enduring monument to man's ingenuity.' He turned back to Rod. 'Put the poor thing out of its misery!'

'Yes,' Rod agreed, turning away, slightly bent over. 'Somebody stick a knife in the poor bastardization!'

Nobody moved. Nobody spoke.

Rod frowned, lifted his head. 'Didn't anybody hear me? I said, kill it!'

He sought out Tuan's eyes. The young King looked away.

Rod bowed his head, biting his lip.

He spun, looking at Yorick.

The Neanderthal looked up at the ceiling, whistling softly.

Rod snarled and bounded up to the dais, dagger in his hand, swinging up fast in an underhand stab.

His arm froze as he looked into the dulled eyes, looked slowly up and down the naked, hairless thing, so obscene, yet so . . .

He turned away, throwing down his knife, growling low in his throat.

Yorick met his eyes, nodding sympathetically. 'It's such a poor, pitiful thing when the power's turned off, milord – so weak and defenceless. And men have done it so much dirt already . . .'

'Dogs!' roared Brom, glaring about at them. 'Stoats and weasels! Art thou all so unmanned as to let this thing live?'

He whirled about where he stood on the dais, glowering at the silent throng before him. He snorted, turned about, glaring at them all.

'Aye,' he rumbled, 'I see it is even as I have said. There is too much of pity within thee; thou canst not steel thyselves to the doing of it; for there is not *enough* pity in thee to force thee to this cruel kindness.'

He turned, measuring the Kobold up and down. 'Yet must it be done; for this is a fell thing, a foul thing out of nightmare, and therefore must it die. *And will no man do it this courtesy?*'

No one moved.

Brom looked long and carefully, but found only shame in each glance.

He smiled sourly and shrugged his massive shoulders. 'This is my portion, then.'

And, before anyone quite realized what he was doing, the dwarf drew his sword and leaped, plunging his blade up to the hilt in the Kobold's chest, into its heart.

The monster stiffened, its mouth wrenching open, face contorting in one silent, simian scream; then it slumped where it sat, dead.

The others stared, horrified.

Brom sheathed his sword, touched his forelock in respect where he stood on the arm of the Kobold's stone chair. 'Good lasting sleep, Sir Kobold.'

' 'Twas an ill deed,' said Tuan. 'It could not defend itself.' But he seemed uncertain.

'Aye, but soulless it was, also,' Brom reminded. 'Forget that not, Majesty. Is it dishonour to slaughter a hog? Or to stick a wild boar? Nay, surely not! But this thing ha' wrought death and was now defenceless; and therefore no man would touch it.'

The cavern was still; the company stood awed by the event.

Yorick broke the silence. 'Well, then, my people's god is dead. Who shall rule them in his stead?'

Tuan looked up, startled. 'Why, the Eagle! Say to him that I would fain parley with him that we may draw a treaty.'

But Yorick shook his head. 'The Eagle's gone.'

'Gone?' Tuan said blankly.

'Thoroughly,' Rod confirmed. 'I saw him disappear myself.'

'But . . . why,' Tuan cried, 'when his people were his again?'

'Because they don't need him any more,' Yorick said practically.

'But . . . then . . . wherefore did he remain when he'd been overthrown?'

'To make sure they were freed from Mughorck,' Yorick explained. 'After all, he's the one who really masterminded my end of the invasion, you know.'

'Nay, I did not. Who now shall rule thee?'

Yorick spread his hands. 'To the victor go the spoils.' He dropped to one knee. 'Hail, my liege and sovereign!'

Tuan stared down at him, horrified.

'Thou canst not well deny him,' Brom said, *sotto voce*.

'Thus hath it ever been – that the victor governed the vanquished.'

And that, of course, settled it. In a medieval culture, tradition ruled.

'Well, then, I must,' Tuan said, with ill grace – but Rod noticed he stood a little straighter. 'Yet how is this to be? I've a kingdom already, across the wide sea!'

'Oh, I could run the place for you, I suppose,' Yorick said, carefully casual, 'as long as you're willing to take the final responsibility.'

'That I can accept,' Tuan said slowly, 'an 'tis understood that thou wilt govern in my stead.'

'Glad to, I assure you! For the first year or so, anyway. But don't worry about what happens after that; I've got a very likely-looking lieutenant who should fit the bill perfectly. He's even learning English . . .'

The prisoners were assembled beneath the High Cave, all four thousand of them. Four soldiers stood on the ledge, two to either side of the cave-mouth. At some unseen signal, they flourished trumpets and blew a fanfare.

Inside the cave, Rod winced. They were beginning to get the idea that pitch wasn't just a matter of personal taste, but they had a long way to go.

Four knights rode out of the cave in full armour, raising their lances with pennons at their tips. They sidestepped, leaving the centre clear. After them came Yorick – and then, just as the sun rose, Tuan stepped out onto the ledge, gilded by the dawn.

An awed murmur ran through the crowd below.

Yorick stepped up a little in advance of Tuan and to his side, and began to bellow in the Neanderthal language.

'I'll bet he's telling them the sad news,' Rod muttered, 'that the Eagle's gone.'

A groan swept the crowd.

Brom nodded. 'Thou hast the right of it.'

Yorick started bellowing again.

'Now he's telling them they've got a new king,' Rod muttered.

'Emperor!' Yorick shouted.

Tuan looked up, startled.

Inside the cave, Gwen shrugged. 'He is, in all truth – and Catharine's an empress.'

'Sure,' Rod agreed. 'It just hadn't hit him before.'

A thunderous cheer split the air.

'I'd wager Yorick hath but now told them that he will rule as viceroy,' Brom said drily.

Rod nodded. 'Logical guess.'

There was a pause, and they could hear Yorick's stage whisper: 'A speech might be appropriate, my liege.'

The pause lengthened; then Tuan cried out, 'I am thy new ruler!' and Yorick bellowed the translation.

The crowd cheered again.

'Now they know it won't be a real conquest,' Rod murmured.

Tuan went on, with frequent pauses for translation. 'I am thy new ruler and will never forsake thee. Yet, since I cannot abide here with thee, I give to you a viceroy to rule in my stead. Thou hast called thyselves the People of the Kobold . . . and did worship a goblin . . . calling it thy god. This god was false . . . and the mark of it was . . . that it demanded thy worship, which should go to the One True Unseen God only. I shall not demand such worship . . . only fealty and loyalty. An thou wilt be loyal to me and my viceroy, I shall be true to thee.'

'He does it well, don't you think?' Rod said softly.

Brom and Gwen nodded. 'He ever hath,' said the dwarf. 'Yet wilt thou, I wonder?'

Rod frowned. 'What do you mean? I don't have to do any speechifying!'

'Nay,' Brom agreed, 'but thou'lt now have to be the mainstay of two nations, the power behind two thrones.'

'Oh.' Rod's mouth tightened. 'Yeah, I know what you mean. But honestly, Brom, I don't know if I can handle all that.'

'Aye,' Gwen sympathized. 'The two lands are more than thirty leagues apart!'

'I know,' Rod said heavily. 'And I can't be in two places at the same time, can I?'